WITCH

Also by Donald E. McQuinn

WITCH

Donald E. McQuinn

A Del Rey® Book
Ballantine Books • New York

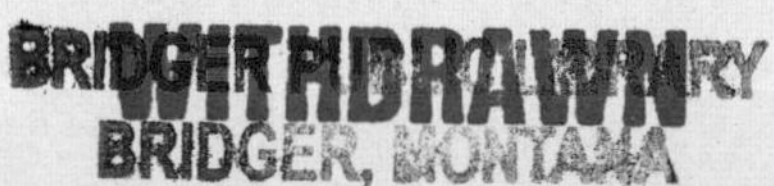

A Del Rey® Book
Published by Ballantine Books

Library of Congress Catalog Card Number: 94-94357

ISBN: 0-345-37841-5

Cover design by David Stevenson
Cover illustration by Michael Herring

Manufactured in the United States of America

First Edition: November 1994

10 9 8 7 6 5 4 3 2 1

To Caitlin and Emmett and Ilana and Alec
With love

WITCH

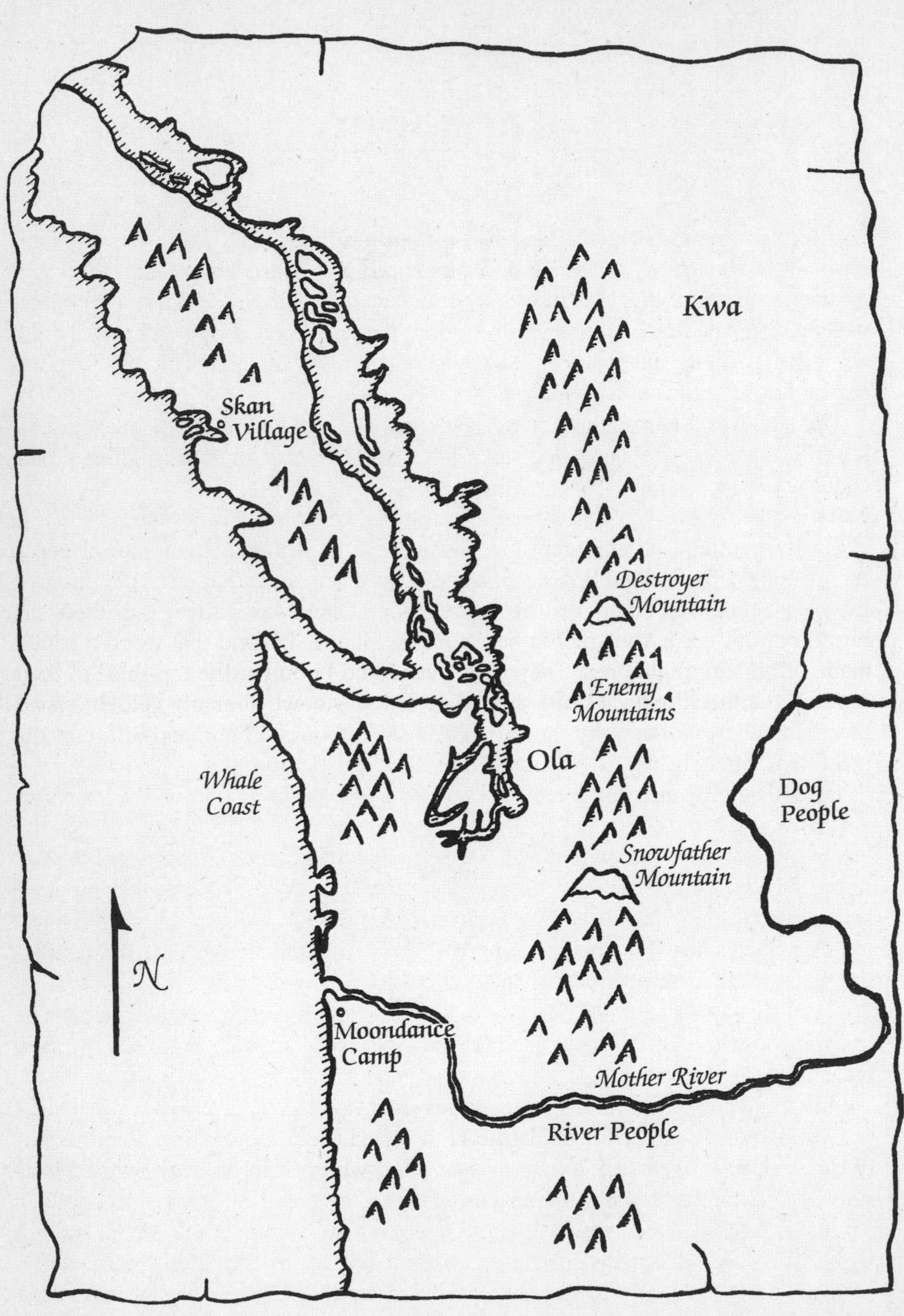
Kwa
Skan
Village
Destroyer
Mountain
Enemy
Mountains
Ola
Whale
Coast
Dog
People
Snowfather
Mountain
N
Moondance
Camp
Mother River
River People

Prologue

In the thundering darkness of storm-tormented night, one tiny fire struggled desperately to survive. Towering boulders caged it within a natural amphitheater, closing it off from land, forcing its light out at the raging sea. Horizontal sheets of flame streamed out from piled driftwood, flames flattened by wind that fanned the coals to fierce incandescence. Sharp crackling conflicted with the spiteful, seared hiss of blown surf spume and driven rain.

The surf was a rearing, glistening black menace. Unending waves threw themselves against the shore's tearing stone teeth and tumbled to ruin in ghostly pale chaos.

A crabbed figure huddled over the blaze. Its back was to the sea.

Slowly, painfully, a hand crept out of the previously inanimate mound of dense furs. Ruddied by firelight, the aged, bone-thin fingers spread apart. They savored the heat before descending to the figure's side. There was a silver cup there, its round bottom nestled in smooth beach rocks. Slightly beyond that stood a tripod made of human thighbones. They were joined and bound at the top third of their span by the metal tentacles of a golden octopus. A bowl, similarly golden, rested in the frame created atop by the short ends of the bones. The outer surface of the metal was ornately chased with a coiling, stylized octopus.

The delicately crazed and cracked interior lining of the bowl was the crown of a human skull.

The frail, ancient hand spidered down to clutch the silver cup, raised it. The hooded head bowed. Drank. The cup was replaced. The hand caressed the fire's warmth lingeringly before edging back under the dark furs.

Suddenly, impossibly, audible song rose from the still figure. Fine as needles, the notes pierced the rumble of wind and surf.

Chanting supplication, the voice wrapped its pleas for conquest and plunder in promises that the god Sosolassa would have his every appetite gratified in fullest measure.

Still singing, the figure rose, turned seaward.

Gusting wind snatched back the hood, revealed the person within. Reminiscent of the froth of broken surf, long gray hair wind-whipped in disarray. Swirled wetness settled on the harsh, eroded features of a crone. Dark, weasel-quick eyes squinted angrily. Downcurved lips, drawn against strong, white teeth, were a wire-thin arc of disapproval. The cumulative impact of the whole defined the woman, however. Her wrinkled face was a chart that traced a voyage spanning generations. She had watched other lives begin, aspire, and end. Time no longer had consequence for that forbidding visage.

The woman's whole being resonated malice.

Deliberately, she replaced the hood. Braced on an ornately carved walking stick taller than herself, she shuffled to pick up the tripod and bowl. Returning to the fire, she placed the objects between herself and the flame. She walked stiffly to the sea with the silver cup. Hiking up her robe, protected by high boots, she waded deep enough to scoop the cup full. Retreating to the bowl, she knelt and transferred that water to it. After assuring the liquid's perfect level, she pulled at a slim gold chain at her throat to draw out a peculiar, curved object. It resembled half of a broad-based beak. Highly polished steel, the pointed end glittered in the firelight. After dipping the object in the water, she lifted it high in both hands.

When she spoke, the voice was a nightmare thing. Rasping, hoarse, it was the rush of dry sand.

"Sosolassa, stalker from the Deep Calm, father of storms, hear the prayers of your slave. I offer myself. Taste, and know I live only to serve you. With this symbol of your mouth, I surrender myself." The woman drew the point of the beak across her left thumb. Expressionless, she returned the beak to its resting place. She held her fresh wound over the gold-encased skull. Blood splattered in the water. Firelight robbed the drops of color, so that only smoky, dark tendrils coiled away from each impact. Satisfied, the woman took up the silver cup and, with the bowl in her other hand, retraced her steps to the high-water line.

Bending painfully in a ceremonial bow, she emptied the sacrifice into a retreating wave. After a pause, she refilled the cup. Returning to the fire, she took up her former position and poured the new water in the bowl.

Once more, the amazingly clear music poured from her lips, this time without words. Rhythmic, repetitive, she sang the same short refrain over and over. Her gaze never wavered from the liquid's flat, steady surface.

The first tremor of her head came some while after she began her hymn. Soon she was nodding, swaying to her own cadence.

Untended, the fire guttered. Sticks collapsed onto the coals, flared their contribution, were reduced to mere glowing embers.

The hooded head slumped forward until it could fall no further.

Abruptly, the singing stopped. The silent woman rocked side to side. The wind grew fiercer. Gusts shivered her small body. The dying reach of waves rolled almost to her feet. Still she rocked. The fur of her wrap stood up in the back, conjuring a wet, angry cat.

Small waves appeared in the bowl. The old woman twitched erratically. Her hands shot out from inside her sleeves, clawed at the beach rocks. The scrabble of their naked whiteness was the panic of exposed darkling creatures. She moaned a low ecstasy. Her torso pitched forward. From within the hollow of the hood spooled a silver string of drool. Wind snatched it away.

The woman muttered.

Another voice—deep, imperious—answered.

Eerily, it came from her. Heavy, brutishly powerful; yet it was the woman's tiny body that birthed it. The words were indistinguishable. Guttural, wet, they caught the sibilance of the sea and transformed it to noisome, bubbling semblance of speech.

When the woman's normal voice came again, she fawned. She bobbed and squirmed in fulsome servility.

The bizarre conversation lasted until the fire was nearly out. Long after that, the woman straightened with the slow uncertainty of waking. Wide eyes struggled to reorient a consciousness obviously strained to dissociation. When the wind slammed another gust against her, she rocked violently, weak and vulnerable. Clutching her walking stick, she propped herself. She lifted the bowl and tripod to the side and bent forward over the muddled black-and-red remnants of her fire, soaking up what warmth the wind and rain allowed her.

Getting to her feet, she extracted a wooden whistle from her robe. The shrill call fled inland on the wind, up, over the enclosing rocks. In moments a man came, running hard around the side of the natural amphitheater. He was half again as tall as the woman, huge in fur hat, cloak and trousers, the latter bound with leggings. His sudden stop sent rocks skittering. When he advanced again, hands joined in front of him, fingers knotted together, his limp was obvious. He bent to speak to her. "I'm here, Tears of Jade. You are finished?"

She didn't bother to look at him. A flicker of hurt touched the man's hard, angular features. Concern replaced it when Tears of Jade's hand sagged, barely retaining her grip on her stick. The man watched, horrified, hands extended in helpless reach as she retched horribly. He never touched her.

When she straightened, he said, "It's the mushrooms you eat to prepare for these meetings. It grows worse. You were dizzy before, never sick. It's too hard on you."

Tears of Jade threw back her hood, disregarding spray and rain. Her face was spectral against black clothes, black night. "Your tongue will kill you, fool. The mushroom is the godfood that lets me hear the words of Sosolassa. You criticize the thing that allows me communion with the god?"

Agonized, he pleaded. "It's killing you."

She gasped. Her voice pitched to a screech. "You speak of death in the presence of he who is death? Pray! Pray, Lorso, before he takes you." She gripped his wrists. "Don't turn. Don't look. Even now, the cold tentacle that freezes the heart may be reaching from the sea. Don't look at the water. To see is to die."

Ashen, shaking, the man closed his eyes. Bloodless lips silently entreated. Tears of Jade stared seaward, alert, unafraid. She could have been some small, weasel-animal, defying whatever threatened her young. Little by little, she relaxed. She released Lorso's wrists. "We're safe. He's forgiven you. For now."

Lorso took several deep breaths. He never glanced at the sea. Formally, he said, "Do I have permission from the spirit woman to touch the holy articles?"

Sure they were leaving, he was already reaching when her rustling "No" checked him. Unbending warily, he waited. She said, "You must hear now. Sosolassa warns me. Enemies rise in the east. I see a man who is all sun, bright and comely. I see a woman. She is dark, but gleams, as the night sea playing with the stars. Flowers of the land bend to her in love and unity. The man is a conqueror, one who overcomes in order to rule, not pillage. Children of prophecy, that man and woman." She paused, spat. "He is landrat, knows not the sea, one of those who dig in the dirt for their salt. The woman is landrat, also, and worse than the man. She is evil. She brings change, calling it love. I sense the curse of knowing too much. She will not follow the laws that ordain what all women, everywhere, must be."

Tears of Jade stopped. Lorso waited, barely breathing. At last, the old woman continued. "Sosolassa says the man who thinks to conquer all will throw landrat soldiers against the Skan—we, who control all that touches the kingdom of Sosolassa. The god lusts to feed on the arrogant dead. Tears of Jade is ordered to destroy the children of prophecy. Sosolassa will be god to all."

Transported, the old woman flung her arms wide, spun in a circle. She drank the tumult and fury of the night.

Knuckles of clasped hands white with stress, Lorso waited until she relaxed. "You who raised me from a child know that I kill for Sosolassa with joy and pride. I no longer have a count of the lives I've sent to the Deep Calm. I already yearn to kill these children of prophecy. But surely, to be named in prophecy, they're under protection. Does Sosolassa say he'll protect us from their god?"

The woman replaced her hood and turned with cruelly slow deliberation. Her eyes blazed up at the towering figure. "Sosolassa makes orders, not promises." Her taloned fingers reached to stroke Lorso's cheek. Only his eyes moved, whites flashing like those of a frightened horse. She went on, more to herself than to the man. "Mighty Lorso. Slavetaker. Was I wrong to choose him as my strength? Is he not grown to make the Skan rulers of the Great Ocean and the rivers that feed it? I seek a man to challenge armies, and my Lorso cringes at one man and a woman. I am old. Weary. Must I raise another boy to take Lorso's place, one that will truly love me and obey our god?"

Lorso dropped to his knees. "I am sworn to you, Tears of Jade. All know it. Order; I obey. I am your weapon."

Tears of Jade took his head in both her hands. "I know, my son. I know. My unfailing Lorso. It was wrong of me to tease you. But I sense ruinous—catastrophic—change coming from these enemies. You can only be one of my weapons. I will need another. Not stronger. Not braver. Wilier. Poison, Lorso. And you will get it for me."

Lorso nodded rapidly, illuminated with devotion. Nevertheless, as Tears of Jade walked away, his hand stole to the hilt of his sword. He looked toward the savaging surf. His expression turned to aching longing, as one who sees a love forbidden him by law and distance. He sighed and shook his head. Picking up Tears of Jade's holy paraphernalia, he trudged after her.

BOOK I

Malice

Chapter 1

The sun's last rays splayed across the darkening waters of the Inland Sea with a cold golden intensity. Penned up all day behind the dead gray of steel-bellied clouds, the light broke free in blinding exuberance. Near-horizontal sheets of pure energy limned the pillared firs and steeply pitched shores of the Sea Star islands. Striated cloud banks gleamed in sudden splendor, burnished to bright, seething color.

The sea shifted uneasily at the swiftness of the transformation, as if it sensed how very short this glory must be, and how very dark the night to follow.

The thirty people around the driftwood fire were too busy to concern themselves. Laughing, joking, willing hands wrestled the last heavy-planked canoe high on the beach. The father and son who manned it held up sleek salmon and, as fishermen must, regaled the gathering with details of the giant that got away. The banter continued as everyone wandered toward camp.

Much later, black-green water slid almost imperceptibly up the beach. Between the camp's flaring fire and the looming forest, driftwood lay in a wild tumble. Limbs reached. Massive, broken trunks showed ends like jagged teeth. Bleached gray by sun and scoured by windblown sand, the mound created a backdrop for the singing, story-telling group. Warped and fragmented shadows writhed across the erratic surface. Sometimes—a trick of fitful flames—the wavering images seemed to take on lives of their own.

Rudimentary hide-and-wicker huts flanked the communal cookfire. The people were For, from the nearby Whale Coast peninsula. Approaching spring occasioned this annual pilgrimage and fishing expedition.

The For religious formality was solidly bound to Church, but their legends blended naturalism with the struggles of the tribe's founders. They didn't exactly worship the life-giving masses of salmon that exploded from the sea to clog the rivers of their land with their breeding frenzy. They didn't precisely consider the orca or the immense gray whale as gods. Nevertheless, their plank homes were covered with painted and carved images of Salmo, the stylized fish that embodied the spirit of the salmon. No fortress was considered complete until the Chief himself had beaten the sacred rhythm on that fort's unique Whale Drum. That music and the accompanying warrior's dance consecrated both drum and site.

Tonight, this and similar blood-clan groups of For were dispersed throughout the Sea Star islands. This was a time when ancestors were honored by feasting, by anticipating spring's burgeoning warmth. Life was good. Now, with the last song sung, the last joke's laughter ringing soft silver into the night, they straggled away to their sleeping huts.

Abandoned, failing, the campfire found enough mischievous energy to dart shards of light at the water. Reflections glittered with startling vigor, like sudden, chilling eyes.

In the slow passage of the night, the temperature dropped steadily.

Slyly, peering around headlands, banks of mist slid silently westward to submerge all but the highest island peaks. Moisture collected on the huts, on the tentative prespring leaves of deciduous trees, on the drooping needles of evergreens. Heavy silence gave way to the sporadic, mysterious whisperings of falling droplets.

In the sea, no more than a few body-lengths from shore, something struck at prey. Splash and swirl muttered primeval triumph and terror. One of the two For guards stirred. The goose down within his quilted clothing sighed sympathy. Soft leather, crushed and stressed, released pungent smells of hide and oak tannin. The guard at the other side of the camp, head bobbing, continued to sleep soundly.

Other creatures stirred the night-cloaked sea.

Lorso whispered commands to his helmsman.

Slim, knife-sharp in all her aspects, the Skan sharker felt her way carefully shoreward. At the end of each propelling stroke, her oars rotated a half turn. Edge-on, they drew back to the starting position. Oiled leather grommets in the oar holes muted potential squeals. Lorso hissed softly to indicate the beginning and end of each movement. The sea chuckled eagerness along the lean hull.

The sharker's carved figurehead was a huge, gaping white bear in attack. Its hungering eyes sought landfall.

Once again, an attack disturbed the waters. The rowers never bothered to look. Skan warriors lived in the knowledge that they were the sea's ultimate predator. The small killings of lesser creatures were inconsequential.

Grating gently, the hull gripped land. Two men lowered themselves over the side with careful speed. They hurried ashore, one uncoiling a stout line of plaited leather. At the stern, an anchor slowly lowered. In moments, the bowline pulled taut. When it did, Lorso led the raiding party's disembarkation.

Dressed in solid black, faces painted for raiding, the men blended perfectly with the night. Each jacket was decorated on the back, however, with a large stylized figure—eagle, bear, mosquito, and others—in white. Using the totem representations as guides, the column, like a deadly, multilegged beast, advanced on the sleeping camp.

Lorso moved in a near-crouch. Despite the limp, he covered ground quickly. Halting abruptly, he raised a hand. The men squatted, alternates facing left or right.

Lorso sampled the breeze from the camp, simultaneously moving his head to analyze the sound that checked him. Scent told him much; the cedar and fir ashes were still warm. The camp had fed on salmon. Something else, too. Seals, probably; warm blood reeked.

The earlier sound was repeated. Settling even closer to the earth, Lorso twisted about, using his side vision for a clearer view. He drew the secrets of the darkness to him, as a spider reads the world through the tingling of its web.

Someone was ahead. Snoring. Retreating to the closest Skan, Lorso pointed at the indistinct heap that was the sleeping guard.

The designated warrior moved to stand over his victim.

Lorso and the raiders moved ahead.

When the huts were only a few paces away, he stopped. Keeping his white bear totem directed away from the camp, he dispersed his men to his flanks. There were twenty, not counting himself.

Lorso rose, his face to the sky. He shrieked. The ululating cascade shattered the night. Before his signal was even half finished, the faster Skan were at the huts.

Each warrior carried a spear and a sword. Their technique was to plunge the spear through the flimsy hut wall. If anyone bolted out the small exit, the sword awaited. Some For warriors were astute enough to lift the entire shelter and roll out. They fought desperately. Hopelessly.

Screams of anguish and terror rose, only to break with the eternal finality. The howling helplessness of children tried to make itself heard. Women sobbed for the lives of those same young ones. Both pleas drowned under hoarse, brutal war cries.

It was over very quickly.

Efficiently, Skan bound and gagged survivors. The fallen were checked to assure none were faking, and hiding weapons. The living too damaged for slaving were eliminated. Lorso glanced at the horrified, huddled prisoners. "Build up the fire," he said. Men leaped to obey.

Most of the Skan were rummaging through the belongings strewn about. Grabbing a particularly tall man by the shoulder, Lorso said, "Get three men. Bring her here."

Even the asymmetrical war paint failed to disguise the warrior's wince. "Why me, Lorso?"

Lorso smiled. It wasn't a warm expression. "Because she likes you. You want me to tell Tears of Jade that you don't like her?"

The warrior whirled, jerked three other men from their searching, and led them at a trot down the beach toward the sharker.

Lorso shouted for more firewood. By the increased light, he picked through the wreckage of a hut with the point of his sword. Flicking open a basket, he discovered a trove of succulent smoked oysters. Sitting cross-legged amidst the destruction as if at a banquet table, he ate. He munched steadily, deep in thought, oblivious to the wailing of children, the rending and tearing sounds of his men ripping apart baskets, sacks, clothing—everything that had belonged to the people of the camp.

Lorso knew these people had nothing of real value.

Save—perhaps—one. He shivered.

Immediately, he shot an aggressive glare about, daring anyone to have seen.

Something moved in the darkness. A backhanded swipe of Lorso's sword tumbled the basket of oysters. He rose. "She comes. Get the prisoners over here in the light." Oar-hardened hands yanked captives to their feet. Unmindful of any injuries or pain, the Skan warriors hastily formed them in a line.

When Lorso faced down the beach again, the firelight revealed his four warriors shouldering a platform. Atop that, there was a chair and a dark figure. The warriors moved in straining, careful unison, using the out-thrust butts of spears for additional stability. Arriving, they lowered the platform to the ground with near-comic delicacy.

Tears of Jade's pointed shoes poked out from beneath the flowing skirt like the black claws of a perched bird. A low-crowned, netted hat obscured her face. Hands hid within sleeves. The robe itself was dark green, shot through with random flecks and swirls of purest white. It was as if the figure wore the sea. From behind the shielding net, she said, "Lorso. Bring them closer. I must see clearly." The voice drifted, dry and soft as smoke, yet within it was a dire dominance.

Lorso's gesture was unnecessary. The Skan warriors obeyed.

Tears of Jade turned by slow, threatening degrees to look at Lorso. "Why do you vex me? Have I told you what I require?"

Lorso stammered a reply. "This afternoon . . . You said household slaves. I thought . . ."

Brittle words cut across his stammer. "You assumed. Get rid of all but those who qualify."

Again, the Skan warriors moved without waiting for Lorso's orders.

The tiny figure looked up at the two traumatized young women left in front of her. Both had the fair skin and dark hair that was the pride of For women. The disheveled long tresses hung tremulous in the breeze. Traditional one-piece knee-length smocks, cut to fit closely, revealed vital bodies cresting from youth into full womanhood.

Something like a growl, visceral and savage, mumbled through the gathered Skan.

The young women were almost close enough for Tears of Jade to touch. Even so, the old woman bent nearer. "You know who I am?"

Terrified, gagged, both shook their heads.

"Tears of Jade is what I am called. You know that name?"

The young women's eyes widened in greater horror.

Basking in their fear, Tears of Jade almost purred. "Spirit woman of the Skan people. Servant to the god, talker to the dead, the knife that cuts the veil that hides the future." Waving a finger, she said, "Release them. Take off the gags."

While two warriors carried out her orders, Tears of Jade went on. "Now you can flee. Into the hands of these men. You are young. Pretty. They would enjoy you very much. They grow bored quickly, however. Then they seek . . . rougher amusements. Best you not run. Smile for me."

The girls stared, too stupefied to move.

"Smile." The tiny body hunched forward. One girl burst into tears. The second grimaced wildly.

"Turn around. Slowly." After their full circle, Tears of Jade extended a gnarled forefinger from the sleeve of her robe. It indicated the taller of the girls. Lorso was in front of that one in two swift steps. Wrapping his hand in the girl's flowing black hair, he twisted her head back and up. A warrior moved to grip her arms from behind. Before she could scream, Lorso's knife flashed across her throat. Her high collar fell open. Another slash opened the dress down to the hem. The warrior behind the girl tore it from her. Naked, too shocked now to scream, the girl stared past Lorso at Tears of Jade.

The earlier sound groaned up from the warriors again, urgent. A bound woman on the ground struggled, shouting incoherence through her gag. One of the warriors kicked her. The strangled cries dropped off to sobs.

Tears of Jade said, "Lorso. We go home. Get clothes for this one." The ancient woman's head swung slowly from one still warrior to the next, pausing at each. Every man's gaze tore away from the naked, vulnerable girl and looked to Tears of Jade. Every gaze went to the ground. Lorso wanted to roar at them that they were Skan warriors. Instead, he cursed himself for not daring those old, terrible eyes himself.

Finally, Tears of Jade continued. "This girl is mine. You will not even think of her." Redirecting her attention to Lorso, she added, "If the woman crying on the ground over there is this girl's mother, save her for me. For the others, the same as before. No prisoners to slow us down. No survivors to seek help and pursuit. We leave when the guide star is there." The small finger pointed.

Lorso snapped orders. "You four—carry Tears of Jade to the sharker. You two—take the dress off that girl, give it to Tears of Jade's slave."

Bending close to Tears of Jade to keep his comments confidential, Lorso still had to raise his voice to be heard over the rejected girl's screams as she was claimed. "You're sure you've found the right one? How can you tell?"

Tears of Jade's laughter rustled. "I know. That's answer enough for you. Your concern touches. You see she's untouched, unharmed. She will be my weapon, just as you. I have names now: Gan Moondark, Rose Priestess Sylah. Gan will rule a kingdom. Sylah will change the spineless religion that calls itself Church. I must destroy them, so that Sosolassa and the Skan people are paramount. I have little time—a year, perhaps two. Then he who waits in the Deep Calm will feast."

"Tell me how to help. I want you to be happy."

Tears of Jade gestured for her bearers to approach and raise the platform. From aloft, she extended her hand down to Lorso. Cold, dry fingers traced his brow, his lips. "Poor Lorso. You never understand. Pleasure isn't the issue. My goal is to destroy the children of prophecy, to make the names Gan and Sylah signify shame and disgrace. When I do concern myself with pleasure, my delight is the perversion of pleasure. That's why I treasure you so." She straightened. A word set her bearers in motion.

Chapter 2

Gan Moondark straightened at the sight of his Wolves' bright banners. Standing apart from the other men gathered with him, he was torn between pride of accomplishment and the soul-grinding weight of responsibility. This was his first complete summer as ruler of the Three Territories. Sometimes it felt like the hundredth.

It threatened to be the last.

First pestilence, and now war. The packs had suffered. When he brought the kingdoms of Ola and Harbundai into union with his own Dog People, peace and prosperity seemed assured. It was not to be.

A new, strange people, expanding to the south, was bleeding his kingdom dry.

He had to stop them.

Doubt tore at him as never before. He wondered what his own people truly thought of him now.

He took stock of his appearance. Tall. Fair-haired. He took more pride than was proper in great physical strength and proficiency with weapons. It was practically a compulsion with him to keep that pride hidden. His wife said he was handsome. He told himself Neela was biased, but secretly hoped she was right. Her own incredible beauty was unquestionable. So was the wonderfulness of their son, Coldar, who sincerely believed that not being quite able to walk didn't preclude being able to run.

That was what was best in life. A family. Simple, good things.

That wasn't the life of Gan Moondark.

He ruled.

Was he good enough? Did he deserve to rule, or was he one of those who rises by luck, only to fall by incompetence?

Impossible. His mother prophesied that he would bring glory to the Dog People. She also said his life would always have two paths. Today was a day of choice.

His oiled chain mail gleamed in the morning sun. The copper handle of his sword—the blade shaped in the spearhead design the Dog People called a murdat—was a killer whale. Tail flukes made a wide buttplate; the blade protruded from a mouth rimmed with inset ivory teeth. Beside Gan lay his brindle-gray war dog, Shara, the massive beast as heavy as most men. This morning the dog wore the wide spiked collar of war.

The Jalail Wolves led through Ola's Sunrise Gate. They marched in a column of fours, singing. Originally a five-hundred-man pack, they were now far fewer. They wore the black and white of Jalail on striped sashes, but as the original Wolf pack, their high-flying pennon carried Gan Moondark's personal red and yellow. Exiting Sunrise's brass-faced doors, the thunder from the first of their huge, cart-borne drums rumbled across the fields. It was as if the shocked air magically hardened, shuddered the very organs of everyone it touched. Gan smiled inwardly, acknowledging to himself, as he could acknowledge to hardly anyone else, his susceptibility to that power.

Gan, who still saw himself as warrior, Nightwatch of the Dog People. He wondered if anyone saw the frightened, unsure man who wished with all his heart he could throw off the responsibilities of his position.

Searching the distant marching column, he noted how many of his warriors limped, how many swung an arm awkwardly. His cavalrymen sat with bowed backs on shuffling horses.

It was barely two weeks since many of these men had risen from sickbeds and met the first invading wave of the Kwa People and their new allies, the Mountain

People of the Enemy Mountains. That first thrust sent Gan's northern packs reeling back onto the fortifications of Ola. Now, two days' march to the east, an even larger Kwa and Mountain army advanced to finish the conquest of the fledgling Three Territories.

A knot of men stood several paces behind Gan. All but one wore black torso armor fitted with steel bars and bosses in personalized decoration. The armor itself was buffalo or wildcow leather. Boiled in oil until pliant, it was molded to the individual, removed, and allowed to harden. It turned most sword strokes and was proof against arrows, except at close range. The apparently fanciful steel arrangements increased protection. Legs were protected by high boots, while the thighs and groin were shielded by a leather apronlike cover, similarly decorated.

The uniquely dressed man of the group was the most intriguing, and it was he who stepped forward to stand at Gan's right side. The huge dog to Gan's left stopped panting, turned and examined the newcomer for a moment, then resumed watching the marchers.

The smaller man wore chain mail, too. The truly unusual aspect of his armor was the split in the skirt on his right side. It allowed unobstructed access to the holstered pistol at his waist. In the face of a culture that was clearly based on the visible panoply of swords, knives, and armor, a firearm was a singular, staggering contradiction. Yet the man seemed perfectly accepted by his fellows.

When Gan finally spoke to him, it was with the familiarity of long-standing friendship. "Well, Louis, everyone's making one last argument against this move. It's your turn, I suppose."

Consternation swept the smaller man's features. Gan laughed shortly. Louis Leclerc drew himself erect. "I won't waste time, then. Defend the walls of the city. Let the Kwa and the Mountains come to us. We've got my black powder. You've got me, Bernhardt, Anspach, and Carter. From on top of those walls, each lightning weapon's worth thirty to fifty men." Leclerc slapped the pistol for emphasis.

Gan raised his eyebrows in silent question. Leclerc colored. "All right, so forget Carter and Anspach. They're opposed to killing because they believe it's wrong, that's all. The point is, Bernhardt's a woman, too, and I believe she'll stand beside me. We can destroy an attack against any wall, anytime."

Gan draped an arm across Leclerc's shoulder. Insistent pressure forced the older man to walk along beside Gan. Keeping his voice low, Gan repeated Leclerc's last word. "' . . . anytime.' I also saw the look on your Bernhardt's face when I said my defense must be aggressive. Never mind; we all do what we believe is best. Which brings me back to defense. Remember, many of these Mountains are survivors of our last battle; they were King Altanar's allies. They've always been the deadly enemies of my Dog People. We don't call them Devils for nothing. Now they're back, with their northern brothers. They'll come at you, believe me. The captain of the Nion boat that docked here ten days or so ago said the Skan are coming in their sharkers. More than anyone's ever seen. They expect to arrive here two days after the Kwa attack. Which wall do you defend then?"

Stubbornly, Leclerc said, "All the more reason to sit tight. Make them come to us, use our firepower to best advantage."

"Firepower." Gan managed a tight smile. "You mean the lightning weapons and the black powder that breaks everything. Firepower. Yes. Your dialect has some descriptive words. But consider; it's past midsummer. Plague made us neglect fields and livestock. If I don't cripple these invaders, they'll rampage across the countryside, slaughter my people, destroy our already-meager harvest. Winter will mean starvation for our survivors. What good then if Ola's walls stand firm now?"

"Why are the Dog warriors sitting east of the Enemy Mountains while you fight a mutual enemy on the western side?"

"My tribe suffered the plague worse than anyone. They're under pressure from the Buffalo Eaters to their east. Moondance nomads are moving north. The Dogs can't help us. I must attack, Louis, before my enemies mass against me. I must destroy the Kwa and the Devils in order to defeat the Skan when they arrive."

"What if you lose?"

Gan suddenly radiated menace. "My responsibility is victory. Slavery is the alternative. I won't have it." His right hand slipped down to grip the hilt of his sword. Blue eyes glinted from palled features. Leclerc thought of the strangely ominous color of glacial ice on Snowfather Mountain. Gan continued. "My wife was stolen from me once. In her, our unborn son. We've talked about that event, Neela and I. Between us, we decided. As a family, we live free or die free."

For a moment, Leclerc couldn't speak. When he inhaled, it hurt. Then, "Well. That seems to settle it." He was almost turned to leave, when he changed his mind. "What about Conway and Tate? If the Dog warriors that rode south to Church Home found them, they should be getting here soon. Can't you wait a while? Tate and Conway are an army by themselves."

Still distant, Gan said, "If they were found, and if they still live, and if they get here in time, maybe they'll make a difference. I have a bellyful of ifs and maybes. I can afford anything but indecision and time, Louis."

"And human feelings," Leclerc muttered under his breath, walking away. Instantly, he repented. Of all people, he himself—and all the friends who'd accompanied him to this rebuilding world—knew of Gan's humanity.

Leclerc rejoined the waiting group. He ignored the irritated glances of the rest of the men, who were clearly impatient to hear what Gan said. His mind jerked back through time, to the escape from the cryogenic crèche that kept the band of survivors from his world alive to discover this one.

There were times when he thought of that gift as the cruelest joke in the insane comedy that destroyed everything he knew.

The world into which Louis Leclerc was born destroyed itself. Nature, in her infinite patience and kindness, had obliterated most nuclear scars, but there remained places where man glassed the very earth. Their gleam shamed those who understood.

Only those from the crèche did understand. They also knew of the nerve gases and the obscenely unnatural genetically engineered diseases. The few humans who survived taught their descendants that everything left over from the holocaust was dangerous. There was truth in the tales. Urban areas harbored concentrations of disease, radiation, chemical pollution. Initially collecting points for fugitives of the nuclear winter, they became pestholes. People shunned man's works. Learning was blamed for creating the world-breakers' arrogance. Education became anathema.

Leclerc and his friends stepped out of the capstone of mankind's technological achievement—a cryogenic facility that suspended them in time for over five centuries—into a world that considered reading and arithmetic so dangerous those skills were restricted to the privileged few. The people of this world mined destroyed cities to salvage metal, glass, ceramics. Paper or anything else with legible writing on it was immediately destroyed under the supervision of Church, the monotheistic religion that seemed to Leclerc to be a mélange of Christianity, Judaism, and medicine.

His thoughts went to his absent friends. Donnacee Tate, their surviving professional military type. And Matt Conway. A transportation manager, Conway survived to become an adept warrior. His acquired skills helped keep his friends alive when the evil King Altanar captured them. Yet the civilized, sophisticated mind behind that new knowledge made Conway a near-neurotic mass of self-doubt.

Only Gan Moondark would let two such fighters as Tate and Conway accompany the Rose Priestess Sylah on her quest for the thing Church called the Door. Especially with their weapons. Those had survived the centuries in the crèche, as well. Infantry small arms, the thing called a wipe, as well as handguns. Leclerc's hand stole to his pistol. He realized with a start that he hadn't fired it once since Gan overthrew King Altanar. Within two days, however, that would change.

Leclerc sighed. He'd hoped to spend the rest of his days in peace in Gan's Three Territories. Foolish dreams. Peace in this world ended at birth. It only returned at death.

If the wipe, the tool this world called the lightning weapon, didn't turn the tide engulfing those Three Territories, Louis Leclerc would learn all about eternal peace.

He was swept by a vision of himself sprawled in a disjointed heap. The feathered shaft of an arrow jutted from his chest. His stomach was slashed, a gaped mouth. It exposed a mass of wet things. Leclerc unconsciously turned his head. Blinking, he cleared the image.

Shocked, he felt the fear creeping insidiously along nerve paths. It sang in the channels of his spine. He held out a hand. There was no tremble. But he knew. It was in him now, like a disease. Almost sobbing, he told himself to hide it, to never let anyone know. That was his only hope. Cowards had no life here.

Acknowledging the other men at last, Leclerc interrupted the muddle of questions. "Murdat must strike. The troops will not be recalled. We, his Barons, his commanders, must assure that Murdat strikes true, that every stroke kills. We will win. We *will*."

A man called Emso, a grizzled, scarred old warrior who was among the first to pledge to Gan when the young man was little more than a wandering outcast, drew his sword. He carried a murdat now, exactly like his leader. Emso battered his shield with the flat of the blade. "Murdat!" he shouted. There was a warrior's wild joy in the shout. He repeated it, louder. The Barons took up the chant.

In the distance, the Wolves heard. Moments later, every man shouted the title.

Torrential, the cadence rolled across the fields, careered off the city's stone. "Mur-dat! Mur-dat!" The chorus continued as the other regiments and their drums moved out of the city.

Gan listened, watching the men stream along the twisted road. Biting his lip thwarted the choking lump in his throat. He wasn't sure if his eyes misted out of pride and love for those men, or fear for them. He knew he wished time could end at this point, and hold him in this moment forever.

Chapter 3

Kate Bernhardt waited at Sunrise Gate when a frowning Leclerc rode up. She wore the ground-sweeping black robe of Church almost exclusively now, as did the other two women who survived the crèche and remained in Ola. The fourth, Donnacee Tate, was their sole female adventurer.

Bernhardt was deeply committed to the Priestesses of Church and their efforts to bring some semblance of civilization to the myriad cultures of this world. Leclerc admired her for it. For that matter, he admired Sue Anspach and Janet Carter, despite their total submergence in Church. They were in danger of becoming more orthodox than their leaders.

Bernhardt waved at him across the level ground extending beyond the city walls. He waved back, the sudden motion causing a pack llama in the train next to him to shy. Leclerc turned to apologize to the merchant for the brief disturbance, recognizing the man as a Jalail by his bold-striped black-and-white sash. The merchant smiled broadly. "Not a problem, Louis Leclerc." At Leclerc's surprise, the man laughed aloud, gesturing with a broad sweep of his arm. "My first return to Ola. Just about a year ago, I was with Gan Moondark when we charged across these fields. Fought under the red and yellow of the Jalail pack. Brag to my grandchildren about that, I will. About the strangers who helped us, too. You're the one who gave us the thunder packages that knocked down King Altanar's doors. Many of us are alive today because of that." He paused, then continued with what Leclerc could only think of as dogged cheerfulness. "As soon as I sell off these furs, I'll join the volunteers on the walls. In case the Kwa force Murdat back to the city. Never thought I'd see the day I'd offer to defend Altanar's old stone box." He saluted good-bye in the Wolf fashion, closed right fist pressed to his jaw by his right ear.

The man's conversation reminded Leclerc of his talk with Gan. It rekindled his irritation. The stone-and-brick city was a series of defendable squares. The walled castle backed against steep cliffs that dropped to the Inland Sea. The landward approach was a flat meadow, allowing no cover from defenders' arrows. Or ammunition. Both city and castle walls were tall, strong, studded with turrets to provide flanking fire. More, the resistance that helped overthrow Altanar built a network of tunnels under the city.

At the gate, Leclerc turned his attention back to Bernhardt. Halfheartedly, he looked for Carter and Anspach. Bernhardt realized what he was doing, and her expression when he looked back to her was rueful. She waved ineffectually to indicate where their friends should be by her side. "I'm sorry. Janet and Sue . . . They're really uncomfortable with you riding off to war with Gan. They think he should try to negotiate, compromise."

"Can't they understand this is a fight to the death?"

Bernhardt came forward, put a hand on the reins of Leclerc's prancing horse. "Calm down, Louis. You're getting the horse all worked up, and you know you don't ride that well."

"The horse is fine. And I'm hardly riding off to war. I'll give some support fire . . ."

"We. We'll give some support fire. I'm coming."

Leclerc burlesqued a huge wince. "You told Janet and Sue? That took more courage than war."

Bernhardt's laughter was in keeping with her appearance and manner. She was a larger woman; not big, but generously proportioned. No one would ever think her beautiful, but there was an elemental femininity to her that was much more attractive than she seemed to realize. Leclerc always thought her expression in repose had a soft, hidden sadness, as though there were something she wished she could share, but could find no way to express.

She said, "I shoot well. I'm strong. It's only two days to the place where Gan expects to meet the Kwa and their allies. We met the Mountains once, Louis. I know what to expect if they win. It's going to be desperate."

"It's not all that bad." Leclerc looked around nervously. Morale was already a problem.

"I worked in the healing house with the Healers. Wounded men and men still weak from plague forced themselves out of bed to return to their units. The Healers say none can remember men so recently recovered from illness being tolerated by men who're well. You know how they normally shun anyone who's even suspected of being exposed to disease. Things are worse than bad."

"All the more reason for you to stay here. We should have trained some of the Wolves to use these weapons."

Bernhardt's lips thinned. "We all agreed. Knowing how to fire the wipes and the pistols is our final insurance in this world. If someone does kill one of us and gets the guns, they can't turn them on our friends. It has to be that way."

Laughing softly, Leclerc dismounted. Bernhardt fell in beside him on the way to his quarters. He said, "We live in irony, don't we? Back in our world, I signed up for the crèche because I thought coming out into the surviving world would be an exciting challenge. I left my world of protein structures expecting to be thawed out to reproduce the exact same culture."

She watched him from the corner of her eye. "I've always suspected you were secretly pleased when we came out of the crèche cave and found we'd been in there centuries, instead of decades."

The earlier fear oozed free once again. He refused to look Bernhardt's way. She might see the death-fearing person he was fighting. He spoke too loudly. "I'm ashamed to admit it: Yes, I like it here. But I'm still primarily a technician." He laughed, the ring of it cheap as brass in his ears. Adding a dismissive flip of the hand, he went on. "I could be a warrior. Not like Tate and Conway. More a planner than a grunt. All my life I dreamed of being a man of action. Living here's taught me my skills are too advanced to waste. That sounds arrogant, but it's only honest. The best thing I can do is improve the local technology. Leave the heroics to the younger guys."

"Oh, stop it. You're just fishing for compliments. You can't be more than thirty; that was the top age for crèche volunteers. You're a good-looking man, with a good smile and a good heart. I happen to think all of that, plus being a first-rate technician, is a lot more important than fighting."

Leclerc shook off the attempted kindness. "Think about it, Kate. Technology increased pollution, it didn't cure it. Terrorism and constant warfare only reflected unbearable overpopulation. We have to understand what our contemporaries taught their children about intellectuals and technology. Look, I reinvented black powder. Have you seen the way women hide their kids when I pass?"

He paused, struck by a perception so startling it approached epiphany. Continuing in an awed, subdued voice, he said, "I never thought. Black powder isn't just about breaching walls, or penetrating chain mail or plate armor. It's one man killing more than one man at a time. A product even these people can produce in abundance. I've moved the whole world from single combat to mass destruction. *They* sensed what I am. No wonder they fear me."

Bernhardt hugged herself, white hands startling as they peeked out of the deep, black sleeves. "You mustn't feel guilty. Gan's not afraid of advances. He directed us to teach all Chosens to read and write and do basic arithmetic, remember."

Leclerc was harsh. "Chosens. Church buys the children the slavers will kill if Church rejects them. That's the real world, Kate—slavery. You forgot to mention that your other students are all Gan's military officers. They learn to read and write so they can communicate better on the battlefield."

"You think I'm happy about warriors being an elite? At least they fight people who practice slavery. Like the Kwa and the Mountain People. Like the Skan. Our Chosens and the warriors will teach others. What if we can create a culture that fights for justice, for fairness for all?"

Leclerc threw back his head and guffawed. Seeing Bernhardt's pain, he broke it off. The lingering smile was affectionate, the voice apologetic. "You're a darling. I wasn't laughing at you, honestly. I was laughing at humanity. Every culture fights for justice, for fairness. It's just that all those vicious fools out there"—he flung an arm in an extravagant sweep—"don't understand that only we have real justice, real fairness."

Only partially mollified, Bernhardt sniffed. "Well, it's true. You're only teasing me because you know I'm right."

Leclerc linked an arm through hers. "The old earth has just about healed from all the damage we did her, but I don't think she'll let us run quite so free this time. Oil was nearly exhausted when the collapse started, remember. Aluminum ore was scarce. Everyone was worried about increasing dependency on low-grade iron ore and coal. Today these people mine what used to be our cities for raw material. New technology's inevitable. We have to guide them in the direction of a culture that accommodates nature and other cultures. And freedom. I think Gan's a necessary step. He's a tyrant, but a benevolent, progressive one. If a democratic polity can evolve here, he's the man to protect us."

Bernhardt pressured his arm with her own. She turned to smile at him, their heads almost exactly even. Leclerc was mildly surprised at how her presence, her companionship, pleased him. There was a comforting quality about her. He decided it was because she was so understanding. A very bright woman, actually.

They were crossing the meadow separating the town proper from the castle grounds. The summer had been gentle in what Leclerc still mentally called the Pacific Northwest. Intellectually, it didn't disturb him that the land was cut up into tiny states that called themselves kingdoms or tribal holdings. He accepted the fact of diverse, warring fragments of humanity, the exoticism of major religions called Church and Moondance.

In his heart, the land was more than geography. At times it spoke to him. A sudden view or evocative scent would set off a nostalgia that left him trembling and weak. It happened once in the evening, looking across the ebon waters of the Inland Sea. The last rim of a fiery sunset edged the Whale Coast mountains. Leclerc saw Puget Sound. The Olympic Mountains. And was nearly crushed by homesickness.

Then there were the times when he brooded. Under his feet—burned, gassed, infected, irradiated—lay the cities of millions. Their names seared his thoughts. Seattle, Tacoma, Bellingham, Olympia. It embarrassed him to think how many smaller communities he couldn't even name. Covered by the detritus of centuries. Some buried in volcanic mud or drowned by diverted rivers when the northwest slope of Snowfather Mountain erupted.

Paradoxically, those were the times when he loved this place with the greatest fierceness. Now, back in his present, he let his view rise west beyond the structure of the castle to the greater wall of the distant Whale Coast mountains. My country, he thought, and the words swelled in him. My land—savaged, wounded, crushed to her knees and changed beyond recognition, but my country still. Neither of us can ever be the same, but I can be wiser than I was. I can love you better, if not more. "You must rise."

"Did you say something?" Bernhardt stopped, puzzled.

Flustered, Leclerc stammered an answer. "Nothing. Thinking out loud, I guess. We better hurry. I've got to load equipment on wagons, get the horses ready, check my own gear, see to—"

"I've got a lot to do, myself," Bernhardt interrupted, her look making it clear she was rescuing him from his own babble. Leclerc nodded agreement. They continued their walk.

Bernhardt swallowed her hurt, wondering why he wouldn't share. Did he really expect her to believe that lame story about equipment? She knew there were changes going on in him. Dark, wrenching realizations and concerns that involved a depth of feeling she'd never suspected of him.

She sensed it all as warning, and winced inwardly. He was a good man, eager to do the right things. Why did she feel that now, when he was most at risk and needed someone to be afraid for him, that she was a bit afraid *of* him?

And why in the world would that make her feel all the more protective?

It was too confusing.

Chapter 4

Stillness mocked the wide valley. Sunlight bathed sprawling pastures, but no cattle or horses grazed the lush grass. Rich fruit gleamed in laden orchards. Strong stands of corn and beans stretched in ripe rows. No farmers inspected the crops, nor did children shoo away the huge flocks of opportunistic pigeons and geese settling to wreak havoc.

Crows, swift black darts across the waiting green, were eerily furtive.

Massive hills, their dark shoulders caped in firs, pressed against the lowlands. Even higher, the Enemy Mountains rose in the distance.

Gan pointed at the closer high ground from his position on the small rise in the center of the valley. "They'll follow those parallel ridges," he said, "keeping inside the tree line. Once they've gotten behind our defenses, they'll close to cut off our retreat, then destroy us."

The grizzled Emso listened in silence. Now he was acidly sarcastic. "If that's the way of it, can I give the men permission to break out all the rations? And pull in the scouts? If we're all going to just squat here and die, we'd as soon be well fed and well rested. *Murdat*."

Even as he turned away to hide a smile, Gan marveled at the nuances the speaker squeezed into the last word. Somehow, it came out a title, a challenge, and a borderline insult, all at once. Shara edged forward to peer past his master. Gan put a hand on the dog's head. "Easy, Shara; it's only Emso."

Emso grunted, shooting a sharp glance at the animal. "Dog, if you had good sense, you'd growl at him, not me. I'm not the one predicting your death."

"I didn't say anything about us dying. I told you what the Kwa leader means to do."

"Ah. Then you have a plan. Do we guess at it? With a prize for whoever gets it right?"

"Testier than usual. Angry. That's the Emso I need." Gan finally faced the older man. "Remember how we dealt with Altanar, flanked him under cover of darkness?"

"Of course. But the scouts say these people are moving on us. We'll be under attack long before nightfall."

"We attack."

Blinking, Emso kept his stare locked on the far distance. "Don't try to stir me like some young fireblood, Murdat. We both know our only chance is to check these people and run, then sting them again. There's no glorious victory here." His color rose as he spoke.

"Exactly. We disrupt and defeat him in pieces—or the whole of his force crushes us. We're outnumbered at least five to one."

"Then why are we staking the ground around this knoll? Why dig pits to trap horses and men, why exhaust the men building that wall?" Emso's pointing finger was an angry spear.

Gan said, "Because this is where everyone but the Jalail Wolves will stand. We're the bait. You're the deadfall."

Some heat receded in Emso's face. Gan called, "Leclerc! Bernhardt! To me, please." They arrived at a run, the wipes clattering against their chain mail. Gan said, "You go with Emso. There's a shallow draw a short walk to the rear. He leads the Jalail pack up the draw onto the ridge to the south. From there, you'll drive east until you run into the Kwa forces advancing toward you."

Drawing his sword, Gan sketched their position in the dirt, then illustrated flanking thrusts and a massive center attack. Muttering, he continued scratching marks. "Scouts and refugees all say the mass of men is in the valley. Other scouts say Kwa warriors are on the ridges. We'll engage the thrust on the north side with our cavalry. Emso, after you've stopped the southern thrust, drop onto the rear and flank of the Kwa main strength."

Leclerc studied the marks in the dirt. Carefully expressionless, he looked to Emso. "If that's what the Kwa propose, this is a good counterplan."

Emso snorted. "Dying in bed's a good plan. Are you betting on it?"

Gan laughed, vastly entertained, and Bernhardt muttered to Leclerc, "How can he do that? I know he cares about all of us, but he enjoys this murderous foolishness. It doesn't make sense."

By then Gan was speaking again. "If my plan works, we hurt the Kwa. We may be crushed, even so. If we meet him head-to-head, we must be crushed. I'm not betting on anything but you, Emso; you and our Wolves."

Emso smiled crookedly. "Your tongue's as quick as that murdat. You want to speak to the Wolves? There's no time to waste."

Leclerc and Bernhardt fell in behind Gan and Emso. Bernhardt said, "I won't be able to keep up with these men."

"They'll make allowances for us." He slapped the stock of the wipe. The sound brought Emso's head around. As if aware of the discussion, he said, "You'll travel mounted, with my reserve. Our footpace is too much for you. I'll assign a man as escort. When we find the Kwa, I'll try to get word to you where I want you to use the lightning weapons. If I can't reach you, let the escort decide where you're to strike."

Leclerc's jaws tightened. His mouth worked, biting off unspoken words.

Unaware of Leclerc's irritation, Emso turned back to Gan. Bernhardt put a hand on Leclerc's forearm. He refused to acknowledge the contact, but she spoke anyhow. "It's nothing personal, Louis. Emso doesn't act offended when you school him on how to use your black powder. He respects your knowledge and skill. All he's asking you to do is afford his assistant the same respect."

"He's telling me I don't belong, that only my weapon is important. 'Warriors to the front. Leclerc to the rear with the women and children.' "

The cavalry was already moving off to the left, keeping well hidden. Without his mounted Dog warriors, Gan had only his heavier Olan farm-horse cavalry. They were, of necessity, both scout and shock unit. The farmers, fishermen, and loggers from the western side of the Enemy Mountains were grim, hard fighters. Their forests obviated the fleet swirl of cavalry soldiering. When they clambered aboard a horse, it was to ride over someone, not around him.

Gan's defense of the knoll relied on the training and techniques of his men. They had portable barriers to disrupt the battlefield. They carried special weapons, extremely long spears, designed to extend beyond the barriers into the attacking force. Shallow trenches circled the knoll near its top. The excavated earth was piled up periodically to form small bulwarks. Archers could move through the trenches protected from enemy arrows, then mass their own fire from relative safety.

The portable barriers were Leclerc's project. They were simple articles. Short poles lashed in a cross constituted the two ends. Smaller poles lashed between provided strength while creating an encumbrance to advancing men. Additionally, the connecting poles were strung with stout cord and metal hooks. No man could fight and drag such an impediment around with him. Nevertheless, they could only be considered a nuisance; small, light, and fairly quickly destroyed.

Leclerc made them deadly. Each barrier carried a small leather sack filled with small rocks, a tightly wrapped charge of black powder, and a fuse that theoretically had a four-second delay. In testing, the fuses lacked perfection. Some sizzled off all too rapidly. No one was seriously injured. Several men acquired a disturbingly intimate knowledge of the sound of rocks overtaking and passing at high velocity. Everyone admired the superior footwork exhibited. Soldier humor leans toward bleak.

Off to the right, the solid blue banner of the Galmontis pack crackled above warriors testing the portable barriers one last time. To the left, the Fin pack worked under their yellow with black stripes. Eleven West and Malten manned the forward positions, ready to delay the Kwa advance before falling back to the knoll. Far to the rear, the Olan units formed a reserve out of sight in a sheltering orchard.

A flash of bright purple caught Leclerc's eye. The Violet Abbess, swirling her cloak about her. Gathered together with her six War Healers, the older woman's brightly embroidered robe stood out against the somber black of the Priestess' garb. Leclerc frowned, thinking how the Abbess had recently been heard harshly criticizing Rose Priestess Sylah, blaming her exclusively for the rift in Church.

There was no time to dwell on that. Leclerc consciously looked away, only to spot a pair of Messengers loitering in the distance, easily identifiable by their garish clothing. Leclerc had no fondness for Messengers, an attitude he shared with Gan Moondark. As Gan said, they were like buzzards, always around in times of trouble. Messengers moved without hindrance across everyone's territory. If one of their guild was interfered with, much less injured or killed, all Messenger service was denied the group on whose territory the deed took place until compensation and punishment were agreed on and executed. In a world where plague sprang up with the swift unpredictability of a spring rain and where neighboring tribes treasured enmities for generations, lack of communication with others was a death warrant. Everyone welcomed Messengers, catered to them. No one liked them.

The Jalail Wolves' marching drum rumbled its assembly call. There was no further signaling. The column trotted through brushy cover into the streambed as stealthily as a brotherhood of thieves. The splashing of their progress turned the creek water into hysterical brilliance.

Leclerc and Bernhardt hurried along in trail. A few hundred yards upstream, their escort announced they were far enough into timber for his wards to mount up. Red-faced, wheezing torturously, Leclerc pretended to weigh the merit of the idea. It offended him to see how gratefully Bernhardt accepted. Lips pursed judiciously, Leclerc was careful to infer he was grudgingly following orders. They soon caught up to the Wolves.

Soon after, Leclerc was shocked out of introspection by an agonized scream. The sharpness of it seemed to actually lighten the forest gloom. The rational part of his mind warned him that this was psychological reaction. The rest of him didn't care.

Roaring commands and the shouts of men in combat struck next. The Wolves ahead of Leclerc and Bernhardt broke out of their column and into squads. Half advanced with notched arrows to their bows. The other half held up heavy rectangular shields on their left arms, while the right hands brandished murdats.

Surrounded by the twenty men who made up the reserve, Leclerc and Bernhardt waited.

The Wolves were forced back. Leclerc was astounded to notice that most of the reserve appeared more anguished than apprehensive. He had to reason it out; they heard their comrades engaged, but were forbidden to help. Murdats in anxious hands twitched like cat's tails. Leclerc suffered no such delusions. He wished with all his heart the Kwa would turn and flee.

Three short and two long whistle blasts sent the pent-up reserve howling forward.

Leclerc kneed his horse ahead. Their lone warrior escort caught the reins. "Not yet. We wait for the signal."

Infuriated at being denied, ashamed of the relief surging through him, Leclerc yanked his reins free. As he did, the first casualties staggered toward them. Leclerc's breath caught at the youth of the pair careering from tree to tree. One had shed his hide armor. Blood pumped from his left bicep.

Leclerc observed the wound coolly, wrote off the arm. His own callousness appalled him.

The second man supported his friend on his left side. The broken shaft of a spear extruded from his rib cage on his right. They barely looked up as they passed. The man suffering the spear thrust mumbled to himself.

The command whistle shrilled again, two staccato notes, then two more.

"Now!" The Wolf escort slapped the horses' rumps, making them rear. Before the animals could recover, he himself was sprinting off toward the battle, murdat drawn. Leclerc and Bernhardt raced forward through the thick forest.

Bernhardt screamed involuntarily at the sight of men simply, industriously, killing other men. The disciplined Wolves fought as units. In pairs, they moved as one, parrying with shields to strike with murdats, deflecting with murdats to smash with shields. The Kwa warriors, wildly painted, fought with heavy, two-handed swords they swung with the cutting, crushing power of axes. Leclerc winced as one battered the shield of Wolf, sending him sprawling. The Kwa poised for the finishing stroke. The downed Wolf's partner struck first. The Kwa dropped, writhing, screaming.

Leclerc was firing before he fully realized it. His mind roiled with inchoate images of brute violence. The awareness that he was bowling over a fellow human at every report threatened to empty his stomach. Beside him, Bernhardt was screaming for everyone to stop. Tears poured down her cheeks, leaping off her chin every time she squeezed the trigger and the wipe slammed her shoulder. Leclerc had hoped that the crashing report of the weapons would send the Kwa streaming for home. They were of sterner stuff. It was casualties that stopped their advance, broke them, and finally sent them into headlong retreat.

It was very difficult to accept that the fighting was stopped. The Kwa, dragging their wounded, filtered through the forest in escape. The injured left behind shared common misery with stricken Wolves. Slumped in the saddles, Leclerc and Bernhardt watched Emso begin checking the fallen for those who could be helped. While the bulk of the force watched for counterattack, others carried their comrades to a central treatment point.

Bernhardt and Leclerc joined in the crude first-aid efforts. They quickly had one man washing wounds and another tearing up cloth to make bandages. Emso smiled grim approval, saying, "I'm sending a man to fetch a War Healer. One man will stay here to care for these casualties. We carry out the rest of our mission."

Leclerc, tying off a bandage, jerked his chin toward the remains of the Jalail pack. "You don't even have enough men to guarantee a safe retreat to rejoin Gan's defense. You can't attack anyone."

It was as if Leclerc spoke an unknown tongue. Emso's strained ferocity rejected him. There was something so unbearably intense in that expression that Leclerc looked away before Emso spoke. "We leave at my word." Emso strode away.

Leclerc started to argue. Bernhardt hissed at him. When he faced her, indignation boiling over, she said, "He has no choice." She returned to her work.

So did Leclerc, but the movements were automatic. Images crowded his thinking. Emso's controlled ferocity. Gan's clipped decisions, like scissors snipping away alternatives, reducing the world to a series of absolutes. He remembered other faces, men he couldn't even name. They all behaved, looked exactly alike. Leclerc agonized: Why did he know they simply felt differently about all this than he did? How could they?

Then came a chilling comprehension. They were at a level of commitment men never achieved under normal circumstances. Nor could any man maintain that level of involvement for long and remain normal.

Leclerc looked into himself. Hunter, camper, skydiver, surfer, car racer. He enjoyed risk. Challenge. He took chances that could lead to serious injury. Possibly death.

These men threw themselves wantonly into a situation where someone *must* die.

None courted death, none challenged it. But they went where death was, and staked their lives on their ability to embrace her and survive.

In that moment he touched the edge of their being, felt the lightest tremor of the blood-race of exaltation.

He loathed that contact.

Louis Leclerc would never be like them. Whatever enabled men like Gan and Emso and Conway—yes, and women like Tate—to bet their lives with an eagerness that counterfeited love, it wasn't in Louis Leclerc.

Leclerc looked up to wipe away sweat from his brow. Bernhardt was watching him. She said, "Promise me; if we get out of this, you'll decide exactly what you want to do, who you want to be, and follow that decision. Will you do that, Louis? Please?"

For one shocked moment, he thought she'd read his thoughts. Humbly, he said, "I promise, Kate. Thank you."

Blushing faintly, Bernhardt returned to her patient.

A War Healer approached, sidesaddle on a small donkey. The animal picked its way past the fallen, groaning men with a heedful, stiff-legged grace. Stoic patience emanated from the small, gray mount and its hooded passenger.

Leclerc moved to Bernhardt's side. He jerked a thumb at the War Healer, snickered. "Did you see her ride up? Right out of the New Testament."

Choking with emotion, Bernhardt rose, backed away quickly from the man she tended. "Have you lost your mind? Do you know what these people would do to us if they suspected you spoke to me of the One who rode an ass? He's forbidden to women. And another thing: remember that self-pitying blather about riding with the women and children? Well, forget it; I don't think you're tough enough to live in third class with us."

She stalked off toward the War Healer, leaving him openmouthed. By the time he recovered, she was in low, controlled conversation with the Priestess. Leclerc swallowed his indignation. Nothing was working out the way he intended. He started toward her, determined to apologize properly.

She saw him coming, smiled a tentative, forgiving welcome.

Emso's hoarse order to form in march column cut off Leclerc's carefully composed speech.

Chapter 5

Emso's intercept force was barely into the forest when the main body of the Kwa advanced on Gan's knoll. Loosely grouped in four large units, they dressed in a wild array of furs and coarse cloth. Like the Wolves, the Kwa covered themselves with hide armor or chain mail. Helmets were motley, from artfully formed brass and copper to towering antlers fixed to leather. Swordsmen carried tall, narrow shields strapped to a forearm; they reached from just below the eyes almost to the ground. Advancing, they pounded the shields in unison. That noise, in tempo with rattling drums and lowing brass warhorns, created a storm-sense. In the

wake of the advance crops were crushed, orchards broken and bent. Pastures were flattened, dusty.

Behind the Kwa, waiting in reserve to exploit any break in the Wolf front, were the Mountain People. Their warriors went to war painted in death masks, representations of black-eyed, bloody-mouthed white skulls. They wore torso armor called a barmal, a shell of black wildcowhide over woven willow wands. When on foot, as today, they fought with short swords known as ma.

A flight of arrows—a nervous-sounding covey of death—arced up and out from Gan's most forward defensive positions. Kwa shields rose almost in unison as experienced warriors automatically defended. Some pained cries erupted. Two black-robed War Healers dragged three, four, then a fifth man to the rear. Other wounded helped each other or fended for themselves. A lesser number lay where they fell.

Organically, the mass closed on itself, healing, dismissing its injuries.

A man trotted to the fore, alone, bold. He wore a steel helmet with a huge span of wildcow horns. Steel bosses gleamed on a shield that, like all others, was painted with a demonic face. Crushing silence fell across the entire Kwa force as the man raised a double-bitted axe. Facing the defenders, his voice swelled. "Yooou!" It lowered, left shivering, ghosting echoes. Then the entire Kwa force repeated the sound.

Hackles rose on Gan's neck. All around him, men shifted, hefted weapons. One Wolf, isolated within his own thoughts, cursed steadily, softly.

One by one, the lone Kwa called the names of the Wolf packs. His men echoed each time. Gan's name came last, punctuated with a thunder of swords on shields.

Two Kwa warriors then hurried forward, supporting a struggling, bound, and gagged prisoner. A bearded figure hobbled along behind. In his long, earth-brown robe, the older man superficially resembled the black-clad women of Church. His walking staff was a head taller than himself. Atop was a horizontal disk. Clear quartz crystals dangled from it. Although heavy clouds threatened to block the sun, the decorations glinted wild, hard sparks.

Gan watched the scene unfold with suspicion. The acrid scent of prebattle tension took on an evil putrescence. Gan noticed that the cursing man among his own troops was quiet.

The brown-robed man moved to stand before the horn-helmeted leader, who dropped to one knee. The bearded figure gestured, his words lost in distance. The entire Kwa host knelt, as well. From under his robe, the older man produced something large and white. Bending to the leader, he put the thing—a mask—in place, and stepped back. The enemy force rose as one; the rustle and clash whispered menace throughout the valley.

Facing the Wolves, the Kwa leader posed in his new persona. The mask was vaguely egg-shaped, narrowing from top to bottom. It extended outward almost to the wearer's shoulders and stretched from the center of the helmet to a handsbreadth below his chin. It curved back toward the ears slightly to allow peripheral vision through down-sloping slot eyes. The mouth was a bent oval, curved toward the chin. There were no other features. The flat white expression was of unspeakable anguish. Gan felt as if that empty, inhuman visage stared into him personally.

Noise brought Gan's head around to see who was behind him. The Violet Abbess said, "The North Wind," and made an elaborate three-sign. Her eyes wandered, the nervous flit of a creature seeking escape. She continued. "It's their god of war. The Kwa People say that, in the beginning, it was North Wind who brought unending cold and rain that killed. The old man is a priest. Watch."

Gan turned. The priest stepped back, touched the bound man with his staff. Raising it to the vertical, he spun it. The crystals circled, glittered. Continuing to back away, the robed figure kept the bright circle rotating.

The two men holding the prisoner stepped to the side, retaining their hold on his arms. The leader raised his axe, chopped. Twice. Yet again.

Released, the slain prisoner dropped, quivering.

The Kwa bellowed.

The Violet Abbess gasped, then, "You brought this on us, Gan Moondark. You and the apostate Sylah and her accomplice, Lanta. You let them go on their foolish quest, and their blasphemy has sundered Church. Because of your sin, the One in All turns His face from you."

The woman's malediction was a clammy hand on the small of Gan's back.

The Kwa charged. Their archers released swishing flights of arrows over the assault units to drop on Gan's defenders. Gan's archers returned fire, giving ground to shelter in the trenches.

Shrill pain ripped the brave fabric of war cries and exhortations.

From the forested slope of the northern ridge, a column of horsemen lanced out, driving at Gan's flank. Gan signaled. A horn blared. A thin white banner rose on a tall pole. The heavy cavalry of the Three Territories galloped out of their hidden position in the streambed to engage their counterparts.

The Kwa hit the portable barriers. Gan exclaimed in grudging admiration as the first warriors simply threw their bodies across them, becoming human pathways for those who followed. Wolf spearmen, surprised by the quick failure of their defenses, fell back awkwardly, the thrusting weapons too clumsy for effective combat.

Just as it appeared the Wolf spearmen must be overrun, the first of Leclerc's black powder sacks exploded. The Kwa warriors checked as if the detonation were a wall. More sacks went off. The charge collapsed. Men howled fear and agony as whining stone tore flesh, burst armor, shattered bones.

Gan signaled again. His huge leader's drum, as long as a man and half that diameter, roared. The paired drummers, one at each end, beat out the command to counterattack. From their shielded orchard position, the Olan force responded. Signal flags directed the counterattack around the knoll's right. The Kwa forces were retreating down the hill when the armored Olans crashed into them from the side.

Surprise was complete. Victory seemed ripe for the picking.

Slanting off to his own left, the Kwa leader directed the bulk of his forces at the Olans.

Shattering reports from the lightning weapons announced the arrival of Leclerc and Bernhardt. Flechette rounds, blistering the air with their velocity, sent Kwa warriors spinning and tumbling like fall leaves.

The Kwa force shuddered. Once again, Gan thought of a single organism. This one, wounded, stunned, was straining to maintain itself. Gan anxiously sought the Kwa leader, knowing that, like himself, that other man saw this conflict balanced on a razor's edge.

Warhorns droned down on the valley floor. To the east, galloping out of a covering wrinkle in the landscape, the Kwa cavalry reserve rumbled into view. They hammered down the southern side of the valley, driving for the lightning weapons.

Rushing to the men engaging the Olans, the Kwa leader, now on horseback, renewed the attack himself. Sheer numbers forced the Olan pack back.

Searching to his left, Gan saw his cavalry successful, the surviving enemy streaming back to the shelter of the forest. Gan's drum summoned his riders, sacrificing pursuit of the broken force to the more pressing needs of the failing defense.

Now was when the training and communications within Gan's forces would be tested to its limits. The men of the Three Territories had never retreated under pressure.

Gan recalled the lectures of his War Chief father. The tradition of the Dog People was lightning maneuver, strike and retreat, wheel and strike again. Trained infantry could do the same, albeit slower.

Gan's drum dominated the battlefield, rode over the smaller unit drums, shrieking whistles, and the unending human voices. Packs charged as units, goring the Kwa mob. As swiftly as they'd come, they stopped, then fled. Invariably, the mauled Kwa cheered and pounded after them, only to be struck from a different direction by a different pack.

Yet the Kwa pressed forward. Always forward.

Gan looked east and south. Emso and his men, with Leclerc and Bernhardt, were held in place. Whatever damage they were doing, they couldn't free themselves to reach the main battle.

Gan Moondark was beaten.

The realization came to him as his Olans were forced back along the shoulder of the little knoll and raging Kwa stormed up the slope. It shocked him, as if someone he admired had whispered something unspeakably obscene in his ear. Disbelief thickened his mind.

Stumbling backward, arms flailing, he stared at the quivering, bloody arrow embedded in his chain mail. The links held the barbs out of his flesh. He jerked the thing free, flung it away with a low growl.

Confusion was gone. In its place was release, the willing surrender to battle-madness. He vaulted onto his war-horse, calling the great hound, Shara. Sword in hand, Gan howled, reveling in the absolute of mortal combat. Gone was the crushing responsibility to direct forces, gone the need to mourn men killed and maimed doing his bidding. Gone was Murdat. Man, horse, and dog flew at their enemies, a trilogy of death.

Ordinary warriors of both factions fell away from the maelstrom of destruction.

Some Kwa, brave beyond wisdom, stepped in front of the team. The horse's iron-shod hooves flailed. Shara's crushing jaws snapped bone. Gan's murdat stabbed.

He sought the Kwa leader. Even when he felt the pressure of the Kwa encircling, he thrust his way deeper.

Near the rear of the Kwa force, the leader's personal guard killed Gan's horse. Riddled with arrows, screaming defiance, it charged into the tight ranks. Collapsing, kicking and biting, its dying fury scattered men. Gan pitched out of the saddle, landed on his feet.

Mere steps apart, he confronted his masked foe. For an instant, the combined mass and might of both opposing forces were as nothing. Two opposed wills were all that existed.

Rolling thunder announced the duel. Ignoring that, and the first splatter of rain, the Kwa leader waited as if acknowledging an expected event. Kwa warriors surrounding the tableau edged away in awe.

Rain came in earnest, heavy drops that ran red off the skirt of Gan's chain mail and formed tiny, jagged streams the length of his sword blade.

A younger man rushed to stand beside the leader. Both men were the same height, nearly the same weight. Heavily muscled arms. Strong men. Calm, confident. The masked leader circled left, both feet always in contact with the ground. The younger man held fast, lowered to a crouch. Each carried a double-bitted axe and the long, narrow shield.

From within the mournful mask, the older man's deep voice had a weird, removed sound. "Us then, Gan Moondark. I am Red Sky. This is my son, Two Fists. Me and my son against you and your son. You have the best of it, I think; your child resembles you even more than mine does me."

Gan smiled easily. "The dog has met his father; that boy can only wonder if he has."

Two Fists took the bait. Screaming, he charged. From the corner of his eye, Gan saw Red Sky jerk, knew it was a dismayed, aborted effort to stop his son's rash move. Then the older man came, as well. Stepping back and to the side, Gan forced Two Fists to turn to follow, putting father and son together in front of him. The move prevented a Red Sky attack from the side.

Shara rose on his hind legs beside Gan, muzzle gaping, forcing Red Sky to shift to a better defensive posture. At that, the dog dropped to all fours and lunged.

Red Sky was very quick. His axe fell with incredible speed. Shara yelped as the blade glanced off his ribs, opening the flesh in a long, ugly flap. Nevertheless, the dog's cry was muffled, because his teeth were fastened in Red Sky's thigh. A shake of the head severed arteries, stripped meat from the heavy, startlingly white thighbone.

Red Sky tumbled to the ground.

Two Fists, having been feinted into missing Gan on his initial rush, whirled to find Gan waiting for him. The son's gaze went to his father's efforts to escape Shara. Blood jetted from the older man's ruined thigh. Two Fists completely lost control.

Pity slipped across Gan's concentration, a swift unimportant whisper. He stepped back, letting Two Fists' axe swish past. Then, sliding to his left, he drove his sword into Two Fists' unprotected kidney. The axe, on backstroke, soared off into the watching warriors.

Two Fists dropped to his knees, toppled onto his face.

Gan turned, crouched. Shara circled Red Sky, who was on one knee, mask askew, struggling to regain his feet. The man faked a move at the dog, then spun to lash at Gan's legs with the axe.

Only reflex saved Gan. He leaped straight up. The gleaming blade hummed under his feet. Gan slashed his attacker as he touched the ground. The murdat severed Red Sky's spine. Tore through the flesh and muscle of the neck. Crashed into the back of the mask. Decapitated, the Kwa leader fell, convulsing. A man's length away, its whiteness fouled with mud and blood, the mask covering Red Sky's face lamented up into the falling rain with empty eyes and silent woe.

Calling Shara, Gan sprinted for the gap created by Two Fists' escaping axe. The priest moved to block them. Unintelligible noise and saliva sprayed from the gray-bearded mouth. The ornate staff rose in threat. Shara exploded past his master, seized the man's whole head in his jaws. Twined together, man and animal fell to the ground. Growling, Shara shook his quarry as a terrier snaps a rat. The crackle of breaking bones triggered screams of disbelieving rage and shock from the Kwa.

Slashing furiously at those quick enough to try to stop him, Gan hurled himself onto one of the horses tied up in the rear. Flattening himself against the animal's neck, he shouted at Shara to attack the rest of the mounts.

Arrows slipped past, dug into the ground around the darting, barking Shara. A spear, seemingly as big as a log, flew over Gan's shoulder, the shaft actually bouncing off the horse's upflung head.

Shara squealed. Gan looked to see the dog snap at an arrow in his side, close to the nasty axe wound. The arrow broke off, and Shara regained his speed in two bounds. He was abreast of Gan in a few more ground-eating strides.

Just as Gan was congratulating himself on escaping, the arrow struck. Then he was holding the reins in one hand, clawing at the thing in his neck with the other.

He gritted his teeth and broke off the shaft.

Turning his head was agony. Distant Wolf signal flags ordered retreat.

The leader's drum sounded. His drum.

Thunder rocked the valley. Rain came in torrents. Small knots of men still struggled around the Wolf defenses, but the flow of the Kwa warriors was toward a large, growing circle of men who stared in mute disbelief at three sprawled figures.

Not all merely stared at the dead, however. A full twenty or more pounded in pursuit. They screamed vengeance. Spray exploded as prey and hunter blasted across a rain-polished bean field.

Clapping a hand to his neck to staunch his wound, Gan felt his strength ebbing. He willed his mind into the stabilizing near-trance of nara, the warrior's hard core of courage and composure.

Shara strained to keep pace now, sorely favoring his injured side. Gan urged him on. Ahead were trees. Cover.

Gan grieved for the lost glory he expected to bring the Dog People and the Three Territories. Into the thick, scented air of the forest. Uphill. Seeking a final stand.

He was not to die on his beloved prairie. It was the thing he'd feared since the day he crossed the mountains.

CHAPTER 6

SHARA'S BREATHING WAS THE SOUND OF A RUSTED SAW. HEAD DOWN, MOVING WITH A strained, off-center motion as his wounded side stiffened, the dog stared fixedly ahead. Gan fared little better. Keeping the horse balanced on the steep, slick grade and its treacherous footing taxed him to his limit. The energy surge of combat had long drained away. He was soaked, chilled, and exhausted. The arrowhead in his neck stabbed anew at every heartbeat, every movement.

Gan thought enviously of his friend and mentor, Clas na Bale, who could step outside pain almost completely. Wounds were an inconvenience for Clas, except for the blood loss.

Concentrating on the inward-turning mental power of nara, Gan mapped the pain, imaged it. He used it to stimulate his senses.

Far below were the voices of his pursuers and chuffing, snorting horses. Around him were smells; wet bark, coniferous needles, ground litter. The unmistakable scent of wet dog. It couldn't be Shara; wind direction precluded it. That meant wolves. The knowledge pleased him. Wolves had entered his life before.

Rain. Enervatingly cold, almost blinding. Gan decided the latter was a blessing. If he couldn't see, neither could his enemies. He twisted to look back down the mountain.

The arrowhead seized at the move, punishing like a live thing. Shock rushed to break his will. Faintly, he heard Clas: "Pain is a killer. Run, and it'll overtake and destroy you. Face it. Let it be what it must. Separate the injury from the rest of you. Wall it off, Gan."

His wheezing horse labored onto a shelf, a high meadow where the earth was luxuriously near level. A few more steps and the animal stopped, head down, legs spread, totally used up.

Gan dismounted quickly. The ground sloped away gently on three sides. To his left the mountain shouldered up into shrouding mist. A prudent man would head downhill and attempt to outrun the pursuit. After all, their horses were exhausted, too.

Gan grinned tightly at Shara. "Even if I could run away, I don't think you're good for much longer, are you, boy?"

Sprawled on the wet grass, the dog moved his tail in weak acknowledgment.

At the juncture of meadow and mountain stood an outfall from ages past, a frozen surf of boulders standing in unmoving waves. The mountain wall was split by several narrow clefts.

A whack on the spent horse's rump made it hunch its back, groaning. When it turned to look at Gan, blood trickled from its nostrils.

Far away, men shouted. A horse whinnied.

"You've got to lead them away," Gan said. "If they find you, they'll know I'm nearby."

The horse swung its head forward again, where it drooped almost to the ground. It shivered violently, coughed.

Gan drew his murdat. If he killed the animal among the nearer rocks, it would probably be overlooked.

The mute, helpless look of the spent horse twisted in Gan's imagination. The face became human. Many faces. Gan saw men fall under his own weapon, more clearly now than when the deed was done.

That was war. Life. That was the way.

The pursuit was closer. Individual voices shouted distinguishable words.

Gan sheathed the murdat and ran. By the time he reached the rockfall the Kwa were just below the crest where the meadow started. Crossing the rocks was leap after leap from one rain-slick boulder to another. Each jarring landing threatened to buckle Gan's knees. Shara alternately growled and whined at his own pain.

Someone shouted discovery of the abandoned mount.

It was impossible to continue across the rocks without being seen. Gan dropped onto his stomach. Shara stretched out beside him. Behind them, the Kwa searched for tracks.

Gan crawled to one of the narrow gaps. Tantalizing, it revealed a cluttered pathway barely wider than a man's reach. Rocks of all sizes formed a haphazard uphill staircase that disappeared in rain and mist. If it ended just beyond the limit of Gan's vision, it was the worst kind of trap. "Not much of a chance," Gan said, ruffling Shara's head. "Up or nothing, dog."

Brown eyes met his, trusting. For a fleeting moment, Gan remembered the horse in the meadow.

The Kwa were combing through the rockfall before Gan and Shara progressed ten body-lengths. A boulder, far larger than it appeared from below, blocked the passage. Gan clawed his way up and over, spurred by the excited calls of the searchers. Shara, on hind legs, was just out of reach. He leaped, tried to scramble up the stone face. Whining pain and frustration, he fell back, time after time. Gan coaxed as he never had.

Shara gathered himself for the effort Gan knew must be the last. Facedown, draped over the boulder, the pain of the arrowhead toyed with Gan's consciousness. The image of the dog wavered, disappeared, returned.

Shara bounded upward. Gan lunged. Fingers looped under the war collar. Whatever happens now, Gan told himself, we end it side by side. We've given too much to each other to separate now.

He was glad Neela would never know he'd made such an incredibly stupid decision.

A spike from the collar poked Gan's wrist. It worked against the flesh as the dog struggled. When the point pierced, the bite of it was actually a relief from the grinding pressure. For an instant. Then the shaft was working back and forth along the bone. Gan moaned through grinding teeth. Little by little, the two of them won. Gan praised the dog. He cursed his great bulk. When Shara got his hind legs under him and pushed up onto Gan's level, they collapsed in one dirty, bloody pile, too exhausted to move. Only when Shara lifted his head, yanking the spike free, did Gan react. He managed to stifle the yell. It took several deep breaths to quell the shaking.

Keeping low, he crawled to the edge of the boulder, peered over. A Kwa warrior squatted at the passage's mouth, examining the rocks. Gan barely ducked in time to avoid the man's upward glance. He and Shara stumbled on, hearing their pursuer shout for his companions.

Gan almost missed the hole. Knee-high, barely wide enough to admit a man. Feetfirst, he jammed his way in. The chamber was so low he couldn't even kneel, but it hid him and Shara.

Shoving the dog aside, Gan searched frantically for some way to hide the entrance. It was partially shielded from the lower approach by a fallen slab. Gan wrestled with another. At his best, it would have been a difficult load. In his present state, it was excruciating.

The narrow chasm echoed with the yells of the Kwa. For the first time, Gan noted that the rain had stopped. The blood trail would be clear.

It ended at the hole.

He crawled uphill a few paces. With his bleeding wrist, he made smears on the walls, on the ground. Then, backing into the cave, he strained at the entry cover until it was in place. He moved deeper, forcing Shara along.

The Kwa stopped outside. A man excitedly reported the blood uphill. Another stopped him. "That's not spilled blood. That's marks, like paint."

"He's falling. Or the dog is. Come on."

The sound of movement, away. Then complaint. "What're you waiting for?"

"Something's wrong." The better tracker spoke. "Look, here: scuff marks. He moved something."

"We've found marks all up this chimney. If you're too tired to keep up, sit down and wait. We'll bring him back for you to look at."

Gan ignored the argument. The emplaced slab left a hole about the size of his two fists. Shadows moved across it. A sword blade poked in and retreated.

Someone laughed. "You think he changed into a marmot? What about the dog? You think it's a mouse now?"

A spear slithered inside, the head gleaming, inquisitive. Gan deflected it to the side. It turned this way and that. Gan continued to force it into the walls. The spear withdrew. The tracker was suspicious. "It seems not to go anywhere. I don't know. You—give me a hand with these rocks. I want to see what's behind them."

Gan extended his murdat in front of him.

Cracking, ripping, lightning shocked the earth nearby. Simultaneous thunder pounded the mountain. Loud shouts competed with the rumble. The rush of rain seemed to swell directly out of the dying roar.

"That's perfect!" The sarcasm was enraged. "Now the blood trail's washed off. If he gets away, it's your fault."

Boots splashed off into the distance.

Gan realized his pursuers would soon discover he wasn't ahead of them. A little more altitude, and they'd be into snow. They'd find no tracks, come back, move the rocks.

Going outside was a tempting possibility. Gan dismissed it. There was sure to be a watch on the horses in the meadow, even if he made it that far without being caught. Once discovered, he'd be overwhelmed. Better to hope the Kwa got discouraged.

Gan shuddered. Killed in a hole, speared like a rabbit. What was it the Kwa said? A marmot. It wasn't a very honorable death.

Shara stirred, pushed against him. Irritably, Gan shoved back. The dog persisted. Gan tried to turn to admonish him.

Then he heard the call. Faint, wavering, unmistakable. Wolves. Howling. Not just one. Many. Daylight calling, in the rain. Practically unheard of.

A horn blew. Two long blasts, then a series of short notes. One didn't have to know Kwa signals to hear the urgency in the signal.

Now, with a chance of survival, Gan succumbed to his ordeal. He struggled against the lethargy rolling through his body, collapsing his strength, his will. Pain, ever patient, drilled through his nara. His heartbeat dropped. Breathing was a burden. The murdat grip slipped from numb fingers.

Noise erupted outside.

Outside. What did "outside" mean? Why were there voices? Angry. ". . . told you he's no ordinary man. Wolves never howl like this. It's magic. If they've attacked our horses . . ."

Quiet again. Peaceful. Sleep.

The dream came slowly, a black mist. Under the mist, a black sea, rising and falling. Gan saw himself on a small boat. Its sails were tatters, its hull leaking.

Something watched him. Under the water. He felt its presence. Cold, slimy. Yet he saw nothing.

"It waits for you, young Gan. You, less than filth." The voice burned with hatred. Its rattling dryness was the scrape of fingernails on slate. Gan struggled to wake. Laughter. Worse than the words. Then, *"I will release you when I've done with you. Watch the dream. Understand."*

Directly ahead of the boat, the sea rose in a mound. There was no other way to describe it. An excrescence, pulling black water with it. Bubbles welled, swirled around its edges. The thing grew ever larger.

The small boat was drawn to it.

Hauling on lines, Gan fought to raise the sail. Every time he pulled, the line snapped. The black thing in front of him towered over his boat now, mountainous. The voice came back, this time from inside that monstrosity. It whispered, enjoying its terrifying power. *"You would test the sea, would you? You don't fear this power? Then see what awaits."*

The impossible thing reversed itself. Subsided. As it lowered, it turned, almost imperceptibly, at first. Then faster. Faster. When it was level with the surface of the water, its massive speed created a dark, spiraling vortex.

Where there had been a mountain was now a huge hole.

Caught, the small boat whipped around the whirlpool, heeling, tipping. Gan caught the mast with one hand, the rail with the other. Far below, distorted by shifting water and dappled light, Gan saw things—indistinct, coldly predatory things—lunge from dark fastnesses. Terrible knowledge told him they waited for him.

The boat rail gave way, disappeared into the vortex. Planks separated along the hull. The mast snapped, speared down into the depths. Gan braced against the canted deck, clawed for a handhold.

In the midst of all that frigid horror, his hand was suddenly warm. Once more he heard the voice, stronger, more insistent with each word. *"The sea waits for you. Come, Gan. Now. Gan. Gan!"*

Another voice contradicted that one. "It's me. Gan! Speak to me."

Light burned Gan's eyes. At the edge of vision, he saw Shara's head across his leg. He wondered how the dog got there. Why were they lying down?

The cave. The Kwa. He reached for the murdat.

"I have your weapon, Gan. Give me your hand." Recognition pierced Gan's confusion. Emso. Gan tugged free the hand under Shara's head. It was wet where the dog licked it.

Memory swam in Gan's mind. Water. Cold.

Emso had him by the hands, dragging him from the cave.

Gan felt himself falling into unconsciousness again. He cried out, chill with the fear that something waited, yearned to catch him when he was helpless.

Emso said, "I've got you. I'm here. You're safe."

Gan heard the waiting thing laugh. Wet. Bubbling.

CHAPTER 7

SYLAH FEASTED HER EYES ON THE MOTHER RIVER, LUXURIATED IN THE MYRIAD GREENS ranging from the metallic water to the riotous plants gracing the banks. Higher, farther from the sustaining moisture, the hillsides were warm golds, yellows, oranges, all glowing proof that, for all the river's power, this was sun country.

Astride her horse, Copper, Sylah faced north. The ground underfoot was hot and dusty. The animal was anxious to reach the water below. Shifting hooves clattered on dry rock.

A small change in the wind brought the river's cold breath sighing up the slope. The gorge of the Mother River created its own climate. Wind from the sea swept its length, modifying the bitter winters. During summer's heat, that same wind could be chill. A midsummer morning beside the Mother River might demand a jacket to hold off fog and chill; afternoon might require the lightest shirt possible.

Turning to her right, Sylah looked north and east. Her heart twisted with pain. Three days' ride—four, at the most—and she could be in her husband's arms.

Should be in his arms. But he demanded she stay away.

Barely discernible in the distance rode the departing Messenger who'd come with the news. With him were the Dog warriors who'd rescued her and her friends from the nomads. They'd been trail companions during the long, hard ride north from the Dry.

Sylah rose in her stirrups, looked south past her four companions. They, too, examined the back trail. No one ever stopped looking over a shoulder when pursued by Windband nomads. Sylah made a three-sign and gave a silent prayer of thanks for escape from the place of the Door.

Escape, with the treasure of her life's quest in hand. The secret of the Door, hidden for generations. It was Sylah's now. The thought exulted her. Reared to be the Flower, the one to rescue the secret for Church, she'd succeeded. Embarrassment touched her cheeks with warmth; she remembered being tempted to use the Door's secret as her personal property. The counsel of her friends saved her. The same friends defeated Moonpriest's attempt to steal the secret. Unfortunately, that evil one somehow reasserted control over the battered, plague-stricken nomad nation.

Plague. It was why Clas denied her. He would risk sickness to reach her. He would go to any length to prevent risk to her.

She loved him for his concern. Nevertheless, after her long, dangerous quest, she was infuriated by his assumption that she was too weak to confront anything he dared.

Ironically, the plague apparently started with Matt Conway, a man as responsible as any for the success of her quest. When her journey started, Conway was a puzzle. Then he seemed a man searching for himself. Now he was assured. Strange: She trusted him completely, yet she knew he lied about his past. As did his accompanying black countrywoman, Donnacee Tate. "We come from a distant land," they told everyone, "far to the east."

Liars. All of them. Seven of the original eight still lived; Conway and Tate, of course, and the four in Ola with Gan Moondark—the man Leclerc, and the three women, Sue Anspach, Janet Carter, and Kate Bernhardt. Then there was the one called Jones. He was now Moonpriest, the leader of the Windband nomads and high priest of Moondance.

They claimed they were from lands so far away that even Church's missionaries were unknown there. Then how did they come to know Church's basic concepts?

Only on the quest did Tate and Conway acquire a warrior's ability to move with stealth, or read tracks even adequately. People like that traveled without being discovered until they came to the Enemy Mountains? Never.

As if those things weren't enough to make them frighteningly suspect, the men treated the women as equals.

Sylah's thoughts diverted.

Clas.

He understood that the search for the Door was her life. Only her man trusted—loved—a woman enough to allow her that freedom, much less admired her for needing it. But what would he say when he discovered that the generations-old secret of the Door was a thing called books? Or that Conway and Tate could read them?

What Tate and Conway did, what they insisted Sylah must eventually do, was blasphemous. Both dared speak the forbidden word, insisting they *teach* her and others to use books. Everyone knew that Church demanded that any words on paper found in the godkills be surrendered to Church, to be ritually burned in the Return ceremony. Everyone also knew the giants that ruled the world in ancient times enslaved mankind. The slaves learned too much, grew pretentious and rebellious. The giants destroyed them, turned their huge settlements into godkills, radpads, and radzones, where terrifying sickness waited to strike the unsuspecting.

Men called Siahs founded tribes wherever the One in All allowed people to survive.

The ability to read, write, and do arithmetic became the privilege of the highest ranking, most feared, most watched people in every culture. Sylah hated such laws. She understood the need, however: How else did Church assure no one challenged the order of things?

The strangers were at ease with books. Sylah still swallowed panic whenever she handled one. So many words.

Still, she embraced her responsibility as the Flower. Her life had been a search for power. Not for herself, but for all women. It was her own hatred for the treatment she suffered that drove her, but her goals were never self-oriented.

Save one precept: *I will not be owned.*

As an orphan, rescued from slavery by Church, she grew to adulthood as a Chosen, a child of Church. Life was regimentation and the privilege of serving others forever. Still, no one endangered any Church woman. To harm one meant the entire tribe was denied Church. No Healer or War Healer would minister to them.

Priestesses were women, however. Even Church women, unimaginably free by the standards of all other women, were crushed by a world that saw them as servants and bearers of children. When Sylah thought of her life, one word demanded primacy: Resentment. *I will not be owned.*

Now, however, the power she sought was hers. If she could keep it. If she could control it.

If she could stand it.

Far, far away, the Dog warriors who'd rescued her and the Messenger who'd sought her out were a last movement on the horizon. It was as if they had never been.

Behind her, Nalatan, the warrior-monk she'd married to Donnacee Tate, said, "We should be moving, Sylah. We know Windband's back there somewhere."

Waving to indicate she'd heard, Sylah's hidden smile was deprecating. To herself, she murmured, "Make a new world tomorrow, Priestess. For today, continue to flee."

When she turned, she was erect, confident. "No sign of them yet, Nalatan?"

He backed his horse until he was beside Tate. Neither he nor the black woman made any overt indication of awareness of the other's presence, but a stone would have noticed the attraction between them. Nalatan answered, "Nothing since we flushed that ambush four days back."

Tate said, "We didn't cut them up that much. It's not like them to back off without one last crack at us."

Lanta, the other black-robed Priestess, spoke up. "Once we're across the river, they won't dare chase us any farther. They're afraid of patrols from the Three Territories."

Conway said, "I think Lanta's right."

Sylah nodded. It was routine for Conway to agree with Lanta. When he couldn't, he said nothing. Everyone was certain he was making amends for something. No one knew what.

Conway went on. "If someone's watching us, they may have signaled the main body that our Dog escort's gone and we're alone."

Tate frowned. "It's a bright day. They could be using mirrors . . ." She stopped abruptly, jerking around to look to Conway with apology plain in her features.

He smiled bleakly. "Yes. Mirrors. The ones I taught Windband to use. One of my smaller mistakes, but bad enough."

"I'm sorry." Tate walked her horse to Conway's side. "I keep forgetting you were in the nomad camp with Moonpriest. I can't seem to put you two together. Not the way he's changed."

"I wish I could forget. Funny; I want to think of him as Jones. I don't want to believe a friend could turn into Moonpriest."

Tate pitched forward, aggressive. "Jones is dead, Matt. Dead. Moonpriest lives instead."

Nalatan said, "We'll all be very dead if we don't get across this river."

Tate turned, mischievous. "My, we're very testy today, aren't we? Don't they teach you not to interrupt in that brotherhood of yours?"

"They teach us to survive." Nalatan was unperturbed, accustomed to Tate's baiting. Beneath the studied calm, his admiring affection glowed like banked coals.

Sylah said, "Conway, ride on ahead, please; make sure the ferry landing's safe."

Conway whistled. Moments later two Dog hounds raced toward him from where they'd obviously been watching the back trail. No one paid much attention, except Tate. Her mobile, high-cheekboned features turned soft, injured, erasing the infectious smile. More than concern, more than sorrow, she registered unspeakable loss. Even when Nalatan put a hand on hers where she gripped her reins, she remained fixed on the dogs.

Conway bent down to scratch the animals' heads. "Mikka beat you, Karda. Slipping in your old age?" The male wagged his tail as if enjoying the joke.

Conway galloped downhill. Karda led, while Mikka, the lighter-colored female, followed the horse.

The remaining foursome fell into their accustomed trail formation. Sylah and Lanta rode with the packhorses. Tate and Nalatan rode drag. Nalatan took the opportunity to sympathize with Tate. "You shouldn't grieve so about the loss of your own dogs. They lived the life they were born to lead. It's good to sorrow for them, because they loved you, but take care you don't tarnish their deaths."

She snapped around, glared. Nalatan continued. "You were sun and moon to them, Donnacee. As you are to me. They died protecting you. Of course they didn't want to die. Nothing gives up life willingly. But such a glad sacrifice is mighty. It gives meaning to everything that went before. Please, try to see that."

"Are you trying to tell me how I should feel if you get killed? Is that the kind of foolishness you're unloading on me? I'm never going to brag about any death. Not the way you brag about those stupid scars, or how your friends have died fighting for Church. Never."

"Brag's a harsh word. Even so, stories of the struggle to survive are a warrior's only victory over death, don't you see? We who live remember. The best part of us—the honest purpose, the honor—goes on."

Tate shook her head furiously.

Nalatan opposed her vehemence with gentle stubbornness. "Tanno and Oshu died for you. I'll praise them forever. I loved them. I love them still."

"So do I!" It was a cry of injury. Tears flooded Tate's dark, wide eyes. "You know I do."

"Then think of them with love. Joy. Whatever they would give you, if they could."

Thoughtfully, Tate studied Nalatan. For a while, he stood up to it. Finally, nonplussed by such unremitting scrutiny, he found a blemish on his reins that demanded close attention. After a while, she said, "I do love you, Nalatan." He colored in response, but continued to look down. She went on. "I wasn't sure I'd ever say that to anyone again in my life. I knew I'd never even think it about a white man. It's happened, though, and it's because you helped me see so many things. About myself, mostly. But I'll never really know you, will I? I mean, I've watched you in action; stood beside you and fought with you. Then you talk about my dogs and warriors and dying, and there's sadness and happiness and mystery and understanding in it that makes me want to cry. You baffle me."

Nalatan looked up at last. "You imagine you're uncomplicated? I'll spend the rest of my life never knowing what to expect from you."

Her normal, impish expression flashed back. She leaned across, kissed his cheek. "What a life we're going to have, lover. Sure beats living in the Dry with all those other monkish brothers, doesn't it?" Her grin was positively lascivious.

Nalatan stammered something about checking the back trail. He yanked his startled horse around by main strength, trotted back up the mountain.

Tate clapped a hand to her mouth, smothering delight at the way the back of his neck glowed. Slowly, the laughing features eased, swirled through a panoply of emotions as brightly unpredictable as the iridescence of oil on water. "What a life, indeed," she said softly. "Who'd think a person could lose a whole world and be so happy in another one?"

Chapter 8

Conway waited in the cool shade of an alder copse. On the group's arrival, he jerked an angry thumb at the River village, a short distance away. "Windband riders got here first. They warned the ferryman to stay clear of us. He says he'll take us, but we have to share the boat with some River traders. They're already frightened of Windband. The ferryman's afraid they'll learn Windband's after us. There could be trouble."

"Why is this ferryman willing to help us?"

Smiling crookedly, Conway shook a small leather sack. It clinked merrily. "Kossiar coin. That's another piece of news. Kossiar units are attacking River villages. They've never been this active so far north before."

Tate said, "We know the slave revolt gutted Kos, and Windband clubbed the Kossiar army. Why this sudden aggressiveness?"

"Replace the slaves." Conway spat the word. "My guess is that Kos finally crushed the revolt. Now they have to replace the lost 'workers.' "

Sylah made a face. "I'll never recover from Kos. Never. I wanted so much to believe their ruler. I knew in my heart the Chair lied about freeing the slaves. I was a fool. I nearly destroyed us all. I hope you can forgive me someday."

At the mention of forgiveness, suspicion flashed in Conway's glance. "Some of us are too worried about our own burdens to add to yours. Which explains why 'forgive' is such a frequent word among us."

Sylah turned to speak. Conway cut her off. "Later, Sylah. Please. The traders are right over there." He nodded in the direction of the gathering. Fourteen adult males, Sylah noted; no women, no children, no elderly.

The back of her neck tingled.

Still, save for ordinary knives at their sides, the traders were unarmed.

The ferryman trotted forward, his skirtlike lower covering billowing in the wind. He wore a tight, sleeveless jacket and, unlike the traders, a sword in an ornately beaded scabbard belted to his left side. The thing that caught Sylah's eye, however, was the band of his floppy, wide-brimmed hat. It was a rattlesnake skin, with the head still attached. The dried, dead creature gaped, the curved fangs extended in biting attitude. The rattles dangled in the back, rustling at the man's every move.

A nervous grin twitched across the ferryman's face. "I know you, Rose Priestess Sylah. All the River People know Sylah, all know her husband, Clas na Bale. I am Saris."

Saris' use of the Dog People's formal greeting style was a courtesy. Nevertheless, there was too much studied eye contact. Mannerisms were too assured. Sylah watched him and his group while she introduced her friends. The men behind Saris were very cool, but not hostile. When Sylah presented Tate, acknowledging the black woman almost undid Saris. "Everyone's heard of the Black Lightning. I confess, I thought they lied. You really are black. I never saw—"

Tate cut him off smoothly. "I know you, Saris. What news can you give us?"

When he answered, Saris was still nervous, but controlling it well. "The Matt Conway one told you I was warned not to help you?"

Sylah said, "He did. We're grateful for your courage."

Saris looked around furtively. "They hate you very much. They say you're outcast—the little Violet Priestess, Lanta, too. Not that I care. All know Church women are never to be harmed, and Saris wouldn't break holy law." The friendly eyes were suddenly cunning, a change almost too quick to catch. "Windband says you stole the treasure of the Door."

Tate said, "Do we look like people carrying treasure? Windband tried to capture us. We fought them off."

Nalatan moved his horse forward. "We killed many. They are Church's enemies."

Saris bobbed his head curtly. He angled closer to Sylah, a move that also distanced him from Nalatan. "We have to hurry. Come."

Sidling next to Conway, Lanta frowned at him. "Keep Mikka and Karda close."

Conway was immediately alert. "What did you see?"

"Deceit. Saris lied. The other Rivers are too unconcerned."

Without further comment, Conway urged his horse forward, calling to the dogs. To say more to Lanta invited argument, and he'd vowed to avoid that. It was beginning to gall, though, this constant deference. How long did he have to do penance? For that matter, how long could he feel penitent?

Lanta said she could forgive, but never forget.

Unconsciously, he glowered. What did that mean? Slowly, the fierceness faded. He wondered if the time would ever come when she could look at him and think of anything but that one terrible, shameful moment.

He loved her. She loved him. Why couldn't that be enough?

Saddles and packs removed, the horses boarded the ferry on planks. Skittery, they took the steeper ramp down into the center well that was the boat's cargo space with stiff-legged hesitance. The dogs followed Conway with a look of put-upon determination.

When Conway and Nalatan finished seeing to the horses, they joined the women on the forward deck overlooking the cargo well.

Saris cast off. The dingy sail blossomed in the wind. Its mast, firmly treed to the keel, rose past the horses down in the hull. The boom was level with the raised decks. When it swung over the horses, the frightened animals snorted and strained at their hobbles and tethers.

On the landward side the rock-strewn bottom wavered, darkening as the water deepened. The current was swift, far faster than seemed proper for such a huge body of water. The mass and power of it, this close, was awesome.

Tate leaned close to Conway. "Did you see that salmon jump over there? Thirty pounds, I'll bet. Easy."

"I knew a guy who fished here once."

"In the Columbia? No kidding?"

"Won the permit lottery. You remember how much it cost to enter; we thought he was nuts. Then he not only won, he used the permit himself."

Tate was impressed. "Wow. They were worth a fortune, man."

Conway went on. "There were more foreigners fishing with him than Americans. They could afford to buy the permits from the winners here, you know? What really cost them were the bodyguards. It could get pretty hairy; lots of people really hated to see what our outdoor experience had come to."

They fell silent for a while, remembering. Tate brightened determinedly. "Your friend—he catch anything?"

"The limit that day was five. He caught the third. It wasn't even noon when they closed the river. Lucky, huh?"

"Boy." Tate shook her head. "I never knew anyone who knew anyone who fished for salmon, much less caught one. Back then." She stared out over the water, then broke that off to stand with Nalatan.

Saris trimmed his craft with economy of motion and practiced skill. Once on a course, an ingenious catch arrangement held the rudder in place, freeing his hands to work the braided leather rigging.

The traders lounged about aft. Some stared at the small group gathered at the forward end. Conway and Nalatan exchanged wary glances when some of the Rivers moved down among the horses. Idly, the traders inspected them, learning quickly to steer clear of the Dog war-horses belonging to Conway and Tate. Those animals suffered no strangers. A River touched the flank of Conway's Stormracer. A hoof lashed out wickedly. The man foolishly leaped closer to the horse's head. Having failed to cripple his victim with a foot, Stormracer tried to do the job with his teeth.

The River cursed and retreated. Several of his friends leaped down, examining him for injuries, glaring at horse and owner.

Conway shouted to them, "You're welcome to look. They don't like being handled."

The near-injured man grumbled under his breath.

A narrow catwalk affair allowed fore-and-aft passage on each side of the ferry's hull. Rivers now eased out onto that, some sitting to dangle their feet, letting spray speckle dusty boots.

Sylah pointed. "Look, there—a burned village."

One of the men on the catwalk followed her pointing finger. "Kossiars," he said. "Slavers. No one this far upriver ever saw Kossiars before. They came in the night."

The voice went on. Sylah heard no more. Her mind filled with disoriented flashes and images. Flame. Father, bathed in firelight from the burning homes of neighbors. Swinging the household axe. The only weapon available when he woke to the terror that was on him. It failed to save him or his family.

Screams. Fire. A child too deep in shock to speak, carried away in a basket with more like herself.

The child had a name, like her slaughtered brothers and sisters. That name died in the hut.

Sylah. A Chosen of Church, forbidden by Church law to have any memory of her childhood. Sylah. So clever. Clever enough that, when her voice came back, she never in her entire life revealed that she remembered loving a mother and father.

"Sylah?" Nalatan's voice broke her reverie. She faced him, blank. He looked at her with concern. "They spoke to you." He indicated the six Rivers clustered on the catwalk and in the cargo hold. Sylah stared blankly. Her mind still roared with memory. She swayed, unsteady. Lanta's calming touch helped; she indicated which River had spoken. The man repeated, "As the friend of Gan Moondark, can you tell us why he refused to help the River People? The Kossiars destroy us. We ask the mighty Three Territories for help, and he refuses. Why?"

There was more than hurt and confusion in the question. Beneath the words was something else. The pleasure of taunting.

Sylah turned to Lanta. Affecting her best simper, she said, "It's so depressing when serious things interfere with pleasure. Remember our nighttime boat trip in Kos? When there was a fire? The same thing happened then."

Without waiting for a response, Sylah returned to her questioner. She maintained the shallow manner. "Gan Moondark is one of my closest friends. His mother was of the River People, you know."

"Stolen." The flat accusation came from Saris. A tremor seemed to run through the Rivers. Sylah saw the story of Gan's mother was no new subject.

Quickly, she replied, "A gift woman, granted. But the beloved of Gan's father all his years. He took no other woman, ever."

Saris laughed unpleasantly. "He had no chance. Everyone knew she was a witch. He thought he was making a good bargain, but we're not traders for nothing. A witch. River People know witches on sight." Saris nodded, confirming his own skill. The snake-head hatband bobbed menacingly.

"Gan should have helped us." It was the original River questioner again, closer now, on the foredeck. Behind her, Sylah felt, rather than heard, the movement of her friends. Addressing the closest River once again, Sylah created a sweet, vapid smile. "Why are we arguing? This is just the way our other boat ride changed. Everyone was so happy until the argument. Even little Jessak."

"Jessak? You said Jessak?" It was Saris. His voice was high. The man closest to Sylah pushed back, forcing those behind him to give ground. "You were *in a boat* with Jessak?"

Innocently, Sylah said, "The name means something to you?"

Fear danced across Saris' features. "All who entrust their lives to water know Jessak. He is legend. He holds our lives in his hands. A god." Saris looked around anxiously. "Church admits no god but the One in All. Only a witch would speak of knowing Jessak."

Laughing lightly, Sylah made a playful slapping motion. It was carefully staged to make her look as dense as possible. "The Jessak I know is just a baby. We rescued him from Kos, when the slaves revolted . . ."

"They said you stole the Chair's son. Jessak? That's his name?" Saris' air of confidence returned. The rest of the men read the renewed manner as a signal. As one, they looked to Sylah and the group at the bow.

Behind her, Conway said, "We've been going upstream a long while, Saris. When do we turn?"

"Soon." The tone stirred the hair on the nape of Sylah's neck.

Nalatan spoke, puzzled. "There's something strange . . . Wind moving just that one clump of trees over there. Just ahead."

Sylah resisted the need to see this thing. She concentrated on Saris. Looking upstream past her, he clutched at his chest and shouted, *"Now!"*

The River on the foredeck closest to Sylah drew a hidden sword, lunged at her.

Conway shouted at the dogs. Karda struck as the River reached for Sylah. Crushing jaws closed on the man's left arm, and shook. Screaming, the man tumbled over the side. The water around him reddened. Another man pressed in, only to be met by a ready Karda; both ended up in the cargo hold. Another River, sword upraised, moved to his yelling tribesman's aid.

Sylah turned away, unwilling to watch the dog die. The concussive crack of the wipe slapped her, left her head ringing. By the time her eyes focused, Karda's second victim was choking his life away through a torn throat. The sword wielder was on his face under the hooves of the hysterical horses.

Conway charged aft through the plunging, rearing horses, followed by both dogs. Sylah turned to find Tate facing forward. Before she could speak, Nalatan had Sylah by the shoulder, thrusting her to the deck. Lanta grabbed her as she sprawled.

Looking aft again, Sylah saw Conway beside Saris. The dogs savaged three more armed men attempting to close with their master. Conway fired with the precision of a carpenter driving nails.

The surviving Rivers sought refuge in the river. Conway, features distorted by the passions of combat, put the muzzle of the wipe to a cowering Saris' head.

Sylah's attention was drawn to the bow again by the hollow report of the lower tube of a wipe, the part called the boop.

Tate's target was a sharker. The appearance of a Skan raider this far upstream on the Mother River left Sylah openmouthed. More than that, the vessel was shedding branches and brush. Whole saplings fell away. Nalatan explained, "The taller trees were lashed to her oars. I saw the first ones fall off as they left the shore. They were waiting for us."

Sylah nodded, still mute.

The ferry heeled dangerously, tumbling everyone standing. Sylah, pressed against Lanta, heard Conway shout, "Hang on! We're turning around, heading downstream. Tate, come on aft."

The women remained in a mashed huddle until the banging, plunging turn was completed. Clutching the rail, Tate clawed her way astern. Watching her, Sylah's eye was caught by the erect, shipped oars of the sharker lowering to the river. The camouflage was gone now, revealing the ship in her slim menace. At the first stroke of the oars, the low, dark vessel leaped appreciably closer.

The rest of the group hurried after Tate. Conway still sat beside Saris, wipe resting on the shaking River's shoulder, the muzzle nestled in his ear. The hat and its intimidating hatband lay on the deck. The snake's head was under Conway's boot.

Conway said, "Nalatan, get some of that leather line. Tie this pig to the rail by his neck, in case he has thoughts of leaving."

Saris begged, "We can't outrun a sharker. Let me stop. I'll talk to them. They know me."

Sylah spoke over Conway's derisive laugh. "Get us to shore, Saris. If we escape, you go free. My word on it."

Nalatan said, "They're gaining. A horse can't run that fast."

Tate said, "I'll slow them down." The boop thudded. A moment later, when the explosive round detonated in the river, she muttered, "If I can hit them." She fired again. Nalatan loyally cheered her closer miss.

Turning Saris over to Nalatan, Conway added his firepower to Tate's. A round hit the hull. Another round landed on the deck. The Skan, true to their reputation for heedless ferocity, absorbed the punishment and charged ahead. Oars went slack and were pitched over the side. Conway and Tate selected white phosphorus ammunition as the range inexorably shortened. Soon smoke boiled up from behind the gunwale protecting the rowers. Open flame appeared. The cries of the wounded accentuated the shrill squealing of the ferry's leather halyards.

Shouting back to Nalatan without taking her eyes off the onrushing sharker, Tate called for a change of course. "Her rudder's gone. Let her pass close; we'll tear her up with the wipes."

With Nalatan's shortknife at his throat for inspiration, Saris performed. At the last possible instant, he brought the clumsy ferry within a body-length of the near-crippled sharker. The Skan vessel skimmed past, smoke boiling from her deck and collapsed rigging. Crew appeared and disappeared in the swirling haze, dashing buckets of water on the flames. Trying to maintain steerage, many rowers still manned their positions. Blinded by smoke, unwarned by any lookouts, they were unprepared. Extended oars were impacted, irresistibly wrenched from hands. Driven by the momentum of the other hull, the handles pivoted forward, transformed to immense clubs. Shattered men were flung from their seats like crushed fruit.

Conway and Tate saw the carnage. They lowered their weapons even before the vessel was past.

The river claimed the sharker. Spinning, wallowing, she swept downstream.

Soon afterward, Saris brought the ferry to a grinding halt against the bank. Sylah and Lanta questioned him while the others unloaded the horses. First, Sylah explained to Lanta, "He reached for his chest when he ordered his men to attack. I want to know why." When she found the thin chain at his throat, she dragged out a flat, silver-shining disk.

"Moondance." Both women made a whispered curse of the word.

Teeth bared, Saris pulled back against the hull. "Moondance will crush all of you, Church as well as witches."

Sylah asked, "Who calls me witch?"

"You ride with those who destroy with lightning. Isn't the Lanta one a Seer? They're all witches, whether Church calls them so or not. Everyone knows the black woman witched the monk, Nalatan. Made him renounce Church."

"They know all that, do they?" In contrast to Lanta's trembling fury, Sylah was introspective.

Committed now, Saris grew evangelical. "We Rivers and Windband are joined with the Skan. We'll make peace with Kos. Gan Moondark will find us coming from all the four holy directions. Waters and mountains will rise against him and all who stand against us. The Three Territories and false Church will be a harvest of slaves."

Saris was unaware of Nalatan's approach. Not deigning to look at the River, Nalatan said, "The horses are landed. If you'll join the others, I'll tend to this. I saw his accursed disk." He raised his sword.

Saris shrieked defiance. "I die to live forever in the moon. I'll be revenged! Moondance. Moondance!"

"Free him." Sylah stepped back.

Ugly with contempt, Nalatan sliced the leather lashing.

Bending swiftly to his ankle, Saris rose with a shortknife from a boot scabbard. Grinning in a transport of religious ecstasy, he struck at Sylah. She saw him, dreamlike, saw her hands rise slowly—too slowly—to fend him off.

The knife filled her vision.

A glinting blur cut in front of her. Saris' jacket stirred. A slit fell open in the material. The shortknife spun away. Shock warped his frenzy. He stopped, not believing the flush of blood staining his chest and forearm.

Nalatan aimed his killing stroke.

Sylah grabbed her companion's arm, held on until he calmed. Then she moved to minister to Saris.

The River had his left arm pressed across his chest, the hand closing the wound on his right bicep. Immersed in fervor once more, Saris regaled her. "You'll see, witch; you'll see. You'll curse the day you spared me. As I curse you."

Nalatan spoke to Sylah. "You give mercy where it's neither appreciated or wise."

Calmly, Sylah rejected Nalatan's anger. "That's when it's most needed."

Chapter 9

Smoke coursed over the top of the stone-and-timber palisade of the Skan fort. Billowing blue-gray mimicked the waves of the hard green sea, an arrow-shot away. Morning's early mist mixed with the smoke, gave the wall a brooding, watchful air.

Lorso limped along the battlewalk on the inner side of the vertical log palisade. He passed archer ports every few paces, tall slits cut at junctures of two logs. At the southwest corner of the square fort, Lorso turned left. The morning sun breaking the horizon warmed his face. Ahead, sharkers nested on the still surface of the natural harbor east of the fort. Looking at the bright gleam of dawn on the water, Lorso thought of a razor edge, heard the erotic whisper of honed steel drawn along leather.

It was his favorite sound. From childhood, it soothed him. Never before had he thought of it as sexually stimulating.

Jaleeta.

If sound could ignite desire, Jaleeta was the one woman he needed to fuel it. Quench it. So contradictory. Like the sharpening. Soothing. Exciting. How could that be?

Jaleeta. He stopped, put a hand to the wall. Beyond the harbor, the log cabins of the town swam in his sight. Yearning stole the strength of his knees. He glanced to the south. There rose the rounded, split peak that represented the beak of Sosolassa, the octopus god of the Skan. Sosolassa, who heard all, saw all, and spoke through his chosen spirit woman, Tears of Jade.

Jaleeta's owner. Jaleeta, the weapon Sosolassa ordered Tears of Jade to find.

Lorso was unable to look at Jaleeta without seeing the naked, fire-bathed form he'd captured. Vulnerable. Quivering. His, by right of strength.

Lorso's stomach tightened painfully. Jaleeta was forbidden, claimed by a god.

But Lorso knew Jaleeta didn't want a god. Jaleeta wanted Lorso. Tonight.

Tears of Jade refused to live within the walls, saying, "Sosolassa gave our sea, our land, to those who had the courage to reject the first Siah and that one's weak ways. Skan walls offend Sosolassa. Skan seek out and destroy trespassers, prey on all who are not Skan."

Rising from the bed in his tiny cabin, Lorso smiled, thinking how the old woman shamed the wall-trusting warriors mercilessly; the Chief, bold as a mouse, and the Navigators, old and worn out. They crept up to her cabin for her unerring counsel and tried to escape before her tongue stripped their bones.

Strapping on his sword, Lorso sobered. Aside from her contempt for the Skan leadership, there was nothing funny about Tears of Jade.

It wasn't right for a man—even adopted—to fear his mother.

Sweat dampened Lorso's palms. He dried them on his coarse, canvaslike trousers.

The solitary window admitted light from a quarter moon. Scudding clouds alternately filtered and exposed its face. The room held a table, two chairs, and a large chest for storing clothes and blankets against one wall. There was a smaller chest opposite the door, by the darker blackness of the fireplace. Lorso's sealskin rain cape and conical rain hat of woven cedar bark hung on a peg driven into the door.

Stepping outside, he closed the door soundlessly.

Through fitful moon shadows, he slipped from cabin to cabin across the town. There was no watch, as such. There were eyes in plenty. Not everyone slept.

There were dogs, too, prowling in packs. Essentially feral, they lived in the forest, occasionally tame enough to hole up in a barn or tunnel under a cabin. Usually that was to birth pups. At night, they slunk in among the dwellings. Wolves wouldn't pursue them into the populated area, and the dogs scavenged freely. They could be very dangerous. At least once a year, someone was badly bitten. Less frequently, a pack killed. When that happened, there was an intense hunt. For a while, dogs were fewer. Soon things were as before.

Lorso often thought he shared a disturbing similarity with them. They belonged to no one, yet found protection because they had utility. Among the Skan, Lorso was renowned, yet ever the lone one. His entire family was taken by Sosolassa. That was why Tears of Jade adopted him.

He reminded himself he was loved. Adopted, yes, but loved. Absolutely.

For a moment, Lorso was unsure if his thoughts of the dogs created the sense of their presence, or if he was actually being followed. Bared sword in hand, he turned.

The pack leader, crouched low to the ground, was no more than a body-length away. Discovered, it settled even farther. A warning growl shivered the darkness. Hair rose on Lorso's neck, his arms.

Slowly, weapon extended, Lorso backed away. Fear of exposure demanded he retreat. Infuriated, he ached to lash out. It was a very large dog, and the pack followed it under good hunting discipline. Aside from the scratch of claws and some panting, they were utterly silent.

Lorso leaned forward, lifted the sword point. Like smoke, the pack rolled back on itself, drifted away.

Once at the fringes of the town, buildings were farther apart. Brush and trees provided better cover than corners and doorways. Lorso relaxed a bit.

Light gleamed through a gap in Tears of Jade's door.

The old woman was awake.

Fear knotted his guts into a frozen chain.

The spirit woman knew.

Panic shrilled in his ears. He clutched his sword in both hands. If he was discovered, he was determined to die fighting rather than provide entertainment for a howling crowd.

Then he heard the soft music from the cabin near Tears of Jade's. The dark cabin. Jaleeta's.

Sweet, intricate, the melody was like the smell of flowers on the night air. A tarn, the deep-bodied stringed instrument of the Skan, chanted mellow chords, background for a voice softened to confiding yearning.

Lorso crawled across the open ground. Carefully skirting her flower beds, he crouched at Jaleeta's door. He tapped gently.

Without missing a beat or changing the tune, Jaleeta melodically sang, "Come in, my love. Make no sound. Come inside. Be still, wait for my touch."

Lorso slipped through the door. Sword still in hand, he hunched against the wall, waiting as bid. His heart threatened to break his ribs. His breath caught in nostrils overcharged with her presence. Woman-scent and scrubbed skin, brushed hair and sweet oil of cedar. Sweat dappled his lip, tingled at his temples.

When the song ended, she said, "We must be careful." The voice was fire; the sighing whisper of movement in the dark raised the heat to an unbearable pitch.

Then there was total silence. Thick, choking. An overwhelming sense of someone—*something*—else nearby threatened to suffocate him.

Tears of Jade's pinched, withered visage claimed his mind's eye. The face hated him.

When something touched his cheek, he flinched. Fingers pressed to his lips. "I'm here, my love. With you. Yours. As this night is ours." Her hand left his face to cover his grip on the sword. Jaleeta laughed quietly. "You won't need this. Tonight you conquer with a different weapon." Then the hand was at his throat, moving down to his blouse, freeing the first toggle from its loop. Sly fingers reached inside to explore his chest.

He lunged forward, reached to enfold her. His embrace closed on tantalizing laughter. Words came from across the room. "I'm here, Lorso. Naked. As you saw me once. As I was when I hated you, as I am now that I must have you. As you must be when you come to me."

Lorso dropped the sword to the floor. Frantic hands fumbled with toggles, loops, belt, laces. Everything fell heedlessly beside the sword.

Crossing the room, hands outstretched, he contacted flesh so soft, so firm, so deliciously inviting he halted in sheer wonder. Jaleeta caught his wrists, denying him further touch. Maddened, he strained forward. She spun away, avoiding his grasp, maintaining her own. A different tone, steely sharp, demanded, "Not yet. The bonding. Afterward . . ." The lone word promised.

Jaleeta released him. A moment later—a moment that seemed forever to Lorso—metal pressed into his hand. He recognized a shortknife. His thumb sought the blade, relishing the eager edge, the one he'd put there when Jaleeta promised him this night. Quickly, he drew a line across both forearms, just below the elbow. Jaleeta's hands traced his muscle there, lingered on the wetness. "Now me," she said. "Hurry, Lorso. Hurry." Two quick inhalations marked the corresponding cuts on her arms. Then she was pressed against him, warm, yielding. He raised his arms over his head, in contact with hers. The razor-thin wounds joined, the flowing blood melded.

"There." The word clung to his tongue like a clawed thing. He forced out the oath. "Blood of one, blood of both. I swear my life to you. Sosolassa hears me."

Jaleeta repeated the bond, bending forward, whispering them in his ear. The plosive sounds were moist caresses, the sibilants drawn out, insinuating. Between words, her tongue played across his flesh. Her body moved against his.

With a throaty, inarticulate rumble, Lorso picked her up bodily, took her to the fur-blanketed bed.

Tears of Jade hobbled into Jaleeta's room with one hand grasping the arm of another woman. In the free hand she held her ornate walking stick. She prodded the curled-up, sleeping Jaleeta. "Get up," she said. The ancient, dry voice was surprisingly light. Amusement danced in it.

Jaleeta immediately rolled to a sitting position, feet on the wooden floor. She drew the bearskin about her.

Tears of Jade smiled, a slash through the myriad wrinkles. Her teeth were blindingly white, their gleam equal to that of her quick, probing eyes. "You seem to have weathered the storm well. My lovely little seabird has caught her first fish. Fully fledged, you are, and on the wing, my darling." Instantly serious, she leaned forward. The silent woman beside her took her weight. "All went well?"

For a long breath, Jaleeta was expressionless. Sleep-deprived eyes stared. The rich, full lips were slack. One hand rose to comb fingers through disarrayed hair. And then she grinned, transformed herself from a tired, just-wakened waif to a lascivious, sated woman. "Well? Wonderful would be a better word. If there is any word." She pouted. "I wish he didn't have to go."

"You naughty thing." Scandalized, chuckling, Tears of Jade detached herself from the support of the other woman, walked to a chair by the window where the first light of day brought hints of color to objects. With the walking stick, she indicated the corner where the other woman should retire. The spirit woman continued speaking to Jaleeta. "I'm not interested in your nasty rutting, young scamp. Show me your arms. He swore?"

Jaleeta held up the thin wounds.

Tears of Jade nodded satisfaction. "We progress."

"Progress where?" Again, Jaleeta pouted, this time seriously.

"That's not for you to know. Or concern yourself with. Have I made your life a good one? Have I lived up to every promise I made you?"

"You treat me like your own daughter."

"Better. Believe me, far better. Because you are the one who will bring the Skan the glory we deserve. With my help, you will rise to rank no woman of Skan—perhaps in the world—has ever known. You will *rule*. I am re-creating me, Jaleeta. A mind as nimble as mine, a body and energy to do the things this old husk will never do again. You live in order that I live."

Jaleeta nodded.

Tears of Jade continued. "The man we need is in our net. Now it's my turn. He'll leave for the Three Territories with two more sharkers tonight. Let his needs ripen a while."

The woman in the corner broke her silence. "The attack on Gan Moondark's capitol will wait for them?"

Head down, the old woman shook her head, gray locks swaying. "The Kwa aren't the allies we need to destroy Gan Moondark. If he is overthrown by this attack, so much the better. In the end, they all work for me." She turned to Jaleeta. "For us. We use their strength, their dreams, their minds. Men are the sea, thunderous and irresistible, terrible. We sit beside Sosolassa, hidden in the darkest, stillest calm. We watch. Wait. Mystery and misdirection deflect mindless greed and brute strength. Like the moon, woman's sister ever, our light is deception, our darkness blinds and snares."

Gnarled, blue-veined hands worked painfully up the walking stick, pulling Tears of Jade erect. When the woman in the corner rose swiftly to assist, a single glance from Tears of Jade sat her back down as effectively as a blow. Shuffling to the door, Tears of Jade said, "Stay with your daughter, Mena. I will call you when I want you."

Long after the older woman was gone, the two in the cabin remained unmoving. Finally, Mena went to the window. Before she spoke, she was careful to turn her face back into the room. "She's gone. Are you all right?"

Jaleeta threw aside the bearskin and stretched luxuriously, a catlike move, enhanced by a satisfied smirk. Then she looked at her mother, and the self-possession collapsed. She clutched the cover to her again, blushing. Lowering her eyes, she nodded. "I'm all right. It was . . . not troublesome."

Mena wrinkled her nose, hurried to a tall cedar chest, its exterior completely covered with carved representations of Sosolassa. Pulling open a door, she reached inside and brought out salve. "It's a good thing your Lorso knows how to use a knife. The cuts are very thin. They'll heal quickly. Tears of Jade says you must keep them hidden, but you can't wear bandages." Her voice caught, and when she turned to her daughter, unshed tears marred her eyes.

"I should have killed myself long ago. None of this would have happened. My poor child."

Extending her arms for medication, Jaleeta spoke wearily. "How many times have we talked about this? Our life is good. Tears of Jade was cruel only until we learned to see her as our friend. You struck me often enough, when we were For. 'To make me understand,' you always said. Tears of Jade only struck harder."

Mena sniffed, dabbed at the injured arm more vigorously than absolutely necessary. Jaleeta barely flinched, then smiled. "You see? Pain. The same as I get from Tears of Jade."

"I don't understand you. I had such hopes." The mother's face crumpled to abject misery. "I punished you for doing wrong things, to keep you from harming yourself. She tortured you. No sleep. Only enough food and water to keep you alive. No one but her to talk to. I prayed for you to die, because I thought your mind would break. Now you act as if she's . . ." Mena choked to a stop.

"My mother?" Jaleeta stroked the wet cheeks bowed before her. Suddenly, the younger was the acknowledged comforter and sustainer. "I was prepared to go insane. Or die. Tears of Jade saw that. It pleased her. Only when she hurt you could she bring me to her side. But her way is the right way. I see it. You heard her. I will rule. What did I, a For girl, have to hope for? More fish? A better canoe? In my whole past life, the only memories I cherish are of you. The rest is nothing. You are the only mother I have, ever will have. But I need some time alone, now. Please?"

Stricken, Mena reached to grip the hand still lingering on her cheek. "Are you hurt?"

Rising, drawing the bearskin around her, Jaleeta turned away, hiding a slow, secret smile. "I'm not hurt. I just want to think."

Muttering, unsatisfied, Mena left without argument.

When she was gone, Jaleeta inspected her arms, as if expecting to learn something from the cuts. "Your plans died under Skan swords, Mother. Tears of Jade's plans are her secret. No one even suspects that Jaleeta has plans. 'You will *rule*.' " The latter was Tears of Jade's voice, the rasping dryness accentuated to burlesque. Even the old woman's appearance was precisely caricatured; Jaleeta suddenly bent, doddering, head wagging. She straightened. Stretched languorously. Her muted laughter was like a warning from the darkest corner of an unknown room.

Chapter 10

A wooden shutter closed the tall arrow port carved in the castle's stone wall. Stirred by the wind, the brightly painted slab shook and grumbled to itself. Stylized wolves, done in the ancient forms of Ola, danced with movement. Under the impact of stronger gusts, the irritable muttering rose to angry complaint.

Halfway across the room, backed up to a fireplace, was a massive table fully two body-lengths long; the legs were leaping salmon, carved of wood, thicker than a man's thigh. Gan slept facedown on its polished surface. A thick, white bandage rose from the back of his neck. Arms flung wide, his hands were tightly clenched. The left was red, swollen; the skin suggested something overripe. The buttoned cuff of a long-sleeved shirt failed to hide another bandage at the wrist.

Occasionally Gan flexed his fists. Every time that happened, the other figure in the room stirred. Even in the grim shadows of the stone castle, the woman's long, blond hair glowed. Under that gold-bright crown, however, beautiful features were troubled. Gan tightened his hands. His body moved in sharp spasms. The woman's own hand flew to her breast and an anguished murmur pressed past lips pursed in sympathetic pain.

That noise was enough. Gan stood as he woke, murdat simultaneously clearing its scabbard. Complete awareness was an instant behind. Embarrassment chased recognition across the sleep-muddled features.

"Neela." He spoke the name as a croak.

Her laugh was light, albeit tinged with relief. "Who did you expect? I'd have wakened you to come to bed, but I knew it was useless."

Gan's rueful smile was lopsided. He put the sword on the table and came to her, taking her in his arms. "I'm sorry." He lowered his head gingerly to bury his face in her hair. "I know you worry."

"I wish I could help."

"I do, too." He stepped away abruptly. "No. That's not true. I wouldn't wish any part of this life on anyone. The Kwa are advancing again. The Skan ships are only days away."

"You'll defeat them." Neela took his face in both her hands. Her eyes sought his with fierce intensity. "Men chosen by fate are required to accomplish, not to wonder why they are chosen. But I won't have you a prisoner of your dead mother's prophecy. If you are to bring glory to our people, do it as Gan, not her instrument."

He stroked her hair, examining it as if it were some new marvel. "Emso's got men spreading rumors among the Kwa, telling them our strength is even lower than it truly is, and that the Skan mean to cheat them out of their share of the spoils. If I can goad the Kwa into attacking without the Skan, we've got a chance. If not . . ." He turned away, fumbled with his murdat, returned it to the scabbard. "Even when the Kwa are beaten, I have to pursue. The Wolf packs are exhausted, but if we don't drive the Kwa ahead of us, they'll burn and destroy everything in their path. They'll see that we starve this winter."

Heavy pounding on the door interrupted. Gan called, "Come," and the door swung open.

A grimy, red-eyed warrior stood there. In leather armor, he carried a helmet under his arm. It was steel, with a carved wooden mask on its crown. Black and yellow, waxed to a high polish, the mask was a wasp's head. Wire antennae swayed. Pieces of inlaid obsidian created compound eyes. "Our outposts are coming in, Murdat. Emso sent me to tell you; the Kwa drums are already talking."

"You were on patrol tonight?"

"Three of us from the Fin pack. First patrol after nightfall. Two Kwa won't bother us anymore."

"You haven't slept."

"Some, Murdat. Ola has a lot of wall to watch. There'll be plenty of sleeping after the fighting."

Gan nodded. "Go tell Emso I'm on my way. Then sleep. I order it. I can't have a man like you too weary to fight."

Closing the door, the man left. Gan turned to Neela. "I won't see you until this is over. Even if we lose the city walls and we have to come back to the castle for a final defense, I'll be too busy."

"I've made my own plans." Gan's eyes widened in surprise. Not only was it unlike Neela to take such a step without discussion, her tone was unique. The word *final* came to his mind. She went on. "Coldar will be in the abbey with Janet Carter, Susan Anspach, and the Chosens. I'm joining you on the walls."

"Neela, be reasonable. The noise, the excitement . . . Coldar will need you. We agreed we'd never be captured, but nothing was said about you fighting."

"I'm a Dog woman, not some castle-bred child-bearer. I can use a bow as well as most men. I fought Mountain warriors beside you when we fled our homeland. My child is here. My husband. You have no one here with more reason to fight. Or win."

For several heartbeats, they held to each other in mutual silence. He kissed her on the lips, a gentle touch of love, a promise. "You're right; we've stood together before. We'll do it again. And win again." He swung away from her. He didn't look back.

Outside, Shara and Cho greeted him with delight. His wince as he wrestled with them, the product of the wound to his ribs, belied his confident, carefree banter. Shara was no more recovered from his injuries than his master. Cho still limped on the injured leg that kept her out of the last battle with the Kwa. When he took their spiked war collars from the wall pegs, they whined and pranced eagerness. He had to scold to still them. When he rode for the eastern wall, Shara gamely strained to take the lead. Cho followed.

The streets of Ola were too crowded with refugees to allow a gallop. Rude shelters propped against walls pushed almost to the center of streets. Children cried in the darkness, and coughs rattled harshly in the narrow ways. The dim, passing faces turned up to Gan were heavy with the desperation of uprooted people. The awful stench of the overburdened sewer system fouled the night.

Worse than that was the indefinable smell of fear. The acrid precombat stink of men was a thing Gan knew well. This was different. The weight of death and enslavement pressed against these children, their mothers, the aged, wringing out an aura Gan had never experienced.

He was sweating when he reached the perimeter street paralleling the wall. Vaulting out of the saddle, he was instantly nauseated. He leaned heavily into the horse. If he fell, his men would see, take fear. He looped an arm through a stirrup.

The wall wavered. He closed his eyes. Looking again, he exclaimed aloud as the stones merged, melted. The faces of the cave nightmare were there, flowing as they had on the malevolent sea-mound. They cried to him for help.

"Come up, Gan. We're here." Emso. Gan drew air into burning, empty lungs.

His strength stormed back. He ran up the stairs to the battlewalk. Shara and Cho bounded behind him. Warriors seeing the trio nudged each other. Backs straightened. Quivers were repositioned just so, swords loosened in scabbards.

To the east, faintly limned mountaintops carved the sky.

The Kwa forces were already in position. The haze of dying cookfires made them a ghostly mass. Emso, grizzled face drawn tight in a scowl, said, "As many as we killed last week, it looks like we hardly touched them."

"Then we'll touch them harder."

"You sound angry, Murdat. It's not like you." Emso inspected Gan with unconcealed concern. And spoke with his usual candor. "We've got men in the healing house who look lots better than you. You fever. You're pale."

As if on cue, the Kwa war drums rattled. A Jalail pack man shouted scorn. Another howled. In a breath, all the packs were howling. Discordant, wild, the baying drowned out the enemy drums.

Emso waited for the din to quiet a bit. "That's why we won't fail. The packs know you're under special protection, Murdat. We'd never have found you without your wolf-brothers stampeding those Kwa horses. By all rights, you should be dead inside that rock, you and Shara, here. If the dog hadn't killed that Kwa priest, they wouldn't have stopped fighting for a funeral ceremony. We wouldn't have had this time to regroup. Those are signs, Murdat; omens. The men know it. So should you. The most important thing we draw from you is faith."

Gan's mind seethed with images. The dream in the cave. The faces on the melting stone wall. That unbearable voice. He heard himself say, "There was a horse. Did you see it?"

"Horse? There were twenty or more. They scattered."

"Did the wolves take any?"

"I told you before. You must have been sicker than I thought. We didn't see any sign of the wolves attacking the horses. Just ran them off, left the Kwa to us." He spat over the wall. "What difference does that make? You're here. We've got a battle on our hands."

"No difference. You're right." It pleased Gan inordinately to think of the tired, beaten little horse, free.

Gan collected his wits, strode along the battlewalk. He stopped beside a dark young warrior with the green and white of Eleven West painted on the back of his barmal torso armor. The youngster acknowledged Gan, then returned his attention to the Kwa.

Gan said, "Where's Baron Eleven West?"

"Where the walls join. He says it's a weak point. Where he should be."

"You don't agree?"

The man colored, kept his eyes carefully front. "I don't know enough to disagree. But it's where I should be. Where the heaviest fighting is." With that, he faced Gan, belligerent.

"There's enough danger for everyone. I hope yours doesn't come from the Mountain People riding with the Kwa. They may be very distant cousins of yours, but they're still blood. If they come at this wall, I'll move Eleven West men, if I can."

"Don't do that." It was a protest. The young warrior swept out an arm, indicating the wall south of him. "The Kwa and our 'cousins' came through the Eleven West barony. My mother is dead. My brother and sister are slaves. My last brother, a child, is here in Ola. We owe those 'cousins.' "

Gan looked away, hand dropping to his sword hilt. "When this is over, we'll arrange to exchange prisoners. I hope we'll get your sister and brother back."

"And my mother?" The man drew his sword. Hatred distorted his youth, made him old and ugly.

"Control, warrior; control. Your enemy's as human as you. Don't confuse the excitement of combat with simple killing. That's a curse."

Thoughtful, the younger man nodded slowly. Gan moved on. Kwa whistles shrilled, and Gan signaled for the Three Territories drums to challenge. The combined Wolf voices roared with them.

The Kwa forces moved to attack positions. As at the battle in the valley, a leader stepped forward, wearing the bull's-horn helmet. He removed it, stripping off an outer cover, exposing highly polished brass, golden in the sun. The Wolves were ready this time, and their jeers and taunts rang against the Kwa's ceremonial preparations.

When the ritual sacrifice was dragged forward, the Wolves' scorn turned to helpless fury. The victim was a wounded Galmontis pack warrior still wearing his red armband. The prisoner hung raggedly on a wooden frame that extended his arms and braced his back.

A brown-robed priest slew him from behind with a beheading stroke.

Baron Eleven West was the first man to break the thick silence that cloaked the Wolf regiments. "To the death, Murdat. No Eleven West man will be taking prisoners this day. Nor live to be one."

Gan gripped the Baron's arm. "I'll be at the north end of the wall, with Baron Galmontis. Use the drum and warhorns to signal; we may not be able to see flags."

Eleven West saluted, then made a formal three-sign. "May the One in All be with us, Murdat."

Gan and Emso took their positions as the first Kwa arrows curved up from the archers leading the massed troops. Selected Wolf archers returned a slow accurate fire.

Slingers moved into position beside the defending archers, laboring up the stairs with leather sacks full of fist-sized slingstones. Shortly afterward, the hum of arm-long leather slings and the wasplike buzz of the missiles joined the more musical twang of bowstrings and arrows. The sound of a slingstone impact was unmistakable. Nothing on the battlefield had the devastating crush of solid rock striking its target.

Leclerc and Bernhardt, each carrying two wipes, lumbered up the stairs to stand beside Gan and Emso. "Where do you want us?" Leclerc asked.

"Right here with me. You prepared the . . . what did you call them?"

"Grenades. They're ready. It took all the black powder." The last was apologetic.

"You've worked hard, my friend. When we've won, everyone's going to sing about the battle-winning warrior who threw lightning with both hands."

"They'll sing that he did it for Murdat's glory." Bernhardt's soft accusation came through clearly. An arrow sighed overhead, underscoring her words. She squinted in reaction, but refused to look away from Gan.

Just as softly, he answered, "We have our differences. I'm happy that you fight on my side. At least you consider me less evil than my enemies."

Bernhardt shook her head. "The word that comes to my mind is 'unfortunate.' It's not you I dislike, it's what you must do."

Gan felt his face warm. "I haven't talked to you about your perceptions enough, Kate Bernhardt. That was an oversight. I'll do something about it when this unpleasantness has passed."

She smiled, a surprisingly bright, challenging grin. "I certainly hope so. For all the best reasons."

Everyone laughed then. Bernhardt looked shyly pleased with herself. Still smiling, she turned and walked away to take a position. Once her gaze took in the restless mass of the Kwa and their allies, she paled.

Leclerc said, "She'll be all right, Gan."

"I know. Your women have some strange ways, though."

A low rumble from the front drew them to the wall. Kwa archers were retreating, save for the ones forever stilled.

When the brass-helmeted leader lowered his sword to start the attack, the impact of the shout from his suddenly charging men sent a visible shudder through the Wolves.

Without waiting for instruction, Leclerc aimed and fired. Using the boop, he blasted holes in the first wave. The Kwa came on. Men staggered, fell, were pushed aside and trampled by those coming from the rear.

Drums blasted. Warhorns brayed. Shrill, nerve-searing whistles shrieked commands. Above all the cacophony supposed to impose order on chaos, there rose the agonized cries of the injured.

To Leclerc's right, Bernhardt fired as she had in the previous battle, weeping freely. Leclerc was astounded to see Neela running up to the battlewalk, long hair flying, bow and arrow in hand. She disappeared among the men manning the wall.

Turning, looking beyond Bernhardt, he watched the green-and-white banner of Eleven West stream to the ground inside the wall. The dying bearer held the shaft until impact knocked it free. Leclerc leaned out, fired down that way, parallel to the wall. The boop round snapped off the legs of a ladder, bringing it down in a tangled mass of broken men and timbers.

Another ladder angled up at the same point, tottered for a moment. A Kwa warrior, literally frothing at the mouth, scrambled up the rungs, forcing it forward until it slammed in place against the wall. The last Leclerc saw of him, he vaulted onto the battlewalk.

Green and blue Olan colors lifted where the Eleven West banner had fallen. Looking to the left, Leclerc saw Kwa warriors forcing Galmontis pack defenders away from a widening foothold on the battlewalk. Ululating war cries spoke of men who scented victory. The Kwa reserves took up a chant.

An arrow plucked at Leclerc's sleeve at the left bicep, broke into splinters against the wall. He thought the arrowhead glinted disappointment as it spiraled away to the ground.

He fired a few more rounds. His arm itched.

Unwilling to believe the evidence of his eyes, Leclerc reached to finger the slit material. He was fascinated by the neatness; no raveling threads or rough edges. Likewise, where the flesh was peeled back, he marveled at the startling whiteness of his own fat. Revealed muscle twitched while red flowed steadily, thickly, past the slack lower lip of the injury. His sleeve dripped messily on the battlewalk.

Bernhardt cried out. He turned to see her slump. She touched a massive raw wound above her eye. Although it bled, there was no gash. A slingstone, then. Once again, his mind rejected the overall, the general, insisting on registering specific details. Her hand, so white, so delicate. Slim, graceful fingers in fluid curves. Suddenly they were shaking. Leclerc wanted to curse the erratic tremors distorting that beauty.

He forced himself to move. Leaden legs dragged, bent under his weight. Before he'd taken three steps, Gan had the wounded shoulder in a grip that made him gasp. He looked up into features warped into a caricature of the Gan he knew. Spattered with blood. Wide eyes ablaze with inhuman passion. Teeth bared in grimace. A butcher's image, a thing given over to murder. The voice grated past blade-thin lips. "We're being overrun. The grenades. Fight. It's all you can do for her."

CHAPTER 11

HUGE FIRS BORDERED THE NARROW TRAIL LEADING NORTH TO OLA. FISSURED BARK AND dense needles absorbed light and sound, shrouding Sylah's group in dim silence. The greatest hazard in such a locale was deceptive openness. Vision extended for surprisingly long distances. A first impression was of a park. In fact, however, the bulking trunks and shaded light were a treacherous combination. Everyone in Sylah's group had seen an entire one-hundred-man Wolf pack trot off into a similar forest and rapidly melt out of sight.

Suddenly, ahead of Conway's point position, Mikka popped out of the forest onto the horse-wide trail. She looked to Conway, then forward again, hackles raised. Conway signaled Tate and Nalatan to join him. The trio drifted off the trail. Sylah and Lanta also moved aside, but they allowed the armed riders to open distance between them.

Abreast of Mikka, Conway stopped to peer ahead. Whispering, Tate said, "I smell smoke."

Nalatan nodded agreement, nostrils flaring. "Not just wood. Leather. Meat."

Distancing themselves from each other, they trailed a wary Mikka. She led them to Karda, lying flat on the bank of a fairly wide stream.

Then they heard the screaming. Animallike yelps.

Conway said, "I'll take the dogs, circle to the right. You two parallel the trail straight ahead."

Conway reached the burning cabin first. The fire was confined to the interior. A woman lay sprawled outside the back door. Smoke streamed past her, coming out of the one visible window, as well. At the far rear corner of the building, two mounted men laughingly struggled over a length of bright cloth stretched between them. One shouted, the words indistinguishable. Other men answered from in front of the building.

The scream rose again.

Conway fired twice. The horses bolted, the shattered riders bouncing out of the saddles.

Calling the dogs, Conway charged. Racing around the near side of the cabin, he broke upon a knot of confused, dismounted warriors. They stared after the stampeding horses.

Two more shots accounted for another man. There was something white and red on the ground in the midst of the group. Conway avoided looking at it. He managed another shot. Leather torso armor collapsed inward as another figure tumbled away. Exiting, the now-misshapen, high-velocity, flechette shrieked insanely.

The most aggressive of the surprised warriors spun to slash at Conway with a long, bloodied sword. Without breaking stride, Karda launched himself at the exposed throat. Momentum and Karda's crushing hold combined to lock warrior and animal in a snarling, choking crash. Then Karda was up, bounding after his master.

An onrushing Tate and Nalatan appeared. Tate was already firing. Nalatan bellowed a war cry. His parrying bar, the peculiar iron rod with its round, convex shield at its center and the heavy ball at each end, was in his left hand. The right hand spun his sword in a silver, hissing circle. Riding into the group as it tried to react to this whirlwind attack, his horse sent two men sprawling while the sword dropped another.

Beside him, Tate killed two more.

When they turned to ride back through, the sole man on his feet threw away his sword and raced into the forest. Nalatan dashed in pursuit. There was a shriek. It ended with a shocking, abrupt closure. Returning, Nalatan hung out of his saddle, sweeping the parrying ball through the forest litter to clean it.

Conway found it hard to believe the incident was over. So brutally quickly. His neck was stiff in the grip of nervous reaction. Nalatan rode to him. Tate bent to examine the small naked figure in front of the house, surrounded by the bodies of its torturers.

One of the downed warriors stirred. Another groaned, moved a hand. Conway sent the dogs to watch them.

Tate rose. At a look from Nalatan, she shook her head. "Too late. Just a little boy."

Sylah and Lanta galloped up. Barely glancing at the fallen warriors, they hurried to the house. The fire was progressing; flame darted out the left window, but the door was still clear. Conway looked in. Through flame and smoke, he discovered two more bodies. A man, still holding a shovel. Another boy. A pitiful little knife lay nearby. Conway moved with Nalatan to the side of the cabin that was shielded from Conway's first view. They found a young woman, nude. Conway remembered the men playing with bright cloth.

The Priestesses turned to the two surviving warriors. Conway said, "You see what they did."

Lanta answered, "Sylah's a War Healer. I'm a Healer. You've done your duty. Now we do ours." The small back turned to him was complete dismissal.

The warrior Lanta treated was a dog's victim, right arm torn from elbow to wrist. Conway said, "What people are you?"

Groaning, the man said, "We're Kwa." He sagged, cried out pain.

Sylah reacted with alarm. "Kwa? But you're from so far north . . ."

Conway's own stomach knotted. "You attack Ola? You came south through Harbundai?"

A hint of triumph touched the pain in the Kwa's features. "We allied with the northern Mountain People. Plague keeps the Dog People in their camps, so they can't help. We take Ola today."

"How many Kwa? What's happening in Ola?"

The man swallowed. His silence told his captors Ola's situation was bad. Nalatan bent to almost touch noses with him. "Looters. Cowards. Left to raid poor folk like these."

The man squealed, backed away.

Sylah pushed Nalatan back with gentle determination. To Lanta, she said, "Bandage him as best you can. I bound the other's leg." She addressed the Kwa. "We'll leave you food and water."

Alarmed, Lanta's patient struggled to rise. "Sharp Rock can't use a weapon. I can't walk alone. Our horses are gone. Someone'll find us." His eyes rolled, trying to see the fiery cabin without turning his head.

Conway said, "Few people live in this area. It's more likely a tiger or wolves will find you. They'll be kinder than you were to this family." Helping Lanta to her feet, he smiled at the Kwa, relishing the acid of it.

Sylah and Lanta insisted on proper disposition of the dead. Nalatan helped Conway stack cordwood for a pyre in a small shed. Nalatan looked speculatively at his friend. "You seem in a great hurry. These Kwa worry you?"

"Plenty. If they're in Ola, Gan's in trouble. Our friends are in trouble."

"They need us?"

Conway smiled at Nalatan's automatic self-inclusion. "I'm afraid so. We have to hurry."

The fire was roaring, billowing black smoke, as they left. Drooping branches of nearby firs rose and fell erratically in the heat. Conway was reminded of the helpless gestures of graveside mourners. The Kwa pair huddled together against the fiery backdrop.

On the trail, Lanta rode ahead of Sylah to be with Conway. He attempted to scold her for joining him on point, but she hushed him. "I want to help you."

"Help me what?"

"With the pain. I can see it."

Conway smiled crookedly, continuing to scan the forest ahead and beside them. "As long as you're seeing with your eyes and not using your power to See my future or past, I can't complain, can I? But you needn't worry; I'm all right."

She shook her head, the tiny features set. "You're a fine man, Matt Conway. I fear for you, though. A thing like those raiders becomes completely personal to you. Caring for those people was right and good, but you mustn't hate so. It'll destroy you."

"Would it be better if I just killed them, like swatting flies?"

"I'd almost prefer that. What frightens me is that you blame yourself. You were too late to stop those men. In your heart, you're angry with yourself, as well as them. Men like that are everywhere, all the time. You can't stop them all. You can't blame yourself if you don't."

"I'm already blamed by others for a crime I didn't commit. What's more blame to me?"

Lanta blanched. Conway averted his gaze. Had he pushed her too far?

Gently, confiding, Lanta put her hand on his. "We're two lives entwined, you and me. Between us, we must untie the knots, put together an honest, seamless weave. I think I can help you. I know I need your patient understanding. Please —be with me."

Conway swallowed hard, then, "I don't want to be anywhere else."

They crested a ridge. Several lower intervening ridges rose between them and where the embattled walls of Ola gleamed distantly in the midmorning sun. Tongues of flame wavered among the clustered buildings. Smoke caught the offshore breeze and flattened to a trailing, mournful pall. Horns and drums carried across the distance.

Nalatan, with his almost-hawklike perception, said, "There's a lull. No ladders against the wall."

"Red and yellow." Sylah interrupted anxiously, clutching at the back of Nalatan's blouse. Her fingernails left scuffs where they gathered the leather. "Gan's colors are red and yellow."

Squinting, leaning forward as though the reduced distance would make a difference, Nalatan concentrated. He straightened abruptly, smiling. "In the center, by that gleaming gate."

"Then we're in time," Tate said, shifting the wipe on her shoulder. "Lock and load, troopers. Semper Fi."

Nalatan looked puzzled. "You've said that before; Sem-per Fi. When you expect trouble. It's a prayer?"

"Whoo!" Tate clapped her hands together, laughed aloud. "Not hardly a prayer, sweetheart, not hardly. Next best thing, maybe." She laughed again. Nalatan turned to Conway, who shrugged helplessly.

Conway said, "Weapons and surprise can give us advantage. We can come on from the rear, tear these people apart before they even know we're there. What d'you think, Donnacee?"

"The sooner the better. All we have to worry about are the ridges. Crossing them will skyline us, if we're not careful."

Nalatan pointed. "There and there. Trees and brush. We go that way. It brings us in on the rear flank, not directly behind. We shouldn't be directly behind, anyhow. When they retreat, we don't want them running over us."

Conway signaled the dogs forward. Streaking across the fields, they disappeared into the first copse. A moment later Mikka was looking back.

When Nalatan and Conway pointedly closed together and rode ahead of her, Tate followed without comment. She was careful to hide a smug smile. Of the trio, she knew she was the best trained, best equipped, to deal with the situation at hand. Either man was stronger, and thus advantaged in hand-to-hand combat. Conway had some tactical experience, gathered during his service with Windband. Nevertheless, neither man had her understanding of firepower and its application. So she let them ride in front, leading and protecting.

They reached the last ridge before the approach to the city without incident. Just beyond, howling, shield-bashing warriors worked themselves into a fury.

Nalatan ducked to lower his silhouette. The simple precaution changed everything for Tate. Ahead were enemies. They wanted to hurt Nalatan. Kill him.

Sharp, nipping bites of fear worried at her resolve.

She loved him. He mustn't be hurt.

He would fight. Combat was the core of his existence. He was the core of hers.

A small voice protested that life was tentative, death ever ready. Tate dismissed it. She and her man were warriors. Born for each other, born for this moment.

No one would hurt Nalatan. She would prevent it.

The rhythmic shouting of the Kwa broke in a crescendo of hoarse voices. Discordant horns brayed.

Tate took the chaos as her own, absorbed it. Sweat bathed her face. She held the ugly, black wipe in a grip that made her knuckles crack. Nervous fingers complicated lashing her horse to a sapling.

The Kwa flank guard was a mere three men. Carelessly, they'd abandoned their post on the south side of the hill. They were fascinated, watching the spectacle of massed warriors streaming past a stone's throw away. Nalatan and Conway were on them, swords flashing.

Tate's voice was metallic. "Nalatan. Good cover for you there. They'll come at us. You keep them off. Conway, we concentrate on the main body. Your sector is from that warhorn north; use your boop. I take the south. When they rush us, I cover the retreat; my horse is the fastest."

Conway nodded, grinning. "Negative your last, sweetheart." He was already prone, elbowing up into a firing position. "You take Nalatan and go first. Without you, he'll never leave this ridge, and you know it." A hard gesture cut off her argument. "Shut up and shoot. They're at the wall."

The crack of wipes and the deeper reports of defending boops on the wall split the din of battle before Tate and Conway joined the firing. Kwa warriors spun and fell.

Tate saw a flash of gold. A helmet. The wearer waved his sword. Tate's boop round opened a hole in the crowd, short of her target. The gap closed immediately. The leader searched for the source of this new threat. At the flash of Conway's next round, the helmeted one grabbed a man and pointed toward the ridge. The messenger ran south, dodging the warriors heading for the wall.

Tate fired at the helmet again. Reloading, she saw Conway arcing rounds at maximum range. He'd done massive damage. The northern wing of the Kwa effort was visibly slowed, staggering forward. Small knots of men were sheltering together under shields, edging rearward.

Cavalry charged toward the trio from a hidden reserve to the east. Some angled to cross the ridge and deny retreat. Simultaneously, warriors on foot peeled off the extreme southern flank of the Kwa force to advance on the newly identified threat.

Nalatan's arrows took their toll unheeded. The running warriors came on, screaming, threatening, dodging from cover to cover. Tate shouted, "Matt! Take the infantry." She joined Nalatan's defense against the cavalry coming up the slope.

She saw the lance strike Nalatan. His pain, his shock, registered *in* her. She *felt* the long, triangular lance head plunge into his right side, felt his disbelief and the swift, organic taste of death.

She ran to him.

For her, the battlefield fell silent. Arrows drifted past, slow, trivial things. Nalatan wrenched the missile free of his armor, flung it down. Sweat sluiced his features. He braced to meet the continuing charge of the rider who threw it. A death-masked Mountain warrior leveled the long sword called a sodal at him.

Tate had no shot. Nalatan blocked her. She screamed. The point of the sodal flew across space. At the last instant, Nalatan leaped sideways to put himself on the side of the horse opposite the Mountain's aimed sword. For the Mountain to use it as a lance, the sodal's sharp edge would cross under the horse's throat.

The Mountain was expert. He whipped the sword over, slashed downward. Nalatan's parrying bar deflected the blow. The Mountain's speed carried him past. Smoothly, Nalatan dropped the bar and snatched up bow and arrow. When the Mountain turned to resume his attack, the arrow was already on its way. It struck just above his mouth. He flipped backward out of the saddle.

Then the rest of the cavalry was on them. Bayonet slashing, wipe firing, Tate stood side by side with Nalatan, backed against a tree trunk. Frenzied Kwa neglected their bows and arrows, charging individually with bare steel, screaming.

From the corner of her eye, Tate saw Conway being forced back. The dogs charged and retreated, savaging attackers. An incredibly tall warrior suddenly appeared, rushing at Conway. He wore a bronze helmet hammered in a bear design, as if the animal held the man's head in its mouth.

The other warriors stepped aside, hearing their champion's roaring war cry as he came in a rush. Conway raised the wipe.

At the report, the brazen helmet exploded off the man's head, flying high into the air. It spun lazily, like an obscene toy. The warrior sprawled on his back. His sword, the point stabbed into the earth, swayed back and forth as gently as a reed.

And it was over. A few shots at shadowy, fleeing foot warriors and headlong cavalry. Disbelief escalating to nausea at the full realization of the carnage. Tate struggled to calm herself. Before she could turn, Sylah was at Nalatan's side, tending to his wound. He smiled at both women. The incredible brightness of his widened eyes revealed what effort his control cost.

Lanta rushed to Conway. "Are you hurt? Did they hurt you?"

Distant, still on the tender edge of madness, Conway said, "Not a mark. Lucky. The dogs—small cuts. Look at them. Lying there. Another job done. That's all."

"Done, indeed." She pointed toward Ola. "Look. The Kwa are beaten."

Grimy, blood-spattered, face drawn into planes and angles that spoke of years lived in hours, Gan spoke to Emso. "Cavalry. Through Sunrise Gate. Give them no rest, Emso, no chance to reorganize. Kill any carrying loot or looting. No mercy. Nonlooters who surrender, treat well. See that War Healers tend them. Compassion for any who'll allow it, Emso. Kill the rest."

Fist to ear in Wolf salute, Emso turned and ran.

Huddled a few feet away, resting against Bernhardt, Leclerc watched. His throat worked convulsively. He said, "Did you hear that? 'Kill the rest.' How do we deal with this place, Kate? I thought I wanted action, excitement. This . . . this nonstop *butchery* isn't what I expected. I don't know . . ."

Bernhardt put an arm around him, consoling. He slumped into the embrace. The side of her face was hugely swollen, the right eye a useless slit. When she spoke, distorted muscles gave the gentle words a mushy sound. "You did more than your share, Louis. No one was braver. But your skills are the real future for all of us. You're our key."

Leclerc knew it was true. He felt much better. Personal risk wasn't warfare. Gan—men like Gan—could never learn that. Intellect. True command required true intellect.

Wounds and weariness were forgotten in the reunion. Wolves on the walls joined the inhabitants and refugees crammed into the city in a tumult that was part celebration of victory, part welcome to returning heroes, part thanksgiving for near-miraculous intercession. It was the latter that Gan addressed first. "You timed it perfectly, Sylah. How did you know we were under attack?"

Sylah put an arm across Tate's shoulder, pointed at Conway and Nalatan with the other hand. "These three discovered Kwa raiders at a farmhouse, and the survivors told us. They're the ones who got us to Ola in time to join the battle. Lanta and I were simply there when it happened."

Lanta said, "If not for the raiders, we'd never have known of the attack, never hurried to help. It's well to consider that good can come of evil."

Gan thought it strange she should look at Conway when she spoke, and even more strange that Conway should react as if hearing welcome news. There was a story there, Gan told himself, and wondered if he'd ever hear it. Oddly, Emso's words of signs and omens plucked at his mind.

Neela started a different conversation. "The Door, Sylah. Tell us. The quest was successful?" Grimy, still perspiring from the exertions on the wall, Neela's face shone with the certainty that her friend won through.

Sylah's chin rose in unconscious pride that would have shamed her, had she been aware. "The secret of the Door is discovered. Its new home is the Three Territories."

Wild cheers were still thundering when Neela bent to Sylah's ear to make herself heard. "You have it with you? Can we see it?"

"There's more to it than the eye can understand at first glance. We must talk. Not merely Sylah and her friend, Gan. There must be understanding between the Flower and Murdat."

"Then we wait to examine this treasure." Gan caught Neela's ill-repressed impatience from the corner of his eye. He spoke with increased authority. "The Wolves and I can only afford a bit of sleep before we march north. The Skan are arriving. Their chance to combine attacks with the Kwa is gone. I must convince them we still have the strength to defeat them."

Tate turned to Nalatan. "You get your wound tended to. Sylah . . ."

Nalatan raised a warding hand. Gan stared in openmouthed awe as Tate stopped in midsentence and waited. Of all the fine things he'd seen that day, Gan decided, seeing Tate defer to this man she called husband was the finest. Nalatan said, "Until I'm satisfied that the Flower and the secret of the Door are safe, my oath is unfulfilled. The wound is no hindrance. I ride with him." He inclined his head in Gan's direction.

Gan grinned at Tate's swift look of pride and love and worry. He turned to Sylah. "Whatever this treasure is, I'd feel much better about it if you'd keep it with you here in the castle until I've settled with the Skan."

Sylah hesitated. She and her friends had been so close, through so much. But Gan was right. She nodded. His pleased response smacked of male superiority, and it irritated.

Trapped in responsibility. The old game was ended, the new one just begun. *I will not be owned.* The words mocked.

CHAPTER 12

GAN WONDERED IF HE LOOKED AS HAGGARD AS HIS COMPANIONS. TATE SLEPT IN THE SADdle, lolling like her bones were melted. Beside her, the quiet, intense warrior-monk named Nalatan rode alert guard; it was as if the ugly lance wound in his side were a scratch. Gan admired Tate's choice.

Secretly, Gan had long wondered if any man that appealed to Tate could put up with her amazing independence. Nalatan appeared to revel in it. Gan hoped he'd get to know him.

Leclerc and Bernhardt slept in a cart, curled up like puppies. Despite their wounds and the arrival of the other lightning weapons, they insisted on making this march. Conversely, the youngster driving was far too excited to acknowledge weariness.

Conway trailed immediately behind, wrapped in his own counsel. Gan continued to marvel at the change in the alien warrior. There was a new, unapproachable quality in his manner that resisted definition. For no definable reason, Gan saw him as despondent.

All the conjecture fled at a jaw-cracking yawn. Blinking, stretching, Gan smiled to himself. After a day of fighting, then marching northward all night and into the day to this point, everyone looked more like a survivor than a winner. Concern for personal situations would have to wait.

The coast road was peaceful enough now. Not like just after dawn, when the column came across a marauding band of Kwa. Unconsciously, Gan grimaced. It was hard to reconcile any goal with executions. Nevertheless, he wouldn't consider mercy for men who slaughtered innocents for their meager possessions. Or fun. One of the looters was a boy, hardly old enough to play with a sword. At least he died fighting, unlike those that surrendered and begged for their lives. Now they could bargain with the One in All. Their bodies were properly burned.

Gan was surprised when Conway saluted those who died fighting. Gan considered his own sympathy for enemy dead a guilty secret. Seeing that behavior in Conway was disturbing.

Leclerc's reaction to the executions was a shallow superiority. He obviously considered them simpleminded vengeance. Gan wished Leclerc had the burden of satisfying the needs of the people of the Three Territories.

The thought caused Gan to look at Leclerc a bit differently. The man was no leader, but he was brilliant. There were better ways for him to exercise his skills. And, Gan thought, everyone would be spared most of this new, unseemly arrogance.

Scouts reported twenty sharkers lying offshore of the mouth of the Sweetmeadow River. South of that boggy delta was a good landing beach. Gan had never fought a battle this size with the Skan, but he'd come to know them from their piratical raids. Fierce, merciless men, who went into battle screaming the name of a dark octopus god. They took slaves in preference to any other loot. There were shuddering rumors of human sacrifice and terrifying rites.

Twenty sharkers could carry up to eight hundred men.

No one had ever seen the Skan in such strength.

Gan straightened with a start. He'd forgotten the scout boat. Peering through the trees, he relaxed at the sight of the lone sharker paralleling the coast. It came from the north at sunrise, obviously seeking the northbound column. There was no hiding from it, so Gan ignored it. Or tried to. He knew the vessel's presence sat on everyone's consciousness. Like a raven, it flowed along in its element, graceful, even beautiful. Signifying death.

Turning in the saddle, Gan looked back at the column. Carts and wagons of every description squealed, groaned, and squeaked. The noise was no problem for the exhausted warriors sprawled in them. Not even the thumps and bumps of the rough road woke many. The ruder shocks pried grumbling curses from the lighter sleepers before they resumed their slumber.

Men who'd already slept and those still waiting for their turn trudged alongside the wheeled transport. They had the careful, stolid tread of men no longer concerned with destinations. Strides were short, feet wide-spaced, arms and torsos pitched forward. Balance was everything to them; they feared the failure of energy or will necessary to rise from a fall.

On turning to the front, Gan found himself coming free of the forest, entering a fairly recent burn. Blackened stumps pointed skyward. Gan thought of decaying fingers aimed at the source of the lightning that caused the destruction. Thick brush already claimed the scorched ground, glowing with vitality, rich with mineral residue from the holocaust that opened the forest to colonization.

Gan welcomed the relatively clear area because it afforded him a view of the Inland Sea. Beguilingly blue and innocent, it seemed to hold out the distant coast and the Whale mountains as an offering. Treacherously, it failed to reveal the Skan fleet Gan knew to be hidden by the blunt peninsula directly ahead.

A rider appeared across the burn at the edge of the forest. Gan halted the column, signaling a rest. Equipment clashed and clattered as the men broke ranks and sprawled. Horses whickered in anticipation of water and grain. There was little banter or complaint from the men. Gan frowned; more than anything else, quiet defined exhaustion.

The scout's horse crossed the burn at a dispirited trot. A hazy plume of dust rose behind it. Dismounting, Gan absently stroked Shara and Cho while he waited.

He looked out to sea at the ghosting sharker and spat on the ground.

The scout came to a halt, touched his right ear with his fist in salute. "No Skan on the beach, Murdat. The boats just sit there, like they're waiting for something."

Gan managed to hide his wince. The scout's choice of words was painfully accurate. Gan was certain that as soon as the land-bound forces were prettily drawn up for battle, the Skan could weigh anchor and race south. There were beaches suitable for landing there, too. Gan would be cut off from Ola, and the city's walls were defended by a thrown-together mass of young, old, and wounded. Yet Gan had to keep Skan away from his people and their harvest.

The invaders had a maneuverability he couldn't approach. The Dog People were feared and respected for their horses and their whirling, slashing, fighting technique. Now Gan Moondark stood with his feet rooted to the earth while his enemy was poised to dart off in whatever direction he chose. Gan's option was to slog along in pursuit.

He'd gambled to find the Skan ashore, intent on pillage.

He'd lost that toss.

There was one left.

He sent for his unit leaders, telling them, "I'm going to negotiate with the Skan, if possible. If not, I want to lure them ashore here. If I fail both objectives, all units except the Ola pack and the original Jalail Wolves are to return to their own lands to defend them."

The wiry, sly-looking Baron Fir shook his head. "The Skan'll never come ashore to talk. And if you go out there, they'll kill you."

"We've no time for argument. All units hold to this high ground. Build fires, more than you need. Lots of smoke. Sound the drums, the warhorns. I want noise and activity, but don't let them actually see our men. I'm going to convince them they can't win."

Baron Galmontis, bearded and scarred, found a tight smile. "I'd rather wave a roasted lamb at a starving tiger," he said, and the others managed grim laughter.

Gan smiled along with them. "I'm going down to the fishing village. I'll need a man who can handle a boat."

Fir nodded. "I've got fishermen." He turned and called a name. A young warrior struggled to his feet and approached.

Galmontis said, "I don't like this. We can back away now, wait for them to land, then attack."

One of the Ola barons bristled. "They're not sitting off your territory, waiting to kill and burn. We fight them here, to a finish, or convince them to leave. There's no other choice."

Galmontis peered through thick brows, more bearlike than ever. "What if we lose Murdat?"

Conway said, "You won't lose him. I'm going with him to see to it."

Gan flushed. Before he could react more strongly, Conway spoke directly to him. "I'll stay in the boat that carries you out there. We'll stay out of arrow range. Let them know I have the lightning weapon. Tell them I'm the one who destroyed the sharker on the Mother River. I can do more, just as easily."

"Take him with you," Fir said.

Grudgingly, Gan agreed.

On reaching the low ground, and out of sight of the sea, Tate kneed her horse forward to Gan's side. She said, "Wash and shave before you go to talk. The troops need time to get into position, and you can't show up looking shabby. We're changing your bandages before you leave, too."

Gan opened his mouth to protest. Tate hushed him. "Don't talk back. Give me that murdat and chain mail. I'll have someone polish it. I'll clean your pennant, too. Conway will carry it."

Looking helplessly to a smug Nalatan, Gan shook his head and dismounted to tug at the heavy chain mail. Conway did the same, grinning at Tate. He said, "Amazing. Ever since you decided Nalatan was okay, you've become completely domestic."

"Dome-*what*?" Tate's eyes widened. Nostrils flared. She had Gan's red-and-yellow banner in her hands. She bent down from her saddle and shook the pennant in Conway's face. "I'll show you domestic. How'd you like this rag shoved up your nose?"

"Ah, ah, ah." Conway waggled an admonitory finger. "No time for sweet talk, you silver-tongued darlin'." He half turned, winked at Nalatan. "She'll always love me best."

Conway narrowly dodged Tate's kick. Laughing like schoolboys, he and Gan trotted off to splash in the river.

Quietly, Nalatan said, "You must be more respectful, Donnacee. The other men might not understand."

"Pooh." Tate was unimpressed. She shouted to a man to bring oil and a whetstone, then set off for another part of the river. Resuming the conversation, she said, "Of course they don't understand. They don't have any reference. But they see Murdat laughing and relaxed. It's got to make them feel better."

Nalatan chuckled. "You're one surprise after another. And you? How do you feel?"

After thanking the young Wolf for delivering the oil and stone, Tate bent to the task of buffing the chain links. "Never mind how I feel. Just stay close to me, you hear? Please?"

Instead of answering, he put a hand on her shoulder, squeezed hard. Then he squatted beside her to sharpen Gan's sword.

Shortly, standing at the edge of the Inland Sea's lapping waters, Gan raised a white flag. A sharker replied in kind. Oars reached out from it, like legs extending from a surface-skimming spider. Swiftly, the boat came to within arrowshot of the beach. It whirled about to lay broadside to. The oars rose to vertical in unison, dripping silver droplets in the sun. Anchors splashed at bow and stern. Shields hanging on the sharker's sides gleamed with savage designs in brilliant colors. Rocking easily, mast and picket line of oars swaying back and forth, she quivered, eager for battle.

Softly, in a voice thick with admiration, Gan said, "Look at her, Matt Conway. She lives. No less than a war dog, or one of our Dog horses."

Conway agreed, more apprehensive than appreciative. Still, watching the carved white bear figurehead nod glaring contempt for the world, he felt the vessel's life, too. It reminded him of Stormracer, and the way the horse believed an army couldn't stand against him.

Gan and Conway ordered their dogs to stay. Nalatan and Tate took position beside them. Tate put a hand on Conway's forearm. "If this operation goes in the dumper, you concentrate on the white bear, there. I'll get Leclerc and Bernhardt up here with me, and we'll give you long-range cover. If we start firing, you head for shore double-time, okay?"

"If I can. I won't leave him."

He refused to turn, waiting what seemed a long time for her response. At last she said, "That's what I was afraid of, I guess." She sighed. "Saddle up, then, sucker. Keep your dumb butt down."

Conway continued to look straight ahead; it was the best way to hide the tight smile pulling at his lips. Tate spoke to him exactly as she would another marine.

He decided it was a privilege he could gratefully forgo.

Conway settled astern with Gan's pennant aloft. Gan stood forward, back against the mast. Four Wolves muscled the boat into deeper water.

The young Wolf at the tiller was deathly pale, eyes startlingly wide. His movements were mechanically correct, but his attention was fixed on the ominous array of vessels. Conway understood entirely. At the moment the rocks of the bottom stopped grating against the hull and they were seaborne, he was amazed to discover how much larger the sharker had grown.

Moments later he spotted archers, arrows drawn to the head, between every shield.

Behind him, ranged in an arc of sound, the hidden war drums of the Wolves bellowed. Conway hoped against hope the Skan heard defiance, and not desperation. As he did.

Chapter 13

Amidships on the sharker, a Skan warrior lifted aside a shield that portrayed a stylized bear paw. Gan turned to look at the young Fir fisherman. "You see where they want us?" The youngster nodded, swallowed hard.

Conway said, "Don't let them talk you away from the side of the boat, hear? I want to be able to see you at all times."

Gan nodded absently. He faced the land, looked at the pennons bright against the forest. Beyond the trees rose the distant Enemy Mountains, patched by snow. He stared past them, let his mind go free.

There was time for nara.

Calm. He listened to his heart, breathed slowly, closed his eyes.

Conway watched his friend, fascinated. Gan's color changed from pale tension to ruddier relaxation. Nervous fingers hung slack. The head swayed, somehow surmounting the stiffness of the wounded neck. The muscles around Gan's closed eyes loosened, easing his expression.

When they were almost in contact with the sharker's hull Conway said, "Gan? We're there," and was, as always, impressed by Gan's instant awareness.

A man leaned over the rail to extend a hand. Geometric red-and-black tattoos appeared to sleeve his arm. Accepting the lift, Gan rose easily to the rail and dropped onto the deck. He listened to the slapping sail and swirl of water as his companions pulled away. A salty dryness filled his mouth. He willed it away.

The man who limped forward to confront him was naked from the waist up. His loose trousers came to midcalf. Soft leather boots rose to a finger's breadth of them. Knives in scabbards hung outside of each boot. Additionally, he wore a short, massively thick sword hanging from a wide belt. His dark hair was worked into tight braids. Gan didn't count, but was certain there were eight. That would match the number of tentacles of the convoluted octopus tattooed on the man's torso.

"My name is Lorso," the man said. His voice was deep, one that shouted unquestioned orders to be heard over storm or battle's roar. The plain features, although young, carried the dark, ingrained patina that only years of wind and sun can produce. Pale blue eyes, almost gray, invited a staring match. He went on. "I know you defeated the Kwa. They're fools. They should have waited for us. Still, they weakened you, or you wouldn't be here to negotiate."

"The Kwa are fools for attacking us at all. Few will see their homes again."

Lorso smiled. The face of the cruel raider showed for an instant. "You sent Emso and most of your cavalry after them. I have almost eight hundred men on these boats. We can land anywhere. You've blinded yourself. Your hand is almost useless. Your head sits uneasily on your neck."

"Uneasily, but firmly. You thought to lure me away from Ola's walls. I kept you in place while my Dog warriors march." Gan saw the twitch of an eyelid. He sensed an opening. He also knew that nothing is as perishable in combat as surprise. He pressed his argument. "The plague is over. You've had a sharker follow us up the coast. You know I've dropped off groups of men all along the way. They can't stop your landing, but no matter where you come ashore, you'll be attacked. There's a reserve hidden in the forest outside Ola. I'll be north of you. They'll be to the south. You'll get ashore, but whichever way you turn, you'll have Wolves on your back."

Gan let Lorso digest what he'd heard, then resumed. "You've never seen the lightning weapons of my friends. Two of them with such weapons were on the ferry on the Mother River. Your sharker attacked them. The lightning weapons destroyed it. Many Skan won't see their country again. How many will never return from here?"

Lorso was almost rigid with suddenly increased tension.

From the corner of his eye, Gan noted the postures and attitudes of the crew. Openly hostile, they didn't seem poised to attack. There was a signal, then, something they knew to watch for.

And Lorso was poised to send it.

Turning his back, ignoring prickling shoulders, Gan forced himself to wave easily for Conway to approach. Then, facing Lorso again, Gan said, "We have nothing to negotiate, Lorso, except the lives of your men. My people are moved inland; you'll find no slaves, no loot. My Wolves wait for you. The lightning weapons are ready."

The sailboat thudded against the sharker. Gan leaped aboard.

Lorso's right hand crept upward. Now the crew stirred. The signal involved that right hand, then. Behind him, Gan snapped his fingers, and was rewarded by the scraping of metal on metal. He knew it as the sound the lightning weapon made when prepared to speak. A tremble of anticipation raced up his spine.

The Wolf sailing the boat heeled it over in a tack that made the rickety mast groan. The rough sail cracked full, threatened to split.

Behind the bucking, straining little boat, the sleek lengths of the sharkers rocked in careless, indolent dance. Gan thought of cats watching a mouse.

Yet nothing happened.

The sharker that trailed the Wolf column up the coast joined the fleet. A signal flag skipped up the mast of Lorso's vessel, and the new arrival rowed alongside.

Gan watched from the water's edge. Turning to his friends gathered behind him, he said, "I told Lorso two lies; that Dog warriors were riding to Ola, and that we left units on the coast trail. I think he believed me. Anyhow, the scout captain's trapped. If he tells Lorso he didn't see our numbers shrink—which you all know didn't happen—he has to wonder if he failed, in which case the Skan fleet possibly lands in an ambush. If the captain says he did see changes in our numbers, Lorso has to strongly suspect he's looking at a hard fight for little gain.

We can hope he'll leave. Nevertheless, I want two-man scout teams along this beach all night. If the Skan come ashore, the teams are to retreat silently and warn us. We'll fight from concealment on the high ground, not down here on the flat. Silence all drums until you hear the command drum. Two men out of every ten awake at all times, sharing the watch. All men and animals fed by sundown. Cold rations. No fires, no lights. I'll sleep with the Jalail pack in the center of the formation." He turned back to the sea, oblivious to the activity behind him.

Later, Tate, Bernhardt, Leclerc and Conway sat together looking out over the black silhouettes of the sharkers. A sinking sun flamed rotund summer cumulus. The peaks of the distant Whale Coast were broken teeth against dying fire.

Bernhardt broke the silence. "You think they'll come in the dark?"

"No." Conway hoped he sounded more confident than he felt. "These Skan come for loot, and Gan hit the right note when he told them there was nothing here for them. No loot, no shoot. They'll go home."

"When?" Leclerc packed doubt into the word.

"Now!" Tate jerked to her feet, almost falling in her excitement. "Look. Sails going up. Everywhere."

Distant shouts came from the ships. Brazen horn signals followed. A drum set an oar pace. More horn blasts shuddered, eerie now that the boats were almost invisible. Stern lamps pierced the darkness, golden against the blackness of the sea. The bobbing lights formed a pattern, four lines of five. They moved in order toward the extinguished sun. Then they disappeared.

"Oh-oh." Tate was immediately apprehensive. "I don't like that. We don't know which way they're going."

Leclerc thrust himself against the night. "They could be going to Ola? Getting behind us? What about Carter and Anspach?"

"Lanta." Guiltily, Conway added, "And Sylah."

Tate put her hand on his shoulder. "They're just giving us a quick twitch. A parting shot."

Each joined in the general mumble meant to reassure. Leclerc decided to turn in. Bernhardt made the same move. Tate, Nalatan, and Conway remained, sitting so close together both men were actually in contact with Tate's shoulders. Again, there was a long silence. This one was different, however. It resonated between the trio, a pregnancy of nebulous, unspoken questions. The baffled need to articulate *something* was almost palpable.

It was Conway who left. Nalatan said, "Donnacee, what's wrong with him? Doesn't he realize Lanta loves him?"

"Of course he does."

"Then why this distance? Why are they so sad all the time?"

She shrugged, the movement gentle against his shoulder. He put his arm around her. She continued to stare after the vanished fleet, speculative. "I don't know, lover. Look how long it took me to realize I was in love with you. It's not always easy."

"I worry about him. A good man, very much alone. Sometimes I think he'd do anything if she'd accept him."

Tate twisted, faced Nalatan. In the night, she could see no expression to help her interpret the last remark. Defensively, she said, "That had a nasty ring to it, as if Conway might do something disloyal. I hope I heard you wrong."

Nalatan made no effort to soften his words. "When a man's dying of thirst, he won't ask the cost of a drink. Conway would never hurt a friend. Intentionally."

Tate's intended furious retort turned sour in her mouth. She swallowed hard, eating words. This man she loved renounced his vows, his entire life, for her. If anyone knew the cost of loving another, he did. She kissed him, telling herself everything would work out. It certainly had in her case. Nalatan took her in his arms. She forgot Conway and Lanta.

CHAPTER 14

THE SOFT GLOW OF TWILIGHT FLOWED ACROSS THE INLAND SEA. BELOW THE CASTLE'S JUTTING balcony, water polished to the sheen of jade carried small balancebars. Sails, lazing under an easy breeze, still drove boats fast enough to purl silver wakes.

Neela broke the long silence holding the group standing around the small table. "I love to watch water curl away from the front of the boat. A silver ribbon that comes from nowhere, glitters, and disappears."

"A bone in her teeth," Tate said, and her gaze was far away. Twice, Neela said, "What?" before Tate heard her. Stammering at her blunder, Tate sought Conway's reaction. His reassuring smile indicated she hadn't compromised their secret past. The other strangers to this world—Janet Carter, Susan Anspach, Kate Bernhardt, and Louis Leclerc—were equally undisturbed. "It's an old expression," Tate said. "We say the boat looks like she has a bone in her teeth."

Neela laughed. "A strange thing to say, especially when you call the boat 'she.' So aggressive sounding. Your boats are always 'she'?"

"Of course. They're beautiful, courageous, thrifty, and no man ever really controls one." Tate winked at her friend.

When the general laugher quieted, Gan observed dryly, "They can be very distracting, as well. We're here to determine what to do about these, not admire the view." He pointed at the table.

Besides his wife and the strangers, there were Sylah, Lanta, Nalatan, and Emso, only that afternoon returned from pursuit of the broken Kwa. Everyone stared at the exposed secret of the Door.

Books.

Fastening his attention on Sylah, Gan went on. "Since the beginning, Church law requires any writing from the time of the giants be surrendered to Church and burned in the Return ceremony. Despite being cast out by the new, false Sister Mother, all who know you understand you're still Church. You're the Flower, destined to find the secret of the Door. But your secret is forbidden. Books are learning. Learning caused men to challenge the giants and be destroyed. It's evil."

Carter, thin and intense as a knife, said, "Knowledge isn't evil. It isn't good. It just *is*. How it's used is what makes good or evil."

Lanta said, "The Apocalypse Testament tells us, 'The foulest deeds are done in the guise of the fairest favor. Truth told by dishonest tongue is the liar's poisoning.' "

Diffident as ever, Anspach couched her argument in more personal terms. "Reading is learning, Gan. You've said yourself how much it's going to help you administer the Three Territories when we've trained more people to read. What's in these books will bring better lives to all your people."

Instead of answering Anspach or Carter, Gan stared hard at Conway, then at Tate. He said, "I'll ask you for the truth now, Donnacee Tate. You exchanged blood with Clas na Bale. You would never disgrace him by lying to me. Of all your tribe here, only you and Conway have seen inside these books. Is that true?"

Tate nodded, wary.

"How, then, do the others know what's in them? How can they say these will help me? Is there witchwork here, Donnacee?"

Tate's mind raced. If she looked to Conway for reassurance, Gan would think they had a story between them. If she tried to explain about the world that died, and the crèche that brought them to this time, Gan would assume she'd gone mad. Or more likely decide they were all witches.

Clas na Bale would never shame Donnacee Tate. Therefore, she must speak the truth.

"We all know what's written in the books." She paused, heard slow inhalation by her friends. She also saw the way Gan and Emso edged hands closer to their weapons. Emso was frightened and angry, a dangerous combination. Gan was rigid. Nalatan looked as if he might be ill. Behind Gan, Shara and Cho sensed the force of the sudden tension and lumbered to their feet. Tate continued. "We don't know everything that's in them, of course, but we all have some of the information. In our tribe, we're made to know about books. No one knows everything. Some know more than others. For instance, among us, Leclerc knows the most about making things."

Gan interrupted. "He's helped us build. He destroys as easily. The black powder is a blessing. It saved us many, many lives. But it is not an honorable way to fight." He stole a guilty glance at Sylah. "The Violet Abbess quoted to me from the Old Book of First Church. She said the Old Book tells that the giants struck men with 'roaring fire that devoured high buildings and smoke that killed without being seen.' I think of those words when Leclerc's black powder kills."

Tate plunged ahead. "You should think of those things. You must always think of the cost of war. Your mother prophesied that your destiny is to bring glory to the Dog People. You have. Your life isn't over, though. There are other people who would join you. They need your strength to resist those who would destroy the Three Territories and debase Church. And you."

"I want no kingdom. I fought Altanar and the Barons of Harbundai because they gave me no choice. I—"

Tate spoke over his protestation. "Want it or not, you are Murdat. Choice? Will the Skan stay away? You never hurt the Skan. They come to kill and pillage anyhow. To the south, Kos hopes to make slaves of you. To the east, Windband prowls like wild dogs. What choice will they offer the Three Territories?"

"We'll fight them if we must." Gan was sullen. That alone showed how well he understood the danger.

Pushing her advantage, Tate said, "You know you must. We'll help you win. With the knowledge in the books. You don't have to touch them. That way no one can say you're—forgive me, Murdat, but I must use the forbidden word—no one can ever say you're involved in teaching."

Gan winced. Emso tugged at his murdat.

Nalatan took a tentative half step toward Tate, then caught himself and made a three-sign. "The thought is forbidden, Donnacee. To speak that word as act, to suggest one human do it to another . . ."

An agitated Leclerc ignored Nalatan's religious concerns. "What gives you the right to tell Gan I'm the one who'll use these books? We're already in trouble just because you brought them here. Now you want to make me the heavy, the guy out front. You want someone to bring science and technology to this world? Do it yourself."

Clearly surprised by Leclerc's reaction and puzzled by the strange, unknown words, Gan immediately moved to restore peace. "I heard Tate's words, Louis. I heard respect. No one here is in trouble. I sense great opportunity." He smiled suddenly, unexpectedly. Walking away from his friends, he drew a candle from one of the pyramidal racks standing about the room. He put some tow into a ceramic box holding smoldering coals and blew on it until he had a flame. Gan resumed his remarks as he moved about the room, touching light to the remaining candles. "Cloaked in every opportunity is disaster. Consider the power of these small, unmoving, unspeaking books. Church is split. The dark religion, Moondance, rushes to take advantage of the confusion. Sylah and Lanta are outcast. Each of you who accompanied Sylah on the quest has suffered loss, been tested to the limit of endurance. Nations, too. Mighty Kos is crippled. The all-conquering nomads of Windband were turned back for the first time. A terrible price has been paid, just so we can look at this treasure. What more avalanche do we unleash if we use it further?"

"Return." Emso's voice was stone against stone. "The One in All will strike, as in the beginning. Return the books."

Sylah stalked to the table, face set, long, black robe swishing anger. "The books are the secret of the Door, promised by Church for generations. I found them. I keep them."

"*You* keep them?" Emso's blunt, lined features mottled, twisted. "Flower you may be, Priestess, but Church herself you are not. Whatever power is in these things belongs to Church, not one person. Murdat must decide for you. Without him and the Wolf packs of the Three Territories, you have nowhere to hide."

Sylah faced Emso, imperious. Gan almost exclaimed aloud. She was transformed into the woman he'd met when their lives first entangled. Sky-blue eyes glared. Thick, black hair flowed and swirled, angry as a cat's twitching tail. He'd forgotten how commanding—and how beautiful—she was. "I know my debts. I know my enemies. I will bring Church to its rightful place."

Conway said, "Not alone, Sylah."

Sylah clearly heard the gently chiding tone under the declaration of loyalty. The haughty manner eased. With a thankful glance at Conway, Sylah looked back to Emso. "Forgive me. I overstep. I see beyond the Three Territories. I see Church as she was, always reaching, always bringing better life to more people. Such a goal needs a leader, Emso, and I am the Flower. I wanted to find the Door, but I never wanted to be more than my own person. Now I'm obligated to bring the power of the Teachers to the world."

Emso's anger softened to his normal expression of general disapproval. He sent an irascible glance at Gan before answering Sylah. "Everyone around here worries about doing good. I say we Return the books because if we don't, every fool who can put together a gang of thieves is going to come trying to steal this 'treasure.' More fools will want to kill the anti-Church that holds the 'treasure.' That accounts for all the fools but us. And we're too few to rule everyone else. Unless your books can stop armies. If someone's going to put a sword in my guts, I want it to be a fight over my land or his, not those silly things." He flung a hand out at the books, then hurriedly made a three-sign, as if the unintended closeness might contaminate. Chin up in defiance, he finished, "I can't even read, Sylah. And proud of it. It's the way."

Softly, Gan said, "I ordered that all my leaders learn reading. We'll discuss your pride later." Emso's glare at the table made it plain where he placed the blame for his predicament.

Gan settled into a large wooden chair against the wall, far from the candles. The faint glow that reached him cast his eyes as dark and sunken. The fist bracing his cheekbone pulled his mouth into an unintentional snarl. Above him, the carved head of the chair featured a scene of a cougar defending its deer kill against a marauding pack of coyotes.

Tate was considering the symmetry of the images when someone touched her shoulder. Turning, she found Sylah indicating she wanted to talk on the balcony. Tate followed, then waited patiently while her friend organized her words.

"You were very brave tonight, Donnacee. No one else wanted to tell Gan what he already suspected. Clas would be proud that you honored his blood."

Tate said nothing, thinking only of the way she'd shaded the truth, bent it to fit her needs. Nor did she confess to the most confidential find behind the Door. Only Tate and Conway understood the importance of the small red notebook that confirmed the existence and general location of the other crèches constructed by the world that had destroyed itself.

Sylah said, "I know you could have told him more than you did. I've had my suspicions about you people from your distant land all along. The feeling's grown stronger ever since we opened the Door. Perhaps someday I'll have my curiosity satisfied." She laughed, then, but as cheerful as the sound began, it trailed away, ended on lingering melancholy.

When Sylah continued, she averted her eyes, looked out to the starred night. "I speak of suspicions because I want you to see I'm not afraid to acknowledge them. Suspicion isn't necessarily distrust. You're my friend. I'm yours. Our goals haven't always been the same. They'll differ again. But I love you as my sister, and I turn to you in need." She paused, gathering strength. "Everything that was said about the danger of books and learning was true. Leclerc's knowledge helped Gan end many lives. What other destruction have I put in Leclerc's hands? Or the hands of others, less good-hearted?"

"Knowledge and wisdom don't always grow on the same tree. People will use whatever they can to get whatever they want. Wisdom would have all of us wanting a mutual good."

"The goal of Church. The mutual good of all."

"Not anymore." Tate turned to rest her elbows on the balcony rail, facing Sylah and the room. Silhouetted against the warm candle-glow and movement of the intermingling group in the room behind her, Sylah was an enigmatic, vaguely mysterious figure, her features obscured within the confines of her hood, her hands tucked into her sleeves. Tate went on. "As long as the Harvester rules as the new Sister Mother, Church will be no more than another piece in the unending power game. If Church is to be a force for universal good, it starts here, Sylah. With you."

"I can't do it. I'm not strong enough. All I wanted was to be free, Donnacee. You know that." Sylah moved forward. In the ground-sweeping robe, she appeared to float across the balcony. A pale hand, appealing, fluttered in the dark, lit on Tate's sleeve. "I want to be safe from orders and obedience. The Door was supposed to free me, give me power to reject the restrictions men put on me, that Church put on me as a Chosen. I'm more of a prisoner than ever. My Abbess, who chose me and helped me, made me into the Flower. Why didn't she just tell me? She couldn't know what it would mean. She wouldn't do that to me, would she? If she loved me? She did love me, Donnacee. I know she did. Why didn't she understand what would happen? I want to go to my husband. I want to be me, not the Flower. Why can't I have that much peace?"

Taking the white, agitated hand in her own darker grip, Tate spoke soothingly, yet with stern purpose. "Look around you. Gan, living out a prophecy. You think he doesn't want to walk away from all this trash and raise a houseful of little Gans and Neelas? Leclerc? Poor man wanted adventure, and now it's got him by the throat so tight he can't spit. You see Carter, Anspach, Bernhardt? The first of the new Teachers. Elated. And scared stiff, 'cause they know how dangerous the job is, and there's no one else to do it. We're all thrashing around like cats in a sack. At least you and Gan have missions. Your freedom can't come until you've made the way clear for others. Oh, you could be free, easy enough. All you have to do is walk. Go to Clas. But you'll never be free inside. Not until you do what you know you have to do."

Sylah wept. There were no sobs, no sniffling. Eerily, on a face of unbearable sadness, tears simply welled and flowed as springwater.

Choking, Tate hugged her. They stood that way until Sylah pulled back. She dabbed at her eyes with a handkerchief. She managed a wan smile, put on a scolding manner. "My mind and my conscience tell me you're right. My heart wishes you'd dry up and blow away."

Tate's answering laugh was confiding, binding. "I'm not that easy to shake. I hang on pretty good."

"My sister."

Before Tate could respond, Gan was requesting they return. He stood beside the chair now, arm draped across the carved back. He spoke to Sylah. "Once again, we run together, Sylah. Something reaches for me from these books. It frightens. It excites. We will make a world, or make a failure in such glory as none has ever seen. Who is with me?"

Shouts of camaraderie echoed from the timber and stone. Laughter and excited conversation swelled among them as they moved to the dining room.

Sylah spoke to one, and then another, steadily falling back until she was alone at the rear.

Church training in reading reactions exposed many things to her.

She saw the angry uncertainty lurking behind Emso's forced smile. She saw the infinitesimal glint of smug self-congratulation in Leclerc's overenthusiastic endorsement. She saw the quick admiration for Leclerc and covert eagerness in the faces of the three quieter women of his tribe.

What tore at her, however, was the covert glance between Tate and Conway. In that swift look a lie was born, a bastard that shamed them, hidden from all others. Every War Healer knew the surest cure for a corrupted wound was cleanliness. And exposure to the sun's healing, to the light brought by the One Who Is Two.

Deceit was an insidious infection that poisoned friendship. Deadly. It must be exposed.

Chapter 15

The rattlesnake whirred brittle threat.

Wedge-shaped head aimed like a dart, it watched the advancing man.

The snake was massive, its muscular length compressed inside the shaded shelter of a rock overhang. The sinuous S-curve of its forward third sat a full handspan above the dry, sandy ground. Fifteen rattles vibrated in a furious blur, as troublesome to the eye as the heat waves shimmering up from the sunbaked earth.

The snake's fangs were as long as a boy's little finger. Behind them, stretching along the roof of the mouth, were the poison sacs. On striking, the mouth would gape, jaws opposed. Impact collapsed the sacs, turned the hollow fangs into conduits for venom.

The snake's toxin reservoirs were full to bursting. Hunting had been bad for some time. The snake was famished. It was hot. It was very irritable.

The man squatted just out of range.

There were other men, far behind the squatting figure. The snake ignored them.

White clothes reflected sunlight that hurt the snake's eyes. Since it relied as heavily on the heat-seeking organs in the pits in its head as on ordinary vision, the heavy, flowing robes confused that function, as well. Heat and sight images were both muddled, indeterminate.

Flickering rapidly, the snake's scent-gathering tongue clearly defined this slow aggressor as man. Strangely, there was a scent of snake, as well. The tongue worked even harder, stabbing aroma from the air, trying to assign a value.

Most troublesome of all, however, was the white figure's refusal to close the minute gap that would eliminate indecision, guarantee an effective strike.

Vibrations tingled across the snake's belly scales. The snake-man thing was making noise. In the snake's world, noise normally meant seek or evade. There was no retreat from the present position.

Flexing its scales delicately, edging forward one grain of sand at a time, the snake gained a tiny advance. With escape impossible, attack was demanded.

A white turban covered the man's head. On his chest, dangling from a silver chain, was a large, polished silver disk. The man's eyes glittered with the intensity of the snake's cold pupils. Still, the man smiled. He bantered, practically baby talk.

"You're afraid, my fat, old brother. You don't recognize me. I am Moonpriest. My mother, the moon, gives me dominion over my brothers who lose their skin, who are reborn as was I. All men must acknowledge me, and so must you." He aimed the disk to throw sunlight directly in the snake's eyes. The animal flinched. Rattles chattered wildly.

Pressing against the ground, it gained another hairsbreadth advance.

Moonpriest crooned, "I need these savages to understand my power. I dislike bringing you pain, but they must see you defer to me. Behold, I have brothers with me." Moonpriest reached inside the robe. When he removed his hand, he held a pair of rattlesnakes. They were almost the size of the old one coiled in the shade. Both rattled and coiled instantly. Moonpriest hurriedly stuffed them back into the leather carrying sack against his chest.

"They hate the noon sun as much as you, my brother." Slowly, Moonpriest spread his knees as wide as he could. With both hands he clutched the robe material at his knees, drawing it tight. Waddling awkwardly, he advanced. Eager murmuring rose from the crowd. Moonpriest's smile flicked to scorn, returned to rapt concentration. Sweat runneled the dust on his brow and cheeks.

The snake struck. Too fast to actually see, its speed cheated the eye.

Fangs punctured the taut white robe between Moonpriest's knees with an audible snap. Moonpriest winced in spite of himself. Behind him, a loud shout, part horror, part amusement, split the hot, bright day.

Caught in the material, the snake thrashed heavily. Grabbing it behind the head, Moonpriest raised the reptile high. The tail dangled below the level of his knees. It took all his strength to control it. The turban was knocked askew. Moonpriest straightened it before turning to face the crowd. There were at least a hundred River warriors and the five Windband nomads. Women and children strained to see past the men.

A hush fell as Moonpriest approached, thrusting the enraged, writhing snake ahead of him. Remnant drops of venom dangled from the needle tips of the fangs, liquid gold that caught the sun and turned the life-giving light malevolent.

A similar color marked the twin penetrations in Moonpriest's robe.

Stopping perhaps three body-lengths from the crowd, Moonpriest dramatically brought the gaping head even with his face. Smiling, beatific, he bent to the animal. He kissed the rough, scaled head.

Moans of disbelief and fear moved through the crowd. In the trained voice of a public speaker, Moonpriest said, "Go, my brother. Tell all our brothers that your ruler, Moonpriest, son of the moon, is here to bring eternal life to all the River People who come to him." Gently, Moonpriest lowered the snake. Aiming it toward some brushy shade, he released it.

The snake hesitated. None of this was within its experience, its instinctual references. Then it fled. With silent muscular sinuosity, black diamonds rippling beautifully against the brown of scales and earth, it whisked out of sight.

Rushing forward, cheering, the River People crowded around Moonpriest on three sides. Everyone was careful to avoid the area where the snake disappeared.

"Bring me Saris now," Moonpriest said. The hubbub dropped to silence. A part in the gathering allowed two warriors to advance. They carried a blanket by the four corners as a sling. Saris lay in it. His skin was pallid. Individual black hairs stood out starkly. The warriors deposited him at Moonpriest's feet.

"I'm here, my son." Moonpriest knelt to put a hand on Saris' forehead. "You have been my major support among your people. I come because you and your people need me. If my mother wills it, I will make you well."

Saris tried to speak. Moonpriest pressed a hand to the bloodless lips. There was no telling what the fool might blurt out. The crowd was completely under control now, and it must remain so.

Saris' wound was far uglier than Moonpriest expected. The blade had opened the chest and slashed across the right bicep. Fortunately, it hadn't cut major blood vessels. The problem was infection. The stench was harder to bear than the sight. Moonpriest gulped loudly.

Saris' hot, bright eyes widened in alarm.

Moonpriest hurriedly feigned dabbing at tears. "How it hurts me to see you injured," he said, careful to keep a clamp on Saris' mutterings. For the merest moment, Moonpriest longed to pinch the nostrils between thumb and forefinger, press the heel of his hand against the chin. He imagined the rolling eyes, the air-starved, heaving chest. It would serve the incompetent fool right. No one gave Saris permission to make his own arrangements with the pagan Skan. Foul savages.

Fool Saris. Useful, though. Moonpriest sighed. He'd try to save the man. Meanwhile, there had to be a way to capitalize on it if the treacherous lout died.

Moonpriest bowed his head.

The River People murmured at such intense religiosity on behalf of one of their own.

Straightening, Moonpriest forced himself to inspect the wound again. Then, loudly, "My mother says it was a great sin for you to deal with the Skan without my permission. She knows what is in your heart, however. She instructs me that, if you repent satisfactorily, you will heal."

Saris' eyes grew even brighter. He reached to push weakly against Moonpriest's silencing hand.

There was no choice but to let the man speak. Moonpriest glowered as the

River warriors crowded closer to hear. He felt himself suffocating. How could he have failed to notice how they reeked? Fish and sweat and muck. Moonpriest waved his arms. The closest Rivers edged away.

Saris said, "I don't want to die."

Moonpriest held back a sigh of relief. If the man was going to be simply banal, there was nothing to worry about.

Straining, fighting for words that came in breathy gusts, Saris continued. "If Moonpriest . . . truly new Siah . . . speak to moon. Save me."

Moonpriest rose, ignoring a knee that cracked indignantly. To the warriors who'd brought Saris, he said, "Take my son to my camp. I will pray for him."

The warriors lifted the sling. Saris groaned. A grizzled warrior in the forefront of the crowd, body mapped with scars, frowned across Saris at Moonpriest. "The High Chief of all River People knew of Saris' plan. He approved. He also looked at Saris' wounds two days ago. He said Saris will die. So say I."

Saris' groan rose in pitch, became a wordless beseeching. Moonpriest gestured for the bearers to remove the injured man. To the graying warrior, he said, "Be careful, my son; you're assuming the power of a goddess. She alone will decide Saris' fate."

The warrior spat at Moondance's feet. "The unseens in Saris' wounds will kill him, not the moon. And don't call me your son. I am Vessash, a River warrior and Church believer, no child of false religion."

Anger warped Moondance's face. "You challenge my mother? Make her angry and she leaves, takes her powers with her." Suddenly suggestive, Moondance put on an evil grin. "You and Saris aren't friends, are you? You'd like to see him dead."

Vessash's grim contempt wavered. Still, he held Moonpriest's gaze. The other tribesmen edged away. When Vessash answered, what was meant to be defiance carried a tinge of bravado. "I argue with all who speak of alliance with the Skan or following a false Siah. Saris himself sent away our one War Healer. The One in All is testing him. I say you and the moon can do nothing for him. Witchwork with a snake won't save a man's life. Once Saris dies, we'll know you for what you are."

"He won't!" Moonpriest shouted. "I have the power. I'll save him." Aware of his own words, Moonpriest stopped abruptly. Frightened eyes swept the crowd. The shift in their attitude was palpable, a psychic eddy that laid a cold hand on Moonpriest's back. They were entranced. The child of a goddess had promised to save a tribesman.

Vessash was waiting when Moonpriest's gaze returned to him. Moonpriest found a smile, fashioned words. Hadn't he said Saris must repent "satisfactorily"? Only his moon mother could judge Saris' repentance.

Vessash struck directly at that argument. "You say you have the power. Saris lives or dies by your hand."

Later, Moonpriest was sitting alone on a bluff, staring down a long slope to the river. Peering around anxiously, afraid he was truly alone, he was relieved to see his Windband escort preparing the evening meal and attending to chores. Affection for them surged through him.

It was sad that affection—*adoration* was a better word—came from such lower orders. Moonpriest faced the river again. In the end, he was always alone.

Conway had understood. Treacherous, back-stabbing Conway. Moonpriest's head roared with rage at the name. All the while Conway worked with Windband, pretended to be a true help, he plotted with lying, soulless *slaves* to destroy the god. It was sickening. Indeed, sickening. Wretched Conway, spreading disease. Disease and lightning weapons denied Windband the treasure of the Door.

Furious, Moonpriest struck his thigh with his fist. Unintentionally forceful, the blow hurt, jarred his thoughts back to the problems of the present.

That other warrior, the old, ugly one—Vessash, that was him. Witchwork, he said.

Saris had to live. But how to manage it?

By evening, Saris was weaker. He craved water. One of the nomads rode out into the dry brush, making no comment. Moonpriest was sure he was deserting. He'd never trusted him; not really. The scar that twisted the left side of the man's mouth into a constant expression of disparagement was indicative. Moonpriest told himself he should have tested the man long ago. Too late now.

Dusk was a soft touch on the heat-tormented landscape when the scarred nomad returned. He extended a handful of leaves to Moonpriest. Moonpriest's continuing suspicion showed in his sidelong manner, his abrupt, "What's this?"

"My mother called it hurtweed. She made a tea for us whenever we were injured or couldn't sleep well."

Moonpriest took the bundle without comment. Features twitching angrily, the nomad watched his ungrateful leader walk away, then yanked his horse around and retreated to tie the animal to the picket line.

The proffered medicine presented Moonpriest with yet another dilemma. If it was, in fact, a well-intended remedy, he still couldn't be sure what constituted a proper dose. The stuff might kill Saris. Accidentally? On purpose?

Betrayal was everywhere. Treachery.

Moonpriest built his own fire, cooked his own meal. The Windband escort nervously watched him eat. He heard them whispering. About him. A god always knew. Their clumsy nonchalance was a shouted lie.

Moonpriest wouldn't suffer alone if Saris died. If they were lucky, they'd be executed in the River way, bound and thrown into the river to drown. Unfortunately, the tribe wasn't above entertaining itself with some painful, if unsophisticated, torture.

Moonpriest would die as a witch. He didn't know what that entailed, but it was sure to be horrible. As a religion, Moondance understood that fear was the very fuel of spiritual life, and a witch was the most feared of all things.

Saris drank the prepared tea greedily, the same way he'd been drinking water all evening. Moonpriest watched him anxiously. It was full dark when he noticed the change. Despite the cooler night, Saris perspired mightily. His breathing turned shallow, albeit regular. He seemed relaxed. Too relaxed? Moonpriest detected only a weak, tentative pulse.

Down at the River's shore camp, a drum sounded. Startling at first, it quickly assumed a compelling restful beat, exactly two-to-three against Saris' pulse.

Moonpriest settled to a sitting position. Slumped over, free hand fisted under his chin, he fixed his gaze where the moon must rise. Evening's stars turned from uncertain specks to hard lights while he concentrated. The moon saved him once, claimed him as her son. Moondance must conquer, and for that, her son must survive. Nodding to himself in the darkness, Moonpriest agreed with his assessment.

Mother allowed them to torture him, though. She let him die. Revived him, to prove his truth and his worth.

He remembered that torment. The exquisite agonies. Days and nights.

Desperate for distraction, he released himself to the drum, to the solace of unchanging rhythm.

Hypnotic.

A word from another time, another place.

Murky, frightening fragments of memory oozed through his mind. There was a place of logic, once. That world transformed reason into argument, confused thought with emotion. Confrontation. Discrimination. Terrorism. Murder.

Violent, racking shivers slammed through Moonpriest's body. He fell into trancelike sleep. The corner of a new moon pierced the horizon.

Chapter 16

After a cautious approach to Moonpriest's resting place, the Windband escort stopped in dread. Moonpriest lay utterly still beside the unmoving Saris. One of the nomads groaned.

The leader of the group rammed an admonishing elbow to the midsection of the complainer. Fear drove the blow too hard; the complainer staggered back.

Another nomad said, "Moonpriest lives. The grass at his mouth moves with his breath."

The leader edged closer.

Moonpriest was curled in a fetal position. His chin pressed hard against his fists. Aside from the dead white hands, his color seemed all right. Deliberately, the leader scuffed a boot across the gritty soil. The noise had no effect on Moonpriest. Coughing was equally unsuccessful. So was calling that grew louder until it approached shouting. Desperate, the leader dared to prod Moonpriest's shoulder.

And leaped back as if burned.

Moonpriest's eyes flew open, focused uncomprehendingly on those of the leader. Moonpriest mumbled, blinked owlishly. Joints cracking, he rolled to a sitting position. Words croaked harshly. "She came to me. My mother. Spoke."

Unnerved, the leader stammered apology. His companions stood away from him. To a man, they all clasped their moon disks.

What Moonpriest saw was men hiding behind Moondance's symbol.

They'd doubted before. He'd seen it. It almost made him sad. How could they hope to understand the honor of being born again as the moon goddess' only child? They understood nothing. Appreciated nothing. Wasn't Moonpriest the one who personally prayed over all the plague victims and saved their lives? These men saw others who questioned Moonpriest struck down by the goddess' lightning. They saw the faithful rattlesnakes kill traitors. Despite plague and battle defeat, Church failed to thwart the true religion; Moondance and Moonpriest still controlled Windband. And these piddling ordinaries thought they could doubt her son, then cower for safety behind a wretched piece of silver.

Moonpriest widened his eyes, hissed, made a rattling noise with his tongue against his teeth. He extended a darting, snake-striking finger, pointing.

The warriors flinched. Moonpriest's laughter pealed across the new day, sent a small bird into chirping, jerky escape. Sobering, he said, "All will be well. Ordinaries doubt. Gods forgive. If it suits them."

The term *ordinaries* lingered in his mind. He turned away from the escort to consider it. It never occurred to him to describe others that way before, yet he'd done it twice already this morning. Immediately on waking from the dream-time with his mother.

How wonderful of her. To give him the exact word, the exact way, to consider those he was reborn to lead.

A nomad's tight voice collapsed the moment. "Saris lives?"

"Certainly." Moonpriest turned to examine the wounded River, smothering a grunt when his stiffened limbs objected. Saris' breathing was no better than before. The pulse fluttered. The awful infection smelled as bad or worse.

Moonpriest steeled himself, pulled aside Saris' blanket. Gagged, swallowed.

And suddenly realized he had no idea whatever of the instructions his mother gave him in the dream.

Panic struck like ice water falling on him from a clear, untroubled sky. Unable to move or speak, he gobbled inarticulate turkey sounds, flapped his hands in meaningless circles. The nomad warriors retreated in unison.

Lurching to his feet, Moonpriest stumbled away from Saris, from the camp. He howled his misery, tore at his robe, thrashed through scrub growth heedless of scratches or rips in his garment. Only when branches threatened to dislodge his turban did he take notice. He grabbed it, holding it securely to his head. Even in this extreme, he refused to expose the pink nakedness on his skull where Sylah had operated.

When he mustered coherent thought, he cursed the moon goddess. This was worse torment than any physical pain. Women. All alike. Vessels of disappointment. He trusted her. And now this.

He lashed out at the passing brush with his fists. He kicked and wailed.

Slinking from cover to cover like coyotes, his escort followed, whispering to themselves of the wonders of divine madness. The morning was cool, but sweat glistened on them.

Moonpriest stumbled over the goat carcass, sprawling headlong onto all fours. Scrabbling about, blinded by the turban that slipped over his eyes, he managed to flail himself free of it. The first sight to greet him was a pulsing mound of maggots.

Choking, Moonpriest threw himself to the side, staggered to his feet. He backed away from the repulsive mess, hands uselessly pushing against the air. What he couldn't allow himself to do around Saris he was unable to prevent now. He fell, crawled like a beast, retching until tears wet his cheeks.

The leader of the escort ran to where Moondance sagged, panting, against a large boulder. The man offered water from a brightly painted, incised gourd. The stopper was a grinning skull. Moondance ignored it until he realized the carved material was bone. Then he was reminded of death. The goat. The obscene, squirming life clustered under his nose. His stomach churned.

The nomad took one look at Moondance's changed expression and fled.

Moondance drank greedily, spat, drank again. Little by little, he felt physical control returning. Filth, Moondance thought; why must he be surrounded by filth? White was his color. Purity. The white of moon, of silver.

The maggots were white.

Moonpriest shuddered, hugged himself, rocked from side to side.

Something whirled across his mind. Something awful. It wouldn't be identified.

He ground his teeth in frustration. *Filth.*

Other words, unclear, struggling to surface. Then, with a clarity that made him exclaim for joy, he had them. *"From what is foul will come that which is strongest. Utmost purity springs up from meanest desecration. Just so, even an enemy is a wonderful tool in the hands of the skillful."*

The words of his mother. He remembered. There were more.

"Demand excess. Only in excess so catastrophic it destroys can true creation originate. Only in the ruination of excess can humans learn the beauty of moderation. Lead them. Force them. To salvation. To me."

Moonpriest understood. His love for her humbled him. He dropped to his knees, prayed a quick thanksgiving. Then he hurried back to the campsite. Storming past the befuddled escort, he showered them with orders and curses.

After a swift bath in the river, Moonpriest changed into a fresh robe and attended to Saris. The River was conscious by then. As one of the nomads clumsily spooned dabs of porridge into the man, Moonpriest explained to Saris what must be done. "The bad flesh must go, Saris. It's full of evil. If that evil claims your body, I lose my grip on your soul. Of all the warriors who fight for me and die and join me in the moon to be reborn again with me, only those who die of evil magic will be denied their rightful place. You must let me cleanse you."

Saris' eyes glowed against the gray-blue color of dying. His words crept past pale lips. "What if you fail? What if I die while you try to save me?"

"Then you belong to me. So long as you trust me, I will save the soul, even if I lose the body. But I know I can save that, as well."

"Help me." Saris' clutching hand was a claw.

Moonpriest inhaled deeply, took Saris' hands in his own. "The sun is sometimes my mother's fiercest enemy, but we must use him. We must have sunlight on the wound. On the clean wound."

"Clean? Unseens claim more of my flesh every day, Moonpriest. No man rots like me and lives." Crystal tears slid along his cheekbones.

Moonpriest took a firmer hold on Saris' hands. The man was weak unto helplessness, but there was no sense in being careless. "I must arrange for the things that feast on evil to eat the evil."

Incomprehension kept Saris calm for the space of a heartbeat. Then he was frantic. He struggled valiantly until his paltry energy was expended. He attempted to scream for help, managing a hoarse wheeze. Then, defeated, "You mean maggots."

"Perhaps it would suit you to let the evil unseens claim your soul. As surely as they'll claim your life."

Saris freed his hands, pounded the earth with fists too weak to raise dust. In the end, he turned from Moonpriest, drew his face tight in a mask of disgust and denial. "Save me," he whispered, hating the words with his voice. "Save my life."

"You'll stand at my right hand when I'm called to my mother." Moonpriest dabbed cool water on Saris' brow, rose, and stepped back several paces to the waiting escort. He fixed each in turn with a stony gaze. "Do as I say, and we live. Fail me, and your children will be cursed for seven generations. I want no River close enough to see Saris. You, on the end; go to the dead goat. Get a double handful of maggots in a basket and bring them to me. You, the one who brought me the hurtweed; I want more of it. I'll want more every day."

The leader asked, "Can you heal him, Moonpriest?"

"I said it, didn't I? Carry out your orders."

The escort scattered.

For the next week, Moonpriest slept beside Saris. During the day, he sat with him, supervising his feeding, adjusting his position so the sun had best access to the wounds. Several times a day, Moonpriest bathed the unaffected skin around the injuries. Flies by the thousands landed on his hands, his face, on Saris' exposed flesh, all volunteering to add to the numbers of maggots. Almost frantically, Moonpriest shooed them off. Some slipped past, nevertheless, and contributed their translucent eggs.

From the very first, Moonpriest forced himself to watch the slimy little creatures go about their revolting work. Concerned only with continuing life, the heaving, liquid-looking mass obliged with gluttonous industry.

Moonpriest was startled and gratified by the rapid improvement in the wounds. Where there had been nothing but rot, clean tissue appeared. The maggots ignored it. Moonpriest constantly dabbed at the exposed good material with a solution made from leaves the herb-wise warrior brought him. Soon there were patches of flesh large enough to be covered by bandages. Gritting his teeth at his proximity to the maggots, Moonpriest regularly massaged the area of the injury. Saris complained of the pain. Moonpriest ignored him; he was sure blood flow was important to the healing.

Several times a day, Moonpriest inspected his tiny herd of helpers for signs of pupation. A twig launched the nonproducers unceremoniously into the surrounding brush. During the night, mouse wars erupted over the unexpected bounty.

Moonpriest had the escort set live traps for the mice. His rattlesnakes gorged in their turn. Fat and content, they were even more docile than normal. When Moonpriest was forced to go to the limit of his camp's perimeter to meet with yet another of the unending River delegations, he carried the reptiles looped along his outstretched arms. The tongue-darting heads rested on the back of his hands, where gold and jet eyes glittered malignant contempt at all who spoke to Moonpriest.

All things contributed to all other things.

In the long stretches of the night, Moonpriest found himself more and more drawn to contemplation of that concept. Whatever one learned prepared one to learn something more. All contributed to all.

And Sylah and her noxious companions had escaped from a library. Church blathered for generations about "the treasure of the Door," and in the end, it was mostly vidisks.

Moonpriest wished it had been only vidisks. What could be more useless than video in a place where a wall plug, mined from a long-forgotten city, was nothing more than a source of reusable copper? No one had heard of TV for at least five hundred years.

The Door hid more than vidisks. Books. Sylah had books. She also had six people from the cryogenic crèche who were literate.

Saris was going to live because of knowledge. Divine knowledge in this case, Moonpriest thought, although the secular knowledge of the young herb-wise nomad was welcome.

Continuing to reminisce, Moonpriest considered that when he'd ordered the library behind the Door incinerated, there were two reasons. Primarily, it was to kill Sylah and her companions. The other reason was to destroy any learning not controlled by Moonpriest.

This episode with Saris proved the validity of the second point. The moon made him know the maggots would eliminate the foulness killing Saris. The nomad showed him the herbs that protected the unhealed flesh from further infection.

The fed maggots fed the mice that were fed to the snakes.

All contributed to all. To serve Moonpriest.

In teaching how to heal one insignificant fool, Moonpriest's mother taught her son the ultimate lesson.

This new, sin-raddled world, with its unending violence and terror, was unready for uncontrolled knowledge. It was wrong that Sylah, that spawn of hypocrite Church, should have access to learning, much less control it. The control of learning was a divine right.

Moonpriest must control.

To control, he must possess. To fully possess, there must be no one to contest him.

Moonpriest scratched names in the dirt at his feet.

Sylah. Conway. Tate. Leclerc. Bernhardt. Carter. Anspach.

Scuffling about in a weird, irrythmic dance, Moonpriest erased the names. He laughed happily, softly. It was as if they'd never been. As their world and its arrogance were destroyed, so must the impious be.

Obliterated. All.

Chapter 17

Lorso stood with fists clenched on his hips, head back, looking up at the semicircular seating of the men's council room. Its proper name was the All. It was a name never spoken outside those walls.

Cedar logs of immense girth, set upright in deep graveled trenches, formed the oval building. Directly behind Lorso, the inner sides of ten logs were carved into faces. Half again as tall as a man, each was artfully sculpted in such a way that all appeared to stare at the same jaggedly irregular rectangle of black obsidian. Roughly knee-high and twice that long, the block lay in a curved swath of pure white sand that reached from the base of the wall posts to the first row of the banked seats. The stone was obviously a speaker's stand.

Lorso, barefoot on the obsidian, was the focus of the audience as well as the frowning glare of the abalone shell eyes of the carvings. Firewood blazed in iron braziers directly in front of each face. Dancing flames sent swirling, changing colors across the iridescent shell. The unblinking eyes lived. Judged.

Lorso ignored the carvings, the false eyes, and the heat of the braziers. The ancestors behind him were long dead, gone to the Deep Calm. Sacrifice on an altar would propitiate them. All forty of the Navigators were here. Alive and angered. If they decided sacrifice was needed, it would be a very different matter.

"It is not enough for Skan warriors to die bravely," Lorso shouted, loud enough to end the grumbling murmur of the Navigators. He swept the entire curve of the audience with a belligerent stare. "Skan always fight well, die well. Did the Navigators name me Slavetaker so I could send the Skan to die and prove their courage? Where is the man who questions the courage of the Skan? Of me?" He surveyed the listeners again.

A shaven-headed older man in the front row got to his feet with studied deliberation. Lorso protested vainly. "Please, Domel; it's not necessary to stand. The formality . . ."

One dignified glance stopped Lorso. Domel said, "Tradition is always important. As I intend to explain." Domel advanced slowly. The blank expression of the weathered face suggested an inner hard darkness as stark as the obsidian speaking block. At his knees and ankles, tight against embroidered woolen blouse and trousers, were bracelets of clam shells. They were painted in a bright rainbow of colors, all in the geometric patterns of the Skan. Lorso stepped down, into his sandals. Shedding his own similar footwear, Domel took the block. His voice was rough, strong.

"Lorso speaks of the reasons for battle. He should. The Skan sent nearly eight hundred men to destroy the Three Territories. They outnumbered the sorry Wolfpack scraps Gan Moondark rounded up to man the walls of his forts. The Three Territories is wounded, bloody from the fight with the Kwa. Yet Slavetaker listened to the boasts of Gan Moondark and called off the attack. The largest force the Skan ever sent to war failed its mission."

Pausing, Domel made a slow, sweeping gesture to indicate the carved faces ranged behind him. Then he pointed at Lorso, not looking at the man. "What would the ancestors say?"

A wind of condemnation rushed through the gathering. In the ruddy fireglow, the confused, active mass of their brightly embroidered, appliqued, and beaded clothing created an image of fire in itself. A tentative shout of "Guilty!" rose. It was repeated, louder. Another voice attempted to argue, and was shouted down.

Raising a hand, Domel silenced the growing hostility. He smiled. Strong white teeth contrasted with the eroded features. Contempt clanged in his words. "What children you are. The Skan fight for gain. We prove our courage, our skills, in combat. What idiot spawned this notion of dying for honor? If a man chooses to fight another for glory or to right a wrong, that's the way of men: we all know it to be a fool's way. But a tribe fights to survive, to destroy enemies. And to prosper. As the first ancestor taught us: 'What we have, we defend; what we want, we take.' Trade is good, pillage is better. But the Skan consider cost. Always. Lorso understands."

When Domel paused for breath, the gathering managed only a sullen murmur. He continued. "The Skan prey on the lesser creatures, as the first ancestor showed us. Now, listen to Lorso."

When Domel was seated again, Lorso removed his sandals, resumed his place on the block. Much more conciliatory, he said, "There were no slaves, no products near the coast. Only Wolves. The Kwa betrayed us, attacked early. They were crushed. They hurt the Three Territories, but not enough. Now we join forces with the more dependable River People and Windband. In the spring, Windband and the Rivers help us destroy Gan Moondark. We will harvest his people and their possessions from north of Destroyer Mountain to the Mother River."

Another man rose, older than Domel. His gray hair was braided in the traditional eight tentacles of Sosolassa. "The Skan have never shared their loot. Skan take. Skan keep." He sat back down.

Soberly, Lorso nodded agreement. "The Skan also use small fish as bait for larger fish. Once the Three Territories are defeated, we've no more need of Rivers or Windband. No one suggests we not attack them."

Cheers replaced the earlier disapproval.

At the doorway, as Lorso was hanging his sandals on the accustomed peg and putting on his ordinary boots, Domel joined him, saying, "The survivors of the sharker destroyed by the lightning weapons say you did well to avoid landing at the Sweetmeadow. I've never seen Skan men more shaken."

"The man escorting Gan Moondark to my vessel carried a lightning weapon. I recognized it from descriptions. But for that, I'd have taken the so-called Murdat. Did the survivors of the Mother River attack tell you this man Moonpriest controls the lightning, just as the strangers who serve Gan Moondark? The Skan must have that power."

"Such a thing will never be given. How do we steal it?"

Lorso smiled tightly. "They say you were the greatest Slavetaker the Skan ever had. I believe it. You'll be the next ancestor."

Domel made a face. "I'm in no hurry to be anyone's ancestor. But your answer: How do you mean to get us the lightning power?"

"We send a sharker to help coordinate the Rivers and Windband. They'll learn about Moonpriest's weapon, how he uses it. As soon as the Three Territories are beaten, they'll steal it."

Domel strode along, head bent in thought. They were exiting the fort by then, passing through the gates. As always, Lorso admired the work there. The horizontal planks were hewn square, thick as the span between a man's fingertips and elbow. The vertical boards were a third as deep, but equally wide. Iron drift pins as big around as a wrist secured the opposing timbers. The gates themselves were tall enough for a man on horseback, with plenty of overhead to spare. Above them rose a squat, six-sided tower, its wooden sides fireproofed with copper sheathing.

The tower, and designated points on the wall, were always manned. Surprise was a favored Skan tactic. They had no intention of being its victims.

Lorso's gaze went to Jaleeta's home. He stared at the window. The translucent sheepskin covering mocked him, a blind white eye that refused to reveal any of the secrets hidden behind it.

They were nearing the market. Wind from the sea caught the scent of cedar chests, of new wool, of herbs, oiled leather, furs. All swirled in his mind, all dragged his consciousness to the maddening, soaring delights of Jaleeta. The cedar and wool scents conjured the rough textured blankets from the chest by her window. Among the herbs were those she used to scent her body. He imagined the indistinct whiteness of her, a spiritlike vision of temptation sprawled on dark furs, the leather straps of her bed sighing as she turned to him . . .

"What's wrong with you?"

Lorso jerked back to reality so sharply his neck literally cracked. Domel looked at him with genuine alarm. "Have you heard anything I said?" Suspicion touched his features. He stepped back. "Are you ill?"

Lorso massaged the back of his neck. "I was thinking how to provision for the trip to the Mother River."

"What?" Domel fumed. "Just ask the man who sent the last one. Are you sure you're all right? This isn't the first time your mind's caught the out tide."

Feigning indignation, fighting free of Jaleeta's presence within him, Lorso said, "I've got many things to think about."

"Think about me talking to you. I said Gan has six people with lightning weapons. We could send a spy among them. Create some dissension. Steal a weapon."

"Even if we could approach those people, which isn't likely, there's something about Moonpriest we have to consider. If he controls lightning as Gan's people do, why is there no religion around Gan's six? It must be because Moonpriest is more powerful. No one worships Gan or his lightning people. Everyone says the Rivers are abandoning Church for Moondance. Moonpriest already commands Windband. All fear him."

"Including you?"

For several steps Domel tried to pretend he wasn't aware that Lorso was no longer beside him. When he turned, Lorso was waiting, pale but composed. Several bystanders took one look at the two men and left hurriedly. A vegetable seller slowly sank out sight behind his stacked merchandise. Lorso said, "A name, Domel. Who says I fear any man? I'll bring you his head."

An infinitesimal smile moved the corners of Domel's mouth. "Come, walk with me again. Can you find a crew as bold as yourself? How many—even among the Skan—can live beside one who controls lightning and not be afraid?"

"They needn't be unafraid. They only have to be patient and daring. All Skan are those things."

Domel remained mild and considerate. "I'm sure we can find the men we need. But you know the For are building sharkers? That seagoing landscum, Wal, has several. And good crews, I hear."

"If they try to interfere with us, we'll sweep them off the sea. We have the best men, and greater numbers."

Domel grinned widely. "I'm sure you can do it."

They talked a while longer, desultory conversation. Lorso thought he detected impatience growing in Domel. He almost smiled, acknowledging that if impatience existed, it was his own. The sun was already far to the west. Soon Jaleeta would be in his arms again.

Domel made a small joke. Lorso forced a polite laugh. At the same time, he stretched luxuriously, relaxing tension, savoring the smooth pull of eager muscles.

Tears of Jade, leaning on her walking stick, eased open her cabin door. The light of the single candle by the fireplace fell far short of the waiting darkness outside. With words dripping the hurtful sympathy of sarcasm, she said, "Is the hour too late, poor Domel? Are we unable to find our way in the dark?"

"Mind your mouth." Domel's utterly silent approach brought his answer shockingly close. Tears of Jade stepped back too hurriedly, almost lost her balance. Domel smiled, crossing her threshold. He said, "It goes well? They're together?"

Tears of Jade made a noise in her throat. "The girl enjoys her work entirely too much."

Domel chuckled. "If you could remember as far back as your own youth, old woman, you'd be envious, not worried. We have the mother; the daughter will do whatever she must."

"Jaleeta's a strange child. Sometimes I wonder if I really know what she's thinking."

"Doubts? The harpoon is thrown, the whale struck. It's too late for questions. What have you done?"

"Don't raise your voice." Tears of Jade was calm, almost dismissive. "The plan will work."

"The future of the Skan depends on it." Domel lowered his face until his nose was practically touching Tears of Jade's. "If he learns what we've done to him, he'll watch the gulls strip our bones clean."

"Yours. Not mine. I'm his mother."

"You're no mother. You claimed him when your sister died to make him your hand. He's your will, your muscle."

"As Jaleeta is my will."

"But you wonder."

"Not about what she'll do. I only wonder what she's thinking when she's not carrying out my orders. She does everything almost too well."

Domel visibly relaxed. "You, nervous. I never thought I'd see it. Well." He lowered himself into one of the cabin's chairs. A yellow mask with impossibly long, black fangs and black hair jutted out from the wall directly above him. Empty, red-rimmed eyes searched the distance. Domel ignored it. "Stormtime comes. If I'm to convince the Navigators that Lorso should head the crew that goes to negotiate with Windband and the Rivers, I must begin soon."

"Has Lorso mentioned sending a sharker to the Mother River?" Tears of Jade took a chair close to Domel.

"Today."

Tears of Jade stroked her chin. Domel looked at the bent, bone-thin finger, the talon nail. He turned his attention to the candle. The woman said, "He'll do what the Navigators require. See to them. What about the Nion? You trust him?"

"Of course not. I'm sure I've identified his price. He's leaving his son as hostage. It seems safe."

"You told this Nion what will happen to his son if he betrays us?"

Domel rose, smiling. "I said I'd give the boy to you."

Tears of Jade bobbed rhythmically, making a strange, coughing sound. Domel's eyes widened before he caught himself. He'd forgotten what it was like when Tears of Jade laughed. He judiciously composed a conspirator's smile. Tears of Jade waved him out. The ancient woman's sounds of amusement followed Domel into the darkness, played cold games across the flesh of his back.

Chapter 18

Lorso paled. "Captain the sharker? Leave here?" The phrases were pleas, rather than questions.

Domel carefully kept a sympathetic, yet firm, expression. "The Three Territories landscum are still cautious about settling near the coast."

"I can't go to the Mother River. Not now. Not when . . ."

"Not now? What makes this time different?"

The secret nearly escaped. Jaleeta's name rose in Lorso's throat. He choked, stammered, "Stormtime comes."

"You are Slavetaker. What the Navigators decide, you do. It's not like you to argue."

"Slavetaker. Yes. And the child of Tears of Jade. We'll see what my mother thinks of your plan." Lorso's head was down, chin tucked in. He looked through his brows.

Domel noted that the ugly red spots on Lorso's cheekbones were gone now. More, the wounded look was replaced by an analytical squint. Domel saw death in that enclosed, retreated face. He felt his own age, a heaviness in his blood. His groin pulled tight. "Not my plan, Lorso. The plan of all the Navigators. It was thoroughly discussed."

"Not by me. Slavetaker sits in all councils."

"There was no council. It was agreed on in general conversations."

Lorso straightened. His look at Domel was speculative. "Naming me to both these tasks was someone's idea. I'll find out whose. For now, we talk to my mother."

Domel tried to make conversation as they walked. Lorso refused to speak.

Pushing open the door to Tears of Jade's cabin, Lorso walked in. Bearskins covered the windows, closing out all light from the sunny day. The old woman sat before a brazier, the four iron legs cast to resemble fanciful dragonlike creatures. In their clenched jaws, they held a fire pan glowing with coals. A swinging arm suspended a small pot directly over the heat. Syrup-thick fumes boiled upward from its depths to pool against the rough slabs overhead. Ropy tendrils extending from the pulsing mass sinuously explored the ceiling.

Without looking up from the crimson glow of her fire, Tears of Jade said, "Close the door. Quickly, before you ruin what you've already disturbed. Sit on the floor by the bed, both of you." She reached into a bag woven of dried grasses lying at her feet. Falling on its side, the bag spilled out wrinkled, nasty stuff. Tears of Jade poked through it with a crooked finger, selecting for the little pot. Lorso noticed how, with the door closed, the smoke now sought escape through the window immediately behind himself and Domel.

Just at the edge of hearing, Tears of Jade talked to herself. "Sosolassa, help your slave. Help me combine the things you've shown me, shown my mother, shown my grandmother. I pray to you, father of storms, stalker from the Deep Calm."

In the darkness of the cabin, the polished masks on the wall glowed softly. Stuffed animals, some in natural poses, watched the proceedings with polished agate eyes turned rubious by the coals.

Lorso sucked in his cheeks, bit down hard on the folds of flesh. This was the stuff of the god, and he knew from experience that Tears of Jade had limited control over such things. Strange potions and powders came of her dealings with the Sosolassa. Never a word was said of how those things were used. Still, Lorso grew up watching Tears of Jade's enemies become her allies. Except for those who wasted and died.

There was something evil in those fumes. Lorso felt it, fought it.

Beside him, Domel wobbled noticeably. "The smell," he said. The words dragged. "I don't like it. It's in my head. Not uncomfortable. It frightens. But I feel good. Friendly. You understand? I want to talk to you, Tears of Jade. You're a good person. Much nicer than everyone says. I like you. When your son and I were talking—"

Tears of Jade reached out to rap his shins with her walking stick. Domel yelped, then said, "You did that because you like me too, don't you?" He turned to Lorso. "Isn't it wonderful how we all like—"

"Shut your mouth." Tears of Jade struck again, harder. To Lorso, she said, "Take the pot outside. Quickly. Don't breathe near it."

When Lorso came back in, Domel was shakily taking down the bearskins. Sunlight bursting through the window's translucent covering formed a rectangular pillar of light in the residual smoke. Lorso watched it coil, rise and fall, infinitely changing and fascinating. He reached into the beam, stirred it with his hand, laughed happily.

He remembered something irritating. Angry. He was very angry.

No he wasn't. Everything was fine.

How entertaining the smoke was! He paddled the drifting nothingness gently. His hand was a fish. It grew a mouth.

The crack of the walking stick on his forehead was like a whip. He sat down hard outside Tears of Jade's door, both hands trying to restrain a growing knot at his hairline. Tears of Jade was standing over him, holding Domel by the ear like a naughty child. She held a bowl in the other hand. Crumbled leaves smoldered in it. Releasing Domel, who promptly sprawled on the grass, grinning foolishly, she sniffed deeply of the new smoke, then thrust it at Lorso. "Breathe. Deeply. Quickly."

Lorso obeyed. The stuff tingled, tasted bitter. He thought of the precious powder that sometimes made its way up from Kos, the stuff called dried orange skin. Then Domel was inhaling the smoke. For a moment, Lorso wanted to laugh at the older man; his shaven head wobbled on his neck like a shiny squash on a vine.

Then Lorso's anger came back. Jaleeta appeared in his imagination, her face maddening with her mocking, challenging smile. As he watched, she diminished, drawing away.

Tears of Jade handed Lorso the bowl, indicating he should dispose of it. He started into the cabin, thought better of it, and set it on the bench by the door. When he turned and straightened, she was waiting. Her hand went to the knot on his head, her practiced touch gentle. "Pain sharpens the mind. I saw you joining the smoke. It frightened me. Nothing must touch you. Nothing. My son."

He looked into the sere, shriveled face. In those ancient, worn features he saw what no one else had ever seen. Love. For him.

He knew the malice, the enmity, the avaricious need for power that lived there. All the Skan knew that face as well as they knew the taste of the sea. Only Lorso knew of her love.

Normally, that face of love nullified fear, soothed frustration. In it, Lorso felt enfolded, protected.

Not this time. Sweat ran down his face. "Something bad has happened." The words came lamely. He longed to take her hand, hold it to his cheek.

Tears of Jade said, "Tell me what's wrong. We've always solved your problems. Let me help you again, my son."

Lorso faced Domel. It was easier to maintain a proper attitude with another male as the target of his emotions. "The Navigators had a secret meeting, excluding me." He summarized the decision, ending with, "Leave the alliance talk to someone better suited. Please, Mother; let me stay here."

Domel, impassive, shifted his attention to Tears of Jade. She spoke to him. "Why was my son not allowed to participate?"

"It wasn't a meeting. Men met informally, discussed the matter. All agreed. They came to me, asked me to instruct Lorso. There was no conspiracy. What was done was done from respect. It was done to assure the glory and survival of the Skan."

Tears of Jade was quiet a long while. Lorso grew more anxious at every heartbeat. Then the woman said, "The decision of the Navigators is the mind of the Skan. The first ancestor said it. My son, Slavetaker, knows this."

Lorso appeared to shrink. Tears of Jade went on, lecturing gently. "Slavetaker is ordered. Slavetaker may resign. There is precedent, and there is no shame."

"Then I'll resign. The Navigators cheated me. Slavetaker fights. Others talk. Thank you, Mother. You show me the way. Thank you." Lorso's voice caught.

Tears of Jade said, "No hurried decisions." She took him by the arm, turned him toward the harbor where the graceful sharkers rocked in the sun like hook-billed birds of prey. "Take a small boat out where the Skan find their thoughts. Listen to sea and sky. Fast. Two days. Then we talk, then you decide."

Lorso opened his mouth to speak. Tears of Jade's look stopped him. She pushed him toward the harbor. Head down, he shambled off.

Domel waited until Lorso was well out of earshot. "This is very tenuous. We're trying to land a whale with a trout hook. I know the smoke softens the mind, makes us hear your thoughts as our own, but I always worry that one time it won't work."

Tears of Jade carefully emptied the pot. She ground the residue into the earth with one tiny foot. "You should worry more that someone may find out how we work together. The tribe would be angry to learn how we influence them. As for this plan, it's sound. It has risks. For the glory of the Skan, no risk is too great. Lorso will do exactly as I wish."

"You control us all, don't you, old woman? Have you ever heard of the Bear Cult among the northern Kwa? They line the walls of their ceremonial house with bear skulls. Some men even keep bears as spirit guides. Like pets, they are, live in the man's cabin and everything. Great silverbacks. I knew one such man. His bear never left his side, did everything the man told him. One day the bear killed the man. Ate the man's head. Gone. Kwa take bear heads, the bear took a Kwa head. Frightened everyone so much they moved the village. We caught them before they got their defenses organized. Forty slaves, that raid was worth. We left no one alive."

Tears of Jade sniffed, disinterested.

Lorso cleared the harbor while Domel was still walking back to the Skan fort. Steering the boat down the coastline, Lorso watched the older man and smiled, despite a persistent dizziness. He was sure Tears of Jade's smoke had something to do with it. She obviously used it to smother his anger. She was very wise.

Both Domel and Tears of Jade thought themselves very wise, skilled in the ways of intrigue. What they'd forgotten was the power of love. Lorso laughed aloud, the sound catching in the sail, riding the wind with him. Two days, Tears of Jade said. That meant three nights.

The sun warmed the wooden boat, bathed him in a luxurious ease he hadn't known since he fished these waters as a child. Humming, he set a course for a favorite spot, a sheer cliff that plunged into the sea. Where a familiar stunted fir jutted from a foothold in the vertical stone face, he secured his bowline.

Rummaging in his gear, he retrieved line and yarn-wrapped lures. Bright yellow material winked and wiggled as it sank out of sight into the blue-green depths. A small fish darted out of a cleft, struck at the lure. The metal lump bounced sideways. The fish lurched back to cover to ponder life's treacherous deceptions. As soon as the line went slack, Lorso hauled in until his bait was just off the bottom. He jerked on the line, knowing that below, out of sight, the lure leaped and fell back, tantalizingly like a crippled fingerling trying to reach shallower waters.

Something struck, hard. Snubbing the line, Lorso let it play out for a while, then reclaimed it hand over hand. Soon he had a thrashing quillback on board, its mottled black and brown scales like a fine working of bronze and iron.

A nearby beach afforded an excellent pullout. Lorso idled away the afternoon. It was dark when he finished eating. Picking his teeth with a bone, he decided it was time to return.

He sailed in the dark with the surety of generations of experience. Each wave told him of a particular shore formation. When the small boat yawed, he knew exactly what underwater current or surge created the movement, how deep the water was, and how long until he cleared that anomaly and moved into the next. In addition, he had the stars and the unmistakable profile of the mountains.

He rigorously avoided looking at the mountain that formed Sosolassa's beak. Telling himself he was challenging Tears of Jade's orders, not the desires of the god, he pressed on. The rumble of distant surf took on the mutter of anger, and he prayed for guidance.

For a man of Lorso's skills, landing the craft and creeping to Jaleeta's cabin undiscovered was no more trouble than a walk in the starlit dark.

She waited for him, a beckoning whiteness against the cloaking night. As he stepped across the threshold he was struck by that perfect image of their love; shadowy, secret forms, hidden from all eyes, hardly visible to their own. Theirs was a romance of darkness, of passion that allowed no visible flame, yet melted away everything. Their time was measured in star tracks, their conversation virtually limited to the incoherencies of ardor.

Tonight, however, Jaleeta's outstretched hands flattened against his chest, held him away. She sobbed. Lorso stepped back so quickly his shorter leg betrayed him and he staggered clumsily. Scrambling forward, he came to where she sat on the edge of the bed. He clutched at her knees, and once again she held him at arm's reach. "How could you do it? I thought you loved me. You said you did. You lied!"

"Lied? Me? About what? When? Of course I love you."

"You say it now. To get what you want. It was the same today with Tears of Jade, wasn't it? All you care about is yourself."

Thoroughly baffled, Lorso settled back on his haunches. "What did she say?"

"She said you won't be Slavetaker anymore."

"So we can be together, Jaleeta. So I won't have to go to the Mother River. So I can stay here with you through stormtime."

"And what happens to me? When you ask Tears of Jade for me, will the Navigators let me go to a warrior? Even a sharker captain? Tears of Jade says the Navigators decide who gets a bed slave, so long as the man pays the slave price. No captain has enough furs, jade, or gold for me. Slavetaker could own me for nothing, because Slavetaker meets with the Navigators. But you don't want me."

"I do. You know I do." He pressed forward. She resisted, making a hushed squeal, rolling off the other side of the bed. She said, "You want me. Slavetaker doesn't. I love only Slavetaker."

Fury, power, pride surged in Lorso like a northwind wave, crashed against his self-image. He rose, prepared to roar. He choked back the sound, compressed all his need into a whisper so urgent it raked his throat. "Whatever you want, whatever you need, I am that man. Whoever says different, whoever says he would touch you, dies. If Slavetaker is who you love, come to me."

The softly blurred whiteness of her stirred. Leather bed straps sighed. As did Jaleeta, taking him in her arms.

Chapter 19

The Nion captain stepped ashore from the small rowboat with the wary step and tense, craning pauses of a buck deer coming to water. It was apt behavior. There were predators hidden from him at every quarter, including Skan swimmers silently maneuvering to cut off the rowboat's escape seaward.

Tears of Jade and Domel waited on the land side of a small fire. Domel sat on a log close to the flames, bareheaded, hands ostentatiously clasping his bent knees. Tears of Jade was farther back, on a proper chair. She wore a black dress of shiny material that shimmered in the firelight. Her wide-brimmed, veiled hat shielded her face, while her hands remained hidden in the folds of her sleeves.

The Nion was dressed for combat. His outer layer was boiled leather. Glossy artwork decorated every part of it. On the chest was painted a ferocious demon, one clawed hand holding a screaming warrior while the other hand raised another warrior to the monster's fanged maw. Hidden on the reverse of the leatherwork were intricately sewn bamboo stalks. The third, final layer was thin steel plates. It was highly protective armor, but heavy enough to slow a man. Two swords, one long and one short, hung in ornate scabbards on the captain's left side. His helmet was gilded steel, artfully formed in the likeness of a crowing cock. The outstretched wings were genuine feathers. The tail, made of steel simulating feathers, was attached to the main element by steel rings; it trailed protectively over the captain's neck.

Physically, the Nion captain wasn't much taller than Tears of Jade. He was far broader, however, with a thick, barrel chest and sturdy limbs. The legs were exaggerated by leather greaves. Exposed forearms showed compact, solid muscle.

Dark-browed, skin burnished to a red-gold by the flames, he continuously looked all around with dark, curiously shaped eyes. Right hand across his body, the captain gripped his long sword.

From behind the veil, Tears of Jade taunted the Nion. "So nervous, Hada? An ancient spirit woman and a man so old he needs help to lace his boots; we frighten you?" In the silent darkness, her rustling, insinuating voice had an earthy quality, as if it issued from the forest itself.

Hada smiled pleasantly. His hand retained its grip on his sword. "It's possible things lurk in the woods that even a spirit woman doesn't know about. I prefer caution to sorrow."

"Always the wisest course." Domel nodded sagely. "The plan satisfies you?"

Hada gestured with his free hand, a flip of dismissal. "What could be easier? I claim I found the girl adrift, escaping from you. I deliver her to Ola. She gives me a token proving I provided safe passage, I return that here to you, and you give me the jade we agreed on."

"And we return the son you leave with me as proof of good faith." Tears of Jade imitated Hada's gesture, the clawlike hand making a slow, almost mocking appearance, then disappearing again.

For the first time, Hada's accent intruded heavily on his speech. Tightly, he replied, "My son waits in the boat. You have the girl?"

Domel whistled. Behind Tears of Jade, bushes rustled. Hada stiffened. Jaleeta and her mother appeared, the older woman in leather leggings, skirt, and blouse. Jaleeta wore a robe similar to Tears of Jade's. There was no hat, but a hood hid her face. Hada relaxed and smiled. "There's no need to cover her so completely. My men obey. She'll be in no danger."

Tears of Jade bent forward, raised an admonishing finger. The flames of the fire suddenly collapsed to fitful, struggling wisps. The coals hissed agonized fury, the suspiration of a dying reptile. All but Tears of Jade recoiled with startled cries. Slowly, the ancient woman forced herself erect. Domel, recovering some of his poise, offered a hand. She irritably pushed it aside. As she rose, so the fire regained its strength. The diminutive figure appeared to lift the flames, blend with them. By the time she pulled aside her veil to glare at Hada, the fire was as it had been. "The Nion care nothing for our god, but I warn you, harm to her is harm to Sosolassa. His is the power of the sea. He quelled the fire so that you may know his presence." She paused momentarily, then, "The exchange, Hada. I would see the boy."

Hada looked to Domel. The Skan said, "We waste time. You need the tide to be clear of here by dawn. We have many hours of travel to the sunset side of the island."

When Hada was on his way to the rowboat, Tears of Jade whispered to Domel. Her gaze remained fixed straight ahead, her lips barely moved. "My orders need no approval from any man, Domel, nor do I give reasons to scum like Hada. Remember who I am."

Easily, Domel said, "No one ever forgets you. You must remember that Hada isn't Skan. He doesn't appreciate your—qualities." His covert smile was quietly smug.

Hada returned with a bareheaded Nion boy of perhaps fourteen, his hair cut in an uncompromising bowl all the way around at the level of the tops of his ears. Facially, he closely resembled his father. He was a shade taller than the adult, simply dressed in a pullover blouse and trousers of coarse twill. His boots were of fine, glowing leather; their tops were covered by heavy leggings. The sword and scabbard at this side were plain. He tried with all his might to look at Tears of Jade without showing fear. When the small woman advanced on him through the fire, rather than around it, he quailed. Had he the presence of mind to look at the adult males present, he would have noted that they, too, were open-mouthed in shock. Jaleeta and her mother clung to each other.

Smoke curled from the neck of Tears of Jade's robe. More swirled from under the ground-sweeping skirt. She circled the two Nions. The boy shivered violently. Deep in his chest, Hada rumbled a stern, wordless warning.

Walking back through the fire, Tears of Jade carefully avoided the fern frond on the ground in front of her seat. It marked the sealskin bladder hiding under its thin layer of soft earth. Thinking of Domel's expression and his frightened yelp, Tears of Jade bit her lip to resist laughter. It was always amazing how a small trick could have such great effect. A bladder full of water and a short length of seal intestine leading underground from the bladder to the center of the fire. A step on the container forced the water out into the base of the flames, temporarily quenching them. And wearing a soaked undergarment to protect one while walking through the fire was uncomfortable, but hardly a major miracle.

Such simple things. And grown men squealed and thought deeply and shakenly of gods and their vengeance. Even poor Domel, who was sure most of what Tears of Jade did was purest trickery, dared not disbelieve.

Tears of Jade glanced sidelong at the sacred peak. Ideas for magic were Sosolassa's gift, sent to her that she might glorify his godliness. Humor for Sosolassa. She laughed with the god. Not by herself. Never.

Tears of Jade faced Hada. "A handsome youth. A credit to his father. And mother." The latter remark brought a minute change to Hada's expression. The old woman's lined face seemed to quiver, as at a private joke. She went on. "What is his name?"

Hada smiled, condescending. Accent even more pronounced, he said, "You could not speak correctly. In your words, Axe." To make himself clear, Hada made a chopping gesture.

Tears of Jade said, "I will step aside to say good-bye to the girl. You may do the same with Axe, if you wish."

"No need." Hada's back stiffened, his face grew hard. "Nion sons understand duty to father."

"I'm sure." Tears of Jade took the silent Jaleeta's elbow, led her to the farthest edge of the firelight. "Cast doubts or fear from your mind. I've told you all we know of those who surround Gan Moondark and the witch, Sylah. Do as I have ordered. You will be richer and more powerful than your small dreams can envision. Betray me, and I shall know it. You understand what I will do?"

"Yes. I know." It was a sigh, a shudder.

Tears of Jade put a hand on Jaleeta's sleeve. Between ball of thumb and the knuckle of a forefinger, the older woman gathered a fold of material and the flesh under it. Tears of Jade pinched and twisted. Jaleeta gasped, shrank away. The grip tightened, generated a low moan of pain. "What do you mean, 'yes' you fool? You can never know what I will do, how I will act. You obey. You do not 'know.' "

"Yes. Yes, I kn—I understand. I'll do exactly as you want. I swear."

"Certainly you do. Because your mother is here. She'll live well, so long as you succeed." Tears of Jade released the pressure on Jaleeta's flesh. Taking the arm in her free hand, she stroked the affected area. "Poor darling." The sere voice tried to croon. Instead, the solicitous words had the nervous whir of wasp wings. "Sometimes I think you hope to trick me one day. Everyone does. Sooner or later. They come to me with their hopes, their dreams, their enmities, all carefully disguised as truth. They think I'll help them. I use them. All of them. As Sosolassa wishes. Now I use you. The god orders. He promises reward. Obey, my beautiful Jaleeta. Obey and thrive. Come. The adventure begins now."

Three days later, under a flat, gray sky that pressed against the earth with dank persistence, the squat Nion trader dropped her sails and wallowed to a stop inside the stone jetty of Ola. Crewmen threw lines to waiting boats, where oarsmen bent to the task of hauling her alongside the wooden dock. As soon as a wooden brow was properly secured, Hada hurried ashore with Jaleeta in tow. In daylight the young woman's robe showed the intricate geometrical patterns of Skan decorative art, red-black on black. Something like a spasm of hatred raced from man to man throughout the entire port area. Every step the couple took toward land was followed by dozens of pairs of eyes. The everyday shouts and sounds of ship commerce dwindled to no more than the sigh of wind in rigging and rub of wood on wood.

Long before Hada and Jaleeta passed through Ola's southern gate, Gan was on the wall. Neela was at his side, young Coldar wide-eyed on her hip. To his right, Sylah, Bernhardt, Carter, and Anspach also watched the confident, strutting Nion approach across the greensward between the castle and the city. Several paces behind him, Jaleeta's bowed, hooded figure hurried to keep up.

Carter said, "That's a woman with him; I'm sure of it. She's practically running. Inconsiderate fool."

Baiting her, Gan said, "Or a boy. In that robe, it's impossible . . ."

"You know better." Carter's grin flashed on and off, quick enough to be missed by the inattentive. Gan thought to himself how that smile typified the woman. A mind as sharp and cutting as a shortknife, the edge of her temper never far from the open. Still, she'd taken to the ways of Church; the young Chosens claimed her total being. Around them, she was loving-kindness personified. Gan couldn't watch her in the company of her wards without thinking of a snow leopard with its kittens. Carter exhibited the same graceful, delicate care and love. Gan also knew how that patience flared into raw ferocity at the slightest suggestion of danger to her young.

Yet he could never forget that Carter had broken under stress once. It was a disconcerting shadow.

Gan shook himself free of thoughts of Carter. Neela, sensitive to her husband as always, looked up at him, a questioning frown on her brow. Gan said, "The Nion's almost here."

Neela grabbed his arm as he moved to leave. He turned with a look of vast surprise. She laughed at him. "You're not leaving us here while you talk to this mysterious Nion and his Skan companion?"

Gan swept them all in a continuing look of total incomprehension. "You're curious? Unimaginable. I never suspected it. Of course you can come with me. Remember, though; proper procedure. Nions conduct no business with women present. They think it's bad luck. I've often wondered—"

Sylah interrupted. "Wonder what your life will be like if you say one more word, Gan Moondark. Just one."

He grinned. "You'll be hidden behind the curtain that divides the room." He pointed at Coldar. "Not him, though. You'll never keep him quiet." Approaching two, Coldar cared nothing for the sense of his father's words. The attention was satisfactorily stimulating. He whooped and grabbed at the accusing finger. Father and son exchanged conspiratorial chuckles. Gan said, "You see?"

Neela huffed mock irritation. "Ladies, you go ahead. I'll find someone to watch this little disturbance, then join you."

Instead, as a group, the Church women surrounded her, leaving with her. They sneered in unison passing Gan.

Alone, the light amusement slipped from his face. He called to Shara and Cho, setting off down the stairs.

Whatever the woman with the Nion represented, it was hard to imagine any good falling from it. The Skan would send no woman to conduct official business. The Nion-Skan relationship was always treacherous. Ruefully, Gan considered that his own relations with the Nions were delicate. They were an aggressive group, eager to defend anything they considered theirs. Worse, they exercised little discrimination in deciding what was theirs to defend.

On the other hand, any relationship with the Skan involved bloodshed. Everyone traded with them for their jade and the pink-and-black sostone. Unlike other people who traveled the sea because it was a way to go from point to point, the Skan treated it as home. Their settlements existed only to reequip returning sharkers. It wasn't unusual for one of their vessels to be gone for two years, trading, raiding, simply chasing the next day.

In his deepest heart, Gan admitted he envied that.

Now, however, he must deal with one of their women. Quite possibly a Nion captive.

A Jalail Wolf, the twin tails of his red-and-yellow armband dangling bright against the black and white of his homespun blouse, waited in the passageway outside the meeting room.

Gan returned his salute, then, "Does this Nion have language, or will I need an interpreter?"

The young Wolf made a face. "An accent, but very good language. Full of himself."

"Really? What's he told us?"

"Not much. It's more his attitude than his words. Says, 'Tell the mightiest warrior on this side of the Great Sea that a representative of the mightiest nation in all the world requests to speak to him.' Got honey in his mouth and a shortknife in his hand, if you ask me."

"I didn't, but I should have," Gan said. "What about the woman?"

"Not a sound. No one's even seen her, all wrapped up in that Skan robe. She must be an eye-burner, to keep so bundled up when it's this warm."

When Gan entered the meeting room from the side, Hada and Jaleeta were in front of the massive table centered before the dividing curtain. The curtain was painted with stylized wolves, each in the color of a pack. Ranged in a semicircle, they glared out at whoever faced the table, white fangs bared.

Gan, flanked by his dogs, called to the Nion, "Know me. I am Gan Moondark."

The Nion faced him, drew himself erect, then bowed from the waist, both hands outstretched. Gan interpreted the latter gesture to indicate no attempt to touch a weapon. The Nion straightened, this time clasping his left fist in his right hand under his chin. He said, "I know you, Gan Moondark. Know me. Hada of the Nion. We are the Island Sword People, obedient to Emperor Mas, the Conqueror." That said, Hada lowered his hands.

Gan said, "I know you, Hada. I compliment you on knowing how we speak. I apologize that I'm not so accomplished."

Hada said, "It's expected, Murdat." Gan heard past the words, caught the implication that Hada would as likely expect a wildcow to sing. Remembering the young Wolf in the passageway, Gan resolved to see that perceptive man promoted. Politely, to Hada, he said, "Your thoughts are understood and appreciated. You're the first Nion I've ever met, the first to ever ask to meet me. How can I help you?"

"I come to help you." Again, the taint of covert condescension grated. Gan wished Sylah were present to analyze the man. Hada continued. "My Emperor knows of your war with the Skan. Secretly, he wishes to help you, but it's very difficult. Complicated? Is that a good word? Good. However, I had good luck at sea, coming here. Just dawn, three days ago, my men saw a small boat. North, between the Skan island and mainland." He jerked a thumb at Jaleeta. "She was in the boat."

"I want no Skan prisoner. You know there are no slaves in the Three Territories. Take her back where she belongs."

Hada smiled. "I do. She belongs to you." He half turned. "Tell him, female. Speak."

Jaleeta shook her head. Her voice, softened by the tunneled hollow of the hood, was timid. "I know you, Gan Moondark. Know me. My name is Jaleeta, a woman of the For." She threw back the hood of her robe, and Gan was sure he heard a stir from the other side of the curtain. It was to be expected. Jaleeta was startlingly beautiful. Green eyes looked at him in hope and fear, while a tentative smile pulled at full red lips. White teeth and white skin complimented tumbling hair the color of best obsidian. "I was prisoner to a spirit woman, an evil thing called Tears of Jade. She serves a false god called Sosolassa. I stole a boat to escape, and Hada found me."

Gan tried to sound fatherly. "I'll get someone for you to talk to, someone who'll make you more comfortable. It can't be pleasant to stand here and tell your story to two men."

He strode around the edge of the curtain, where the entire group from the castle wall, plus Leclerc, waited for him. Gan gestured them to silence, indicating they should get back from the curtain. When he'd restored some order, he said, "Neela, you come out with me. Take her to the side, see what she says."

"Don't tell me you suspect that poor girl?"

"I suspect nothing, I accept nothing. I simply want to know more."

Neela swept past him. Gan turned to the others for some sign of understanding and hurried away to escape their chill disapproval.

Hada waited patiently. Neela and Jaleeta were already in close conversation, seated on chairs as far from the men as possible. Gan indicated a seat at the table for Hada, joining him. Hada eyed the curtain suspiciously before untying the strap holding his sword scabbard to his belt. Ceremoniously placing the sword and its leather-covered carrier on the table, Hada grabbed it at the middle in a clenched fist. Gan watched with open curiosity.

Hada said, "This is how a Nion warrior swears he speaks the truth—with hand on the most important object in his life. I lied to you. The female stole no boat, never escaped. She was given to me to bring to you. For trade things."

"The Skan paid you to bring her here? Is she sick?"

Blanching, Hada squeezed the scabbard tighter yet. "I don't think so. I didn't think . . ." The monstrousness of the thought choked him off.

"Why tell me now?" Gan asked.

"Skan think Nions only traders, have no honor, do anything for trade goods. I think female is a spy. Gan Moondark is a good man, strong warrior. I help you. One time. After this, you are Murdat, I be Nion. There is honor between us, but not friendship. But you say nothing yet. Tears of Jade holds my son until you take female."

"Your son? Hostage?"

Hada shrugged nonchalantly, but his pride shone through. "Nion. Brave."

Gan said, "Jaleeta's a For. They're traditional enemies of the Skan. Anyhow, how would she get information back to this Tears of Jade? It's impossible. Jaleeta couldn't be a spy. " He absently tugged an ear lobe. "Unless there's someone here already in the pay of the Skan. Even so, what could she learn?"

Hada said, "I know nothing more. I must leave." He rose, putting on his sword. "Now I speak to the female. She has token for me. I give it to Tears of Jade, she gives me my son."

Gan accompanied the Nion to Neela and Jaleeta. Neela acknowledged the men coldly. Jaleeta smiled her gratitude. From a pocket of her robe, she took out something, handed it to Hada. She said, "It's all I have to offer. Not payment. A keepsake, from someone you rescued. Please, if you ever trade with the Skan, tell them this: 'Jaleeta of the For People puts her curse on the Skan forever.' " Gan was surprised at the sudden hardness of the features, the glaring intensity of the green eyes. Hada's stern composure wavered. Jaleeta finished with, "Please remember exactly what I said."

Hada took the token. After a short semibow for Neela, he left. Gan accompanied him to the door. Out of sight of the women, Hada held up the token for Gan to see. It was a small, golden octopus. He grimaced and pocketed it.

When Gan returned to the pair, Neela was holding Jaleeta's hands in her own. Without preamble, Neela said, "Jaleeta's staying in the castle. She's deathly afraid of that woman, Tears of Jade." Neela shivered. "What a terrible name. So cold."

Wide-eyed, innocent, Jaleeta said, "I confessed to Neela. I didn't escape. Tears of Jade paid the Nion to bring me here. She holds his son as hostage for my safe arrival. I'm to spy on you. She said if I don't find a way to live here, in the castle, she'll punish my mother."

"How will she know where you live? Can she see so far?" Gan heard the distrust in his voice, saw Neela's disgust.

Jaleeta accepted it as due. "Someone will contact me. Maybe tomorrow, maybe moons from now. I must be prepared. But what I want to do is destroy Tears of Jade. All the Skan. They slaughtered my family. Everyone. Tears of Jade says I'm her weapon, that her horrible god gave me to her to come here and weaken you, so the Skan and the River People and someone called Windband can enslave all the people of the Three Territories." Suddenly, emotion overwhelmed the young woman. She refused to break completely. She sobbed, just once. Stubbornly, she set her jaw, chin up.

Neela was bitter. "Can she go now, Murdat? No more tests of courage or honesty?"

Gan shook his head, waved a hand in silent, unconsciously rude, dismissal. Then, belatedly aware of what he'd done, he wondered if the rudeness was instinctive.

Chapter 20

Leclerc stared at Jaleeta's retreating form as she swayed down the hall beside Neela. Gan took the opportunity to study the man, glad to occupy his mind with something other than the foreboding set off by the strange newcomer.

There was something indirect about Leclerc, a suggestion that he observed the world obliquely, instead of head-on. Gan wondered if that elusiveness was what convinced him there was more to Leclerc than his amazing ability to make things.

Permitting himself a grin he knew would go unnoticed, Gan made a silent wager that, at this precise moment, Leclerc was thinking of how to cleverly arrange an introduction to Jaleeta. Any other man who was that staggeringly smitten would walk through a wall to introduce himself. And let others worry about picking up the pieces.

Sylah remarked once that she always felt an air of loneliness around Leclerc. Neela agreed immediately, adding, "I think he's lonely, but I don't think he knows it." Gan laughed at that. The women had given him that withering cut of the eyes that says men comprehend nothing more complex than dog slobber and horse sweat.

Perhaps complexity was what made Leclerc different. It was interesting how he favored white in his clothing. It reminded Gan of King Altanar's former police, the men ironically called protectors. Gan was sure Leclerc never imagined any connection between himself and those devils. If anything, the clean look indicated Leclerc's awareness of the better things in life. Only the finest smoke-cured deer hide had the creamy color and texture of Leclerc's favored shirts. Today he wore one of them, and tan homespun trousers. Both were embroidered with small, bright designs. Boots, always black, were the best buffalo hide. In keeping with custom, he carried them in a bag indoors, wearing soft elkskin slippers.

Suddenly impatient with his own mental wandering, Gan called him. "Leclerc? You said earlier you wanted to talk to me."

Leclerc jerked as if burned. "Oh. Yes." He colored, frowned. "I'm sure you remember what everyone said about the thing they call the wallkiller in Kos; the thing that throws a heavy weight long distances. I've been thinking about something to allow us to throw the black powder. I want to build a different version."

"Different?"

Flying hands cutting pictures in the air, Leclerc explained. His preoccupied manner was completely gone. "We don't need anything as big and clumsy as the wallkiller. I don't want to make a simple large bow, either. The weapon has to be mobile, something the Wolves can take apart and move from place to place." He stopped, grinned. "How'd you like to shoot arrows as big around as two thumbs and long as a man's arm? Shoot them at least three hundred paces? Hit hard enough to rip that door like a dead leaf?"

Cloaking rising excitement in deadly seriousness, Gan said, "I'd like that very much. You say this thing will throw the black powder, as well?"

A frown almost like a wince etched Leclerc's forehead. "That's a little more difficult. I think I can do it. I don't remember very much . . . I meant to say, I don't promise very much. I've never built one."

"If anyone can do it, you can. We're going to need every advantage we can find. A harsh winter may keep raids to a minimum. But when spring comes, so will our enemies. The Three Territories are weary. The Wolves need you and your friends. You're our hope."

Leclerc shuffled a bit, embarrassed, then, "If I have the authority, I'll start the project. I need to requisition materials."

"Use anything you want."

Leclerc threw a glance down the hall where Jaleeta disappeared, then left through the opposite door.

Gan thought about the new weapon. Three hundred paces. An arrow heavier than a Dog warrior's lance. His stomach rolled uncomfortably as he remembered his loathing and disgust on seeing the carnage caused by the black powder. Magic was no way for a man to strike down another.

The Gan Moondark who ruled the Three Territories embraced the magic. Hated it, and hoarded it to him as a miser hoards wealth.

He was in a foul mood as he left the room. Ever sensitive, Shara and Cho fell in far behind. Taking the stairs two at a time, he hurried to the soak on the same floor as his quarters. He was unprepared to find Neela there. She, on the contrary, smiled a ready welcome. Despite everything else on his mind, his blood quickened at the sight of her naked in the large stone-walled tub. Rising steam further distorted the muted image of her submerged body; he needed no clearer view. Indeed, the hazy vision of her seemed to ignite greater excitement. She said, "I've been waiting for you."

"Waiting? I didn't know I was coming here until a few moments ago."

She laughed easily. "This is where you usually come to work out problems. The girl, Jaleeta, is a problem. Coming here was a logical step for both of us."

Closing the door behind him, he said, "That means I'm going to get advice, doesn't it?" He began disrobing.

"They killed her whole family, Gan. Her mother's that old woman's hostage."

"What old woman?" He sank in the tub, leaning back so his ears were submerged.

Neela lifted his head by the forelock. "Keep your ears up here where I can talk to them." She explained about Sosolassa and the Skan religion, as well as Tears of Jade's place in it. Then she told of Jaleeta's capture and life with the Skan. She finished with, "If someone that cruel had your mother captive, wouldn't you pretend to do everything you were told?"

Eyes closed, Gan said, "I never knew my mother. How can I answer . . . ?"

Neela dunked him. He rose, snorting and coughing. When he cleared his throat, he surrendered. "Your superior persuasiveness has overwhelmed me. I have an irresistible urge to tell you why Jaleeta makes me suspicious. It's because she hasn't told us the full truth about herself or why she's here. She lived with the spirit woman—Tears of Jade, you said? Strange name—for almost four years. Did she tell you what work this old woman made her do? I thought not. And doesn't it strike you as strange that a woman so beautiful wasn't claimed by a man? One more thing." Gan held up a hand to forestall what promised to be a furious outburst, then continued. "Oh, she says Tears of Jade sent her to spy on us and relay the information through some unknown contact, but what information? Our conversation? Our eating habits? Our favorite colors? Consider this unknown conspirator; if I believe Jaleeta, I must suspect everyone who comes in contact with her. That suspicion alone aids our enemies."

"She's already promised me she'll identify whoever comes to her." Neela's superior smile had the gleam of a knife.

"From what you tell me of this Tears of Jade, and from what I know of the Skan, it wouldn't surprise me if they planned to sacrifice a false contact in order to protect the real one." The silence in the misty, apple-scented room stretched out uncomfortably. When Gan reached to take Neela's chin in his hands, she was unresponsive. She averted her eyes. He said, "What is it? What did I say?"

She shook her head as much as his grip allowed. "Not what was said, but who said it." She raised a troubled gaze to his. "The Gan I fell in love with, my Nightwatch, my loyal dreamer, would never conceive of such duplicity. Now you must think of such things. You grow accustomed. What have we done to you?"

"No one did anything. I did what I was supposed to do. A man of the Dog People rules three kingdoms." He released her, sat back, eyes closed.

"The prophecy—"

Gan cut her off harshly. "The prophecy. I remember you telling me you didn't care about my mother's prophecy."

"I said if this isn't what you want, walk away. I'll be beside you."

Contrite, Gan leaned his shoulder against hers. "I'm caught. The Harbundai Barons—Fir, Galmontis, Jalail, Malten, all of them—have been battling each other in one alliance or another for generations. One of the few things they have in common is a traditional distrust of the Olans, and for good reason. I'm the only one they all trust. If I leave, they'll go back to squabbling among themselves, and be slaughtered as soon as spring weather brings the Skan, Windband, and the River People."

"Their fate's not your responsibility."

Gan pivoted, looked down at her. "Look me in the eye and say that."

Neela looked away, made as if to leave. Gently, firmly, he held her by the shoulders. Steam from the soak mocked their tension, its amorphous, aromatic tendrils drifting in careless coils. At last, Neela said, "It's not fair."

Gan's sigh eased through a half smile. He bent to her, kissed her cheek. "I'll tell you what's unfair. I'm alone behind a barred door, naked in a soak, with my beautiful wife, and we're *talking*."

Her eyes flashed at him, then away again. Her jaw tightened. "That's . . . That's so exactly like a man. We have to talk about those things. It's serious."

"I was never more serious in my whole life."

"No, Gan, I mean it. Stop that." She reached to grab his wrists where his hands were sliding off her shoulders. She started to rise, preparatory to getting out of the water, then realized by virtue of Gan's gaze exactly what part of her was breaking the surface. She sank back quickly.

For a moment she was genuinely angry, telling herself there was a time and place for everything, and being alone and unclothed had nothing to do with truly important matters. Or it certainly shouldn't, anyway, and someone had to be aware of such things. Or certainly should be.

She was aware of him, after all. Nuzzling her hair. Pressing against her. It wasn't too late to be firm, push him away, insist they talk out this problem.

Not that he didn't confide in her, ask her advice. He did. Trusted her.

They really did have too little time to simply enjoy . . .

That was a dangerous word. Appreciate. Not enough time to appreciate each other.

Enjoy was better. It really was. A person might as well be honest. And he was so handsome. Strong. Strong? How did his hands get there, with her holding his wrists so tightly?

She pulled her head away, where her face had inexplicably found its way to his shoulder. She looked up at him. "You're sure the door's barred?"

He grinned. Winked. "First thing I did when I came in."

She knew she should be angry again. He was lifting her, going up the steps out of the soak. She wrapped her arms around his neck, but feigned a pout as a matter of form. "You really have become deceitful."

His grin broadened. "So exactly like a man."

* * *

The following morning, Leclerc scribbled furiously, bent over Bernhardt's table. His writing utensil was a quill. The surface he busily covered with rough sketches was hide. He grumbled to Bernhardt as he worked. "I hate working on leather with this miserable charcoal-and-water stuff. I'd sell my soul for a pad of paper and a ballpoint pen."

Patting his back, smiling sympathetically, Bernhardt chided, "Watch your language, Louis. People here would see that soul freed of earthly concerns for just that sort of talk."

"I know." Angry resignation burdened the words. Mercurially, Leclerc brightened. He straightened, jabbed at the picture with the quill pen. "That's got it. Yes, that'll work. It's the way I remember it. Sinew's wrapped around these shafts, and that's what pulls the crossarm back, see? It'll take a winch to do it, of course, but that's easy. It's the release that's going to be a problem."

Another voice intruded. "What's got you two so intrigued?" Followed by Sue Anspach, Janet Carter forged into Bernhardt's small cell in the Iris Abbey. The presence of four adults in the space effectively cut off cross-ventilation between the slit of a window and the doorway built into the stone walls. Furniture was meager and rough; a narrow bed, a table barely large enough to hold its wash-basin, pitcher, and Leclerc's work. There was a solitary chair. A box under the bed was the sole point of storage. A tall candelabra, its three tapers unlit, sat on the floor in a corner. Directly behind it, impossibly anachronistic, Bernhardt's wipe hung from a wooden peg.

In their black Church robes, the new arrivals seemed to absorb the limited light. Bernhardt said, "Conway told Louis about Moonpriest using an oversized bow to shoot arrows. Louis says the best catapults were different. He's going to build some."

Carter addressed Leclerc's bent back. "I thought you were showing people how to build arches. Better roads. Aqueducts. Conway and Tate make war; let them work on this catapult thing."

"Believe me, I'd rather not design weapons, but none of us pursues any goals if Gan's overthrown. You remember the Harvester? Picture what she'd do to your little Chosens who've learned to read and write."

Anspach spoke up. "All Janet meant was that you're too good a man to be wasting your time. There's so much this world needs. You could provide it."

"Thanks, Sue. I can help; I know that. This is important, though. Come spring, the whole world's going to drop on us."

Carter refused to be persuaded. "Bigger and better weapons will make a difference? What about negotiation? Logic and self-interest?"

Pivoting slowly, Leclerc abandoned his sketches. "It takes two. Gan already sent Messengers to Windband and the Skan asking for conference. Nothing will come of it. Look at Church's own Violet Abbess, right here in Ola. She hates Gan. He's doing more for Church and the Chosens than anyone in history, and half of Church hates his guts."

Anspach interceded. "We just hate to see you doing this."

"I don't." There was a diffident, embarrassed look on Bernhardt's face, overlaid by determination. "Louis is doing what he has to do so we can all do more of what we want to do." She spoke with her gaze studiously fixed on the other women. Still, she edged closer to him.

Thanking Bernhardt with a glance, Leclerc said, "There's almost no tradition of arbitration in any of these cultures; not as we understand it. Discussion, if there is any, comes after the fight, not before."

"We're going to change that." Normally the least outspoken of the trio, Anspach stuck out her chin. "The Chosens of the Iris Abbey are growing up educated. When they leave here as missionaries of Church, they'll be more than Healers and War Healers. They'll carry learning with them."

Leclerc said, "Gan insists his officers all learn reading and writing."

"Not a completely happy situation," Carter said, her face darkening. "We've seen the power elite in every tribe we've contacted. It frightens me to think of weaponry and education consolidated in the hands of a few. That's a recipe for caste."

"Of course." Leclerc was conciliatory. "We're the ones who have to take the responsibility of assuring fairness. Sweetness and light won't do it. Leadership and sheer strength are the only safe bet."

A Chosen, demure in her miniature version of Church robes, appeared at the door. "Murdat's wife comes," the little girl said, all wide-eyed solemnity. "She brings the Jaleeta one."

Bernhardt thanked the child and sent her back to the abbey. The foursome elected to meet their guests outside, where the weather was fine. After getting acquainted, the group strolled to the abbey herb garden, with Jaleeta exclaiming at every step at some new wonder. "Everyone says how grand Ola is, but it's more. No one ever saw walls so high and thick. And the size of these gardens. So many flowers."

"What about the Skan village?" Carter asked. "How do they live?"

Jaleeta's eyes darted at her questioner, the features momentarily hard and wary. "Cruel people. They say other people live to serve the Skan." While the others walked the garden paths in silence, Jaleeta told of her capture. On describing the torture inflicted on herself and her mother at the Skan village, she wept.

Everyone gathered around immediately, sympathizing, assuring her there was no need to continue her tale. Jaleeta insisted. "How else can you understand why I even pretended to agree to betray my people, to spy on the one man who can help me and my poor mother? You must know what they're like. They worship an octopus they call Sosolassa, a religion of fear and terrible magic. The spirit woman, Tears of Jade, is old, old, old. And ugly. She never knew love, and hates anyone who does." Suddenly, Jaleeta reached for the closest arm, that of Leclerc. "Please, all of you, my new friends; I trust you. I know you'll protect me, and I'd give my life for you. Never let her have me again. Kill me, first. I'll kiss the hand that strikes, I swear."

"No more of that." Neela swept to Jaleeta, pushing Leclerc aside. "We have our own magic. We have Louis Leclerc. He has more secrets than there are stars in the sky. These women know the way of reading and writing. Conway and Tate are great warriors. Our Church friend, Sylah, is the very Flower promised to us for generations." Neela held Jaleeta at arm's length, smilingly confident. She tossed her head, and sunlight glowed hot on the golden sway of waist-long hair. Something beyond Jaleeta caught Neela's eye. "And we have leaders like that."

Jaleeta and the others turned. Neela waved, beckoning for Emso and Wal to join them.

"The scowling one is Emso," Neela explained. "The black-bearded bear is a For, one of your own people."

With a scream of delight, Jaleeta broke away from Neela, raced to embrace Wal, reaching as far around him as she could. Wal froze, stunned. Emso howled laughter. Finally, laughing and crying, Jaleeta turned her face up to Wal. Barely coherent, she said, "Wal Stonebeach. Sea raider, trader. I'm Jaleeta, daughter to Narom Sailman. Don't you remember me?"

"You're dead." Wal's eyes, already huge with shock, bulged even farther. "The spring renewal . . . The Skan . . ."

"I escaped. They captured me, gave me to Tears of Jade. I escaped." In broken phrases she summarized her story. The tears finally stopped, leaving only the smile. At her story's end, Wal whirled her in a mad dance. Her hood flew off, releasing a cascade of hair, black and hard-shining as a raven's beak. "Look at you!" It was an exultation. "You were a skinny little wave-racer, eyes too big for your head, all giggles and wiggles. No one would know you. And you live."

The excitement bled away from Wal's voice. He saddened. Interpreting his look Jaleeta said, "Only me, Wal. And my mother. Tears of Jade holds her to assure I don't betray her."

Wal nodded, grim. "We'll protect you. When we crush the Skan, we'll save your mother, too."

"No one can make that promise." Jaleeta put her hands on his arms. She pushed herself free of his grip. "They may kill her any day. The Skan don't even need a reason to kill. I've seen. Make no promise. Except revenge. I ask that."

"You'll have it."

Carter interrupted. "Jaleeta. There's another man here you have to meet. Emso. He's been with Gan from the very first. Emso's the only man besides Gan who's commanded the forces of the Three Territories."

Emso colored. A smile sat uncomfortably in place of his normal dour look. He nodded politely. "What Wal told you is true. You'll be protected here."

"The Skan will come. In the spring. I'm not supposed to know."

Emso's eyes flicked toward Wal, then back. "We're preparing for them."

"They know the sea. They have many, many sharkers, warriors. They expect the River People to help them."

This time Emso's look at Wal was much longer, more meaningful. The black-bearded For moved closer. Emso asked, "What do you know of the River People?" His voice was uncharacteristically soft. Narrowed eyes betrayed concern.

Jaleeta stepped back nervously. "Tears of Jade has an adopted son, Lorso. He's Slavetaker. That's like a war chief. She sent him to the Mother River to talk to the River People and Windband."

Wal said, "You told Murdat?"

Jaleeta appealed to Neela. "No one asked me anything except about myself. Did I say something wrong? Why is everyone angry with me?"

"No one's angry." Leclerc came forward, frowning disapproval at Emso and Wal. "You're telling us things we didn't know. It's not good news." Seeing the alarm flash across Jaleeta's features, Leclerc hastily added, "It's very important news, though. We have to tell Gan. All of it."

"Will you be there?" At his nod, she turned before he could speak, pointed at Emso. "And you? Janet Carter said he trusts both of you, and he doesn't know me."

Emso answered, "Of all the people in the Three Territories, you're the one with the least reason to lie to us about the Skan."

"Thank you. And thank you, Neela, for bringing me to your friends. I felt safe before I met all of you. Now I feel I can even fight back, if only in my woman's way."

The three women in Church black watched the others hurry toward the castle. Bernhardt turned to walk to the abbey, halting at the sound of Carter's thoughtful musing. "That's a very complex, shrewd article. Did you see the way she broke all three of those men to harness? I've seen some feminine wiles in my time, but that was rock-solid Eve-at-her-best stuff."

"Oh-h-h." Bernhardt drew the syllable out into a descending note of disdain. "She's young and pretty and frightened. No man can resist that."

Carter turned to face her. Taking Bernhardt's elbow, she pushed her gently toward the abbey. "Two out of three won't do it. She's not frightened."

Anspach disagreed. "Sure she was. I saw it."

"We saw something. Like, when Louis mentioned talking to Gan, she was all right until he said to tell Gan 'all of it.' I'll swear she winced. Maybe not winced, exactly, but something happened. It was quick. A twitch. But I saw something."

"Nuts," Anspach said. "Kate's right. The girl's scared. It's that simple."

Carter refused to give ground. "Wrong, wrong. Not scared; not the way any of us would be. And I'll tell you something else: If you believe our dark charmer is a mere child and not a sexually sophisticated young woman, you better spend a few hours out in the meadow observing the birds and the bees. Trust me on this."

Kate Bernhardt was amusedly sarcastic. "So when did you become the expert on lost innocence?"

Drawing herself erect, the wiry Carter strutted. "You're looking at a woman whose own perfection has driven several men into the consoling arms of women exactly like Jaleeta." Carter spun, flaring her robe, arms outstretched. "Presenting Janet Carter, new to this world, but nevertheless *the* authority on the timeless principles of how to screw up a romance. I know a succubus when I see one. If that bimbo has her way, we're all doomed to eternal spinsterhood."

Anspach and Bernhardt fell on her with mock blows. Grabbing her arms, they hustled her along between them. Bernhardt carefully avoided eye contact with her friends.

Jaleeta stood in the center of her room, hands clasped at her waist. The angle of her bowed head precluded her looking at anything higher than the maid's waist. Even so, the other young woman's patronizing voice underscored the scornful expression Jaleeta couldn't see. "Neela said you should be given this room for permanent quarters. When Altanar was king—when I first came to service in the castle—all this was servants' quarters." Jaleeta saw the woman's floor-length skirt hitch, and knew she'd made some large hand gesture. Tempted to look up and discover exactly what "all this" signified, Jaleeta forced herself to maintain her mouselike humility. The maid went on. "Some day the rooms'll be much nicer. For important guests."

The carelessness of the insults irritated Jaleeta. The woman knew her charge was under Neela's personal care, and still she hadn't the wit to watch her words. It was very disappointing. The maid was too stupid to be a source for all but the most insignificant gossip. A two-edged proposition, at best. Tears of Jade insisted that anyone who carried tales in one direction invariably carried them in the other. Jaleeta wasn't certain that was true, but Tears of Jade had been right about everything else.

The maid described the room, tone clearly implying that Jaleeta needed help in appreciating such luxuries as a down-filled mattress and a pieced-glass window that actually opened on hinges to provide ventilation. The woman completed her circuit at the single door. Head still down, Jaleeta asked, "Where's the locking bar?"

"When Altanar was king, the only rooms with bars were his. No one needed protection. We had the protectors, then. All dressed in white. Everyone was afraid of them, but we slept easy. No one went creeping around at night when the protectors were on guard."

"Is the castle dangerous now? People creep around?"

"I never said that. I was just saying how things used to be." Fear rippled through the words. Jaleeta murmured understanding and apology. She amended her earlier evaluation of the maid. There was resentment in her. Was it isolated? Reinforced?

As soon as the door was closed behind the departing servant, Jaleeta flung back her hood and raced around the room. Touching the polished wood of the two chairs and table by the window, she made low, sensual sounds of pleasure. She examined the ceramic pitcher and washbasin, the copper-decorated wooden clothes cabinet. A tall candelabra made her smile, thinking of such a wealth of candles instead of a stinking fish-oil lamp. Flinging open the window, she exulted in the dizzying two-story drop to the cropped lawn and neat gardens. A westerly breeze stirred late summer's heat. The air came laden with alien scents: hot stone and mortar that made her nose wrinkle; many horses; turned earth, and the sultry aroma of sun-washed flowers. Over everything, though, familiar and insistent, was the sea. Jaleeta leaned across the deep windowsill and inhaled luxuriantly.

The knock on the door startled her. Whirling, she faced the sound.

The knock came again, followed by an imperious, "Jaleeta. The escaped For girl. You're in there; I heard you."

Jaleeta took a deep breath. Raising her hood, resuming her subdued manner, she opened the door.

The Violet Abbess waited, arms folded, hands hidden within voluminous sleeves. Bright green and violet trim enlivened the sleeves and lower hem of her black robe. The hood, thrown back, carried identical decoration; deep within the hood, invisible unless intentionally exposed, was a gleaming green lining. Sweeping in, the Abbess literally knocked Jaleeta aside. From the center of the room, her back to Jaleeta, the older woman said, "I am the Violet Abbess. You were captured by unbelievers. Tortured. Lived with a spirit woman. Are you still loyal to Church? Tell me the truth. Lie, and you'll be cast out. Confess your sins freely and your punishment will be lightened accordingly."

"Please, Abbess." Jaleeta appealed to the Abbess' back. "I refused their god. They couldn't make me worship. I am loyal."

"Ah!" The Abbess whirled, stepped away in order to extend an arm and an accusing finger. "Loyal to whom? Even the Skan know Church is split, fully half our sisters in open rebellion. Whom do you support?"

Eyes downcast, Jaleeta pondered. This woman was power. Authority. Jaleeta had survived that once. She snatched at the Abbess' hand, clasped it to her forehead, and dropped to her knees. The unexpected move pulled the Abbess off balance. Jaleeta wailed, "She beat me! They hurt my mother, and made me watch! She said she'd give my mother to the Deep Calm. But I never worshipped, Abbess. Never. I swear."

The Abbess reclaimed her hand. Shrewd eyes examined Jaleeta's face. Their intensity frightened the younger woman, made her feel the very pores of her flesh might betray her. Tears came easily.

Cupping a hand under Jaleeta's chin, the Abbess said, "Your fear tells me you still have honesty in you. But you haven't answered my question. Which faction of Church do you support?"

"The Skan know only that the Rose Priestess Sylah discovered the secret of the Door, and that the new Sister Mother has cast out Sylah. They don't know why, so I don't, either. But they say Sylah is the most powerful woman in Church. I guess I support her."

The sound of the Abbess' palm against her cheek shocked Jaleeta more than the blow hurt. In the small, stone-walled room, it was like the crack of a whip. For a moment, her eyes blurred. When they cleared, the Abbess' hands were back inside the robe sleeves, arms crossed again. "You guess wrong. How can Sylah be 'the most powerful woman in Church' when she's cast out? She is anti-Church."

"She's a War Healer. If she keeps men alive, how can it be anti-Church?"

"What is a person who performs Church's holy offices, but who is not Church? What name do we give those who do magic?"

Jaleeta's eyes widened. She shook her head, denying what the Abbess demanded of her.

"Say it. Say it, child. Say what Sylah is, or be cursed with her."

"Witch."

"Louder." The Abbess shook Jaleeta, snapped her head back and forth. The hood fell away, released a wild tumble of shining black tresses. "I want to hear your heart speak. And I will know. The Violet Abbess will know."

"Witch. Witch! *Witch!*"

The Abbess released her, examined. Jaleeta felt that cold presence stalking her mind, prodding, peering.

The Abbess said, "You're afraid. Good. To call Sylah a witch should frighten you. If it didn't, I'd know you were lying. She is a witch, as is her little Seer friend, Lanta. But Church will triumph over them. There will be pain. Fire cleanses all."

Jaleeta saw the infinitesimal change of expression then. It was one Tears of Jade made familiar, a blend of hate, anticipation, and joy.

It stirred Jaleeta. It was the same face Tears of Jade wore when she described her plans for poor, foolish Lorso. Poor passionate Lorso.

The Violet Abbess thought herself harsh and cruel. Jaleeta wanted to laugh aloud. Tears of Jade made her look like a milk-fat kitten. Lorso would cut her throat for sport.

They all had much to learn of Jaleeta.

The Abbess sat in one of the chairs, gesturing for Jaleeta to do the same. "I'm going to trust you," the Abbess said, "because I have no choice. You've been given access to the castle, to Neela, even to Gan Moondark and the rabble that supports him. Church will bring them down, reinstitute Church order. You will help me."

Jaleeta recoiled. This was treason. "Murdat took me in, Abbess. Neela befriended me. The others . . . "

"Enemies." The Abbess rose, advanced. The hand that gripped Jaleeta's chin and forced her head up was hot, dry. "When you've told them all you know of the Skan, they'll abandon you, marry you off to some old man who'll use you until he tires of you. They betrayed Church. They'll betray you. I am your only hope."

Jaleeta shook her head. The harsh grip moved with her. Then, suddenly, she was released. The Abbess resumed her chair. Her features softened to sadness. "I've spoken too cruelly. I'm old, Jaleeta, accustomed to my way, accustomed to loving Church and being surrounded by those who love her as I do. Strife and pain have made me older than my seasons, as bitter as failed harvest. Now I come upon you, a young doe, weary and confused. My crude eagerness may startle you into the path of wolves. I fear for you, as I fear for Church and her rightful place. Church is beauty. Jaleeta is beautiful. You think your knowledge is the prize they treasure. You are horribly wrong. They'll twist your knowledge from you quickly. Draining your beauty will entertain them for years. One of them will enjoy it; the rest will be amused. You will know the agony of utter helplessness and abandonment. All because I failed you." Rising painfully, the Abbess walked toward the door, stopped. "Consider Emso. Old and ugly, I grant you, but the only one of Gan's circle who resists the preaching of the witch, Sylah. Church will deal more kindly with him than any of the others. Say nothing, however; to repeat a word of what I've said dooms him."

Covering her ears with her hands, Jaleeta backed against the wall. "I don't want to hear."

Managing a wan smile, the Abbess nodded. "I've been heavy-handed again. I mustn't mislead you; never think Emso's disloyal. He's merely old-fashioned and opposed to this new learning Gan loves."

"Church is still strong, and she'll be stronger yet. I'm too small, too weak, to be involved in these things, Abbess. I'd do more harm than good. But I love Church, and believe in her. In the end, she'll win. You'll see."

"Thank you. Your faith is as good as it is great. I learn from you." The Abbess let herself out, closed the door softly. Shuffling down the hall, she turned the corner. At that point, she stopped and straightened, stretching. When she smiled, she squinted, as one does when peering into the furnace where rough iron is tormented into steel.

At the same time, in Jaleeta's room, the younger woman stood by the window again. She threw her head back and laughed. There was hardly any sound, giving her amusement a sinister cast. After a moment, she positioned her hands in front of her as fists, the right ahead of the left. She appeared to study an imaginary long, slim article that extended some distance in front of her. Laughing again, she leaned back, jerked both hands upward. "Hooked," she said, exulting. "Well and truly hooked."

This time her laughter pealed loud into the sunshine.

CHAPTER 21

THE MESSENGER SWEPT INTO THE AUDIENCE ROOM WITH A FOPPISH SWAGGER. TWIN SPOTS of bright red leaped to the seated Gan's cheeks. Standing beside him, Emso extended a discreet hand, barely touching Gan's arm.

Gan spoke with careful neutrality. "You have a message for me?"

The Messenger bowed. He wore a soft leather hat that formed a limp cone, a full forearm long. Whipping it off as part of his greeting, he slapped it on the floor. Straightening, one leg cocked, he invited admiration. His shirt was of red, white, and green vertical panels, the trousers green with red checks the size of a man's palm. "I have the honor to bear a message for Murdat, ruler of the Three Territories."

"Know me, then. I'm Gan Moondark, called Murdat. Speak."

"I cannot. My sender instructed me to deliver the message to Murdat." The stare for Emso was deliberately insolent. This time Gan's restraining hand steadied Emso.

"Emso is my most trusted friend. He knows what I know. Speak."

"I cannot. A message must be spoken as the sender instructs."

Gan let go of Emso, rose slowly. "I hold nothing from my friend. Now, speak."

"My orders are clear." Confidence rapidly crumbling to consternation, the Messenger fumbled with the leather hat. His voice pitched upward. "Anyone who interferes with a Messenger . . ."

"Stop." Gan spat the word. Emso preempted further argument. "I'll wait in the next room. I don't mind. Really." He sent the Messenger a smile that drew a wince.

As soon as they were alone, the Messenger stepped closer to Gan. After collecting his wits, the Messenger's voice changed completely. His words came in a hoarse whisper. Gan recognized the voice of the woman who was now Sister Mother. "We have our differences, Gan Moondark, but nothing two practical people can't overcome. I am offered alliance by one sworn to destroy you. Weakness demands I accept. Unless you counter that offer with your own. Church must be one. It cannot be without you. Do not force me to choose against you. Do not force me to destroy you along with my enemies."

For a significant moment, the Messenger remained stiffly erect, features contorted by the intense effort to reproduce the message in its correct phrasing, tonality, and inflection. Sweat studded his forehead. Shivering, he slipped back into his own persona.

"That's all? That's the entire message?"

"Every word, as it was spoken."

"You've said nothing about this to anyone? One of your guild, perhaps?"

Drawing himself up haughtily, the Messenger said, "We are trusted because we reveal nothing, not to sender, not to receiver, not to anyone. I would never reveal anything about you."

It was a well-deserved rebuke, and Gan accepted it in frustrated silence. He managed to dismiss the man with courteous, if short, thanks. Then he called to Emso. As his friend returned, Gan made a face, gestured palms up. "He spoke the truth. The message demands my silence. I wish I could discuss it. I think your answer to the sender would come easily, and your judgment has never failed me. I apologize for excluding you."

"Everyone has secrets. Gan has some, Murdat has more. Even I have one or two. I think. Sometimes I don't remember so well." Emso winked, enjoying himself.

Gan laughed. "You always understand. I always wonder why."

"I've wondered myself. Sometimes I think it's the fear." Emso was suddenly deadly serious. "There's a smell of desperation around you. I can't explain. It's as if every time you make a bet, it's for everything you own. You understand? Those who love you find ourselves having to make the same bets as you."

Gan made a rare two-sign, invoking the One whose name was never spoken. "I want loyal friends around me, of course. I lead, Emso; I don't order. When I command the Wolves, it's because we're all fighting the same fight, fighting for the same goals."

"Men follow you because you give them hope. Even now, surrounded by tribes that mean to exterminate us, weakened by plague and warfare, the people of the Three Territories know Murdat will bring them victory, peace, and plenty. They'll fight to the death believing the survivors will see it. Me? I know war's a game that never ends."

"Why fight at all, then?"

"I was a beaten man, fighting for a defeated land, waiting only to die when you came to Jalail. Something told me you, a beaten, outcast boy, would find a way to save us from Altanar. I didn't want to believe. I had to. You gave me more than life. That's why I fight."

"You owe me nothing."

"No one spoke of debts." Emso's voice sharpened. "I'm grateful to you, but not so grateful that I live for you. I live as I choose, Murdat, and I'll die my own way. My life is mine. Again. And forever."

Gan's smile started as a slight movement of his lips, spread to encompass and illuminate his entire face. He put his right fist to his right ear in the Wolf salute. "I hear. I understand. Emso is his own man. Let the Messengers go forth in all the directions, spreading the word."

Emso mumbled and huffed, then finally found a tight grin that acknowledged Gan's jest. "Well, it's a serious matter. I don't talk about it easily, and that makes me gruff. Gruffer. I won't talk about it again, I promise you that. Once is enough. But I will say almost every man in the packs feels exactly the same."

"Are they afraid of my 'desperate' behavior, too?"

"I see more concern than fear. There's something eating your mind, something you fear more than defeat, more than death. I expected your charge against the Kwa, you know. I've seen men go into combat resigned to death, seen men use combat as a way to die. There's some of that in the way you act now, but it's not the same. When I first saw you, you fought for right, and for hope. Now I only see hope, and I don't understand what you hope for anymore."

"I hope for freedom. I don't want the responsibility. I never guessed what it could be like, how much of it there is."

"If you were a simple power-seeker, another Altanar or like that Chair person Conway tells about, it wouldn't bother you. As it is, I expect it to kill you." The latter phrase came with a dismissive nonchalance that snapped Gan's head around. Unperturbed, Emso continued. "You won't know when to stop. Even if you try, the prosperity you create will draw new enemies. You'll always respond. For your friends, for your people."

"That's the cruelest thing anyone's ever said to me." Almost imperceptibly, Gan settled into an aggressive crouch.

"Killing me won't change the truth. It'll only mean you've lost a friend."

"Don't say that." Gan straightened quickly, as if denying the tense moment ever occurred. "I depend on you."

"Good. Now, back to where we were when the Messenger came in: Everyone's sent for. The Barons arrive tomorrow. So does that For pirate, Wal. Conway, Tate, and Leclerc will be here. Is there anyone else you want?"

"That's everyone. We don't dare deal with so many enemies without everyone knowing everyone's responsibilities. Coordination, Emso. It's what makes the Wolves unbeatable. It's more important now than ever."

Emso moved to leave. "I'll make arrangements for tonight's dinner."

"See that there's entertainment. Tomorrow we'll argue. Tonight we'll enjoy ourselves."

Snorting, Emso slammed the heavy door behind him.

Soon he was standing in the doorway to the huge kitchen that served the needs of the castle. The woman in charge came to greet him. She wore the red-and-yellow belt of the castle staff over homespun blouse, slacks, and apron of off-white. When the woman brushed her hands on the apron, small puffs of flour leaped from the material to precede her, as if declaring her calling. "Good morning, Emso. How many join Murdat for dinner tonight?"

"Are there no secrets in the Three Territories? I just came from Murdat."

The woman shrugged. "The son of the woman who brings me greens was sent to fetch Baron Galmontis. My second baker's daughter is . . ."

"Stop." Emso raised a hand. "It's bad enough knowing we have no security without hearing how every gardener and dough-squeezer in the land is shouting our business."

"The only one shouting is you. You don't seem to feel my cooks and suppliers are so dangerous to you when you sit down to my table."

Emso opened his mouth to explore the connection between eating and state secrets, and despaired of penetrating the logic involved. Instead, he mumbled the number and turned to leave, trying to avoid the appearance of slinking.

Neela adroitly sidestepped his retreat. Emso came to a clumsy halt. Reaching out to assure he didn't bump her, he inadvertently hit Jaleeta with a forearm. Further nonplussed, he grabbed Jaleeta's shoulder to help her keep her balance, forgetting his own. Staggering, practically embracing the young woman, he lost whatever composure he had left. Leaping as if Jaleeta burned him, he slammed into the wall behind him.

Emso disliked sympathy. Hearing it chopped up by unrestrainable laughter was almost unbearable.

When Neela choked out, "What brings you to the kitchen?" he answered with a wounded dignity that almost set off another round of hilarity.

"Murdat's dinner arrangements. And you?"

The cook answered for Neela. "I'll be ready to show you and Jaleeta the kitchen as soon as I check on my bread, Neela. I was coming for you when Emso came." She gestured at rising loaves on a table, and Neela nodded understanding. The cook hurried away. To Emso, Neela said, "I'd completely forgotten the Barons are all coming. It'll be a chance for Jaleeta to meet them. We'll be having entertainment, too, won't we?"

Jaleeta shrank back. "I can't come."

"Why not? You're my guest, mine and my husband's. The Barons are just men. Sylah will be there. Lanta and Tate, too. Of course you can come."

"That's not it." She sent a furtive glance at Emso.

"Gan and I trust Emso as we trust each other. So must you."

"Thank you." Emso nodded his appreciation to Neela, expressionless. He repeated the gesture for Jaleeta, who flashed a bright smile of relief and acceptance that quickly broke, replaced by the troubled expression. Addressing Neela, she adamantly rejected the invitation again. "Don't you see, Neela, I can't repeat anything I don't know, or make some innocent remark later that reveals something important. Let me help Sylah and the Church women with the Chosens. Tears of Jade will suspect I'm shirking, but I don't care."

Emso glowered. "How's she to know?"

Jaleeta edged closer to Neela, her wide, vulnerable eyes fixed on Emso. Neela spoke before Jaleeta could. "Jaleeta was told she'd be contacted. Someone in the Three Territories is a spy, expected to carry whatever she learns back to this Tears of Jade and the Skan. Don't bully Jaleeta; she has no idea who it is."

Bridling, Emso tried to soften his expression. The result was close to grimace.

"I was going to say I think she's very wise. And very brave. Being from the sunrise side of the Enemy Mountains, you and Gan don't have much knowledge of the Skan. Over here, to sunset side, we know Tears of Jade's name too well. Mention evil, and you mention her." Emso turned his gaze on Jaleeta. "Take no chances. Do as Neela says; go to the dinner. You'll hear no secrets, but you'll be able to impress your contact with your knowledge of our activities here. We'll see you have some pretty tales to tell, never fear."

A smiling Jaleeta extended a shy hand, pulled it back in a flutter of embarrassment. She faced Neela. "I don't know if I can do it, Neela. I mean, meet this person, tell him what I'm supposed to say. It'll mean lying. I've already proven I don't do that very well." She blushed.

Emso bent forward, reassuring. "Don't you worry. We'll give you easy things, and we'll go over it with you until you've got it right."

"You're very kind. No wonder Gan and Neela think so much of you. I'm glad you're always close. Sometimes I wonder what could happen if Tears of Jade learns I betrayed her. Or if she just decides to get rid of me."

Emso glowered. "You're one of us, Jaleeta. We take care of each other."

Neela read entreaty in the grateful, touched look Jaleeta sent her. Turning Jaleeta toward the kitchen, she told Emso, "I promised Jaleeta I'd show her the kitchen. Excuse us, please."

Neela was surprised to realize the gruff warrior looked more solemn than cross. When he saluted to leave, his eyes lingered on the partial profile Jaleeta turned to him. What Neela saw in the crags and scars of the hard-used features then gave her a feeling that went far beyond surprise.

Chapter 22

The sharker fought the current. Wearily, bow crashing through a battering chop, it strained past looming cliffs, towering trees. Progress was a grim plod; like a temperamental, high-strung horse the vessel sometimes reacted to the confused swirl of wind and current with what the crew could only consider a display of temper. The boat reared, shaking and twisting its entire length, spilling its sails so they refilled with thunderous slaps. The crew winced at each outburst. They feared and distrusted the unknown spirits of this rushing, relentless sea of fresh water. More, they knew the peril of sailing an angry boat.

The men had more problems than the river. Sea-raiders, they were unable to accept a horizon they had to lift their chins to examine. The gorge of the Mother River imprisoned their vision, loomed over them with awful silence. The crew had discovered, however, that the silence was preferable to most of the sounds that came from the dark forest cloaking the river's banks.

Two days after the wrenching experience of crossing the bar at the river's mouth, Lorso realized that Tears of Jade's view of the political situation along the river was seriously flawed. There were great distances between the villages of the

River People, and even greater differences in their allegiances. Many rejected affiliation with Windband; that was Lorso's first shock. The hostility of the non-Windband adherents was an even more unpleasant awakening.

The most disturbing revelation of all, however, came from the most unexpected direction.

Traditionally nothing more than a source of slaves, the tribe living south of the Mother River who were known as Smalls was suddenly a force to be reckoned with. The reclusive forest dwellers had always been far more ready to flee than fight. Lorso was shocked to learn the Smalls had expanded north onto forested land claimed by the River People. Those River villages opposed to alliance with Windband actually welcomed the incursions, since the Small presence created a buffer between themselves and the pro-Windband faction. All of this was forcefully brought home to Lorso and his crew when they attempted an evening landfall on territory newly occupied by the Smalls.

Typically, the Small attack wasn't pressed. They merely wanted to drive off the intruders. Even though three Skan died under arrows shot by their invisible enemy, the Skan regarded the ambush as proof that the Smalls were inept. Instead of exterminating the crew, the Smalls had only inflicted casualties. The Skan vowed to return.

On Lorso's present signal to make for shore, the crew hunkered down behind the raised gunwale, bows and arrows ready. Once in the quieter waters of a large eddy, they launched small boats, one fore and one aft, to carry ashore mooring lines and shore guards. Cooking and eating was done aboard, and the fire doused before darkness. Men moved to their assigned guard positions. Despite the damp chill, the protective hide sleeping cover normally stretched from gunwale to gunwale was left stowed in the hold. A bit of discomfort was much preferred to waking in the dark, under attack, trapped under the confining leather.

Then it was the time Lorso hated. Without the demands of sailing to occupy his mind, the mission's weight swept down on him, full force.

Tears of Jade had no concept of the difficulty of maintaining communications with anyone as far upriver as Windband. She merely set a certain time to reach them. What she couldn't anticipate was that the length of the Mother River seethed with new alliances and multiplying intrigues.

Church and the schismatic Rose Priestess Sylah had their adherents. This settlement hated Kossiars, that one hated Windband. An unsettling number of villages—particularly those on the north bank—openly favored the Three Territories in the fighting they expected to erupt in the spring. On the south bank, the presence of the Smalls assured harassing attacks on Skan sharkers approaching their holdings. Every landfall brought new tales of joinings and separations. The whole thing swirled and looped in Lorso's mind.

In the darkness after the last meal, Lorso rejected all of that political concern. Sleepless, watching the stars, he listened to the mumbled conversation of his boat and the river. He was alone, by the tiller, as was correct for the captain. From there, the lovers' talk that passed between the vessel and the water was heard best. In theory, only the captain was privileged to listen. Everyone did it, though, straining to detect the querulous whine of jealousy that meant planks working loose, or the irritable grate of a mast wearing away at the tree. The relationship between boat and water was always delicate; far more dangerously balanced than that between men and women.

Stretched out on the deckboards, Lorso heard every whisper, felt the least tremor in the supple keel. To him, the boat was ultimate femininity, one moment shy and graceful, the next straining and fiery in her needs. But always beautiful.

And so he thought constantly of Jaleeta. Blood howled passion through pulsing arteries that cared nothing for gods or spirit women or the fate of nations.

A repetitious dream haunted him when he managed to fall asleep. The sharker fled, galled by clouds of arrows. One arrow, a huge thing, called his name. It was the same as always, dark against moonlight. Horribly, the thing had a face. The features were human, distorted by battle-rage, gnashing, gleaming teeth and mad, fixed eyes. The face shrieked his name, arced down, down. Pain swallowed him. And cold, black water. Blackness.

Lorso woke, choking.

The Lorso in the dream knew the name of that face.

Making his way to the rail, Lorso relieved his bladder. The splashing brought a guard, sword drawn. The man grinned acknowledgment on seeing what was happening. Lorso told the man to ready the signal to bring in the shore watch, ending the conversation. When certain he was alone again, and with his back to the rest of the ship, Lorso drew a small knife and nicked the tip of a finger. Head bowed, he squeezed out symbolic drops of sacrificial blood. Dripping it into the river, he begged Sosolassa's favor.

Tears of Jade assured him that all river gods were subject to Sosolassa and his limitless sea. Lorso believed. Nevertheless, the god of this one was an insubordinate fury. Tears of Jade never saw the bar at the mouth, where fresh water stormed unendingly against the supreme god's domain. Of course the river lost, was smothered. But what death was that, that knew no end of struggle, no cessation of life?

Running a thumb along the tips of all his fingers, Lorso reaffirmed they were all healing quickly.

When he turned, the men were stirring. The tenor of their waking was even more surly than usual. Lorso frowned. Shipboard life was too close to tolerate temper. The last friendly village estimated the sharker would reach the place where Moonpriest waited in five days. Today would make the sixth, and no sign of a settlement.

The mood of the men suggested relaxation was in order. Lorso ordered the cook to prepare oatcakes, and to open one of the honey kegs. As soon as the men saw the great iron griddle plate unpacked and lowered onto the firebox, they brightened. A hot breakfast in place of the standard cold sausage and hard bread excited everyone. Honey was a treat reserved for special occasions.

As the steaming fragrance of cooking rose to fill the boat, Lorso addressed his crew. "It's been a tiresome voyage. You've handled it well. I'm proud of you, but I know that's not enough to satisfy you. We should reach Moonpriest today. If we don't, we keep going until we do. Sosolassa orders it. After my business with

Moonpriest, however, we're on our own. We've taken too much abuse from these mud-sucking landscum. Deblo, you're in charge of storage spaces; make room for slaves. Be sure we have plenty of strong line."

It was exactly the message his Skan needed. Additionally, the rising sun brought a stiff breeze. By midmorning the bow lookout shouted news of a village. Colored banners hung in the trees. The raw-throated blare of a horn rolled downriver to them, echoing hauntingly from the enclosing mountains. With a cheer, the Skan leaned harder into their oars. Eager youngsters darted out into the river in canoes and on the peculiar one-man sailboats. The latter seemed to fly across the surface, and the men piloting them were amazingly skilled. A favorite display was to build up speed, catch the crest of a wave, and fling their craft up, airborne. As soon as the sharker was secured with lines to the shore, the Skan crowded the rails and applauded the acrobatic sailors.

Lorso went ashore in a short whitebear cape over cream-colored woolen trousers and shirt of the finest, lightest thread. The shirt, a simple design of front and back sewn together, was decorated by a gray keystone pattern running back and forth in horizontal lines. Trousers were tucked into piebald sealskin boots. A thin jade amulet, as long as Lorso's hand, hung from a gold chain around his neck; it depicted a leaping killer whale.

The most striking thing was Lorso's hat. Woven of dyed cedar bark, a full two handspans tall and gleaming black, it represented a raven's head facing forward, golden eyes agleam. The rear was a snarling animal face, again with golden eyes, but with the addition of pointed dentalium shell teeth. Bristling seal whiskers, set into the hat's weave, extended outward. Tiny silver bells at the tips of the whiskers chimed an almost inaudible chorus at Lorso's every move.

Greeting him in his immaculate white robes, turban, and silver moon disk, Moonpriest looked positively austere. "Welcome, Lorso, to my humble camp. Our scouts only warned us of your coming last night, so please forgive the lack of proper welcome."

Despite Moonpriest's modest demur, bright, fluttering cloth pennants decorated the trees. Everyone in view seemed to be dressed in new finery. The place was a blur of colors, feathers, flowers. Best of all, a smoky richness of cooking lay across the camp in an enfolding aura.

Back from the river, directly behind Moonpriest, sat a massive white tent Lorso was certain belonged to his host. A wide avenue led to an open entryway with a shading awning. Moonpriest, half turned, waiting for Lorso to join him. Walking toward the tent, Moonpriest said, "Arrived a few days ago. The old one burned. Many in Windband lost tents that night. A punishment. We welcomed an imposter, nurtured a man who claimed to be a brother, child of the moon, as I am. He murdered my war chief, destroyed our camp. He was sent by Gan Moondark and the Church witch that calls itself the Flower." He stopped, faced Lorso just outside the tent. "I seek allies. My interest in loot or slaves is small, only enough to offset my losses, expenses, and the fair demands of my warriors. All else Windband and Moonpriest renounce. But the witch must be mine."

"Traders spoke of the damage to your camp. I'm instructed to express the sympathy of our Navigators. Also the sorrow of our spirit woman, named Tears of Jade. Because she's another religious, like yourself, she understands the great pain that comes of a breaking of faith."

The faint glimmer of annoyance that slipped across Moonpriest's features was well controlled, Lorso thought, but sufficiently revealing. Moonpriest didn't like being considered "another" religious. Secretly, Lorso was very pleased. Whatever Moonpriest might be, and it was obvious he was a leader of a fierce people, he believed in false gods. There would be no divine guidance for Moonpriest as there was for Tears of Jade, so the triumph of Sosolassa was assured. Difficulty might delay the inevitable; it wouldn't stop it.

Before entering the tent, Moonpriest faced west. It was shortly after the sun's high point, and Moonpriest lifted the silver disk at his breast, tilting it to catch the sun. It angled light onto a nearby ridge. Immediately, a ululation rose, a wavering spiral of sound that raised the hair on the back of Lorso's neck.

A sound of distant thunder followed the echoes of the call. It grew louder, finally erupting from behind the ridge as a charging wave of horsemen. As they hit the crest and descended they bellowed war cries, some roaring deeply, some screaming high and wild. Command pennants snapped in the wind.

Horses and riders—Lorso was sure there were hundreds—stormed past. Some came within a handspan of his nose. The wind of their passing stirred his clothes. That was as nothing compared to what the vibrating earth did to his insides.

Slung across their backs, the horsemen carried short, recurved bows of a type Lorso had never seen. Each brandished a long, steel-tipped lance. Every saddle sported a sword in a scabbard. Lorso had no knowledge of horses or riding. He had an appreciation for armor, and noted how many of the warriors dressed in chain-mail shirts that draped low enough to protect almost to the knee. Helmets were universal, as well. They appeared to be metal over padded leather. Fittings in the back carried small, colored pennants. They streamed in the wind, dividing the riders into groups—white, red, yellow, and blue.

The last of the riders finally whooped and yelled departure from within an obscuring cloud of dust. Lorso inhaled hugely, albeit distastefully, hating the stink of dirt, fresh animal droppings, and sweat.

Inside the tent, a hidden stringed instrument and a high-pitched metallic-sounding drum combined to play soothing intricate melody. Overhead, a long, rectangular fan stirred the air, which was thick with floral scent. Slaves hurried into the room carrying trays of berry syrup in ceramic containers. A larger, far thicker bowl with a similarly heavy lid held chipped ice. Following Moonpriest's example, Lorso mixed the syrup with ice and water from the large bowl. He almost gasped with pleasure, suddenly aware of exactly how hot the cape and woolen clothes were.

Moonpriest said, "Feel free to take off the cape. We've no need to be uncomfortable, you and I. We'll be friends. My mother has said so."

It was on the tip of Lorso's tongue to retort that he'd had no such message from Sosolassa, but he decided it was impolitic. Besides, this outlandishly dressed little man with his tight face that looked like it was made of dried fish skin was almost pathetically eager to please. Lorso determined to accommodate him. Shedding the cape, he said, "I'd be honored to be counted a friend. Your reputation has brought you great respect among the Skan. Our Navigators will match your accomplishments in the east by attacking from the west."

Suddenly, the ingratiation of Moonpriest's smile acquired a bite; Lorso caught himself thinking of the white-cold country far to the north, where an uninitiated man could lose the skin of his hand simply by picking up a piece of exposed iron. "Windband's attack will drive up from the south. We need several sharkers to keep renegade Rivers away. We ask little, as I'm sure the Skan want to attack the most populous areas, near Ola and Harbundai, in order to acquire slaves and loot."

"The Skan are warriors, not caretakers."

Moonpriest shook his head. "Only the Skan fight on water as well as land. If Windband attacks the Rivers, they hop in their boats and float away from us. We need cooperation against attacks in our rear."

"The Mother River is still just a river. If Windband had some boats . . ."

"Windband admits it knows nothing of boats. Would the Skan care to ride into battle on our horses?"

Hiding a shudder, Lorso said, "I'll discuss the matter with the Navigators. Perhaps we can spare two or three sharkers to help you here."

"You see?" Moonpriest was completely affable again. "Didn't I say we'd be friends? Our first problem, and we solved it with no trouble at all. Now, let's consider exactly when we should attack. You'll have to concern yourself with tides, currents, winds, the phase of the moon."

Lorso cupped his chin in his hands, bending forward to watch Moonpriest's darting hands draw a huge map in the dust of the tent floor. As lands he'd only heard of were sketched and related to each other, he realized Moonpriest hadn't solved their first problem. On the contrary, he'd won their first argument. A small thing, but an inauspicious start.

A disquieting dryness invaded Lorso's mouth and throat. He cursed his fate. Raised by a religious, then sent by that one to argue with another. If he gave too much or lost the alliance, Tears of Jade would punish him for failing Sosolassa.

He wouldn't fail. Tears of Jade sent him, and she was Sosolassa's presence on earth. Lorso eased into calm assurance. The power of the god was with him.

CHAPTER 23

TENSION WHINED IN THE COOL NIGHT BREEZE STIRRING THE TORCHLIT PENNANTS OF Windband.

River boys, filled with pride, guarded the heavy shore lines binding the sharker to the beach. Windband and River warriors mingled easily, if not warmly, with the Skan crew. Responsibility for flirting with the exotically tattooed Skan fell entirely to the River women. They were known for their beauty, and aware of it. They applied themselves to their social requirement with laudable industry.

That, of course, was the root of some tension.

The men of this particular subgroup of the River People were celebrated for their combat skills. Equally, the nomads of Windband considered warfare a way of life. A mere look at the Skan crew identified them as fierce fighters. Now all three cultures sat in community, eating and drinking. Weapons were admired, passed around, hefted. Fletching was discussed, the advantage of waterfowl feathers compared to those of other birds. Cautious thumbs traced the razored edge of swords.

Contributing to the stiff behavior and set jaws, singers and taletellers from each group dueled with their counterparts.

Moonpriest was acutely aware that one overenthusiastically demonstrated thrust and one excessively excited parry could bring bloody chaos. He smelled danger, acrid as steel held too long to the grinding wheel.

Joining Lorso at a huge trestle table, Moonpriest smilingly gestured at the man accompanying him. As that one sat down, Moonpriest introduced him. "Lorso, this is my right hand. More than that, my brother, my truest friend. Fox Eleven, former Manhunter of the Mountain People, now War Chief of Windband." To Fox, Moonpriest added, "Our friend Lorso is the adopted son of Tears of Jade, the spirit woman of the Skan. Although we worship differently, we're agreed that Gan Moondark is a mutual enemy. He protects the witch, Sylah, who would raise Church to challenge all men."

Fox and Lorso exchanged controlled nods, quiet greetings.

For a moment, Moonpriest despaired; even his most senior lieutenants eyed each other like dogs across a bone. He forced himself to continue as if nothing threatened.

"What everyone must understand is the terrible power of the secret of the Door. Women are bidding to control that power. Sylah simpers and claims she desires only equality for women. As if that weren't enough! In plain fact, she intends to make Church and its women the overlords of all. Men will be servants. Women who aren't Church will be even worse off than now. Imagine a woman with privilege. We all know how deceitful and spiteful they are. Imagine yourself slave to a female."

A touch of color tainted Lorso's weathered features. Moonpriest cursed himself for underestimating the hold the woman called Tears of Jade must have over her adopted son. He spoke quickly, glossing the error. "I'm sure you never hear Tears of Jade insist that women rule your people."

"Tears of Jade would never suggest such arrogance." Images flicked across Lorso's mind as he said it. Men who'd disagreed with Tears of Jade. Men who'd been foolish enough to desire young women Tears of Jade wanted given to men she favored. Lorso remembered incantations. Potions and powders created in deepest secrecy. The god's business. Sosolassa could be very cruel. Men died in indescribable agony. A sharker commanded by a man who offended Tears of Jade disappeared at sea.

Sternly, Lorso reminded himself that Tears of Jade never sought personal power. Power rested with Sosolassa. What happened was his doing.

Fox asked, "What do you think of our River allies? One of your men told me you were attacked frequently, coming upstream."

Pulling at a long braid, Lorso's answer was almost a challenge. "In the end, it'll be helpful to us that they're divided. Once Gan Moondark is crushed and Sylah dead, the Skan see little need for the Rivers."

"Many would agree with such argument." Moonpriest's lips barely moved. "If two allies suddenly turned on a third, however, it might prove very difficult to form other alliances later in order to overrun Kos."

"If the third ally turned on its friends, those two would be right to defend themselves." Lorso shrugged hugely.

"Exactly." Fox leaned forward, peered around Moonpriest at Lorso. The lean, leathery Mountain warrior was outfitted in finery typical of his adopted nomad brethren. Fire opals set in silver disks were sewn in large-petaled floral patterns on his shirt; smaller versions decorated his sleeve. Larger opals dangled from his ears on long gold chains. He reflected small firelights in myriad directions. Fox bunched his fists on the table, continuing, "I mean to mount Gan's skull on my battle pennant. I'll make a spirit flute of his leg bone and a cape from the skin of his dogs. But I will give up all of that if Moonpriest orders, because he is a god. He must—"

A hand shot out with a swiftness surprising from one as apparently nonphysical as Moonpriest. It clamped down on Fox's wrist. He finished the sentence for Fox. "He must never forget that others can't be forced to acknowledge his holiness. We know what happens when power is abused."

Moonpriest released Fox, leaned back from the table. His eyes lost focus. His voice took on a haunted tone, yet there was menace in the dry scrape of it. "A god who lends his power to another is punished. Conway is an agent of Sylah's Church. His evil destroyed Windband's camp, destroyed many lives. He brought the curse of sickness to Windband, helped Sylah cheat me of the Door. If not for Fox and the elite fighters called Blizzard, my nomads would have been scattered. We survived rebellion and apostasy. We're stronger than ever. My power is stronger than ever. As you and your men will learn. But enough storytelling. Our host indicates entertainment."

The music of the River People struck Lorso as effeminate. He was used to the skirl of whistles and the hypnotic thump of heavy drums. The four River musicians plucked at strings stretched over long-necked hollow boxes, producing complex, supple sounds that wound across the crowd as delicately as smoke. It was much like the earlier music in Moonpriest's tent, even to the insistent little metallic drum in the background.

Somehow, though, the music stirred Lorso. Thoughts of the mission struggled to remain uppermost in his mind, but sank under visions of Jaleeta. As if to mock his weakness, a lone River woman moved out into the open ground formed by the three dining tables. At the dancer's appearance, a gusting exclamation swept the crowd of over two hundred men gathered there. In the taut silence that followed, the instruments seemed to grow louder. The song became a goad.

The woman, bold as a jay, strode the front of all three tables. Dressed in a long, white deerskin skirt and close-fitting sleeveless jacket of the same material, her black, gleaming hair was a cloud that swept below her buttocks. The white leather was embroidered in green, yellow, and blue, rippling lines that spoke of the life-giving river and sun. Belled anklets and wristbands tinkled as she walked. Lithe, she smiled at her audience with the confidence of a woman who knows precisely how tempting and dangerous her beauty is, and who revels in the knowledge. With her circuit of the tables complete, she gestured in the direction of the River women and nonwarriors beyond the fire at the fourth side of the banquet area. A girl darted out with a mask, then ran back.

The mask was a tiger. Pure white fangs bared in a snarl, it was amazingly life-like. The tempo of the music increased, the volume subsided. Intricate melody gave way to a simpler, repetitive refrain.

The woman breathed life into the image. For quite a while, she stalked. Those watching felt her press against shielding rocks, knew the rough touch of bark as she eased around trees, sensed the twigs and rocks underfoot that must not be broken or rattled.

She portrayed a hunt, projected the full atavistic emotion and imbued it with sensuousness. Utterly silent, the warriors were transfixed.

The twanging little drum raced now. The string music shivered with anticipation.

She sprang, an incredible athletic move that began with four running steps to reach foot-blurring speed. Soaring high, she straightened horizontally, flew directly at the head table, at Moonpriest, Lorso, and Fox. At the last instant, when it appeared she must fall facedown, she drew her feet under her, landing on the ground, facing them in a triumphant crouch. Rising swiftly, she posed, arms outstretched, demanding admiration. Then she was racing to disappear among the mass of her people.

"Isn't she splendid?" It was Moonpriest, flushed and grinning.

"A very attractive dancer." Lorso heard the tension in his voice, cursed it.

The music was drowned out by the rough, raucous laughter and shouting of stirred-up men.

One of Lorso's crew appeared at his shoulder. Sweat ran down his face. Bits of food clung to his cropped whiskers. "Windband's got women," the crewman said. "They said we can come with them to the wagons, outside the village. Come with us."

Lorso looked to Fox, who winked. "Captives. Some Smalls, mostly Kossiars. A few Rivers from hostile villages. None as pretty as the last one."

Moonpriest added, "We can't ask our warriors to live like monks. No one's allowed to damage the women. It's all very well managed. You and your crew are welcome guests."

"No. I can't. I took an oath. My mission must be accomplished." Over his shoulder, addressing his fellow Skan, Lorso added, "Go without me. I never should have sworn . . ." He forced a laugh. It jangled in his ears like broken shells.

No one else seemed aware of the falsity. The crewman hurried off. Feeling foolish, vulnerable, Lorso got to his feet. "I'll sleep aboard," he told Moonpriest. "Thank you for your hospitality." Then, embarrassed not to have asked sooner, he said, "Why didn't someone from the River People join you and Fox and me?"

Moonpriest laughed easily. "I asked Saris to give us this afternoon and evening alone with you. I explained that some persuasion was needed to bring the Skan into complete alliance. You understand?" A sly grin assumed complicity, and Moonpriest added, "Tomorrow you'll both meet. Saris and I have more entertainment scheduled. Uncommitted Rivers from many villages are coming here. I will convert them to Moondance. They'll see you and your vessel, hear you describe the power of the Skan. We'll strengthen our force by many, many warriors."

"I speak to them?"

"Just tell them who you are, how many sharkers you can send into battle, that sort of thing. Can you do it?"

Lorso straightened. "I speak to our Navigators. I'll have no trouble here."

"Good man. We're going to rule, my Skan friend." Moonpriest clapped Lorso on the shoulder as the latter waved and turned away.

Once Lorso was out of earshot, Fox spoke. "He didn't even see the dancer's look for him. Maybe he's not a man at all."

Moonpriest led Fox away from the table. "Lorso has another woman. At home. I'm sure of it."

"Then the plan failed. You wanted Lorso involved. 'Increase our hold on him,' you said."

Irritably, Moonpriest increased his pace. "Use your mind. You, who can track anything anywhere; can't you see the importance of his refusal? As a tracker, isn't it as important for you to see what actually *is*, rather than what you *expect*? Lorso denies himself. We have our opening."

"I understand about the tracking. I don't understand about Lorso."

"Good." Exasperation made the word a weapon. "Just leave the thinking to me. Good night." Moonpriest broke off toward his tent.

Lorso, picking his way along the bouncing board connecting the sharker to land had no thoughts for Moonpriest or Fox. He focused his mind on Jaleeta. He thought of her hair. Like the dancer's. Of her grace. Dancer's grace. Of her rich, full body.

With his eyes closed, cedar and lilac seemed to flood his nostrils, the scents she favored. The pressure of her embrace forced air from his lungs, and his body tightened with the tactile memory of warm, soft skin pressed against him. No matter how hard he tried, however, Jaleeta's face evaded his mind's vision.

He discovered a drowned friend once, dead on the bottom in water only waist-deep. The day was perfect, cloudless, the sun a benevolence. Light joined with the wind-ruffled water's surface to disguise the features, mottle them, turn them this way and that, so Lorso didn't know if the mouth grinned or grimaced, didn't know if the wide, sightless eyes begged for release or winked in macabre jest.

Why would Jaleeta come to him with the same wavering, unsure features?

Chapter 24

The next morning, Lorso stood at the bow of his moored sharker and watched a matched team of six black horses pull a massive wagon onto the level stretch just beyond the rocky riverbank. He sneered. Horses. Eyes rolling, clomping about on huge, hard feet—they could cripple a man just by stepping on him in their smelly excitement. Disgusting.

The wagon load was covered. Idly, Lorso wondered what needed protection on such a fine day.

Behind him, Moondance said, "Good morning, Lorso," and the Skan started. When he turned, Moonpriest and a River smiled apology from down on the shore. Moonpriest said, "Didn't mean to startle you. I came to introduce Saris." Moonpriest tilted his head to the side, indicating the River, gestured at the team and carriages. "This is all part of the demonstration planned for today. What disturbs you?"

"Nothing. I was wondering what they're doing."

Saris said, "Moonpriest has wonders to show us."

"Wonders?" Lorso moved aft to where the gap between hull and shore narrowed and vaulted over the side. Moonpriest laughed aloud, entertained. "Very acrobatic."

"What?" Lorso asked. He noticed the River, Saris, was as puzzled as himself.

Moonpriest blanched, appeared to choke. "A word from my past," he said. "From before I was claimed by my mother, and born again. We called a person who could leap and turn that way an 'acrobat'; what they did was 'acrobatic.' I forgot you don't have the word."

Saris nodded, looking wise. "Would you call our woman who did the tiger dance an acrobat?"

"Not exactly."

Lorso was too sensitive about his limp to endure the subject for long. "Where is this land of yours, Moonpriest? The Skan trade wherever land meets water, even as far as the country of the Nions. No one we trade with knows this place. We know your friends came to Gan Moondark—"

"Never say that!" Moonpriest's visible discomfort over questions about his homeland escalated to rage at the remark about Gan Moondark. Inwardly, Lorso exulted, delighted to have irritated one so pompous. The notion that he'd angered a god chilled him momentarily. When he considered that he was under the protection of his own Sosolassa, he relaxed.

Moonpriest raged on. "I was an ordinary man once, and I come from a place more distant than you can imagine. I came with other men and women. That much is true. I never joined Gan Moondark, as the others have done. They're fools, under the influence of Sylah." He broke off, literally panting in his fury.

Lorso watched the man's color suddenly alter. The bloodred of anger weakened to an exhausted, blue pallor. Moonpriest recovered, then resumed, icily calm. "This day you'll see my power. You'll know how unfortunate it is to lose my affection." He stalked away.

For a moment, the two men shifted awkwardly. Finally, Lorso managed a small grin. "Perhaps I irritated him. A little bit." He held up thumb and forefinger, almost touching.

"More than that, I think." Saris' answering smile was tentative, the quick cut of his eyes toward the retreating Moonpriest cautious. "He's very dangerous."

Making conversation, inviting Saris to share something to eat, Lorso examined the River leader. The tight, sleeveless jacket showed a well-muscled torso. One arm was seriously injured. Full, bloused trousers looked too skirtlike for Lorso's taste. Unlike the clothing, Saris' hat looked quite new. The wide brim was excellent weather and sun protection, the crown high enough to protect against the sun's heat. It took a second look for Lorso to realize the hatband was a snake, with the head extended forward, fangs at the ready.

He recoiled. Saris saw and understood. More assured now, he swept the hat off, extended it toward Lorso. A taunt lurked in his words. "I'm told there are no poisonous snakes where you live."

Lorso positioned his feet for a sword stroke. His hand went to the weapon's handle. "You were told right. They kill people. Why wear one?"

Saris laughed easily. "Snakes are the spirit animal of Moondance. This snake, the one that warns, is Moonpriest's spirit animal. Only men chosen by Moonpriest are allowed to wear the skin of the sacred one."

"If a man is chosen, must he wear the skin?"

Pondering a moment, Saris grew serious. "Moonpriest never said that."

"Good. Skan have their own spirit animals."

"Moonpriest respects these things. He allows anyone to worship any way they choose, as long as they acknowledge Moondance's supremacy. He says all gods and spirits answer to his mother."

Sweat prickled along Lorso's spine. He wished Tears of Jade were present. How could he reconcile Sosolassa answering to the moon mother? If he denied the rule, the alliance must collapse. If he accepted it, Sosolassa would claim him. Adopted son notwithstanding, Tears of Jade would take the sad walk to the ceremony rock and sing the song of curses for Lorso. Spirits burdened with the song of curses lurked in the sea, just under the surface, always wet, always cold, always reaching out to draw down the living.

Saris shrewdly guessed what caused Lorso's concern. "If I were troubled by a conflict between my religion and Moondance, I'd say nothing. If Moonpriest doesn't demand that you accept the moon mother, why bring up the subject?"

Tears of Jade warned that intrigue would be as ordinary as rain in the course of the alliance. Lorso already saw the negotiations as more like stalking prey; the advantage wasn't with whoever played the game fastest or hardest, but most quietly.

He changed the subject. "What is this wonder you spoke of?"

The River's reaction was unexpected. Saris' eyes widened momentarily. Lorso was certain he saw a touch of fear. "Moonpriest's surprise. Later, just before sundown. We need time for the people to gather." He indicated upstream. Lorso looked to see a pair of previously unnoticed River boats approaching. The grayed wood hulls and dusky tan sails blended admirably with the greenish-brown water and the sunbaked cliffs of the north shore. That was the best thing Lorso could say for them. Heavy, stolid, the vessels were built for work. They carried traders, cargo, livestock, or fishermen. Lorso hid his contempt, picturing how easily his sharker would slash past such a waddling hulk. He asked Saris, "How many people will come to hear Moonpriest?"

"Hundreds. The River People are a large tribe, even if we are divided over Moondance. Not everyone who comes will accept Moonpriest. Many will. Moonpriest says that for every one that goes away committed, that one will bring us two."

The notion intrigued Lorso. The Skan approach to other faiths was quite simple: If it was any good, it protected believers against the Skan and Sosolassa. If Sosolassa prevailed, his power declared the losers slaves. Those were plain, demonstrable facts.

"What do we do until this grand demonstration?" Lorso made no effort to hide his impatience. "Is it so necessary for me and my crew? I should be discussing the time of our attack, the goals of our forces. Moonpriest knows no Skan is going to fall in a faint and declare him a god. We came here to talk about war and loot."

Looking as if he'd bitten into something rotten, Saris kept his answer calm. "You're stronger than your men, Slavetaker. Your crew spent all night with the Windband slave women. Many are still there. I doubt their minds are on war and loot."

Inwardly fuming, Lorso satisfied himself with a curt nod. He walked in the direction Saris indicated. By the time he spotted the wagons drawn up in the wide, pleasant valley, he was sweating. He knew of the massive, high-wheeled wagons, so was prepared for his first sight of them. Even so, when a Skan hopped out of one he exclaimed aloud at the fact that the spoked wheel was a good head taller than the man.

There were at least twenty wagons. Lorso was sure the ten fancifully decorated ones were for the women. The cloth tops, stretched across frames, were painted. One was a moon over a chain of mountains. Another showed a tiger leaping after an escaping deer. A third was nothing but roses, large and small, red and yellow and white. The wheels and yokes were painted, as well. Lorso noted all this while pausing against a large rock outcrop.

He felt eyes.

As nonchalant as possible, he feigned examining his boot, and inspected his back trail. Maintaining the same casual mien, he scanned the slopes on his flanks. Trees were thick on both, but well spaced, with little brush between them. There were uncountable places to hide, but nothing shouted of danger.

Brush crowded the path leading into the valley and wagons. Normally a horse and game trail, the weeds and brush showed the scars left by the huge wheels. Telling himself he was behaving like a frightened fawn, Lorso pushed aside the eerie feeling of being watched and stepped out toward his men. At the same time, he knew he'd seen or heard or smelled *something*, and he'd failed to identify it.

The arrow meant for his chest passed in front of him so close it sliced open his billowing shirt. Not to be entirely denied, the razor-sharp head nicked the underside of his right upper arm on its way to a clattering stop in the brush. Yelling, Lorso dove for cover in the brush, clamping his left hand on the nasty little cut in his arm while the right drew his sword. Cursing himself for not carrying his own bow and arrows, he lifted his head slowly, cautiously.

Far up the mountainside, a man ran away. The distance startled Lorso. It wasn't surprising that the arrow missed; it was amazing that it even came close.

Lorso's shout had been heard. The Skan crew and several women tumbled out of the wagons. A few Windband nomads made an appearance. One swung onto a horse, not bothering with saddle or bridle. Whacking an open hand against the animal's rump, he galloped to Lorso, arriving in a skidding halt.

"Is it a bad wound?" the nomad asked; then, without waiting for an answer, "Who did it? A River?"

The newcomer's face fell when Lorso admitted he had no idea. Joy replaced disappointment when Lorso added that the man was fleeing up the mountain, and pointed to the figure clambering across some rocks. "A hunt!" the rider exulted. "A man. Best game of all. Sorry about your arm. Doesn't look like much. We'll get him for you, though. I got to go get the others." He left at the run.

The first of the Skan arrived shortly after the nomad raced off. Lorso's wound was inspected and bandaged with practiced expertise. Long before the last Skan straggler reached Lorso, however, a pack of mounted nomads streamed up the mountainside. Their whoops and screams resounded through the valley. The Skan watched with the stoic interest of men analyzing a danger that might one day demand attention. The tough, barrel-chested horses of Windband seemed to defy gravity. Lorso wondered if these improbable animals had claws instead of hooves, the way they scratched and gouged their way uphill. Their riders clung to them like demons, only to leap off just when it seemed the beast must pitch over backward. On foot, the riders helped the horses. Sometimes they pulled them up by the bridles. A few actually tucked in behind the mount, shoulder to the horse's hind end, and hoisted them forward to the next firm purchase.

Simultaneously, another Windband party howled around the eastern side of the mountain. Lorso guessed they'd make a long circle to cut off any escape to the south.

He almost felt sorry for the fool who'd tried to kill him.

CHAPTER 25

MOONPRIEST SUFFERED NO ABSTRACT SYMPATHY FOR LORSO'S POTENTIAL KILLER. LISTENING to the tale, he appeared to burn with a quiet, mad rage. Long after Lorso finished, he sat immobile, gaze fixed on a point far beyond the tent walls.

Watching him made Lorso uncomfortable. Tears of Jade had much the same habit. Lorso took the opportunity to examine the tent. Rather, that room of the tent. Four standard Skan cabins would fit in that one room. The white material admitted a filtered, muted light that was bright without heat. Rugs covered almost the entire floor. Where they failed to meet across the flattened, pounded earth, slaves had strewn thyme, mint, and other herbs. All those aromas mingled with the thick smell of warm beeswax, the primary waterproofing agent.

Seating consisted of ornately carved chairs arranged in a semicircle facing a slightly raised platform. Moonpriest sat on the latter on a long, padded object. Lorso was told it was a sofa. It, too, was white, so soft Moonpriest appeared to be absorbed. A dark purple-blue screen was backdrop. The color of the cloth was eccentric, lighter in some places than others. At the top center there was a hazy moon that shimmered confusingly, but which dominated the screen, nevertheless.

The thing was merely a piece of luxurious prettiness to Lorso until he looked away, then looked back. Suddenly, he saw its significance. The moon drifted in twilight. The paler colors indicated stripes of cloud. Moonpriest sat immersed in the scene, a creature of the sky.

"Sylah." The solitary grating word jerked Lorso out of his inspection. Unmoving, Moonpriest repeated himself, louder. "Sylah. It has to be Sylah. Not even Gan Moondark inspires the fanaticism to attempt such a foolish, useless act."

Bristling, Lorso rose. "Foolish? Useless? Me?"

"Sit down. You hear insult where there is none." Moonpriest gestured impatiently, so preoccupied with his own thoughts he failed to encompass Lorso's anger. "The Skan sent their finest warrior to me to create an alliance. Gan Moondark knows killing you would infuriate your people. Your own men would testify no treachery was involved. The schismatic devil Sylah understands nothing as well as she understands murder. You'll see. The man will tell us."

Lorso scoffed. "First you'll have to catch him."

"If the man flies, Fox will scent him in the sky. If he swims, Fox will track his ripples in the stream."

"Even so, he may die before he confesses."

Moonpriest laughed. The expression that accompanied it lifted the back hair on Lorso's neck. "If his faith serves him well, he'll die resisting capture. When we get our hands on him, he'll confess. Oh, my, yes. You'll see."

Reluctantly, Moonpriest admitted to himself his rudeness toward Lorso. He inquired solicitously about Lorso's wound, clucking concern over possible infection. Lorso's demeanor was impressive; he was more concerned about the damage to his shirt. Not until Lorso's explanation did Moonpriest realize the material was linen, and not cotton. The further revelation that the dye that made it such a rich blue was indigo was even more impressive. Seeing Moonpriest's interest in those things, Lorso launched on a description of linen manufacture.

Moonpriest groaned inwardly. Hastily, but tactfully, he interrupted. "This is something I very much want to learn, Lorso, but I must always be working on newer, better weapons for our victory."

Watching Lorso leave, Moonpriest wondered if the ignorant savage had any comprehension of just how important those new weapons would be. The Skan were no better at siege operations than the nomads of Windband. Both cultures struck without warning to loot and pillage, then disappeared. One faded into the vastness of the sea, the other into the equally accommodating spaces of the Dry.

That had to end. Raiders could spearhead conquest, but trade and industry were the basis of empire.

Moonpriest bent forward, cupping his chin in his hand, contemplating. After the disaster with Conway, with its terrible fires in the Windband camps, there were many who declared him a false god. That number multiplied when the attack on Church Home failed, and plague fell on all Windband. Yet he overcame. Living proof that his mission was blessed.

Empire. There must be a base. Church and state in one place. In one man. In one man-god.

No empire could flourish without assured access to the sea. No religion could be secure without barricades for defense against unbelievers. The fortified cities of Ola and Harbundai offered solution to both problems.

Moonpriest rose with swift decision, swirled outside in his full white-and-silver shirt and trousers to mount his white horse. A slave steadied the animal until Moonpriest was well seated. Moonpriest accepted the action as a courtesy; he was a far better horseman now. One traveled with Windband mounted and at high speed, or got jounced and battered dizzy in a wagon that took forever to get anywhere.

Riding south, Moonpriest soon reached an indistinct trail that branched off the well-traveled route paralleling the river. It appeared to head directly into the face of the towering mountains, but instead, it led to a narrow valley.

A little farther on, his goal stood revealed.

Raw wood shining against the dusky background, alone in its clearing, a massive catapult, the type properly called a trebuchet, waited to be tested.

Moonpriest listened to the nervous slave in charge of its construction. "She's sound now, Moonpriest. We can take her apart in a morning, put her together again in the time between second meal and darkness. She'll throw a stone as heavy as a big man as far as the best arrow flight."

"How long to build another?"

The slave's visible tension soared. "Sometimes the wood's flawed, Moonpriest. Or the bull-hide lines aren't as strong as they should be."

"You'll meet my requirements or die."

"Four days. Five, in rainy weather."

"Three. And part of the fourth. Damn the weather. Now, make this thing work."

The slave ran to the machine and his crew. The long arm, with its basket made of thick leather strapping, lowered backward as men heaved on the winch handles. The stone-weighted end raised. Streaming sweat, the workers twisted the wheel. The basket dropped. At last, four men heaved a bulky slab of stone into the mesh.

The men released the winch. The basket rose. The weight fell, came to a slamming, booming stop. The long end whipped forward impossibly; Moonpriest doubted his eyes. The timber bent like a reed. The stone cut the air with a noise like falling water. When it struck the cliff wall, the thrown stone shattered explosively. Great shards of living rock blasted away from the cliff, leaving a discolored, jagged wound. Pieces even slipped free after the main damage was done.

The grinning slave in charge said, "I told you. We have it. Do you want to see how we take her apart now? Or throw another rock? It doesn't take long."

Moonpriest was satisfied. He reined his horse into a whirling turn and trotted off.

The sun was low in the sky, gilding the restless surface of the river, when Fox and the search party rode into the camp. Whoops and shouts announced success. Stopping in front of Moonpriest's tent, they called out their news.

The battered, bloodied man leashed to a horse swayed in their midst. His face was scraped raw, his shirt torn from his shoulders to hang in shreds across his belt. The skin of his chest and stomach looked burned from being dragged. It was hard to tell if the blood puddling where he stood was from his lacerated bare feet or if it flowed there from his other injuries.

Moonpriest stepped out to examine the prisoner. To Fox, he gave a curt "Good work," then circled the man slowly. The man panted, gaze fixed on the ground in front of him. "Give him a drink," Moonpriest ordered, waiting until the gulping, straining man took all he wanted.

Moonpriest spoke gently. "You tried to kill my friend. Tell me why."

It took two tries for the man to form words. "Skan. Important Skan. Pink-and-black stone, sostone. Thought he'd have lots. Rob him, sell stone."

"Why lie to me?" Moonpriest reached out, jerked the defeated chin up, twisted to make the man look him in the eye. "I only ask you questions so you may answer with truth, and lessen your punishment. I am Moonpriest, the man who is a god, the god who is a man."

"Truth." The man tried to gesture with the hands behind his back. "Wanted to rob. Please. Don't kill me."

Fox said, "He's a Peddler."

Moonpriest smiled. "Give him more water. Food, if he wants it. He'll be useful this evening. Lorso should be happy to see we take the attempt on his life as a serious matter."

Fox said, "When he finds out it was a filthy Peddler who shot at him, he'll take that very seriously, himself."

Later, as Lorso and his crew approached, nomads uncovered the large wagon, now resting in the center of a roped-off area. Hundreds of Rivers pressed against the barrier, and they emitted a collective sound of wonderment and awe as the device stood revealed. The Skan ranged behind Lorso muttered among themselves. One called out: "Is that what everyone talks about, Lorso? The god's lightning wagon?"

Spinning around, Lorso's stiff leg caused him to pitch to the side. Caught by surprise, one man failed to get out of the way, stumbling into a companion. There was a series of bumps and curses. The group came to a shuddering halt. Lorso snarled at them. "We serve our own god. I've told you; no Skan challenges Moonpriest, this Moondance thing, or any other false beliefs. We defend ourselves if we must. But I'll hear no more about other gods. Is that understood?"

An older man said, "Everyone understands. It's just that—"

Brusquely, Lorso talked over the explanation. "Stay together there, at the near corner of the roped-off square. If there's treachery, fight back to the sharker. Who cuts the mooring lines?"

Two hands went up.

"And if they fail?"

Two other men signaled.

"Good. I sit at a special table with Moonpriest, Fox, Saris, and some Rivers. Be alert. Remember, you're Skan."

Still irritable, Lorso suffered through introductions to several River chiefs and dignitaries. After the first two, they all looked alike; floppy trousers, floppy hats, self-important floppy faces. They favored feather decorations. Colorful, but they swayed and bobbed and jittered, adding to his general feeling that these weren't substantial men.

Once protocol was observed, Moonpriest took the Skan leader's arm. "Come. I want you to see my mother's altar."

The two of them walked all around the device. Moonpriest said nothing until they returned to the front, which was identified by highly polished copper stairs leading from the broad bed of the wagon to the top of the altar's platform.

Moonpriest enjoyed the irony of the situation. Lorso had no faith whatever in the power of the moon mother. The supreme jest was that if the principle of a static generator were explained to him, the bloody-minded savage would transmute the hard science of it to magic even as he heard it. Playing the game to its limit, Moonpriest pointed out the most obvious features of the device, giving them explanations Lorso could accept.

"The actual altar is the table in the middle of the wagon bed. The two ceramic disks are called moon disks. You see how they're separated by that large piece of framed leather? Actually, they're mounted on the same axle—you can see it sticking out of the center, braced on those two triangular stanchions. The two disks are kept separated to signify the moon we see part of the time, and the moon hidden to us part of the time. Big, aren't they? Just about as far across as from your fingertips to your shoulder."

Badly feigning polite interest, Lorso said, "It's pretty. I understand the four painted columns on the leather in the frame; each column represents a changing phase of the moon, from full to dark, and so do the metal images stuck to the top of the frame. The metal rays pinned to the face of the disks must signify a harvest moon. They're copper, and we call the red moon the Time of Harvest. It probably means good harvests for all your followers."

Sarcasm tainted the words, a mere wisp of scorn. Moonpriest heard it as clearly as brass. A flush inched up his throat. "The rays show how my mother's power flows in all directions. She blesses all seasons." Moonpriest reached to stroke one, from its narrow inner point to the rounded, fatter end that reached about a handspan from the disk's outer edge. The ridged form was mirror-smooth. Even the copper pins holding them in place on the disk caused no appreciable surface roughness. Moonpriest let his hand wander to the two thin rods projecting from the triangular axle brace. One extended to the upper left of the disk, one to the lower right. Brushes of copper wire at the ends touched the copper rays.

Forgetting his guest entirely, Moonpriest fondled the rattlesnakes carved into the nearest of the two posts flanking the disk-separating leather screen. Facing out on both sides of each post, one snake stopped just short of the ball carved at the top of the post, while the other reached only halfway up. The lower held a comb in its mouth. The copper teeth of all four combs thus mounted were perpendicular to the disk, almost touching the copper rays.

Moonpriest checked the stability of one of the copper rods attached to the closest pair of snake-held combs. The rods plugged into horizontal holes in the closest carved pole. Directly below that hole, a copper chain came out a similar opening; the lower end coiled on the wooden part of the altar surface. A copper wire tied to the farthest pair of combs dropped to a copper slab atop the altar; the metal sat on several thicknesses of waxed wildcow hide. From that, twin copper rods, like bannisters, spanned directly to another copper slab on the floor of the wagon bed.

The altar was perfection. Only Moonpriest knew its truth. Even those fools who sided with Sylah, and the weak-boweled preachings of her ineffectual Church, couldn't control his mother's power. Only Moonpriest. They might understand the generation of electricity, but could they duplicate his construction? Who but Moonpriest could build such a device that allowed him to destroy the unworthy and spare the needed? Moonpriest. *Moonpriest.*

"Moonpriest?" Lorso's puzzled call violated Moonpriest's inner soliloquy. He spun around. Lorso was pointing to the far end of the wagon. "Those things; are they part of your religion?"

"Yes." Moonpriest collected himself, composed explanation. He gestured for Lorso to follow. Handing the Skan two tubular, flat-bottomed copper pots, he said, "See how well these sacred objects are made." He bent to pick up a porcelain jar, swiftly taking something from inside it, slipping it behind his back. Ingenuously, ignoring Lorso's attempts to get a glimpse of the hidden object, Moonpriest said, "See how seamless the copper pots? Now, look how the porcelain jar slips neatly into the larger one?" Moonpriest lowered it into the pot in Lorso's right hand, continuing, "Now, put the smaller copper pot inside the porcelain one. There; finest porcelain, completely sleeved in purest metal, save where the porcelain extends this little distance at the top. Three strengths are needed, Lorso. Three. This is the collector that holds my mother's power, waiting to judge the true and the false. Set the containers on the metal slab, just as they are."

There was command—and mystery—in the suddenly harsh voice. Resentment twitched at Lorso's mind, but his body moved as if that new voice controlled it. When Lorso straightened, Moonpriest whipped the previously hidden thing from behind his back, thrust it in Lorso's face.

"The Man Who Is Death." Moonpriest intoned, chin tucked against his chest. Slitted eyes peered upward. Slowly, he retracted the cast copper figurine. It was an elongated man standing on a circular base. The arms were pressed to the sides, fists clenched. The thin, bony legs were stiff. Huge, round eyes of white quartz stared. Bone teeth gleamed in a tiny, gaping mouth that screamed eternal, silent terror.

The piece went into the smaller copper pot. Head and shoulders extended above the top. "You will see." Moonpriest's words were northwind's hiss in icy rigging. Transfixed by the bright inhumanity of the figurine's glaring eyes, pierced by Moonpriest's voice, Lorso's thoughts scattered, his heart raced, his knees felt unsound.

Tears of Jade. Only she spoke and stole his strength. Only her.

Until now.

Chapter 26

Lorso never spoke until he was safely returned to the torchlit riverbank and seated at the official table with Fox, Saris, and the River dignitaries. By the time Saris rose to introduce Moonpriest to the newly arrived Rivers from their distant villages, he was berating himself for allowing Moonpriest's posturing to disturb him. At the end of Saris' surprisingly short speech, Lorso was sufficiently recovered to sneer at Moonpriest's back as the white-clad man left the table. Every Skan knew Sosolassa raised the moon to pull the sea higher onto land; that was how the god peaceably showed man his strength. Sosolassa's angered strength was a thing best not thought about. What power could a scrawny landscum like Moonpriest squeeze from clay and copper?

Tears of Jade would grind him to powder.

Moonpriest gathered himself to make his about-face. Taking hold of his robe with one hand, he started his turn, then flung the material so it billowed. Torchlight picked out the silver wire artfully woven into the cloth. When the swirling subsided, he bowed to his River hosts. Rising, he caught Lorso's eye. For a moment, he considered a bold, conspiratorial wink for the Skan leader. Lorso's expression quashed that idea. Disappointment touched Moonpriest's eagerness. He was certain he'd seen a glimmer of fear when he confronted Lorso with the Man Who Is Death. Now Moonpriest sensed hostility.

Which made the game that much more exciting. What the savages didn't understand was that they couldn't win.

Gods play. Men gamble.

With the moon altar to his back, his audience to both flanks and the front, Moonpriest spoke. He opened his true mind, the god's mind, and his mother poured beguilement through him. Reason flowed from his mouth, coated with sweet cajoling, spiced with wit and humor. Moonpriest soared within himself, intoxicated by his own words, no more conscious of their source or sequence than a plant analyzes the component nourishments of the earth.

Lorso strained against the compulsive voice that exhorted and then lulled, only to stir his heart again. No warrior could hear of eternal life gained through death, of a life after death in a land of honor and pride, without yearning.

Lorso pulled back. His own god had ears. Punishments.

He looked to his men, scowled. Those who caught his glance quickly lost their foolish, gawking expressions. They elbowed the men next to them, surreptitiously indicating Lorso's black disapproval.

Moonpriest saw it all. The god within him floated free, looked down at Lorso, laughed happily. Bringing such a one into the correct faith would be more rewarding than attracting a hundred weak-willed fools.

Then, while the god that was Moonpriest hovered, unseen by mortals, enjoying the vibrancy of the words coming from the man that was also Moonpriest, something disturbing happened.

The man who had become Moonpriest looked into the eyes of the man who had become the god called Moonpriest.

The god reeled at the revulsion in the man, at the desolation and abandonment. Moonpriest the god felt exposed, violated.

With dire determination, the god resumed his rightful primacy. The last mote of the deceitful, willful man's thinking must cease.

Moonpriest halted his oration. He signaled for Windband nomads to deliver the prisoner to him. Then he waved Lorso forward.

Taking the Skan leader by the elbow, Moonpriest led him atop the wagon and positioned him at the far end, beyond the altar.

Two nomads in ceremonial dress brought the prisoner. The guards wore tight jackets that exposed the arms from the shoulder, and loose, baggy trousers. The front of the clothes was solid white, the back solid black. The prisoner now wore a rough robe, white, sleeveless, that reached midway between knee and ankle. The guards hoisted him onto the wagon, standing him on the copper plate on the wagon bed at the center of the altar. The man showed neither fear nor hope. Still, he swayed, and gripped the copper railings with both hands.

Lorso saw the venomous look Moonpriest flashed the prisoner, and deduced the man had somehow thwarted Moonpriest. The assumption was verified quickly.

"See this wretch," Moonpriest thundered. "He came to murder the friend of Moonpriest. Only the foulest of men claim the name of Peddler. Only Sylah would force any man, even an ambush murderer, to pretend to be one. This man had no pack animal, no goods to sell. Still, he refuses to admit that he is of Sylah's Church. Denial will not save him. My mother will prove he lies."

Moonpriest did the unimaginable. He indicated Lorso should join him on the wagon.

Stunned, Lorso didn't move. The Skan crew stirred, made ominous noises of fear and warning. Moonpriest waved again. From the corner of his mouth, Saris urged compliance. "Go, Lorso. It's a great honor. Many of my people will lose their own fear if they see you have none."

Lorso's hand went to his sword. There was a hint of accusation in Saris' tone, an inference that fear contributed to Lorso's immovability.

"He startled me." Lorso rose quickly. A glance silenced his crew. Head up, Lorso paraded to the wagon. Ignoring the steps, he leaped smoothly to take his place beside Moonpriest. Many in the crowd made sounds of admiration.

The prisoner looked at Lorso with undisguised contempt. It was hardly the expression of a defeated man, and Lorso speculated about defective questioning technique. Then he noted the hand gripping the copper banister. Flesh at the ends of the fingers oozed. The nails were missing.

Moonpriest said, "I will show you that this man lies, that he is the enemy of Moondance, the enemy of all friends of Moonpriest." A quick nod from him, and the nomad guards assumed seats on the ends of a long beam running perpendicular to the moon disk frame. There were crank handles in front of the seats. The men turned them. Leather belts set the disks to turning, slowly. They muttered, making Lorso think of distant surf. The wagon trembled.

Taking the statuette of the Man Who Is Death from the receptacle on the altar, Moonpriest lifted it high. In the darkness, the polished copper figure glinted. Eerily, the hollow eyes seemed to suck light from the torches and swallow it. The agonized grimace swept the crowd. A low hum of anticipation rose.

Waving the wandlike figure, Moonpriest spoke softly to Lorso. "I have a surprise for you tonight. There's a deceiver among us. Saris says one of the River leaders at our table belongs to Sylah's upstart wing of Church. He's the true target of my mother's fury. You'll see."

Addressing the crowd again, Moonpriest replaced the figurine. "Many of you question if my mother strikes those I choose, or if she truly strikes those who lie to us, or mean us harm. Let one of you ask this prisoner a question to which we know the answer. Which of my friends will test our enemy?"

"Me!" A short, thick warrior ducked under the restraining rope to posture bravely in the forbidden area. "Ask him if he's afraid."

"Ask him yourself." Moonpriest smiled benignly. Lorso smothered his own grin, knowing the questioner was planted. Tears of Jade used the same technique.

After the question was repeated, the prisoner answered with a shake of his head.

The black-and-white guards increased the speed of the moon disks. The noise level rose. The wagon seemed to be trying to speak, its boards and fittings moaning in disorganized chorus. Raising his voice, Moonpriest spread his arms, gripped the decorative knob atop the carved post. "Take the Man Who Is Death from his place," he said, moving to stand away from the frame. Lorso made room for him.

Gingerly, favoring the ruined fingers, the man reached. Fear danced across his features, but his jaw remained clenched. He grabbed the cast copper piece and lifted. For a moment he swayed, unsure if he still lived. Then he scowled.

"Put it back. There are other questions." Moonpriest jerked his chin at the interrogator-warrior, who responded eagerly. "Prisoner! Are you a Peddler?"

Once again, the Peddler acted out his part of the entertainment, answering, lifting the figurine, replacing it. Other inane questions followed. The crowd was involved by then, enjoying themselves, asking if the man could fly, or lived under the river. Finally, Moonpriest quieted them.

"Answer me, now, failed murderer. Answer my mother. All have seen you speak the truth. And live. I will ask you my question." He flung out his arms, steadied himself by grasping the snake-carved pole. "Those who accept

Moondance and Moonpriest become as my spirit brother, the snake, able to shed this life as a skin. My brothers will be born again with me, to return to the world from the moon and live in paradise."

The guards worked harder. Sweat dripped from their chins, stained their clothes.

The copper rays were a shining, solid wheel.

Lorso caught an aroma, something he'd never smelled before. Clinging, demanding, it made him think of heat, but there was no sign of fire, except that of the torches.

Sound picked at his ears. A sizzle. Malevolent. Connected with the bad, sticky smell. Lorso didn't know why he knew that.

"Are you sent by Church?" Each word rang.

The prisoner smiled. An enigmatic, self-confident smile, as if there were a joke taking place, and only he comprehended. His voice was loud enough for those on the wagon and no one else. "I failed Church. She didn't send me." He turned his head, shouted over his shoulder at the seated dignitaries. "I was not sent by Church!"

The bloodied, tortured hand shot forward toward the silent scream of the Man Who Is Death. A spark, startlingly bright blue-green in the dim ruddy light of torches, leaped to meet the grasp. There was an earsplitting crack. The prisoner gave a cry, indefinable.

Lorso knew he would hear it for the rest of his life. Men died all around him all his life; none ever made that sound.

None of them were killed by a god.

The prisoner bolted erect. The outstretched arm went rigid as steel. Then, in the same instant, he flew backward. Flaccid, the body landed in a confused tumble.

For the space of two or three heartbeats, a time that felt like seasons, no one stirred. Then, simultaneously, everyone erupted. Noise rolled across the night, across the river, echoed back. Someone called Moonpriest's name. The crowd seized it, made it a chant.

Moonpriest basked. He preened. He paraded the length of the wagon.

Lorso refused to yell with the rest. He could refuse that; he couldn't deny the roaring in his ears, the ripping beat of his heart. Moonpriest pulled him to the steps leading down from the wagon. Lorso stumbled along behind, elated and shamed at the same time. Moonpriest said, "We'll speak to my traitorous River infiltrator now."

Moonpriest watched Lorso's reaction carefully. Lorso's silence during the spontaneous cheering only reinforced the conclusion that this was a leader, a man controlled by his own mind.

It was exactly what was needed to counterbalance Fox, Moonpriest thought. Not that Fox wasn't extremely bright, but he responded to emotion first. Thought came later. A man like Lorso would provide a perfect complement; a fighter—even a god—needed two hands.

Moonpriest forced himself back to the present. He stopped in front of the accused spy. The mindless thunder of the crowd's enthusiasm dwindled.

Looking directly into the River's eyes, Moonpriest said, "I know your heart. You are Sylah's."

The River raised a hand, a defiance that made Moondance laugh aloud. Before the River could speak, Moondance continued. "Look at the false outrage. Liar. I demand you touch the Man Who Is Death." Moonpriest stepped back. Projecting, calling on the trained voice, he spoke over his victim, past him, went directly to the crowd. "All have seen that my mother treasures truth. Speak honestly, and you are one of us. Lie, and your soul is burned."

"I can't." The River's eyes rolled. A cottony swirl of spit speckled the corner of his mouth. "I mean I won't. No one can question my honor. I'm an honest man. Just ask." He stopped abruptly, seeking one who would vouch for him.

Each former friend showed the face that denied: sad, furious, ashamed.

Moonpriest said, "I need good men. Confess. Be forgiven. Join me. Help me."

Awareness of abandonment seemed to brace the man. "I will never be tested. No man questions my integrity."

"No man is. I am. Moonpriest. The god who is a man. Take my test, or be proven guilty for refusing."

The bare challenge was out. The crowd sighed anticipation.

Breathing heavily, the River stared into Moonpriest's eyes. His lips tightened. His words sounded as if drawn through ice. "I'll take your test. Then I leave. I won't be offended this way. You've made an enemy."

While everyone around the River relaxed, something told Moonpriest that this was a most dangerous time. He signaled his men to turn the moon disks.

The River dropped his sword belt on his chair, then moved to the front of the table.

Moonpriest led his victim toward the altar. He saw a River woman open her mouth as if to scream. Her eyes rounded. Hands clapped to her cheeks.

Moonpriest dodged, dropped like a stone.

The lunging River, knife in hand, tripped over Moonpriest's feet, tumbled past.

Lorso was thrusting at the spy before he could actually fall down. The sword took him just above the belt from behind. The impact drove him forward, out of control, bent at the waist in parody of age. A slash hacked into the unprotected nape of the neck. Almost decapitated, he wobbled on, three, four, five incredible, terrible steps.

He ended facedown, arms reaching toward the moon disk altar.

A strange sensation of separation filled Lorso. To his left, nomads and River allies encircled other Rivers, clearly those formerly commanded by the figure lying at his feet. People cheered, screamed, shouted. It was no more than a worrisome buzz in his ears. Moonpriest held him at arm's length. Lorso watched the mouth work and heard nothing. Suddenly, however, words broke through.

"It was as my mother foretold. 'Keep Slavetaker at your side. He must know your power before he will consent to protect and ally with you.' For this you stood with me at her altar. For this you stood with me to confront the traitor."

Lorso suffered the rest of the night's events as a dream. Later, alone, he sat by the sharker's tiller. Downstream, a dying moon plunged its curved blade into the horizon. Under Lorso's dangling feet, the unceasing river whispered urgent journey.

Lorso clenched his fists, closed his eyes in a compressing scowl. He repeated the name of Sosolassa over and over.

Chapter 27

Shara and Cho stirred simultaneously. In tandem, both great heads lifted from between forepaws to sniff the air. With a smooth grace that denied their bulk, they rose from their comfortable doze. Gan ignored them until Cho leaned into his right side. He smiled down at the top of her head. She pushed that way when she was disturbed enough to want his attention, not disturbed enough to growl or bark. Grabbing a floppy ear, Gan gently pulled her head back and forth. "What's this? Pretending there's something dangerous out there, so you can lean on me?"

The heavy tail wagged lazily. Neither dog took its gaze from the doorway leading from the roof down into the castle's interior.

Certain this calm curiosity merely signaled the approach of someone unexpected, Gan watched the door, nevertheless. It was unlikely anyone meant to attack Murdat on the roof of his own castle, Gan thought wryly, but men who reacted only to what was probable didn't grow old.

He turned from the crenelated wall where he'd been staring out to sea. A twinge of resentment drew an unconscious frown across his forehead. The Inland Sea fascinated him. Not just its ever-changing surface or the beauty of its mountain-ringed shores and islands. Gan saw more. He saw a path leading wherever courage would take one, a field of maneuver where skill matching valor must be the living heart of any battle. He saw a road, horizon to horizon, endless, that should carry trade in all directions. Trade. The soul of empire.

Emso appeared, followed by Conway, then Tate, and finally Leclerc.

Pretending to scold, Gan pushed down on both dogs' heads. "Frauds, both of you. You knew who it was all along." Bright eyes and canine grins called to mind impertinent children. Contributing to the image, both dogs lay down with gusting, self-satisfied sighs.

Conway said, "Cho seems completely over her injury. She looks good."

"Where are your own dogs?"

"Back in my quarters. You know how Shara and Karda keep wanting to test each other. I'm afraid if they get into it, we may not be able to separate them."

Gan grimaced. "The idea of stepping into a fight between those two . . ." He let the sentence fall away.

Emso grunted. "Forget the dogs. We're in the middle of something lots worse. That's why we're here."

Dryly, Gan said, "Maybe someday you'll come to me with something cheerful,

Emso. There's a surprise that could kill a man." Gan looked to the others. "What brings you up here with my croaking raven?"

"Ideas." Leclerc spoke, glancing around uncertainly. When no one preempted his beginning, he continued. "Everyone knows Windband, the Skan, and many of the River People will attack us as soon as winter ends. The three of us have been telling Emso the Three Territories can't withstand that pressure."

Bristling, Gan turned back to the sea. "No one is required to stand with me. You came to me of your own will. You can leave when you choose."

"See?" It was Tate, scolding. "Didn't I tell you he'd be nasty as a boar hog? Didn't I say, 'Just tell him what we've got, and see what he says.' Didn't I tell you that?"

Keeping his back turned, Gan fought a grin. He wanted desperately to watch Leclerc and Conway try to dodge Tate's barbs.

Leclerc's words tended to run together. "Tate's right, of course. I didn't mean that the way it sounded. Of course. The thing is, we have some ideas. Ways to offset numerical superiority."

"That's better." Tate was grudgingly forgiving.

Gan faced the group again. "I was too quick to be offended." He wanted to say more, but he decided against it. In plain fact, he was never sure how much to say to these strange people who'd become so important to him. For all their fine qualities, they shared one troublesome trait in common.

Secretiveness. Whatever they did, whatever they said, there was a distance around them, an air of things known and unsaid. Gan always sensed an eerie melancholy behind their most joyous moments, as if they each understood something very unpleasant about each other.

Gan corrected the last thought. The little Seer, Lanta—there were times when he had the feeling that she knew of things inside Conway. Gan also knew Lanta's love for Matt Conway assured no secret of his would ever pass her lips.

Right now, dressed in leather trousers and woolen shirt, with a spotted calf vest for extra warmth against the early fall chill, Conway looked exactly like any warrior from Jalail, Harbundai, or Ola. So did Leclerc, although the briefest glance assured he was no fighting man. And then there was Tate. With her catlike grace, high cheekbones, and exotically slanted eyes, she'd have been unusual in any case. Combine those qualities with black skin and a face that expressed her thoughts as clearly as clouds foretold the weather, and you had someone who defined *different.*

Gan admired her gaudy red short cape, embroidered with its bright yellow emblem of an eagle, wings spread, clutching an anchor. Like her, contradictory; what would an eagle want with an anchor? But the symbol drew the eye. There was strength in it. And weren't the colors the finest, those of his own clan? Although he himself preferred the plainest of clothes, Gan delighted in her swagger and vitality. Unpredictable; more dependable than rock. Independent; as deeply concerned about others as anyone he knew.

More than any of her companions, he liked her most. And knew her least.

Conway spoke. "The truth is, Tate and I do have to go away for a while."

Nodding, Gan accepted the statement without comment. That wasn't good enough for Emso. " 'Religious matters,' they said. Maybe you can get more out of them."

Tate grinned. "I don't ask you about your beliefs. You don't ask me about mine."

Emso grumbled under his breath. Gan thought he heard something that sounded like "frog sweat." Unmistakable concern and guilt flooded Leclerc's face before he turned away. Gan had no time to puzzle over it. Conway was saying, "I didn't want to go, at first. She's right, though; it's necessary. But now I think she should stay here to help train the Wolf recruits. Nalatan's upset that she's leaving. He's mad enough to bite through steel. Maybe you can talk some sense into her."

"I've got enough sense for all of you." Tate's widened eyes and set jaw were defiant. Her words were for Gan, but her fiery look was directed at Conway. "This is something only Conway and I can deal with. Together. Just because I'm married now, he and Nalatan think I should run off into the kitchen and knit socks for the rest of my life."

Conway buffed his nails. "I've eaten your cooking. You go in the kitchen, knitting might be the safest thing for you to do."

"Don't smart-mouth me. I'm not letting you go back to our . . . out there in the mountains alone, and that's that." The short pause after the word "our" told Gan that Tate stopped herself because she was about to say something she shouldn't. Reacting to Conway's teasing, her defiance had acquired a gloss of amusement. Then came sudden reticence. Again. With the recurrent and unwelcome feeling that one of the strangers silently expressed thoughts with complete confidence they would be understood by other members of the group. It was a too-intimate knowledge. It made Gan's neck tingle.

Oddly, it was Leclerc who spoke into the sharp silence. "Give up, Matt. In the first place, you'd be a fool to go alone. You can't make Tate stay home. If her husband can't convince her, what chance do you have?"

Tate accepted the victory magnanimously. To Gan, she said, "Use Nalatan in my place. He's more like you and Clas na Bale than anyone I've ever seen. There's not a better warrior in the Three Territories or anywhere else. And I'll fight anyone who argues."

Gan struggled with the return of the earlier smile. It escaped, cracked wide open, turned to laughter. Shocked, Tate tensed. "You laugh at my husband?"

"No, no." Gan held up a warding hand. "I was just thinking that if you two have children, I hope they're all sons. Pity poor Nalatan, living in the same house with more women like you."

Tate sniffed and turned her back on the group.

Gan looked to Leclerc. "You said you wanted to talk about ideas. Like the arrow-thrower you described? I'm getting reports that you're working with wildcow tendons. The word *witchcraft* has been heard."

Leclerc made a face. "It's giving me more trouble than I expected."

Careful to keep concern from his voice, Gan said, "There are other reports. The

Moonpriest one has catapults. More than the one he used in the battle at the Door."

After a quick, dismissive sound, Leclerc moved forward. Unaware of the speculative look of the hounds at Gan's feet, he became enthusiastic. His hands danced, described pictures in the air. "Moonpriest's weapon's an overgrown bow. It'll wear out too fast in combat. Its bowstring won't handle rain well. Mine uses corded sinew, drawn taut. Larger arrow, better accuracy."

Emso interrupted. "If we ever get it. Moonpriest's weapon is here. Now. It works."

"Mine'll be better."

Gan reassured Leclerc. "Emso's always impatient. Believe me; when you've perfected your weapon, he'll be first to complain we don't have enough of them. You'll never satisfy him." He laid an affectionate hand on Emso's shoulder.

Tate said, "We have other ideas. Nothing we can talk about yet. We've been looking into the treasures of the Door. That's going to save the Territories."

Emso threw his hands in the air. "The only thing that can save us is fighting well. Murdat, we took a bunch of beaten men and untried boys and turned them into the Jalail Wolves. We didn't jabber about Doors or cata-things or 'ideas.' We built a fighting unit. We can do it again."

Tate rounded on him. "I was there, Emso. Me. Remember? Who improved the murdat all the Wolves use now? And the shield?"

Conway put a conciliatory hand on Tate's arm. She jerked free of it, too offended for easy mediation.

Gan addressed Emso. "As Leclerc said, we're overwhelmingly outnumbered. We need every advantage we can find. How can you argue?"

Red-faced, Emso struggled for words. The plain, rough features managed regret. "I'm sorry I made you mad, Tate. I don't like all these new things. Changing the look of a sword, or the way a man uses a shield is one thing. Even what Gan did with the kites was good, in a way. But the black powder. And the cat's . . . cata . . . that other thing. And the lightning weapons. It's *things* killing *people*. It's not right. What are we doing? Not to the Skan, not to the idiots of Moondance or that evil scum, Moonpriest; they'll all rot in the Land Under in due time. But what happens inside us?"

There was no quick retort. The thoughts were Gan's own. He never saw the havoc of the lightning weapons or witnessed the crushing, blind ferocity of the black powder without feeling soiled somehow. It made his flesh crawl.

Emso put words to the heart of it, made it accusation: What happens inside us?

Searching for reaction among his companions, Gan spied the looks that passed between Conway and Tate and Leclerc. What he saw there jolted him. The three strangers, who shared a commonality that linked them intimately while separating them from all but their own, were all filled with shame.

Chapter 28

"You're beautiful." Sylah stood back from Lanta, fists on hips, head cocked to the side. "I'd love to see you dressed in the bright cottons the Dog women weave, or the doeskin and linen the women of Harbundai fashion. It's the penalty we pay for being Church. Black, and more black. If we live long enough and rise high enough, we get a piece of colored trim to show off our rank." She made a small sound of disgust, then sighed. "Now I'll have to ask forgiveness for the sin of vanity. Followed immediately by prayers asking forgiveness for lying. Never mind; we set out to make you a robe that befits a woman trying to catch the eye of a lover, and we've done it to perfection. You helped a bit extra, providing such a nice figure."

The small Seer blushed. Sylah teased further. "The poor man's lost, of course. I expect a delightful scandal when he charges across the room tonight and throws himself at you."

The color threatened to break into open flame. Delight wavered under the strain of apprehension. "Do you think so, Sylah? Really? He knows I love him. I thought when we got back here, everything would be all right. But he seems confused." She ended with a weak wave.

"Why won't you talk about it? Neither of you will admit what all your friends know; something happened between you, something dreadful. Obviously, you both want to put it behind you. Let your friends help."

Lanta shook her head. "Whatever I say hurts us both. I thought he'd be more . . . more forceful, I guess. Maybe I see something that really isn't there."

Sylah put her hands on Lanta's shoulders, gently turned her so they were face-to-face. "I've seen how he looks at you. I don't understand what keeps you apart." At Lanta's sudden stricken look, Sylah pulled her friend to her for a quick embrace. Then, stepping back, she continued, conciliatory. "The important thing is that Conway holds himself responsible for what happened to Tee, as well. He's convinced she never would have gone looking for the escaped slaves in Kos if he hadn't goaded her into it. And, of course, if he'd been with you all along, he couldn't have influenced her."

Lanta gestured helplessly. "It's so complicated. I've loved him from the very first. Why couldn't he see that? What was I supposed to do?"

"Ask me to number the stars. Or explain the weather. Don't look to me for answers about love."

"But you and Clas are so happy."

Too late, Sylah tried to hide her hurt. Lanta raised hands to her cheeks. "Oh, Sylah. How could I be so stupid? I make a mess of everything."

Sylah managed a smile that felt like something twisting across her face. "We seem to say the wrong things. My remark stung you."

"Vulnerable." Lanta's tiny features darkened. "That's the word for women. We're always so vulnerable."

"Not all of us. We can't forget the Harvester. After all, she's Sister Mother now. How vulnerable is she?"

Refusing to rise to the change of subject, Lanta went on. "I worry about myself and that vulnerability. It's natural to see men as protectors, to some extent. All those muscles should be good for something. When it goes beyond physical help, though, are we practicing vulnerability? Do we use men? If he marries me, the act makes him a Church defender. Is that honest? Do I really want him, or is some part of me luring him into marriage because I feel that terrible vulnerability for what I am as well as who I am?"

"You said you love him. If you do, exactly how much choice do you have?"

For a moment, Lanta was quite still. Then, as if relieved of a great weight, she beamed a fresh, uncomplicated smile. "None. Of course. You have to be vulnerable to fall in love, don't you?"

"Exactly. Now, one last question on that matter, and then we talk about something else: Have you noticed the way Leclerc looks at that For girl, that Jaleeta?"

Lanta's momentary lightness evaporated. "No, I haven't. I've seen her look at other people, though. Like she's figuring out how useful they might be. Why's Neela so fond of her? You'd think Jaleeta's her little sister."

"Neela grew very lonely while we were away. There were few people for her to talk to. None she trusted as she does you, or me, or Tate. Now we're back, but we're all very busy. Jaleeta's an ever-present companion. We're not. Even if we were, Jaleeta makes Neela feel needed."

"She's got her baby. And Gan tells everyone how important Neela is to him. Gan asks Neela about the Barons, about negotiations, about helping the wives of Wolves who died or are wounded. He's made her his valued partner. How many men would do that?"

"Precious few. But would you want it? At the cost of all the other questions? If Gan's not riding off somewhere to supervise one thing or another, he's talking to other people about their problems all day and into the night."

Lanta touched Sylah's sleeve with pained delicacy. "You would see that, wouldn't you? With your Clas off to the east with the Dog People. It's like you, to worry about others when you've got more trouble than all of us."

"You give me too much credit." Sylah squeezed Lanta's consoling hand. "Actually, I'm just a nosy gossip, watching what everyone does. We have work, though. Not enough to keep you from your Conway, but something you mentioned before. Jaleeta. I think she can hurt Neela. Leclerc, too."

"You think she really is a spy?"

"It's possible. You mentioned how she watches; have you watched her?"

"Why? What should I expect?"

"Just do. Let me know what you think."

Nodding, Lanta looked eager. Sylah glanced out at the sun. "It's near evening meal. Kate, Janet, and Susan are making a presentation, something to do with the books from the Door and the Chosens. It's a good time to start paying close attention to Jaleeta. Sit by me. We'll compare what we see."

Far away, the first streaks of sunset registered above the snow-tipped crowns of the Whale Coast mountains. Lanta appeared unaware of that beauty. "Are you going to have me use the trance, See her future, if I can?"

Anxious fingers twining, Sylah answered with a firmness she simply couldn't make herself feel. "If I'm what Sister Mother says I am, a schismatic, I have every right to claim to represent Church and ask for your powers. I don't believe I'm a schismatic, though. I just want to do what's right, and we know Sister Mother's evil. But if I ask you to See, and the Tenders of the Abbeys decide someday I did wrong, they'll punish you. I couldn't stand that, Lanta."

"We won't worry about it. Not now. Let's go get ready for evening meal. We'll have enough there to keep us busy."

"Especially you. Flirting with Matt Conway." Sylah rolled her eyes. Lanta reached for her. Sylah dodged, and the two of them hurried away, forcing their way past their cares to share a few moments of carefree laughter.

Later, sitting in the dining hall, Sylah found herself remembering that lightheartedness and comparing the present with the days of Altanar. The room arrangement was the same, with a short table against one wall, where Gan sat at the center in place of the dead tyrant, and two longer tables ranging down the two flanking walls. The gathering wasn't as large as she'd heard some of Altanar's were. Still, there were at least sixty people present.

Large fireplaces, set into the walls, backed up each table. That illumination was augmented by a square chandelier holding three tiers of candles, as well as smaller candelabra on the tables. Small windows, little more than slits, allowed hotter air an escape near the ceiling. In spite of that ventilation, there was smoke in the air, and the light created by the flames had a roseate, muted glow.

Sylah liked it. It gave the warmth of the sprawling room a visible component that suggested snugness. She felt it as a rather familylike atmosphere. Everything was clearly visible. Expressions and animation were undisguised, colors were unsullied. Still, Sylah had a sensation of softness, of a place without edges.

Gan wore elkskin with understated stitched decoration. Beside him, Neela was lovely in a dark-blue robe that offset the gold of her hair perfectly. Jaleeta in light leather blouse and trousers, sat on Neela's left. She kept Neela engaged in conversation, the two heads bent close. The young For woman challenged Neela's bright, sunny loveliness with her own dark beauty. Like Neela, she wore little distracting decoration; an obsidian square, held around her neck by a silver chain, and pearl-ornamented comb to hold her rich, black hair in place. Sylah recognized it all as Neela's.

On Jaleeta's left, Leclerc sat hunched and twisted awkwardly to keep his face to her. Sylah thought he looked like an injured heron.

On the other side of Gan, Emso held the place of honor. Like Gan, he dressed plainly. Emso's clothes, however, seemed chosen to underscore his rough, almost crude, personal manner. The woolen shirt was undecorated; even from her place at one of the long tables, Sylah noted worn cuffs. Elbow patches were commonplace, but Emso's were polished with wear. Sylah had to smile at his rough, shorn-sheep haircut. In a city that featured a plenty of barbers, that scraggly mane was pure affectation. Older than his Murdat by several years, he was loyal to a fault. Sylah's mind drifted away, brought back an image of Clas na Bale. She shrugged it to oblivion, unwilling to let her husband's absence destroy another evening. It relieved her a little to think that Gan had Emso to watch his back, even if Clas couldn't be there for him.

Or her. Clas' image persisted at the edge of her vision.

Conway came next. Sylah remembered his original garb, the peculiar, splotched design on unbelievably tough, weather-resistant cloth. All of the strangers wore identical clothes, then. Now Conway dressed more like a Dog horseman than anything else, although not so gaudy as those dashing warriors.

Tate sat beside him. As always, she set her own style. Tonight she was in a black, close-fitting blouse, with a black jacket featuring silver buttons. She also wore obsidian-and-silver earrings. Her trousers, with their finger-wide white stripe up the side of each leg, were hidden under the table, but Sylah knew they, too, were form-fitting. No man in the castle was unaware of Donnacee Tate.

Not that any would trouble her. Tate's own martial prowess was enough to discourage the most unbalanced of aggressive suitors. Nalatan's ferocious skills were legend.

Sylah reminded herself that tonight was supposed to provide good food in good company. The concept drew a wry smile. No matter what entertainment Bernhardt, Carter, and Anspach had planned, there was amusement aplenty in store, Sylah thought. Jaleeta was on full display for the first time. Neela had prepared her well, a nervous hen with her chick. What made that particularly comical was that Neela was the elder by perhaps two years.

Oddly, Jaleeta looked the older. Not aged, by any means, but accomplished. Smooth. Calculating. Her eyes were swordpoints, bright and undeterred.

Servants brought trays of food. Musicians filed in. The latter took up places on a small raised stage to the right. The servants distributed crockery bowls full of greens and the last of summer's tomatoes. Pottery bottles placed on the tables held herbed oils and vinegars. In moments, the room was thick with their redolence. Shortly afterward, heavy plates were distributed, each laden with slices of baked ham. Vegetables—corn, beans, potatoes—circulated in serving bowls. The buzz of relaxed dining struck Sylah as another major difference between this gathering and Altanar's court. In those times, more food was wasted than consumed; excess was quality. Now, with shortages facing his people, Gan insisted the castle's regime consist of adequate rations and nothing more. Also, in the past, the music of the dining room was metallic, horns that brayed and piercing bells, rather than the melodic strings and subtle small drum rhythms of the present. People in Altanar's court forced laughter, admiration, awe. The air trembled with falsity. This was communion, people immersed in fellowship.

Suddenly, like a doe sensing a hunter, Sylah stiffened, head up, alert. Logic told her there was nothing untoward for her to see in the midst of conviviality, nor anything to scent through the richness of food and drink.

Movement at the edge of her vision drew her attention. The Violet Abbess rose from her seat across the room. The exposed green lining of her thrown-back hood gleamed jewel-bright in the fireglow. As if aware of Sylah's scrutiny, the woman stopped. Standing behind the unconcerned diners at table in front of her, she turned slowly, deliberately, and looked directly into Sylah's eyes.

In that moment, Sylah was aware of no one else in the room. She lost the thrum of conversation, the melody of instruments. There was only the hostile presence of the Violet Abbess.

Chapter 29

Pulling her hood over her head, the Violet Abbess retreated into its enfolding fastness. From a face transformed to pale, shaded malevolence, her gaze continued to burn across the room. It pinioned Sylah, held her as the jewel eyes of a snake hold a bird.

Anger released Sylah, however, a warming flood that quickly became a liberating torrent. She caught the look of the other woman fairly, and held it with confidence. The message from the Violet Abbess demanded submission, one will to another. This was irreversible confrontation, beyond theology. Sylah smiled mockingly into that arrogance.

The Violet Abbess broke. Resuming her original course, she proceeded as if nothing had happened.

Pleased with her small victory, Sylah settled back in her chair. A touch on her forearm brought her completely back to reality. Lanta's whisper trembled. "I saw. That look. She's never been so obvious. Church has already cast us out. We've haven't challenged that, or confronted it. Why show such hatred so clearly now, of all times?"

"The very question," Sylah answered absently, automatically. She was in the grip of a growing storm of feelings. Startling. At the same time, she was exhilarated. With each beat of her heart, she realized a transformation was taking place. Her mind worked with awesome clarity. What she saw in her inner vision was so cold-bloodedly precise, so analytical, that it literally repelled her.

Images.

Tate always swung her left arm away from her body before lunging forward with her murdat.

Gan always made an almost-imperceptible nod before giving his dogs a command.

The Violet Abbess always blinked twice immediately after making a statement she knew to be false. She licked her lips before uttering words intended to injure.

Why now? What use were those observations?

What was the unknown, irresistible force building in her? It had a purpose; she sensed that. If it had a goal, what was it?

Strength. Will. Cunning.

Qualities, not sensations. Yet she felt them within herself, thought this must be how the earth felt the stirring of seeds. She looked at her hands. They carried healing, repaired the damaged. Sylah, War Healer, stood for life. Her enemy was death.

Once again, an image. Her beloved Clas. Different; wrenching. The feral look of him when he surrendered himself to the mistress she hated so fiercely, yet dared not challenge. She saw him with his eyes widened, his jaw set. Thick muscles drew smooth, like steel bending. Impassioned. She felt that passion, felt his terrible fear and joyful exultation, as he embraced his demonic lover.

Sylah finally understood. All her senses, every part of her, understood. The silent, dire challenge posed by the Violet Abbess broke Sylah through all normal levels of comprehension.

Sylah knew suffering and struggle, knew the magic that floods the heart of one who escapes maximum peril. This new sensation was entirely different. This was embracing existence in a manner beyond the understanding of those who only fear death and never tempt it. The stakes soared immeasurably higher than life against life. The victor in this battle would define good and evil for generations to come. It was overwhelming responsibility. Yet Sylah exulted. Her whole being sang with glad, living anticipation.

As Clas' must sing, when he faced his enemy.

Sylah looked to Tate, her oft-envied friend, who knew that wild sense of mortality. Her mind cleared itself of that distraction quickly, bringing her focus back to the one who generated these thoughts.

The Violet Abbess.

Here began the real war to control Church. Now.

At risk were the souls of people unknown and uncountable, but people who deserved a faith that taught hope, not obligation. There could be no compromise. Sylah wondered if there could be mercy. Pity.

The Apocalypse Testament. "The choice between defense of Church and the celebration of peace among men will test the souls of all who love Church. Church cannot and will not die, but better she be lost to men a hundred years than her love for all be forgotten for the blink of an eye."

Sylah resolved to never forget that admonition.

Halting at the point where one table joined the other, the Violet Abbess wedged herself into a dim corner, her robe compounding the darkness there, rendering her almost invisible. Lanta hissed like a small cat, then, "She's going to make a scene, Sylah. What can she be planning?"

Sylah shook her head. "I have a feeling I know. What puzzles me is her timing; you mentioned it yourself. When we first arrived in Ola, she was chewing her bit she was so anxious to confront us because we were cast out. We've been here quite long enough for her to declare the personal animosity we just saw. Why now, indeed? Look; what's this all about?"

Interrupting the final moments of dinner, Kate Bernhardt, Janet Carter, and Susan Anspach ushered in two columns of Chosens. Sylah joined the other women in an involuntary exclamation of sheer delight. Then the room fell expectantly quiet. The girls swept in, exuding the almost angelic solemnity enabled only by the innocence of childhood. Full black robes hid their feet, drawn hoods enclosed all but the bright, excited faces. The tiny figures wore soft indoor slippers.

Soundless, they floated magically past the thick, iron-banded doors, across the stone slab floor that suddenly seemed coarse and ugly.

Forming a semicircle at the open end of the rectangle defined by the two longer tables, the twelve children waited. Susan Anspach stepped away from her two friends. In their robes, the adults looked huge beside the Chosens. Anspach cleared her throat. "Murdat. Friends. Since our sister, Rose Priestess Sylah, returned with the treasures of the Door, many have said that only evil can come from them. Others have said they're useless. We, of the Iris Abbey, believe great good is within books. We believe learning is good."

Several people gasped audibly. Many more frowned, casting uncertain glances at Gan, who continued to watch inscrutably. Anspach continued. "What Healers do comes from learning. Is there one who objects to his or her life being saved? Those who build, or tan leather, or make steel are able to do so because they learn. Is it evil to live under a roof, wear shoes, cut firewood with a sharp axe? No one says so. Evil is the fault of people, not learning. By refusing to learn, we deny ever greater accomplishment to good people. If we deny such good, do we not encourage evil?"

At that, there were many clear objections. One man half rose, only to be jerked back to his seat by a clearly terrified woman next to him. Sylah recognized the couple as a Baron left over from Altanar's reign. There were several such nobles in Ola; many were considered less than completely trustworthy. The wife of the pair obviously feared having her husband included in that category. Sylah wondered if there were other reasons for the woman to worry.

Anspach swayed, as if facing up to a wind. Sylah wanted to applaud her resolution when she continued. "The Iris Abbey wants to make learning available to all. We believe the Teachers hid their treasure for our Sylah, whom all acknowledge is the Flower, to discover when the world was ready. The time is now. To help you, Murdat, the first thing we suggest is that you decree the way we measure things. Uniformity of measurements will improve many things. It will improve the value of the books." Another frightened, angry buzz moved through the gathering until Anspach held up a slim bar. "We suggest you call this length a 'unit.' It's divided into twelve sub-units. If you do this, everything in the Three Territories can be measured in units. A man can tell you a wall is fifteen units high, and you know exactly what that means. We ask permission to demonstrate two advantages."

Gan nodded shortly. It was a troubled response, and Sylah winced at his faint frown. Her heart went out to him. He was being asked to contradict the laws and conventions of generations. He already permitted female children to violate those concepts by learning to read and write, and now Anspach was proposing something even more daring.

Kingdoms—and kings—had been destroyed for far less.

Anspach moved to the table and helped herself to one of the large serving bowls, now empty. She carried it to where the Chosens waited, and raised it for the diners to examine. "You all see this bowl. If you want one exactly the same size around, how do you tell the potter?"

A man called out, "Anyone can do that. You just look at the first one and make another."

Another corrected him. "Not if you want the same size. You use string. Lay it around the top, cut it off where the ends touch. Give that to the potter. Another piece of string tells him how deep to make it. Even women can manage that."

Muscle bunched in Anspach's jaw. "If the string doesn't shrink. Or get broken. Or lost. But what if you want ten, twenty, a hundred potters to each make a pot exactly the same size? A piece of string for each? Perhaps. But watch how the Chosens do it."

From inside the robes, the children produced tablets, slabs of wood layered with wax. Sharp scribes served to mark the surface. In turn, each girl used the unit to carefully measure the diameter of the bowl. They calculated the circumference. Anspach carried the tablets to the table, displaying them. "For those who can read, observe: The Chosens spoke no word among themselves, yet each one writes the same numbers in the wax. The size of the mouth of the bowl is known in unit measurements. We can send that number anywhere in the Three Territories, and a potter with an identical unit bar will make a bowl with a mouth the same size."

The uncertain, angry grumble followed her progress along the table, moving with her as the sound of growing flood in a stream. Nevertheless, there was curiosity, too, and many of the audience were impressed. The ban on learning never eliminated intelligence, and there were agile minds in the crowd, speculating on the advantages of the proposal.

A woman raised a timid hand as Anspach reached her. "They didn't measure around. The Chosens. Only across. How can you know . . . ?" She shrugged helplessly, straining to avoid looking at her husband's glare.

"Anyone can learn. Let me show you our second demonstration." Enthused now, Anspach turned to her wards and clapped her hands. While Anspach hurried toward them, she whistled shrilly. A single Chosen walked awkwardly into the room, burdened with a large box in her arms. She put it on the floor. The girls reached into it and hauled out a motley lot of sticks and cord. They proceeded to build with the articles. The gathered diners rose. Some climbed on chairs. A few, perhaps overly appreciative of the beer served, pushed things aside to stand on the table amidst the crockery for a better view. In short order, the Chosens stepped back from a model suspension bridge.

Leaving the children, advancing on Gan, Anspach boldly put her hands on the edge of the table and leaned forward to talk directly at him. "Murdat, what happens to most of our bridges every spring?"

"Happens? They wash away."

"This won't. The ends rest on high ground. Nothing touches the water. Leclerc can build this, Murdat. Because the treasure of the Door tells us how. People can move things to market. Messengers can travel without waiting for water levels to fall. Think about the spring, Murdat. Windband will come from the south. No one thinks you can move swiftly to meet them. Leclerc can't bridge the Bear Paw or the Deer or Shad rivers where they're too wide, but he can bridge any of them somewhere. Mobility, Murdat." Anspach backed away. As she did, Carter and Bernhardt moved forward to join her. Linking arms, they faced him. Anspach continued. "We believe you are Church's best hope to survive the conflict to come. We work with Leclerc. We promise you power. We promise you loyalty. We offer you the full treasure of the Door. For a price. The Iris Abbey must become the new home of the Teachers."

Sylah was stunned. Emotions boiled through her mind, a stew of astonishment, resentment, confusion. Gratitude.

If Gan rejected the proposal, the lives of the three women were dangerously jeopardized. All the change-resistant citizens of the Three Territories would consider them people without standing, less than Peddlers. Worse, no matter what Gan did, Sister Mother would never accept this insult. She would declare the strangers anathema. With the former Harvester now the Sister Mother, that was a death sentence.

Sylah also realized that the strangers knew exactly what they were doing. They'd kept their intentions totally secret because they didn't want Sylah or Lanta or their friends involved. It was an incredible risk, heroic.

Dangerous for Gan, as well. Acceptance of the proposal was absolute rejection of Church Home. Gan would create a working counter-Church.

Movement drew Sylah's gaze. The Violet Abbess edged away from her retreat in the dark corner. Her sudden reappearance brought back all of Sylah's earlier feelings of commitment and involvement. Nevertheless, she kept still, watching, waiting.

From the junction of the tables, the Abbess raised a pointing finger. Even before she spoke, the naked force of her rage silenced the rumble of argument. "Murdat!" Her single word snapped like breaking bone. The Chosens scurried clear of their model bridge, huddled against the three strangers. Carter and Anspach knelt to draw them close, enfolded them. Bernhardt placed herself, shieldlike, between the group and the Abbess.

Again, the older woman called out, "Gan Moondark! Hear the word of Church. And obey."

A Messenger strode into the room on cue. He doffed a flat scarlet hat, bowed with a flourish of matching elbow-length gauntlets and cape. Straightening, he scanned his audience quickly and read it well; he wasted no more time on preamble. He closed his eyes. His features grew harsh. Spine rigid, shoulders back, he opened his eyes and spoke. "I address Gan Moondark, and all who would follow him."

The Messenger paused. Lanta hissed in Sylah's ear, then said, "It's the Harvester. How do they do that? He looks and sounds exactly like her."

Sylah nodded impatiently, unwilling to miss a nuance of sound or gesture. The body language and intonation captured by a Messenger could be almost as revealing as that of the person being imitated. The man went on. "The woman formerly known as Rose Priestess Sylah was cast out by mistake. The responsibility is mine alone."

The room hummed with excited whispers. Neela grinned broad relief and congratulation. Sylah saw from the corner of her eye, but instinct insisted she concentrate on her enemy. The Violet Abbess' hate-warped features had taken on a gloss of satisfaction.

The Messenger continued. "The Sylah one is known to have caused a mountain to burn. She caused the wife of the Chair, the ruler of Kos, to commit suicide. Not, however, before Sylah conspired with dark forces to make the Chair's wife name her infant firstborn son Jessak, after a known evil spirit. Sylah brought plague. Sylah's associate is a renegade Seer who prostitutes her Seeing for her own benefit and for Sylah. The Sylah one marked me, the Sister Mother."

At that accusation, the appalled silence of the gathering broke in a hushed sigh. Sylah caught herself looking away from the Violet Abbess, trying to literally see that sad, horrified sound.

Again, the Messenger. "The use of the marking sign is forbidden to women. All know this. Sylah knows. Yet she did it. For all her sins she was cast out. In communion with all the Tenders of Church's Orders, it has been decided that the punishment was insufficient. All who would be healed or cured or blessed or forgiven by Church, hear me. Sylah! Hear me while you may. All who associate with you are cursed. All who help you are cast out. Church will seek you. Church will destroy you as ritual commands. I, Sister Mother—I pronounce you witch. *Witch!*"

BOOK II

Poison

Chapter 30

There were those in the room who actually strained toward Sylah like dogs on a leash. That image was underscored by the way they checked and growled when confronted by her proud defiance. She saw Gan rise to his feet. Sylah relaxed. The few men and women eager to earn Church's favor by attacking a declared witch would be the kind to need assured approval. As much as Sylah feared witchcraft, she feared cowardice more. Witchcraft required skill, and even then was undependable. Cowardice was another matter. A coward would always find a turned back.

Sylah's personal philosophy also rejected Church's dogma that witches must be killed. Until this moment, she believed they should be rejected, treated as sick, allowed to come in contact only with Church's Healers. It felt very different to suddenly understand that such isolation might well be the very kindest fate she could hope for. The faces of the witch-killers in the room were eloquent testimony that, in their minds, life in any guise was too good for her. She saw more than religious conviction in those expressions, too. She saw lust; covert, shamed yearning for the opportunity to kill with impunity, with pleasure. A witch could be killed as horribly as the imagination allowed, so long as the body was properly burned afterward. There were those who maintained that the dying screams of a witch carried the name of her killers to the Land Beyond, to the eventual benefit of her torturers.

Sylah made careful note of those faces.

Gan vaulted onto the table, kicking plates, mugs, cutlery away in a crashing, breaking clatter. His hand rested on the handle of his murdat, and his look dared anyone to vex him further. Shara and Cho bounded to their feet. They dodged under the table, coming out the front to take guard positions. Hackles up, teeth bared, they emphasized Gan's presence. Once satisfied that no one held notions of further irritation, Gan addressed the crowd.

"Rose Priestess Sylah is my friend. She shared my exile when my own people rejected me, ministered to me when I was near death. She shared Altanar's cells with my own Neela. After daring a dangerous quest, she came back to the Three Territories triumphant, bearing the treasure of the fabled Door. She offers a new, brighter world, and asks only for safe haven. The Harvester one attempted the death of my friends, betrayed Sylah in her quest, and usurped the leadership of Church. I should have expected this insanity. She names my friend and my guest a witch. I spit on this false Sister Mother. I say Sylah is pure. If there is a better one in Church, show her to me."

Gan paused. Still swinging his head from side to side, a tiger inspecting a flock, he examined each person in the room. None matched his gaze for long. "These three women with the Chosens, far from their homeland, worked with Sylah to arrange a better life for our people. They represent what Church must be: the agent of benevolent change. I grant their wish. The Three Territories is now and forever the home of the Teachers. Where I rule, whatever improves the lives of those I rule will have my full support. Some will say I rule with Church or for Church. They lie. I rule. I help Church so long as she helps me. Let there be no mistake; Church is supreme in the Land Beyond. In the Three Territories, Murdat rules. Tell all your friends and families that the world is changed, and we lead the way. A testing is on us. Faint hearts will desert, and good riddance. Go from here now and choose your side. Go." The last word was a roar. The murdat whispered out of its scabbard and sliced the air with a murderous hiss.

The crowd poured out of the room like a multicolored liquid gushing from a jar, leaving only Gan's family and closest friends.

Except for the covey of frightened Chosens.

And the coldly unmoved Violet Abbess.

Ignoring the older woman, Gan smiled at Kate Bernhardt. Softly, he said, "You can stand aside, Kate; I won't eat the children." He waited until she did so, then vaulted lightly from the table. A hand signal settled the dogs in place. He advanced on the small knot of Chosens. They hung onto Carter and Anspach, still not sure of this shouting, frightening man. Even after he sheathed his weapon, none of the huge, round eyes left his face, never blinked. He knelt, hands to his sides, making no move to contact. "I'm sorry I frightened you. Do you ever get excited and talk too loud?"

One girl blurted, "Not *that* loud," and Carter choked on laughter that boiled out in snorts and gusts until she simply let it go. Others joined her, including Gan. After a bit, he went on. "It's bad manners, isn't it? So I apologize. But I'm very excited about what the Priestesses are doing. The things they're showing you will change the world, they tell me. Do you want to help them? And help me?"

Some of the children nodded. Most simply waited. Gan wasn't entirely accepted. Not yet.

The Abbess said, "I forbid. Chosens are the property of Church. What you've done here tonight curses you eternally, Gan Moondark. You will not corrupt our Chosens. Nor will your condemned friends. All of you will be cast out. Cursed."

The room drew in on itself. Gan answered calmly, but his lips were pale as he rose to full height. "You speak fairly. We have made game pieces of these innocents. This war is between those who hold Sylah's vision of Church and those who hold yours. But the fighting will be done by those who have no hope of power, or desire for it. You'll lose, old woman. There are many reasons why you must lose, but the one that will destroy you utterly is the one you'll never understand. The Teachers will grow and flourish and triumph because they aren't property."

The Abbess laughed scornfully. "Brave talk. A warrior, surrounded by his lackeys, insulting an unarmed female. I know I can't physically take the Chosens from your control. Not now. I will defeat you and your weapons, however. I am Church. You cannot strike me. Eventually, Church will have what belongs to her."

"And welcome to it, Abbess. But nothing else. I assume you'll leave the Three Territories now, and take all Church Healers with you. My Wolves will see to your safe passage to the lands of the River People."

The Abbess stalked away, turning to stand under the massive lintel. Outstretched arms almost spanned the doorway. "Church has no quarrel with the people who suffer under your rule. You cannot dispossess us so easily as that." To Bernhardt, the Abbess said, "You. The Bernhardt one. You and your friends play with the souls of helpless children. Keep them from the spell of the witch, Sylah, and those who support her. I command. I warn." She turned and was gone, the black figure an eerie swirl of shifting, erratic shadows.

One of the children pulled on Carter's sleeve, bent the small woman down to her even shorter level in order to whisper in her ear. Carter's face flamed. She straightened jerkily, painfully. Still her answer was gentle and soothing. "No, little one, you're not going to die, or be taken from us. The Abbess is wrong about what we're doing, so we have to show everyone we're good people. You understand?"

Another child ventured her concerns. "We don't have real mothers and fathers. We have to go where Church says. The Abbess is more important than you. She can make us do anything. You, too."

"Never again." The words were hard, decided, but Carter's hand on the child's tousled head was loving. "That's what she was talking about, dear. There are two Churches now, ours and hers. We have to decide which one is the right one."

"Murdat; whose side is he on?"

"Yours. There are things we must do for him, but he wants us to be happy."

"He's scary."

"I know. Sometimes men are like that."

"The Abbess isn't a man. She's scary, too."

Carter nodded calmly enough, but her eyes flashed dangerously at a suddenly smug Gan. "We won't worry about her."

The girl inspected Gan. Then, "You promise we can stay with our Priestesses? And Rose Priestess Sylah and Violet Priestess Lanta? In our own Iris Abbey?"

Gan returned the examination with full seriousness. "You promise to listen to them? To be faithful to their trust and instructions? They're my friends, and I expect you to make them proud of you. Will you promise to try?"

The girl swallowed. "I promise." As Gan's gaze swept his tiny audience, they each managed, "Me, too." Some answers were more like small squeaks, and one broke like thin glass. Gan remained stern. After the last response, he said, "You have the word of Murdat. You'll stay with your friends. They're your family." He turned to face the adults, and seeing some faint smiles, he darkened. "This is serious business. These are the new Teachers. If I die, I task you, all of you, to see my promise carried out." Then, reluctantly, he left the children to go to Sylah. "You are many things. War Healer. Rose Priestess. The Flower. Wife to my closest friend. My friend. Now you are Church." The hard, forbidding set of his features shifted momentarily. It was a change none but a particularly astute Priestess would catch. For a fraction of time Sylah saw the incomprehension of a trapped animal looking at her through the eyes of a man.

That instant threw her back to the night of fire and sword, the night her parents died and she became worse than an orphan. A thing, a possession.

Owned. Gan was owned.

Softly, Gan told her, "We become what we must. We are different strengths, you and I. Fire and water. Darkness and light. When you pray, ask that we never conflict."

Impulsively, she reached for his hand. Her massive gold bracelet slipped out of her sleeve to glint brightly between them. Gan withdrew from the grasp, returned to his wife's side.

The three Church women hurriedly ushered the Chosens out. In the lull that accompanied their departure, Sylah examined the small group of adults remaining in the dining hall. She almost smiled at the way each one struggled to disguise or deny reaction to the things they'd seen. Except Neela. Always open, practically incapable of dissembling, Neela's thoughts came through her expression more clearly than words. And Neela was afraid.

Conway and Tate were grim. They recognized the full extent of the threat thrown at them by the Violet Abbess. Conway and Tate knew the power of Windband and Moonpriest. They saw the Skan sharkers schooled off the vulnerable coast of the Three Territories.

Beside Tate, Nalatan was protective. His look for her said the world, Church and all, would do well to avoid troubling her.

Sylah ignored Lanta, quite certain she knew exactly what her small friend was expressing. Lanta was responsible to forces beyond herself. And Conway. They demanded her first consideration.

The remembrance of mute pain in Gan's face struck at Sylah. She felt lightheaded. She wanted Clas na Bale. The touch of him, the scent of him and him alone in her nostrils. The tingling, moist warmth of his breath on her throat.

Leclerc bent toward Jaleeta. The movement broke the spell of Sylah's yearning. Jaleeta smiled at him. Sylah was deeply disturbed by the artificiality of it. Slyly, the young woman's gaze eased past Leclerc's determined good cheer to Emso. There was a physical quality to that look, as though she used it to touch, to arouse.

And then it was over, and Jaleeta was fully attentive to Leclerc again. Confusion tightened Emso's face. Turning away, unsure of what had actually happened, the tough, harsh features struggled through several changes. In the end, Emso startled Sylah.

Anger. The least expected reaction of all. Then she realized there was something else. Fear. Why? What could make Emso fear Jaleeta's look? Or was his mind on something, someone else?

Her mind drew her back to her earlier thoughts of the dinner, the camaraderie, the laughter, the sharing of good food, good music, good company.

All despoiled. Ruined.

The shrill giggling of King Altanar rattled at Sylah in the clatter of plates being cleared from the table. Candles guttered in a sconce just by her head, the tiny sound suddenly reminiscent of the cruel, smirking whispers of his followers. A dropped spoon clanged, echoed from the cold stone, and she heard the slam of the dungeon door that closed her away from light and life and love.

That imprisonment cost her a price she couldn't bear to think about, even yet. Now she felt imprisoned again, and the power of evil was gaining strength before her eyes. Had she sacrificed so much for nothing? Could she escape again?

CHAPTER 31

THE HONOR OF GUARDING THE CASTLE'S INTERIOR FELL TO OLAN TROOPS WHO WORE THE traditional armor of the former kingdom. Conical metal helmets and metal torso plates weighed them down, as did chain-mail skirts and more plate covering the front of the legs. Their mobility was heavily curtailed, but they could absorb terrible punishment. They stood at all ground-level doors, at selected watch windows on the upper story, and patrolled the crenelated roof.

Emso stalked them this night. He moved silently, with the peculiarly solid grace of a fighting man, continually poised to deliver a fully leveraged blow. The guard normally welcomed his appearance. His inspections were considered hard but fair, and he usually made conversation to help pass the time. Tonight was different. With every minor infraction, Emso's anger erupted. No detail escaped his eye. The slightest nick in a sword blade brought down inordinate wrath. No man's armor was satisfactorily polished.

Sadly, Emso knew he was being unfair, yet he was powerless to help himself. The thing eating at his conscience gave no respite.

Outside the castle, he sought relief in walking. Rounding the walls, he headed for the dock and its attendant warehouses. There would be no one there at this hour. He could sit and think through his troubles.

Preoccupied as he was, he failed to notice the shadow that detached itself from the darkness to follow him until he committed to the downhill grade. Whoever lurked in the darkness understood that once Emso started in that direction, the only reasonable route of return was by the same roadway. There was nowhere else for him to go except the beach itself. The obscured figure melted into the smothering blackness of the castle's base.

Sitting on the dock, feet dangling just above the water, Emso examined his dilemma. He knew the real Church was right in this matter of the Teachers. The name alone was deadly. His mother, a good, decent woman, constantly warned her children that what she called "high notions" was a form of moral decay. A soup ladle wielded like a war club made it clear that Church knew all that anyone needed to know. "If rich merchants and nobles feel the need to do numbers or make letters, that's between them and Church. And the local Baron, of course: A thing as treacherous as learning wants leadership from nobles as well as Church." Emso's scalp tingled in remembrance of throbbing knots the size of walnuts. They saved him from sin.

So why wouldn't Gan let him alone? If it bothered a man to go against the right and proper ways of his childhood, what authority did Gan Moondark or anyone else have to push him into something else?

Especially a man who'd served loyally. Who'd saved Murdat's life. That should be worth something.

Nothing seemed to be enough. No matter what old custom died, Gan seemed determined to root out another. Progress, he called it. So did that weasel-eyed alien, Leclerc. Change; that's all it was. It was one thing to devise new weapons, or fighting techniques. But putting women to work, making them think they could be independent? Craziness. Emso swelled his chest with pride. Did he complain about making the women arrogant and vain? No. Not once.

Teachers. That was too much. Did he dare think the word? Yes. Betrayal. Betrayal of all the old ways. Learning was doom. Everyone knew it.

Emso painfully admitted to himself that Gan wasn't merely mistaken about this Teacher thing, but willfully wrong. He was setting himself above Church's rightful hierarchy.

Emso shivered so hard his shoulders threatened to cramp. He rose swiftly. Mist surrounded him. A thrill of fear ran up his back, a childhood thing of bad dreams and creatures that lurked, unseen, eager to rend, to devour. High above, the light of the castle wall torches was diffused, so that each appeared as a round, orange-yellow eye. The two of them visible from his angle wavered, seeking, trying to focus on him.

As if Murdat watched in the night, peered into the souls and minds of those who served him.

Emso tested the ease of his sword in its scabbard. He checked the fit of the holstered shortknife up his sleeve. He savored the sinister scrape of metal on metal. His step was confident as he began the climb back up the hill.

At the top, just past the bend where the road turned to parallel the castle's southern wall, there was a place where no shard of light penetrated the darkness. The very road was almost indistinguishable, its flagstone surface an irregular, pale deception underfoot.

Someone waited.

What sense, or combination of senses, warned Emso he neither knew nor cared.

He froze. Silence was his best friend. Slowly, fighting the urge for speed, he drew on the murdat. The blade's voice was less than a mosquito's song.

"Emso." Urgency shrilled in the whisper. Emso said nothing, bent toward the voice, pulled his blade free. Raised it like a woodsman's axe.

"Emso." Calmer, confident now, the speaker had lived to call out again, and believed the danger was past. Emso flexed his arms. One step away. Perhaps a shade more. The speaker was close enough to be killed.

"It's the Violet Abbess."

The murdat was moving, thirsting. Emso almost screamed with the horror, the effort, of checking the killing sweep of his weapon. He stumbled, bumped a figure that was unprepared. They both tumbled to the ground amid muffled feminine cries of distress. Emso rolled to his feet, sheathing his murdat, hoisted the Abbess to her feet. He tried to apologize. A voice like a striking whip cut him off.

"Quiet. Fool. Did I creep out here in the night to be beaten? Exposed to our enemies by your witless clumsiness? I'll have bruises tomorrow."

"I didn't know . . ." Emso's whisper trailed away in bewilderment. "I thought . . ."

"It's all right." Forgiveness came grudgingly. Then, completely befuddling Emso, the Abbess was suddenly ingratiating. "You responded as the warrior we need, and it gladdens my heart to see it."

"Me?"

"I said you." The acerbic retort stopped as if the Abbess lopped it off with her teeth. Sweet reasonableness followed. "Yes. Exactly like you. A man who understands the needs of those you defend."

Emso straightened. He was too battle-wise not to recognize a trap. "This conversation is unacceptable, Abbess. I'm Gan Moondark's man."

"My point exactly. No one loves him as you do. It was Emso who guided him to success in creating the first Wolves. Emso saved his life only days ago. Emso fought to destroy Church's enemy, as well as Gan's deadly foe, and to free the imprisoned Neela. These things are known."

"Because they are known, you insult by coming to me in the night this way. I say nothing against Murdat."

"Nor do I wish you to. Church loves him as you do. Church mourns his waywardness."

"Church wastes its time. There were Teachers before. He brings them back. It cannot be wrong. Church itself says there were Teachers. Their mission must have been to . . . They were allowed to . . ."

"Teach. You can't say the word, can you? You speak the title. Teacher, like Abbess or Murdat or Baron. But you can't say *teach.* Because it's wrong. In your heart, you know it."

"You plant doubts and confusion in my mind."

"Your mind? Dear Emso. I seek your heart. Your eternal soul. And I seek to save your friend. Church's benefactor. How can I prove this to you?"

"Leave me alone. Don't interfere with Murdat."

"So be it." Emso blinked at the swift ease of her answer. He stepped back, smelling treachery. The kindly voice flowed on. "I ask you to do nothing, save that which you are committed to: Protect your leader. Help him, loyal Emso. Remember who he is, what he is, what he must be. His mother foretold his destiny. He's to bring glory to the Dog People. Now Church feels his path is flawed. He was good, and will be good again. Be with him. Guard him, guard his reputation, guard his soul. As for the so-called Teachers, do you think Church would injure innocent children, particularly Chosens? Think a moment, Emso. Chosens belong to Church, body and soul; would Church so wantonly and wastefully wound herself?"

"No. But I can't go against Murdat. Church should help him, for her own sake."

"He's been turned against us. We bear no malice. Church ever forgives. I beg you to help us help him."

Emso opened his mouth to respond, and a hand as soft as the mist rolling up from the sea settled on his chest. "Say nothing more. Be patient. Your good, true heart will lead you in the path of righteousness. Go. My blessing is on you."

The barely palpable hand pressed lightly against Emso, and he heard the heavy breath of robes swirling in retreat. Mist mingled with sweat on his brow. He wiped at it with a hand that trembled. Squaring his shoulders, he resumed his way. The guard who admitted him executed a perfect salute and greeting that went completely unnoticed.

Knowing the Violet Abbess' words would deny sleep, Emso walked aimlessly through the castle. In common with Gan and Neela, he shared a dislike for the simple weight of the place. The angular precision of the walls made him feel encased, rather than enclosed. At night, their dark bulk was friendlier, like the irregular press of forest trees or the solid affirmation of hills. His aimless wandering took him past a side door. It opened into the yawning cave that was the King's Hall. The name was a holdover from Altanar's time.

A glow of fire startled him. He almost called alarm before he realized the source was one of the square firepits that ranged the long axis of the room. Flickering light played across immense timber posts. They supported the soaring roof, invisible in the darkness overhead. The pillars were carved to represent men standing on each other's shoulders, three tall. Their faces were contorted.

A small figure knelt at the knee-high wall around the firepit. Natural caution tempered curiosity, and Emso advanced quietly. There was a suggestion of feminine grace in the form, and the size indicated a woman. Still, Emso stopped a safe distance to the left rear. A right-handed person would be disadvantaged drawing a sword, forced to strike awkwardly. "Who are you?"

Cat-quick, the figure whirled away. Jaleeta faced him, shortknife in hand. Emso noted that her jaw was firm, despite eyes rounded in fear. Her ferocity amused him. "I only wanted your name, child, not your life. I won't hurt you."

"You say it. The knife guarantees it."

Emso eased his weight onto the balls of his feet. "If I meant you harm, you couldn't stop me. Tell me why you're here."

Unwavering, the knife held aim directly at his navel. "I don't have to tell you anything. I'm under Neela's protection. I go anywhere I want, when I want."

Emso stepped forward, turning to his left at the same time. When Jaleeta reacted, thrusting, he was already halfway around, so his right forearm slammed into hers. The knife penetrated the air where Emso used to be. Still spinning, he elected not to drive the point of his left elbow into her ribs in the usual crippling stroke. Instead, he merely pushed her further off balance, then caught her from behind. With her right wrist firmly in his grip, he tightened the left forearm across her throat. She struggled momentarily. When he lifted, leaving only her toe-tips in contact with the floor, she stopped. Her plea came in croaking bursts. "Can't breathe. Let go. Please." The knife dropped, the steel ringing unconcerned gaiety.

Released, she stumbled forward, ignoring the weapon at her feet, holding her throat. Facing him, defiant through tears, she said, "I never thought it would be you. That cruel-looking monk, Nalatan, perhaps, or the Conway one, who pretends to see only his little Priestess. Even Gan. Not you."

"Not me what?"

Jaleeta sneered. "I know what you mean to do."

Understanding crowded into Emso's overworked mind. He shook his head. "You're more of a fool than I suspected. I have no interest in you, except to discover the name of someone crazy enough to sit by a fire alone in this huge room this far into the night. Go to bed. And don't forget your nasty little toy." He swept past her to sit on the firepit wall. Lowering his head to his hands, he reflected on a world saturated with nonsense. Several heartbeats passed before he realized he wasn't alone yet. Peering up through his eyebrows, he looked into Jaleeta's sorrowing eyes.

"I misjudged you, Emso. How can I apologize?"

"Go away. If one of the guard patrols finds you, they'll have to put you in a cell until morning. You'll have to explain to Murdat what you were up to in here, all alone. What *were* you doing in here?"

"Praying."

"What? Here? Why?"

Jaleeta smiled, a forlorn, apologetic thing. "Sylah came here to ask King Altanar permission to go to the Dog People. Her quest started right here." She stopped abruptly, looked away.

Emso said, "You admire our Sylah that much?" He was quite certain Jaleeta's admiration for Sylah was only a corner of her concern. If so, she'd want to correct his error. Long ago, he'd learned he had no talent for asking the right questions. Silence usually generated more pertinent answers, anyhow. So he waited.

"It's not just that I admire her so much. I'm alone." She could have been talking to herself. The words made Emso think of the night's mist, soft, seeking, drifting without hope or purpose. Involuntarily, he stepped closer. Two steps, before he even realized it. He was close enough to see the delicate tracery of veins in sheltering, lowered eyelids, close enough to see how the firelight stroked color across the raven gloss of tumbled hair. He felt her sadness enmesh him.

How truly the Abbess had spoken, he thought, awed. He really did understand those he must defend.

CHAPTER 32

JALEETA PINCHED EVER HARDER ON THE SOFT FOLD OF INNER LIP BETWEEN HER TEETH, AND still the smile struggled to break free.

It was almost too much to bear. Emso was the one Tears of Jade feared.

Pride surged through Jaleeta. The famous Clas would pose no more problem than ugly Emso. No man would. Dangerous they might be. Stupid they certainly were.

She reminded herself that Emso was cunning, for all his foolishness. And violent. One mistake, and he'd kill her as quickly as he'd squash a mosquito. Jaleeta imagined an enraged, wild-eyed Emso, his murdat slicing toward her. Even as she shivered with fear, she pictured the sadness that would pierce his heart.

Forever sure of his duty. Forever sad for what damage he did. Perfectly masculine.

For a terrible moment that daydream was replaced by a vision of Tears of Jade. Jaleeta returned quickly to the surer subject of men.

Bull seals, all of them, roaring, ripping everything and each other apart. For what? To claim females that waited helplessly to be driven, bitten, crushed, impregnated. Used and discarded as soon as their season ended.

Tears of Jade said a human female used a man's mad strength, his insensate need. The spirit woman made it clear that as a small piece of cloth captured the power of the wind to move a heavy vessel, so a woman used the strength of men to avoid the shoals of her oppression.

Sometimes Tears of Jade explained more than she meant to, Jaleeta thought. The one fact Tears of Jade never mentioned was the most important: At any cost, Jaleeta must live.

Repressing a shudder, Jaleeta looked around quickly, momentarily unnerved by her own temerity. Putting her own survival before Tears of Jade's goals was risky. Somewhere in Ola, the ancient hag had at least one agent. Who? For the briefest moment, Jaleeta mourned the terrified For girl she had once been. That child never knew evil, never felt the need to look over her shoulder.

She set her jaw. Jaleeta must live. Live well. Fate threw her into this cauldron of hatred and duplicity. Fate would bear the responsibility for whatever followed.

Mere survival would never suffice. Jaleeta knew all too well what happened if a woman merely survived. A man who had nothing but his life to cling to had no reason to curse every minute of every day. Every man believed himself destined to be free. Grimly, Jaleeta thanked the Skan for making her understand that a woman's servitude was predestined. They made her know that long as she was full of promise of service or full with child, she was cherished. As a prize. Father, brother, husband, son were judges. Ordinary women hoped for men who treated them decently, hoped for children who were allowed to flourish, hoped to eat frequently, if not regularly. Joy was brief, humanity denied.

Ordinary women survived. The ruthless succeeded.

In her reverie, she forgot Emso entirely. Alarmed, she looked up, wondering what he must think of her extended silence. The craggy features smiled sad understanding. "You're not alone here. We're strangers to you now, but everyone regards you as very brave. You're admired."

"Everyone's been kind. I suppose I'm being ungrateful, but I feel . . . oh, never mind. It's foolish."

"You're not a fool." Jaleeta flinched at the harsh declarative tone. It could be accusation. She relaxed when she saw his continuing sympathy. He went on. "A fool couldn't have survived the Skan as you did. As for gratitude, we're grateful to you. You've given us insight into our enemy. Now tell me what's troubling you. Let me help you." He took her arm, led her toward the inconspicuous side door.

Demure, eyes lowered, Jaleeta went meekly. She sighed, then, "I feel strange, talking to a man this way. It's all right, I guess. Your honor's unquestioned. I don't know why a young woman, especially an inexperienced one like me, should trust a man like you, but I do. Is that foolish, too?"

Emso's oblique response addressed the part of Jaleeta's speech that affected him most. "It's natural for you to trust me easily. I'm much older. You don't see me as some young man eager to get you out of view so . . . That is, my interest in you isn't just that you're a beautiful young woman. Even if it were, you'd still be primarily someone who can help my leader. Gan Moondark must conquer, and I was born to see that he does."

Jaleeta recoiled, pulled her arm free. "Prophecy?" They were outside now, with nothing but starlight for illumination. Unable to read Emso's features, she reached for him as she spoke, the way Tears of Jade had demonstrated. A finger touched the blood-beat surging at the underside of his wrist. Her thumb rested, mothlike, on the back of his hand, alert to the slightest movement. Emso's hand tensed. The tempo at his wrist increased dramatically. He twitched, as if he'd pull away. But he didn't.

Emso was slow speaking, thoughtful. "No one's placed a prophecy on me. It's Gan. From his mother. He's destined for glory, bound to raise his tribe to triumph. The thing is, he creates a single tribe of all of us. Just as I'm drawn into Gan's personal rise, along with Sylah, Tate, Conway, Neela, Lanta, so tribes and nations are drawn into the rise of his kingdom. More than any of the others, his fate is mine, my life is his."

"You love him very much."

"He gave me back my manhood, saved my people. I'd love any man for that. He trusts me, gives me command of men. What conqueror does that for a used-up farmer? He chose me, Jaleeta. He gave me the opportunity to make myself more than I ever dreamed I could be. He looked at me and *knew.* I would die for him."

The last words sounded sad to Jaleeta. She released the wrist, noting that the blood-beat was slower now, and steady. She probed the seemingly selfless devotion. "Anyone can see how loyal you are. If I were Gan, though, I'd wonder if all my friends were so true."

Surprisingly, Emso laughed. There was a condescension in it that made Jaleeta bless the darkness, because her face burned, and she frowned angrily before she could stop herself. Blind to all of it, Emso went on. "You've put your finger on his weakness. Both of you have the same sort of innocence, but you have the wit to recognize it. Gan's trouble is that once he gives his trust, he can't imagine taking it back."

"Why should he? No one's given him reason to distrust."

Emso disappointed her, ignoring her carefully cast bait. Impatiently she suffered through more blather. She wished he'd choke, but he went on. "Those like myself protect him. We know his enemies."

At last. Jaleeta wanted to sing and dance. The old man did have a bone in his throat. Someone. Who? She opened her mouth, snapped it shut again. She trembled with the need to hear the names of those enemies, real or suspected. Fear of exposure jangled warning. She remembered Tears of Jade: "I send you to the Three Territories to destroy Gan Moondark and Church's witch, Sylah, as one sends poison to an enemy. Poison is guile, deceit, treachery. *Be* those things, my Jaleeta, and all you want will be yours. Is it love and courage that keeps you alive among the Skan? Are those qualities what allows an old woman to control our strong, bloody warriors? Or is it watching, waiting, turning that man against this one, using the strength of others to achieve your own way? Go with my spirit, with my wisdom. Think of what awaits your success. Then think of me, and what awaits your failure. Kill them, my poison. My beautiful poison. Bring them writhing to the ground. Slyly. While we shall stand away, hidden, laughing."

That was Tears of Jade's good-bye, given the night before the long walk across the island to meet the Nion. Jaleeta hugged herself with satisfaction, comparing that cold, hard knowledge with the foolish prattle of Emso.

Emso said, "When you first came here, I wasn't very pleased." They were at the door of the abbey by then, under the glare of flaring torches, and Jaleeta peered up quickly. His warm look slipped to a more quizzical inspection. Still, his voice remained light. "I'm not much of a one for change, unless it's something that helps us win battles. Even then . . . well. Anyhow, when Neela took to you, that meant a change, one close to Gan. It bothered me. Now I see you for the person you are, a brave girl, but still traditional. You behave the old way, with courtesy and respect. You're the sort of person Neela needs. Link to the virtues. You know. Everyone's too eager for new things and new ways nowadays. Neela needs someone around to help him—I mean her—remember the way things were. Ought to be."

"You're a good man. Gan's lucky to have you as a friend. I've only been here a little while, but I already know he loves you. So does Neela. All Gan's friends do, because they know how important you are to him."

Instantly, Emso was the grim, forbidding warrior Jaleeta remembered from her first, inauspicious sight of him. The moment passed quickly, then Emso was saying, "We're all very close. We've been melted together like steel in a furnace, you understand? Still, we have our differences. They don't matter. All that matters is that Gan Moondark fulfills his destiny. We live for that."

Turning, placing her back to the heavy planks of the abbey's door, Jaleeta studied Emso. She pulled up the hood of her cloak, relishing the sense of disappearance. Emso remained exposed in wavering firelight; she was hidden. She took his hands in hers, amused at the sudden wash of confusion that made him blink. He stiffened. Swift dampness coated his palms.

Jaleeta smiled. Another secret of Emso's was exposed. He'd called her "girl." The image in his mind now was "woman." Jaleeta saw it excited him.

Smug Church women could brag all they wanted of their ability to read messages in the movement of an arm, or the appearance of a blood-beat where none existed before. They were so arrogant about their special training. Jaleeta had no need of their self-important skills. A real woman created messages, she didn't read them. Nor did she care about a witch's craft in seeing the future. A real woman created the future.

As poison creates. It gets inside and twists things to suit its own purposes. Poison whispers softly. Deliciously.

"I hope we can be friends, as well," Jaleeta said, squeezing the sweaty hands. "I trust you. Please don't shame me for what I'm going to say, because I must. It's very, very important for me to tell you. I need the strength of someone mature to advise me. I'm alone here. Everyone's been nice, but I'm unsure of myself. Will you help me? Can we be friends?"

"Of course. There's no shame in what you say. There's a great difference between being brash and being honest. It's honest for you to admit to weakness. You're stronger than you think, but I understand how you feel. You can depend on me." He pulled his hands away. Jaleeta let them go, delighting in his reluctance, deliberately trailing her fingers across the hard, callused palms.

"Thank you, Emso. I feel you're someone I've been looking for. I know we'll be even closer, as time goes by. I hope someday my friendship can warm you, make you as happy as yours has made me tonight." She whirled. Ran inside.

Chapter 33

Jaleeta woke the following morning to gray, cold rain. It was already quite light. The realization that she'd slept so late came as a shock. She lurched out of bed, more asleep than awake, and yelped when warm, bare feet missed the wolfskin rug to land on raw stone. Two frigid steps across her small room brightened her mind to full consciousness.

No Tears of Jade stood over her, switch in hand, to punish her for failing to stoke the cabin fire. No mother hovered nearby, wringing her hands and wailing that her daughter neglected her morning prayers to the One in All.

That Jaleeta was dead.

This Jaleeta must live. Must live properly.

Throwing herself in an abandoned leap, Jaleeta crashed back onto the bed. The rope suspension squealed outrage. The heavy frame banged off the stone wall. Giggling, Jaleeta burrowed back under the warm furs, curled into snug, secret darkness.

So it should always be, she told herself, squirming about in luxurious self-indulgence. Scent tickled her nose; the wild, outdoor aroma of bear hide tanned to silken suppleness in the secret way of Neela's Dog tribe. And the lanolin smell of the wool blanket, woven by the same tribe. Crisp linen sheets made by her own For People gave off a scent that made her think of fields touched with sea mist and the sharp stink of the soaking process that was part of curing the flax.

Languorously, she thought of other smells, absent from this bed. Exciting, excited smells. Not smooth, like linen or fur. Rough. Dizzying, strong as the forbidden leaves and twigs Tears of Jade strewed across brazier coals when she sought communion with that world that no other could comprehend.

Jaleeta forced away the image of the old woman's bent figure cranked over her smoldering mess. She pictured Lorso, looming. Her fingers tingled with the memory of his eager, sliding muscles moving under her touch while his hands sought, explored, caressed. His breath touched her cheek, her ear, made her tremble with tiny messages of yearning.

"Enough!" She shouted the word, flinging back the covers, rising quickly. Ignoring the cold stone, she hurried to the small metal stove at the room's outside wall. Stoking kindling inside drew her mind away from dangerous thoughts. Opening the ceramic jar next to the stove, she poked at the coals she'd packed inside before going to bed. A few bits of dried leaf, powdered in a mortar, smoked immediately when poured into the jar. She blew the powder to a dainty flame, quickly feeding it small twigs. Once they were burning, she dumped it all onto the waiting kindling. In moments the stove fire was warming the room. Fortunately, the ceramic chimney drew properly. When the wind was wrong, it backed badly, turning the room into a veritable smokehouse.

While she waited for the water basin on the stove to warm, Jaleeta wrapped herself in the woolen Dog blanket and stared out the window. Her room faced east, with a clear view of Snowfather Mountain's shattered northwest face. Looking at it made her shiver, but not from cold. It was generations since Snowfather exploded in rage, but the tales of death and horror were as fresh as yesterday. The same was true of Destroyer's fury, to the north, but no one cared so much about that one because only Kwa and Mountain People were hurt by it.

Jaleeta paused to make a three-sign. She felt foolish doing it, because she no longer believed in its power. Still, it couldn't hurt to go through the motions.

Tears of Jade called those mountains earthbreakers, instead of volcanoes, and she said Sosolassa controlled them, as he controlled the sea. Jaleeta wasn't sure she believed that, either. Tears of Jade also said she spoke to whales. Jaleeta's own people hunted the whale, and none of them ever made such a claim. The secret singers, the men who spoke of salmon gods and whale gods in defiance of Church's rules against such things, sang to those spirits, but no spirit ever sang back.

"Tears of Jade." Once again, Jaleeta spoke aloud in the silent room. This time her voice was barely audible, even to herself. She tasted the name, moved closer to the open-shuttered window. She spat to clear her mouth. Frothy whiteness fell away, losing itself against the rain-soaked ground far below. Lifting her gaze, she contemplated the mountains. Because the clouds were so high, the view was clear. The peaks around Snowfather appeared insignificant at this distance. She'd never been to them, but everyone assured her they were almost as high as the Whale Coast range of her native country. Snowfather towered over them. This morning there were mists in the hollows and valleys, pale against the silvery black of wet forest. Closer at hand, the fog was alive, filtering in and out of the folds of the earth. Sometimes, even as she watched it, it shimmered away to nothing, like a thing sent to trick and bewilder.

Repelled, fascinated, she stared out at the teasing maneuvering. There was something about the way the mist's veil slipped across the terrain that frightened her. Her mind told her mere fog had no power. Still, the unceasing waves and invisible currents reminded her of Tears of Jade's tales of the god Sosolassa.

Did the land harbor a similar occult menace? The image of Tears of Jade dabbling in the coiling tendrils of her spirit-smoke caught at Jaleeta's mind once again.

Deliberately, Jaleeta concentrated on Lorso. Eyes closed, brow furrowed with intensity, she hugged herself tightly and brought up memories. To her dismay, they wavered, fled. The harsh, carved face of Tears of Jade demanded full attention. Then the old woman's image laughed, the hacking rasp Jaleeta knew too well.

Opening her eyes, Jaleeta inhaled deeply. Rain continued to paint the landscape with its gleaming sheen. Clouds prowled sluggishly eastward. Snowfather brooded in monumental indifference.

Retreating to the stove, Jaleeta stripped off the shapeless nightgown and washed carefully. That done, she reached for a wooden object cunningly carved to represent an opening rose. An almost-invisible line marked where the top was fitted. Opening the container, she dipped a finger in its ointment. A smell of roses filled the air. She rubbed the perfume on a comb. Using a polished copper mirror, she experimented with minor variations on her hair as she stroked it, organizing and scenting simultaneously. She was replacing the comb when someone knocked on her door.

"I'm not dressed. Wait." Jaleeta leaped to the wooden clothes cabinet. After pulling on linen underwear, she yanked out a goatskin blouse, the cloth-thin leather dyed bright blue, embroidered with twining green-leafed vines and red roses. The cotton lining was a darker blue. For trousers she selected heavy, dark-green wool. As she buttoned and adjusted, her anger grew; whoever knocked was being very rude by not stating an identity. She jammed boots into her shoe-carrying bag and got into indoor slippers. Flinging herself into a chair, she began wrapping ankles and lower legs with multicolored leggings. "Come in." She barked the order, making no effort to hide her irritation.

The Violet Abbess flung the door open. She was every bit as angry as Jaleeta. Arms folded across her breast, she glared down at the younger woman. "No former slave, not even a favorite of our most-noble Gan's charming Neela, keeps an Abbess of Church standing in a drafty hall. You assume. You offend."

A sharp retort burned Jaleeta's throat, but she quelled it. The Violet Abbess lacked real power, now that Sylah had Gan's favor, but there was nothing to be gained by irritating her. "I would never offend Church, Abbess. I was too well raised. Even when I was a captive of the Skan spirit woman, I found ways to say proper prayers."

"Did you?" The Abbess' question was a cold knife. Her eyes held Jaleeta's. "And your mother? She prayed, too?"

Jaleeta's memory darted through her conversations since her arrival in Ola. Had she mentioned her mother? What had she said?

Jaleeta felt a trickle of sweat under her arm. "My mother's faith saved us both. She is truly loyal."

"You are not?"

Suspicion. Accusation. Jaleeta heard, and tensed. The way the Abbess asked her questions, the way she held herself, spoke of hidden knowledge. And testing.

"I believe." As proof, Jaleeta executed a three-sign in the manner of her branch of the For; left fist to right breast, right fist to left breast, both fists to abdomen, then to forehead. "I'm not so worthy as my mother."

"Your mother would have been entertainment for Skan warriors for a short while, then slaughtered. She lives because of you. Don't lie. I know more than you imagine."

For the first time, the touch of fear found Jaleeta. The older woman took a quick step forward into the room, her smile positively wolfish. She bent forward. The heavy cape swept open, winglike. Jaleeta imagined a bird, violet, green, and black, swooping. The Abbess' crackling demand was a rattle of hard feathers. "Tell me the truth. Tell me all. Tell me honestly. You *must* not lie to Church. The true Church. You understand?"

Jaleeta needed time. She pretended confusion. "But Gan said . . . In the dining hall, when you—"

"Gan Moondark is cursed! And the obscene witch Sylah, her that he calls Church in his Three Territories." Spittle danced on the thin, quivering lips. The flickering wetness fascinated Jaleeta. She stared, remembering how she'd spat Tears of Jade's name into the rainwashed morning.

Jaleeta stood. The movement forced the Abbess to rise with her, then take a grudging step backward. "What is it you want from me, Abbess? If I was rude to keep you waiting, it was an accident. Trying to frighten me is intentionally rude. I survived the Skan. You think to shout at me and make me nervous? You expect me to weep and confess? Confess what? You expect me to somehow betray Gan Moondark after he sheltered me? I'm not such a fool. Neither are you. Speak plainly. What is it you want?"

For several long breaths, the women held each other in unyielding grips of sheer will. Jaw muscles tightened. Small, excited blood vessels writhed, in tight, scrawling messages of tension. And then the Abbess laughed.

Head back, mouth agape, hands clasped under her chin, the Abbess howled delight. Quieting momentarily, she gripped a startled Jaleeta by the shoulders, shaking her gently. "I see it. I see now. The witch, the Tears of Jade one, she saw it too. It pulses at your temples, draws your hands to fists. The ambition, the irresistible sense of self. The lines at the corners of the eyes, the mouth. The dark, watching pupil, unchanging, uninfluenced." The older woman sobered. She dropped her hands from Jaleeta's shoulders. "I forget myself. Pleasure numbs the brain, opens the mouth."

"Tell me what you saw." Jaleeta didn't try to disguise her excited curiosity.

"Only what Tears of Jade saw."

"You weren't there. No Church was there. Nor in the Skan village."

"Skan travel. They talk. Church listens. I know how dutifully you worked for your mistress." The Violet Abbess was again accusative.

"I did what was necessary to save my mother's life and my own. I never denied Church."

"Or yourself," the Abbess added dryly. Then, "Church also knows how fortunate you were to escape."

After a long dueling silence, Jaleeta finally said, "I asked you before, Abbess: What is it you want?"

"Help Gan find his way back to Church. Speak only the truth to him, to Sylah, and all the others. Tell them that I'm forbidden to cross this terrible gap between us, but I yearn to see them cross it and rejoin Church. Take no action. Tell me only what you feel is helpful. But be diligent, child. Remember, the Skan are coming. So is Windband. All who die without the blessing of Church face the Land Under. I beg you to help me draw Sylah and the rest back into Church's love."

Jaleeta broke away from the fixed, piercing eyes that seemed to poke into her head. The fine, delicate hair at the back of her neck was erect, sensitive to the faint breeze swirling through the open window. There was a sensation of tiny creatures crawling across her flesh. "I can't inform. I won't. Anyhow, I'm alone, a stranger. They'll tell me nothing. If I say I'm trying to help you, they'll ignore me, maybe even send me away."

"You're not alone. All admire your courage. Emso especially admires your character. He mourns Sylah's mistake, fears for Gan's immortal soul. Trust him. Between you, you may rescue Gan Moondark from sin."

Jaleeta's mouth fell open. Her eyes formed rounds of surprise. "Emso hides his true face from Gan Moondark?"

"You injure. Emso stalks his friend's soul through a forest of evil. He is cautious, not devious. Gan is as one blinded. Startle him, push him, and he will strike out of fear and misunderstanding. You must help Emso; he'll help you."

"You're sure it's right? You think I'm strong enough, smart enough?"

Too swift to be denied, the Abbess stepped forward, embraced Jaleeta. A gasp clawed at the younger woman's throat as the dark wings of the cloak closed out the world. A faint tinge of wood smoke clung to the Abbess' robe; an amethyst clasp was pinned to her breast. As the cloak enfolded her, Jaleeta smelled the Skan bonfire and the consumed beach huts of her murdered family. In the deep sparkle of the purple gem, she saw the flicker of flames, the cold of honed steel. Memory of capture, shame, and terror ripped at her.

The Abbess released her, held her at arm's length. Alarm, and then a strange sort of triumphant sympathy flowed across the lined features. "Poor child. You do see the enormity of our challenge." The Abbess' face turned upward. "Bless this child, that she may deliver the sinner to grace. Deliver the enemy to vengeance."

Jaleeta swayed. The Abbess smiled again, confiding. "Are you all right? Do you need me to stay with you a while?"

"I'm fine. I know what I must do. Depend on me." She kissed the Abbess' hand. Letting it go, she kept her head lowered, watching the hem of the robe to assure herself that the woman was, indeed, gone. Then she slammed the door and wedged the single chair against the handle to hold it shut.

For a long while, Jaleeta fed wood to the stove and huddled over it, warming a body that shivered in spite of fire and massage. She mumbled to herself, "Wants me to deliver a sinner, does she? Yet she speaks of Gan and Sylah and all their friends as sinners. So her eye is on only one, and that one is Sylah. What of Gan? 'You must help Emso,' she said. 'He'll help you.' Ha!" Scornful strength echoed from the stone walls in the last. Jaleeta unfolded, rising slowly. Color returned to her features. As she brushed at her clothes, straightening them, even they seemed to brighten.

"Our dear Abbess and our upstanding Emso think to use me to bring down Gan Moondark. How Tears of Jade would laugh. Not only has she delivered her poison to her enemies, the fools are fighting for the chance to feed it to each other." Jaleeta leaned out the window until she was balanced on her midriff, straining to look as far north and west as she could. Rain streamed down her face, dripped from her chin. Long, dark tresses hung heavy with water that cascaded free in a constant stream. Her grin was mad, her whisper hoarse. "Tears of Jade. Hear me. We're winning." She rocked dangerously, brimming with power and confidence now, daring fate to take her.

Tiring of that, growing cold again, she hauled herself inside. Shedding her blouse, she rubbed off vigorously with a drying cloth, then donned a similar top, this one featuring yellow and red. "We're winning," she repeated, then, "*Jaleeta's* winning, you crazy old witch. And there'll be plenty of poison left over for you." She laughed happily. Holding up the copper mirror, she combed her long, glistening hair until it smelled rose-garden sweet and glowed black as ocean night.

Chapter 34

Tate gestured at the rough silhouette of the distant Enemy Mountains. "A Peddler came to the town market yesterday. From up north. He says there's activity. Some Kwa, some northern Mountain People, some of the surviving Mountains who ran away after the war with Gan. Small groups, filtering in. The Peddler also says the first snows are here already, up high on the northernmost peaks."

Conway took another bite of his bright red-and-yellow apple. He sent Tate a long suspicious look, chewing thoughtfully before asking, "So?"

Tate ran her hand across Karda's wiry-coated head. The dozing dog instantly recognized the touch as not his master's. He jerked awake. An angry snarl raised his lip as he turned toward the offensive liberty. Seeing Tate, he stopped abruptly. Confused now, the animal looked to Conway, who ignored the byplay, then back to Tate. A wag of the heavy tail served as apology.

The whole action took only a moment, and then Tate was saying, "So I think we ought to move out as soon as we can. To beat the snow. It could take a long time to find it, you know?"

"The crèche." Conway's voice was as sharp as the crack of the bitten apple. He looked away. "I've been hoping you'd let it rest."

Tate dismissed his disapproval with a hard smile of her own. "We've talked about everything under the sun lately. Except the crèche."

"Because I don't want to argue with you. I think going back is a mistake."

"Spit it out, Matt. You think me leaving Nalatan behind is a mistake. You know we need what's in the crèche." Tate rose with her usual lithe grace, so well coordinated she seemed to drift into the new posture. Fists on hips, she glared down at her companion. They were alone on an unbroken beach of smooth gravel that spanned away, left and right, until it disappeared around distant headlands. Shattered, abraded drift logs, some as thick through as a tall man, littered the shore. Here and there one raised a broken branch stub in supplication. Against the dull earth colors and the leaden fall sky, Tate blazed in bright green trousers, shining black boots, and a poncho of blue and green, done in alternating stripes of random width. Her headgear was a wide, floppy beret that matched the trousers.

Still seated with his back resting against the log they'd shared, Conway stretched out his legs lazily. The black-and-brown wildcow hide that made up his shirt and trousers sparkled with minute droplets of condensing mist. Farther out on the Inland Sea, denser fog advanced in a sluggish wall.

After tolerating Conway's silence as long as she could, Tate made an irritated sound, then went on. "My husband's not the issue here. Survival is. There wasn't any disagreement before. We talked about it on the way back from the Door, before we got to Ola, even. 'We were lucky to find that ammo,' I said. 'We've got to make it last.' "

"And I still agree. But things are different now. I've got a bad feeling. I'd rather wait for spring." He moved jerkily, almost as if he were squirming.

"We can't take a chance on running out of ammunition. What's coming down this spring is going to be lots worse than anything we've seen yet. Moonpriest is building catapults. What if he builds a wallkiller?"

Conway made a face, nodded reluctantly.

Tate went on. "That gives Windband an edge in mobility and missile power. The Skan can control the coast. Maybe Gan's For allies can hurt the Skan at sea, but they can't stop them."

"You think the ammunition in the crèche—assuming the whole cave hasn't fallen in—is necessary?"

"Nobody goes into a battle with enough cartridges in his belt. There's Hy-Pex in there, too, remember. A lump of that the size of my fist is worth pounds of Leclerc's black powder. And more weapons. We can't wait for spring. We've got to hit Moonpriest before he hits us. We intercept him. We can be anywhere ahead of him, on his flanks. We choose the battlefield, prepare it to our advantage. Attrition, Matt. We can cut his warfighting power in half. Maybe more."

A quick shake of the head expressed Conway's view. He went on, however. "We could do a lot of harm. Not that much."

"Think about it. Windband depends on mobility. They have to concentrate forces to come at us, they have to get close to cut at us. I know about their horseback archery. I won't tell you I'm not afraid of dealing with them, but I'll tell you I don't like to think what we'll do to them with our firepower. It'll be slaughter."

"I rode with them, remember? Imagine yourself facing a charge ten times, thirty times, larger than we fought off."

It wouldn't have surprised Tate to see apprehension in Conway, or even a certain sadness over past mistakes, and the need to fight men he'd once fought beside. What she saw, however, was a deep, brooding pain. The silence that wedged between them was grayer than the fog, and far colder.

Conway finally broke it. "Slaughter's the right word. You're as sick of it as I am, aren't you? The killing."

"I was sick of it before I ever did it. Every time it happens, I hate it more. If I thought we could talk sense into Moonpriest, I'd go that route in a minute. He'll never quit. He wants it all."

Conway turned away, still darkly contemplative. "And Gan? The man we serve? Doesn't he want exactly the same thing? And what of our friend Sylah? All she wants is the soul of every living person on this burned, blasted, primitive planet. What are we, if we're not their star killers?"

"What you say is true. But ask yourself if we're on the right side. What happens to those lives, those souls, if we don't do what we can? You watched Windband capture villages. You told me about it. The Skan are no better. What do we do, Matt?"

"Better men than me have gone crazy trying to answer that one." A lopsided, deprecating smile tried to lighten the mood. "This business of thinking is too hard. I believe I'll have to give it up."

"You'd be a pretty sorry specimen if you didn't wonder about it all. You're okay."

The grin lost some of its sardonic twist. "Soaring praise, indeed. But speaking of good men, I still think you should take Nalatan with you. He's twice the warrior I am."

"I can't take him to the crèche. We don't dare let anyone know about the equipment there, about what and where we came from."

"We keep having this same argument."

Uncharacteristically, she refused to meet his gaze. Looking out over the water, chin high, she went on. "If I ever let Nalatan know what I am, where I'm from, he's got to live with the same secret—if he doesn't run away, first."

"That's the dumbest thing I ever heard." Conway strained to sound properly indignant, remembering Lanta's Seeing that exposed fragments of his own life. That episode was a wound that wouldn't heal. "Nalatan wouldn't run away from hell itself, if you were there. The only thing that'll send him away is if you push."

Tate stiffened. His view of her was a profile, and he saw how her jaw muscles hardened to small knots, how a pulse leaped to life in her throat. She closed her eyes, breathing with slow, structured poise. Conway tensed. He knew she was thinking of his twisted, tangled relationship with Lanta, and that she was fighting the urge to remind him of his own folly.

Only when Tate was relaxed again would she face him. "It's probably best if we don't question each other's judgment on something so personal. Nalatan isn't invited, okay? The sort of danger he'd protect against isn't what worries me. We've got a much larger problem than a few Mountain People or Kwa raiders."

"Moonpriest." The single word was a curse, a warning, a realization. "You're not concerned about us running short of ammunition, you're afraid he'll empty the crèche himself. If he does, we're dead."

"Not good stuff to think about."

"Look, I'm not trying to restart our argument about Nalatan, but we could use another pair of hands. We can't pack all that gear out of there, just the two of us."

"We get it out of the crèche; that's priority one. What we can't bring here, we relocate."

"The snow could be a real asset. It'll hide the new cache. I imagine Moonpriest is thinking pretty much the same things we are, right now."

"He has to be. And he's on the same spot: Who does he tell? If he wants those weapons, he almost has to come for them himself. If we see him, I'm taking his ticket."

"Jones? Kill Jones?" In his dismay, Conway fell back on the true name. "He's one of us." He walked several paces to lean against a weathered log. With a weight measured in tons and life of centuries, its gray inertness seemed to mock anything as swiftly transitory as a man's grief.

Still, the taint of accusation in his tone hurt. Tate answered with a coldness she regretted, even as the words flew. "Would it be better if I cried? I nursed him when he was still Jones, when he was dying."

"We're arguing again. A couple of great partners we are. If we unload the crèche before Moonpriest shows up, all of this is pointless speculation. Let's get on with it. The sooner the better."

"You've told Lanta?"

Conway met Tate's gaze. "What's this? Taking turns? I'll explain to her." A bitter aside, more for himself than his audience, slipped out. "Not that my explanations seem to have much effect on her."

"Whatever happened, she forgave you long ago. The woman loves you. Anyone can see it. You've got to move close. I think she's waiting for you to tell her you're both wasting your lives. Step up, man."

Conway jerked, like a horse reacting to a sting, or a dog stepping on a burr. It took a moment for him to recover. "You worry about your monk. Lanta'll be just fine. I can leave in the morning."

"If that's the way you want it."

"That's exactly the way I want it."

Unperturbed, Tate continued. "I'll meet you in the stables. We ought to move out prior to first light. The fewer who see us leave, the fewer to talk about it."

Neither was ready to quit with such discord swirling around them. They moved about aimlessly, each making a great show of studying beach rocks, driftwood, seaweed. Any subterfuge that prolonged the togetherness was seized on. When they caught each other at the game, they broke into spontaneous laughter. Conway said, "We really are great partners. You give lousy advice to the lovelorn, but that's a minor flaw, I guess."

Tate looked fierce. "We don't even want to start on flaws, my man. Life's too short for me to explain your failings to you."

"Be serious a moment. You're sure Nalatan's all right?"

"I told him the trip was a holy obligation." Tate looked away.

"You told the truth." At Tate's swift uncertainty, Conway added, "Maybe not the sort of holy Sylah would agree with, but close enough. If Moonpriest gets that stuff, Gan's not the only one who'll fall. Moonpriest believes in that whacked-out religion of his. With that kind of power in hand, he'll be pure evil."

The two stood mute, aware of the other's thoughts. In the world they'd left behind were evils unknown to this one. Here the streams now ran free and clean, the earth's wind carried no killing compounds. Nature was harsh, even cruel, but she was fair and honest. Men had failed to purify similarly.

Conway said, "A while ago you asked me to think about whether we're on the right side or not. I can't answer that the way I know you want me to. I've seen too much. Any side that solves its problems by killing can't be the right side. My heart tells me so. My heart also tells me it doesn't want to die."

"We're protecting innocents."

"I know. I'm sure what I'm doing is right. What's it costing us, though, Donnacee? How do we do what *they* do, and not turn into *them*?"

Tate laughed, the sound a cold hand that gripped Conway's spine. "All soldiers know that one. The right fights end when the noise is over, and you're still standing; the wrong fight ends when you do."

She reached out, took both his hands in hers. Conway marveled at how they combined supple strength with feminine warmth and delicacy. She said, "I'm glad you're with me. You're a brother. Come on, now; we have work."

Together, they walked away from the sea. Behind them, the fog slipped ashore. It hesitated, gathered itself. With a gray, damp shudder, it swept over the tiny, lapping waves, smothered them, and moved in pursuit of the retreating humans.

Chapter 35

Nalatan's ill-concealed anger cast a pall over everyone gathered around the front firepit of the King's Hall.

Sylah looked away from him and the circle of friends, scanning the crowd behind her. She remembered how she'd felt the day she stood in this same huge room and confronted King Altanar, asked permission to go to the Dog People as a missionary. Now, on the raised stage where Altanar used to hold sway, one of those Dog People waited for the crowd to subside before he addressed them. Gan was dressed plainly in gray woolen shirt and trousers, in contrast to the gaudy splendor affected by Altanar. The only finery he displayed was a remarkable dagger dangling from his belt, the handle and scabbard ablaze with jewels.

Torches burned in sconces attached to the hall's carved tree-trunk pillars. Despite the fires in the huge pits and the torches, the distant walls eluded the light. There was a shadowed, menacing darkness along the blunt stone surfaces. So it was with Nalatan. One felt the fire and heat in him, yet behind that, one sensed cold danger lurking. He hovered near Tate, as if daring intrusion or insult. It was very unlike him, and frightening. As a warrior-monk, he could strike swifter than thought, faster than apology. Sylah hoped Tate could keep him calm.

Lanta broke in on her thoughts. The smaller woman whispered, her lips barely moving, "Look at them. I recognize too many of Altanar's former Barons in this crowd. They make me think of coyotes watching a crippled deer."

"Not yet, sister." Sylah soothed her friend. "They know they end up slaves if Gan loses the war in the spring."

"Unless they help overthrow him." Lanta's elfin face was clouded with worry. "I don't trust any of them."

The fire crackled. A thick log fell. Sparks cascaded upward, swirled out of sight into the copper smoke hood and thence into the chimney. When Sylah spoke, it was a musing sort of speech. "Sister Mother brands me witch. I know I'm not. I'm rebuilding the Teachers, creating a new Church, one that blends learning along with its other ministries. Shouldn't I be allowed to call on your Seeing? If your talent is accessible to Church, isn't that us?"

"I'm not sure, Sylah. I agree, but what if we're wrong? It's a sin."

"Church determines what's sin and what isn't. If I'm Church, I'll absolve you."

"The One in All determines." Lanta's jaw jutted, and her gaze held Sylah's.

Sylah's face burned. Her throat was suddenly dry, achingly tight. Words came with difficulty. "Never leave my side. Never. You're my conscience. How could I say such a thing? If my poor Abbess heard, she'd die of shame."

Lanta's features softened. Her manner was unrelenting. "You wanted power. You thought power would make you free. Now you know: Power imprisons."

"What can I do?"

"What you were born to do, what the Iris Abbess raised you to do. You're the Flower, and you bear the seeds of the new Church."

"I could become like the Violet Abbess. The Harvester." Horror tainted the last, and she looked stricken.

"Whatever comes, it must be from within you."

"You'll help me?"

"Any way I can." Suddenly wry, she added, "We're both cast out. If we fail to re-create the Teachers, we'll at least be the most learned Priestesses in the Land Under."

Eyes rounding in shock, Sylah was speechless for a moment. Then she giggled, the sound totally inappropriate to what had gone before. Both women realized it, and laughed all the harder.

Jaleeta's words caught them by surprise. "Well, at least some people here haven't forgotten how to enjoy themselves." When Sylah and Lanta turned to face her, she was waiting with a mischievous grin. She nodded surreptitiously at Nalatan. "Tate's pet tiger has a real burr under his tail, hasn't he? Even Gan was tiptoeing around him. You'd think Tate was leaving him forever."

The Priestesses nodded in unison. Sylah said, "He's devoted to her. The trip could be dangerous."

Growing serious, Jaleeta said, "I wonder why only two of them are going? I mean, if this is a holy obligation for Tate and Conway, how come it's not for the other women and Leclerc?"

Sylah looked chagrin at Lanta, and got the same back. Sylah told herself she'd have to pay more attention to young Jaleeta. For now, she merely said, "It may have something to do with warrior status. Tate and Conway do most of that for their group."

"That's what I've heard," Jaleeta said. She sniffed. "I like Tate; she's nice. But a woman who fights men? And wins? It's not natural."

Lanta attempted to deflect the conversation. "They're all very different. Louis Leclerc has already changed many things here. Like the strange oven he made for turning coal into what he calls coke. The coke burns so hot it makes the best steel we ever had. Yet he knows nothing of the smith's art."

"I wonder what other secrets he's got?" Jaleeta focused on Leclerc with an intensity that had the two Priestesses exchanging glances yet again.

Tartly, Sylah said, "If he has any, he'll share them with Gan Moondark."

"Good." Jaleeta nodded firmly. "I hope he knows lots of ways to beat the Skan." She faced her black-clad companions, and Sylah thought how colorful the younger woman must look standing next to them. Jaleeta wore a long cream-and-yellow robe, floor-length, tight at the top and hips, full at the bottom. It defined her lush figure perfectly, and the swirling skirt gave her a light, floating appearance. The firelight cast myriad shifting hues across the material, glowed wildly in her rich, black hair. It baffled Sylah that so many people accepted Jaleeta's self-description of herself as unschooled woman. It also occurred to Sylah that envy colored her own view of Jaleeta's sound knowledge of how to present herself.

A blare of trumps stopped conversation. Everyone looked to the platform at the left front of the raised stage. It jutted out from the wall, illuminated by its own torches as well as the room's general lighting. As the noise of the trumps dwindled to echoes, other men sounded warhorns. Made of copper and brass, the latter instruments tapered through two full circles, from flaring bell mouths to a metal mouthpiece. The musicians draped them over the left shoulder, holding the loops against their ribs with the opposite elbow. The bell of the horn was directly above the musician's head, slightly forward. The noise they made was staggering in the confines of the hall. Basso, brazen, they raised a haunting thunder that crashed off the walls, shivered the huge columns, squeezed hearts.

Then came the drums. Nothing like the size of the Wolves' regimental drums, they were massive, nevertheless. Their voices were the singing of mountains, and as the people leaned forward into that storm, the horns and trumps blared once more.

Silence fell like a physical weight. Gan raised his arms. His words were plain. "The Three Territories are faced with destruction." He lowered his arms, stepped forward, as if speaking directly to each person present. "I've heard the rumors. Some say I bargain for my kingdom. Some tell stories that I would exchange gold and slaves for permission to rule the Three Territories. Hear the truth. If I could bargain honorably with our enemies to save lives, I would do so. Our enemies are implacable. The Skan and Windband want us for slaves, our lands for their own. What faces us in the spring is extermination."

He paced back and forth, letting his declaration take root. "I know the Territories are ripped by uncertainty. I know there is dissension. There are those who wish to see me deposed. It may come to pass. But understand this: Any man living here who turns his hand against the Three Territories when the Skan and

Windband mount their attack will be given to them. Naked. Alone. Such a man may live, but without family, clan, tribe, or nation. He will depend on the mercy of our enemies. He will cease to exist for all of us."

A strange sound, almost a whistle, shimmered through the crowd. In a world where one's entire life was tallied by one's relationships, such a sentence was more horrible than any death. Sylah repressed a shudder, thinking how even a slave could identify an owner, and therefore feel he belonged. Gan's dictum crushed even that cruel prospect. Sylah noticed Neela's face. Determined not to embarrass her husband by admitting her own horror, Neela was steeled to immobility.

Intrigued, Sylah deliberately checked the reactions of the aliens. None showed the least concern. It was inconceivable to her that anyone could contemplate such loneliness without pain. Either the strangers were far better at hiding their feelings than she ever suspected, or there was something terribly wrong with them.

Gan continued. "Tomorrow morning riders will range the Territories, with orders for all men between sixteen and fifty to report to the local Barons. Emso and selected officers from the Wolves will train the new recruits. Others will raid Windband and their allies among the River People. Pausing, Gan scanned the crowd. At last, he pointed. "Back there. Baron Fir, come all the way from our northern boundary; do you see any fools in this gathering?"

The crowd looked to Fir expectantly. He was momentarily nonplussed, and then the tight, shrewd face wrinkled in a grin. "No fool great enough to admit to foolishness."

Light laughter moved through the crowd, and then Gan was pointing at another man. He shouted at him, "Otter South. A valiant warrior of the Eleven West barony. How about you? Any fools here?"

"No, Murdat." Otter South was a tall, whip-lean man, and he growled his answer.

Gan said, "Then I tell you all this. Only a fool speaking to fools would promise victory in the war facing us. If I die, I die a free man, leading free men. Murdat abandons no wounded, Murdat trades no man or his property for advantage. I promise all who come to my Wolves one thing only: Honor."

There were cheers. War cries. The instruments on the band platform blared mad song.

Some Barons and nobles of Altanar's former kingdom were far more restrained. They registered their cheers, applause, cadenced war cries. A closer look caught surreptitious glances. In one instance, Sylah detected that most frightening display of duplicity, the covert smile.

With a hand on Sylah's shoulder, Lanta pulled her down while rising on tiptoe. "You saw? Baron Ondrat. He smiled."

"I saw." Sylah cut her off, indicating Jaleeta with her eyes. Then, loud enough for the younger woman to overhear, "I thought he sounded wonderful, too. We will win. We'll crush the Skan. And Windband."

Conviction rang in Jaleeta's agreement. "We must. If the Skan win, they'll destroy the people of the Three Territories the way a weasel destroys roosting chickens."

Lanta bristled. "They won't win. And they'll find they've attacked eagles."

Sylah said, "I wonder how the Skan and Windband will react when the closeness of their relationship is tested. In defeat or victory, I think those two will find a way to avoid loving each other."

"You only need concern yourself with one," Jaleeta said. "If they lose, you'll have the pleasure of watching them tear each other apart. If they win, they'll go after each other, but only after they've torn us apart."

"Don't you have any friends among them?" Sylah asked, extending a sympathetic hand to rest on Jaleeta's.

The reaction was explosive. Jaleeta's face, her neck, her ears, all burned crimson, displacing even the glow of firelight. Her eyes narrowed, her lips tightened. Pure hatred gleamed in her expression. Sylah was fascinated to see how ugly the young woman became, and how quickly she reestablished control of herself. Mere anger took the place of malice, cold judgment took over for emotional excess. To Sylah and Lanta it was like watching an exquisitely played game. Jaleeta's response was short. "The only human among the Skan is my mother."

It was a lie. Dilating pupils shouted duplicity, the surging blood-beat under Sylah's fingers mocked the false words.

The knowledge created more questions than answers. Could Jaleeta's emotional connection with the unknown Skan person be helpful?

Movement at the corner of her eye ended Sylah's contemplations. Louis Leclerc approached wearing an uncharacteristically broad grin. He moved past Sylah without a glance, stopping in front of Jaleeta. "I had to tell you how glad it makes me to see you looking so well. We were all worried about you when you first arrived. You'd been through a lot. Tonight you look wonderful."

Jaleeta lowered her eyes decorously, gave shy thanks.

Turning her back in order to shield her words from Jaleeta, Lanta whispered, "Look at how she's looking past him. She's looking for someone."

Preoccupied, amused, Sylah had missed what Lanta described. When Nalatan and Tate exchanged good-byes with Emso, Jaleeta appeared pleased. That reaction solidified as the couple advanced on her. Jaleeta looked at them, rather than Leclerc.

Greetings were exchanged. Leclerc remarked again on Jaleeta's beauty, eliciting another pleased, flustered smile. Tate's reaction was a speculative stare for the man.

Nalatan remained glum. His conversation was monosyllables and grunts. Tate rolled her eyes at Leclerc and Jaleeta in silent apology.

Jaleeta said to Leclerc, "Is your work going well? Will you make more things, so Gan can beat the Skan?"

Leclerc answered gravely, "Well, as Gan said, no one can promise victory. Still, I have some ideas that should help. New weapons."

"Weapons don't fight." Nalatan glowered at everyone, but no one in particular. "Donnacee's trip into the Enemy Mountains has something to do with weapons to save Gan Moondark. I know it does. I'm tired of talk about secrets and I'm tired of thinking about my wife risking her life for someone's kingdom." His blunt belligerence was like a cold deluge.

Tate took his arm in hers. She said, "I love you, too," and the hard, frowning monk looked down at her and melted. He almost smiled. "I finally did it, didn't I? Made a fool of myself."

Tate cocked her head back, tilted it to the side. "I love you for it. That's my burden."

At that, Nalatan did smile. He pressed Tate's arm to his side. Oblivious to the others, he led her away. She turned to wave, sent her friends a small expression of resignation, and shrugged.

The others laughed, the tense moment past. Leclerc invited Jaleeta to visit his workshop the next morning. The two of them walked off, conversing animatedly. Sylah and Lanta waited a moment, then trailed after them, part of the crowd moving into the night. At the door leading outside, Jaleeta turned.

Sylah shoved her friend aside, hiding with her in the shadows. Lanta understood immediately. Together, they watched the couple.

Jaleeta's back was to Leclerc, who stood beaming, waiting patiently. The young woman's gaze swept the room's occupants as a hawk scans a roost of songbirds. She watched Emso, chatting with Gan and a circle of Barons by the firepit nearest the stage. She sought out Nalatan just as he walked through another door with Tate on his arm. A faint, contemplative smile moved Jaleeta's lips. A startling pink tongue, shining like a jewel, slipped between them. Lazily, sensuously, it slipped from side to side, wetting her lips until they, too, appeared enamel-bright. Then she laughed and turned back to Leclerc. Silvery peals spangled the air behind her as she disappeared into the darkness with him.

Chapter 36

The young Priestess stood in the middle of Sylah's sparse quarters. She towered over Sylah, trembling nervously, her robe literally moving with her body. White hands, peering out of the deep sleeves of her crossed arms, squirmed like two mice trying to retreat into grain sacks. She stammered as she repeated her story for Sylah. "The one who told me to come to you is the War Healer on her way from Church Home to the White Bear People. She's been with us since just after you and the others came. We all thought she was bad Church, but she was just finding out who liked you and who liked the Abbess, so . . ."

"That's the second time you said 'bad' Church. There is no such thing. We're divided, but we'll come together. As sisters, not as victors and vanquished. Now, go on."

The apologetic Priestess bobbed industriously. A glance at Sylah's mounting irritation started her tale again. "As soon as the War Healer was convinced I favored you, she gave me the folded paper. She said you'd understand when you opened it. Then she told me I had to bring you a message." The gawky woman stopped. She swallowed hard, then, "She said for you to be at the street of the potters tonight between first and second watch. If you can't be there tonight, then tomorrow night. The one who's to meet you said: 'The marked one sends harm.' "

The Priestess looked questioningly at Sylah, consumed by curiosity about the trenchant words.

Sylah gestured at the leather flagon hanging on the back of the door. "There's wine in that. Drink some. You need it." Looking away then, Sylah pursed her lips. The "marked one" could only be Odeel, the former Harvester who now claimed to be Sister Mother. Remembering the night she'd put the forbidden mark of the cross on Odeel, Sylah repressed a shudder. Once more, she saw barbaric ceremony, unspeakably cruel execution. She marked Odeel because she was part of that obscene performance.

Fury burned in her. A Church official—now the most honored of all Church officials—part of that. It was unacceptable. Wrong.

Sylah turned to the Priestess, who was just putting down a ceramic cup. Sylah said, "What do you know of this traveling War Healer?"

"Nothing I haven't told you, Rose Priestess." A swift twist of reservation marred the young woman's features. "I didn't want to tell her I favor you over the old Church ways. I didn't want to bring you that folded paper, nor any message either. She wormed things out of me. Then she bullied me. She's mean, sister; smooth as cream, tougher than bull hide."

Sylah had to laugh at the other's righteous indignation. She moved to her, put an arm around her waist to walk her the few steps to the door. "There's need in our garden for every blossom. We need her for what she is. We need you just as much for what you are. Go back to your abbey. Forget what's happened." After a significant pause, Sylah added, "My friend."

The tall Priestess turned, transformed. The awkward posture disappeared, the taut mannerisms ceased. Her face, heretofore plain and not particularly becoming, was wreathed in a bright, confiding smile. Her steady gaze held character. "I am your friend, sister. Oh, I'm afraid, and I know I'm not clever or quick-spoken, but I still want to help. I'm a strong, hard worker, and I think I can be as brave as anyone. I'll try, anyhow. Because you're good. You work for all women. You say the garden needs us. Most of all, it needs our Flower." Abruptly, she stopped, bent to kiss Sylah's forehead. And was gone.

Slowly, bowed with the weight of her thoughts, Sylah pushed the door closed. She made her way to the chair by the small table under the shuttered window. Despite the midday hour, inclement weather afforded no chance to open the place to more light. The room was dull, its few touches of color muted. A candle on the table jittered. Rags jammed into the spaces between wooden shutter and stone wall failed to eliminate the tormenting draft.

"Prisoner." In the silence of her thoughts it was just a word, a description. Aloud, it resonated off the stones, the structural timbers. "So much hope," Sylah whispered. "So many people, so desperate for someone to show the way. Why me? I'm unworthy. I'm afraid. So lonely."

I will not be owned.

Unbidden, unwelcome, that old credo hammered at her inner being. Tears burned her eyes. "Does that mean I must be denied my husband's arms? Does that mean I must always be the one to resist, to stand up? Is it too much to simply be me? I want to know life, not service. I want to live."

A meeting with an unknown person. A conspirator. A need—a demand—for secrecy. If Sylah was to live, she would spurn such a plan without pause. It promised death.

So many enemies. So many friends.

The Flower was Sylah. The Flower had no choice.

Who would wait in the darkness?

Sound distracted her. A crackling, crisp noise. It took time for Sylah to realize it was the small paper envelope, crushed in a clenching fist. Blinking back tears, she opened the neatly folded paper. Inside was a flower. Fragrance rose from it, sweet, enticing. A rose, one of the plain ones the gardeners called first roses, saying all others descended from the type. Sylah held the paper close, savored the fragrance. Roses. Someone nailed roses to her door once. It seemed generations had passed since then. Those roses had been a warning.

The pressure of watching eyes worried the back of Sylah's neck as insistently as the chill mist forged into the dark cave of her raised cowl.

She stopped abruptly, whirling to catch whoever followed her. The bottom of her flowing robe, sodden with rain, flared out like a black blossom opening against the night. Heavy cloth expelled arcs of water with a scornful hiss. A distant shadow, darker than the darkness—something confused her eye, tricked her mind. There was nothing conclusive.

One of the new communal baths Gan required in every poor neighborhood was just at the end of the block. Only a while ago this same street would have been busy with people. This late, long after the evening meal, few people ventured into a cold, windy rain.

Sylah resumed her walk. Experience warned that she heed the odd, tingling sensation of imminent danger. She smiled ruefully in the depths of the hood; she might not have Lanta's Seeing talent, but she had a bird's sense of nearby predators.

Someone in the darkness stalked her. Her warrior husband lectured that the predator misses far more often than it kills. Wary prey survives. Usually.

"The marked one sends harm," the War Healer from Church Home said. Grimly, Sylah remembered how freely the new Sister Mother dispensed harm.

The thought added speed to Sylah's progress. Instinct demanded she run, but the pursuer's stalk decided her against that. Whoever it was, he hung back. Ever since she crossed the open ground outside the castle walls and entered the town proper, he had been there. Too far to harm, close enough to become dangerous quickly. That suggested someone ahead, as well. Waiting.

Hanging wooden shop signs rattled and banged erratically at unpredictable wind gusts. Rain whispered against the brick walls and stone streets, drummed on the tile roofs. Few lights broke the oppressive blackness. Sensible people were indoors, warm and dry, shutters drawn against the increasing violence of the storm. The odd lighted window filtered the ruddy touch of open flame through pieced, multihued glass panes. Jewellike, they provided color, not illumination, reinforcing the unworldliness of the narrow urban canyons.

Sylah determined to lose whoever followed her. They were in the poorest section of the city. Buildings were much closer together. Some of the precise geometry of Ola's street pattern suffered a bit of freehand diversity. Heart pounding, she darted through warrenlike alleys. Once she found herself in a dead end. Shaken, she huddled for long moments, straining to hear the footsteps that meant entrapment. When none came, she made her way back out. Her course was generally in the direction of the street of the potters, marked by random twists and doublings.

The meeting site loomed unexpectedly, the orderly rooflines of two arcades. She hurried under the nearest, out of the rain at last. Cautiously, feeling her way from support post to post, Sylah crept the silent length of the arcade. Distant lightning flashed. The brief light was welcome. She hated the ensuing thunder because it might cover the sound of surreptitious approach.

Immediately after one flash, before the thunder came, she heard her name. A high voice, strained. Female? A man disguising his normal tones?

Sylah answered, "I am Sylah. Who calls?"

"A friend. I come to warn you." The speaker had an odd speech pattern, rising and falling tones that reminded Sylah of the Kossiars, far to the south.

Sylah said, "The message warned me already. Tell me who you are, where you're from."

"I'm here to give you names of our enemies."

Sylah peered into the darkness, fixing the location of the speaker. "Anyone can speak names."

"They're not to be spoken aloud after I give them to you. The only other people who know them are Sister Mother and her Seer. I also come to warn you of two plots. One is against you. The other is against Gan Moondark."

Frowning, Sylah turned to the right. The speaker seemed to have moved a few paces. "Only two? Surely we're worth more."

"Probably. The Seer spoke of two." The voice was unperturbed by Sylah's sarcasm. More than that, it was moved, off to the left. "For Gan Moondark, the Seer spoke to Sister Mother of poison. She saw trust. Affection; almost love. In a moment of great triumph, she Saw the poison do its work."

Lightning flashed. Sylah blurted questions. "He dies? Gan Moondark dies? Who? When?"

The voice was directly in front of her. "The Seer saw no more. Gan Moondark knows poison and knows death. The Seer is certain."

"And me?" Sylah tried to sound calm.

"Of the plot against you, I speak with more authority. Sister Mother orders your death. More, she has tasked the Violet Abbess to assure it. In return for success, the Violet Abbess will be raised to rank as Harvester."

"You said Sister Mother's Seer was involved. Does she See my end?"

"The Violet Abbess appeared to the Seer wearing the robes of Harvester."

Something hard and sharp leaped to life in Sylah's breast. Her words were almost panting. "The Teachers. Do I succeed? Will there be Teachers? Does Church endorse them, support them?"

"The Seer told that wearing the robes of Harvester, the Abbess disappeared into a darkness filled with evil."

The shock of such a vision drew Sylah's thoughts away from her own fate. "What does that mean? How can such a thing be?"

"What a Seer Sees is always true, but it is not always accurate. You know that. The darkness may be a symbol. The robes, too. We know what happens. We don't know exactly how or why. But names are names."

"Yes. Names. You promised names."

"Hear. Remember. There are four. Remember. Ondrat. Krevelen. Byrda. Mull. They plot against Gan Moondark. Church Home knows, and will support them."

"Proof. Give me proof, so I can convince Gan."

No answer was forthcoming for a long moment, and then the voice responded from afar, hushed. "Someone comes. Flee."

Without hesitation, Sylah obeyed.

Black robe and hood made her part of the darkness, drew the night around her in protective folds. Yet someone else was there, as well. Slinking along a wall streaming rainwater, Sylah hoped desperately it was a friend.

She stepped on something, felt it give under her weight. Time tantalized her, let her dread the entire sequence of foot bearing down on a pottery shard, unable to stop. A convex curve pressed against the resistant leather of her shoe sole. Stresses built. Fired clay cracked, a report like two hands clapped together. Rubble crunched.

In the manner of all hunted creatures, Sylah became one with her background, wished herself invisible.

Sound. From behind her. Following. Scraping? Dragging? She twisted her body in that direction, unwilling to move her feet. Sluicing rain washed away all other sounds, blurred vision.

Something moved. Treacherous clay fragments grated. An indistinct figure advanced with definite purpose. Sound pricked at Sylah's ears again. Steel on steel.

Straightening, Sylah drew on her training, put her entire being into authority. "Stop! Whoever you are, beware! I am Church, a War Healer. Begone!"

The figure was close now. Someone bulky, short. Crouched. She raised her right arm, pointed. "Leave here while your soul is still safe."

A rough, incoherent expression, like the snort of a bull, presaged the figure's charge. In the darkness, in the befuddling rain, the hurtling body took on the immutability of landslide. Sylah heard herself make a shrill, surrendering cry for dying.

Sparks flew from the impact where steel drove through her sleeve and struck the stone wall behind it. Sylah leaped away. The thick cloth caught the sword blade. For a moment predator and prey struggled to escape each other. Then, with a defeated sigh, the material sheared. Staggered, Sylah caught herself, spun away in headlong flight. Dodging from post to post, weaving, feinting, she felt the slashing weapon cutting air behind her.

In the diffused light forcing its way through a waxed hide window, something glittered at the edge of her vision. From the corner of her eye she saw the forepart of the blade descend. A rising scream degenerated to a gasp that clotted in her mouth. The force of the blow made her stumble. Reflex pulled her to the left, away from that gleaming horror.

Momentum carried the attacker past her. He whirled. Agile despite his bulk, he poised to stab.

The savage will to survive functioned in Sylah when fear and exhaustion crushed everything else. Without conscious thought, her right hand slipped into her left sleeve, drawing her shortknife. Instinct turned her sideways so the plunging sword passed harmlessly in front of her, right where her stomach had been. She whipped the shortknife at the snarling, snorting face. Caught in his forward posture, the man could only arch backward. The move exposed his throat.

Sylah felt a tug on the blade. It caught, slowed in its arc.

The man coughed. Called out startled, wordless protest. He raised both hands to his neck. The sword clattered wildly on the stone street. He slumped forward, coming so close to Sylah she could see the dark, lost holes that were his eyes. He gurgled, wheezed. His weak, clutching hand dragged at her sleeve as he fell.

Sobbing, screaming, Sylah bent to the body lying at her feet. "What have I done? Someone, please, help! Bring light, bring cloth. A man is dying. Help!"

A door flew open. Light spilled out, first here, then there. Voices came with them, querulous, afraid.

Lightning flashed. A searing, crashing bolt, and then another, turning the night into flickering, metallic day. Sylah looked around. There was someone behind her, above her, hands raised, carrying a mace.

He struck.

CHAPTER 37

MUSIC.

The sound of chings, the flat, round disks used in Ola as percussion instruments. And as vicious throwing weapons. Metallic notes coiled intricate rhythm and melody through Sylah's straying consciousness.

Smoke. Acrid. The smell was unpleasant, but there was release in it. Pain hovered out *there* somewhere, dislodged.

Pain? Why was there pain? Why couldn't she think, and why should her head hurt at all?

And then Sylah remembered.

Her eyes opened. The disembodied hurt seized the opportunity to claw its way through that opening. Sylah cried out, tried to roll away.

"Be still." It was Lanta, ordering, pleading. "You'll hurt yourself more. Be still. Please, please."

The music was gone. In its place was an iron clash of agony. And Lanta's soothing voice. "It's all right now. It's all right. You'll be fine."

"Will she live? Is she truly saved?" Gan's voice. Loyal, dependable Gan. Friend to Sylah, friend to Church. There was something he had to know. A secret. *What?* Important.

The music started again. The unpleasant, wonderful smell came back. The pain retreated, growling like a whipped animal.

Music. Lanta played the chings, a high and a low, a four-beat and a six-beat, weaving through each other.

Ondrat. Krevelen. Byrda. Mull.

Names. The chings rang their names.

Conway's voice broke in. "The guards who stopped Tate and me at Sunrise Gate said if that Baron hadn't gotten there when he did, they'd have killed her. We're staying here until we're sure she's all right." So many friends, such worried voices. Sylah felt her mind sliding away. She fought to hold it.

What Baron? Who'd he save?

Gan spoke again. "You can't know how ashamed I am about that. Of all the old Olan nobles, he's the one I trusted least. Now he's given me the life of one of my dearest friends. How do I apologize?"

"You don't," Conway said. "He doesn't know how you felt; why tell him? Thank him, and let it go at that."

Someone knocked at a door. Neela spoke. "Baron Ondrat. We were just talking about you. We owe you so much."

Sylah strained to hear this new voice. When it came, it was bluff, hearty. "There's no debt. As a matter of fact, I was cursing the luck that had me out in that storm when the lightning showed me what was happening."

Eyes closed, mind drifting like dust on wind, Sylah fought to remember, fought to comprehend. The figure that struck her was faceless in the night. Was it Ondrat? He continued to speak, the words pulling her back from the soft pleasure of unconsciousness. "She was finishing off the first attacker . . ."

"That's not true." Lanta's interruption was offended, shrill. "I saw the wound. The man was standing when it struck. She must have been kneeling, trying to help him, when the other man hit her."

"Of course. Forgive a warrior for leaping to a warrior's conclusion, Priestess. I only made the assumption based on what these old eyes told me. As I was saying, she was bent over, and the second man struck. A blink of an eye quicker, and I'd have spitted him before he could do his dirty work. Will she live?"

"More than we can say for the man you cut down, Baron," Gan answered. "I'm forever grateful."

"Glad to serve you, Murdat."

The conversation subsided to a faraway drone. Lanta's voice traveled through fleecy clouds, rushing waters, to reach Sylah. "My dearest friend. Take in the smoke. Let it smother the pain. You'll be fine."

"How long? When hurt?"

Swift as ever, Lanta understood perfectly. She spoke softly, directly into Sylah's ear. "That night, the next day, and last night. It's the second morning. A War Healer examined you. You're bruised. No detectable break in the bone."

"Who?" Sylah's question caused Lanta an audible intake of breath that brought Sylah's eyes open again. Lanta's face was above her now, the earlier concern warped by fear. "A former slave, a godkill miner. And a Peddler." She barely mouthed the last word.

Sylah's stomach threatened. Peddler. That was important. Why? Disorientation tore at her mind, brought on harder, heavier throbbing pain. Whatever made the Peddlers important, she couldn't stay awake any longer. The soothing smoke called. Lanta stroked the lulling chings again.

Ondrat. Krevelen. Byrda. Mull.

Lies. Someone lied. Who?

Then the worst realization of all crashed in on her. Memory. And truth.

Sylah, Rose Priestess of Iris Abbey.

Murderer.

Sylah tried to cry despair. Blessed unconsciousness claimed her.

Leclerc looked over his shoulder. A few more paces, and the tiny, distant walls of Ola would be out of sight. Good riddance, he thought. And especially good riddance to people who thought they knew everything. He sniffed, then glanced around anxiously to see if Jaleeta heard.

She had. Her expression was quizzical. "Why did you make that noise? You're thinking about that silly argument with Nalatan, aren't you?"

"Well, yes. I am. He's got no right to keep us cooped up in the city."

Prim, Jaleeta nodded agreement. "You shouldn't dwell on it. But I'm glad you told him so. If he wants to tell someone what to do, he should start with his so-called wife."

"So-called? Sylah herself performed the ceremony."

"The real Church . . . I mean, the Sister Mother, not the real Church, cast out Sylah. She can't marry people. And Tate's more of a man than most men. It's no wonder Nalatan's irritable."

"Tate's a fine woman. And all his talk about roving outlaws was just to scare us. Locals and traders and trappers use the roads and trails every day." Leclerc looked back. The trail itself was the only sign of human presence. True, they'd ridden since shortly after sunrise; even so, he couldn't adjust to the incredible isolation that surrounded one so quickly in this world.

Jaleeta said, "Let's let the horses run. To that big rock, up there." Without waiting, she whooped and whipped her mount to a gallop. Leclerc pursued gamely.

Leclerc disliked horses. Horses bit. They kicked. When you got on them, they schemed to shake you off or brush against trees. Or rocks. Or another horse. Always, they bounced. Chafed your crotch. Pounded your rear. Mushed your brains.

Riding at speed multiplied all of that.

But it was worth it. To be this far away from the interference of others, to be alone with Jaleeta. Leclerc gritted his teeth.

By the time the race was over he stood in the stirrups, as if that would distance him from the fire consuming his afflicted parts. Turning to Jaleeta, he said, "That was fun. You ride well." Settling back into the saddle, Leclerc partially stifled a yelp. His first attempt to speak was a strangled croak. He coughed over it, then, "We could eat over there by that burned snag. There's grass and moss. It looks soft. And cool."

"Cool? Of course, silly. There was frost on the ground this morning. It's not cool, it's cold."

Leclerc forced laughter. "Did I say cool? I meant comfortable. Here we are, both of us wearing wool and fur, out to enjoy the fall colors, and I'm talking about being cool."

Reining her horse around, spurring it toward the tall, blackened spire, Jaleeta made a sound of delight, pointing. "Look, right down there. A stream, with a rocky little beach. We'll eat here, and then we can walk there." She bounded out of the saddle. Singing to herself, she unlashed the saddlebags holding their lunch.

Leclerc worked his way to the ground. Walking normally was a test of will. Gaily, Jaleeta called to him, "Start us a fire right over there, Louis. There's good dry driftwood. You brought an axe?"

Chopping wood, Leclerc decided, had to be on top of the preferred list of tortures. Vibration shot up his arms, sent tremors racing down his spine. Tenderized nerve ends exploded. Sweat sluiced his face when he returned with the fuel.

Jaleeta sympathetically helped him unload, then mopped his brow with her sleeve. "You shouldn't have worked so hard. We're here to enjoy ourselves." She ushered him past the hobbled horses. One whickered; Leclerc was sure he detected malicious humor.

As she cooked and they ate, Jaleeta spoke of her life. Leclerc was an avid listener, pleased that she confided in him. With the meal finished, she brightened, bubbling with energy. She whirled, headed for the tumbling creek and rocky beach she'd remarked earlier. "We don't have to leave right away. Who cares if we get back after dark? Come with me."

Planting each foot carefully, Leclerc followed. He laughed, more at himself than in accompaniment to Jaleeta's oddly wild amusement. He was happy.

From navel to knees, he was a throbbing, burning concentration of pain. His brain screamed with desire he wasn't allowed to acknowledge, much less express. The prospect of the ride back to Ola was exquisite torment worthy of the most perverted mind.

And he was happy.

Face alight with excitement, Jaleeta clambered atop a large rock, then leaped to another farther out in the stream.

Leclerc protested, shouting against the roar of the waters. Fear raised his tone. "Don't do that! Come back, right away."

"It's not far. I'll jump from rock to rock." She demonstrated. She failed to consider that her target, with a surface barely above the stream, would have a slippery coating of moss. For a moment, she appeared to stand firm, so that her small squeal carried more surprise than fear. She teetered atop the midstream boulder, feet churning for purchase. Arms flapping wildly, she fixed huge eyes, still not believing, on Leclerc.

"Help?" It was a question, asking why he didn't make the whole situation disappear. She screamed in earnest as she toppled. The torrent swallowed the noise.

Leclerc was already moving toward her. The rushing water was so cold it hurt, striking to the bone with the force of a club. His feet were leaden, yet unstable on the treacherous, slippery bottom.

Lunging, he caught her leg. Smooth boot leather slipped between his fingers. Jaleeta thrashed wildly, her lovely black hair now a fanned mass, flaring downstream. Her face broke the surface, coughing, sputtering. Water pounded up her nose, into her open, screaming mouth. Current seized every fold, every wrinkle of her heavy clothing. Gagging, she submerged again.

Leclerc heaved back, gained against the pressure.

His feet lifted.

Instantly, both bodies whisked away. The world was bludgeoning rocks, blood-freezing cold. And sound. Tossed to the surface for a breath that granted life, they were assaulted by thunder. Plunged back into black-green suffocation, there was the terrifying muffled rumble of tons of living force.

Despite panic that already rendered him nothing more than a life-form struggling for survival, a corner of Leclerc's mind marveled at the fact that he was dying in a stream no more than five feet deep. If it were still, he could stand and laugh at it.

The thought flew away when he impacted. There was pain. Then realization; he was pinned. He put out an arm. His hand struck something soft. Jaleeta. The lovely features under the surface, distorted, bubbles streaming from mouth and nose.

Her foot was caught in the crotch of a branch and the trunk of a downed tree. He was pinned against the trunk and a different, vertical branch. The pressure of their bodies caused the whole issue to roll. Jaleeta's features disappeared, her face a drowned smear deeper in the stream.

Leclerc threw his body out and up. The current caught him, tried to sweep him away. He screamed at it, hooked a hand under Jaleeta's foot. The other hand reached to pull them both free. They went downstream together.

They struck a shelving, cobbled beach. Leclerc braced himself on hands and knees, Jaleeta's limp form lodged against his upstream side. He wrapped a hand in her hair, hoisted her head out of the water. Slowly, like some baffled beast, he crawled through the shallows onto dry land.

Hacking, convulsing, Jaleeta was sick. It was nauseating. It was proof of life, and wonderful. Leclerc laughed, a wheezing croak that attracted the interest of a shoreline-stalking crow. It tensed, gauging the potential danger of the large creature crouched over its kill. For a moment, the bird considered waiting for scraps. It ruffled hard, black feathers against the cold and resumed its own search.

Leclerc struggled upright and discovered a twisted ankle as he dragged Jaleeta into a narrow gully. She shivered horribly. Arcing across her pale features, the wing-curve of dark brows made Leclerc think of ravens, of battlefields, and wasted life. He massaged her unresponsive cheeks. Her hand, splayed limply across her breast, was stark white; veins—ugly, wormlike—netted the back of it. Her fingernails showed the same pallid blue as her lips.

Leclerc remembered a hut on the trail, some farmer's opportunistic settlement on a burn. He had a dim recollection of cornstalks. He'd paid no attention to anything but Jaleeta on the way up into the mountains. He couldn't be sure exactly where he'd seen the place, or if people lived there.

Resignation played across his turmoil with gentling concern. A small voice sighed, said the hut was too far. And how could he walk on a sprained ankle? There was nothing to be done.

A cramp clenched leg muscles into an iron knot. He squealed, leaping to his feet, stamping, massaging. It seemed forever before he stood still, panting. Pain, although less than before, seemed determined to break him.

"The hell with it." He spoke aloud, the defiant declaration puny against the cruel reserve of mountain, forest, stream. Nevertheless, he repeated himself, louder, building to a shout. "The hell with it. I won't just sit here and die."

Limping, he moved to Jaleeta. Her eyelids fluttered when he lifted her. Leclerc told himself that water draining from her clothes would make her lighter as he walked. For perhaps fifty paces he tried to believe it.

It was much farther than that to the trail. Leclerc promised himself the hut was around the next bend. When it wasn't, he promised himself it was the next. His ankle became a distant agony, so constant he couldn't imagine a life without it.

Then the small voice was back, whispering from the growing darkness, "Why punish yourself? You'll never reach the hut. If you do, what difference? You have no way to make fire. Is it worth this effort to die on rotting straw, a feast for fleas and lice, just to have a roof over you when I end your misery? Please, be kind. Stop. Hold Jaleeta to you as you've dreamed. Sleep. Let me give you ease."

"No. As long as I can see, I'll walk."

Seduction coated the voice of despondence, made the words sweet. "Well, then, I'll bring the night. Why not wait here, let the daylight pass? I'll do my task gently. Kindly."

"You lie. Cold. Hard." Leclerc trudged on.

The abandoned hut finally appeared. Leclerc limped and staggered to the shoulder-high doorway, dragged Jaleeta inside. Daylight's waning efforts threaded between rough boards. A hole yawned in the roof. The black maw of a small fireplace mocked him, round and empty. He imagined silent, knowing laughter.

Leclerc pulled Jaleeta's fur coat over her nose and mouth, so she breathed warmed air. Beyond that, he was helpless, ignorant. He was sure massage would be good, but pressing the cold, wet clothes against her seemed wrong. To strip them only exposed her. He decided to simply hold her to him and share what little warmth they had.

The snap of jerking awake sent pain stabbing down his neck. At first, he thought the dim light meant dawn, and he exulted at having survived the night. Then he realized it was still dusk, and despaired.

Until he realized he was looking at people. Men on the trail. Staring at the ground, then at the hut. Hope energized him. He lowered Jaleeta, dropping her in his eager clumsiness. A hand groped at the wall, found a fingerhold. He strained to rise, drew breath to shout for help. He imagined the men with fire in their pockets, in their packs. Fire. Life.

There were five men, eight horses. Four riders handed their reins to one man. That man retreated. Leclerc recognized his gray, Jaleeta's golden mare. The four men now on foot spread out, advancing, darting from cover to cover. Raiders.

Infinitely slowly, Leclerc forced stiff, stone-cold fingers to draw out the holstered pistol. He had to brace it against the pounded dirt floor to jack a round into the chamber. The clack of the receiver slamming forward sent the four outside to earth like rabbits.

A voice called, "In the house. We're travelers, lost. Can you help us?"

Leclerc said nothing. He faced the door with his knees raised, arms on his thighs. The position damped his shivers.

The voice cajoled, "We saw your tracks. Were you fishing? Fell in? We have fire makers. Food."

A man rose, little more than a shape against darkness. The others got up. Leclerc shot at the leader.

The explosion inside the tiny hut was a physical blow. Dirt cascaded from the roof. The flash from the muzzle dazzled.

Terrified shrieks preceded howling retreat. Echoes rumbled up and down the valley. When they stopped, the night was utterly silent. With no more action from within the hut, the raiders took heart again. "One of the aliens, aren't you? Belong to the Church witch, Sylah. You and your lightning weapons. Good. We'll see how long your magic can keep you alive after your swim. Here's what we have for you if you come out." An arrow hissed through the door, punched into the opposite wall.

Leclerc slumped again. How long ago was he so happy? Two hours? Three? Pointless to count; only six other people in the world knew what an hour was, and he'd never be able to tell them of his brief joy because soon he'd be dead. Strength and consciousness irresistibly drained away.

A slow, careful thumb moved in the dark, examined the pistol. Chambered round. Cocked. He put the muzzle just under Jaleeta's chin. He hoped there'd be time to use the second shot on himself.

An eruption of sound and light brought him clumsily awake. Only when he saw the torch at the door and tried to squeeze the trigger did he comprehend his helplessness. A hand squeezed his wrist. The pistol dropped from paralyzed fingers. Leclerc tried to struggle. Brute strength brushed him aside like dust.

"It's me, you stonebrain." Nalatan shoved his face into Leclerc's. He held the torch so Leclerc could see. Leclerc ignored the man, worshipped the flame. He formed a word. "Jaleeta."

Neela piled through the tiny door. One glance told her what she needed to know. Over her shoulder, she shouted, "Get wood. Quickly. Someone get water. Nalatan; your jacket. Now. Get Louis' clothes off, get dry clothes from the Wolves. Hurry."

Leclerc's head swam at the whirl of action. Nalatan yanked the sodden clothes from his body. From the corner of his eye, he saw Jaleeta, white, naked, and then Neela was covering her with her own cloak, followed by shirts and jackets passed through the door. A fire leaped to life in the fireplace. Neela heated water, demanded Leclerc and Jaleeta drink. After the second mug, Leclerc managed to speak, the words slurred. "How'd you find us?"

Nalatan was grim. "You were seen riding this way. There are only three trails. Toward late afternoon, Neela insisted Gan send out patrols."

"I should have listened."

"I know." Nalatan gingerly tucked Leclerc's pistol under him with the toe of his boot. "First Sylah risks her life. Now you. Doesn't anyone here understand ordinary caution?"

Leclerc swallowed. It made a hard, hollow sound. He explained what happened, blaming himself for the accident. Nalatan listened, made no comment. Leclerc looked away. The warmth of the fire and the gentle glow of the hot water in his stomach brought back sleep. He surrendered willingly.

Nalatan stepped outside.

Almost simultaneously, Jaleeta stirred. Her eyelids trembled, flew open. Uncomprehending, she looked into Neela's warm, relieved smile. A frown etched her brow. Then, suddenly, her eyes were open wide. She bolted upright, the piled clothing falling away, unnoticed. Clawing hands clutched at Neela. "Sosolassa. Water. Pulling. Cold. Choking. Help me."

Soothing, crooning, Neela managed to calm her, bundling cover over her once again. "You're all right. You fell in the stream. Nalatan and I thought this was the most likely trail to check. So here we are."

Jaleeta smiled. "Nalatan. Rescue." Then she slept, pale features relaxed in repose, rather than exhaustion.

Chapter 38

Jaleeta wished she could cast a spell on the candle, turn it into a wall of flame separating her from the stony visage of the Violet Abbess. After living with Tears of Jade, she doubted that any other woman could genuinely frighten her. Even so, the Abbess had power, as her dry laughter presently suggested. She said, "You do well to suspect that Emso might discuss any relationship between himself and you with Gan Moondark. You do well to suspect everyone, child. But don't concern yourself with Emso. Emso is mine."

"Then what purpose does it serve for me to be nice to him?"

"He'll say things to you he'll never say to me." Grotesquely coy, the Abbess simpered. "At least, I should hope he'd never say certain things to me."

Jaleeta stifled derision. "What would he tell me that he'd keep from you?"

"His plans, silly. If duty tears him away from you, he'll arrange for your safekeeping. If work wearies him, he'll complain to you, so you can properly sympathize. When Gan resists his arguments, he'll tell you so you may console him. And when Gan confides in Emso what the witch, Sylah, intends, he'll tell you because you'll understand and agree with his opinions. Do you see now?"

At Jaleeta's rapid nod, the Abbess smiled grimly. "And when Gan speaks of defeating the Skan and Windband, you will tell me exactly what Emso says of it."

Rising so swiftly she tumbled her chair in a rattling fall, Jaleeta stepped back from the table. "You ask me to help the Skan defeat the Three Territories? You know what the Skan will do to me if they catch me."

"Indeed I do." The Abbess patted a chair. "Come, sit down."

Jaleeta hesitated. Awareness of her actual inexperience and vulnerability rolled over her in a wave.

The Abbess saw only disobedience. She snarled, "Sit, I told you. *Sit.*" The style that cracked the wills of uncounted Chosens jerked Jaleeta into her chair. The Abbess leaned forward, face hovering just out of the candle's heat. "My instructions carry no element of choice for the likes of you." Rising, the Abbess took the candle from the table. Moving to the window, she removed the draft-defeating blanket hung over the closed wooden shutters. Then she opened the shutters themselves. Cupping the candle behind her hand, she raised it to the window. Three times she exposed the flame to the night. With the shutters closed again, and the blanket replaced, she turned to Jaleeta. "Put some more wood on the fire. It's cold in here. And make tea. Enough for three."

Jaleeta did as instructed. No one spoke to her that way, she told herself. Except Tears of Jade. This crone assumed too much.

Preparing a perfumed brew of chamomile and dried raspberries, Jaleeta entertained herself with images of her revenge. Not until she was setting out the cups did it occur to her to wonder at the third one. When she asked who was coming, the answer was a silent, superior smile that set off a fresh round of fantasized humiliations for the older woman.

The tea was warming in its ceramic pot on the charcoal brazier beside the empty cups when there was a soft knock on the door. With startling swiftness, the Abbess moved to a position where she'd be invisible to anyone looking into the room. She whispered to Jaleeta to ask for a name.

When Jaleeta said, "Who is it?" the response was another knock. Three sharp raps, then two more, deliberately separated. The Abbess moved away from her hiding place, nodding for Jaleeta to admit the newcomer.

Baron Ondrat swept in. He took two long steps and spun about, inspecting the room, hand on sword hilt. A black, rain-soaked cape swirled. More rain dripped from his equally black wide-brimmed hat. Raindrops on his dark beard caught the candlelight. Satisfied, he moved a chair close to the crackling fire and sat down, carefully flipping the cape over the back of his seat. Hanging that way, it trapped and held heat while it dried out of contact with the wearer. His right hand remained on his sword hilt.

This was the man everyone in Ola was talking about. Jaleeta was intrigued. A big man, she suspected he was more bulk than strength. His movements were ungraceful, although forceful. Dark eyes, too close together. Thick black hair. The hand on the sword hilt was huge, the fingers unusually long. His nose had been broken, and a welted scar ran diagonally across his forehead, extending back into the scalp.

The Abbess sat in the remaining chair. "Baron Ondrat has a message for you, my dear," she said. There was triumph in her voice, and a grating malice. Still, her expression of importance crumbled at Baron Ondrat's swift disapproval.

"I'll speak to the girl in my own way, Abbess. Don't interrupt." Then, to Jaleeta, smoothly, "One who wishes you well asked me to say you are remembered. Even missed. One sends you congratulations for becoming the companion of Gan Moondark's ruling clique."

"You? You're the one who . . . The one I . . ."

"We are united against our enemies, Gan Moondark and Rose Priestess Sylah of the new Teachers."

Disbelieving, Jaleeta moved with infinitesimal slowness toward the door. "I don't understand you or your message."

The Baron smiled again. "The old fool isn't aware she's helping Church—the right Church. But you will both help. Certainly."

There were at least two ways to take the Baron's words. Jaleeta sensed that her best defense was offense. "You'll rebel against Murdat? His Wolves will leave your bodies for ravens. Who'll fight by your side? Her?" Jaleeta jabbed a rude thumb in the Abbess' direction, ignoring the older woman's shocked sputter.

Ondrat darkened. "My alliances are secret. Yours are not. I know you were sent here. I know your mission. You'll carry it out as I direct, or be exposed as a spy."

Defiantly, Jaleeta interrupted. "Who'll expose me, Baron? You, Tears of Jade's own fishhook? If Gan Moondark learns you plan revolt, I'll be treated gently compared to what happens to you."

"Stop it, both of you." Tension made the Abbess' command brittle, but it had the desired effect. Ondrat and Jaleeta fell silent, glaring like two trapped cats. The Abbess continued. "We depend on each other. Murdat and that unspeakable Skan witch are threat enough for both of you. Jaleeta, you report all you learn of Gan's plans to us. The Baron will get the information to the Skan. In turn, they inform Windband."

Jaleeta held up a hand, stopped her. "Don't you understand what Tears of Jade plans for you?"

Ondrat answered, "Her plans are nothing. Once the Skan, Windband, and Moondark have exhausted each other, the rightful rulers of this land will plunge our blades in their backs. Olans will rule Ola. All heretics will be destroyed."

"But the greatest heretic of all is already out of bed, walking. You saved her life. Explain that."

Paling, eyes narrowing, Ondrat half rose from his seat. His sword hissed out of the scabbard. Jaleeta cringed. The Abbess made placating noises. Visibly trembling, Ondrat hesitated. His voice was raw. "As badly as I need your help, if you ever try to tell me to explain anything again, I'll cut the heart from your living body. Am I understood?" He extended the blade, rested the bright, eager tip between her breasts.

Transfixed, Jaleeta nodded. Her throat ached.

Reluctantly, the sword retreated, went back into its hiding place. Baron Ondrat said, "Sylah lives through no kindness of mine. One superior to our esteemed Violet Abbess orders me to eliminate the anti-Church. But you two will bear witness: My hand never struck a blow. Not directly. I obey. If the misbegotten slave owned a sword, like the Peddler, the witch would be dead. Once Sylah cried for help, though, I had to get rid of them. They'd have told everything to save their useless skins. If Sister Mother criticizes me for not finishing her, you'll testify that witnesses interfered."

"We'll be glad to verify." The Abbess leered.

The Baron grunted dubious appreciation, then went on. "Nevertheless, young

Jaleeta, we accomplished much. I'm accepted by the fawning filth that surrounds Moondark. Two men died and one witch should have to gain me free access to you. Fail to cooperate, and think what the Skan will do to you and your mother. Or think what life will be for you once we've won. You'll find us extremely generous."

A murderer's friendship. Jaleeta didn't hesitate. "I've already promised the Abbess I'd work with her." She turned to the other woman, hung her head. "I couldn't tell you about Tears of Jade. I was ashamed. I didn't know what to do." Readdressing Baron Ondrat, she went on. "There is a man you should fear even more than Tears of Jade: her son, Lorso. If he discovers that I'm here because she sent me here, he'll give us to Sosolassa. He is Slavetaker, and his look is death." She paused, letting her companions absorb what they'd heard. She finished, "Whoever rules Ola isn't important to me, but Church must be saved."

"Of course." Ondrat rose quickly, nervously. When he caught the Abbess' look of cold disapproval, he forced enthusiasm. "Church is all to all of us." He made a mechanical three-sign. The other hand checked his cape for dryness.

At the door, he turned for a final look at Jaleeta. "You have great beauty. I may claim you for myself, when this is all over."

The last took Jaleeta completely by surprise. Discreet coughing from the Abbess reminded her to respond. Demure, Jaleeta murmured, "I deserve no such honor, Baron, but I'll do my best to earn your approval."

Ondrat grunted. "That's better. I thought there was a well-trained woman under all that loud blather. Very good." The heavy door thudded shut.

The gobbet of spit Jaleeta sprayed after him hit the wood like a glistening dart.

The Abbess exclaimed wordlessly. Jaleeta rounded on her. "You said I worked with you. Now you expose me to that creature."

"Not I. The Skan chose him as the man to contact you."

"I won't bear his children. Prevent it."

"He's no danger to you, although any other woman in Ola would consider him a prize. All the Barons will want you when Gan's gone. You won't be able to choose, of course, but I'll be at your side to help as much as I can."

"A prize? Scum. He tried to kill a Priestess. Oh, she's cast out. Ask yourself if he's capable of killing any one of you, if he thinks he won't get caught. There's your 'prize.' And ask yourself how he and his murderers knew Sylah would be out that night. For all that, why was she out? You call him prize? More like penalty. Sister."

The Abbess bid a hasty good night. She moved hurriedly down the narrow stone hall. She kept her hood back, chin high, reminding herself that a Church woman had nothing to fear. Gan Moondark enforced the old rules. Never mind that evil-tongued snip.

Gliding along in her silent indoor slippers, the Abbess reviewed the meeting. All in all, things had gone well. The girl was truly snared. The Baron? The Abbess sneered. A maddened wildcow bull. There was a certain low cunning in the man. Controlling him was a constant problem, but manageable.

The girl was the key.

The Abbess lifted a hand to straighten her hair, unconsciously preening. A smug smile twisted the normally severe lips. The Baron mentioned ownership. Jaleeta beholden to Church to protect her secrets; Jaleeta firmly placed in an important house. An excellent prospect. Church Home would look kindly on one who arranged such things.

On reaching the stairs leading to the main floor of the castle, a minute hesitancy interrupted the Abbess' self-congratulation. She gripped the railing.

Throughout the evening, it was clear Jaleeta was distracted about something. Probably a man. Emso was practically in her hand. Leclerc seemed entranced, but he was an alien, and one never knew what to make of one of them. Still, there was no indication either of those two were more than amusements. Who, then?

Deep in thought, the Abbess descended.

Jaleeta, seated at the table in her room, sipped the tea that no one else wanted. Tears of Jade's voice filled her head: "You can never succeed by yourself. Strength rules. Alone, you are doomed." Until the Baron's direct declaration about claiming her, Jaleeta thought only of bending men to direct their efforts to her own goals. With that one statement, Ondrat made her realize she needed a male defender. Emso was too set in the old ways. Anyhow, if the Baron won, Emso would be the first of Gan's friends to die. Louis wouldn't be far behind Emso on the death list, either, although Louis seemed more like a man who'd retreat, find a place to survive. Such a smart man. Devoted, considerate. Boring. Jaleeta wrinkled her nose.

There was one. True, he had a woman, and seemed to want no other.

No man was totally steadfast. Tears of Jade said so, and the old woman knew.

Jaleeta wound a gleaming black tress around a finger, absently coiled and uncoiled it. She sipped more tea. She needed someone who'd kill Ondrat if necessary. One loyal to Gan, to assure Murdat's sympathy in case of trouble. A warrior who protected others. A man who needed solace.

Giggling, Jaleeta muttered aloud, "A passionate fool."

Memory called up Lorso. She frowned, distracted. He would come someday. To claim his "escaped" Jaleeta, to assure Gan and Sylah died. Jaleeta wondered once again if Tears of Jade really did the right thing by tricking her son. Old hag. She was safe. Jaleeta was the one in danger. But Lorso could be controlled. If he ever really came. Another passionate fool.

She remembered waking in the hut to see Nalatan, gleaming in the firelight. Once more, she remembered soft furs, shrouding darkness, embers red on a hearth. Shadowy figures. Skin gleaming with a sliding, fiery sheen.

Some problems were wonderfully easy.

CHAPTER 39

SYLAH ROSE FROM THE GARDEN BENCH WITH THE TENTATIVE CAUTION OF ONE NOT COMPLETELY sure of recovery. Everyone insisted she was coming back with remarkable speed. To her, each day's sun moved too slowly, brought too little change. The women's merchant organizations needed her help; food shortages and the common knowledge of oncoming war created a hoarder's dream. The wives of the Wolves were determined to run honest businesses, and relied on Church to maintain moral order. The Violet Abbess refused to help. Then there was the matter of the Chosens. The alien women were good with them—as good as anyone could hope—but Sylah didn't know them as well as she felt she should. More, many people still whispered about them.

There was so much to do, and she was so useless. Each morning, facing the sun, she ended her obligatory religious rites with a private prayer for greater strength.

She also begged forgiveness for taking life. Her mind knew there was no choice. Her heart mourned. Her role was to repair and protect the living, never considering risk. She felt soiled. Still, she couldn't find it in herself to wish she'd died in her attempted killer's place. Confusion was far more troublesome than physical damage.

The injury brought little pain. Obstinate dizziness refused to go away. She raised a hand to the heavy bandage. Every time she touched it or looked in a mirror, she thought of the loathsome Moonpriest and the white head-wrap he called a turban. Not only that, there were times when the bandages felt heavy as a blanket, seemed determined to tip her over. It embarrassed her to wobble and sway. Even now, anxious eyes followed her movements with near-frightening intensity. Emso and Tate kept their distance. Lanta stood close, an ever-faithful shadow.

She hated that look. It always reminded her of the Priestesses who selected the Chosens. They, too, felt love. Concern. And pity. Sylah tried not to see.

Lanta's hand fluttered at Sylah's shoulder, rested where the Peddler's sword struck. Neatly executed white stitches glared against the plain black of the thick cloak. Sylah insisted on that contrast. Bold thread marked the attempt on the life of a Priestess.

Emso caught Sylah's frown. He said, "We've talked about it before, Sylah; that sewn-up cloak makes trouble. The Church people close to the Violet Abbess resent it. It frightens all the people who believe in Church to see such plain evidence of dissension. It even bothers Gan. He said so."

Straightening, Sylah composed herself. "The thickness of the cloak saved my life. That, and bad aim. People must be constantly reminded that a sacred ban was broken. The Violet Abbess is resentful? She has good reason. Church was profaned."

Coloring, Emso said, "They didn't know you were a Priestess. They were thieves. You were just a victim . . ."

"I called out clearly, yet they tried to kill me."

"Baron Ondrat said the blow was falling as you spoke. There was no way the second man could stop his swing." Emso's square, honest face compressed in a mask of stubbornness.

Resignation softened Sylah's voice. "The Baron knows what he saw. I know what I saw. My cloak will forever tell what happened."

Any answer Emso intended was overruled by Tate. "Let it go, both of you. Anyhow, Emso, look at her. Except for those little bitty stitches, the only accent the poor woman has is that tiny embroidered rose. I don't care how holy she is, a woman's got to have some color somewhere. It's a rule. You just train your troops. Leave fashion to us. And you, Sylah: Why don't you give old Emso a break? He's just trying to keep the peace."

Lanta's high laughter was sharp. "Was there ever peace? Will there ever be?" When she saw the reaction her cynicism created in Tate, the small Seer's hand flew to her mouth. Immediately, she extended it toward Tate. Too far away to actually make contact, the gesture was clearly apologetic.

It took a moment for Tate's smile to break free. It was a weary effort. "I've seen little enough peace. It seems we find more reasons for fighting than for not fighting. I've never understood it."

Emso said, "People have to learn respect. Maybe what happened to Sylah did have something to do with Church. Some fanatic, maybe. That's not the point. The problem is the society. There's no respect for anything anymore. People don't even consider the cost of things they do. If Baron Ondrat hadn't killed those filthy murderers, all the Three Territories would be without Church help until they were caught and punished."

Moving toward the entry of the enclosed garden, Tate said, "Well, you all try to get along without my peacekeeping. Now that Sylah's doing so well, Conway and I are on our way. Tomorrow morning, in fact. I've got to get my gear in order."

Facing Sylah, Lanta said, "Will you be all right? I want to go with Tate." Tate waited, curious.

Sylah made a face, exasperated. "Say what you mean. That's the whole problem: You want to go see Conway, but what you say is you want to go with Tate. You and Matt love each other, but you say anything else to avoid that one simple phrase. It's killing you and it's driving all of us crazy."

After a blushing glance at an equally nonplussed Emso, Lanta said, "I want to tell him, Sylah. I did, once . . ." The sentence slid off into dejection.

Heartily brusque, Tate said, "What we need is a plan to break that bad horse Conway to harness. Not that he deserves you, but Sylah's right. He's been happy and single long enough. We're going to stop that. It's the right thing to do."

For a moment, Lanta stared, openmouthed. Then, her blush practically incandescent, she burst out laughing. Emso simply stood as if clubbed. When Lanta recovered, she moved to Tate's side. "You're terrible," she said, more laughter denying the accusation. Sobering slightly, she went on. "Don't you take anything seriously?"

"I take everything seriously. I just don't let it get a hold on me. But that's me, not you. What we've got to do here is make Matt understand what's troubling you. He wants to. He just doesn't know how." The sound of their voices dwindled. Tate's arm draped over Lanta's shoulder as they walked away.

Sylah smiled to herself at the two heads, conspiratorially close. Lanta was too smart to think of a man as a trophy. Her problem was that she failed to think of herself as having value.

Chuckling sounds from Emso brought her out of her contemplation. He was looking after the departed women. Seeing Sylah turn toward him, he said, "Looks like poor Conway's a goner. A man might be smart enough to dodge one woman, but two? He's finished."

The laughter was real, but when he faced Sylah, a quick hint of something different swept across his features. It was too fast for her to categorize. Emso went on. "Lanta was worrying about peace. Seems she ought to be worrying about the war men and women fight all the time."

"You don't have a wife, do you, Emso? No children?"

His face was suddenly so devoid of expression Sylah would have sworn he was schooled in Church's techniques of control. "Had one. She died. Sister raised our children." Sylah accepted that there would be no further information.

"I hope you find someone else," she said. "You're a good man. Most women would be proud to have such a fine husband."

"At my age? You think so?"

The unexpected, eager queries caught Sylah completely off guard. She scrambled for a response. "Well, I . . . Of course. That's absurd. You're not old."

"Yes I am." He shook his head, looking at the ground. "Seen too much, done too many things. You heard Tate call me 'old Emso.' Anyhow, it's like she said about Conway; I've been alone too long. It wouldn't be fair to ask a woman to put up with me."

Soft laughter brought Emso's head up with a jerk. Embarrassed anger narrowed his eyes. Sylah said, "Women put up with men all the time, Emso. It's the way things are, like the forest putting up with lightning and the mountains putting up with storms. You're full of noise and mess, but we love you, no matter. We know how to find the person behind the uproar and care for him."

Emso smiled rueful acknowledgment. "A woman'd have to be willing to work hard to see a good man inside this beat-up hide."

"Nonsense. You're a wise, warm man, whether you want to admit it or not. Many men resent me because I mean to be as free as they are. That doesn't mean I don't like the sense of protection and security that comes from having a strong man at my side. I think I can be brave, but I know I could be a lot braver if Clas were here."

"You think so? Someone younger might want to have someone like me around?"

"Will you stop asking silly questions? The Three Territories are full of such women."

Emso was silent for a long moment. When he spoke again, it was with a sidelong, corner-of-the mouth manner. "I'm sorry Clas can't be here. Have you heard anything? About the plague, I mean?"

"There was a Messenger two days ago. Clas said only that the disease is less damaging than it was. No details. And the tribe is wintering farther north and west this year."

"He gave a reason for that?" Emso failed miserably at nonchalance.

"Windband. Moonpriest." One word was a curse, the other a condemnation. Sylah raised her arm, pointing east. Her sleeve fell back, revealing the massive gold bracelet. "Church must show them the right path. Vengeance is not the way."

Emso's eyes bulged, as if he watched a spell being cast. Unnoticed by Sylah, deep in her own thoughts, he surreptitiously reached to draw his forefingers across his eyes. As a male, Emso's secret two-sign solicited the protection of the One Who Is Two, denied to women. That One was son and sun, redeemer, bringer of warmth and life.

Had Sylah seen the sudden gesture, she would have realized a treasured friend saw in her such a danger that he must call on his most powerful spiritual resource for protection.

Self-conscious about her moment of melodrama, Sylah turned slowly to face Emso once again, smiling shyly. "I just felt I wanted to reach out, to make Moonpriest know my thoughts never leave him. He is the worst of the anti-Church."

Emso swallowed hard. "Conway, Tate—all the aliens—they say he was a good man, once." Nervous feet seemed anxious to take him elsewhere.

Sylah was looking east again. "He was. Before he was injured. It might have been better if I'd let him die."

"You *did* heal him, then?" Emso leaned heavily on "did," burned it with accusation.

Preoccupied, Sylah merely nodded. Sweat beaded on Emso's lip, denying the chill wind swirling about the enclosed garden area. Sylah said, "I've grown into a weakling. The first smell of frost in the air and I need a hot bath and a fire. Will you walk me back to my quarters?"

"You're sure you wouldn't rather go to the healing house? Are you all right?" Emso had her by the elbow.

Sylah smiled thanks, patted his steadying hand. "What a friend you are." Her expression turned sly, teasing. "This is the man who thinks no woman would be interested in him. Silly. If you have a fault, warrior, it's that your loyalty's so strong it makes the rest of us feel inadequate. And every one of us hopes you'll never change."

Bloodred color exploded across his face. Sylah leaned against him, using his sustaining strength to lessen light-headedness. She longed to tell him how comforting it was to have a forthright friend, one she could even disagree with violently, yet never doubt. She wanted to confide in him about the War Healer and the message in the night-shrouded market. But what would she tell him? The secret of the Peddlers? Never. Or that she'd been betrayed, and had no idea who to blame? That would only involve and endanger him.

They were at the abbey then. Although she knew the swift move necessary would bring on a dizzy headache, she whirled and kissed him on the cheek before he could object.

Inside, leaning against the cool stone, she smiled through the expected pounding hurt, treasuring his blushing, spluttering reaction. Such a fine man. Such fun to tease.

Chapter 40

Jaleeta fell against Leclerc so hard he exclaimed surprise and hurt. She spun, forcing him backward, almost tumbling the two of them. Her face was bright with concern. "Oh, did I hurt you, Louis? I'm so sorry. I twisted my ankle." She pressed him against the stone wall of the castle. Her weight rested heavily in his arms.

Suddenly, she glanced around nervously. Stepping back, her look up at Louis tantalized, a seductive merriment. "If we're not careful, people will think we're misbehaving."

"I wouldn't care. If it were true."

Jaleeta swatted at him playfully, then bent to massage her ankle. The move gave her the opportunity to peer around the corner of the stone wall. Emso was still leading the bandaged Sylah in the opposite direction, away from the garden. Jaleeta relaxed. The last thing she wanted just now was a confrontation between Emso and Leclerc. Straightening, she pretended to test the ankle. "It's not really hurt. It startled me, more than anything."

"Startled you?" Leclerc laughed. "I thought the dreaded Skan were coming over the walls, or something."

"Don't joke about them. You don't know. Gan was lucky when he bluffed them into leaving. They'll find out how weak he was. They'll spend stormtime telling themselves they were cheated and shamed. When they come, the Three Territories will know the smell of death."

"You'll be protected. You have my word."

Jaleeta turned away, head down. "You're nice, Louis. No one should promise to hold off the Skan, though. Please, if they win, if it looks like they're going to capture me . . ."

"Stop it." Leclerc forced her to face him. When she continued to look at the ground, he lifted her chin. For a moment he savored the beauty he held, then said, "The Skan won't get near you. Nor Windband."

Stepping away, Jaleeta resumed their course toward the enclosed garden, pulling Leclerc with her. "You make me feel better. When you reassure me, I even feel stronger myself."

They were entering the small garden by then. Fall's iron touch was evident. Gardeners had trimmed out everything but the hardier plants. Instead of denuding the beds, however, they left selected specimens to go to seed. The result was a shadow garden, a place that suggested the loss of summer and a new cycle's beginning. Stark seed-bearing stalks contrasted with the permanent enamel green of ivy festooning the walls. The crystal gladness of the waterfall and pool clashed with bare-limbed shrubs

Twirling, Jaleeta spread her red-orange skirt in waves of flame around her. Shining black boots sparkled across the close-cropped grass. She threw back her hood, the white doeskin interior cradling rowdy black hair that fought to escape and dance in the pale, filtered light straining through newly arrived cloud cover.

Laughing delight, Leclerc said, "You're wonderful. A moment ago you were frightened. Before that, you thought your ankle was sprained. Now here you are, dancing. I never know what to expect from you."

Dancing close to him, then away, she bent and curved and swayed, taunted with her eyes, with full lips burnished red by cold. "Expect the unexpected. It's how I stayed alive. It's how I'll live my life. Jaleeta must live." She stopped abruptly. Her skirt snapped to a stop, settled primly back down to her ankles. She pulled up her hood. When she faced him, she inspected his features with demand that took him aback. As swiftly as it came, that mood was gone, and she was ebullient again. "I'm going to be happy. Why shouldn't I be? You promised me everything would be all right."

"Oh, no," Leclerc protested with a defensive gesture. "I promised they wouldn't get you, and that we'd destroy them. We will."

Intrigued, Jaleeta walked to him, standing close. "You're very sure of yourself. Everyone says you know magic. You made the black powder. You have magic against the Skan?"

"Not magic; we have plans."

"Tell me." Jaleeta coaxed like a child. Nevertheless, there was a full-blown woman involved, one assured of her allure. The effect on Leclerc was earthquake. His superior smile melted to a fatuous grin and braggadocio. "I had to ask Tate a few questions about weapons. I'm building something for Murdat. Windband has a similar weapon, but nothing as good as I can make. Murdat's men will shoot arrows almost as long as a man, and they'll go farther than any arrow ever has. The Skan will fall like this." He swung the edge of his hand at the sere, dead stalk of tall plant. It broke with a weak snap, the seed head spinning off to slap in the pond.

Squealing excitement, Jaleeta grasped Leclerc's hand, held it to her cheek. "You're wonderful. I don't think Tate helped you at all. I think you know all these things, but you share with your friends." She blinked. Then, almost as if disappointed, "Windband and the Skan have so many more men than Murdat."

"There's something else. I won't talk about it. You'll see, though. You'll brag to your grandchildren about it."

For a moment Jaleeta considered pressing him. She reminded herself she had the rest of fall and winter to get more details. Tears of Jade said it well: "Bait only brings the fish to the hook. The fisherman must do the rest." Pushing the severed seed head with a careful toe, she said, "You understand so many things, Louis. Everyone says so. Murdat talks about you to Neela all the time."

"I try to be helpful."

"That's what he says. You're always there to help him."

"Friends are supposed to do that. You help me. Because you're my friend."

Wide-eyed, she was dubious. "Me, help you? I don't do anything."

"No one else makes me feel the way you do. Excited. Alive."

"I'm glad." She looked away, studied the water. In the muddy, leaf-littered bottom, something scurried from cover to cover. Her boot flicked out, stirred up waves that obscured the creature. "Even here, I know what it's like to have no one to talk to. I mean, everyone's nice, but I don't have a real close friend, you know? I used to have, when I was a little girl with my tribe. I never had any friends with the Skan. Just Tears of Jade, and she didn't really like me."

Tentatively, Leclerc moved to stand immediately behind her. He inhaled the smell of her hair, rich with rosewater and the scent of wet, chill fall, yet warm with her energy. He savored the soft curvature of her shoulders, the unconscious grace of her bent neck. "I'm even more your friend than Murdat's, Jaleeta. I want you to feel the same about me. I want you to want to share with me, as I do with you."

She remained bent away from him. His heart crashed against his ribs. He pictured himself a thinker cast adrift in a warrior world, exposing his thoughts to ridicule. There was so much more he wanted to say, so much capacity for care that he wanted to reveal.

A tiny shudder traced her body under the bulky clothes. Leclerc had an impression of indecipherable actions and hidden meanings. He told himself that was exactly how it was within himself, the mysterious attraction of one person for another.

"I do want to talk to you, Louis. Not because you saved my life when I fell in the stream, but because a woman like me needs a man's help. I can't ask for much of your time, because you're so important to Gan. But there are things I can't answer, things I don't know how to react to." At last, she faced him. Her pain was his.

"Tell me what it is. We'll handle it together."

A wan smile shone through the trouble. She lost it, looked past him as though she might see where it had gone. Slim, strong fingers caught up a fold of her cloak and kneaded it incessantly. "Tate tells me that, where you come from, women are free to choose whom they marry. Here a woman has no choice. She must be careful to offend no man. Lately, I've realized that two men . . . like me. They'll be near me a lot. I want you to know they don't interest me. I must be pleasant. I must be accommodating. I must be a proper woman." The last was tainted with shame.

Leclerc longed to take her in his arms, to make her know exactly how much woman she truly was. "Tell me their names. I'll see they don't bother you."

Alarmed, she put her hands to his chest. "You mustn't. Their attention won't bother me, so long as I know you understand."

For a few pained moments they argued. She remained adamant, finally taking refuge in a classic pout. She hinted that Leclerc was no different than her persecutors. He heard himself saying, "I'm not like that at all," and knew he was defenseless in that instant. He surrendered gracelessly. "All right, all right; I'll do what you think best. I don't like it, but it's your life."

"A life I owe you. I haven't forgotten. I never will. But I understand my culture. Seriously, can you imagine me having any interest in two men like Emso, or Baron Ondrat?"

"Emso?" Leclerc felt betrayed. Emso was a friend, a member of Gan's intimate circle. And *old*, Leclerc thought. At least five, maybe seven, years older than me.

Scarred. Worn out. Leclerc shook his head. It was pathetic the way some men responded to age. As for Ondrat, Leclerc felt a surge of gladness in the knowledge that he'd never really liked the man. A pompous, shifty-eyed toad. Not too bright, either. If he'd captured the Peddler who'd attacked Sylah, instead of hacking him to death, the man might have had something interesting to say.

Jaleeta broke in. "I have to go back to my quarters. Neela's taking me to the women's pottery works today. Will you come to the castle with me?"

"Anywhere." He offered his arm, smiling. She pressed her cheek against his shoulder. They walked to the entry, where she flashed a conspiratorial grin, whispering, "We have to be careful. Proper performance is all. For us, everything we do is going to be perfect."

The quick cut of her flashing dark eyes and the innuendo fired Leclerc's imagination. He shrugged away the turmoil in his mind and body, sternly reminded himself that this was a young woman who'd experienced horrible trials and deprivation. She needed care and understanding, not masculine pressure. He wasn't like Emso and Ondrat. He'd prove that to her.

Completely involved with his own thoughts, Leclerc felt his departure was like drifting. He wished he could recall something poetic about leaving a lover. He never considered looking over his shoulder and up at the distant battlewalk.

Kate Bernhardt watched the couple. Inner vision put her next to Louis Leclerc. Too tall to snuggle her cheek against his upper arm, Kate Bernhardt would have to bend uncomfortably even to lay a cheek on his shoulder. She smiled to herself; the discomfort would be nothing. Nor would a strand of Kate Bernhardt's hair trail naughtily, darkly over her shoulder, shifting in the wind. Kate Bernhardt wore her hair in a practical, if fetching, shorter cut. And if it wasn't as dramatic as Jaleeta's ebony, it was a rich brown, smooth as dark honey. Nor was Kate Bernhardt proportioned in an image of delicate sensuality, a thing of spring steel and scented flesh. Kate Bernhardt's beauty was the inconspicuous attractiveness of good features, a body of subtle promise, a graceful carriage that spoke of pride in femininity and all its strengths. More, her beauty was the mysterious, indefinable inner glow that marks a woman who knows love.

Kate watched Louis stroll lightly toward an exit through the castle wall. At the last few paces, the harsh west wind caught her by surprise. It burned her eyes and brimmed them with something hatefully like tears.

CHAPTER 41

"YOU'RE MAKING ME LOOK LIKE A FOOL."

Tate recoiled at the underlying desperation, the forbidden plea struggling in Nalatan's words.

She knew her actions were well thought out. She knew they were correct. Still, she understood her husband well enough to know that logic and correctness weren't always enough. Perceptions and the assumed perceptions of others must be addressed. In order to preserve image, Nalatan was perfectly capable of destroying reality.

The knowledge frightened Tate. The awareness thrilled her. The twin sensations were like winds blowing across her heart. Soft breeze or raging whirlwind, she loved him.

And she must risk that love. She must dare it to survive.

Nalatan lay beside her on his back. The erratic glow of weakening flames reflected in his staring, unfocused eyes. It made Tate think of distant muzzle flashes, of a firefight where she was needed, but couldn't reach.

Her hand on his chest went ignored. She rose on an elbow, looked down at him. "Who would call Nalatan, my Nalatan, fool?"

His eyes were suddenly alert, fixed on hers. "I *want* someone to say it. I know what to do about that. I don't know how to live with the sideways looks, the hidden smiles."

"Because I go with another man? Is that it?"

Nalatan closed his eyes again. "My concern is your safety. The other is an irritation, the yapping of small dogs. But it galls. No man accepts slander easily, especially when it is about his wife."

"Let them have their smirks. Who cares?"

"I care. Not because they say it, but because it's a lie about your character."

"You haven't heard anyone actually say anything. You've got to let it go. Keep this up, and you'll kill someone."

His eyes took on the hard shine of steel. "Yes."

"Don't do this to me." Tate lowered herself onto him, cheek pressed to the steady rise and fall of his breathing. Under her ear, his heart worked with a steady, dispassionate regularity. Tate found that all the more disturbing. She knew a man of passion, of fires in his soul. This cold savage wouldn't fight because the cause was just or the situation demanded it. This man wanted to kill.

Tate made herself go on calmly. "Promise me you won't let anyone goad you into fighting while I'm gone. Please. I don't want to have to worry about you."

"Am I to not worry about you, then? You have no end to your requests?"

"Of course I want you to worry about me. I love you. I want you to love me. I want you to care what happens to me, and I want you to care enough to know that I don't even breathe without thinking of you."

"Then tell me I can accompany you. We can worry about each other together. Better yet, send Conway alone. We'll both worry about him, instead."

"You're not even trying to understand."

"That's not true. I understand entirely. I hate it, that's all."

"I told you it's a religious thing. A mission. To strengthen the Three Territories." Tate shifted, nervous with the lie.

As if reading her thoughts, Nalatan said, "You've taught me much about the true meanings of Church's words. You, Sylah, and Lanta. Church was my life before I met you. It still is, but my place in it is changed. So I do understand. You can't ask me to be happy when my wife rides off into great danger."

Tate focused on the last word. Rationalization put confidence in her voice.

"There's no more danger in those mountains than there is in the streets of Ola. No roof tiles fall out of the trees, no runaway horses trample people."

"Can you think I haven't thought of that? I'm the one staying in this anthill. I'm the one who'll be surrounded by unending whispers and scheming. There's no room here, no air. Without you . . ." She felt movement, and knew he'd turned his head to the side. The window was in that direction. Unless wind actually drove rain through it, he flung the shutters wide every night when they went to bed. Carefully, keeping her head still, Tate rolled her eyes as far as she could. She peered past the edge of the down-filled comforter. At the farthest edge of her vision was brittle darkness. Stars were out, myriad chips shining against the void of night.

Rising, looking down into his pale, blurred features, she said, "Don't think about me being gone. Think about my return. Think how happy I'll be to see you then. Think how much I'll want you then. No separation can hurt us, can hurt my love for you. Think of how you want to remember me while I'm gone. How you want me to remember you."

Slowly, almost as if afraid to move too fast, his arms rose to encircle her. Tate threw aside concerns, worries, doubts. She drew up her knees, arched her back. So braced, she stiffened momentarily, resisted the smooth power of his arms. Then she surrendered, exulted in the strength that pulled her deliciously to her lover, her husband.

The night guard stood in formation, having been properly relieved by the smaller day guard, and waited as the new shift ceremoniously threw open Sunrise Gate. The routine crowd was gathered there, camped beyond arrow range, as required. Quenched fires hissed and lifted clouds of steam. Mules brayed. Horses whinnied. Goats, sheep, chicken, cattle, contributed their vocalizations to the sudden wall of sound that flung itself against the city's defenses. Above all rang the cries of herdsmen and drovers. Disdaining the furor, pack llamas hauled themselves upright with expressions of disappointed surprise. As if influenced by their animals, rather than the other way around, the llama herders moved their charges along with quiet commands and easy gestures; they contributed little to the racket.

Tate nudged Nalatan, who sat stolidly on his horse between herself and Conway. "I've always liked those things." She indicated the llamas with her chin. "They're the classiest animal there is."

"I wouldn't want to ride one into battle," Conway said.

Tate shot him a vexed look, then smiled at Nalatan. "You see why this'll be a fast trip? Who'd put up with that attitude for long?"

Nalatan's smile was strained. "It can't end too fast. I wish it weren't happening."

" 'Tan. We talked. We decided." There was hurt in Tate's voice.

Nalatan winced at her public use of the pet name. "We talked, but you decided. Never mind. You do what you must. But hurry. Please."

"I love you." She bent to him swiftly, kissing him full on the lips before he could react. All around them, there was a sort of group intake of breath, and then spontaneous cheering and applause. Voices called out the names Black Lightning and Nalatan. Tate pulled back, eyes fixed on Nalatan's. Her husband's color went direct to crimson. Then, grinning wickedly, he kissed her in return, a long, fiery embrace that pulled her halfway out of her saddle. The crowd howled approval. This time, when they separated, Tate appeared distracted.

"Maybe we should go now." Conway's suggestion came in a dry, practical voice. It snapped Tate out of her bemused state. "Yes. Go." She seemed to have trouble articulating. Nalatan looked smug for a moment, but when her horse moved forward, the expression crumbled to solemn resignation.

The horses breasted into the last of the entering crowd, picking their way along the narrow pathway that opened for them. Karda and Mikka shuffled along behind the horses, their occasional glance up at the passersby creating a perceptible widening of the route. From the corner of his mouth, Conway told Tate, "Don't look back. Not even once. This hurts him enough, and a lot of waving good-bye will just make things harder."

Feeling very sorry for herself, Tate was hostile. "I don't think you're in much position to give out advice on how to deal with relationships."

Conway blanched as if struck. When he rounded on Tate, he opened his mouth, then clamped it shut.

"Oh, Matt." Tate hung her head, tried to shake away a sudden rush of burning tears. Her voice caught. "I'm so sorry. What a positively bitchy thing to do. I wasn't thinking. I hate myself."

"Forget it. I can imagine the heat you got from Nalatan. The shoe could just as easily be on the other foot. We're both wrapped about four turns too tight."

"I have to ask. Did you and Lanta have a chance to talk? About yourselves, I mean?"

They were at the limits of the cleared area immediately outside the city walls by then, about to enter the first stand of timber. Conway looked at the towering trees and sighed. Tate had the feeling the action was an acknowledgment, more for himself than her. "I asked her to marry me."

Clapping, Tate laughed happily. The echo sang back from the trees. Only as it died did the melancholy of his manner strike her. Her heart sank. He went on. "She said she knows I love her. She said she loves me. But after what happened on Trader Island, down in Kos, she's afraid. She says I didn't believe her, didn't trust her, when all our lives depended on it. She's not sure I'll ever trust her. She doesn't know if she can ever trust me." Conway's monotone broke. Then he exploded with pent-up bitterness. "What's she want from me?"

Tate realized the question had no pat answer. Worse, Nalatan might be asking the exact same thing.

The soft shuffle of the horses' hooves in the damp litter of the forest trail was like speculative muttering.

It was four days later that Conway and Tate saw Mikka suddenly break her shambling progress along the high country trail with a sideways leap into the forest. Without hesitation, the man and woman yanked their mounts to opposite sides of the trail. As they sheltered behind huge tree trunks, they unslung wipes, each silently scanning a full half-circle. The horses, alert, eyes rolling, betrayed excitement only with an occasional twitch of ears pricked high and well forward.

Far away, a raven croaked. Mountain wind soughed in the trees.

Thin high-pitched fluting spiked the cold, clear air. A single note, crystalline. It froze Conway and Tate as effectively as a shout of alarm. When the sound broke, transformed into shimmering trills, the change was almost visible, as if the music suddenly turned to glittering splinters.

Then it was gone.

Mikka remained hidden. Karda, even farther ahead, failed to appear or sound off.

Worried, Conway signaled he was going forward. Tate moved to accompany him. He frowned, shaking his head in a negative. He pointed at their back trail. Grudgingly, she nodded.

Conway advanced on foot. Mobility was less of a concern than stealth in such heavy forest. If needed, a whistle would bring Stormracer at a gallop. Gliding from tree to tree, Conway closed in on the point where he'd last seen Mikka. He flipped the wipe's safety.

The dog blended almost perfectly with the rock outcrop where she sheltered. She was aware of Conway long before he saw her. Nevertheless, she held her position, staring off uphill in a manner Conway could only consider confused. The hackles on her neck were raised. Conway thrilled at the fierceness of her when she glanced his way.

Karda drifted into sight. His dark bulk slipped from cover to cover as lightly as fog. Conway was disturbed to see that, like Mikka, the big male was uncertain about the presence above them.

Incongruous, unwanted memory twisted and squirmed in Conway's deepest consciousness, demanded presence. He saw a grove of trees, carefully tended. A Church grove, holy. Lanta walked there, sad and alone, playing a flute. But that was a long time ago. The melody and tone were different. Conway shook his head, made an inarticulate sound of dismissal. Lanta was in Ola, safe from exactly this sort of testing puzzle or any other danger.

Bringing the dogs to heel, Conway returned to Tate. "I'll go see what I can find. Some rocks up ahead will give you good cover while I'm gone."

"Forget it. I'm coming with you. Whoever that was, he knew we were here. I feel it. He was a long way off, for that flute to sound the way it did. He's been watching us. He just let us know it."

Deciding against argument, Conway described the odd behavior of the dogs. "I've never seen them like that," he finished.

Tate merely nodded, falling in with her companion's departure. The route was directly up the slope, which grew steadily steeper. Snow gleamed dully where they finally spotted the still, waiting dogs. Dismounting, Tate and Conway again thoroughly checked their surroundings. To the flanks stretched unbroken forest, majestic trunks melding distantly into impenetrable walls. The mountain was quite narrow at that point, and the slope of Snowfather Mountain was visible beyond the left shoulder. Not far above the dogs, the trees on their own mountain ended. The landscape became stone and snow, a brooding, disapproving presence.

Leading the horses, Conway and Tate pressed forward. The dogs watched them come. Karda, indicating his unconcern, sat down and scratched busily.

Footprints were perfectly clear in the new-fallen snow. Someone walked out of the forest directly to a comfortably flat rock. Flattened snow showed the imprint of a seat. Conway said, "He wasn't worried about us catching him. Look at the strides. Even, heel and toe; no hurry."

Tate used her foot to measure. "Not a big man. Shoe size about the same as mine."

Straight-faced, Conway said, "Some people would question that deduction."

Tate's eyes narrowed. "Some people might mourn a man who made snotty remarks about the size of a woman's feet. I wouldn't."

"Point taken." Conway moved to trace the mysterious flutist. Tate followed. The dogs ranged ahead on the flanks. They were relaxed. At the edge of the snow, Conway's tracking abilities fell short of further pursuit. He said, "We can put the dogs on him."

"Why? He did no harm. And if he wants to draw us into an ambush, what better way? Anyhow, we've got our own fish to fry."

"I guess you're right." Conway rubbed his jaw. "The dogs certainly don't know what to make of this. What bothers me is knowing there's been someone on the back trail. This could be connected with that."

"We don't know someone's following us. We saw a fire one night and smoke the next morning. That's it."

Stubbornly, Conway disagreed. "No one lives up here. Or hasn't since the Mountains were crushed. And you've seen the way the dogs keep dropping behind us, sniffing like crazy every time the wind blows from the west. They know."

"They know doodly. Have they gone on alert, the way they did when they got wind of our flute player? No. Because there's no one back there." Gesturing at the rectangular carrying case lashed behind Conway's saddle, she went on. "Even with the scope on the sniper rifle, we saw nothing. An hour scanning, at least, and all we proved is that the solar panels still drive the computer sight."

"We'll see. You're right about one thing; we have to get moving. I don't want to get caught up here when the bad weather hits."

They were halfway back to the trail when both dogs warned of a presence ahead. Again, they behaved as if their hearts weren't in their work. They shifted uncomfortably. Hackles remained down. Dark eyes flicked continuously between Conway and the unseen intruder.

Conway readied his wipe. Over his shoulder, he saw Tate do the same. She moved into position abreast of him. At Conway's signal, the dogs led, ghosting from cover to cover. The riders followed, weapons ready.

A lone figure waited. For a moment, Conway thought he was looking at a bear. Only when the person shifted did he realize he saw a bearskin draped over someone hiding among the rocks. It was the same place Mikka had used for shelter.

Tate leaned against a tree, braced to provide covering fire. Conway dismounted, moved forward.

The figure jerked. Reflexively, Conway flung up his wipe. An instant before firing, he was amazed to realize that whoever was wearing the bearskin cover was fighting sleep. Now that he was closer, he saw the general outline of a drooping head, a body sitting with knees drawn up, arms folded across them.

Tate had spoken of ambush. Conway realized his vulnerability. The dogs were preoccupied. Tate was so close she'd be involved, couldn't provide backup.

Piercing, the flute called. Closer. The singular note again broke apart into warbling variations. The figure stirred.

The dogs watched Conway. Panting, eyes round with expectation, they crouched. White fangs framed lolling, red tongues.

Conway decided. If this was to be an ambush, he'd trigger it on his terms, not his opponent's. He launched the dogs. Roaring, they charged. Long, pistoning legs devoured the ground to their victim.

The bearskin robe flew to the side. Disbelief twisted a face pale as the snow of the mountain. Hands outstretched in pitiable plea, Lanta shrieked terror.

Chapter 42

Conway screamed at the dogs to break off the attack. Karda planted his forelegs, locked the knees. Mikka was fractionally slower. Her bulk slammed into the larger male. She bowled him sideways. Unable to regain her own balance, Mikka tumbled onto her side, skidding through the forest duff.

With both huge animals scrambling to their feet, jostling her, Lanta's screams choked to a breathless stop. Conway was with her as fast as he could move. Barely in time, he caught her as she gave way.

Clumsily, he lowered her to a sitting attitude, Tate, not troubling with discussion, adjusted Lanta into a prone position, feet raised. Rushing to her horse, she yanked a heavy blanket from a saddlebag, returning to swaddle the small, still figure. Little by little, color returned to Lanta's cheeks. Pale lips regained tone.

Conway's gaze locked with Tate's. They stared at each other across their patient. Almost inaudible, Conway said, "I almost killed her."

"Don't be ridiculous. You had no way of knowing it was her."

"That's the whole point. I had no idea who it was. But I set the dogs on her, anyway. Just to be sure. What am I, Tate?"

Tate bowed her head, busied herself tucking the blanket under Lanta. "What are you? You're alive. And unless you want to become dead, you'll keep on doing what you did. These aren't called the Enemy Mountains because people ran out of names. We don't have any friends here."

"Lanta's not a friend?"

"Don't play games with me. You did what was right. It won't be Lanta, next time."

"There won't be a next time. I'm taking her back to Ola."

Tate was cold. "Whatever. Leave the sniper rifle."

"I have to take her back. She's cast out. No one'll hesitate to kill her, now that she doesn't have Church protection."

Tate didn't trust herself to speak further. Feelings raged through her, whirlpools of frustration, anger, confusion. Of all people, Conway should understand the importance of denying the contents of the crèche to Moonpriest. Instead of leaping at the opportunity to help, he'd been unenthusiastic from the start. Now he was being obstructive. It wasn't fair.

She'd left Nalatan because this mission was so vital. Her marriage might be mortally wounded. Yet Nalatan stepped aside for her. Lanta broke that bond of mutuality between Conway and herself, and all Conway wanted to do was protect her. The best chance Church—and a reasonable civilization—had was the survival of the Three Territories as a haven. Lanta was endangering that concept.

Lanta was with her man, in spite of everything. Conway was creating a romance while Donnacee Tate might very well be destroying hers. It wasn't fair.

Eyelids fluttering, Lanta inhaled deeply, exhaled in a long sigh. She looked up at Conway. A delicate smile brushed across her features. Suddenly, her eyes flew wide and she lunged upward.

Tate and Conway restrained her. Conway said, "It's all right. You're safe. Unhurt. You fainted. You're all right now."

Craning about, Lanta located the dogs. They returned her frightened stare with studied disinterest. Karda yawned. At the sight of the teeth, Lanta hastily looked away. She focused on Conway. Her voice was shaky. "I was afraid to follow you up the mountain. I heard something—music—up there. I knew you'd come back down. I waited. I must have fallen asleep. Why . . . ?" Her gaze went to the reclining dogs again, making it unnecessary to finish the question.

"I'm so sorry." Conway put his hand to her cheek. "The bearskin cloak confused me. I was afraid of an ambush. I'm ashamed."

Lanta's protest was alarmed. "No, no. You were right. If I hadn't fallen asleep, I'd have heard you, called out. It's my fault. But we're together now. Everything's all right."

"We'll be back in Ola in a few days. We'll always be together."

Lanta insisted on rising. Conway and Tate watched uneasily until she was fully erect, braced against the rock behind her. Voice steadied, Lanta said, "I'm here to go with you."

"Impossible. No one outside our tribe can go where we're going. It's forbidden." Tate's words grated. Her look at Conway demanded he concur.

Conway addressed Tate. "It makes no difference. I told you, Church's life protection doesn't include her anymore, so I'm taking her back to Ola."

"I won't go back." The calm assurance broke the confrontational pressure building between Conway and Tate. Lanta continued. "I must go with you, Matt Conway. I care nothing for your secrets. I care nothing for the edicts of a false Church that denies me my due. My life is unimportant, unless I live it as a complete person. I can never be that until this matter between us is resolved. We're one, or we're not. This mission of yours will tell us."

Harsher than ever, Tate said, "You Saw? Peeked into the future?"

"If I knew the future, I'd have no need to be here. Nor would you."

Furious, Tate glared. The unshakeable determination of the smaller woman fueled her resentment. If Nalatan had been so quietly insistent, would it have made a difference? If he suddenly appeared, as committed as Lanta, what could she do about it?

Words burned on her tongue. Just as they were about to be unleashed, Tate truly saw the other woman. The cruel, barbed phrases died. There was something in Lanta's pinched, pale features that dashed the angry things she yearned to shout. Tate realized she was seeing the gamble of a person whose emotional losses demanded one final try. Lanta, the woman everyone half-feared because she might already know their future, was betting her own.

Conway said, "Tate's right, Lanta; there are too many good reasons for you to stay in Ola. The most important one is, I love you."

Tate stifled a groan. If either Conway or Lanta heard, they gave no sign. Lanta said, "The risk is to our life. If you go without me and don't come back, what do I have? If you go back to Ola with me, what value is your friendship to Tate? If you refuse me the right to come with you, what does it say of your confidence in me?"

Like a fighter unable to fend off all the blows aimed at him, Conway could only blink and dodge. Wearily, he concentrated on the one thing he felt he could contend with. "I'm worried about your safety."

"And I told you I care nothing for it. I don't want to die. But I'd rather that than go on loving you and fearing you and loving you and fearing you and . . ." She turned away. A tear ran wet silver down her cheek. She brushed it off with a distracted, jerky motion.

Conway looked to Tate.

Tate wanted to speak to him as badly as she'd wanted to berate Lanta, earlier. In truth, the heat of resentment still brought hot, smoky words of criticism to her mind. She pulled free of them. Nevertheless, she forced herself to confront Conway's beseeching with a face like stone.

At last, he turned back to Lanta. "Have you thought what it'll do to me if you're hurt?"

Lanta balled her fists. "Will you never understand? We must do this together. This is our test."

"I don't need any test. I love you. I want to see you safe."

"And I love you. For us, though, love isn't enough. We've hurt each other too much. Can't you see I can't be safe inside myself until I know I trust you, that you trust me? Without something to share, we'll never heal the wound that holds us apart. It's like cautery; no matter how badly it hurts, sometimes it's the only cure we have."

Conway's gaze dropped. Slowly, he turned from Lanta. His shoulders rose and fell in a long, time-consuming breath. He walked away bowed, legs working stiffly.

Tate watched, still silent, thinking how worn out he looked. Lanta, on the other hand, was taut. Birdlike, she appeared poised for flight. Tate's mind went to the huge rafts of ducks that banded together on the lakes of Ola. Just before migration, there was a nervous energy in those flocks that one could feel. Tate remembered watching the birds only a few days before this trip, thinking how one sensed in them that trembling urge to simply go.

Tate's earlier anger collapsed. Quietly, unwilling to disturb Conway, Tate eased up against Lanta. The smaller woman's expression didn't alter, nor did her focus leave Conway's back. Still, there was an almost-imperceptible responsive lean into the contact.

Conway said, "I don't see how this can help."

Tate felt a shock of defeat run through Lanta. Fumbling, she reached down, took Lanta's cold hand in her own.

Conway continued. "The dangers are too many to list. We can't let you know exactly what we're doing. But if you believe it's what we need, I'll do anything."

Lanta seemed to fly to him, reaching to take his face between her hands. "I told you, I don't want to know anything. Except about us."

A wan, baffled smile lifted Conway's features. "Why couldn't we be like everyone else? Why couldn't we just fall in love, be silly, say stupid things?"

Examining Conway's features as if he were some exciting new discovery, Lanta answered. Wonder and love overshadowed the prim Church-teaching of her words. "There are reasons for things that we can never comprehend. We are tested in order that we may succeed. We fail in order that we may learn to try again. There is a goal for each of us."

"You're my goal."

Lanta blushed. She smiled, a radiance of joy.

Tate cleared her throat before attempting to speak. "We've lost a lot of travel time. Can we move out now?"

Lanta whirled to face her. "My horse. I forgot. It's hobbled, down the trail."

Conway was already on the way to his mount. "Stay here with Tate. I'll get it." He trotted off, the dogs racing to precede him.

Lanta moved to stand in front of Tate. "I know what you're thinking."

"What about? You two?"

"That. And about Nalatan." She winced at Tate's frown, but plunged ahead. "I almost asked him to come with me to find you and Matt. Oh, you and Nalatan don't have the trouble between you that Matt and I have, but you feared something about Nalatan when you felt yourself falling in love with him. Maybe you're answering a question of your own with this journey. I don't know. But I know I'm your friend. What you want for you and your husband is what I want for you."

Resentment flared anew, red-raw, uncaring. "What if I want you to keep your ideas about my life to yourself? What if I want you to straighten out your own messed-up romance and leave me and Nalatan alone?"

If Lanta was affected by the hostility of Tate's response, she gave no sign. "I wanted you to know. I want you to forgive me, to help me, so I can help you."

Tate retreated to her mount, cinching the girth with a jerk that made the poor animal snort with surprise. It turned to look at her, the huge, dark eye round with wounded disbelief. Under her breath, Tate muttered, "Don't you start, horse. I'll take it out on you if I want to. I'm riding into who-knows-what with Miss

Lonelyhearts and Sir Gala-stupid-had; I don't need sad-eyed trash from some slope-shouldered hay furnace. How can she say a dumb thing like that? Nalatan and me. How can she think there's any problem with us? She wouldn't know happiness if it was a rock the size of a barn. On her foot. Without a shoe. Crazy little twit."

The sound of conversation brought her up short. The others rode to join her. Conway and the dogs led. Tate dropped back to rear guard.

Tate mulled over Lanta's remarks. Was it possible there was something in her manner toward Nalatan that suggested stress? Distrust?

Impossible. She loved the man. Completely. Unquestioningly.

Black woman. White man. Pounding in her head. *Black woman. White man.*

Was that why she insisted he stay behind? Did she, in her heart of hearts, need to test him?

Something checked her internalizing. Ahead, Conway was stopped. Concerned, he looked back past an equally disturbed Lanta, on beyond Tate herself.

The flute. Behind them, close. The tone was lower than before, richer. Gentle melody sighed through the forest, told of loss, dismay. Rising in the stirrups, Tate sought the source. There was only the music.

The end came as a rising, spiraling sound that stretched upward, upward, until it was a shrill, stabbing whistle. And then, achingly abrupt, it was as though it had never been.

Chapter 43

Tears of Jade hugged herself under the whitebearskin cloak. She wore boots and hat of the same material, the latter with flaps that covered her ears. A band across her face covered everything but her eyes. They blazed at the storm-racked sea. Wind scratched their tenderness. Features compressed in blinking pain.

When she forced her lids open again, sea and horizon melded into a gray blur. She murmured nervously when that nothingness was suddenly shot through with light dazzles.

Occasionally, when her true sight was blinded, she saw other things.

Tears of Jade decided not to be frightened this time. Huddled in her warm clothes, she abandoned herself to a preening, snug pleasure. Visions were, after all, a gift of the god, and he was far more jealous than generous.

Tears of Jade smiled. Many thought her mad. She heard some of the whispers. Informants seeking favor scrambled to expose others. All the insectlike skittering only proved no one could be trusted.

Only the god.

As if expressing approval, the god drew her attention to the sea, gave her vision through the waves, into the deep. There, in the swaying kelp and seaweed gardens, she saw the obscene revels that presently beat the ocean to wild frenzy. Ugly, deformed things frolicked, dancing around huge underwater fires of ice that lofted rolling plumes of freezing water. Tears of Jade thrilled, knowing that she was a favored one, that the horrors being visited on the victims would never be hers. Still, the monsters laughed at her, hated her. Reached. Tentacles. Claws. Red, pincer-mouths. Hands of rotting flesh. The sea clouded, closed her out.

Another vision. A sharker came dead east, driven by a storm that sang death in harp-taut rigging. Skan sailors, men who knew the sea better than most men know a lover, crouched against the gunwales and listened to water and wind wrenching their ship apart.

Tears of Jade's inward-turned gaze brought her the bow of the sharker. The figurehead. Lorso.

For a moment she thought fear transfixed him, but a second, closer look showed fury. Eyes bulged. Jaw jutted. Fists of ice, blue-white and glistening, battered his way through a towering wave. The next wave was larger; he clawed his way up the face of it, dove headlong down the opposite side.

Behind the man-ship Lorso, cowering in the hull that was his body, the crew called his name. Lorso himself bellowed into the storm. The power of his voice blasted wavetops into silvered spume. Shattered waves fell toward him, only to cleave and let him pass.

Pounding her walking stick into the scant soil crowning the overlook, the old, bent woman whirled away from the apparition.

She cautiously opened her eyes to the real world. All was as ordinary people saw it.

What did the vision mean? Never, ever, had she seen Lorso so suffused with wrath. Not even when he was transported with religious fury, killing for Sosolassa.

Painfully, the twisted figure pulled itself fully upright. Aching joints and brittle tendons conformed to indomitable will.

A blast of wind howled in from the sea, nearly bowled her over. From within her thick furs, her night-dark eyes sparkled. She crooned softly, the wordless singsong of a mother jollying an infant. Another gust, weaker, buffeted her. She laughed happily, reeling at the thrust. Loving Sosolassa. So wise. Willing to be playful with a slave.

Far to sea, Tears of Jade thought she saw a wave crest move at a wrong angle. Cupping a hand at her brow, she stared. A sail. Reefed, little more than a speck against the tumult. Quartering across the wind, driving from the southeast.

"Lorso." The single word reeked pride. "The son of Tears of Jade. Only my son could survive." She stopped. There was such a thing as too much ability.

Tears of Jade made her halt way down from the overlook. Men gathered in the trees at the base of the knoll shifted uncomfortably as she drew closer.

Domel broke the apprehensive silence. "Does the god choose to instruct us?"

Indicating her ornate sedan chair with the walking stick, Tears of Jade waited for two of her bearer team to come help her into the seat before answering. "Lorso comes. We must hurry. I must be there when he arrives."

Domel bowed silent assent. He cut his eyes at the sedan-chair bearers, saw the apprehension. Their burden was painfully heavy. Being slaves, they knew what was in store if their pace faltered on the long return to the harbor. What would happen to all of them if one stumbled, much less fell, didn't bear thinking about.

Tears of Jade shouted orders. The eight bearers shouldered the chair. The slave at the right front called a cadence. In a short distance, they were moving at a surprisingly swift pace. The men accompanying Tears of Jade followed on horseback.

The longitudinal poles of the sedan chair rested on massive pillows. That, combined with the peculiarly loose-kneed stride of the runners, provided a jolt-free ride. Still, a constant barrage of criticism rasped through the fur curtains enclosing Tears of Jade's compartment. Sensitive to every nuance of the men's movement, she criticized each by position, even though unable to see them. "Second forward left. You're a full half-step off first forward's rhythm. You, left rear leader. I feel you bending away from your share. Get your shoulder into that pole, or I'll have it broken for you. Heave! Lazy piece of filth."

Sweat poured off the straining bearers. Expressionless, precise, they churned along the trail back to the Skan village.

On arrival at the harbor beach, they slowed to a careful stop. The leader called hoarse commands. Pivoting in unison, each bearer grasped his pole in both hands. When they bent to lower the chair, they sank into clouds of steam rising from their bodies. Second right forward and right rear leader pulled back the curtains to lift their passenger free of her chair. Exiting, Tears of Jade inspected them. They stood erect, eyes straight ahead. Their limbs trembled, and their chests rose and fell rapidly. One struggled to contain a cough. To Domel, she said, "Grain them well tonight. Put a flax poultice on right forward leader; he's trying to hide a limp. I want them cooled out right, and then rubbed down. By a man. They're treacherous brush stallions, and I won't have them wasting their strength on some slave mare unless I want them bred."

Domel turned to one of the boys gathered to watch the group. "You. Take this team to Tears of Jade's stables."

The boy, bold-eyed as a jay, leaped to obey. In fact, he vaulted to the roof of the sedan chair. From his perch, he grinned at Tears of Jade, a shifting, nervous mix of daring and trepidation. Domel tensed. The bearers started, gawked.

Tears of Jade deliberately removed her veil. Then she laughed, a rustle that bared her teeth. "You'd test your luck, would you? Get away. Take good care of my stock."

Shouting commands in a cracking voice victimized by hormones and excitement, the boy drove off the team. His smile for his friends was triumph. Still, he kept a wary eye on the bent old woman. Tears of Jade spoke to Domel. "Get that brat's name. I want to know more about him. Now, where's my son?"

As if in answer, Lorso's sharker surfed into the entry of the narrow coastal indentation leading from open sea past the mouth of Skan's protected harbor. The Skan called the channel the Throat. With the wind flogging her, the sharker sped down its length as if, indeed, being swallowed. The steely waters leaped and tumbled in a welter of crosscurrents. Under Lorso's sure hand, the sharker danced along as if the Throat were mere play. She heeled over to dash into the quiet waters of the harbor with a flip of her stern.

Domel said, "He handles her gracefully. You must be very proud."

She turned, peered up at him. He smiled, sent a small gesture toward the ship. "The hand of Sosolassa is surely on him. Stormtime is always deadly. He always survives. People say he's blessed. It must be comforting."

"You can't imagine." Tears of Jade smiled, looking away to assure Domel couldn't catch the sarcastic twist of it.

The beaching went smoothly. Slaves lay smooth logs in place while others waded out to attach lines to the hull. The fat beachmaster, grizzled and wrinkled from a lifetime of outdoor exertion, slashed speed out of his workers with a heavy sealskin whip. A multiple pulley system, one of the many fixed to tree trunks buried in the earth, greatly facilitated outhauling the vessel on the log rollers. As the sleek vessel rose from her natural element, suddenly tentative on her narrow bottom, the roller-placement crew returned with long, forked poles. These fit the oar holes, and the slaves holding them kept the sharker upright. When she was sufficiently clear of the water, the poles were wedged into the earth. Braced, her seaweed-cloaked, barnacled hull dripping, the sharker's ferocious bear figurehead was suddenly no more than a carving, frustrated and helpless.

A crane swung over the side, dangling a large net. It was a short distance to the ground; nevertheless, when the line snapped and the cargo thudded to the rocky earth, Lorso bellowed anger. Slaves rushed to release the net. Open, it spilled its cargo of humans. Most struggled to rise, their bound wrists and ankles entangling and dropping them once more. The beachmaster sent his crew among them, separating one from another, pitching them free of the thrashing pile like ears of corn.

Lorso's dissatisfaction was reserved for his crane operator. "Any injured come out of your share." The order still hung in the air as Lorso leaped over the side. He moved among the slaves, poking, prodding. There appeared to be little damage, and he left with no further recrimination. After embracing the unresponsive Tears of Jade and exchanging properly formal greetings, he told her, "Twenty adult males. Puked their brains out all the way from the Mother River. Call themselves River People. Don't know any more about water than a rock." Lingering excitement made his words staccato. Energy shone from his face like a fire devouring its last splinters of fuel. "Where's Jaleeta?"

Domel said, "Congratulations on a safe voyage, Lorso. I'll see to the slaves, and leave you with your mother." He had to pass Tears of Jade to reach the slave barracks. His departure had the rigid precision of a man who dares not run.

Tears of Jade clutched Domel's sleeve. He froze. Taloned fingers hooked in the material, she said, "Domel knows all about what happened."

Disbelief swamped Domel's features.

Completely unaware of the older man, Lorso repeated himself. "Where's Jaleeta? I don't see her."

"The girl betrayed me. She betrayed the Skan." Tears of Jade freed the stunned Domel. She turned to lead Lorso away. He grabbed her shoulder, spun her around. Ignoring her quick, bright fury, he snarled his questions. "Is she all right? Where is she?"

Tears of Jade looked deep into his eyes. A curled, dry hand moved to disengage his grip. Lorso's hard, callused fingers peeled back without resistance, limp as seaweed. She said, "No one has ever tricked me so. Hurt me so." She ducked her head. Drawing erect after a moment, she was the proud, injured spirit woman. "I trusted her. So evil, Lorso; she never warned her mother. I had hopes for her. I'm old. Perhaps too old. She was so young, so beautiful. I hoped . . ." Emotion overwhelmed her.

"Where? When?" Lorso's words were more like groans.

Domel was rigid. Afraid to leave, he acted as if immobility might make him disappear. Tears of Jade went on. "Somehow she escaped. Stole a boat. We know that. My spies tell me she's safe in the castle of Gan Moondark."

"Safe? With our worst enemy? He'll kill her when we move against him. He'll make her hostage."

"Hostage? One who's betrayed us? Who here, besides me, could ever care what happens to her?"

Lorso gaped. The weight of his sin, his deception, his lost love—all coalesced in one instant into a huge, unbearable mass. His eyes rolled up, nothing but whites showing. Skin turned gray as ashes. Tears of Jade planted the foot of her walking stick firmly, slammed it forward. Lorso yelled, grabbed his battered forehead. Pain restored awareness.

Tears of Jade said, "It's not necessary to mourn so, my son. I know how you love me, but you must not be so distraught because a slave abused my affection. Yes, I was fond of her, but now I must think of the Skan. She knows little of our plans, and my pain at her deception is unimportant. Only I cared about Jaleeta, only I am shamed in the eyes of good men such as Domel and all the rest of the Skan. Isn't that true?"

Lorso looked into the eyes of the woman who spoke to a god. "She betrayed. You trusted her. She betrayed love."

No longer able to watch, Domel looked away. As much as he feared Lorso, there was something in this new agonized manner that repelled him.

Tears of Jade saw only a creation responding perfectly. She smiled at the self-hatred in Lorso's voice. She told him, "Never mind. If Gan Moondark, or one of his followers, thinks he can use her, we know how foolish that is. Anyhow, we'll recapture her when we crush the Three Territories." She paused, brightening. "What if we can recover her? And punish her."

From the corner of her eye, Tears of Jade saw Lorso's hand twitch toward the hilt of his sword. She wanted to sing her joy. All her years of training was condensed into that one gesture, barely noticeable even to the most observant. Only Tears of Jade understood its significance.

Lorso wanted to kill. *Yearned* to kill, as he yearned for the brainless slut who unwittingly bound him ever tighter to the one who understood his true destiny.

The god was good. Sosolassa blessed.

"Come to my cabin. We have many things to discuss."

Lorso, panting, followed eagerly.

Chapter 44

Domel, having escaped to shelter in the slave barracks, watched Tears of Jade lead her son away.

The stink of danger burned his nose. In his mind, he heard Lorso's eager question: "Where's Jaleeta?" Two words. A thunderclap. Expected. Unnerving nevertheless.

At that moment Domel comprehended the mesh of the treachery that now ensnared him. Stomach churning, he cursed the old hag's duplicity, his own unquestioning stupidity. His face wrinkled with self-contempt, remembering the seductive words of Tears of Jade as she described how Lorso would be eager to recapture Jaleeta.

Lorso was besotted. He wasn't mindless. Sooner or later he'd discover Jaleeta had help escaping. Blood would splash the earth in waves.

Domel berated himself. He'd let himself be flattered by Tears of Jade's wheedling insistence that only a man of his wisdom could assist in her plot. Fool. He'd thought to please her. And profit. Shameful. Words rang in his memory: "You're the only one I can trust, Domel. It will be the same with my son. No one man can rule the Skan, and he'll need your sure counsel. Help me, and I'll know you and your sons are the ones to stand beside Lorso."

Domel's hand crept up to stroke his chin. He stared at the distant treetops in deep contemplation. No one was more influential among the Skan than himself. There was reason to be apprehensive about her plans for him, but to become paralyzed by that fear was as dangerous as to pretend the plans didn't exist. In fact, she might not be as clever as she thought. For all her powers, for all her hold over the Skan, she was very much alone.

Alone. A woman. With a secret not even she dared reveal to her son. Nor could she afford to have someone else bring it to light.

Rock-hard muscles slid toward relaxation. Whatever schemes Tears of Jade was hatching, she'd need help to bring them to life.

Domel turned to face the inside of the barracks. Through his preoccupation, he saw the whites of terrified eyes. The curved roof arched high over the heads of the huddled slaves and the bored guards squatting against the walls. In the dusky light piercing the rents in the hide walls bared swords had a dull, sullen gleam. The smell of hopeless fear mixed with the stench of seldom-aired bedding and infrequently washed bodies.

Domel's attention locked on his own situation. Things weren't too bad, he told himself. Not as long as he knew such a fearsome secret. A crooked, bitter smile lifted a corner of his mouth. If there was something worse than knowing a secret that could harm Tears of Jade, it was *not* knowing such a secret.

A good dagger would cut with either edge.

Domel realized the guards were watching him, puzzled by his prolonged inactivity. He strode forward, growled orders. The bound captives were hurriedly formed into two lines, facing each other. Accompanied by two guards, Domel walked between them, determining crafts. Two woodworkers. One potter. One leatherworker. They were marched off. The rest identified themselves as fishermen, farmers, loggers.

Domel's next inspection was more meticulous. Guards ordered mouths opened. Some were pried open with knives. He checked teeth. Pinching, prodding, he examined muscle tone. Feet were lifted, examined. Fingers were counted, bent to evaluate strength and flexibility.

Sixteen slaves watched Domel's every move. He spoke to a guard. "Timberworkers first. Chained, working in the forest tomorrow. You understand?"

The guard nodded. Domel faced the prisoners. His finger darted from one to another, each movement defining a lifetime's servitude. "You. You. You." He chose eight. Guards herded them away. "The rest to the sea-slave barracks."

Once again, bound, subdued men were led off.

Watching them stumble out under the blows of the guards, Domel permitted himself a pecking nod of approval. That was how things were done. Decisive. Unhesitating. Prudence and caution were major factors, but one didn't let them interfere with getting work done.

Following in trace of the departed slaves, the faintest of smiles touched Domel's features. Tears of Jade admired his wisdom, did she? Well she might. And well she might have remembered that her dupe, Domel, was Slavetaker, once. Far too old and slow now to confront Lorso in combat. Still, no man aged among the Skan without a certain cunning.

The timberworkers already squatted in front of the smith's workshed, except for one. He stood with his right foot raised onto a stump. Raising his heavy hammer, the smith brought it thudding down to flatten the rivet that would secure the anklet and chain to the slave until his death. The man groaned. One of those waiting turned away, weeping.

Tears from a man offended Domel. "Get that weakling out of the timber stock. He'd never last. He'll get another slave injured. Exchange him for one of the sea-slaves."

Not looking back, knowing he'd be obeyed, Domel led the way to the sea-slave barracks. On arrival, the accompanying guard shoved the weeping slave to the ground in front of his new group, simultaneously yanking a replacement from among the others. Domel walked to stand over the cowering man, saying, "This is where you belong. You'll fish for us, work here on the boats and on the docks. You won't be troubled by frightening sights."

The guard with the exchanged prisoner snickered aloud. The eyes of every slave darted to him, then returned to Domel. At that moment, however, another distraction appeared. A burly man leading two younger men, equally bulky, came around the corner of the sea-slave barracks. The leader greeted Domel, then added, "I came as soon as I heard. These eight are for me?"

"They look to be a fairly healthy bunch. The fair one there looks strong. He ought to be able to lift shrimp traps all day."

"They all will." The burly man laughed hugely. His assistants, still behind him, pitched in.

Domel aimed a careless kick at the slave lying at his feet. "Be careful of this one. He's sensitive. The sight of one of his friends being chained made him cry."

The burly man's amusement vanished. "I'll see he works, Domel. Don't worry."

"I'm sure of it." Domel looked down at the man. "We chain timberworkers so they can't run away. You won't be chained. The weight would take you straight to Sosolassa if you fall over the side, you see, and we mean to keep you. We have a better way to stop your running away." He jerked his head in the direction of the waiting trio. "A man can haul traps, catch fish, repair nets—all manner of things—without any need to look at his work. And a blind slave never knows which way to run to get away."

With a purely visceral movement, the slaves packed together against each other. A confused, indistinct sound of horrified disbelief rose from them. Beyond Domel, the two assistants moved forward. They carried leather bindings. The burly man drew a short, ugly little knife. Jutting from his thick, gnarled fingers, it glimmered.

The celebration of Lorso's return was lavish. The site was a longhouse, set on a knoll not far from the Skan port. Despite being hidden in a grove of ancient cedars, it afforded views of the sea and Sosolassa's sinister hook-beaked mountain.

Barrel-roofed, the first impression of the place was of a half tube, its apex twice the height of the tallest man. Long horizontal planking ranged its length, suggesting a ship hull. There were no windows. The long axis was north-south, with doors at each end. Midway along the length were two additional east and west doors. All doorjambs and lintels were elaborately carved and painted with totemic and magical symbols. The thick planks of the eastern entrance featured the finest carvings, highlighted with inset stonework of polished jade, garnet, onyx, and the intriguing pink-and-black sostone. Representation of Sosolassa's mass and fury dared entry. There was a plaque on the right side of the path a few paces from the door; as tall as a man, and as wide, it was rather like a signboard. Well greased, it resisted the steady drizzle. There was something about it that suggested dim antiquity. Oddly, and completely out of context with any other visible aspect of Skan culture, its sole display appeared to be a deformed mushroom. The stem was elongated, the crown irregularly bulbous. The color was a sickly gray, save for the bright red base.

Lorso and Domel approached the eastern door on foot, beside Tears of Jade in her sedan chair. Some distance away, the bearers stopped. They remained behind as the two Skan continued, supporting the old woman. Just before reaching the strange painting, Lorso and Domel released her. Right hands raised to the right side of the face, bent to the left, all three literally slunk past the decorated board. Safely beyond it, Tears of Jade took their arms again, swept inside with them.

Skan warriors were crowded inside. Grandly carved and painted ceremonial bowls, each representing a clan, rested on a line of trestles down the middle of the building. All held aromatic, steaming soup or stew.

Long tables burdened with the finest seafood, fresh and smoked, flanked the bowls. There were few vegetable dishes, but a large variety of baked dried fruit concoctions. Vats of beer loomed along the curved walls. Slave women rushed through the west entrance of the longhouse, still distributing food. Some carried cedar-root baskets filled with smoking hot rocks, leaving a trail of pungent, peppery scent. The rocks were lowered into the carved bowls, replacing those which had cooled.

Domel managed to make himself heard over the general hubbub, shouted flattering remarks about Lorso from the east side of the longhouse. When Domel called for a cheer to celebrate the alliance with Windband and the River People, the response was as brief, if enthusiastic. The gathered warriors clearly respected Lorso. They equally clearly wanted to get on with the festivities. Domel stepped aside. Tears of Jade took his place. Silence moved through the gathering the way spreading oil damps waves. Loud, raucous voices broke off. Laughter sputtered, choked.

Tears of Jade spoke. The dry, peculiarly carrying voice insinuated itself into every cranny. "I thank the warriors of the Skan for allowing a woman to speak at a warrior banquet. We have greater reason to celebrate this new alliance than any of you can know. The Skan are on the crest of the wave that brings us to domination. Sosolassa has shown me Church, broken and defiled. The god has shown me Gan Moondark wrapped in the god's dark tentacle. The witch Sylah will be a toy for the men of the Skan. I saw the Mother River choked with the dead of Windband and the River People. There will be killing as the Skan have never seen before, slaves enough to fill the hold of every sharker."

Bellowed approval surprised Tears of Jade. For the briefest instant, it showed in her drawn lips, stiffly raised chin. "Sosolassa demands the Skan act as one. Trust all, trust none else. Treat our new allies as brothers. On Sosolassa's order, strike them all." She paused, spread palsied arms. The material of her extended cloak trembled in the fitful light, giving her the look of a tiny, eager wasp. "I, Tears of Jade, trusted an outsider. Learn from the folly of an old woman. All know of Jaleeta. Learn, men of the Skan. She was not of us, and she betrayed us, used magic to trick these weary eyes. I will be avenged. As Sosolassa commands that all Skan always be avenged."

The assent from the crowd was different this time, a low, feral growl.

Surveying the entire room, Tears of Jade finished, "Eat. Drink. Enjoy. Make your life here as it will be when Sosolassa calls you to your final honor. Live as Skan, that you may properly die as Skan."

A step back took her to the east exit. She passed through it with astonishing quickness. For many of the rapt warriors, their view impeded by the crowd, she literally disappeared. A thick, uncertain quiet enveloped the room. Only the crackle of the fire and the dancing flames lived in that moment. Then Lorso's voice rang out. "Eat! Let's hear singing! Otter Clan; do you have voices?"

Activity exploded. The rhythmic Otter war chant, a boast of deeds set to the beat of racing sharker oars, hammered across the rising laughter and shouting.

Before Domel could finish the food on his wooden platter, the first trouble started. Munching a doughy confection of dried apples, raspberries, and honey, he merely glanced up when a serving slave raced past, screaming. Crunching sounds, the unmistakable crackle of breaking cartilage, demanded closer attention, however. Domel turned to see an irate Sea Lion Clan warrior glaring down at a seated Otter. The latter's eyes lacked focus. His nose was seriously rearranged, bent left. Copious blood emphasized the recent completion of that novel alteration. The Sea Lion man said, "You know that's forbidden in here. Anyhow, if you want a woman, use your own slaves. That one's our property."

A second Otter's fist expressed exception to that hypothesis. It dropped the property-proud Sea Lion in a snot-bubbling heap. Howling merrymakers from other clans flailed at their closest neighbor. The serving slave slipped away.

As did Domel. Bent over a brimming container of beer, he nimbly dodged revelers until he was against a wall. Enjoying his brew, he watched the ebb and flow of the melee.

Since weapons were forbidden at a Skan banquet, there was little chance of serious damage. True, there were those occasions when someone was brained with a wildcow thighbone, or had an eye gouged with a spoon, but Skan law decreed that no injury sustained inside during a Skan longhouse banquet could be pursued further in any way. Skan social cohesion needed forgetfulness.

By the time Domel finished his third—or fourth—tankard, former combatants sprawled on the tables and the floor in all directions. Among the conscious, arms draped over shoulders. Heads lolled together. Clan intertwined with clan. The low hum and hiccup of mumbled war stories soothed the ear.

Domel was mildly surprised at how swiftly the evening had scampered past. He leaned back against the wall, luxuriating in the sensuous weight of eyelids that shuttered slowly, slowly downward. The fire's failing flames cast a soft, roseate glow across the dreamlike expanse of abandoned food, discarded utensils, and twitching bodies. Domel admired it all proudly.

He'd been a fool to worry about Tears of Jade. Not that she wasn't a formidable woman. Her spirit powers were undeniable. A little frightening. That word again. *Frightening*. Ridiculous. War. Conquest. Skan life, that was. Kill the allies when they were no longer useful. Clever. Perhaps a bit more beer was in order. He forced amazingly heavy eyelids open the merest slit.

Lorso stood two body-lengths away. Watching.

Domel held himself still, like a newborn fawn smelling wolf. Like the animal, Domel knew his life depended on being something he was not. He pretended sleep. Even through the hazed vision of near-closed eyes, beer, and smoke, Domel saw vengeance.

Lorso left.

Domel's breath came in gulps. His skin tingled. Rising, kicking the beer container aside, he picked a way through the litter. He was amazed by his swift return to sobriety.

Chapter 45

Pressed against the sodden cabin wall, Domel blamed his bone-rattling shaking on the weather. His heart knew it was more than cold. If Tears of Jade or Lorso ever suspected he spied on them, death would be a kindness.

The young Domel was a braver man. A better man. The one huddling in the darkness like a crippled dog sniffing for scraps was a fool.

Domel thought back to other uncomfortable vigils. The blood ran hot, then. Those nights he welcomed misery because it sapped the strength of his prey. That Domel feared only failure and dishonor.

This Domel dabbled at greater power, allowed himself to be tricked. Tool of a woman. A spirit woman, but a female, nevertheless.

For a moment, Domel thought he saw a way out of his dilemma. If he stormed into the cabin and told Lorso exactly what happened, he could at least die quickly. After the explanations, the sword stroke would be swift and clean.

Shaking his head, Domel acknowledged the futility of that effort. Tears of Jade would deny everything, and be believed. Domel remembered the expression on Lorso's face in the longhouse. That face would kill slowly. Appreciatively.

Domel crept farther along the wall, daring Lorso's predator's senses, getting closer to the window.

"He didn't see me, didn't know I was there." The words were muffled; Lorso, defensive.

Tears of Jade's words were clear, like a knife blade slipped between the cabin logs. "You tell me you stood over him, looked down at him, and he didn't see you?" Domel recoiled. Bile burned his throat, almost choked him.

"He was drunk. I watched him. Eating, drinking. Alone. He has no friends."

"People like Domel and me need no friends. We have knowledge. I pray the god grants you some. Someday. Every important Skan alive owes Domel for something. He's woven a net of debts. That's why you will not kill him until I say it's time."

"How long must I wait?"

Domel's stomach rolled at the yearning in Lorso's plea.

Tears of Jade soothed. "Soon, my son. And control yourself. Such a frightening glare. Remember, I'm the offended one, not you. You didn't care for the girl. I did. I had hopes for her. You certainly didn't."

When next Tears of Jade spoke, demanding Lorso give her time to think, her voice was thoughtful. It puzzled Domel that despite its softer quality, it sounded even clearer; then he realized she'd changed her position. In his mind's eye he saw her, away from the fire, seated in the chair by the window. With the black curtain drawn, she'd be almost invisible, a small, dark interruption against a larger blackness. Chin resting on a twiggy hand, as if crouched. If the fire burned brightly enough, it caught in her eyes, glittered. Sometimes she sat like that for so long one wondered if she still lived.

Domel chewed on a knuckle. If Tears of Jade called on the god to punish him, death was only a passage from this world to eternal suffering. If he could be free of her, however, he'd be free of Sosolassa. The god wouldn't strike at him without her encouragement.

Musing speech interrupted his thoughts. Tears of Jade spoke. "Perhaps it would be best to eliminate him as quickly as possible."

"Tonight." Lorso's urgency conjured a shark scenting blood, bending back on itself in its eagerness.

The spirit woman continued, unheeding. "I'm not sure I can make him reveal all the people under obligation to him. Torture would probably work, but it could take a long time. I can't trust you not to do something foolish. Nor will you be able to concentrate on your duties while he lives; I see that now. Once I tell everyone the old fool wanted Jaleeta since she came here, that he intended to escape with her, the Navigators will send him to Sosolassa immediately."

"I send him." Lorso made it a demand. "He hurt me. You, I mean. It must be me."

Tears of Jade was considerate. "He must drown, go direct to the god. You shall be in charge."

"I want to feel him die on my sword."

"That's exactly what we cannot have. You, with your eyes full of killing, your face shining with hate. Who knows what tales he'll tell to spare himself?"

Sighing, Domel accepted the last as the final blow. Now Lorso would expect denial. He'd hear the truth of his mother's treachery as the squealing of a coward.

Lorso spoke again. "If I'm as obvious as you say, maybe he'll run away. Or maybe he actually will start telling lies about Jaleeta."

In the whispering rainfall, Domel waited along with Lorso for an answer. None was forthcoming, and when Lorso continued, he was defensive.

"He'll try to make her running away look like your fault, tell everyone you were cruel to her. Some will believe him. Jealous people."

Tears of Jade simpered. "Some envy you, as well, son. You're too modest. Yes, some will believe Domel's raving. The sooner we're rid of him, the better."

"Now?" A chair's scrape signaled Lorso's eager rise.

"In the morning."

Domel pushed off the rain-slick logs of the wall. Partially erect, he paused. Someone was speaking again. He dared not leave without hearing what was being said, yet to stand there, a handsbreadth from Tears of Jade and all her malevolent power, was devastating.

Tears of Jade said, "Again, you're right. Take him tonight. Bring him to me. I've suspected him of witchwork for a long time. By morning, I'll have him ready to confess his sins to the tribe."

Lorso sounded frantic, the blood-fury forgotten. "Witchwork? You've known? Why didn't you do something long ago? What if he's done something with . . . with the girl?"

"I told you she's in Ola, with Moondark. Sometimes I get the feeling you're more concerned about her absence than all my injury."

"Never, Mother."

"Well, then. Now, eat something. I don't want you out in this weather on an empty stomach. I have a few things to prepare. When I'm done, you can fetch him to me. No, don't argue. Eat, then work."

Delicately, carefully, Domel straightened. A ligament caught in his knee. To straighten it meant to make it crack; to walk on it as it was meant excruciating pain. Domel limped until he was safely out of earshot. The pinched ligament came free with a brittle pop. He sighed relief and struck out for his cabin at a careful trot.

Suddenly, he was aware of a presence behind him. Stopping abruptly, he whirled, drawing his sword as he did. Years notwithstanding, the old techniques still worked. The bared blade hissed through the drenched night, a swift, deadly arc.

The leader of the feral dog pack scrambled backward, upending followers. Several set on each other, growling and snapping horribly. The leader sidled to Domel's left, away from the sword. Low to the ground, snarling in a nervous, high tone, it looked for an opening. The rest of the pack, its slender discipline shattered, milled about in disarray. Domel backed away. His heel caught on something, almost tripping him. It was a large rock. Squatting, keeping the sword pointed alternately at the leader and the pack, Domel picked it up.

Instantly, the dog ran, tail between his legs. Domel flung the rock with no hope of doing damage. Resuming his trot, he muttered, "Time to get another hunt together. They get bolder every night. We'll lose another child soon."

Domel made a face. There'd be no more wild-dog hunts for him.

That life was over. It would end with honor, at least. Domel was suddenly aware he still carried his sword bared. Lashing the weapon back and forth, plunging it into the darkness before him, he hurried his pace, invigorated.

When he came through the door into the firelit room, his wife sat in a chair to the right of the hearth. Leaping upright, she clasped both hands at her breast. Fear contorted her features. On the other flank of the fireplace, Domel's youngest son kicked back his chair. He rose quickly, snatching up a sword. For two hammering heartbeats, the trio stood frozen. Domel broke the silence. "It's me, you fools. Who did you expect?"

His wife went on the attack. "You startled us. What's the matter with you?" Her accusatory gaze went to the sword in his hand.

Covering sheepishness with a display of irritation, Domel slammed the weapon into its sheath. "Dogs. Attacked me. Worse every day." He dropped into the chair vacated by his wife, put his hands to the fire's warmth. "There's worse trouble than that, though." He paused, reaching down to unlace soaked boots. His son seized the opportunity to speak.

"We know." The two words drummed like an ultimatum.

Domel masked inner turmoil. "What do you know?"

The son flinched. His mother was made of sterner stuff. "Rendo saw the way

Lorso looked at you tonight. What have you done to offend him so? Rendo said he looked murderous."

"Nothing. I did nothing. It was Tears of Jade." Domel stopped, looking from one to the other. Their rejection was palpable. The import broke over him like a god-wave, the legendary roaring wall from the sea that crushed all before it. "They're going to kill me, send me to the god. We can't stay."

His wife choked, finally made words. "We've done nothing. We made no sin."

Not daring to shout, Domel could only try to project his urgency. "Do you think either of them cares what you've done or not done? Didn't you hear me? They mean to send me to the god, then rule the Skan between them. They'll kill Rendo and his brothers next. Lorso is coming. Tonight. *Now*."

Rendo stepped back. "I can work with Lorso. So can my brothers. They don't even live with you anymore. We haven't offended him." Domel's wife scurried to stand beside her son.

Domel was surprised and pleased at the clarity of his thinking. Sorrow for departure was only the deep, familiar pain of a wound. Shoving wife and son aside, he jammed extra clothing in a waterproof bag. To his wife, he said, "Tell them where I've gone. It may save your life. I'm going to the sacred mountain, claiming sanctuary. Remind Lorso no one can touch me there."

"You'll have to come down for food. He'll wait."

"It's my only chance." Domel shouldered the bag, rushed to the door. There was no reason to peer out. If there was anyone there, he'd find out. If anyone was coming, the flash of light from the door would only warn them of his presence. He faced his wife and son briefly. "My crime was to listen to Tears of Jade. My sin was ambition. Trust was my mistake. You, Rendo: Pray you live to understand."

The door thudded behind him as he dove forward, rolling to the side. The soggy ground absorbed his fall. Rain deadened the faint sound of impact and his scrabbling crawl away from the cabin. He stopped. His sword reached into the darkness, seeking.

Pursuers weren't after him yet. He rose. Moving in a crouch, he set out. Soon, he slowed. His wife was right; even if he reached the god's mountaintop, starvation would eventually force him to confront Lorso.

What good was a god's sanctuary if it merely delayed the will of men?

The trail to Sosolassa's mountain paralleled the arm of the sea that reached to the Skan village. Blasphemous thoughts would reach the god. There would come a tentacle oozing up onto the beach. Inland. Black as night. Domel's mind saw it. Toothed suckers trembled at the thought of warm blood. The tentacle was probably already ahead, waiting. Tears of Jade would never let him reach sanctuary provided by the very god she spoke for.

That didn't make sense. Why didn't she strike when he was listening outside her window? And what did she care about his carefully woven net of obligations and secret knowledge? Couldn't the god tell her what was in everyone's mind?

Every step shriveled Domel's faith a bit more. All his life, the demands and rewards of the god, as spoken through Tears of Jade, provided a satisfying existence. Now that the god's demand was for his life, Domel examined his devotion with a somewhat enhanced focus. Had he wanted to believe? Or followed a code that served his needs?

The whole thing made his head hurt.

If the god was there, he was already sentenced to be weighted and thrown to the sea and Sosolassa's slave barracks. If the god was fallible, why should a Skan warrior stand and wait to be butchered for him?

Domel's heart pounded with a heady, daring rhythm. There was excited purpose in his step when he turned toward the harbor. Soon he was close enough to identify small balancebars nodding sleepily on the restless waters.

There were guards, of course. Slaves, chained to posts, required to sound warning horns and alert the Skan to any raids or unexpected storms. Alertness was life to the slaves. Raiders killed them in order to preserve surprise; if the slaves failed to warn the Skan, they died for their failure.

Foul weather helped cover Domel's stealthy advance. Knowing where the guard would be, he came at the huddled figure from landward. Before striking, Domel hesitated. There was something disturbing about the indistinct form. A helmet. Under the rags the man affected to keep out the weather, he wore a helmet. Domel cursed under his breath. There was probably a leather vest, as well. It all combined with the man's curled-up position to complicate a silent killing stroke. Slowly, gathering himself, Domel came fully erect. The sword climbed higher, hanging in the night like an axe.

The cloth bundled over the helmet dulled the clash of metals. The shrill screech of steel cleaving steel could have been the dying gasp of small night prey. The brittle rattle of the dead slave's chain sounded offended.

Pitching his bag into the closest balancebar, Domel slashed the mooring line. The rocking, rolling hull stirred memories, reflexes. The coarse rasp of braided leather line paying out through a fist filled him with reminiscence. Brine-soaked cedar smelled intoxicating. The wild, terrible sound of his war cry strained in his throat. He pictured himself washed by the resounding echoes.

For one flashing instant, he thought of his family. There had been good years there.

The boat yawed. The mast creaked, a seductive whisper. The outrigger eased back into the water with a barely audible kiss. Domel paddled out to the Throat. He released the yards, hoisted the sail slowly, steadily. There was no pop of wind-stressed cloth, no warning splurge from sudden acceleration. Stealthily, the balancebar knifed seaward.

Domel thought he was just about abreast of his own cabin when the unmistakable gold-gleaming rectangle of an opened door split the night. Light skipped across the water's chopped blackness. Domel slid behind the gunwale, even as he jeered at himself. He was far beyond anyone's vision.

Except Tears of Jade's. And Sosolassa's. Doubt crowded his mind. And fear. He remembered things. Terrible. Inexplicable.

Ahead, churning silver marked the waves of open sea. Laughter shrilled in the rigging. Heavier chuckling, the sound of secret knowing, drummed from the sail.

The balancebar skimmed along. A different scent came to Domel, the unmistakable smell of the full, awesome ocean, its waters free as sky, massively indifferent to land or man.

As the small boat approached, the curling, crashing crests became white forms against the blackness. Some were blunt, irregular. Some were pointed. Domel thought of them as teeth grinding and gnashing in frenzy.

Sosolassa's sea.

Chapter 46

The device gleamed in the sun. Polished brass and copper vied with waxed oak. Spoked iron-shod wheels seemed eager to roll.

The crowd surrounding it at a respectful distance stared. Reactions were varied; some faces showed amusement. Most displayed nervous apprehension. There were a few, however, who seemed to need to share their opinions. They moved with furtive hostility, always intent on Leclerc. Speaking softly, quickly, then passing on, they left a wake of troubled thoughtfulness. Occasionally blatant hatred surfaced, like some putrid bubble bursting.

Leclerc fussed over his newest creation. For all its bright, shiny beauty, the apparatus was an odd-looking thing. Essentially a low-slung, long wagon, the bed was actually a rectangular, pitch-sealed wooden box, slightly less than knee-deep. The box was full of water. A leather hose leading to one of the many wells on the castle grounds assured a ready resupply.

Two tanklike structures, one at the front and one at the back end of the wagon bed, stood with their bottom third in the water. A slimmer, tubular article rose vertically to one side of them; it was centered at the edge of the box. Between the shorter twin tanks—they were about waist-high—stood a sturdy oak stanchion about a third taller yet. A beam was centered on an axle near the top of the stanchion. There were long handles near the ends of the beam. Dropping vertically from the same beam were two vertical posts; these were attached to the top center of what appeared to be lids fitted inside the twin tanks.

The single tube centered between the tanks had unusual features, as well. It was actually two pieces. The narrower top was sleeved into the larger bottom half. A leather gasket sealed the joint. At its upper limit, the slimmer tube became two branches that reached out and then turned back toward each other, creating a flattened circle that looked like two opposing horseshoes. Where the branches joined each other, a nozzle pointed at the sky.

Copper pipes, under the water, connected the bases of the two large tanks with the base of the narrower.

Platforms at the back and front of the shallow wooden tank were obviously intended for someone to stand there, with access to the beam-end handles. A similar platform projected from the side of the wagon next to the tall, slim tube.

Gan and his party arrived. They circled the entire thing curiously. If he noted the whisperers in the crowd he gave no sign. He touched a copper tank. Smiling apology at Leclerc, he wiped away the resulting fingerprint with the tail of his leather vest.

Nalatan came to the rear of the wagon, reached a hand up to one of the horizontal beam handles. He voiced the obvious question. "What is it?"

Instead of answering directly, an excited Leclerc said, "You'll see. I want you to stand on the platform at the front end. I'll get on the back. When I say 'push,' you push down on that handle as hard as you can. That'll raise this end. See how it pivots on that stanchion in the middle? Once your end is down, I'll pull mine down. Then you do the same. Understood?"

Nalatan looked dubious. "We make the beam go up and down?"

"Exactly."

"Why?"

"You'll see." Leclerc's nervous gesture sent Nalatan up onto the forward perch. Leclerc himself moved to the narrow tube. Gripping the top, he twisted. It pivoted until it was nearly horizontal. He hurried back to his handle. At his signal, Nalatan pushed down. Leclerc's end rose. He pulled it down. The vertical arms attached to the beams lifted smaller diameter copper tubes from within the larger tanks, then plunged them back. Wet leather squealed. The machine wheezed, shuddered. Hollow burbling sounds rumbled from the twin tanks. The single narrow tube trembled. There was a sudden gelatinous cough, a monstrous hawking.

Crammed into the confining nozzle, pressured by all the power Leclerc and Nalatan could muster, water erupted from the machine. It jetted over the crowd, splattered against the castle wall, and peeled back as spray. Yelling people dashed to escape. Leclerc raced for the nozzle. Laughing uproariously, Nalatan continued straining at his work. Leclerc pushed the nozzle so the water arced up over the castle wall. On the other side sheep registered startled disapproval.

The dry part of the watching crowd applauded and laughed excitedly. The reaction of the sprayed participants was more mixed in nature. Gan, dripping, guffawing, hurried to Leclerc, slapping him on the back. "You said it moved water, but I'm still amazed. How do you do it?"

Glowing with pride, Leclerc explained. "It's just a pump. The two things that fit inside the large tanks are pistons. Make them go up and down, and they force water into the third tank, then out through that nozzle. Compression does the trick. Imagine four men on a pump like that. Or six."

"What's the purpose?" Emso crowded to the front of the spectators. He was wet, and not amused.

Leclerc answered easily. "Putting out fires. A few of these and we're in less danger of having the place burn behind us while we defend the walls."

"If we're defending the walls, who's going to work those handles? Anyhow, Ola's mostly brick and stone. You've wasted our best metalsmiths' time for weeks. They could have been casting arrowheads, making chain mail."

"I showed you how to make more, better steel, remember? My coke oven made that possible. The men who made this pump learned things; circumference, diameter, radius. This device started a whole apprentice program. You'll have arrowheads."

Emso looked ill and angry at the same time. "You made them learn? What are those things you said? Did you do to the smiths what your friends are doing with the Chosens? You did that to men?"

"I taught them. Is that the word that's choking you? Yes, I taught. To help us all. Even you." Leclerc couldn't resist throwing a taunt into his confession.

Pale, expressionless, Emso stared into Leclerc's eyes for several heartbeats. The entire gathering held its breath. As Emso exhaled, the collective sigh of the crowd was audible. Then Emso said, "Because you are friend to Gan Moondark, I won't use the name we put to magic makers. But I warn you, never say you help me. Not me." His glance flicked at Gan, too quickly to be called a defiance.

Distressed by conflict between trusted companions, Gan saw only the most obvious part of the problem. He hurried to Emso. "Careful, old friend; be calm. Leclerc only did what was necessary to build his . . ." He checked, looked helplessly to Leclerc.

"Pump." Leclerc spat the word.

Gan turned back to Emso, repeated the word. "His pump. I know it's against the old ways, but look what the new ways bring us. Fire's the worst thing that can happen to town or castle. We can fight it better."

Emso was inscrutable. "You're my leader. Since you came to this side of the Enemy Mountains, I've followed you. Ever you make changes. Ever you've been right."

Gan's laughter was relieved. "I've been right because you made it so. Now, tell the truth; if Leclerc had brought us some new weapon, wouldn't you be more enthusiastic? What better weapon than something to save lives, buildings?"

"There are many ways to lose even such a large thing as a city." Emso's glance at Gan was as cryptic as his remark. Still, his lips moved in a tight smile. "But I think only of combat, of spring and those coming to destroy you."

"We'll be ready. Even this new thing may be a weapon."

Emso bobbed his head and left, examining the crowd. There were those who met his eye. Something passed between them. Leclerc could only think of it as approval. He jumped when Nalatan spoke behind him. "You've angered Emso."

"Emso's always angry. You know that."

"Angry at the world. When such a man concentrates on one person, it's a heavy force."

Leclerc was determined to keep the conversation light. "The rest of you should appreciate me, then." He moved to disconnect the pump hose, hoping Nalatan would take the hint and go about his own business.

The move failed. Nalatan joined him, hauling in the leather hose, coiling it. "Emso's confused. He holds to the old ways. Your tribe breaks the restrictions imposed by generations before us."

"You don't seem to mind all of us." The words were gone before Leclerc thought of their full import. He stammered, "I'm sorry. I wasn't thinking. I promised myself—everyone did—we wouldn't say anything that might make you think about . . ." Dismay closed off the words.

Nalatan acknowledged the mangled apology. "I understand, Louis. Truly. You think I'm not aware that no one mentions Donnacee? Or Lanta? Do you really believe I don't see the smirks, hear the whispers?"

"How can you stand it?" Leclerc threw down the hose lashings in the now-empty wooden box, abandoned pretense. "What keeps you from killing some of these idiots who think what's happened is funny?"

"Those contemptibles? I would shame myself." He flashed a smile. Leclerc felt the frustration behind it like a cold edge laid across his throat. He was grateful for Nalatan's continued explanation. "When I left Church to marry my Donnacee, I changed myself. I thought that was so for her, as well."

Watching Nalatan, so outwardly contained, so inwardly agonized, made Leclerc wish he could grab Tate by the shoulders and shake some sense into her. No one should treat another person the way she was treating Nalatan.

In the same steady voice, Nalatan said, "She's much like Emso, you know? He's completely caught in what he believes. Donnacee doesn't see herself that clearly. Emso wants to protect his beliefs. Donnacee wants to find what her beliefs are."

"You're a very understanding man."

Thoughtful, Nalatan looked off to the east. "I understand Donnacee. I don't care if anyone else does. I tell myself I don't care what anyone says or thinks of me, of us. But sometimes the questions come. What if something happens to her? What if I wake up some morning and I *do* care what someone says? What will Nalatan say of the old ways then? What of Nalatan's soul?" He walked away without looking back, leaving Leclerc to wonder if the words were meant to be heard at all.

Finishing the cleaning up, Leclerc drifted through the crowd. Soon he was aware of Bernhardt. She spoke to Carter and Anspach. The two of them cut a furtive glance at him. Then Kate approached him. He pretended not to notice. Jaleeta was missing from the gathering, which was troubling enough, but he was particularly concerned that she'd suddenly appear while he was alone with Kate.

Irritation combined with guilt and set him on edge. Kate Bernhardt was a friend, an ally from the crèche. There was no one in that group he liked as much.

The truth of the last thought was a revelation. It made him all the more cross. Now, if Jaleeta put in an appearance, he'd feel even worse for dismissing Kate.

It was her own fault. He never asked for her company. If she got hurt, it was on her own head.

Kate said, "We've only got a moment before someone interrupts. I wanted to tell you how proud I am. Our contribution to this world hasn't been all that wonderful. You're the one who's been the most constructive. This antique-style fire engine is your best idea yet. Congratulations, Louis. And thanks."

Her expression was warm, admiring. If Jaleeta saw that, she'd think something really stupid. Leclerc said, "It's just a pump; I'm hoping we'll find other uses for it. Anyhow, you three are the ones who're doing the real work. Teaching a new generation of Teachers. That's progressive. I just make toys."

Laughing lightly, Kate put a hand on his arm. Leclerc didn't move. In his mind, he cringed. The touch suggested intimacy, shared feelings and attitudes. Any number of things. It was exactly like her. Somehow she managed to create a sense of calm. Why couldn't she understand he had every reason to be nervous as a cat? He hardly heard her good-bye.

He wished he'd been more welcoming. More polite, anyway. It wasn't that he didn't enjoy Kate's company. He just wanted to be with Jaleeta more. Why couldn't Kate understand?

When Gan retired to the castle the crowd slowly broke up. Working to hitch up the horses and move the pump wagon back to his farmhouse provided Leclerc with time to think. Oddly, his thoughts went to Nalatan's discomfort. It was a short step from there to Lanta and the buzz of scandal when it was realized that she'd ridden off to join Conway.

It was Kate who finally convinced Sylah that Lanta was in no danger of having her religious faith sullied. Forcefully persuasive, Kate's combination of warmth and quiet intensity swayed Sylah, persuaded her that the "religious" aspect of Conway and Tate's trip wouldn't impact on the small Priestess in any way. Leclerc clucked at the two-horse team; for such a reserved woman, Bernhardt could be amazingly compelling.

"No danger." Leclerc voiced the words aloud later as he guided the team into the barn. He wasn't sure exactly why the phrase popped into his mind, but it served to break the oppressive silence, and that was what he needed. The farm was deserted, everyone gone for the regular market day. He unhitched the animals and led them to their stalls. He just finished graining them when he heard the approaching horse.

He wondered if Jaleeta was finally coming. She'd want to see how the pump worked. How would he fill the water reservoir box? Could the two of them power the machine?

The rider appeared in the barn door. Late afternoon sunlight cut across the figure, obscuring it. Craning about, Leclerc advanced. Kate Bernhardt's voice came at him. "I have to talk to you, Louis. I know I'm intruding, but it's important."

As always, she confused him. Her voice was soft, heavy with an urgency that gave it several nuances of intrigue.

Now what if Jaleeta showed up?

"I've got a lot of work to do, Kate. Couldn't whatever's troubling you wait until tomorrow?"

Color flooded her cheeks. "This isn't easy. I'm bringing you news you're not going to like, but I have to talk to you about it. Or go to Gan."

"Me or Gan? It must be important." Leclerc hated the stain of sarcasm, hated himself for not holding it back.

Kate's urgency gave way to exasperation. "They're talking about killing you. Right now I'm trying to make up my mind if I'm warning you because you're important to Gan and the Three Territories, or if it's because I give a damn if you live or die. In fact, I don't think I do."

Yanking on the bridle, she peeled her horse up onto its hind legs and into a pawing, head-tossing turn. Snorting surprise and indignation, it came down running. Before Leclerc could move, Kate was thundering out of the barnyard.

Chapter 47

Just as Leclerc abandoned hope of recalling Kate, he thought he saw her horse slow. He started running again, knowing how foolish he looked, puffing and panting down the muddy track. His strangled yelling sounded equally silly.

Turning in the saddle, Kate stopped. She laughed uproariously. Leclerc swallowed the last part of a shout and nearly choked. Salvaging shreds of dignity, he slowed to a walk. He wished he could look menacing. No one could manage a threatening mien when his feet were slithering about in ankle-deep mud like two pigs in slop. Balance alone demanded near-total concentration; there was none left over for manly posturing.

Kate trotted back. She looked contrite. Amusedly contrite. "I'm sorry, Louis. I lost my temper. You were pretty snotty."

He wished she wasn't so considerate. It blew all the anger out of him. Worse, it made him feel odd. "You caught me at a bad time."

Understanding lingered in Kate's smile, but it threatened to turn sharp. "You made that clear. I thought maybe something happened at your demonstration that troubled you. Or maybe something didn't happen."

Leclerc had the feeling he was being sliced like bacon. He reminded himself he mustn't be short with her. That's how all this got started. Or was it? He wasn't sure of anything anymore. He said, "Come back to the house. Tell me what's up." He reached to the saddle cantle where it flared up behind her. Assuring his balance occupied him for a moment. When he looked back to Kate, he was startled by the change in her manner. She was bleak, brows drawn close, forehead cut by a deep frown.

"I'm afraid, Louis."

"Of what? The war this spring?"

She shook her head, eyes still straight ahead. "I don't know exactly."

Leclerc tried to lighten her mood. "You'll have to do better than that. You said someone's out to kill me. I can't run away until I know which direction is safe."

The weak joke earned a weak smile. "Running won't do it. That's the problem. We've got enemies inside the walls."

"In the castle? That can't be."

"I can't say for sure there's anyone in the castle. I know there are people in the Territories who actively oppose Gan. And us."

"We've known that all along. What's happened to frighten you? And don't you think it's about time for names?"

Kate blushed furiously. "It's gossip. Some of the Violet Abbey sisters aren't completely controlled by their Abbess. They tell us bits and pieces. Some people here are terrified by the things you do: We see invention, they see perversion. They hate us. They're really afraid of you. The Violet Priestesses say four Barons seem to be working together a lot. Priestesses have overheard conversations. Nothing incriminating, but suggestive."

"Come on, Kate; everyone in the Territories knows those old aristocrats miss their good old days. It's the same old story; the rich always know what's best for the poor."

"They love power, and Gan took it from them. The Priestesses say men trade with the returned Mountain People. And there's talk that fishermen go out at strange times and won't tell anyone where they've been. Some say they deal with Skan."

They were at Leclerc's place by then. He tied up Kate's mount while she stepped to the ground. Walking across the raised stone porch into the house, he said, "No one's ever stopped trade, Kate. I know, I know; the Priestesses suspect some sort of spying going on. Don't you think Gan's got his own spies working that territory? He's no fool. And Gan's ordered everyone to put away as much food as possible for spring. I'd be suspicious if the fishermen weren't going out. They're doing what they've been told."

While Leclerc threw kindling on the coals and fanned up a flame, Kate moved to a chair. She decided to wait for him to finish his chore before arguing further. Looking around the room, she allowed herself to mentally step away from her deeper concerns for the moment.

It was unmistakably a bachelor's cave. Equally, it could belong to no one but Louis. A desk stood piled with drawings and plans and pages of notes. Kate thought of her small Chosens, straining to grasp the simplest arithmetic. One day he'd make them aware of angles and diameters, of levers and pulleys, of friction and gravity. Pride swelled in her. Sylah brought the treasures of the Door, but it was herself and her friends who could teach the Chosens.

She snuggled deeper into the absorbing warmth of her leather armchair, telling herself to remember to get the name of the man who made them. They were Louis' design, she knew.

Leclerc turned from the fireplace. She reluctantly straightened, surrendering her chair's comforting embrace. "Everything you say is true, Louis, but you're only putting a different face on the same facts. Anyhow, the Violet Abbess herself has said some things about 'when Church discipline is reestablished.' Last week she was openly wondering what Church would do with the 'ruined' Chosens. I think she'll cast them out if she ever gets the chance."

Leclerc shrugged. "Probably. She's mean enough. That doesn't prove—"

Kate cut him off. "Think, Louis. You cast out Chosens, you withdraw the protection of Church from orphan children. Where do you think they go? To lunch? They've got one future: slavery. She knows that."

"Oh, someone would take them in." Leclerc blustered, waved his arms. "Anyway, it's just an old woman, shooting off her mouth. You see a threat to Gan? Really?"

"You bet I do. Not just Gan. Let me give you another of the good Abbess' pithy observations: 'Cut off the branches, kill the tree.' Does that suggest anything to you?"

"Does it make any difference? You're going to educate me anyhow."

"I can educate children; a fool may be beyond me. Didn't you hear the fear and anger in Emso today? All the things you've given Gan have marked you. I've seen your face when women hide their children from you. They call us Teachers witches, too. We speak of equality and we teach girls. Those are unforgivable crimes. But you. You do things no one can explain, make things no one's ever seen. In your case, they *believe*."

A rack of fire tools hung from the stone face of the fireplace. Taking the brass poker, Leclerc shuffled it around in the coals. The end of the instrument was cast in the shape of a man's head, mouth open, eyes wide. When Leclerc lifted it, with sparks swirling around the end, it looked as if the tiny face spewed fire and ash. For a moment, Leclerc stared at the thing. He jammed it back into the rack, nearly dislodging the other tools. When he faced Kate again, his jaw was set. "I won't let a lot of rumors keep me from perfecting things that mean progress."

Kate shook with anger. "Don't lecture me. I knew I shouldn't have come here. You wouldn't listen to me if I told you two and two is four." She whirled. The heavy Church robe flared in a warning circle. On her way to the door she flung a last remark over her shoulder. "You'd be safe if your enemies knew you as well as I do. Just an overgrown boy, smart enough to build lethal toys and way too stupid to be a witch."

The door was cedar planks, steel banded. A full two inches thick, it was proof against the strongest arrows, built to hold off a man with an axe for an appreciable time. When Kate slammed it, she put her back into it. The entire house shuddered. Leclerc yanked the door open again.

Kate sat her horse, backing away from the hitching rail. She matched Leclerc's glare. A blink multiplied her ire. Blinking was weakness. But she had to. The tears would have come, otherwise, and that was even worse. She told herself she had to avoid breaking the delicate thread that was once the rich fabric of their friendship.

He held out both hands. "I didn't ask to come to this world, Kate. No more than you did. But now that it's happened, I'm going to be everything I can be. Everything. I won't be distracted."

Kate's heart closed like a fist. He didn't understand anything. "Oh, forget it. Just forget it." She pulled her horse's head around.

To make her humiliation total, she looked up to discover Jaleeta a stone's throw away. Kate turned to see if Louis knew of the other woman's approach. Instantly, she regretted it. Leclerc stood on the porch, so tense he might have been impaled.

This was the second time this had happened; Kate wondered what miserable fate planned her life. Still, the sight of the other woman eased the fire burning in her. By the time she reached the gate, her departure and Jaleeta's arrival literally simultaneous, there was nothing left but cold, bitter ash.

Jaleeta smiled too sweetly. "I heard you were coming this way. I hoped we could talk. Do you really have to leave? I suppose you must. It must be terribly demanding, being a mother to so many children. And not a father in sight." She laughed merrily.

Kate found a smile. "It's work. Not as tiring as trying to make a father out of every man in sight." Kate intended her laughter to have a sneering ring. Instead, it raked at her ears as a grating cackle. Jaleeta's composure actually cracked. Back straight, head up, Kate rode on. Inwardly, she worried. Behind that shining beauty she'd seen an even brighter evil.

Kate slowed. She should go back. Not even Jaleeta would seduce a man in front of a witness. Then Kate asked herself why she should bother. She couldn't be present all the time. Nor did she want to be. She heeled her horse into a ground-eating trot, suddenly anxious to get home. She couldn't compete with Jaleeta. If there was to be a struggle for Louis, something besides physical beauty would have to win it for Kate Bernhardt, she told herself. It was a heartrending admission.

Jaleeta bubbled with enthusiasm. "Everyone's talking about your new machine. They think you're wonderful." Her teasing smile hinted at how much she agreed with them. "I want to see it myself. Will you show me? Please?"

Jaleeta was dressed in a formfitting blouse with overlying vest, and matching trousers caught up in ornately decorated calf-high boots. The vest material was heavy linen, the blouse of the finest cotton. Both were a very pale beige, simply decorated. The window behind her was pieced glass, salvaged from godkills, and she made a perfect foil for the multicolored light. Jaleeta could never have explained the effect, that of a polished ivory figurine serene against the clash and vibrancy of hue and visual tension. She sensed it, however. She moved across the window, displaying.

Leclerc rushed to grant her request. Leading her toward the barn, he pointed out his large flock of chickens, indicating the effects of controlled breeding. Similarly, he drew her attention to the horses, cattle, and sheep roaming the adjacent fields. As they approached the barn, she linked her arm through his, gazing up at him. "You do so many things, Louis. Doesn't it bother you when someone says you do magic?"

"You mean Emso?"

She looked away.

Leclerc grew expansive. "Emso doesn't like to think about change. I want to change everything." He swung his free hand in an all-encompassing arc. The other clamped harder on Jaleeta's. "Where my friends and I came from, people had a name for me. I was called a 'tinker.' I liked to work with things, fix what was broken, make stuff. And I like excitement, too. I like challenge."

They were entering the barn, then, a huge, dim place. High in the rafters, sparrows chattered constant aggression and complaint. Directly ahead, the pump gleamed softly. Jaleeta stopped, looked away from the machine. She wrinkled her nose, distracted, and aimed a questioning, unpleased look at Leclerc.

He hesitated, puzzled, then smiled broadly. "That smell bothers you? Hides tanning. I use a lot of leather, so we make it here. And the black powder uses sulfur and other things, too. Then there's the coke ovens, off there in the distance. Lots of smells. A price of progress." Quick, distracted irritation touched his features. When he spoke again, it was defensive. "I've said it before, and I meant it: I'm going to be everything I can be. It didn't exactly work out that way for me before, but this time it's going to be different. I'm in the game to the last card. No more tinker, no more fixer. This time it's builder. Creator."

Without realizing it, Leclerc had turned during his speech. He faced Jaleeta. His hands gripped her shoulders. The pressure of his attention caused her to take a rearward step. He leaned closer. A second step followed, and then another. An object stopped her abruptly, painfully. She exclaimed aloud. Leclerc paused. Awareness softened his features. Still, he maintained his grip. He spoke softly, confiding. "It's appropriate that you should bump into this thing. A symbolism. This is power."

Looking at the device, Jaleeta tingled with an inexplicable understanding of his meaning. The rough oak was rock-solid, but there was life in it. And death. Her eyes devoured the thing, its rough, plaited cord, the geared wheel and handle on its side. Brass gleamed, and cold iron's sullen gray-black called for her to touch its menace. She reached, both hands caressing. Inhaled, taking in oiled wood, soft leather, hammered metal.

Satisfaction honeyed Leclerc's voice. "This is where it comes from, Jaleeta. Power starts with this. And this." He pointed to the catapult, then to his head. "Power isn't a man's arm, or clever schemes, or daring deeds. It's knowing. And I'm the one who knows. There are more wonderful things to come. Each of them a step forward for me. And you."

"Please. We have to talk. While we can. I promised we'd see each other. You know how I feel toward you. But I lied when I came today. I didn't just come to see your new magic. I came to say we can't be together the way we . . . I hoped."

He stared. "You have someone else?"

Mute, she turned away. She shook her head.

"Tell me. Who?"

"No one. I can't."

"You have to." He came to her, put out a consoling, pleading hand. He stroked her hair.

Covering her face with both hands, she shook her head. "It's a secret. I'm not supposed to know. I don't dare tell."

"You can tell me. You must. I'm here to protect you. I promise."

"It's too dangerous. You'll get hurt. I couldn't live with that. Louis, please: I owe you my life. I can't risk yours."

"No one's going to hurt us." His gentle embrace pulled her close. She calmed, taking strength from him.

"Gan has to make stronger alliances, protect the hold he has on the Territories. He wants to . . . to use me. A gift."

Sick with disappointment, with disillusion, Leclerc denied the possibility. "We won't let it happen. It's savage." Almost as an afterthought, he asked, "Has he told you who?"

Her head moved against his chest in a small, sorrowful negative. "He never said anything to me. Only to Neela. She told me. But it's a secret, Louis. She's been so good. I can't cause her trouble. Please, promise you won't ever tell."

"Certainly. But who does Gan have in mind?"

Silence fell over them, a thing Leclerc felt he could reach out and tear apart.

He gripped Jaleeta tighter as her arms stole up to wrap around his waist. Clutching him as if he anchored her to hope, she finally spoke. "Emso."

Chapter 48

The voice of the north wind in the rigging sang of cold. Sometimes it crooned, in a low throbbing that spoke of muscles so chilled they cracked when forced to move. Another song was faster, stronger, its message one of hopelessness, of icy wind and water draining a man's will so he sagged, waiting for death. Worst of all was the shrill wailing of the stormwitches. Every Skan had a tale of the invisible women called stormwitches. Their evil hands tangled the lines, ripped the sails. The worst were from the north. Their breath turned flesh and blood to stone, their voices numbed the mind.

Grunting incoherent pain, Domel leaned into the tiller. Stormwitches knew he steered by sound and feel; they redoubled efforts to confuse him. He put a hand in his mouth, bit hard on the fingers. The pain helped him think; the touch of warmth restored a moment's flexibility.

North wind drove the sea down on his stern. What he felt for was the reflected wave, a counter to that force. Only a man who'd tested waters all his life would feel it at all. Even to Domel, it was almost indistinguishable in the flow and thunder of the torn sea. Not quite quartering, almost exactly three heartbeats apart, the echo deep in the water came to him.

During those brief lulls when the stormwitches paused for breath, he heard the boom of breaking waves. Those, too, told him where he was.

Instinct was his timekeeper. Without a horizon or stars, he could only guess how long before dawn. Not that it would be very bright. The storm had the smell of the far Ice Ocean, a promise of somber days, opaque. Domel searched his conscience, asking himself if he was considering a run for land because it was time, or if he was simply beaten. He decided it was time.

Both mornings since his departure, sharkers beat the coastline, looking for him. For two days he'd sheltered in tiny clefts before resuming the sea at night. Again, he needed a secure hiding place before sunrise caught him out in the open.

Thinking of Tears of Jade's revenge warmed his blood. He worked a bit more smoothly, changing course, edging closer to land.

He knew exactly where he wanted to touch. There was a small bay, with a narrow, almost hidden entry. It featured a place where a creek ambled through a marshy valley before feeding into the sea. Sharkers used the bay from time to time. Hauling the balancebar inland would be a struggle, but it had to be done.

He wanted to call up a young Domel, the one who knew that three freezing nights and two days without sleep or food were nothing. In spite of everything, he laughed aloud. Time rearranged memory most kindly, but there were some lies a man couldn't even accept about himself.

Domel set his course. Making this landfall was the greatest challenge yet. Sosolassa would send waves like mountains. Stormwitches would scream in his ears, cut him with ice knives. But he must try. Without rest, fire, warm food—soon—the race was over.

He searched the blackness so hard his eyes watered. The god lifted waves ahead of him, disguised the tattered white tops to look like the rocks marking the harbor entrance. Wind caromed off the land, set up swirls and eddies to confuse him. Domel sneered. The god couldn't disguise the sound of the right surf, couldn't make the wind do anything Domel didn't know about. These were Skan waters, and Domel exulted in his knowledge of them.

Skepticism and sheer, raw arrogance warred with religious fear.

The headland loomed suddenly. Dim, menacing, it roared challenge: Execute the turn properly and live to chance the chaotic winds of the tiny bay; miss the turn and go down. To the lusting god.

The balancebar skidded around the guardian rocks. Domel hung on, shouting defiance, muscles afire with effort. The sea crashed around him, over him, clawed at his hand on the tiller. Taking one last risk, he aimed the prow for what he believed to be the creek mouth. At full speed, he drove across the small bay. Wind-whipped reeds slashed at him. The dread grate of hull on rock failed to sound. Then branches clutched at his clothes, screeched along the hull, grappled with the rigging. Their presence meant he was past the marsh itself. The boat lurched to a halt. The actual stream channel was a boat-length to his right.

Snuffling with exhaustion, Domel fought collapse. There was work. Drop the slatting, banging sail. Lower the mast. Raise the balancebar. He cursed pain, his awkward, cold-stiffened body. Paddling, he moved upstream. When the hull scraped bottom, he stepped out, pushed inland. At last, tying off to a tree, he staggered away. In the lee of a downed log, he sagged to his knees. He was asleep before his body hit the ground.

The next morning, wrapped in soaked hides, shivering under the lash of continuing rain, Domel held his breath as the sharker prowled the inlet. The sight brought a pained, grim smile. Tears of Jade and Lorso must be mad with fury, he thought smugly. Nothing else would force sharkers out in this weather, or spur them to search so diligently.

Approaching the mouth of the creek, the slim hull seemed to tense. Domel watched with a mix of fear and heartbreak. In the depths of his being, he felt the living hull. Sharkers were predators, like their masters; Domel believed that. Right now the vessel whispered to its captain. It smelled prey.

While oarsmen steadied the boat, others manned the side, scanning the reeds for signs of passage. The few broken stems at the mouth of the creek were scrutinized, dismissed. Slowly—reluctantly, Domel believed—the vessel slid back out to open sea.

Domel knew he was seeing the last of his life as Skan. He thought of cool mornings, with wisps of fog draped across valleys. Evenings, rich with the sounds of his people and aromatic coils of smoke from driftwood fires. He closed his eyes to savor memories of the rough beauty of his mountains, his cragged coast.

The search would last perhaps another two days. He was confident he'd avoid it, now. This place was good shelter. The storm would end about the time the searchers tired of looking for him.

It was time to consider exactly what he'd done. Sosolassa's spirit woman herself wanted him dead. To escape her, he'd dared the god's sea, the wrath of the god's stormwitches.

He lived. And planned. He would have fire. Food.

For the first time in many, many moons, Domel felt the prickle of bloodlust jitter across his skin. He grinned, teeth white against gray-cold flesh, wild eyes blue-bright as ice. "Skan. I live. To kill. Again."

Chapter 49

"He was very aggressive." Jaleeta looked away from Emso's fierce glare. The toe of her boot drew a formless squiggle in the damp sand of the beach. Holding her breath made her face red, exactly as if she blushed. "I wasn't really afraid. I don't think he'd hurt me, really. I'm just a girl. Maybe it's all my fault. I don't understand men."

"How was he aggressive? What's he done?"

Jaleeta took a quick half step that almost put her in contact with Emso. "He didn't do anything exactly improper. It's just that . . ." She turned away, hugged herself. "He acted like he could do anything he wanted. Like I didn't have anything to say about it."

"You never should have gone there. Especially alone. I hate to sound like your father." Emso swallowed audibly. Stiffly formal, he resumed. "I know what I'm talking about. Stay away from Leclerc. In the future, when someone acts as if he's interested in you, tell me. You're a beautiful woman, and far too trusting."

She frowned darkly. Her voice quivered. "Why do you insist on talking about your years as though they shame you? First your words tell me I'm a woman. Then they tell me I'm too young to think of myself that way. Your age makes you attractive, gives you character and strength. Other women tell me I'm lucky to be able to walk with you, talk with you, because you're my friend. They speak freely because they see how you think I'm just a child. They embarrass me. Am I so insignificant?"

Nonplussed, Emso stammered. A crescent-shaped scar by his right ear contrasted whitely with his red, sweating face. "You're the most significant person alive. I mean . . . what I said . . . the thing I meant is that I don't want to see you hurt. You're too important. You mean too much to me." The last ended on a rising note of surprise.

Jaleeta seized on it. "To you, Emso? Not to Gan Moondark?"

"Gan? What's he have to do with this?"

"Nothing." Once again, she turned away. She hesitated, head down, then walked off, shoulders slumped.

He was beside her in two long strides. He forced good humor. "Whoa, there;

I expect straight answers from my friends. And I expect them to answer like adults, not like little children that the other women tease."

Her smile forgave. "Everyone says you're so harsh, so ferocious. I wish they could see you as I do."

"Never mind the flattery. I want to know why you mentioned Gan."

"It's nothing. Everyone knows how you love him. Everyone knows men like you know what's best for the Territories, what's best for all of us."

"I never said I know what's best for everyone. Neither did Gan." She shot him a sharp, disbelieving look, and he went on hurriedly. "He rules. He doesn't tell young women how to live."

Walking again, she said, "Rulers have to do things other people don't. Or can't." She sounded bitter.

Stopping, Emso called, "Wait." When she turned, he went on. "I don't understand hints and sideways remarks, Jaleeta. I speak my mind. I don't deal with those who don't."

Jaleeta ran back, embraced him impulsively. "What a loyal heart you are. The Territories will never know how fortunate they are to have you. You make my small troubles seem so unimportant. But they're important to me, and I do want your help." She tilted back, turned pleading eyes on him. He waited. At last she continued, with the faintest touch of asperity, as though Emso missed a cue. "We talked about Louis taking me for granted. Don't you think he might have a reason?"

Coloring yet again, Emso nodded. "It's the way men are."

Irritation swept away the beseeching manner. "Do I have to shout? I think he expects Gan to give me to him. Oh, he'd never say it out loud—and I forbid you to ever say a word—but we both know Gan's in Louis' debt for the magic things he makes. A king rewards those who keep him in power. Just as they forget to reward those who brought them to power."

"That's uncalled for. Gan's never forgotten his friends, nor will he. He doesn't give away humans, either. He's no slaver."

"That's not what I meant. A woman can be pushed into a marriage very subtly. He'll push Louis on me, make it impossible for me to talk to other men. Eventually, I'll have no choice."

"Your imagination stretches too far. Gan's said nothing. Leclerc's said nothing. Yet you have your whole future planned out."

"I knew that's what you'd say. You do think I'm just a child. Or a thoughtless woman, good only for breeding. I think through a problem, and you call it imagination. See if I come to you for any more help."

Jaleeta flounced away, remembering to throw her hips wide at each step. She listened confidently. When his hands dropped onto her shoulders, she was ready, stopped instantly. Emso's momentum brought them into hard contact. When he rebounded, she pressed back against him. She affected a tiny catch in her throat, saying, "Oh, Emso, hold me. I'm so confused. I don't want to belong to a man I don't want. I don't want to offend Gan, who's given me such a good life. I don't want to quarrel with you."

For a space of several breaths, he said nothing. The silence ground into Jaleeta.

Had she pushed too hard? Was his loyalty truly that solid? The false sob; was it too much?

Emso's words rumbled. "I have to think. But while I live, no man will have you against your will."

Spinning around, she clung to him, hiding the irrepressible delight and triumph that consumed her plans in an instant.

The Violet Abbess twitched the reins, moved her horse as close as possible to Emso's. In a confidential near-whisper, she said, "Don't frown so, my friend. You did well to come to me."

Emso shook his head. The confounded buzzing refused to go away. "When I told you I had a question, you said you'd no time to talk, that you were on your way to a meeting. When I insisted, and you listened, you said I must come with you. Why the change, Abbess? And why so reluctant to discuss a simple matter like Jaleeta's future?"

"I'm a Healer, Emso." Her look was arch. "My art is to comprehend symptoms. What you tell me of Jaleeta's situation is merely one symptom. Others have seen different ones. They also seek my advice."

"I know nothing of illness. I'm not going anywhere where someone's sick."

"There are many sicknesses. Jaleeta's problem is one kind."

"She feels pressure from Gan that may or may not be real. How is that sickness?"

The Abbess sighed. "For all the harm Sylah's done, she's right that Church must lead the way in assuring that women can't be bought and sold. Gan should realize his attempt to force Jaleeta into marriage is a sign of disrespect for Church."

"We don't know he's forcing her into anything. And Gan is Church's truest defender. Where else is Church as free as in the Three Territories?"

"Nowhere. And we all pray for him because of it. What we fear is the apostate Teachers. His understanding of Church becomes warped. The very love he has for us is used against the true Church. See how he's forcing Jaleeta."

"You don't *know* that." Emso's temper forced words through clenched jaws.

"He's certainly not going to shout it, is he?" The Abbess reached to pat Emso's clenched fist. "What would you say if I told you it was Gan's suggestion that Jaleeta visit Leclerc?"

"She told you that? Why didn't she tell me?"

The Abbess ignored the question. "Such an act is a knife aimed at all women's status. A threat like that is a threat to Church, yet Gan says he is Church's protector. He never lies. What are we to make of these contradictions?"

Sullen, Emso sought relief in reminiscence. He remembered the early days in Jalail. Those were bad days, full of fear, torn by loss. But they were men, then, bonded together like boards nailed one to another. One leader, one goal.

One goal. Even then, Gan knew his fate. He faced anything, knowing he must conquer or die. He was a true leader, one who knew the friends who raised him to his place, who would gain him ever greater glory. But gaining glory was the easy part. Simple courage and daring answered all questions. Being a ruler was more, meant holding power the way a rider grips the reins of a horse. Or the handle of a sword. Murdat.

The Violet Abbess broke his meandering. "I'm taking you to another friend of Church. A man who loves Gan as I do. He's had his differences with Gan, granted, but they stem from Gan's senseless rush to accept Sylah's outlawed version of Church. Other than that, he idolizes Gan Moondark and wishes him only good."

"And who would this fine man be?"

"Baron Ondrat."

Emso goggled. "That old Olan? He'd rather die than allow women any freedom or Church any influence. Are you making fun of me?"

"I was never more serious. It's only Gan's new arrogance that keeps him from seeing how much Ondrat's changed. Has Ondrat asked a solitary favor, even a change in attitude toward himself, since rescuing Sylah? He's too proud. Also, he knows how many of the old Olan nobles hate Gan, and how many of Gan's other friends distrust all Olans. Ondrat is a more thoughtful, better friend than Gan knows." She glanced around, dropped her voice even lower, forcing Emso to lean toward her to hear. "Again, I must fall back on my experience as a Healer to make my point. It's very simple: The patient rarely knows what's best for him. To grow well, the patient must be made to understand the nature of the illness. Only then can there be effective treatment. Gan must be made to see himself as others see him. You understand?"

Nodding, Emso drifted away from her.

It was very unsettling to discover that someone else was concerned about the changes in Gan. Just as he was trying to put his own thoughts in order, the Abbess touched on the very qualities he was afraid to consider.

Loyalty. Trust. Humility.

Emso worried his lip between his teeth. Gan was supposed to help Church, not split it. Ondrat was too slippery by far, but he understood the necessity for one united Church. That was the way it used to be, the way it must always be.

Equality. The word was destroying Gan Moondark, undoing all the good he'd accomplished. No one quarreled with equality for men, and intelligent men understood that women deserved some. What Gan couldn't understand was that the Teachers destroyed the difference between men and women. It was one thing for a woman to know how to work leather or make pots, or anything else that earned her a living. The trouble came with reading and writing. Once women got their hands on that, they'd all want to be merchants, with the power that money brings, and they'd want to teach more women, so pretty soon all of them would be reading and writing and doing numbers. Then who'd watch the children? Who'd take care of the homes?

By helping destroy Church, Gan undercut the one force that could keep social balance.

Grudgingly, Emso conceded that the black powder was a good thing. Still, like reading or numbers, it was something that had to be understood for exactly what it was. At least Gan realized it was a weapon. Leclerc was brilliant to create it, a fool to think ordinary people could use it to break ordinary rocks and so forth. A stupid concept. Then he made things worse. The coke, for making steel. Cut the ground right out from under the charcoal makers, that did. Worse, it made it too easy for just anyone to get his hands on better steel. Smiths were turning out far more quality material.

Now it was a pump. Typical. No understanding of people. Anyone could see; once people knew there was a way to put out a house fire, everyone'd want a pump for his part of the city. Or one for every neighborhood. Or more than one. There'd be no end to it. They'd get careless. Whole place would go up.

Emso felt ill. It seemed everything conspired to move Gan farther and farther from the truth. Farther from the real Gan.

Chapter 50

Emso bristled at his first sight of Baron Ondrat's fortified village. The ugly heap shouted presumption, squatting broadly on its knoll, lording it over the small walled town. An ostentatious banner flew from the castle's central tower. Emso conceded there was a certain rightness in the design, at least. Whichever ancestor chose a boar's head as the Ondrat totem must have anticipated his presiding descendant.

The outer defensive wall was made of huge vertical logs. Emso sniffed. Although they'd require great heat to ignite, once aflame, they were certain to set off the buildings behind, which were far too close. Secondly, the rank vegetation growing in the fields around the walls was untrimmed and ungrazed. There was abundant cover for a surprise attack. Grass even hung over the outer edges of the downed drawbridge, proof that it hadn't been raised and the mechanism checked for a long time. There weren't even guards on the wall. A muddy trail led from the east gate to a mounded midden at the edge of the forest. Rats scampered on the accumulated offal in broad daylight. Emso muttered, "This kennel belongs to the man who thinks to correct Gan Moondark? Agh! Ten hungover Wolves, that's all I'd need. Flatten this festered wart before breakfast. Needs burned just to get clean."

"You spoke?" The Violet Abbess fixed him with a challenging glare.

"Only thinking what to say to the Baron when we discuss military matters."

"We're here to speak of helping Gan. There won't be any need of that."

"Oh, there may be," Emso said easily. Ondrat's slovenly barony was the only hopeful subject to come along all day, he considered sourly. More, it was the first thing he'd completely understood. And now there was going to be more discussion, more argument. He fell in listlessly behind the Abbess. She led the way across the drawbridge. A lone guard, slouched inside the wall, picked his teeth with a twig as they rode past.

Despite the general decrepitude of the buildings, despite the litter cluttering the streets and narrow alleys, Emso smiled, tried to appear friendly. The people of the town who bothered to meet his gaze did so with blunt curiosity. Emso felt it as half antipathy, half repressed hostility.

A man bellowed angrily. Emso turned to see him standing over a woman. Disregarding a veritable rain of shouted abuse, she scrambled on hands and knees, snatching at a spilled basketload of apples that bounced and rolled brightly in the street rubbish. Another woman, accompanied by a man Emso assumed to be her husband, bent to help. Her escort yanked her upright. She yelled at the pain, but that was all. The man making all the noise looked to the husband, who smiled openly. "All alike," he said, jerking a thumb from his wife to the other woman. "Always in the way. I saw what happened. You all right?"

The angry man grunted. "Ran right into me. Lucky I didn't get juice on me, or something. Ought to put them back in the women's market, where they used to be." He obviously had more to say, but he caught his new friend's warning lift of the chin. Turning, the offended one looked directly up at Emso. He set his jaw in sullen defiance before turning away. At his feet, the market woman was struggling to rise. He said, "It wasn't my fault. You should have looked where you were going." With a sidelong squint in Emso's direction, the man strode off. The husband and wife beamed smiles for the Abbess and Emso as they, too, left.

The woman, finally upright, and with most of her apples back in her basket, bowed low to the Abbess. Freeing a hand, she made a clumsy three-sign. The Abbess acknowledged it with a tiny nod. The woman said, "I tried to get out of his way. I really did. He was too big, going too fast. I think my skirt's torn." Distracted, her head swiveled constantly as she tried to combine propriety and the search for lost fruit.

"It's the price we pay for equality." The Abbess edged her mount closer to the woman. It lowered its head, nuzzling aside a noisome pile of decaying cabbage. After a loud snuffle, it rose with an apple. The fruit disappeared in a satisfied crunch. Pretending not to notice the market woman's expression, the Abbess went on. "Equality means men no longer protect us from other men. It means if you wish to sell your apples in what used to be the men's market, you should expect no favoritism. It's wrong for women to be unequal, of course, but now that we have equality, we must be careful to be fair. We're not as strong as men. It's our responsibility to remember, and avoid conflict."

The woman paused in her search. A minute gleam flicked across her eyes. "I was trying to avoid conflict. I was trying to keep from getting dumped on my a . . . apples."

"You must forget the incident, remember the principle. Without equality, you wouldn't be allowed to sell here, where the men have traditionally been. Equality means you share the best selling place, and the hazards thereof."

"The old place was a muddy sinkhole. No one came to buy. What good's this equality thing if all we get is more work and more abuse from the likes of that hog that knocked me down?"

"Oh, that's beyond me, beyond Church. The rule of the land says it must be so, and I can only try to explain to those Church used to protect."

Thoughtfully, the woman nodded. The Abbess spurred her horse forward.

Coming abreast of her, Emso said, "I never thought of that, what you told that woman. With someone like Gan to make sure equality worked, it seemed flawless. There are problems I never thought of."

"That's not your responsibility. Sylah and her alien friends started all this when Gan first assumed power. That was in your own home; Jalail, wasn't it? Your traditional Baron died. Or was killed. Something."

Before Emso could respond, they were at the gate of the castle. The encircling defensive wall was a simple raised mound of dirt with a few rock-faced emplacements. The best Emso could say for it was that it was commanded by arrow slits in the stone walls of the castle itself.

Two towering doors, painted red, decorated with black boars' heads facing each other, admitted directly into the great room. It was cold, dank, dark. Tattered banners and weapons hanging from the walls and cross beams celebrated past Ondrat triumphs. Emso noted their age. Victory in battle appeared to be a thing of memory. The nearest wall held a collection of armor, in the Olan style. The heavy metal torso pieces and leg shields were suspended from hooks. Above them, polished helmets with flowing horsetail plumes sat on a shelf.

Smoke backdrafting from a series of fireplaces thickened air already cloyed with mint and soap. Emso smiled to himself; Ondrat was making an effort to live up to Gan's insistence on cleanliness.

Ondrat entered at the far end of the great room. He greeted his guests warmly, dressed in surprisingly formal attire. His russet wool shirt was clean, quite probably new. Over that was a gleaming leather jacket, well-oiled and rubbed. Boots complemented the jacket's quality workmanship; they were laced up the side, highly polished. Wool homespun trousers were tucked inside in order to display the striking circlet of blue jay feathers at the top of each boot. On his left wrist, clamped outside the shirt, was a huge silver bracelet. It featured the same boar's head as the flag. On his right wrist was another bracelet, steel, large enough to be considered an arm guard. In fact, Emso noticed with increased interest, there were several deep scars in the metal.

Once the Abbess and Emso were comfortably seated in soft leather sling chairs in front of the largest fireplace, Ondrat carefully inspected the entire room. It took long enough to try the patience of the Abbess. "Surely you don't suspect disloyalty from your house people?"

Finishing, Ondrat said, "I don't suspect, Abbess; I expect. That way all my disappointments at least have a pleasant aftermath."

The Abbess took charge of the conversation. "I've already told Emso about your concern for Gan and Church. You know Emso. You, a warrior and a noble, can most appreciate the loyalty that's made his name the most honored in the Three Territories." She looked directly into Emso's eyes. "I say these things not to embarrass you, but to emphasize the purity of what we discuss here today. Of all men, you are the last to tolerate any mark on the honor of Gan Moondark. We mean to lift him to greater glory. We mean to bring him to Church."

Emso looked away. "I love Church, Abbess. As does Gan. And, in her way, so does Sylah." At the Abbess' recoil, Emso stuck out his chin. "Your feud with the former Rose Priestess has spilled over into your relationship with Gan, and that pains me more than I can say. There's good reason for Sylah to be uncertain. Disaffected, even. The one called the Harvester, who rules Church as Sister Mother now, tried to kill Sylah. Not after Sylah was cast out, but when she was still a Rose Priestess. The Harvester tried to kill Violet Priestess Lanta when she was still one of yours."

Tenting her fingertips under her chin in a prayerful attitude, the Abbess shed anger, grew solemn. "Corruption at such levels as Sylah and Lanta occupied is unique in the history of Church. It shattered the Sister Mother. She reacted badly, and has repented at great length." Then, shifting expressions with dazzling speed, she was confiding. "But what repentance from Sylah? She who sullies the souls of our innocent Chosens, leads our beloved Gan to contaminate all the old ways. When you see her and the alien women, with their unknown ways and histories, who else do you see? Leclerc." The Abbess sat back in relaxed triumph. "What friend for a witch if not another witch?"

This time Emso didn't bother to hide a jerky, darting three-sign. Still, he refused to abandon a friend. "I know Sylah. Gan trusts her."

Ondrat showed a feral smile. "Without trust, there can be no closeness. Without closeness, no betrayal. What witch admits her condition?"

"Or her conversion." The Abbess' sly suggestion made Emso blink. She attacked. "When Sylah led Lanta, Conway, and Tate south, her quarrel was with the Harvester, not with Church. Since returning, however, has Sylah ever affirmed loyalty to Church? Church was—is—her only family. Is that a natural thing? Sister Mother said what she's become, and Church speaks truth. Eat the pain of the truth, admit the truth. Witchcraft."

Emso shook his head, mute, miserable.

The Abbess looked to Ondrat. Her nod was almost infinitesimal. He said, "There's proof, Emso. If you've the heart for it."

Red-rimmed eyes fixed Ondrat with a look of murder. The Baron took a quick step backward, raised the hand with the steel wrist guard. "I meant no wrong word, friend. What I can show you is harsh. I want your word you'll draw no weapon in my castle."

"So long as I'm not attacked." The words could have blown in from a cave, chill with implication.

Ondrat spun on his heel, practically trotted to the door. Flinging it open, he gestured for someone to enter.

Domel stepped into view.

"Skan." Emso spat the word as he rose, hand to sword.

Waiting for just that move, the Abbess reached to check him. "It's all right. He's one of us, now."

Emso made a growling noise deep in his chest. The Abbess tightened her grip. As Ondrat approached cautiously, she continued. "Listen to Ondrat. Meet this man. He's come to help us, risked his life for us."

Domel stepped forward. "My name is Domel, a Navigator of the Skan People. Baron Ondrat tells me you are Emso, right hand to Gan Moondark. Yours is a name all Skan know."

"There'll be a lot fewer to know it after the battle this spring."

Domel held his composure. "I tested my god. I rejected the god's spirit woman.

I put to sea in a boat that weighs little more than your horse, and I dared the god to take me. I beat him. His wind and waves and his stormwitches failed. Do not try me. Not until you've bested a god, as I have."

Ondrat, nodding furiously, grinning, forced his way into the discussion. "A family of clamdiggers brought him to me. They found him on the beach, more dead than alive. I . . ."

Emso cut across his contribution. "Your name's Domel, you said. Very well. Why come to the Three Territories, to Gan Moondark? Skan have no friends here."

Visibly relaxing, Domel answered in a confiding manner. "When I made landfall on Baron Ondrat's coast, I was so weak I thought I must die. But I made land: You understand the significance? I defeated Sosolassa and his sea. Healers, including the Violet Abbess, saved me. If I'd been able to fight, I'd have killed the fishermen who found me, but I lived, robbed of my tribe, my honor, my family. Why help your Murdat? To help myself. To bring down those who chained me to a false god. Just as Gan Moondark is humiliated without knowing it."

"Careful." Emso's word was a growl.

Imperturbable, Domel continued. "You doubt? Know, then. Our war leader is named Lorso. He made alliance with Windband and most of the River People. They mean to finish the work started by the Kwa. Devastation. Slavery. Once that task is complete, Sister Mother will be killed. A new Sister Mother is to be empowered."

"Who replaces her?"

"There is the master treachery. Do you really believe that three warriors and two Priestesses defeated the nomads of Windband without witchwork? Can you believe that these aliens, who kill with thunder and lightning, are satisfied to give away all their power to further Gan's ambitions? My friends, the Violet Abbess and the noble Baron Ondrat, tell me there is an alien named Leclerc who creates strange things, things no man has ever seen. Can you believe this power, like the knowledge being forced on the Chosens, exists solely to benefit Gan? Witches roam your lands. Imagine a witch as Sister Mother."

The Abbess interceded. "We're not without hope or resources. Gan Moondark's heart is without actual sin. We may save him yet. You may."

Emso looked to her. She smiled. "The Skan sharkers won't mass to strike us until spring. Domel volunteers to lead a strike against the main village."

"To destroy his own people? With what forces? What boats?"

"My boats. My men." Ondrat threw out his chest. "We are more than fishermen, Emso. Once Ondrat sailors roamed as fiercely as the Skan." He turned, indicating the aged trophies.

He missed the quick dismissal that passed between Emso and Domel. From that mutually attuned glance, Emso seemed to take strength. He straightened, so slowly it was almost unnoticeable. The minute, gloating smile that touched the Violet Abbess' lips was proof that she saw. And understood.

Emso asked Domel, "You're sure it can it be done?"

"With luck. Once I've disposed of Tears of Jade and her usurper son, the Skan will know that the old god is overthrown. They'll come to Church. I'll cancel the Skan attack on the Territories."

"If I work behind my best friend's back, even to his advantage, I trust nothing to luck. I will know every move, every decision made. Nothing is done without my approval."

Ondrat and Domel looked at each other, turned to the Abbess. She clapped her hands, childlike in her glee. The angular face crackled into myriad lines of laughter. The sound pealed through the room, echoing wildly. "Wonderful, Emso. Oh, wonderful, my staunch friend. But now I have better news. Hear Domel."

Sitting down, Domel waited for Emso to do the same. Then he said, "I arranged escape for the girl Jaleeta. I'm a recent convert to the true Church. She always believed. She must not know I'm here. She can't reveal what she doesn't know, and I fear for her if Sylah learns her true faith. Of all of us, she is bravest, risks the most. Who would dare deceive a witch like Sylah, live in her very shadow? Jaleeta confirmed that Moonpriest and Sylah conspire to replace the real Church. Remember, Moonpriest is an alien, too, yet I'm told Sylah even saved his life, once. There was no real escape with the treasure of the Door. It's all treachery, lies within lies. Once we eliminate the Skan attack, Gan will turn all his attention to Moonpriest. The cowardly plans of Sylah and the anti-Church will be forced into the open. You'll be waiting for them. To save Gan from himself."

Domel leaned back, satisfied.

A gnarled, scarred hand worried at Emso's kneecap. He studied it as if it revealed deep truths. "Everything fits. Except Nalatan. He's a warrior-monk. He's no alien. He may be bewitched by Tate, but nothing else. If there was no fighting, no escape, how do you account for him? Are you saying he's a traitor, too?" He looked up at last, sharp, predatory.

The Violet Abbess answered before Domel could. "Only a few breaths ago, you defended Sylah. We've demonstrated how viciously cunning she is. We know what she's done to poor Gan's mind. You realize now what she's done to yours. What horrible things have she and Lanta done to that monk? He knows nothing of women. Or witches."

"Tate loves him. And him her. There's no mistaking that." Emso gripped the edge of his chair as if that hold were the only thing keeping him from falling off the earth.

The Abbess nodded, kind. "Wouldn't you have to be witched before you'd let your wife go off into the mountains with another man? Poor Emso. You want so much for others to be as trustworthy and loyal as you. It cannot be, my friend. There are none like you, and you have fallen among the worst of the worst."

"But Conway and Tate said their trip was a religious thing. A quest."

Domel broke in. As he spoke, his eyes flicked at the others. Quick, erratic, they were like twinned, glittering insects. "Religious, indeed. Moondance. Lorso said all the aliens living under Gan Moondark's protection are Moondance."

The Abbess sent Domel a look of approval. "There you have it."

"Gan's a good man. Good." Emso's jaw jutted. He turned away.

The Abbess suffered with him. Tears misted her eyes. "We must get him back, Emso. He belongs with Church. We can save him."

The trio watched in eager silence as he rocked back and forth.

* * *

From atop the castle tower, the Abbess and Ondrat watched the lone rider wend slowly down the track to Ola. Emso was almost within the forest, more than two bow-shots away. Ondrat still whispered his question. "Do you really trust him?"

Not bothering to look at her companion, she said, "Trust him? Of course not. He's using us, just as we're using him. In good time, we'll destroy him. Or he'll destroy himself. I don't believe I ever saw a man so full of hate."

"Him?" Ondrat pointed, startled.

The Abbess rounded on him. "Emso? Of course not. How could you ask? That fool's a trussed hog. No smarter than the sword on his hip. Mighty warrior, hah." She turned back for one last look as the forest absorbed the rider. "Watch Domel. He's the one. Befriend him. Keep him hidden. And above all, keep a sharp knife at his back."

Chapter 51

Tate came on Conway silently. He leaned against a tree, staring into a fiery dawn. Far below, coursing the valley as if pulled along by its tumbling stream, a wedge of ducks sped past. The oddly heavy bodies blended almost to invisibility against the green-black backdrop of forested mountainside. Without turning, Conway waved over his shoulder, then pointed directly overhead. Chagrined at having been detected so easily Tate ignored his gesture. "You're getting as spooky as Nalatan and Gan. You couldn't hear me coming."

He faced her, grinning. "I knew someone was there. The dogs' ears have been jerking around. They stayed relaxed. It was either you or Lanta."

Tate walked to the animals, ruffled a huge head with each hand. "Big old tattletales." Karda accepted the affection stoically. Mikka wagged her tail. Twice. An extravagant display. Tate asked, "What were you pointing at? You see something in the clouds?"

He nodded, pointing. Small, soft puffballs hurried along busily, generally southwest to northeast. "Rabbits, Gan calls them. They roll through first. Then come the wolves, the big clouds. It's a weather front. We'll get the wind soon."

"We've got warm clothes. We'll be all right."

"Snow makes it hard to travel. It could get dangerous."

Tate made a derisory sound. She whistled softly, the tune of the mysterious flute music of a few days prior. "This trip's already dangerous. Anyhow, it's too early for snow."

"Tell the clouds. And my nose. I smell it."

"We'll be all right." She faced east, stretched, took in a huge breath. The lithe body twisted and turned, luxuriating in the easy flow of muscle, the stimulated rush of blood. Sagging against a neighboring tree, she said, "Dangerous or not, it's glorious. That's what you were doing, isn't it? Just looking?"

Conway chuckled. "You got me. I was trying to remember an overture."

"A what? You?"

"Don't be smart. I liked classical music. I was thinking of Berlioz's overture to 'Les Francs-Juges.' This dawn is that music. The strings seem to mourn. Chilling, a sense of women lamenting. The brasses come in then, heavy. Tubas, trombones. The strings are absorbed, you know? The deep, heavy notes surround them, sound as if they're crushing the orchestra, the audience." He colored slightly. "Anyhow, that's what I was thinking about."

Tate's smile broke open slowly. "You and Nalatan. Like two butter patties, slick as you can be. Just when I think I've got one of you all figured out, you slip something like this into the game. I'm out here in the middle of Woods-R-Us, wound up two turns tighter than the manual allows, and you've taken to hearing symphonies nobody's played for five centuries."

Conway's laughter mingled with hers. He called the dogs, started back toward camp, Tate beside him. A noise like a sigh drifted lightly down from the distant tops of the trees. Continuing to match his stride, she put a hand on his shoulder to steady herself while she craned upward. "I believe you called it," she said. "I think I just heard your violins."

Lanta looked up from the firepit as they arrived. A pot of water boiled over the flames. Pale smoke gently angled northeast. It dissipated before it was as tall as Conway.

Tate said, "Conway's predicting snow. What do you think?"

Pouring a fine powder from a leather bag into three wooden cups, Lanta nodded. "It could be heavy." A gust of wind far above grunted agreement. A gray-and-black bird, somewhat larger than a robin, ghosted through the trees to land sideways on a huge fir. The deeply fissured bark, cracked like sunbaked mud, provided excellent footholds for the tiny, needled feet. It squawked. The dogs watched it intently.

Tate said, "Here he is. First boldeye of the morning. Good name for the greedy beggar. Listen to him."

Lanta added water to the powder in the cups. Frowns marked her audience as the fire's smoke verified greater wind strength. Conway said, "Let's get moving. I'd like to be down the mountain when the weather breaks."

Everyone picked up the pace of breaking camp. Instead of heated porridge, the meal of choice was a thick slab of bread and cheese, with pemmican. Conway sawed off chunks of the latter. The shredded meat, heavily herbed, was mixed with fat and smoked after it was packed in the cleaned gut. Its sharp scent saturated the campsite. The dogs begged with dignified eloquence. Conway threw them each a chunk, then sliced up leaf-thin bits for the half-dozen boldeyes now fluttering eagerly from tree to tree nearby. They called constantly, anticipating. Conway flipped morsels that were adeptly taken in midair.

Lanta scolded. "It's bad enough to spoil the dogs. You shouldn't spoil the birds, too."

"I want them close. I listen for them. If something disturbs them, they'll make noise."

Tate paused in loading her packhorse to send him a surprised look, then went about her business. Lanta was more forthcoming. "I thought you were just amusing yourself."

Conway grinned. "Well, some of that. There's no harm in some fun."

This time Tate's look was outright astonished. In a voice only her horse heard, she said, "That's the very limit, that is. Until she showed up, he was all business. Now he gets up in the morning to listen to symphonies no one else can hear. He makes nice-nice with our woodsy friends. What a change. The big question is, does he know it?"

Conway called to her, "What're you mumbling about, Donnacee?"

"The meaning of life. Mind your own business. You ready to go?"

"Whoo. Touchy." Conway mounted smoothly, gestured Karda ahead, sent Mikka loping down the back trail.

Tate moved to help Lanta with her problem pack mule. This morning it was suspiciously docile. Now, heaving on the cinch looped under the animal to secure the packsaddle, Lanta's exasperated wail announced the devilment the beast had in mind for today's trial. "She's breathing. Like before. I knew she was being too quiet. Dumb *mule*." The last was imprecation.

Tate grabbed the leather strap, pulled with Lanta. The mule grunted. "Maybe it'll exhale if we wait." Lanta's suggestion carried no hope, and Tate answered accordingly. "This hammerheaded oatburner will stand here with a gut full of air, taking teeny-tiny breaths, until we buckle the cinch and start walking. You know it. I know it. The mule knows it. We'll get five steps down the trail and it'll breathe out in one big 'whoosh,' and the whole load'll be in the dirt." She gave Lanta a look of resignation. "I'm going to have to do it again."

"Are you sure?" Lanta put a feather-light hand on the mule's flank. The skin quivered. "It seems so harsh."

Tate sighed. "It does to me, too, but it doesn't seem to bother the mule as much as it does us." Tate bent her knees, bringing her shoulder level with the mule's belly. Lanta grasped the loose cinch, planted her feet. Rising swiftly, Tate drove an elbow into the mule's side. Compressed breath exploded from the animal in a lip-flapping, nostril-flaring rush. The other end of the creature erupted in a ghastly, burbling bugling.

Both women yelped dismay, but gathered themselves quickly to yank on the cinch. It drew several holes tighter. The mule danced, an intricate piece of footwork that took it absolutely nowhere, but brimmed with immense self-satisfaction. Then it turned to fasten a sardonic, one-eyed gaze on Tate and Lanta. Moving so quickly the animal had no time to escape, Tate had it by the nose, opened its mouth. She peered inside. Wide-eyed with disbelief, Lanta asked, "What are you doing?"

"Looking for the problem." Tate let go, stepped back. "This brute's too mean, nasty, and crude to be just an ordinary animal. There's got to be a man in there somewhere." For a long moment, Lanta was frozen. Then, blushing wildly, she clapped her hands to her mouth. Laughter squealed past.

Continuing to break into repressed giggles from time to time, they mounted quickly and set off after Conway.

The descent soon turned sharply steeper. They saw where Conway's horse slipped, ripping chunks out of the forest duff, and dismounted.

They came to a point where the grade was easier. Two small streams joined to create a third, larger and more boisterous. One felt the air now, a pulsation that labored along the ground, forging passage through the massive trunks.

Conway's marker, a broken branch, indicated his path. For a while they paralleled the stream. Soon, however, they were directed across. The grade of the slope eased more. Lanta and Tate remounted. It was darker. The sky was a shroud of black, plodding clouds. Thunder muttered. Under her, Lanta's horse shied nervously, pecking at the soft forest floor with quick, erratic hooves.

When the snow came, it whirled through the branches on a suddenly raging wind that made the forest groan. Lanta looked back. Something moved in pursuit, a shadow against the snow-hazed darkness. Her heart leaped, a cry of warning seized in her throat. Then she recognized Mikka. Lanta waved at the dog, feeling foolish.

After that first roaring gust, the wind trailed off a bit. The snow continued, a swirling beauty that denied its deadly capabilities. The women admired it as they feared it, riding in silence, hunched over. The posture was a mental response; their fur, wool, and leather clothing could withstand far worse conditions.

Still, it was the bent attitude, with eyes cast down, that saved Lanta's life. Had she been erect, attentive to the trail ahead, instead of her mount's forefeet, the footprint would have escaped her attention. It was a large track, a man's. No heel detail showed in the snow. A running print. A moccasin. Clear, only now smudging with soft, downy flakes.

All that information reached Lanta's brain and was recorded and analyzed practically instantaneously. She threw herself onto her horse's neck, digging in her heels. Startled, the animal bolted forward.

The arrow that sang out of the snow plucked at her robe. She pulled her racing horse aside, hurtled past Tate. The latter was already slinging her wipe into firing position. She charged in the direction of the archer, shrieking above the wind. Lanta whirled, saw a man struggling to reach cover behind a tree trunk. Before Tate could fire, her horse was on him; the man went down in a tumbling mass, trampled. Tate spun to return to the attack. Lanta saw there was no need. Heels beat the ground. Hands and arms stroked in a macabre swimming. Snow rushed to cover accusing blood.

Lanta slowed, dismounted. If there was life in the man, it was her responsibility to tend to it.

She heard the blow before she felt it.

There was a sound of exhalation. Then metal on metal, high-pitched; chain mail. A burst of pain, bright and sharp as the strike of a noon sun. Blessedly, that was gone as quickly as it came. It left a dull ache that sucked her strength away. She reached for her horse for support. She watched, dumfounded, as useless, dead fingers slid along the glistening flank.

Her knees buckled. Kneeling, she looked into Tate's terrible expression. Agonized, helpless. Lanta wanted to tell her friend it was all right. It wasn't as awful as everyone said. Only sad.

The face that wouldn't let itself be seen earlier came back. Hateful as ever, it remained hidden. But it laughed.

A scream drowned that noise. It embarrassed Lanta. She'd meant to go bravely, silently. Or had it been poor Tate, watching a friend's going?

No matter.

Chapter 52

Lanta cried out against consuming black heat.

Coolness touched her forehead. It was marvelous, sustaining. She reached to capture it. Her hand moved, but it was slow. She wanted to scream that the cool touch wasn't needed just for the head, but for the whole body. Tears of joy filled her eyes when she realized the goodness was moving to her face, her neck.

"Her hand moved. I'm sure of it. And look; tears." Wonderment mixed with relief in Conway's voice. "Can you hear me, Lanta? It's me, Matt. We're right here, me and Tate. Can you hear me?" Her hand was swallowed in his. He practically shouted. "Donnacee! Donnacee, she's squeezing my finger. She's coming back."

Lanta heard deep, unintelligible rumbling, more vibration than anything. Good feelings came with them. The lovely coolness continued on her burning skin. She felt something else, too, a pressure on her hand. Whatever it was, she wanted it, needed it. With all her strength, she clutched at it.

A horrible, mocking face tried to force itself into her mind. Before she could fight it, she heard the bass rumble again. And then there was another face. Indistinct as the first, it was kind, and worried. Loving. The bad one snarled, catlike. The good one persevered. The bad one withered. She was exhausted. But protected. Safe enough to let herself drift away.

Tate rose from her position against the wall of the tiny dome-shaped hut. Halfway erect, her head touched the sea-smelling For cloth ceiling. Its odd quiltlike construction was good insulation. Irregularities dimpling the inner surface indicated the camouflaging fir boughs outside. Stepping around the three small candles that provided illumination, Tate knelt beside Conway. Taking Lanta's other hand, she bent close to her ear. "Welcome back, little buddy," she said. It was a crooning, lullaby sound. "You scared us half out of our minds, you know? You took a bad, bad hit. It's over now. You're all right, hear? We're with you. Everything's fine. Under control."

Tate rocked back on her heels. Lanta's released hand sank slowly back to her side. "See that?" Tate pointed. "Yesterday that would have just flopped wherever you dropped it. She's lots stronger."

Conway maintained his hold on Lanta. His face was wounded when turned to Tate. "This makes three days. All she's had is drops of water on her lips."

"We're doing what we can." Tate was transparently brusque. "She's in good shape, strong. She's coming back."

"It's just that seeing her like this . . ."

Tate patted his shoulder. "Do us all a favor. Take the dogs, scout around. Get some air. Make sure no one's looking for us. Or the two warriors."

Glum, not arguing, Conway busied himself getting ready. At the entry, he started out, then pulled back in, replacing the cloth door. "Snow's melting fast. By tomorrow we won't leave tracks."

"Not in snow, maybe. You said those two warriors were Windband. Are they good trackers?"

"They've got a few."

"That's who'll come looking for their missing scouts, then, isn't it? So we're going to be followed."

He shook his head. "Of all the lousy luck. If we'd been a little earlier, just a little later."

"If wishes was wings, frogs wouldn't bump their butts when they hop. But they ain't, and they do. So that's that. But we've got to get out of here. We're probably very lucky we didn't have to use a wipe. I'll bet there are people close enough to hear."

Conway looked away. "They must have heard the one screaming, then. The one Mikka killed."

"You feel sorry for him?" Tate scowled. "I saw his war club go up, man. I saw it come up for the second shot, saw it hang there, aimed to kill her. With a horse between me and the man raising it. There was nothing I could do but watch. If it wasn't for Mikka, she was gone. Your Lanta. So what if the man died hard? He had it coming."

Conway was quiet a long time, his gaze fixed on the tent entrance. When he spoke, the words were careful. "You're right, of course. We all do, though, don't we? Have it coming, I mean. Except the ones like Lanta and Sylah. Kate, Janet, Susan. They want to help everyone. Improve lives, save lives. But the ones who do the killing are respected warriors. The good people, they're the ones everyone hates the most." He was outside before Tate realized that was all he had to say.

Remaining crouched, Conway took three ungainly steps into the presunrise twilight before rising to full height. He continued to move, even then, turning, scanning the surrounding forest. Exiting the shelter made him feel vulnerable. He knew that if he discovered such a hiding place, his own action would be to wait, kill the first man out, then attack.

There were no boldeyes at this lower altitude, but Conway still cultivated the presence of birds. Several crows perched in surrounding trees, shifting and muttering guttural expectation for the routine handful of grain. They weren't completely dependable as guards. They'd already scolded once. Investigation revealed an intruding bear's tracks. Fortunately, it was a black, and not one of the fearless prairie bears. Those monsters had no respect for puny humans.

Rising from the piled boughs Conway put together to keep them off the muddy ground, the dogs stretched and yawned hugely before presenting themselves for an early-morning ear pull. Conway obliged, whispering a special thanks to Mikka. Her dark eyes adored him before she rubbed her head against him at the hip, almost pushing him over. For a moment, he thought of that immense bulk and power howling through the air at his throat, and the hair rose all over his body.

Contradictory laughter forced past lips that carved a cold smile. His own world had been infinitely more destructive. And no less primitive. Gangs, religious fanatics, and political morons killed savagely in that disappeared existence.

Conway was startled to realize he was happier here.

Happier wasn't the right word. It was more like a satisfaction. That was it, he decided. He was more at ease confronting this world's dangers. And its injustices. Things had an accessibility here they lacked in that other legislated, regulated, overpopulated place.

Yet he thought of one man dying under Mikka's crushing, tearing jaws, and shuddered.

He wondered if such thoughts ever troubled Nalatan. Or Gan. Or doughty old Emso. Or—most intriguing of all—the remarkable Donnacee Tate.

He shook his head, threw off the whole conjecture. They were all soldiers. Warriors. By instinct. Matt Conway was a product. Not like them. Not at all.

By that time he was ready to ride. The dogs were calmed down, but they continued to watch him with an air of puzzled expectancy. He sent them out with a signal to scout.

The sun was at midpoint when the dogs spotted the wolf. It took a moment for Conway to see the animal, a minute speck working its way across a bare spot on a ridge. Suddenly, it was running. Other wolves appeared, previously hidden on the opposite side of the rise. Conway estimated ten, in full flight.

He reached behind his saddle for the sniper rifle. Opening the rectangular carrying case, he exposed the interior's solar cells. After connecting the wires leading from the power source to the computerized telescopic sight, he put the rifle to his shoulder and sighted on the ridge.

Several things could send a wolf pack running. Tigers and prairie bears attacked wolves when the mood was on them. An angry wildcow or a grumpy buffalo could scatter them. Only one thing moved a pack to simply create ever-increasing distance between itself and that presence, however.

One by one, the riders who frightened the pack reached the skyline. They moved in a loose column, eight in all, with three packhorses. A long-range patrol, then. Possibly hunters, less likely a war party.

At this range, even with the scope, little detail was discernible, but these men dressed brightly. Highlighted by patches of snow, they were as gaudy as tanagers. Windband.

The telescope crosshairs settled on the leader. The laser aiming feature spoke to the small computer. Miniature motors adjusted the sights. A small blip appeared on the scope. Even at this great distance, the heavy spent-uranium slug would splinter bone, disintegrate tissue, send rips along the length of blood vessels as if that tough, resilient fiber were no more than sunstruck cotton. Conway said, "Turn away, stranger. Just turn away."

Karda yawned, a sign of tension. Mikka looked to Conway, then to the column of riders, then back to her master. She wagged her tail and panted.

The riders plodded toward Conway.

Dusk's long shadows cloaked the valley when the nomads arrived at the swift little river's eastern bank. For a few moments they milled about indecisively. The prospect of splashing across a frigid stream to camp cold and wet held no attraction. Now that the men were closer, their fatigue was evident. All sported unkempt beards. The horses stood hipshot, slumping where they stopped.

The apparent leader of the group was a small man, markedly more active. He urged his mount up and down the stream. Directly opposite Conway, he rose in his stirrups, searching. The narrow valley that wound back into the foothills where Lanta and Tate rested interested him. When he returned to his sagging men and addressed them, he gestured over his shoulder in the direction of that draw. The single gesture condemned Conway to action he'd hoped to avoid. It also confirmed his worst fears.

Only Moonpriest would order Windband scouts so far north. There was only one thing they could be searching for.

The crèche.

On higher ground some distance from the river, the nomads set up camp with practiced speed. A trio tied off the horses to a picket line.

Afoot now, covering behind a tree, Conway dined along with the men he watched. His meal consisted of a slab of coarse cornmeal bread and a chunk of pale yellow cheese so hard he had to gnaw it like a beaver. He cut the last little bit of cheese into two pieces, ridiculously small stuff for the dogs. They accepted it appreciatively, nevertheless.

The nomads put out no security on turning in, save a man by the fire. Wrapped in thick blankets, that one huddled over the remaining coals. For a while, the faint light washed across his indistinct form. Conway found it hard to look at, eerily deceptive. Later, even that was gone.

Leading Stormracer down into a narrow draw, Conway hobbled him, then patted his cheek. "Just be quiet, now. We'll be back in a little while." Satisfied all was in order, Conway whispered to the dogs and moved out.

Naked, clothes held high in a bundle, he entered the river above the nomad campsite where a jumble of driftwood provided an eddy. Although the current was swift, it was quiet, which meant immersion must be slow, to avoid splashing. The water was frigid, a thing beyond anticipation. It chilled his legs and feet to near lifelessness on contact, and when he took a deep breath, submerging groin, stomach, chest, he thought the shock would suffocate him. Swimming one-armed was a clumsy, inept joke. The current toyed with him, flung him downstream.

Chapter 53

His mind got Conway to the opposite shore. He drove himself, raged at the enervating cold, cursed the heedless current. When nerveless fingers touched bottom and a looming, dark indistinctness promised to be the river's bank, he almost cried out relief. Forcing caution, he edged onto dry land. There was no snow to mark his exit. Conway wasn't sure he had the will to delay leaving the water, if he'd been forced to search for such a spot.

Wedging his tongue between his teeth stopped their clattering. It took an eternity to dress. Numb fingers refused to cooperate. Retying calf-length soft leather boots was ferocious. Places where water splashed on the clothes during the swim clung to his flesh. Cold like that didn't ache, he discovered; it burned.

Beside him, the dogs shivered violently. He rubbed them. It was the only solace he could offer.

Stalking the camp helped warm him. Aching joints assured he moved slowly. Deadened feet schemed to make him clumsy, endangering stealth. The dogs moved with him, Karda right, Mikka left, occasionally close enough to touch him. He envied their rapid recovery.

The nomads' picketed horses snuffled weary unconcern on scenting his approach. Still, when he slashed the first lead line, the released animal whickered softly.

Conway pressed against a tree trunk, then lifted an arm across his face. If the horse's reaction brought anyone to investigate, there must be no glaring whiteness to draw the eye. After a wait, he returned to his work.

The dogs disturbed the horses. Conway retreated, stationed the pair to the west. It was important that the horses, once released, run east, away from Conway's own direction of escape. There was small likelihood they'd try to charge past the dogs.

Cutting the rest of the lines progressed well until the dogs growled. Freed horses edged away. Conway faded from the picket line. He crouched beside Karda and Mikka.

Light flared by the nomad shelters. Voices. One crackled anger. The other was muzzy with sleep and excuse. The flame brightened, moved. Words became distinct. Conway heard accusation. "If you were awake, you'd have heard it."

"I wasn't asleep. Dozing, maybe. Nothing happened."

The angry one lifted the torch high, breaking through the brush. "You hope nothing happened. This country's overrun with bears and tigers."

Conway held his breath while the small leader and the careless guard approached. Four horses remained unreleased. Four mounted nomads would round up the lost mounts quickly. They'd track whoever raided their camp. So far, the nomads had no reason to suspect their problems were caused by anyone except a Dog warrior. Conway had to keep it that way.

The leader said, "I know I heard something. These horses are too tired to be moving around for no reason."

One of the horses chose that moment to leave. The torch bobbed as the nomad leader hurried to investigate. Firelight sprayed through the growth. Conway heard a sword slide from its scabbard.

Exploding from his cover, Conway was on the leader before the weapon cleared. A killing slash failed to prevent his dying shout of alarm. In any case, the second man had ample opportunity to scream before Conway's whipping backhand cut his throat.

Conway cut the tethers holding the last four bucking, rearing animals. The barking of the dogs stampeded the entire herd eastward. Nomads boiled out of their shelters, hornets from a hive. Conway led the dogs in a dash for the river. At the sight of that black coldness, with its ghosting white surface swirls, he seriously considered trying to hide or make a stand. Good sense prevailed. He stripped hurriedly, wrapped his clothes. Gritting his teeth, forcing himself to avoid splashing, he set out.

Against the diamond-hard stars, the forest was a jagged silhouette. The chuckling, killing-cold river dragged him downstream.

This time he hauled out even more clumsily. When he stood, he collapsed, crawled, finally rose to lurch forward in ludicrous semblance of walking. As he dressed, mind and vision conspired to trick him. Trees moved. Shrubs suddenly shot up in front of him, only to be somewhere else when he dodged to avoid tripping over them. Paralleling the stream back toward the tethered Stormracer, he relished returning warmth even as it brought torture to his joints. He was about to turn away from the river when he heard the nomads reach the bank just opposite.

"Flea-bitten, thieving Dogs. You heard the barking. And the horses ran east. Didn't I say they'd track us, keep out of sight, then hit us when they were ready? Didn't I say that?"

"What does it matter what you said? We lost two men and all our mounts. I saw someone running toward this river. I'm not leaving here until we punish him."

"In the morning, then. We're not finding anything in the dark." Conway listened to them move way from the river.

Hurrying to the waiting Stormracer, Conway clambered into the saddle. He wrapped himself in a blanket, massaging constantly. High up the mountainside was a windfall fir he remembered. He was lucky enough to ride directly to it. Jamming down against the base of the circular wall created by the earth-encrusted roots, he built a fire. Whittled branches formed a frame to dry his clothes. Tea water soon boiled in a small pot. Cocooned in his blanket, Conway luxuriated. Both dogs crowded close. Steam rose from wiry coats, blended with coiling smoke. Conway mixed some tea, downed it in a blistering, wonderful gulp. He leaned back.

He woke with Karda's nose in his ear and a grinding pain between his ribs on the right side where a root pressed into his flesh. Pushing aside the conscientious dog and his highly necessary, but unwelcome, wake-up call, Conway rubbed his back and took stock of his situation.

In the predawn darkness, the remains of last night's fire was warm ashes. That was important; the nomad camp was a considerable distance, but the smell of smoke traveled much farther than the sight of it. Nalatan remarked once that a man's sense of smell seemed particularly acute in the early morning. Conway believed it. That meant a cold meal on a cold morning. At least his clothes were dry. Memory of the previous night's swim struck like a fist. A tearing shiver hammered through his body.

Dried fruit and freezing water wasn't a feast to linger over. Stormracer was quite content with his nosebag of grain. The dogs accepted their dried-meat ration eagerly, then stared at Conway with the invariable expression that said that today, certainly, was the day he'd double the amount. He never did. They never stopped hoping.

Rubbing oil into his boots as he rode, Conway arrived at his observation point above the nomad camp before they were fully active. Two appeared to have assumed joint leadership. While the rest of the patrol stumbled sleepily through their morning activities, the pair examined the ground. Initially pleased, Conway saw them confused by the welter of footprints. Pleasure gave way to disappointment quickly. One man bent low, then gestured sharply to his partner. Moments later, they were on their way to the riverbank, pointing, excited. Conway caught himself pushing forward, his chin almost directly above Stormracer's head, trying to hear a conversation far beyond earshot.

Back in camp, the pair gathered their companions. Arms waved. Fingers pointed. Conway smiled when they formed two distinct groups to eat. He patted Mikka. "We did some good, girl. Two men gone, no horses, and split into two groups."

Mikka wagged her tail. Her gaze remained fixed on the distant warriors.

The patrol broke camp. All six moved out toward the river. On arrival there, however, another subtle split took place. The bulk of the group moved downstream, separate from the argument between the two self-appointed leaders.

The patrol formed up again. Three men stripped and swam the river, clothes and bows held high above their heads. As soon as they were safely clear of the water, the other three moved off south. Conway enjoyed watching the departing trio, remembering the grinding training of the Wolves. In a similar situation, Wolves would have automatically fallen into their fast, mile-eating shuffle. The nomads trooped off with the vague unease of all true horsemen when afoot.

The trio on Conway's side dressed quickly. Weapons were checked. In spite of himself, Conway was impressed. These three were alert, sheltering behind trees, constantly scanning their surroundings. Each tested his bowstring, then inspected his arrows to assure no warp-inducing moisture in quivers.

The nomads picked up his tracks from the night before. They weren't particularly adept. Progress was slow. One man did most of the work. The other two flanked him, watching, moving from cover to cover.

Conway hurried back to his campsite. approaching from the side. Dismounting, he covered his return trail. That done, he tossed some small, dry twigs on the ashes, then blew them to flame. Remounting, he maneuvered Stormracer to a position on the far side of the tiny fire, then heeled him hard. Surprised, the animal dug its hooves into the soft surface litter, leaping ahead. The dogs sprinted to catch up. Conway kept at a run for a short distance before reining in. Stormracer snorted and pranced, incensed by such erratic goings-on. Conway gave him a distracted pat on the neck. "Stage setting, pal. They'll think they almost caught me sleeping. They'll see where I made you take off at a run. If they believe I'm scared, they'll hurry. Careless."

For a while, Conway maintained a fast pace directly away from the camp. Soon he came to a steep slope. It led into a narrow valley. Heavily forested, it slashed toward the larger river valley, but its lower end hooked north, where a spur of the mountains created something much like a wall. The small stream that drained the formation hit that obstacle head-on, rearing high before flowing north a short distance. It soon broke back to the east, though, tumbling on to join the river.

Conway spoke aloud. "We'll take them down there somewhere. The valley's almost closed off; it should confine the sound of the wipe. We need a good ambush point. Before that, though, we need one more thing to convince them they're right behind us."

Before descending, he rode back along his own trail. Where he stopped, he sawed on the reins, once more irritating the horse. It danced about angrily, digging up clods, whickering. That done, Conway forced it into a hard turn, then galloped for the point of descent. He pulled the horse in a tight circle, as if listening to pursuit. Headlong, he dropped downhill through the trees, breaking branches, leaving a blatant trail. At the bottom, he assured that the horse splashed across the creek. Unlimbering his wipe, he leaned down from the saddle and rapped Stormracer's foreleg at every step. The animal suffered the indignity badly, jerking the leg away.

Almost any tracker would swear he followed a lamed animal.

When he determined he'd gone far enough, Conway recrossed the stream. Circling back, he moved uphill before paralleling the valley floor. The horse moved easily, pleased to have no more knee tapping. Conway halted some distance downstream of his original crossing point. Tethering the horse, he moved into position on foot and sent the dogs to scout out the nomads.

Both animals were back in surprisingly short order. Hackles raised, gleaming eyes darting glances back over their shoulders, they came to stand beside him. Heads down, wide-legged, they growled at the still-unseen enemy. Conway quieted them, placed them behind him.

The nomads read his trail exactly as he planned it. Faces streaming sweat despite the cold, they came downhill almost at a run. The trio slowed to look at the stream. Water glistened on the rocks where Conway crossed. Only a man fleeing in fear would be so careless.

Unless he planned an ambush.

After a muttered, brief exchange, the nomads advanced more cautiously. One took a covered position, arrow nocked to bowstring, covering the continued advance of his companions. At the stream, a second man took cover to support the third. That last man crossed the stream, tense, reading signs, watching for attack.

The trail satisfied him. In pantomime, he signaled his friends, whipped an imaginary horse. He took a few steps, lifting one foot high in imitation of a limping mount.

The nomad closest to the stream crossed, joined the tracker. Together, they squatted behind trees, scanning a full circle. They gestured the farthest man to proceed.

When he rose, a squalling magpie flew out of the tree directly above Conway.

The nearest nomad jerked around. He looked directly into Conway's wipe. Amazingly blue eyes somehow mingled in Conway's senses with the hard crack of the weapon.

Conway swung around to fire at the other two. The instant of distraction provided by the bird was all they needed. Both were in motion. The one facing downstream was already moving in that direction. Conway shot him first. He assumed the third man would follow, which meant he must turn completely around. Slowed, off-stride, he'd be the easier target.

What should have been Conway's last shot nicked a branch, glanced away uselessly. The man dropped his bow and arrow and ran.

Conway sent the dogs.

The nomad shrewdly anticipated that. He sprinted for a jumble of boulders and rock slabs. The huge animals closed amazingly. Long, powerful legs devoured distance. The man screamed, scrambled up the rocks like a squirrel.

Karda tried to follow, leaped, clawed at the smooth surface, fell back. Jaws snapped fury and frustration. Mikka circled, picking her way, getting above her quarry.

Helpless, the trapped nomad watched Conway advance. At point-blank range, Conway lifted the piece to his shoulder.

The man compressed himself against the rock. He wept, shook his head in denial. Hands, palms out, gleamed with sweat. Bright sunlight silvered their trembling, gave them a strange tenuousness. Conway thought of the winking, whispering leaves of aspens.

Gushing wetness discolored the man's leather trousers, ran in a staining wash down the face of the rock. He didn't bother to look to see his own shame and terror. He managed to form words. "No. No, please."

Conway lined up the front sight between the man's eyes. They were dark brown, almost black. There were small hairs clustered between the brows. The man had to die. Free, he'd run for his companions, tell them that the raider was no Dog warrior, but Matt Conway.

Karda stopped trying to reach the nomad. He looked back over his shoulder. There was something in the dog's manner that made Conway pause. Belatedly, Conway understood. The pack had treed. The leader's responsibility was the kill.

The nomad sobbed, closed his eyes.

Conway said, "Take off the sword. Lay it beside you."

Untrusting, the nomad opened his eyes, squinting. Sensing he might live, he scrambled to obey. The weapon clattered on the stone.

Conway remembered Windband. Storming towns, villages. Vicious. Cruel. Men who killed for pleasure, took captives for profit. And amusement. Men who made death a mercy. The image before him wavered. When it cleared, the wipe was again aimed between the burnt-brown eyes. Conway focused on that point, remembering.

The man tried to speak, choked.

"Go." Conway called off the dogs, then repeated, "Go. I give you your life. Tell Moonpriest that while he lives, I hunt him. So long as Moonpriest leads Windband, I kill every Windband man I see. One day I'll kill Moonpriest. Tell him. Tell them all."

The man inched forward, then retreated, gaze locked on the wipe. Conway shook it, shouted, *"Go!"*

Leaping down past Conway, running, stumbling, falling and rising, the nomad fled. Once, with plenty of trees between himself and Conway, he turned to look over his shoulder. There was a gleam, a flash. Conway was enraged to think it might be a grin. Doubt curled up in his stomach like a malevolent, self-satisfied cat.

The dogs sat a few paces off, staring at the place where the freed nomad was last visible. Conway walked to them. Mikka seemed almost to be leaning away. Conway ruffled Karda's ears. The male glanced at him quickly, then resumed his watching. Conway left, half afraid the dogs wouldn't follow. They did, loitering behind. "I did what was right." Conway spoke aloud, a crushed whisper. "It won't do any harm. Killing him wasn't necessary."

He pictured the Windband patrol, waiting a short distance away. If they heard the shots, they'd already be returning. They'd find the trail, follow it to the camp where Lanta and Tate waited.

They'd tell Moonpriest. Moonpriest would pay any price for Lanta and Tate. And Matt Conway. To take them alive.

Another secret. To be kept from Tate. And Lanta. They mustn't know the danger he'd created.

Mistake. Weakling. The words whined in his ear.

He flung himself into the saddle. Memory conjured the horrified man pinned against the rock. He saw the narrow, targeted flesh between the dark eyes. Saw the sight lower, lower. Surrender.

"Damn you!" he shouted. The words rang the valley like clashing brass, repeating, mocking. "Damn you!"

He wasn't sure who or what he cursed. Or why.

Chapter 54

The following afternoon Tate pointed at the ground and said, "That's where we found the cast bronze arrowhead." She turned in her saddle, facing the looming mountains to the west. "That's the spur we followed down to here. The crèche is up there."

Across the small stream to their right, a cock pheasant crowed from its hideaway in the scrub. Rasping, sharp, it had a mad sound.

Tate went on. "The nomads you ambushed won't know their raider was you, instead of a Dog warrior, which is good, but they're going to want to do something about their losses. I wonder how much time we have?"

Conway ached to confess. Something slimy in the back of his mind laughed at him as he answered, "Not much. Those scouts mean Moonpriest's coming."

"Moonpriest? Coming here?" Lanta, riding up from several paces to the rear, caught Conway and Tate by surprise. They had no wish for her to overhear their concerns. Lanta's voice was high. "I thought . . . You said this journey had to do with your religion?" The intonation was part question, part fearful accusation.

"Not exactly religion." Conway gestured, reaching for explanation.

Lanta leaped into the pause. "You said religion. Now you say Moonpriest is coming."

"We're here because we want to help Church. The Territories. Moonpriest knows about certain secrets here. We think he's coming after them."

"Like the Door. If he gets the secrets, will he be stronger than you? How does he know of these things?"

Tate stepped in. "Moonpriest has never had a chance to get here. Neither have we. Now it's a race. We have to take as much power from here as we can, and we have to assure that Moonpriest never gets any. What we're doing is like a pilgrimage. To us, the place we're going is almost holy."

"Almost holy?"

Conway said, "Like an abbey. The place isn't, but what it represents is."

Lanta was dubious. "I want to see it. Take me with you."

"No. It's too powerful."

"I saw . . ." Lanta bit off the sentence. Her mind filled with the dreadful images she remembered from Seeing Conway's memories. She didn't understand them. Nevertheless, they froze her blood. Her gaze went to him. He was ashen. She was sure he was remembering, too, and hating her for Seeing inside him. She looked away.

Conway said, "We'll all go up the mountain. When we're close to the secret place, but far enough away for you to be safe, we'll make camp. Tate and I will do what needs done. Then we leave, fast."

Lanta nodded, unwilling to speak.

Single file, with dogs scouting ahead, they moved out. Conway thought about the trip down the mountain the day they ventured out of the crèche. Each step was an adventure, with the very air an unknown quantity. Did the breeze carry radioactive contamination? Was the earth toxic with chemicals? Or bacteriological vectors? Was anyone else alive? Anywhere?

Conway watched Tate. His heart lifted at the way she sat her horse. Loose, flowing with the animal's movement. Her eyes sought in all directions. Her head was raised, listening, sniffing. She cradled the wipe, ready.

Campsite was a perch on the shoulder of the mountain, a steep walk from the crèche. Most importantly, the crèche entry was hidden from view; the terrain required one to go south, then resume climbing to reach the actual location. With practiced ease, the trio settled in. A small hollow under a boulder the size of a house provided basic quarters. Branches and the For cloth supplied weather protection.

At last, straining for nonchalance, Tate broached the subject. "We've got some time before dark; think we ought to look things over? Nothing special. Just check. You know."

Too quickly, Conway said, "Might as well. There's no hurry, really. But it can't hurt, I guess."

They took a packhorse. The dogs led.

Alone, Lanta busied herself tending to the tethered horses. Moving from one to another, Lanta stroked the muscular, arched necks, ran her hands across the smooth, warm sides. Even the Dog war-horses responded to her. She was proud of that. She told herself that animals understood more than people. The horses didn't care about the blessed curse of Seeing. They didn't flinch away from her touch.

The way Matt Conway did.

She reached the obstinate mule. Her hand, tracing the long sweep of a jawbone stopped, forgotten. The animal's soft eye blinked reproach.

Matt Conway didn't flinch from her touch. He luxuriated in it. He avoided her, but when circumstances created physical contact between them, she could see he enjoyed it. Her face warmed; she enjoyed it, as well. There was no point dissembling about that. After all, she'd run away from Ola, forced herself on him during this quest. What sense was there in denying her love?

The mule nodded vigorously. Lanta laughed aloud at the timing. "You do understand, don't you? Even you." She tugged on a flicking, black ear, then resumed petting the animal's muzzle. She soon left the animals, strolled to the shelter entrance. Sitting down, back against the looming boulder, she drew herself into a snug, warm ball, tucking her heavy robe and coat around her. Overhead, a breeze poured through the branches, the liquid rush of it soothing. Lanta pulled up her hood, retreating further. Weariness settled on her. Not the sort that normally came at the end of a day, but an odd, compelling need to close her eyes. It was as if the comfort that pulled her deep into her warm wraps now tugged even more urgently, drawing her away from this place.

This place.

The Seeing. It was coming after her, not waiting for her to call to it.

Thinking about Matt Conway. That was the way it happened before.

The black curtain of the Seeing fell. Claimed her. Fiery words streaked and flared across a void.

"The Lanta one will be torn from the garden of the Flower because of the Matt Conway one. The Lanta one demands complete trust given and returned. Who dares such without total knowledge and understanding? Hear, and weep."

The flaming words disappeared, left only darkness. Then Lanta heard the crying. Voices, uncountable in number, all weeping. Every conceivable misery washed over her, threatened to drown her. Then, the words once more.

"So it was with the Conway one. That was the end of the life he knew. As was this: Feel, and wonder."

Rhythm. Immediately, Lanta knew it was a heart, beating fearfully. She felt its helplessness, a moth's dust-fragile wings battering stone. It stilled. Then came cold. Something was dead, yet feared death. In blackness.

The return of the flaming words brought heat that was beneficence. Lanta wanted to reach for them. Until the horror of their message struck at her.

"That is what the Conway one brings to wife. A man who knows the inner rooms of death, who cannot grasp what he is. A man who knows the fear of too much knowledge, yet a man driven to know more. The man desired of the Lanta one. The Lanta one will have what she wishes most. To be here, the Conway one has become what no

man should ever be. If you are to be one with him, you must become what one such as you must never be. The decision comes. The question must be answered by the Lanta one: Will you have him dead once, to live more, or dead forever? Think, and tremble."

She woke.

There was a spring a short distance away. She rose unsteadily, running to the clean, pure water, anxious to pray.

Although Conway and Tate knew where the crèche was, it took a few worried moments for them to locate it exactly. Using his knife, Conway pried the camouflaged door open. There was no flow of air to meet them. Instead, when they stepped inside, it was to feel themselves sinking into a chill, repellent atmosphere. Conway struck sparks with flint and steel from a small leather box that also held fluffy tow. Transferring the small glow to rags spread with pitch and tied to a stick created a torch. They advanced slowly. The immense steel door that originally sealed the cave and maintained its nitrogen atmosphere hung drunkenly where the trapped survivors had blown it open. Dulled, freckled here and there with patches of dark corrosion, it saddened Conway. The metal seemed to be asking to decay in peace.

Tate found her voice first. They were past the circular, vaultlike door. "It smells dead. There's a bad feeling, like it ought to stink worse. There's just mostly dampness."

Conway knew her imagination saw what the torch wouldn't reveal; the hundreds who'd died farther back in the cave and were left, coffined in their clamlike cryogenic capsules, entombed forever. Neither of them would speak directly about that. He offered compromise. "We don't have to go all the way in. The supply area's between the door and the—other areas." He cursed himself for the minute hesitation, the unspoken acknowledgment that only a few yards away in uncaring darkness lay people for whom cryogenic suspension eternally failed.

At the edge of the torch's ruddy light, Tate was a dim, bent figure, moving in a crouch. "Over here."

The supply room was an eerily disorderly jumble. Precise aisles and shelves were an earthquake-smashed landscape of refuse. Light barely reached the corners of the square concrete room. The blackness of the rough vault overhead was vague, threatening. Wavering shadows suggested lives that resented trespass.

Conway picked up a camouflage jacket, only to drop it with a wordless cry of revulsion. "Mold. Mildew. Nasty stuff." His voice thrummed imperfect echo. The offending cloth sighed when it landed, collapsing on itself. Thin, powdery clouds puffed into the stillness.

Tate grimaced. "Let's hope the weapons aren't ruined."

"And the Hy-Pex. We'll want to seal off this place for good when we're done with it."

Tate looked wounded when she nodded affirmation.

All cloth was ruined. Some articles were already disintegrated, identifiable only by buckles or zippers or buttons. More came apart at a touch. Food supplies, never intended to be more than a measure to feed crèche volunteers until they were transferred elsewhere, were ruined. Tate mourned their loss. "There were rations for three days for everyone in the crèche. They weren't much, but we could have used them. We wouldn't have to hunt on the way back to Ola."

Conway picked up one of the food packets. The plastic film container was swelled taut. Idly, Conway punctured it with the tip of his knife. Noxious glop oozed out. He hurriedly dropped the mess. "Well, they're garbage now."

"Always were, buddy." Tate sighed, nudged the vast mound with her foot. Packets slipped and slid in minor avalanche. "The dried fruit wasn't bad. And the burritos. First, you added some Tabasco, then . . ." She stopped. Resumed sharply, "Let's get to the weapons."

Wipes, pistols, grenades, masses of field equipment—all were strewn wildly. Rummaging, Tate gave a running commentary on her findings, each comment more depressed than the last. Finally, holding a tubular article in both hands in front of her, as if presenting an offering, she faced Conway. The device was perhaps a yard long, four inches in diameter, capped at both ends. A boxy apparatus Conway assumed was the sight rested atop the thing. When he looked from the sight to Tate, he was surprised to see fierce, unshed tears glistening. She spoke harshly. "This is antiarmor rocket, sabot, laser-guided. Aunt Sally, the troopers called her. The ones who died here. They never even grew up. For what? We said it was for living space, for enough food, for clean air and rivers, for freedom. We almost exterminated the race and the world it lived in. All of it's forgotten. And here we are, getting ready to send more young men and women to their deaths, babbling the same old things. Words. None worth one young life. You hear me? Not one. None of it." She was shouting when she finished, sweating. Echo rolled through the cavern.

Conway answered very quietly, "We can make a difference here, Donnacee. We have to try."

Like fire dying, the rage faded away. She looked tired, sounded worse. "Right. We have to try. Put that down with the rest of them: 'Damn the torpedoes; full speed ahead.' 'Come on, you sonsobitches. You want to live forever?' 'Today is a good day to die.' If it wasn't so sad, it'd be funny. The hits just keep on coming, don't they?" She spat. A tiny billow of mold rose where it landed. Tate watched the miniature cloud as if it were of supreme importance until it disappeared. Absently, so softly Conway was sure it was intended only for herself, she added, "What sorry fools we are. If it weren't for love, there'd be nothing good in us at all."

Immediately, she was brisk again. "Some of the wipes are in reasonable shape. Most of the wipe ammunition, too. And grenades. Each trooper had a unit of fire —that's enough for a day's combat. We'll need all the horses to haul the stuff. We'll go on foot."

"Where's the Hy-Pex?"

"Over there. There's more mold and crud on the cases. I never thought this place was so damp. Remember how some of us talked about staying here?" She shuddered, looking around.

"Is there any point in trying to salvage the Aunt Sallys? Or anything else?"

She shook her head. "Not really. They worked off batteries or hand generators, and they're all shot. Explosive junk; might as well use them to blow the place."

"That was my thought. What if we hide some wipes, take the firing pins? That way we ride, instead of walk."

Considering, Tate stroked her lips with a finger. "Good point. Speed's important. And even if Moonpriest finds the weapons cache, we'll have all the ammunition."

"All the ammunition. Not a happy thought, exactly. When it runs out, the Black Lightning and the White Thunder are just a couple of bozos lost in the wrong world."

Tate laughed, shook a warning finger. "Speak for yourself. This world or that, nobody calls Donnacee bozo. Now let's get busy. That torch's getting low. We better find a hidey-hole for this stuff."

The westering sun was low when they stepped outside. Near-dusk softened the rolling lands stretching eastward, suffused late fall's cool gray with a blue that suggested iron and steel. Unspeaking, Conway and Tate reached out to each other. Hands gripped, withdrew. Conway's dogs trotted to rejoin him.

Lost in thought, Conway and Tate moved downhill in companionable silence. Suddenly, Tate stopped. Her head went up, alert. Incongruously, Conway's surprise at her manner was blunted by a sudden incongruous awareness of her attractiveness. Curiously tilted eyes swept the forest, bright, lively. High cheekbones accented the full mouth, now downcurved with stern intent. Her hair was an ebon frame for features done in rich, dark tones. Beauty and grace surmounted the blunt, ugly wipe in her hands.

"Did you hear it?" She continued to seek, turning. Conway looked to the dogs. They were alert, disturbed. He listened with more purpose.

Music. The flute, melodic; haunting delicacy drifted through the forest.

"Where's it coming from?" Hair prickled on Conway's neck.

Tate set off down the hill again. "I don't know. But it complicates the problem of hiding anything, doesn't it?"

The music stopped in midphrase. The abrupt silence stung like scornful laughter.

Chapter 55

Lanta was pleased to be distant from the others and their secretive muttering. She felt a certain resentment at being so completely left out, but consoled herself that the discussion was probably religious.

Her mood darkened as evening's cold seeped into her bones. The memory of the Seeing crowded into her consciousness. Twice now the Seeing warned her about Matt Conway. It told her she and Conway could be one. That should have been joy. Instead, the message carried menace.

The return of the dogs from a routine patrol of the area underscored the melancholy thread of her thoughts. They came in slowly, almost reluctantly. Both animals flopped down and curled up right away, pretending sleep. Twitching ears and bright, nervous eyes betrayed them. Lanta sympathized, even as she smiled at them. She wondered if she was so obvious.

Tate's voice ended Lanta's self-involvement. "I apologize for the way we've been excluding you. I hate it, but we don't have any choice. Please understand."

"We've talked about it before. All tribes have their secrets. Church teaches us to accept what we can."

"What if you can't accept something?"

Worry tainted the question, made it more than intellectual curiosity. Lanta was careful to disguise her awareness of the fact. "Custom that causes no harm can be accepted. Pain of any kind cannot. We try to show it can be avoided." She rose, and the two women walked together in the night. Tantalizingly close stars glittered overhead. The dogs lay back-to-back just outside the shelter entrance. Both great heads rose briefly, then settled, wreathed in a white fog of chilled breath. A horse snorted, creating another small cloud, this one swift and boiling, dissipating so quickly the eye wondered if it truly saw.

Lanta felt Tate's controlled inner pressures. Intuition told her that whatever was troubling Tate, it was something to be shared between them. Alone. And it likely had nothing to do with religion.

Tate's words confirmed the insight. False unconcern beribboned the words. "We always end up trying to show them the right way, don't we? Men, I mean. Women do. Oh, you know."

"It's always been that way. And it's never worked." Lanta was surprised by Tate's hastily hidden look of dismay. She laughed nervously and hurried to cover the potential awkwardness. "I've always admired how frankly you speak to men. The people of your culture treat women with more respect than any I know, even the Dog People."

"Independence isn't always easy. Or helpful."

"And I complicated yours by insisting on accompanying Matt Conway while you left Nalatan in Ola."

"Never think that." Tate stopped, faced Lanta. "I was upset when you showed up, that's for sure, but what happens between Nalatan and me is entirely our doing."

"I want to be part of what happens to Nalatan and you. I'd like to be one of the friends who helps make you both happy."

White breath added poignancy to Tate's resigned sigh. "It's the stupid honor thing again. I know Nalatan trusts me with Conway, but I'm afraid someone back there'll say something stupid. He could get hurt."

"I'd worry about who offends him. He'll be fine."

Lanta resumed walking. Tate fell in beside. Although the forest was parklike, with very little undergrowth, it was so dark that trees had a disconcerting ability to materialize directly in one's path. Tate said, "I can't imagine ever coming back here again."

Shocked, Lanta said nothing. Holy sites demanded attention, repeated rites. Foreboding scratched across Lanta's surprise. Was Tate really trying to say the trip, the site, was a ruse? If so, what of Leclerc and the mysterious, wonderful things he made? He never spoke of religion. Even the alien women who joined

Church accepted ritual, participated in observances—and said nothing more than required.

Magic avoided religion.

Tate said, "I'm ashamed for being so nasty when we found you, back there. You did the right thing. I should have said so then."

"You think so?" Lanta seized the change of subject gladly, yet puzzled as to where it was leading. "Has Matt said so?"

"He'd tell you long before he'd tell me, honey," Tate said dryly. "The thing is, I hear what he means and I hear what he says. They're not the same, exactly."

"I don't see . . ."

"Men have their own language. Should, too. They think they think. It's like Nalatan; he's not as worried about his own honor as he is mine. He won't want to walk away from someone who insults him, but he can do it. If someone insults me, he'll take it a lot harder. Same thing with Conway. I don't know exactly what happened, but I know he feels he hurt you, and he knows you're unsure of him. He can't let himself push himself on you. In his mind, you have to come to him."

Lanta leaned against a tree trunk. "If he loved me, he'd ask me how I feel, tell me how he feels. We'd talk."

Tate laughed softly, the warm sympathy gentle against the unhappy tenor of the conversation and the growing cold of the night. "You and Conway are like you and me, right now—bumbling around in the dark. None of these trees is going to reach out and whack us, and even if we bang into one, we're not going to do ourselves serious damage. So we make progress, but we're walking very, very carefully. Maybe you and Matt are being too careful, Lanta. You two hit a tree. You've got to get past that. How can I help?"

"Just be Donnacee. Be my friend."

"You drive a hard bargain." Tate chuckled, then, "Maybe you can help me when I have to deal with Nalatan. That's going to be one fast dance."

"I'm not sure I understand what you mean about dancing, but I'll do whatever I can."

"I hurt him a lot."

"Remember what you told me. It's going to be all right."

"Long as we stick together." Tate extended an arm, gave her small friend a quick hug. They were back at the shelter by then. "We better get inside. Conway'll think we're out here talking about him."

Sleep came surprisingly easy for Lanta. She woke with a start, however, eliciting fuzzy complaint from Tate, whose eyes remained firmly closed. Lanta made her way outside where Conway was on watch. In the intense predawn darkness he blended with the rock he sat against, differentiated only by the thin wisps of condensed breath. The dogs lay beside him. Noses buried in harsh fur, they gave off no telltale clouds.

Conway gestured her forward. In deference to Tate, he whispered. "Early as always. Go back in. I'll wake you."

"I'm awake. I have morning prayers. Anyhow, I enjoy sunrise."

He laughed. "Me too. I just hate getting up."

"You'd make a poor Chosen. Our Abbess would have switched you until you were glad to get up."

"Switched? All you little girls?"

"Of course. It was the way. Sylah won't allow it in the Iris Abbey. The Violet Abbess says that's another of her sins."

"And that's why you wake up before dawn every morning? Because someone whipped you into it as a child?"

"Because I greet the rise of the sun. Because I believe in why I greet the sun. Perhaps the threat of punishment made it natural for me to wake early. I don't know. But my prayers are not a trick to deceive the Abbess. You insult." Lanta felt she should be able to see the cruel silence between them, ugly and raw.

Conway apologized. "I'm sorry. The thought of someone striking you angered me."

"The memory angers me still. I blame the Abbess and the Chosen system, however, not the One in All. Surely you understand. Your religion makes you do things that trouble me. You say you came here in the face of great danger, to perform a deed to help Sylah and Church. You say it's a religious matter and I accept that, but there's more. I feel it."

"I want to tell you." He started so urgently, then stopped so abruptly it frightened Lanta. She held her breath. When he spoke again, his whisper was just audible. "You know so much about me, and understand so little. You understand so much, and know so little. How do I balance those things? How do I explain me?"

"Why do you feel you must?" Lanta got to her feet. Cold muscles and tendons ground against each other like dry rope. Once erect, she felt better. She made her way uphill to her prayer vantage.

The rest of the morning's preparations went smoothly. Neither Conway nor Lanta referred to their exchange. In fact, she found him unusually cheerful. He joked easily with Tate, wrestled with the dogs. He talked eagerly of finishing their "chore" as he put it, and getting started for Ola.

It pleased Conway that no one asked him why he felt particularly chipper. Lanta's question still chimed in his ears: "Why do you feel you must?" It had the simplicity of genius. Why, indeed? And if there was no need to explain himself in the present, why should he even think about explaining his past? True, Lanta's Seeing made her aware of some of the horrors of the world he'd escaped, but he was part of this one now. The new Matt Conway was a better man. Flawed, but a good man. One who deserved a good life.

He was whistling to himself, a thin, tuneless noise as he and Tate started for the cave.

Tate said, "You never told Lanta we heard more flute music yesterday. Why not?"

"Why trouble her?"

"Because she ought to know."

Conway pursed his lips judiciously, then, "The watcher was by the crèche, not the shelter. Close, in spite of Karda and Mikka. If whoever it is wanted to harm us, we'd know. Anyhow, you could have told her yourself."

Tate considered that retort, visibly irritated. Then, "What about the equipment?"

"I'll have the dogs keep our flute player away long enough to do the job. Then we collapse the cave. If we hustle, we can make it to the valley by dark."

When they arrived, the forbidding aura of the cave was unchanged. Tate complained, "Is it me, or is the air in here worse? It's like inhaling mud."

"I'm puffing, too. I thought it was from the climb up here, but now I think it's this dust we're stirring up."

Tate lifted a wipe, brandished it. "It can't be dust. The place has gotten clammy since we left. I think we're just out of shape."

In spite of himself, Conway snapped response. "I must be in really bad condition, then, because my eyes hurt, too."

"Don't yell at me."

Conway knew he should break off the staring match, knew his infantile petulance was wrong. Dangerous. She spun away, snatching up an armload of wipes. Embarrassment flooded over him. Perversely, he remained silent.

It was all very confusing. Even his coordination seemed to work against him. Clumsiness was a function of the miserable light conditions, he decided. He gathered up a load of weapons and followed Tate outside. Dense clouds, barely clearing the mountaintops, made the day gray and dull. Even so, it was so much more welcoming than the cave that something like euphoria lifted him. Then, crushingly, depression weighed in, made him want to abandon the entire project. It took a strong exercise of will to continue.

On reaching the narrow crevice where they meant to stow the weapons, Tate dumped hers with a careless clatter. "This is really dumb. Moonpriest's never coming back here. What's it to us if he does? Who cares, anyhow?"

"Me. You, too. How do you know what Moonpriest'll do? Come on, we've got work to do."

Tate glared. Her concentration failed quickly. The angry gaze wandered off.

The remainder of the morning passed in similar fashion, but the biting exchanges grew fewer. Much later, Conway wiped a film of greasy, unpleasant sweat from his upper lip as he deposited the last load of wipes. Simultaneously, he noted how heavily Tate perspired. They were ridiculously tired. Extracting the bolts from the weapons in order to hide them separately should have been nothing. Instead, it was demanding.

Outside, the dogs worked hard, practically running away to obey every search command. Conway berated them anyhow. He couldn't remember them ever looking so nervous. Hangdog, he thought; they look hangdog. He yelled at them to search. Shouting at their departing forms, he told them to get some spirit. The effort made him cough. That, in turn, made him even angrier.

Removing the ammunition and the bulk of the Hy-Pex dragged. Setting the remainder of the explosive and the Aunt Sallys to collapse the cave became a comedy of errors, albeit one that garnered no laughter. Tate confessed her schooling in demolition was rudimentary. Conway's was nonexistent. Bickering constantly, fumbling sensitive blasting caps with the intense ineptitude of drunks, they finally determined the burning time of the fuse and actually attached it to a blasting cap without blowing themselves apart. By the time they inserted the cap into a block of Hy-Pex and stacked the supply of Aunt Sallys on top of the demolition charge, both ran rivers of sweat. Conway found himself rubbing burning, watering eyes constantly. Carelessly, he dropped the waning torch to the floor of the cave. It bounced, rolled toward the mound of explosives and rockets. He leaped for it, startled by his uncoordinated floundering. Tate's best drill-field expletives soared. He picked up the coil of fuse, unwinding it as he walked toward daylight.

They ignited it with a torch. The irony of that primitive tool initiating an irreversible closure of his connection with the world of his birth hammered Conway. Tate seemed to feel the same. Tears welled in dark, troubled eyes as the sizzling flame sputtered down the length of the shiny orange cord.

The dogs loped into view. Conway yelled at them to come running. He directed them to shelter and made them lie down. Ashamed of careless neglect that could have killed them, he avoided looking to see Tate's reaction.

The blast was anticlimactic. The ground heaved. A fierce storm of dirt and dust shot from the entry, followed very quickly by a hard, brittle crack. Then came a deep, resonant rumble. A billowing, tumbling wall of dirty gray smoke and debris rolled out. As if cut by a knife, it was reduced to nothing by the collapse of the roof at the entrance. Deep inside the mountain thundered the muffled boom of ongoing destruction.

"It's collapsed," Tate said. "It's over. All gone. Everything's gone." She wept facedown on the ground. Clawed fingers dug into the gritty soil. Conway thought of a mourner, sprawled across the body of a lost loved one. He wanted to join her. To rest. His stomach rolled menacingly.

"Get up." He spoke roughly. "We have work. Then you can cry." Rather than the poisonous anger he anticipated, Tate merely pulled herself to her knees. Unsteady but determined, she rose, put one dogged foot ahead of the other.

Conway couldn't remember working so hard. His joints ached, his muscles were like molasses. Covering the smaller cache of working parts was challenge. Hiding the larger crevice holding wipes and Hy-Pex was devastating. It required large boulders to close and disguise the gap. Piled up small rocks would literally shout for investigation.

Twice, both had to stop and seek privacy, where they were violently ill. Speculation about what could be the cause was listless, as if they spoke of strangers.

A massive slab to cover everything was the finishing touch. Blood and sweat from barked knuckles, torn palms, and stressed bodies stained it. At last, it balanced delicately, ready to be lowered into place. Conway said, "Hold what you've got, right there. I'm changing my grip; I'll lower it when you're clear."

Shuffling around, Conway positioned himself. "Let go." Tate stepped away, brushing her forehead with the back of her hand. Conway thought he saw her sway. "Another step," he said. The slab pulled at him. "If it gets away from me, it might break off splinters. Stand clear." Tate did as ordered, expressionless.

Conway edged the stone forward. It had to set just right, or rain and snowmelt would get past it, ruining the weapons. The weight of it drew his strength, sucked the wind out of his lungs.

"Watch! It's slipping this way." Tate reached to redirect the weight. Missed.

The stone's momentum overwhelmed Conway. It dropped onto Tate's outstretched hands. She screamed, a thin lance of sound, drenched with pain.

The stone tilted. The crushing edge rose. Tate fell backward, sat down. Moaning, rocking, she folded her body over the mangled hands. Conway rushed to her.

Crooning a rising, falling melody of hurt, she held out her injury. The skin was badly ripped. No bone showed. When he reached to touch her, however, she hissed and jerked away. "Lanta. Get me to Lanta. She'll know."

"I'll help you up."

An elbow struck at him. "Leave me alone." Saliva trailed from the corner of her mouth.

He caught her as she toppled. Rolled-up eyes revealed nothing but whites. He looked away, telling himself that many unconscious people looked like that. More, he needed all his concentration to pick his stumbling, erratic way over the rough ground.

Fat, lazy snowflakes loafed across his vision. Plump whiteness softened the threatening teeth of distant mountains. He hugged his unmoving friend to him and plodded on.

Chapter 56

Lanta jerked upright. One hand inched out of her tight, warm huddle, edged open the shelter's flap door. Snow blanketed everything, including the dogs. Tucked in tight curls just outside, they blinked away snow to stare back.

Karda's stomach rumbled discontent. That was what wakened her, Lanta realized. She wished she could help. There was barely enough food to nurse Conway and Tate, none to spare for the poor animals.

The valley floor was curtained off by another snow flurry, but in her mind's eye she saw the deer, elk, and wildcows congregating, homing on their traditional wintering grounds. The dogs could hunt there. There were other predators, though; the groaning call of a tiger the previous night, a prairie bear bawling the day before.

Three days, with only slight improvement for her friends. Back inside the shelter, she reexamined them. Happily, color was better, pulses stronger. Breathing was improved, slow and regular. Bending close, Lanta sniffed at each neck, then smelled the breath. The skin was fresh, the exhalations free of the peculiar cloudiness. Lanta grimaced, thinking of it. The stink made her think of something ropy, slimy. The thinnest smile moved her lips; both of them could use a good toothbrushing, but at least they smelled human again.

A while later, Conway stirred as she spooned broth into him. She was wiping his chin when his eyes flew open. They were bright, clear. Startled, she rocked back on her heels, exclaiming aloud, nearly dropping the precious broth. He continued to look directly into her eyes. The first words came with difficulty. "You all right? Not sick, like us? Tate. She all right? Her hands." He tried to gesture. After three days of immobility, muscle was flaccid, coordination chaotic.

Lanta stroked his cheek, brushed hair back at his forehead and temples. He lay still, and she knew he was filling his senses with her, absorbing everything about her. He closed his eyes, sighed contentment. She felt his happiness, the love in him. Her kiss on his forehead was light as breath, but through it she tried to tell him of her joy in his recovery, her joy in his presence. The gentle caress was promise. In her heart, she felt it as the glad surrender she yearned for.

Grating memory reminded her that the Seeing warned of unknown choices and changes. She closed her eyes, chanted softly. Trance came quickly. Deep concentration enabled her to quell hunger pains, fight off depression and weariness. This time, however, the impact of that gentle kiss intruded, interfered with her planned thought path. Instead of the secure comfort the trance normally brought, this one was a mad pattern of heat and cold. Heat when she thought of Conway. Cold when she thought of the Seeing's threats.

Words came to her.

"The Apocalypse Testament said: Love is not acquisition, but divestment. The greatest love is that which gives without thought of compensation. The highest love is that which finds the courage to free the beloved. The highest love may mourn, but it cannot deny.

"The Apocalypse Testament said: Answer your heart. It is where the One in All lives in all people. The laws of man are written to be obeyed, for the law affords respect to mankind and the mind of man. The laws of the One in All address the soul and are paramount. They are carried in the purest blood of the heart."

Lanta surfaced reluctantly, her head a clamor of unanswered questions. As full consciousness pressed her out of the trance, Conway's eyes were twitching open. He groaned.

Anxiously, her hand went to his pulse once more. Reassured, she smiled at him, then turned to Tate. The woman gave no sign of regaining consciousness. Conway spoke again, more confident. "Her hands. How badly are they hurt? I don't remember getting here. I didn't drop her, did I?"

Describing his return to the shelter with Tate in his arms filled Lanta with a pride she made no effort to disguise. In fact, she surprised herself a little, glossing over how he'd slumped to the ground as soon as he saw her approach. Nor did she tell him it took all her will to leave him while she dragged Tate the remaining twenty paces or so into the shelter, or that she dragged him, too. When he asked, she told him they'd been unconscious two days, adding, "Donnacee's badly hurt. No bones are broken, but she won't be much help for quite a while." Lanta lifted a bandaged hand for inspection. It was freakishly huge inside its wrapping. Swelling puffed the normally smooth skin into taut ugliness. Fingernails were missing. Splits shone red and raw in dark, stretched flesh.

Conway looked to the door, back to Lanta. "The dogs? The horses? How soon can Tate travel?"

"Get well. Then we'll talk of other things." Stifling his argument with a spoonful of broth, Lanta earned herself a moment's respite. After swallowing, Conway said, "Tomorrow I have to work. You'll have to help me. We have to get away from here."

"We'll see." Exasperated, and paradoxically pleased by this aggressive approach to recovery, Lanta wished she could distract him. The dogs provided her answer. Ecstatic at the sound of their master's voice, their barking and howling demanded attention. Somewhat ashamed of herself for not including the faithful animals, she opened the shelter flap and gestured them in. They nearly trampled Conway, pushing muzzles into his face, tongues licking like red, wet towels. Too weak to fend them off, delighted to see them, Conway protested and flailed as best he could. Lanta tried to pull them back. An action that normally would have earned her a threatening growl and a close view of lethal teeth went completely ignored; the dogs seemed aware of every nuance of the situation.

Satisfied at last, they obeyed Conway's command to go back outside. Lanta had to laugh at their contented air. Backs to the prevailing wind, they looked to her, wagged their tails one last time, and settled to wait. Lanta reached to touch their heads, whispering, "He is worth it, isn't he? You understand."

The following morning Conway was sitting up, waiting for Lanta when she returned to the tent from greeting the sunrise. She frowned at him. "What's this about?"

"I told you. I have work. We have to leave."

"Impossible. You're too weak."

"Maybe so. We're going to do it, anyhow."

"Do what? I can't intrude on your religious rites. If Tate—"

"No rites. No religion. To help Church, that's as close as I can get."

"We shouldn't leave Tate alone. There are animals about."

"If another Windband patrol comes to look for us, animals won't count."

"It's dangerous. We should wait until she's better."

"We can't." Straining upright, he waved off Lanta's offered hand. Once on his feet, he steadied. By the time they were on their way up the mountainside, he was walking with determination, if not grace.

The boxes of ammunition and explosives were stacked safely distant from the former cave mouth. With their light snow blanket, they were almost part of the landscape. More to himself than to Lanta, Conway complained of the need to leave so much. Still, he exhausted himself merely separating out the new amount. Lanta convinced him the actual loading of the horses would have to wait until the next day.

Just as they were leaving, Conway slowed, fixed a strange, speculative look on Lanta. He led her to a huge tree, had her sit down and lean back against it. He handed her his wipe, saying, "Tate won't be able to use one of these for a long time, will she?"

Lanta couldn't take her eyes off the sleek, horrid object in her lap. There was something reptilian about it. She shook her head, fearing the prospect his question suggested.

He said, "You have to know how to use this."

She shook her head again, violently, not trusting her voice.

"It could mean life or death, Lanta. There's nothing to it. No magic, no great religious experience." He bent to her, close enough for the scent of him to crowd her lungs, close enough for his warmth to caress her exposed face. His hands on the sleek weapon were supple, knowing. He took hers, led them across the smooth, cold surfaces as he taught. Dimly, she heard words: trigger, safety, selector switch. Like bright, glinting glass, they struck at her mind, lodged there.

"I can't." She loathed her denial of him. "I'm Church, Matt. Please. I'm a Chosen, saved by Church to serve Church. A Healer. A Seer. I can never kill."

He was as gentle as possible. "Church tried to kill all of us. They cast you out. You're absolved. Free."

"I was never not free. I believe." She made that point defiantly. His silent insistence forced her back to the real issue. "I live to save."

"I want you to be able to save yourself. You're cast out, vulnerable. If something happens to me . . ." His expression was concern that went beyond fear. There was plea. And a yearning she suddenly felt in her own breast.

When she extended the weapon to him, rejecting it, he took it without a word. She raised her face, stretched toward him. More than a kiss, she savored him, lips brushing his, then each eye in turn. She kissed his mouth.

He stepped back, face suffused, eyes curiously unfocused. His words were rough, from deep in his chest. "We better move now. We're losing time, you know? And don't worry about the wipe. I understand." He turned away, spinning on a heel. The boot cut a swirl in the snow. He said, "I love you for that. For everything. Because you're who you are. We're going to work it all out. We will."

Lanta picked up her share of the load, followed. Snow started again, making the descent that much more difficult.

Halfway back down the slope, Conway gestured Lanta to a stop. Before she could ask his reason, he signaled for quiet. She followed his gaze to the dogs. Both animals, originally beside them, were several paces behind. They stood with hackles raised, looking uphill. Putting her mouth to Conway's ear, Lanta asked, "Men?"

Frowning, Conway shook his head. He whispered, "I don't know." The dogs came instantly on command, although both warily glanced back up the mountainside. Faint breezes came from that direction. Snow distorted vision, suggested movement where none existed. Conway ordered the dogs ahead, but kept them within sight. Both animals continued to turn upwind occasionally, wet noses testing the air. Nervously, Conway and Lanta also scanned the back trail.

Camp was a welcome sight. One of the horses whickered a welcome.

Karda stopped as if frozen. Mikka was fractionally slower. Deathly silent, they raised their heads, scenting. Very slowly, still sniffing, they backed toward Conway and Lanta. Neck ruffs raised, stiff-legged, they moved as if expecting attack. Still, they favored no particular direction. On reaching Conway, they pressed against his legs, Karda to the left, Mikka to the right.

Lanta ran to the shelter, her light footsteps further buffered by a handspan's depth of snow. She disappeared inside.

When she came out, her hood was thrown back. She clutched at her breast. "She's not there." Disbelief pitched her words just short of hysteria.

Conway couldn't accept it. "She has to be. She must have come to, just stepped out." He was rushing forward as he argued, searching for tracks. Even before he reached Lanta, he saw them. He laughed, "See, there's her . . ." The words died. The laughter choked.

Not one set of tracks, but three, led away. Smudged by new snow, they were nevertheless unmistakable. New tracks. Too large for Tate.

Conway shoved Lanta against the rock, hard. A cry of surprised complaint had no effect; he pushed her all the way to the ground. At the same time, he dropped to one knee, his back to her. Facing out, the dogs beside him, he leveled the wipe. It searched back and forth, menacing.

Mocking laughter rolled out of the forest. Twisted by the wind, muffled by whirling snow, it came from everywhere. Nowhere.

The dogs searched frantically, furiously, growling constantly.

"I know you, Matt Conway." The voice tormented. "You remember Fox Eleven?"

"I know you, Fox Eleven. If it's really you. The Mountain warrior I knew faced men. Who is this who hides in the trees like a woman?"

"Should I show myself to the White Thunder? After I've stolen his black friend? Not today. Better if you come to me; she needs your Healer."

"She's sick, Fox. Covered by unseens."

There was a pause. Lanta held her breath, sure she heard low, intense muttering.

Fox was a bit less sure of himself. "It's infection from the injured hands, not sickness. You've become quite clever, but not clever enough to fool Moonpriest or his servants. We would have found you much sooner, but for this snow. It hid your tracks well."

"Braggart. The man I let go told you where to find us."

"I knew you'd be here long before those clumsy Windband wildcows crossed your path. Moonpriest said you'd come here. He knows all. He sent me to find you, Matt Conway. He wants you."

"You'll have to kill me."

"It would please me. I am told to avoid that. I'm allowed to cripple you."

An arrow whistled out of the surrounding forest, struck into the snow within reach of Conway. A rock under the snow deflected the shaft. Exploding away in a flurry of thrown snow, it caromed into the silent trees. Conway's involuntary jerk backward nearly toppled him.

Fox said, "That could have buried itself in your knee. I would enjoy your screams. But Moonpriest prefers you unharmed. I am told to make you understand. Safe passage to his camp if you surrender."

Conway sneered. "Where we'll be tortured to death for the entertainment of filth like you. Kill us now."

"It would be so, left to me. Moonpriest sees more, knows more, than the rest of us. Serve him, and he grants you life and honor. To deny him proves you are all witches. See if I can persuade you. Listen: I think I can wake the black one. I'll tell you what we're doing to her. I want you to know what's happening."

Lanta clutched at Conway's back. "Don't let them do it. Attack them. Death is better." He turned to look into her eyes. Her head moved in an almost-infinitesimal nod. Magically, a shortknife appeared in her fisted right hand. The left rose to touch his cheek. It explored the corner of his eye, where the brow tapered to an end. From there, it drifted the length of his jaw, building memory. Then she touched his shoulder. The gentle pressure of that loving hand insisting he rush to certain death was a supreme irony. Her throat worked before words actually formed. "I know what I must do. Don't look back. Please."

CHAPTER 57

FOX'S LAUGHTER WAS QUIETER THE SECOND TIME. IT SPUN CONWAY AROUND. FOX SAID, "I think the little one believes death is a better choice than serving Moonpriest. Listen to her. Loose your thunder, send your lightning. When you're dead, I'll make a necklace of your teeth, yours and those mangy dogs'. My women will make a blanket of their skins. With my own hands, I'll make a spirit flute of your thighbone, a spirit drum of your skull. The rhythm of your brain will be mine. Your bones will give me your strength, to serve me in battle. I'll own your soul, to serve the sons of my sons. Forever. The witch-Priestess will probably kill herself before we can reach her. Perhaps not. Perhaps you'll both live to see our games with the black one."

Lanta's pressure on Conway's back increased. "We can't escape. Don't let them hurt her."

Over his shoulder, Conway answered, "They intend to kill us when we reach Moonpriest. I know that. But Moonpriest wants to watch me die. It's a long way from here to there." He rose, ignoring Lanta's pleas. Speaking to Fox, he said, "If I surrender to Moonpriest, you take us to him? No abuse? No danger to the women? No harm to my dogs?"

"You sound like a man trying to bargain. Weakling. Peddler. I told you what my master has said. Safe conduct. To serve."

Slumped, Conway leaned his wipe against the rock. Lanta's protestations went unheeded. He added the pistol, then his sword. Karda and Mikka rose swiftly, gathering themselves as three figures ghosted toward them. Conway's command checked them. The men walked carefully around the belligerent animals to gather the weapons. Bands of white material wrapped around ordinary hides and woolens camouflaged the Mountains. With Conway's weapons safely in hand, the trio hurried back to cover.

Fox came forward to confront his prisoners. Ignoring Lanta completely, he smiled arrogant pride at Conway for a long while before speaking. "I always knew it would end like this. Your powers are nothing, compared to my master's. You are no man at all, compared to me. Luck kept you alive this long."

"Maybe Moonpriest will let us decide that. A duel, you and me."

Shifting ever so subtly, Fox's smile was suddenly hard, a mask that glistened with cruelty. "That would be my choice. My master promises that you live, however, if you serve honestly." He gestured. Men appeared, disappeared, flowed through the dim forest and the whirling snow. Something dark and massive loomed higher on the slope, making its way down. Fox pointed at it, laughed. "That's what confused your stupid dogs. We killed the bear for its skin. That man circled, got upwind of you. It was too easy. Your wonderful dogs never suspected."

Conway cursed himself. The dogs had tried to warn him. They smelled bear. They knew something was wrong with the smell. Poor fools. They relied on their master.

When Conway faced Fox again, warriors flanked the Mountain leader. They carried two poles, each half as long as a man, firmly attached to each other at one end by metal fittings and several links of stout chain. Additional lengths of chain dangled from the opposite ends of the poles. "You'll wear this. The poles bound to your arms, the dogs chained at your wrists."

Stepping back, Conway fumed. "Safe conduct? This is Moonpriest's promise of 'long life and honor'? "

"You'll try something treacherous. Between us, I hope so. Once you do, you're mine." Unexpectedly, Fox's gaze swept past Conway, rested on Lanta. "Put the shortknife away, woman. You can't use it."

Lanta pointed the knife warningly. "I am cast out. The law of Church doesn't bind me any longer."

"Church's law is your heart. You can't kill."

Impasse held them all long enough for the small tableau to take several breaths. Finally, as defeated as Conway, Lanta lowered the blade. At Fox's signal, a warrior stepped forward to take it from her.

They trussed Conway to his twin poles like a pheasant displayed for marketing. Bound at wrist, elbow, and biceps, he could move his arms from the shoulder, but not bend them. The chains snubbed the dogs right up against his hands. Lanta's hands were tied behind her back. For extra security, the line was looped around her waist and drawn tight.

Fox himself inspected the bonds. He kept behind the dogs. Conway's control over them was stretched to its limits when the Mountain warrior came close. The animals twisted and snarled constantly.

Fox gloated. "Who else but my master would design such a man-holder, or would know to send me with it to bring you and your foul animals back to him? His mind is above everything, and he himself said I was the only man who could find and capture you. When you're on your knees in his tent, he'll see how I worship him."

"No one will see me on my knees."

Coloring, Fox seemed about to speak. He hesitated, then smiled. Lanta studied it, and wished he'd whipped both of them. The flesh crawled on her back. Fox said, "We'll talk about your knees when the time comes. For now, do nothing foolish, and the journey won't be too hard."

"How do I sit a horse, wrapped up like this?" Conway moved his arms. The dogs tensed and growled hopefully.

"You walk. And we start now." Turning away, Fox gestured for men to take control of the horses tethered near the shelter. As soon as a stranger reached for Stormracer's tether, the animal neighed angrily and lashed out with a forefoot.

Nimbly, the man dodged. The horse continued to display, bobbing its head, quickstepping about, tugging at the line.

Fox shouted at the warrior. "What sort of woman are you? Can't you control a horse? Get him loose, lead him down to our mounts. Now."

The man flushed. The rest of the nomads snickered when he glanced around at them. He leaped to obey Fox.

Thoroughly aroused, the horse was waiting. It threw itself sideways, knocking aside the unsuspecting packhorse tied next to it. The man, hand raised in expectation of grabbing a bridle, found himself bounding into fury. He checked his rush. Too late.

The horse's teeth scissored the man's left shoulder, sheared muscle. The grating crack of the collarbone disappeared in the scream. Shaking the man like a terrier shaking a rat, Stormracer savaged him. Dropping his victim, the horse reared on its hind legs. The man squirmed helplessly. Stormracer bellowed rage, forefeet ripping the air. Blood discolored his muzzle.

The first arrow thudded into his flank. The barbed head struck bone. There was little penetration, but much hurt. The horse screamed.

Turning its head, it looked directly at its master.

Conway's heart turned to ice. Stormracer understood. He was going to die, and would die fighting.

Flailing hooves clubbed the fallen nomad.

Arrows came in a storm. Stormracer reared, bawling. The tether snapped. Free, studded with arrows, he bit at one. Ears back, teeth bared, he charged. One man slipped. The horse bowled him over, skidded to a stop to come back. A warrior darted from behind a tree. A sword flicked, came away red. Blood spurted where the hamstring was severed. Falling, Stormracer reached to bite his tormenter. Another flurry of arrows struck him. Swift, sleek birds, they buried themselves in his heaving body. Rolling onto his side, he snapped at the air, kicked in protest at dying.

The man who'd been knocked down advanced warily on the weakening animal. Raising his sword, he drove it at the throat. The blow was true. With his last bit of life, Stormracer lunged, sank his teeth in the man's knee.

Dead, the valiant animal would never know it crushed the kneecap.

The dogs howled mournfully. Obeying Conway's orders to hold back from the fight, they twitched in aborted tugs against the chains that bound them. Lanta faced away, unable to watch, unwilling to look at the aftermath.

Fox snapped orders. Tate's war-horse was given no chance to inflict similar damage. An onslaught of arrows dropped it in its tracks.

Stonily, Conway stood unmoving, save when the overwrought dogs pulled at him. He stared at Fox. Neither man spoke. Neither acknowledged the cries of the crippled warrior, or the excited running and shouting of the others. The moment, and the promise it contained for both of them, was theirs alone.

Lanta was astounded to realize how each man cherished their hatred. There was no other word for it. There was a stench of obscenity about it.

A nomad called to Fox, repeating the name until his leader grudgingly left off the staring match with Conway.

Moving to Conway's side, Lanta said, "I'm sorry, Matt. I wish I could say something that would help."

A quick look of appreciation, and he was staring at Stormracer again. "We saw a lot together. Remember the day you named him? I'd just gotten over being sick then, too. Gan says they never name war-horses, because they know they're going to be killed. It's supposed to be easier to accept if they're not named. That's not true. I'm glad you named him for me. It was the best name. Best horse. Good companion, loyal friend. I let him die."

"There was nothing you could do."

"That doesn't help, either." He turned, gave her a wan smile of apology. "Don't listen to me. I'm feeling very inadequate just now. I'll be all right. I have to be. There's a debt to pay."

Ordering men to gather the casualties and captured horses, Fox set a grueling pace downhill to where a small security detail watched over the patrol's mounts. Conway was surprised to see how many there were. More nomads drifted in from the forest. Their white wrappings gave them a disembodied look as they made their way through the trees and falling snow.

Conway protested loudly at the sight of Tate, draped across a saddle. Her injured hands dangled free, swollen, angry-looking. Conway was sure he could see them throbbing. Lanta demanded to be allowed to minister to her friend. She started forward, and a nomad grabbed her roughly, pulled her back. Tate went untended, jouncing and jerking downhill.

At the nomad camp on the banks of the creek that drained the valley, Conway noted neat little tents in neat, straight lines. One cookfire at the end of each row. A quick count indicated thirty riders. Two tents stood apart from the rest. Conway assumed they were for Fox and the man who'd normally command such a unit.

Fox saw Conway's inspection. He said, "Moonpriest says warriors must have a system, or control is weakened." Underlying defensiveness robbed his words of authority.

Conway understood exactly why. Fox was uncomfortable. This wasn't Fox's way of fighting. He was a man who went into battle as an individual among individuals. Measured rows and stepped-off intervals denied everything in his nature. Nevertheless, Fox knew about survival in hostile territory. It was dusk when the scouts began to appear. Six altogether, they came at a trot from their various directions, reporting directly to Fox. Unable to hear, Conway knew by Fox's expression and manner that no scout reported anything disturbing. As further proof, Fox indicated a point downstream where he wanted wood piled for the dead nomad's cremation.

Three men off-loaded Tate, dumping her hard. She rolled, limp. One of the men said something. Coarse laughter cut across the hubbub of low-level chatter and occasional shouts. The sinister amusement clashed with the innocent whicker of hungry horses anticipating end-of-day grain. The trio of guards around Tate glanced in Conway's direction. On eye contact, they looked away quickly. Their expression was puzzling. It wasn't gloating, or mocking, or unusually cruel.

Conway expected something of that nature. This was different. Suppressed. These men hoarded a secret and feared that Conway might discover it.

Axes ringing changed the direction of Conway's thought. He watched, morbidly fascinated, as a pyramid of logs rose around a platform holding the dead nomad.

The eerie rise of a wolf's call marked the first leaf of flame to dance among the kindling. Conway recognized the ceremony that followed as a Long Sky People observance. Each warrior approached the growing flames with a handful of grass or leaves. Although the fire wasn't hot enough to require it, the men carefully shielded their faces on approaching. Flinging their offering on the pyre, they backed away, still pretending to avoid searing heat.

More wolves joined the original singer. Howling chorused up and down the valley, dropped into it from adjacent peaks and hills. Always distant, discreet, the sound seemed part of the rite.

Later the pile of logs collapsed. Sparks cascaded up into darkness, danced mad celebration, winked out. Dark anticipation pressed down on the valley.

CHAPTER 58

CONWAY STRAINED AGAINST THE LEATHER ROPE BINDING HIM TO A SAPLING SOME FEW PACES from the fire. He appreciated the warmth. More cold air settled in the valley at every heartbeat, it seemed. The young tree was only about a handspan in diameter. He sat on the ground, bound so he seemed to embrace it. His extended feet were tied together. The same line secured his hands at the wrists. A second line looped around the tree and behind his back to keep him tightly upright. The dogs, attached to the ends of the chain-pole yoke, barely had enough slack to lie parallel to their master's outstretched legs.

Beside Conway, similarly lashed to another tree, Lanta shifted nervously. "They're planning something, Matt." The purling creek a few steps behind them almost overwhelmed her words. The patrol, huddled on the far side of the fire, was too far to overhear.

Conway ignored his own foreboding. "It's your imagination. Hardly anyone's even looked at us."

She jerked her head to indicate where Tate's tumbled form lay close to the gathered nomads. "None of these men has ever seen a black woman. You know what Windband does to female captives. Have they treated her so?"

"Well, no, but . . ."

"They look at Tate, they look at me. They pretend they don't see us. They're hiding something. So are you." She looked away from his offense. "I'm sorry, Matt; I truly am. It's my training."

"If you're seeing so much, what're these people saying to you?"

"Fear. And eagerness. Something they want desperately to keep hidden."

"They're not bothering us. We're all right."

As if overhearing, Fox put down his wooden eating dish, rose languidly. The eyes fixed on Conway consumed. Mute, the Windband men watched. Condensed breath was a diffuse haze around them. The ruffling of the bonfire was the only sound in the camp as Fox advanced. Karda and Mikka tensed, forward-leaning pressure pulling on Conway harder against the tree's rough bark.

Fox stopped, wide-stanced, hands on hips. The fire behind him threw his face into shadow. Darkened eye sockets and deepened hollows under his cheekbones replicated his people's death's-head war mask. "Moonpriest said you and the Black Thunder look for a cave here, a place sacred to him. He said you would profane it, steal the lightning weapons he has hidden there. In the morning, you'll lead us to it."

Relief rolled through Conway. Fox didn't know the cave was already emptied or that it no longer existed, didn't know that his bearskin-clad scout almost caught them carrying a share of the ammunition. Conway's first thought was to deny everything. He reconsidered instantly. The cave entrance was obliterated, the weapons and ammunition safely hidden, all tracks covered by snow. Fox would never believe Conway didn't know the location. Better, then, to admit to having been there, but claim it was destroyed before they could reenter it. Accordingly, Conway acted depressed, regaling Fox with a tale of disappointing discovery.

Fox listened patiently. When Conway finished, he spoke impassively. "You lie."

Conway feigned anger. "I'll show you where it was. You can see for yourself."

"You're afraid to enter, because it's sacred to Moonpriest. You'll take me there. You'll get the lightning weapons for me."

"The cave's not there anymore. I said I'd show you."

"And I said you're a liar." Fox bent forward belligerently. The dogs leaped to attack the perceived threat. The chain joining the two poles slammed into the back of Conway's neck. Light and darkness flicked across his vision. Shoulder joints cracked under the strain.

Fox leaped back. He was a full two paces away when Conway's strangled cries finally quieted the dogs.

The involuntary retreat broke Fox's careful facade. Hatred and rage surfaced. "Moonpriest wants those weapons. You'll get them for him."

"I can't. They're buried under the mountain." As he spoke, Conway looked to the nomads. They were more eager than ever. Deathly silent. Expectant. Cold fear seized Conway's guts.

Far away, an owl sounded. The five notes, all the same key, had a demanding, confident sound. A dissociated corner of Conway's mind identified the bird as the huge, horned one called night tiger.

Fox continued. "Moonpriest said you'd lie. He gave me permission to force the truth from you."

A stir ran through the watching, listening men. Conway had the impression they were closer. He said, "The cave's collapsed. Gone. You can see for yourself."

"Moonpriest is never wrong."

"I escaped him once, Fox. He was wrong then. Now he's caught me. Would I dare lie to him, to you? Now?"

Livid, Fox literally stammered. "You escaped because all of you combined your witch power together. He listened to you. Believed you. Traitor." Fox turned, faced the warriors. "Is it time?"

They exploded. Some actually leaped up and danced, whooping.

Beside him, Lanta exclaimed involuntary fright, a tiny, despairing sound.

Fox quieted his men, though basking in their response. He told Conway, "When you see what these men and I do to your women, you will beg to get the lightning weapons for me."

Conway blinked, unbelieving. When the full impact of the perfidy struck, he went out of control. The dogs, caught in his insensate anger, did what instinct and training demanded, fighting to reach their foe. Fox backed up before parading back and forth in front of them, taunting. At one point he pulled a burning brand from the fire, poking it in the faces of the lunging, straining animals. Mikka snapped at it, yelping pain and frustration when it blistered her tongue and mouth.

That cry brought Conway back to reality. Slowly, almost reluctantly, he crawled out of a pit of madness. Neck and shoulders throbbed from the action of the dogs. Both sides of his face bled from battering and scraping against the tree bark. Reluctantly, the dogs ceased charging.

Addressing his warriors again, Fox raised a fist. Their uproar stopped. Fox said, "You saw? He never suspected. You saw his face? Look at him. Think how he feels. He gave us the women, both of them. You did well, all of you. I warned you not to spoil the surprise. You see why? I told you it would be a wonderful moment. He never knew. Imagine his pain, knowing he'll watch us enjoy them. The witches are ours. Moonpriest promised to crush their power, and he has." Cheers erupted again. The men pressed forward.

Fox stopped them with a gesture. They flanked the fire, with no one behind it, so that when Conway looked, there were avid, cruel faces, then the roaring flames, and then more faces. Beyond them, a few illuminated trees, stark and stolid. And blackness. Fox continued. "This will be done right. Tonight we play with the black one, to make her speak. Watch how skillfully I keep her alive until we have the lightning weapons." To Conway, Fox said, "When the sun rises, you'll take us to the cave. If you do your work well, I'll kill her quickly and cleanly. Then you'll show us the way of the lightning weapons. The witch-Priestess will encourage you. Like the black, she dies easily or very, very slowly. You will choose."

Conway twisted his head to the side of the tree that allowed him to look at Lanta. Tears stained her face. Crying had already passed, however. She wore a determination that couldn't hide fear, but refused to surrender to it. Fox stepped back, enjoying his prisoners' shared anguish.

Lanta's look for Fox spoke of the stench of filth. The look changed when it reached Conway, turned to pleading. Straining to make him understand meaning beyond her words, she went on. "Our lives are ended. Finished. Look at him. There's no mercy there. He's enjoying how we look, what we say, savoring every shade of our misery. He's an obese beast, sniffing and drooling before it feeds its ugly mouth. Nothing you can do will change anything. Unless you live. So live, my love. Remember me. Know that your love is the only thing I leave unwillingly."

Conway shook his head. Before he could speak, Lanta raised her voice, begging. "My life, my death, are meaningless if you don't live. Don't let us die for nothing. Think of me, think of all your friends. Live that they may love you as I do, as I will love you even in the Land Beyond."

Suspicion closed Fox's features. He stepped forward, backhanded Lanta. The casual power of the blow drove her head sideways against the tree trunk. She bounced, slumped momentarily. When she pulled herself upright, defiance disregarded the already swelling cheek.

To Conway, Fox said, "There was a signal in what she said to you. Don't try to outsmart me. You'll get me the lightning weapons. The women will pay for every heartbeat of delay, every moment of displeasure."

"You unspeakable piece of vomit. You and that snake-dropping you worship. Your turn's coming. I swear it."

"Good. Good." Fox's teeth gleamed. "My master told me to bring you to him in good health. He can't complain if you resist, force me to restrain you. Fight me. *Fight me*."

"Matt." It was Lanta, appealing.

Conway subsided. His chin fell to his shoulder. Karda lay his head on Conway's thigh, ears back, snarling. The dog's dark, knowing eyes never left Fox, not even when the Mountain picked up a fist-sized rock and hurled it against the animal's ribs. Karda grunted, then growled.

Conway felt his own heart speaking through the dog. There was fury, of course; a pulsing need to tear and crush and kill. But there was despondence. And defeat. Conway constantly guarded against assigning human values to his dogs, as much as he loved them. Still, he knew them to enjoy, to suffer, to care. He knew they lived in pride. He didn't believe they could anticipate death. He did believe they understood it. In Karda's repressed, hapless snarl, Conway heard the animal mourning the ignominy of this ending.

As Conway did himself.

To watch the women die at Fox's hands was unbearable. To give Fox what he wanted in the hope of sparing them agony was unforgivable. The pitiless brutality of the choices was impeccable. Neither woman escaped torture. The duration of it was Conway's decision. Dying was the only escape.

The night tiger owl called again. Mikka raised her head. Conway flinched at the seared flesh of her muzzle, the oily slick on her throat and breast from constant salivation. The bird's resonant hoot had hardly ceased when a small animal's shriek pierced the darkness.

Two men half carried, half dragged Tate from her resting place. Conway was astounded to see her remain on her feet when they released her next to Fox. She swayed drunkenly, silhouetted against the fire.

The nomads bunched tighter, edging closer. Eyes gleamed. Tongues darted brightly, wetly. Conway shivered. Fox spoke to him. "You heard the owl. A young, unsteady one, from the sound of it, yet good enough to kill. You heard the prey dying? Cherish the sound. The Tate one will make you remember it as pleasant as laughter."

Tate mumbled. Conway strained to hear. Standing closer, Fox heard her clearly. He stiffened at her words. His head jerked backward as if he'd been struck. Clutching one of Tate's battered hands in both of his, he squeezed.

Both dogs twisted and squirmed against their bindings. To Conway's astonishment, they scrambled to escape Tate's scream. In doing so, they bent his arms back at the shoulders. He yelled at them to stop, got them to lie down.

Tate was on her knees, bowed forward, face almost in the dirt, when next Conway looked. Fox straddled her from behind, holding her hands separately in his own. He squeezed them both, twisting as he did. For a long breath, Tate was almost silent, making only a soft, worried panting. Suddenly, her head flew back. Her raised face was a sweating corrugation of pain, the eyes squinted to slits. Her mouth gaped to the cold night sky. The lips shone ruby, bloody from her attempts to bite back the shriek that exploded past them. Conway closed his eyes, not aware of his own screams until the pain of his aching throat made him cough.

He was unable to stop looking. Fox still held Tate's hands, but in one of his. With the other, he drew the gleaming ma from its scabbard. Inserting the point under the back of her jacket at the waist, he began to slit the leather. Slowly, lasciviously. He looked to Conway, smiling lazily. The men watched, transfixed. Steam rose from them, breath and perspiration.

Conway knew then there was a hell, and that one need not die to find it. He opened his mouth to curse them all.

A nomad toward the rear of the crowd leaped in the air, came down slapping at his back. He shouted pained annoyance. Companions turned to look, puzzled. He said, "Something stung me." Anxious to stop the interruption to the entertainment, a man beside him said, "It's too cold. There's nothing—" His disagreement ended on a sharp yip. Others turned to see what this one complained about. A rod, like a small, thin arrow, perhaps as long as a man's arm from elbow to hand, protruded from both sides of the man's neck.

The first man howled, scrabbling and twisting to grasp the thing at his back.

The remainder were paralyzed. It was all incomprehensible. There was no musical twang of bowstring, no whisper of feathered shaft. The darts had no tail at all, save a piece of white fluff on the butt end.

The last man wounded grabbed the thing in his neck. He wrenched it free in one superhuman heave. Blood gushed from the entry and exit wounds, from his mouth. He swayed, toppled. The first man wounded cried for help, an effort that ended in wracking coughs. He sagged to his knees.

Men shouted, searched wildly.

Whistling exploded from the forest. Shrill, nerve-burning, it came from everywhere, nowhere. Trilling signals struck with a psychic impact as demoralizing as the silent, deadly darts. Then there was a storm of the missiles, enough to create a trembling blur around the expanding, yelling group of nomads. Fox yelled, grabbed at his head, fell to the ground. He pawed at the steel thing sticking out of him as a dog flails at a porcupine quill.

Conway felt hands on him, felt the release of his bindings before he saw anyone. Hands as nimble as insects plucked at the chains holding the dogs. Almost miraculously quickly, they fell free.

Asking no questions, Conway leaped into the battle. Almost all the nomads were wounded. Many were down. From the darkness, more silent darts sped at the survivors. Now there were arrows, as well. Heavier, they whirred from short, heavy recurved bows and struck with sodden impact. Men appeared, clad in dark, tight leather. They moved with weasellike efficiency. They were silent now, their whistling war signals unneeded.

Conway scooped up a fallen ma. The rescuers flowed around him everywhere, carrying long spears. A ma slashed at one of the ungainly-looking weapons. The man seemed to move the spear the merest fraction. The ma hissed past harmlessly. A blindingly fast counterthrust plunged into the nomad's stomach. The spearman stepped past him with dancing grace.

Shouting release, Conway struck at a nomad face. It disappeared. Again and again, he struck, feinted, thrust, slashed. Beside him, his dogs roared and bit. Bones cracked. Men screamed. The battle was a blur, a mélange of noise and exhaustion.

It ended as all combat actions, in a lull pregnant with exhausted panting, the suffering of the wounded.

Lanta moved into Conway's peripheral vision, a tiny, dark figure hurrying from one fallen warrior to the next. She carried a water gourd. Some accepted a drink, and she lingered, tending wounds. Some men were past thirst. Lanta examined them, then moved on. Conway noted that when she left one of the latter, she appeared even smaller. More fragile, somehow.

As if waking, he looked around, expecting to see the odd victors of the attack gathered together, aiding their wounded, already telling tales of their personal experience. For a moment, he had the insane feeling that he was entirely alone with Lanta and dead or wounded nomads.

The men who'd come from the night had returned to it.

Conway barely made out four at the edge of firelight. They were obviously posted between the hidden main group and the bonfire. A man stepped between the guards, advanced on Conway. Like the foursome, he was short, sturdily built, clad in tight, unadorned leather shirt and trousers. He wore a leather skullcap. A flap in the back protected his neck. It suddenly occurred to Conway how short all these newcomers were. Memory pulled at him. It faded, pushed aside by the present.

The man kept the fire between himself and Conway. There was something in his hand, long and round. Like a cane, without the curved handle. He raised it to his mouth.

Conway remembered the silence of the darts, the peculiar white tuft on the dull ends. Blowguns. He braced himself.

Sweet, familiar music flowed from the long flute, poured melody on the wrecked bodies strewn about the campsite. The aftersounds of combat quieted. A man cried softly. The nomad closest to Conway sighed infinite weariness. A glance told Conway he was gone.

Lanta came to Conway. He put an arm around her waist, pressed her to his side. They moved together to stand over Tate, who sat, leaning forward, elbows braced on her knees. She acknowledged her friends with a grimace they understood to be a smile, then leaned back heavily against their legs. Karda and Mikka lay down on Conway's side opposite Lanta, tongues lolling, chests still heaving. The five of them—man, women, dogs—waited.

CHAPTER 59

THE MAN LOWERED THE FLUTE. WHEN HE SPOKE, HIS VOICE WAS CLEAR, BUT WITH AN UNsettling ventriloquial quality. "We followed you far, Matt Conway. We watched the Fox one stalking you. Our debt is paid now, I think."

Lanta found her voice first. "Smalls. You're Smalls. You're the strangers in the Enemy Mountains, come north of the Mother River. How many are you?"

Smiling, the man said, "Lanta. Companion to Sylah, the Flower. All Smalls know how you saved our children. All know Matt Conway also helped the Flower, and was kind to one of our sisters who was a slave in Windband's camp. It was decided we were obliged to get involved in outsiders' troubles. We couldn't let the Fox one have you."

Conway blanched at the accuracy of the man's language. He said, "We never felt we were owed. If you did, any debt is paid and overpaid. Thank you. I remember clearly now. Bizal. And young Tarabel. How is the boy? Will you tell us your name?"

"Gladly. Tinillit is my name." He touched two fingers to his forehead. "Tarabel is healed. Bizal sent us north. The Smalls seek a place where we can live in peace. We know Gan Moondark dispersed the Mountain People from this country. We wish to settle where they were. We think we can be better neighbors."

Tate pulled at Lanta's robe. She bent to her friend, listened, shook her head in amused exasperation. To the waiting Tinillit, Lanta said, "Tate says you can be her neighbor any time you want." At Tate's repeated tug, Lanta added, "She said to tell you she'll bake a cake."

Tinillit laughed. "She's brave. You all are. Few resist Moonpriest."

Conway said, "And you?"

The laughter turned bitter. "We are Church. Not that it helped us with the Kossiars, or the River People. Windband is even worse. All would make us slaves."

Tate stirred. Conway put a calming hand on her shoulder. He said, "If you stalked Fox without his awareness, you're very good. I'd think you'd make unlikely victims for slavers."

"Forest is our home. It protects us. Still, we need land to grow crops, raise livestock. We are hunted, Matt Conway. Whenever we stop to rest, to create a home place, we live in the knowledge that soon someone will come for us."

"Enough talk." Firmly, Lanta pulled away from Conway. "Tinillit. You have casualties?"

"None serious. We tend our own." Again, Conway felt rejection, a distancing. There was nothing unpleasant in the Small's voice, no change in posture or expression. Still, Conway knew he was being told to stand clear. The impression was so strong it made him a bit unsteady. Unobtrusively, he felt his head, wondering if he'd taken a blow without knowing it.

Lanta bored ahead. "I'm a Church Healer. I can help."

"We have healers. Generations ago, we watched such as you. Now we even have medicine of our own."

"Have it your way. I'll tend to the Windband injured. Matt, help Donnacee to a place where she can rest. Would you help me, then?" Lanta's response was querulous, totally unlike her. Conway nodded absently, surprised by the peculiar behavior. She turned away, busying herself immediately.

Tinillit said, "We have food. My companions are cooking. We'll bring you some."

Hunger, once acknowledged, tore at Conway. He hurried to make Tate comfortable. As he tucked furs around her, she beckoned him close. "Careful."

He searched her features. Her eyes wandered, uncertain. Her breath rasped. Conway said, "Careful of the Smalls? They saved us, Donnacee. Saved you."

Her nod was painfully slow. "I know. Strange. Something 'bout him. Tin . . . whatever. Careful. Please."

"I promise. Can I do anything for your hands? Some warm water to bathe them?"

"Sleep. Jus' sleep, buddy. You—careful." The deep-set, exhausted eyes closed. Conway marveled at the classic beauty, the contradictory placidity of her repose. He thought of the tongue-lashing he'd get if he mentioned either to her, and smiled to himself. Signaling the dogs, he positioned them to guard her.

Then he remembered the weapons.

Fox had placed them in his own tent, exactly as Conway expected. Carrying them over his head in triumph, he hurried to show them to Lanta. She sniffed. Chastened, he leaned both wipes against a tree, put the holstered pistols beside them, and strapped on the sword. Lanta asked him to move some wounded closer to the fire's warmth.

The first man Conway reached for was covered with blood. Steeling himself, Conway stood across the man's torso to grab the relatively clean shoulders. He never saw any movement until the tip of the ma was at his throat and two earth-dark eyes were fixed on his own.

His stomach curled in on itself. Breath caught in his throat.

The supine man said, "Bring Fox Eleven. Here." The order was strained, but clear.

"He's dead." When Conway swallowed, the ma's point picked at his skin.

"I saw them take him away. Bring him." The ma twitched. Conway felt wetness trickling down his neck. From the corner of his eye, he saw the dogs rise. Suspicious, they cast their heads warily, scenting for a danger they couldn't quite identify. Conway knew that if the animals moved, he died. A hand signal stopped them. He called Tinillit's name, then, "Do you have Fox Eleven? It's important."

There was a silence. Conway sensed movement on the other side of the fire. Bent forward, held by his jacket, he twisted grotesquely to see clearly. The ma remained at his throat. Fox came into view, with Tinillit and another Small following, weapons drawn. A large bandage covered the right side of Fox's head, including the right eye. His left arm was heavily wrapped, as well.

When Fox was visible to him, the man on the ground said, "The White Thunder doesn't even recognize me, Fox." His chuckle was a sour, biting sound.

Conway turned his head slowly, accepting yet another razoring cut from the ma. He blinked, not understanding

The man said, "You should have killed me when your dogs had me trapped. You're soft. That's why we'll kill all your kind." His gaze went to Tinillit. "Free Fox."

"No. If you kill Conway, we kill Fox. Then we kill you. You gain nothing."

"I regain my honor. And you lose one who knows the lightning weapon. You won't pay that price."

Tinillit's feet moved in a tight fidget. "Fox is too injured to travel. His eye is destroyed. He may lose the arm. We can care for him."

"Make him a slave, you mean. Free him. Give him a horse. When I'm sure he's far enough away, I'll give you my weapon."

Lanta came into Conway's vision. She knelt at the limit of her arm's reach, extended a hand to the man's forehead. "I promise you no one will be made a slave. Please, in the name of Church, let Matt Conway go."

"Don't touch me!" The man jerked his head from under her touch. Then he jabbed the ma into Conway's neck. Conway grunted, fought to avoid pulling away. The man panted, forcing words. "Touch me again and I kill him here and now. Fox. Tell Moonpriest I've earned my place next to him in paradise. Tell him."

Fox shrugged out of the grip of his captors. "I will. I want my sword. A good bow and some arrows. And food."

Tinillit signaled for the items. Smalls brought them, put them on the ground between Fox and the horses. Tinillit said, "Choose a mount."

Fox scooped up the material with his good arm. To Tinillit, he said, "I'll remember. Refused to touch me. Made me bandage my own wounds. We'll see who gets touched, when next we meet." Despite his injuries, Fox cleared the camp swiftly. The sound of his horse dwindled. Tinillit listened some while after the last noise disappeared. Carefully quiet, the Small spoke to Conway's captor. "Give me the sword now. You won't be hurt."

"You think you can hurt me? After this one stole my pride?"

Conway interrupted. "Don't be a fool. There's no shame in losing a fight."

The eyes looking into Conway's flew wide. Spittle flecked the man's lips. "What would you know of shame? Weakling. Afraid to kill. You can't recognize courage. Don't you want to know why I didn't try to leave with Fox?"

Conway said, "I'd be more interested to know why he didn't offer to take you with him. Or thank you for freeing him."

The man snarled, "He's too smart to burden himself." He stopped, suddenly sly. "My secret. You don't know. None of you."

Tinillit said, "You can't move your legs."

"No." It was a wail of disappointment. The face that had been craftily resolute collapsed in loss. "It won't change anything. It's your fault. So small. Not a decent arrow. A stick. No noise." He looked around, pulling down on Conway's jacket, forcing the ma into his flesh once again. The pressure was harder. Conway coughed.

Out of Conway's sight, Lanta said, "Please. You're hurting him. Please. Don't."

Conway tried to turn to look at her. The man shouted, "Don't turn away. I want you to see me laughing at you, see me bathing in your blood. I want to watch your face while I—"

The rest was lost on Conway, overwhelmed by the roaring in his ears. He saw everything magnified, slowed impossibly. Flesh tightened at the corners of the nomad's eyes. The pulse in the wrist of the sword hand leaped, a writhing snake. Sinews bulged in the hand, the forearm. A crystalline drop of saliva oozed from the edge of lips stretched pale in a rictus grin.

Rising, slicing, the icy metal of the blade opened Conway's throat. Pain was giant teeth, tearing, parting flesh.

The ma twisted, pulled sideways, tore instead of penetrating.

The wound was more than hurt. It was sound. Thunder, rolling and throbbing.

Conway flew, yelling. He landed on his back, hands clutching his throat. Tumbling, babbling, he scrambled to his feet.

Cradling the wipe, staring through wisping smoke curling from the muzzle, Lanta looked at the dead nomad. Rigid as stone, she focused on the tidy, insignificant-appearing hole in his upper arm. Stark black against the blue-white pallor of death, it featured one tiny ruby of blood. Moving to her, Conway breathed a silent thanks that she couldn't see the exit wound. She should never know how the wicked little round, still cased in its sabot, penetrated the arm and entered her victim's rib cage almost sideways, continuing to whirl, devastating whatever bit of flesh and bone blocked its path until it erupted out the far side of the victim's body.

Conway looked into Lanta's eyes and wondered if she would ever know anything again. Gingerly, he took her finger from the trigger. When the wipe was safely on the ground, he took her in his arms. He spoke, reassuring, consoling. Her eyes remained lifeless as polished stone.

Tate joined him, stroked Lanta's brow, trying to erase at least a portion of the unresponsive stare. Failing that, weakening herself, Tate withdrew. The dogs settled against Conway.

Constellations followed their steady way across the sky while he sat with her in his arms. The fire dwindled, occasionally exploding in an eruption of sparks as one of the Small night guards fueled it.

Talking past Lanta's unseeing eyes and unchanging expression, Conway sent his soul searching into the frozen, dissociated figure. Every indication declared that Lanta's life ended when she saved that of the man she loved. Conway could not accept that. He talked softly, confidently, endlessly. He described the Smalls, how they moved through the darkness like wraiths. He talked to her of the sound of yet another night bird, the one he knew as screech owl, called darksinger by Gan's people. He spoke of his hopes, his fears.

Convoluted, complicated emotional barriers fell. In moments he shattered the stone that had confined his heart for so long. He spoke of fools and love. How could he have been so wrong? How could she not understand that his greatest fear was that he might hurt her, and his greatest shame was that he'd done so? Of course it was wrong of him to feel it necessary to prove himself worthy.

He marshaled argument. He cited example. In the silence that followed his brilliant summary, he reviewed everything he'd said, then whispered to her that, yes, he'd been a total fool.

He told Lanta of caring, of needing, of wanting. He spoke of the warmth of sharing, of the strength of two who support and stand as one. He promised her the time of trouble between them was past. "We have a new life, just waiting for us. You have to be well; you have to. I can't be—don't want to be—anything without you. I love you."

Lanta remained rigid, unchanged. But she closed her eyes. Soon Conway did the same. And they slept.

CHAPTER 60

CONWAY WOKE TO THE TOUCH OF FINGERTIPS BRUSHING HIS TEMPLE. IMAGES OF A PAST LIFE he could barely recall melded with scenes from the night just ended. He didn't know if he dreamed or remembered.

His neck hurt. Burned. He thought of fires, of whole cities aflame. He thought of a sword, seeking his jugular. Did either happen? Touch identified bandages at his throat. That was reality.

In the crepuscular predawn, he looked up to find Lanta's face just above his. She examined him with a look of stricken wonder, an expression that was at once joyous and full of trepidation. He'd been afraid to open his eyes before. Now he feared he'd break a spell.

Lanta lowered her hand from his temple, took his chin in her hand. She smiled almost imperceptibly. "Whiskers," she said. "Does a woman ever get used to them?" She talked to herself, looking deep into Conway's eyes, still acquainting herself with this wondrous new discovery. "So many new things. A creation to be accomplished. Together."

Taking her hands in his own, Conway kissed the palms.

Her smile was brighter, fuller. Yet Conway sensed pain, knew it was rooted in the death of the nomad the night before. His thoughts raced back over the obstacles he and Lanta had created for themselves and for each other, and he swore to himself that it wouldn't happen again. He held happiness in his hands, and he was determined to keep it.

Before he could speak, Lanta said, "I waited for you to wake. I've been practicing saying it. Now I can. I love you, Matt Conway."

"I love you. I will forever."

Lanta rose, the lithe quickness of a startled animal. It was an entirely inappropriate action. She seemed as surprised by it as Conway. She looked down at him with apology. "I have to tend to Tate." The words were flat, clumsy. "I wanted to tell you, to say I love you. I have to do my duty, though." She gestured, a limp, aimless movement.

Conway looked to the east. "You don't have time. Your sun-greeting prayers."

The pain was there again, and gone, the wisp of an insect's wing. Conway rose, took her shoulders in his hands, forced her to meet his eyes. "You saved my life. You were the only one who could."

"I cannot . . . A Priestess cannot kill. All I was taught . . . Everything."

Hugging her to him, he waited for her sudden sobs to slow. When they were no more than shuddering breaths, he spoke. "I know little of Church, but I know she forgives. Forgive yourself. Church's will come when you ask."

"I can't be a Priestess. I can't call myself a Healer, wear the robes. It's not allowed. Even if I'm forgiven, I have to leave my abbey."

"Abbey and Church left you long ago. It was Sister Mother's ally who meant to kill all of us. What about Sylah? She didn't give up everything. Look, Church's present rulers are responsible for hundreds of deaths. That's why Church is split, why women like you and Sylah are going to build a new Church. Let those corrupt old women say what they will. You're beyond them. They can't hurt you."

Lanta shook her head. "You spoke the heart of it. Can I can forgive myself?"

Solemn, he held her at arm's length. "I'm asking you to forgive yourself. I'm begging you. Give me reason to care that you saved my life. You're the only one who can. Help me."

"I want to. I need to think."

Conway's smile turned rueful. "Always a dangerous proposition. But I guess it can't be avoided. While you're thinking, however, remember; I'm thinking about our marriage in Ola. As soon as we get there."

Blushing, suddenly more shy than troubled, Lanta slipped out of his grasp. She went to Tate with a quicker step than was really necessary.

A faint noise behind Conway drew his attention. Tinillit smiled apology. Once more, Conway marked the distance between them. The two exchanged greetings and small talk. Conway took the opportunity to study the Small's spear-blowgun. He was surprised to realize it wasn't simply a length of hollow cane. Instead, it reminded him of pictures from an old book he'd seen before his world destroyed itself. Men made fishing rods in that manner once, the book said. They split the finest cane and shaved it to precise thickness and shape. Then they glued it back together, creating a slender, tapering artifact that combined great strength, light weight, and flexibility.

Conway's mind drew up another memory; driving a freeway along a riverbank, watching miles of closely supervised fishermen, practically shoulder to shoulder. Rods flashed endlessly in the bright sunshine as they worked to catch one of the handful of fish left in the stream. Game Monitors, linked by radio, ranged their assigned length of the human chain, keeping count, as well as order. Fights over tangled lines were common. Riots sometimes erupted among dissatisfied sportsmen when the permitted catch was exhausted and further fishing suspended. He'd always found it ironic that fines levied on poachers and those who trespassed in Controlled Access Nature Preserves contributed so much to financially support what little was left of sport fishing.

Tinillit was saying, "Are you sure you're all right?"

Conway felt his face warm. He spoke with embarrassed, choppy words. "I'm fine. Just thinking." He jerked his chin at Tinillit's blowgun and extended a hand. "I've never seen a weapon like that. Can I look at it?"

Tinillit looked very uncomfortable. He didn't move, yet Conway had the distinct feeling the man retreated. Tinillit said, "I must explain some things about Smalls. When you return to Ola you can explain to Gan Moondark."

Lowering his rejected hand, Conway tried to hide his offense. Coldness marred his voice, regardless. "What is it you want me to tell him?"

More disturbed than ever, Tinillit hurried on. "Please, don't be angry. We know of your ways. We only want you to know of ours." He pointed at the wooden food bowls where Lanta and Tate sat side by side. "Didn't you wonder that no one reclaimed those? You noticed we don't get close to you; I saw it in your face. You think we insult. Would we risk our lives for people we want to anger?"

Grudgingly, Conway conceded. "I guess not."

Lowering the point of the spear-blowgun to the ground, Tinillit went on. "To all people there is a Siah. Ours came when we lived where the forest joins the sea, far to the south. We were without enemies, without war. Strangers came, though. From the sea, and from the land to the north and south. Many, many Smalls were killed. The rest were driven like deer. We traveled into strange lands, not knowing where the godkills and radzones waited for us. Sickness came. Always, we fled. Our Siah died. We were children, lost without our father."

Pausing, Tinillit looked off into the mountains. When he continued, he was stronger. "Our Siah taught us to worship correctly. We look to the sun, bringer of light and warmth. The symbol of the One Who Is Two wakes the world to the One in All. It is so with your people?"

At Conway's nod, Tinillit continued. "Our people sought the sun. From high in the mountains, we saw it before any. Warmth reached us before any. When the winter came and stole the light and heat, our suffering was to purge our sins. We know this, because in spring the One in All brings the good weather back. So we live as we do. In forest, in mountains."

"And you avoid contact with other people."

Tinillit beamed. "You understand. Still, we are changing. Before we were like the marmot. We hid from every danger, considered winter a protection. Now we think more like the bear. We den through the winter, but it's not wise to disturb us. We won't be as we were before. We protect ourselves. But there is penalty. That's why I came to you. Everything that happened here is unhealthy. To be men again, we must cleanse ourselves. Because we want to live in peace in the Three Territories, we offer you our cleansing. If you would be welcome among us, that would be a first step. It will heal you."

Lanta rejoined Conway at that point. He indicated her. "How does your cleansing affect Lanta? Remember, she's Church. Does the ceremony intrude on her beliefs in any way? What about Tate?"

"Excellent questions. The cleansing isn't religious. It requires belief, but not religion. What sort of wounds does the Black Lightning one have?"

"Her hands; you see the bandages. Mostly, though, she's sick."

Tinillit practically leaped away. His hands flew in a three-sign. From the corner of his eye, Conway saw movement. Smalls advanced, slowly, uncertainly.

Karda and Mikka materialized beside Conway. Mikka whined. Conway looked down, amazed. It was a sound he couldn't recollect hearing from her before. Either unaware of his look, or too intent to change her focus, she remained fixed on Tinillit.

Tinillit found words. "Sick? Unseens?"

Lanta answered, "Not disease. More like poison. The cave you heard Fox speak of is evil. Tate's sickness is from there, and can claim no one else."

Conway's muttered "Of course!" went ignored by Tinillit. The Small stared at Lanta. "You swear this, Priestess? By Church?"

"I swear by all the knowledge I have. I won't swear by Church, because this is nothing I've ever seen before. But Conway was affected and is better. Tate is recovering. You see me, unaffected. It's nothing for you to fear. And both of my friends are injured. If you know healing that I don't have, I ask you to use it."

"We'll talk." Clutching his spear-blowgun in a white-knuckled hand, Tinillit spun away to join his tribesmen. Conway called the dogs and retreated to join Lanta and Tate. The animals fidgeted strangely.

The argument among the Smalls was fierce. Tate said, "Looks like I messed things up pretty good."

Hunkering down beside her, Conway picked up a twig, chewed on an end. "Mold," he said, and Tate shot him a look that clearly questioned his sanity.

Repeating the word, Conway expanded on it. "It used to happen where we lived before." Keeping his back to Lanta, he rolled his eyes for Tate. Her head moved in an almost-imperceptible nod. He continued. "All that dampness, so much inorganic material. When it was attacked by molds and mildew and whatnot, it decomposed into some really exotic pollutants. We were doing a lot of heavy breathing in a literally toxic atmosphere."

Lanta said, "You use words I don't understand. Is this how they describe things that are evil in your land?"

"Exactly," Tate answered. Her concentration remained on Conway. "We didn't want to tell you, but there was lots of evil in there. If Moonpriest had gotten control of it, life would've been just about impossible for the rest of us."

"You were even more brave than I thought." Lanta came forward to wrap Conway's arm in her own. She hugged it, looking down at Tate. Conway said, "You sound a lot better, Donnacee. Look better, too. You making some sort of rally?"

"What d'you mean, rally? I was just coasting for a while, letting you do some work for a change." She struggled upright. The gaping slit in the back of her jacket reminded them all of the horror of the previous night. In a moment, Lanta produced needle and thread. She was almost finished sewing when Tinillit's call interrupted. He gestured for the trio to come to him.

Lanta whispered to her companions, "Be careful. They're afraid. Angry."

"You can tell that?" Tate was dubious.

"No mistake. Their posture; they're unsure if they should run or attack. Tinillit most of all. See how his feet are spread, the knees bent? His head's back, pupils of his eyes wide. He's almost . . ." She searched for a word. "Desperate."

The Small leader raised a hand to stop their advance. Conway tried to edge in front of Lanta, but she resisted, forcing him to be satisfied with merely crowding close. The anxious dogs panted loudly next to Conway. He said, "We want no trouble. If your men fear sickness from us, they're mistaken. We'll leave peaceably, if that's what you want."

Tinillit used his spear-blowgun to gesture. "We want peace, Matt Conway. It's why we left the lands of our ancestors, came into this dangerous place. We want to make a home among friends and allies. We are a people who trust no others, avoid all others. If we had dared come closer when you were on the top of the cave mountain, if we had known the Tate one had sickness, we would have fled."

Lanta assumed the role of spokesperson. "It's wise to avoid the ill. Healing is the work of Healers. But you said you had medicine of your own. I believe you. I can feel it."

A subdued mutter like the ruffling of heavy wings passed through the Smalls. There was the sound of surprise in it. Conway tensed. Uneasy men, surprised, was a bad combination.

Tinillit inclined forward, ever so slightly. "Exactly what do you feel, Priestess? Tell us."

She folded her hands in front of her. A thin frown scored her forehead. "Distrust. Fear. Anger. I think some feel that we lied to you, or tricked you. That's wrong. However, what I feel most is hope. Even those who are most angered hope they are mistaken. Let's concentrate on hope and help, then."

Slowly, taking breath between her teeth in a long, pained inhalation, Tate raised her hands. The dirty, stained bandages were like beacons, pointed at the overcast sky. "More Windband may come seeking us. There are Mountain People moving back into the Enemy Mountains from the north. Violet Priestess Lanta has done all in her power to make my hands better. If you can help me, I need you. Your power."

The last word reignited the earlier debate. Ignoring the trio, the Smalls turned to each other. Men shook weapons, gesticulated. Tinillit's sharp whistle stilled them. He addressed his men firmly. "The Priestess senses the minding. If we are to have friends, we must be friends. We will bring them into the cleansing." Another mumble started. He stopped it with a look. "They will receive, not join in. Maybe one day we can accept others in the cleansing. Not yet. They aren't ready." Turning to the trio, he said. "Sit here, by the fire. Face the sun. No weapons. No words. No movement. If you wish, keep the dogs with you, but they must not move."

Conway saw the glisten of sweat on Tinillit's upper lip. He looked into the Small's unblinking intensity. Then, inexplicably, Conway was relaxed. He didn't know what was going to happen, and he was a bit concerned about that, but content he was doing the right thing.

The three non-Smalls seated themselves. Guards trotted into the forest. The dogs sprawled next to Conway. Karda looked to his master, tongue out, mouth open as if grinning in knowing expectation. Then he flopped over on his side.

At first, Conway didn't know what was making the persistent new sound. Thin and taut, it seemed too penetrating to be a percussion instrument. Much like Tinillit's earlier speech, the quick rhythm seemed ventriloquial, with no specific origin. Looking around for it, Conway almost missed the way the Smalls parted, opening a lane through the middle of the group.

Two men, each holding a cone-shaped drum under one arm, danced up that aisle. They wore shapeless black robes, more like bags than clothes, and small black caps. White cloth hung from the edge of the caps. Fine enough to permit vision from inside, the white material completely cloaked face and neck. The simple costume altered the shuffling, swaying figures to not-human obscurities. Leaden forest light further softened the men's outlines.

By snapping their fingers against the drum, rather than using arm or wrist, they gave the impression that the quarrelsome bark of the instrument was independent of the musicians. Tinillit played his flute. The song was sad, lonely. Melody drifted plaintively through the metal snappishness of the drums.

The dancers moved to the drum rhythm with short, chopping steps. Lithe body action reflected the softer melody. On reaching the fire site, the two dancers separated to circle it in opposite directions. One by one, Small warriors drifted away from the group, falling in trail of one or the other of the costumed dance leaders. The pace quickened. The flute sang as softly as before.

Warriors danced with heads hung forward, bobbing. When the two dance leaders met in their circuit of the fire, the columns wove through each other with the untroubled acceptance of crisscrossing pond ripples.

Acceptance.

The word resonated in Conway's mind. He sagged, wanting to believe. Believe what?

His eyes smarted, demanded rest. He thought of the dancers, so relaxed, so calm. He felt them.

An impossible knowledge told him that, awake, moving together, the Smalls reposed together. He sensed minds expanding. Yet simultaneously they were all taking in. Accepting.

Accept.

Conway thought of Lanta. He was fading, abandoning her. The Smalls were taking his mind. He wanted. Feared. Sweating warriors swayed in front of him, steaming in the cold. Unseeing eyes stared out of slack faces. Hair hung lank and soaked. The music shrilled. Conway retreated from it. His eyes fell shut.

He couldn't leave Lanta. Not with such powerful mystery dragging him away.

He looked up again. The warriors were replaced by the costumed dancers. They held spear-blowguns to their mouths, distorting the cloth masks into ill-formed skulls. Chests swelled as they inhaled. They aimed the weapons at Conway.

He struggled to rise, to shout. There was no strength in him. He heard laughter. Carefree, unrestrained. There was a voice behind it, speaking. The words sounded as if they came through a smile.

Accept.

He had to.

CHAPTER 61

CONWAY REACHED TO SCRATCH HIS NECK. HIS HAND TOUCHED CLOTH. THE ITCH WASN'T bad enough to warrant disturbing the bandages. It was barely noticeable, actually.

He didn't want to waken. Sleeping while sitting up shouldn't be so comfortable, he told himself. The cold was there, too, of course, but not a problem. It felt strange, as though it hovered around him, not quite in contact with him.

There was a reason why he shouldn't sleep. Like a small, frightened animal, the memory skittered across the back of his mind, always just out of reach.

It was important. It was time to stop being lazy, time to reenter the world.

A strange thought; sleeping was hardly leaving the world.

Masks. Blowguns.

Conway jerked awake. He rolled forward in a swift, smooth rise that brought him upright with hands outstretched to defend. Ten paces away, Fox crouched, pure malevolence. Conway lunged for his throat.

Lanta's shout checked the unthinking charge. Coming to an awkward, off-balance halt, Conway struggled with both mind and body. Limbs reacted slowly. The earlier lassitude and well-being alternated with the burning hatred and aggression.

Once more, Lanta called to him. Reluctant to take his eyes from the strangely immobile enemy, Conway was startled to realize Fox was bound. Looking for Lanta, he was further astonished to discover her within arm's reach, smiling easily. More than that, Tate was next to her, flashing a grin almost as mischievous and bold as ever.

His head swam. When it cleared, the change was instant. He was alert, confident.

Lanta's smile broadened. Conway understood she'd read the change in him. He laughed aloud. "All right. As always, I'm the last to know. What's going on?"

"Minding." Lanta pointed. Following in the direction she indicated, Conway saw Tinillit. The Small leader's grin was pleased, but diffident, almost shy.

Conway looked back to Lanta. "What's 'minding'? It has to do something with that dance; I'm sure of that."

Tinillit answered. "The dance. The music. More; the mind. All of our minds." He swung an arm to include his group. Pride rose from them almost palpably. "Smalls dance healing. That's part of minding."

"I do feel better." Conway's hand went to his throat. The bandages were there, but the pain was almost gone, replaced by a faint itching sensation. Awed, he said, "The wounds are already healing. I can feel it."

Tate interrupted. "Look at my hands, Matt. Can you believe the difference?" She displayed them proudly. The fingers were stiff, fat in their bandaging, but they moved. Conway was even more impressed by her manner. She was clear-eyed, strong. It was as if the debilitating sickness never existed. He faced Tinillit again. "How do you do this?"

For a moment, Tinillit stared. He guffawed, then, "Ask me how I see. Ask me how I think." He tilted his head to the side, birdlike. "Yes. Ask me how I think. Minding is thinking. It's sending the mind to another place. It's hearing the mind of another."

Chill touched the base of Conway's spine. If Tinillit believed what he was describing, he was inferring an entire community of telepaths. Logic refuted that notion, however. True telepaths would certainly never be enslaved; who would capture them?

Tinillit explained more fully. "Smalls don't see inside the mind of other people. There have been some . . ." He frowned, let the sentence die. "Intrusion is rude. Worse, it's wrong. You remember I told you forest is our friend? We live off forest's animals. Because they are gifts, we thank them for giving us life. When we pass among the animals, we make them know we mean no harm. When we hunt them, however, we must never do that. Hunting and killing are done with an empty mind. The hunter thinks, but he does not hate. Or love. The one who kills must go outside himself, become that which is not. To kill, one becomes the most vulnerable of all. To remain a real person, one must be forgiven."

Conway said, "Anyone regrets killing, but it must be done. You're saying a man should do it like a falling tree, without anger or fear or anything else. I can't accept that."

"When you woke from the minding sleep, did your mind know peace?"

Grudgingly, Conway nodded. Tinillit remained stoic. "The minding dance is community. It cleanses. No soul can live where the mind is fouled."

Faceless men wavered in Conway's mental vision. He thought they beckoned. He blinked away the image.

Tinillit was saying, "For us, the greatest warriors of our tribe are the dance leaders. They take us to a place where we all become one again. They see who is closed, who cannot reopen. You and your friend Tate have never allowed yourself to be cleansed. The dance leaders even used weapons to drive out the harsh thoughts in you both. They asked me to apologize for not being completely successful."

A twinge of expression, too quick for Conway to identify, slid across Tinillit's face. Conway asked, "What of the leaders, then? I mean, they clean warriors who kill men. What happens to the dance leaders who fight and kill the things troubling the warriors?"

"They move in honor among us. Dance leaders are the most respected and most humble of the Smalls. Their lives are short." His quick glance at Conway was pregnant with accusation.

Understanding, Conway said, "They spent a lot of energy on us, didn't they? On me and Tate."

It was a visible effort, but Tinillit recovered most of his good humor. "They told me they'll recover. You and your friend puzzle them. One of them said you both regret what you do more than almost anyone. He also said you swallow regret as if it were food, and, like food, it strengthens hatred and violence. The ferocity of your emotions grows ever stronger with every conflict."

Conway looked to Tate. Her grin was self-conscious now, apologetic. She shrugged. "When he's right, he's right." Then, to Tinillit, "What do we do about all this? After all, we're fighters. And what about yourselves? You did a pretty good job of un-cleansing yourselves right here, just last night."

"If you were Smalls, you would grow up learning the minding and the dance. Perhaps you could, still. But we are Smalls. We keep our distance. I don't believe your path is to join us, live as one with us. The minding is not any one person. It is *us*, the Smalls. We fight, just as you. You honor the killing. We forgive it."

Irritated by Tate's clear discomfort with Tinillit's answer, Conway was abrupt. "You might ask yourself sometime if the dead forgive it." Instantly, he was sorry. He tried to make amends. "I shouldn't have said that. What I really want you to know is how grateful we are for the healing. I don't exactly understand what you did for us, but we appreciate it very much. You saved our lives, you took a great load from our minds. We're indebted to you."

"We wanted to help. The dangers facing the Three Territories threaten us, as well. We know nothing of the Skan, except an occasional Peddler's tale, and who can believe those people? Please, tell Gan Moondark we would be friends. Perhaps even allies. He'll let us live in the Enemy Mountains in peace?"

Conway laughed. "Anyone who can ambush Fox is too good to question. He'll welcome you. But tell me, were you the owl I heard? And the wolves, so far away? How could you fool a man as experienced and cunning as Fox?"

"We know the animals better than any. We don't sound like them; we become them. We wanted to be closer, but Fox is very, very dangerous; he sees everything."

"Not everything. He never saw you, never suspected last night's attack. You did it to him, didn't you? Somehow you 'minded' him, and all the others."

Suddenly uncomfortable, Tinillit colored. "Sometimes we can affect our enemies. We can't make them see what isn't there, but maybe, sometimes, if conditions are right, we can possibly suggest they look somewhere where we aren't."

"Or not look at all." Tate's wry suggestion featured a broad wink.

Squirming, Tinillit's head jerked in what could have been an affirmative nod. Or just a tic. An arm flew out in flailing gesture. "Our riders overtook Fox. We give him to you."

"We have to cross the Enemy Mountains. The first snows are here. Two of us are injured. What can we do with Fox?"

If Tinillit was distressed before, now he was outright agitated. The slight pink of minor embarrassment flared to bright red. He swiveled to send mute appeal to his companions. They met his gaze with resolute refusal to help. Fox's rasping laughter broke the impasse. "All that jabber about killing requiring an empty mind, and souls that go wandering off when it's time to strike down your enemies. Look at him. See how he hates. Oh, he wants to kill me. He's afraid to. Look at them. Rabbits. They can't explain me away with their woman's weeping about dirty souls. What frightens them is they know they'll enjoy it." He whirled on Tinillit, spittle flying from his lips, unshaven, soiled features poisonous with rage. "Weak-hearted little dung maggot. Think how your soul will sing to see me coughing my blood out. Imagine the way I'll jerk, how my heels will hammer. You like it. Admit it. For once in your miserable, slave life, be a man. Kill me. Enjoy doing what a man does. Enjoy!"

Conway found no pity for the Mountain's obvious discomfort, his crablike scuttle as he shouted at Tinillit. Before Tinillit could speak, Conway interceded. "You'll die because you deserve it. Come to that, a quick death's better than you deserve."

"Ah, you see? You want to do it, too. Make your new friends happy. Why not give me my ma? I'll fight you. You're a warrior. Not like these little lice."

Lanta stepped forward. "Matt. Don't listen. He has nothing to lose. You have nothing to gain." To Tinillit, she said, "My friends aren't executioners. You yourself said they have much to learn about cleansing themselves. You can't ask them to do this."

"It was our only hope. Usually we can cleanse what happens in the heat of battle. Anything else is very difficult. Windband has caused us so much suffering. To execute Fox may be too much for the dance leaders to overcome."

Softly, Conway said, "So you decided that since my soul's already torn up, one more little trick wouldn't hurt. Is that it?"

Tinillit hung his head. "Until I saw the pain. Until the dance leaders fought for you, and mourned over how little they could help." When Tinillit looked up, it was with sorrow and defiance. The mix gave him an oddly appealing look, like a man who needs another's approval, but isn't sure how far he dares reach to achieve it. "I made a mistake."

"Your mother made a mistake." Fox's snarl sullied the air.

Tinillit sent him a glance of yearning hatred, then looked back to Conway. "We can't just kill him."

Once more, Fox laughed. The forest rang with triumph. "I knew it. Cowards, all of you." Crafty, cruel, he waggled the hands bound behind him. "Cut me free. You can't just kill me. I'll curse you for a dozen generations. A hundred. You'll never get your souls back, clean or dirty. I'll need a faster horse, too. The last one was slow as a badger."

One of the Smalls moved up on Tinillit's signal, prepared to cut Fox's bonds. Conway stopped him. "Wait. Get him mounted, first. Hobble the horse." The Small hesitated until a nod from Tinillit approved. Fox swung into the saddle confidently, smirking. In an aside, Conway told the Small holding the reins, "Hold on tight. Be ready for trouble."

Moving swiftly, Conway grabbed a looped leather throwing line from a nearby saddle. Before Fox could properly react, Conway wound a loop around Fox's closest ankle, binding it to the stirrup leather. By then Fox was alert to his danger. He kneed the horse viciously. Restrained as it was, the animal jerked about as best it could. Conway darted around to its other side. Fox kicked at him. Conway quickly had that foot secured like the first one. Smalls raced to help him draw the line taut.

Fox was bound to the animal.

Coolly, Conway tossed a loop around Fox's neck, then hauled him backward until he was bent across the saddle's cantle. Handing off the line to two Smalls, Conway drew his knife. Fox was rapidly turning purple. Slits opened Fox's trousers, sleeves, and the sides of his jacket. With a few tugs, Conway stripped away the leather and coarse homespun. He signaled the Smalls to slack off on the throwing line.

Gasping, Fox rose, sucking in air. Once he could breathe well again, he straightened. He looked at Conway, baleful. Conway said, "Go back to Moonpriest. Without your men. Naked. How Moonpriest will brag of his war chief. His naked, tied-like-a-market-hog war chief."

Disgrace seized Fox's mind. "This is worse than killing, Conway. I'll be waiting for you in the Land Under. My curse on you."

Conway stepped back. Lanta moved to his side. "Matt. There are tigers. Bears. Remember, the horse can eat and drink. He can't." Conway continued to stare at Fox. Lanta pressed ahead. "What Tinillit said is true. You run the risk of becoming as evil as he is. I couldn't stand that. Not now."

Tinillit said, "Matt Conway."

Conway turned. Tinillit's gaze was locked on Fox. "Remember the nomad you freed. Remember what his gratitude cost you. Remember what Fox planned for all of you. And learn something from me: Do you remember the Small girl you met in Windband camp? The blinded one?"

"Certainly. She drowned. I always thought she was murdered."

"My aunt's daughter. I watched her grow up. Until Windband captured her. There have been many like her, Conway." Tinillit pretended to be hard. Still, Conway saw more pain than vindictiveness.

Conway stepped forward, removed the horse's reins and bridle, then the hobble. He slapped the horse on the rump. Fox rocked as it leaped forward.

Suddenly, unexpectedly, Fox managed to stop it. Rising in the stirrups, he twisted to face the camp. "You're the same as me, all of you! For all your talk, you enjoy my pain, my humiliation, my dying. Pray that I die, because if I do, you need fear only my spirit. If I live, you'll learn how Fox Eleven pays his debts."

Using knees and feet, he turned his mount and rode south.

Only after the forest swallowed Fox did Conway speak to Tinillit. "Life has many debts, doesn't it? Many recoveries."

"Yes. You've risked much. For us. Our dance leaders are too weak for another minding. Perhaps one day soon."

Conway was abrupt. "Perhaps. We have to go, anyhow. The passes are already difficult."

Tinillit said, "Until you're on the sunset slope, some of us will screen you. Others take our prisoners to Windband, exchange them for Smalls. "

Lanta came to speak to Tinillit. The Small was barely the taller. She said, "You know Church's trouble. You know Sylah has revived the Teachers." Nervously, Tinillit nodded. Lanta went on. "Church will survive. It will grow. Our Teachers can help your people. We'd like to learn more of the minding."

"The tribe must decide. But I have seen powerful things here, and I will speak of them." Tinillit straightened as he faced Conway. "Many will say what you did was vengeance. Some will say justice. I say necessary."

"And I appreciate your understanding."

Before leaving to salvage the weapons and ammunition, Conway and Tate agreed that once they reached the passes, everything the three humans couldn't carry through the snow must be off-loaded and hidden. Leaving Lanta and Tate with the Smalls, Conway took three packhorses to load the equipment. He was back by nightfall, and the evening passed quietly.

Breaking camp went smoothly, despite Tate's still-clumsy hands. The dogs seemed to sense they were going home. When Conway sent them ahead to scout, they frolicked like puppies at first, settling to business almost reluctantly.

Much later, with the sun below the crests to the west and darkness honing the cold, Lanta trotted her horse forward to join Conway. He waited patiently while she wrestled with whatever it was she meant to say, trying not to smile too obviously at her inconsequential small talk. Finally, she blurted her question directly. "Would you have killed Fox, if Tinillit directly asked you to?"

"No."

"What would you have done if Tinillit wasn't there?"

"We'd all be dead now. Or wishing we were."

"That's not what I mean, and you know it. If Fox were your prisoner, after what he almost did to Tate, after everything you know, would you kill him?"

At last, he turned, looked her in the eye. "I wanted to. I don't know if what I did was right or wrong. I let a man live I could have killed. I'll be feared for what I actually did, instead. All I'm sure of is, Tinillit's right. Combat risks a man's soul even more than it risks his life. As much as I want to live, it's more important that I can live at peace with myself. I need you for that. You hold me in place."

Rising in the stirrups, she brought her face close to his, a hand on his shoulder. In perfect accord, they stopped the horses. Their kiss was a bond. Neither had a thought for anything else in that moment, so neither saw Tate. Behind them, she averted her gaze. Her initial sharing smile withered quickly. What took its place compared with the small, blasted plants of summer still clinging to the frozen cliff.

Chapter 62

Emso settled into the tub in the castle's bathhouse. The square, stone form stood on a tall base. A small fire burned under it in an inset fireplace. The water steamed a rich aroma of cedar. Emso sighed luxuriously as heat dissolved the ache in cold bones.

Moments later he was splashing violently, lunging for a drying cloth. From the open door, Jaleeta watched his thrashing modesty, pealing silvery laughter. Craning to see backward over his shoulder, Emso finally found his voice. "Scandalous! You shock, Jaleeta. You shouldn't sneak up on a man in his bath."

Ignoring him, face alight with a daring, teasing smile, she angled to the side, taking some of the strain off his twisted neck. "Emso, be serious. Our heads are at the same level. You're in a stone box. Whatever would I see that would embarrass either of us?"

"Not the point." The last word was accentuated; accumulated water on Emso's lips spattered, triggering more laughter from Jaleeta. Emso's indignant glare collapsed into indulgent resignation. "You're a spoiled little fox kit. I hope you're not so careless around the young men."

Shocked, Jaleeta advanced, but not so far as to further disturb Emso's composure. "How can you even think such a thing?" She tossed her head, sending heavy tresses flying in a gleaming arc. "Anyhow, you know my situation. With Louis. And Gan. You're the only one I can talk to. I hoped you understood."

"I understand. Too well. I've tried to draw Gan out on the subject. He won't discuss it. Pretends he doesn't even know what I'm talking about."

"He's afraid. He knows his old friends would be ashamed to know he's becoming a tyrant."

"Never think he's afraid."

Downcast, Jaleeta edged forward. "Isn't there something that can be done? It's Sylah; she controls him."

"You don't have the years to judge him. Be careful what you say. What can you know of a man being owned?"

A fiery wash raced across Jaleeta's features. Intuitively, she turned away, aware that anger such as she felt at that moment was transfiguring. Emso must never discover that his little girl could resemble a vengeful demon.

Emso saw only the reddened skin of her neck. "I've made you blush. I apologize."

"There's no need. I know I'm not as wise as you. I lived with Tears of Jade, though. I've seen her control. I understand witchcraft."

"Take care. Such accusations are for Church. You can't use the word *witch* and not expect to be challenged."

Jaleeta straightened. "I owe my life to Gan Moondark. If no one will speak for his soul, then I must."

Emso turned away from her. The severity of his frown etched his brow. Despite that, he seemed more contemplative than irritated. Long after Jaleeta's flouncing departure, when he started scrubbing, it was with a peculiar detachment.

Jaleeta waved to the Chosens playing outside the Iris Abbey. In no time she was the center of a laughing, shouting, crowd of children. From a pocket of her robe, she drew a section of bamboo. One end was fitted with a removable cap of polished bone. The tube itself was deeply carved with the image of a boar. Opening it, she produced a tightly rolled sheet of material, slightly thicker than a leaf and a dark, wine red. When unwound, it stretched a good arm's length. She held it aloft, dangling it. Sunlight turned it into sheeting flame.

"Strawberry leather!" The cry from small throats echoed from the abbey's stones.

"Enough for everyone." Judiciously, Jaleeta tore off pieces of the sun-dried puree, handing it out carefully. The Chosens might be wards of Church, and therefore holy in many respects, but they were children. It wasn't outside their scope to stuff a fair share of sweet into a secular mouth while extending a consecrated hand for more. Finally, there was one piece left, and one potential customer. A small girl, shorter and slighter than all, hung back. Not until the little one was jostled and half-turned by a departing older child did Jaleeta see the birthmark. On the right cheek, just in front of the ear, the small wine-red stain was an irregular blotch, with a short, jagged line issuing from the bottom. Jaleeta thought of lightning breaking from a cloud.

Jaleeta waved the fruit leather, smiling, enticing. Solemn, the girl stared back.

With supple grace, Jaleeta caught the child by the hand before she could get away. Jaleeta's sultry whisper cajoled. "I understand. Really. Some of us are always alone, no matter where we are. Because it's that way for me, too, I'll always be your friend. You don't have to be my friend if you don't want to. It's all right. But I'll be yours. Now, take your strawberry sweet. Jaleeta wants you to have it."

The little girl's head remained averted. The small hand reached. Like a newborn puppy, it moved with blind determination, seeking a bond transcending nourishment. The hand touched Jaleeta's fingers. It stopped instantly. Jaleeta felt the connection. The hand drifted to the fruit leather, closed over it. The girl scampered away.

"That was lovely." Jaleeta rose swiftly, met by Janet Carter's delighted smile. "Jay Six is so shy. She doesn't play with the other Chosens. Not even the ones from the Mountain People." Inflection made it known that Jay Six's tribe was a particular test.

Standing beside Carter, Sylah and Kate Bernhardt wore smiles of considerably less warmth than Carter's. Bernhardt nodded. Sylah spoke. "The children look forward to your visits. It'll take poor Susan forever to calm them down." She gestured over her shoulder, where Susan Anspach shooed them to class.

"I didn't mean to make trouble."

Carter hushed her. "Don't apologize. They need laughter. You bring it. Sometimes it's too easy to forget how important smiles are. I know I do."

Jaleeta said, "They'll appreciate your work a great deal more than a tiny piece of fruit leather. Little moments like this won't even be remembered."

Bernhardt's smile was thin. "Appreciation always waits in the future. Pleasures like sweet things and childish laughter may be temporary, but they're here now."

Sylah said, "Please, excuse Jaleeta and me? We have to talk."

Carter winked at Jaleeta. "We'll help Susan. She'll need it. Come on, Kate."

Bernhardt's fixed smile didn't alter. She nodded before turning to follow.

Sylah took Jaleeta's arm, led her away. "I think it's time for us to speak plainly to each other, Jaleeta. Why do you dislike me so? Do you believe I'm what Sister Mother calls me? Or is it me, personally?"

"I don't dislike you."

"Stop it." Sylah was quietly firm. "You're a very skilled young woman, but you're no match for me. I'm trying to be your friend. I know something of being a stranger. I know what that can do to a person's mind. Especially a woman's mind, in this man's world. You're using them, aren't you? That's a fool's choice. Eventually, they'll ignore you. Worse, they may discover what you're doing to them. There's nowhere to hide then, Jaleeta. Now, then; why this dislike?"

Jaleeta's brain raced at a pace threatening to outstrip her heart. She bought time with silence. Head down, watching each slow, reluctant step, she remembered the words of Tears of Jade. The old woman warned that Sylah would interpret her face and body the way Skan warriors interpreted the sea. Jaleeta fumed, but quickly recovered. This conversation was too vital to permit remorse or anger.

"I'm afraid." Jaleeta complimented herself: Tears of Jade said that if you must lie to a Priestess, start with a truth. Come to the lie slowly, gently. "I'm afraid to think of anyone as a real friend. I remember my family dying when I was captured. Since then, my life is lies. And threats. I use the men. Yes. One protects against another. I don't trust any of them." She met Sylah's eyes, bold. "Anyone. Now you'll tell Gan Moondark and Neela. I don't care."

"Of course you care. You need them. Look at me." Sylah stopped. Jaleeta had to turn to face her. Sylah put a hand to Jaleeta's neck, just under the jaw, saying, "You have ambitions. You mean to use us all."

Jaleeta opened her mouth. Sylah pressed against her jawbone with a thumb. Jaleeta's teeth clicked together. She inhaled sharply. The hiss was clearly audible. Sylah's smile burned with contempt. Sure, controlled force hummed under her words. "Your eyes, your muscles, your blood, all tell more truth than your tongue. Listen. You know nothing of obligation. You feel none. I do. Gan Moondark and other friends saved my life. They offer me sanctuary and support for Church. Church will flourish and expand. I must provide the first nurturing. I am commanded. That can only happen here, in the Three Territories. Nothing will interfere. Nothing. Come to me as a friend, and I will protect you. Threaten Church, or the Teachers, or the Three Territories in any way, and I am your implacable enemy."

When at last Sylah released Jaleeta and stepped back, Jaleeta's eyes remained fixed for a heartbeat, then rolled. Whites gleamed. She steadied. "I'm a guest of Murdat himself. I'm trusted."

"How well I know. You think you're looking straight ahead into an exciting future. I tell you you're looking down. Into horror. Let me help you."

Turning away, Jaleeta walked. Sylah followed. After a while, Jaleeta stopped. She looked up into Sylah's face, hand to her throat. "There are things you should know. Things I've been told. Everyone in the Territories is in danger. I want to tell you. I fear, Sylah. I'm not a bad person. I fear."

"I know. I can wait. Come to me when you can. There are many forces working here. Youth and beauty are very weak weapons in such a struggle, Jaleeta. They'll win you much less than you think."

Inwardly, Jaleeta triumphed. She'd anticipated a lecture of some sort. "I've behaved very foolishly."

Sylah reached out again, stroked Jaleeta's temple as if the fingertips felt the mind inside. She said nothing. Jaleeta cursed the older woman's enigmatic smile that left her confused and somehow ashamed. Sylah turned and left without speaking.

Jaleeta wanted to scream at the straight, unyielding back drawing away from her. No one dismissed Jaleeta. Not without paying for the insult.

Slowly, relishing her anger, Jaleeta made her way to the stables. A gull shrieked laughter at her. Pigeons in her path flurried aloft. Their glittering eyes stared down on her in mindless wonder. After assuring no one was watching, she pitched a stone at them. Their panicky flight failed to brighten her mood.

A young groom hurried to get her horse and saddle it. She basked in the boy's bumptious admiration, posturing for him. He stumbled and floundered comically. Satisfactorily. She moved to stand beside him while he adjusted the gear. He was fair, sturdy; she thought of new whaling boats, the rough strength of newly hewn wood. Crisp, golden hairs gleamed on bare, thick arms whenever one of the spears of light coming through the barn's gaps and knotholes glanced off his flesh. Close-shaven, scrubbed, he smelled of strong soap. Under that, as shy as the boy himself, were warmer, elusive scents.

Pulling the cinch tight, the stableboy finished. When he stepped back, he turned deep blue eyes on her. For a fleeting, tingling moment she saw past that diffidence, down into the raw, unexplored maleness of him.

Foot in the stirrup, she reached to brace herself on a brawny shoulder. He quivered like a fly-plagued colt. She chided herself for enjoying him too much. An abrupt move swept her up into the saddle. Without looking back, she urged the horse outside at a jarring trot.

There was no time for idle games. The passes were heavy with snow already. Spring, bringing the combined attack of the Skan and Windband, wasn't that far away. No, dawdling at amusement was not only inappropriate, it was potentially fatal. It was time, instead, to assure that the fools destroyed each other.

A song of excitement reeled through her mind, sending her carefully organized thoughts spinning off. She felt challenged. Strong.

They thought to hurt her, couldn't imagine her cunning. All of them. Sylah; empty threats. Lorso; muscles and lust. Gan Moondark and his sickening sweet wife. Emso; laughable. Tears of Jade; far away. Old. And doomed.

Nalatan.

Yet again, orderliness collapsed. The vision of the warrior-monk was suddenly intertwined with that of Lorso. Emso. The stableboy. Lassitude touched her, expanded within. It was heat, and a secret, straining eagerness.

She slapped at the horse's rump with all her might. The sting of her hand and the startled animal's headlong gallop cleared her head. Hair streamed behind her. She blended with her mount's racing rhythm, blood pounding to that exhilarating tempo. Raising her chin, she shouted laughter at the world. She knew. *Jaleeta* knew.

The greatest magic in the land was Louis Leclerc.

He was a sword of unnamed, mystic power.

He wanted Jaleeta. He would have her. Possess her.

Exactly as the leopard, innocent in its ferocity, claims the bait in puny man's clever deadfall.

Chapter 63

Some distance from Leclerc's farm, Jaleeta reined to a slow walk. It wouldn't do to arrive all disheveled on a sweat-frothed horse. Louis was a fool, but one exercised care, even in managing fools.

She wondered what the farmers along the way thought of her raucous laughter as she pounded down the narrow road. They'd probably tell anyone who'd listen. She shrugged, smiling lazily. It was too late to worry about that. Soon they'd have plenty of tales to whisper about the wild Jaleeta. If they dared.

Rested, but still full of life after its run, her horse tossed its head and pranced approaching Leclerc's house. Jaleeta knew she was a pretty picture, long hair tousled across the back and shoulders of her down-filled jacket. Glossy black complemented the bright blue and its orange trim. Her beige leather skirt flowed smoothly to glossy ankle-high boots. The horse, a muscular gray, with proud, arched neck, was the perfect seat to display her beauty.

Off to her left, naked apple trees stood in neat rows, scraggly branches jerking about in the wet wind. To the right, winter crops flourished in long, narrow beds. She recognized the frail green of hardy lettuce, almost overpowered by the robust verdance of spinach. There was broccoli, several beds of onion-things—garlic, shallots, leeks—and other crops she couldn't identify.

Leclerc grew vegetables in ways no one else considered. When he succeeded, he shared the knowledge freely. Farmers accepted with smiles and thanks. But they whispered about strange practices. There were stories; a man's cousin saw something. Or a nephew did. Not actually saw, perhaps, but the cousin or the nephew knew a man who had. After all, Leclerc was the man who claimed that ashes mixed with sulfur and pigeon droppings was the secret of the roaring black powder that knocked down walls and tore men into pieces no bigger than a cat.

It frightened Jaleeta to think of controlling Leclerc.

It frightened her even more to think that someone else might.

He came out to greet her. The aura of jealousy around him was like an intoxicating cloud. "It's been a long time. I wondered if you'd ever be back."

"I hoped you'd come to Ola. I look for you every day."

He shook his head. "Unwise. I don't want to see you if I can't be honest with you. With myself. I thought you felt the same way."

Sadness marred her explanation. "I don't feel safe riding so far alone. I wanted to, though. Neela's always so busy with little Coldar. The Teacher women and Sylah have responsibilities. I don't really know anyone else." Again, the most delicate hesitation, the significant glance. Then, "There's no one I want to be with."

Hurrying to her, he handed her down from the saddle. A waiting boy ran to lead the animal away. Once they were alone again, Leclerc was friendly, but she felt his tension. He asked, "Has Gan said anything more about you and Emso? Emso's not forcing himself on you? Did anyone say you couldn't visit me?"

"No one's said I shouldn't come." She lowered her eyes, cut him another glance, appealing. "I'm a guest, Louis. I know my place, my obligations to hospitality. Those people, your friends, are very clever. They make someone like me understand, and they don't have to use words. Not the way I do. I'm too ordinary. Not like them."

"And what might 'like them' be?"

They were at the door by then, and Jaleeta stopped, back pressed against the jamb. "They want to control things. People. I only want happiness. And security. A woman needs that."

He hung her jacket on a wooden peg on the back of the door. The heavy wood drummed comfortingly when he closed it, as if commanding the cold to keep its distance. He was curt. "Yes. Women should be protected."

Jaleeta twisted, peered sharply at him, but he was turned away. She moved to one of the cushioned leather chairs, sat down. "I've been watching Gan. It's shameless of me. He's my host. But he's the strongest man there is. He's not the largest or tallest. Why is he the leader? I think it's because he's smart and strong."

"Of course." Picking up odd bits of disarray on the way, Leclerc made his way to the stove. A long-spouted kettle steamed at the back. He moved it to a hotter location, fumbled in a cabinet for a ceramic jar of herbal tea. After measuring the dried product into a teapot and setting out two copper mugs, he rejoined Jaleeta. He pulled a chair close, leaned forward. "You're a perceptive woman. I think you see more, understand more, of life in that misbegotten castle than you let on."

The language was not to Jaleeta's liking. She smiled noncommittally, waiting. Leclerc went on. "Leadership is intelligence. It's guidance, and only a moral person can supply guidance. Without moral honesty, it's not leadership. It's driving, making your followers nothing but workers in your behalf. Or it's deception, making followers believe in something that's not true."

"I'm confused. I was talking about Gan giving me . . ."

Leclerc interrupted. "Gan's hurting more people than you alone. He's betraying the trust we all had in him."

Alarm raced through Jaleeta, a cold warning. Talk of betrayal could mean revolt or desertion. Either meant destruction to her plans. Leclerc must understand that his first task was the elimination of threat to the Three Territories. Everything must take place in order. "He's Murdat, Louis. We all need him to defeat the Skan and Windband."

"And we will. I promise." Water bubbled out the spout of the kettle, sizzled on the stovetop. Leclerc went to prepare the tea. Jaleeta snuggled deeper in her chair. At last the conversation was moving in the right direction. She hugged herself.

Someday the castle of Ola would be filled with soft leather chairs. Everywhere she went, they'd be waiting for her. And slaves. Good things to eat, and fine clothes.

The spring-meadow scent of chamomile blended with the tang of raspberry leaves and the perfume of roses. Steam wafting from the mug Leclerc handed her brought images of a child harvesting herbs with her mother. The child was happy. But ignorant. And stank of fish and hut smoke.

She leaned forward almost imperceptibly. Delicately, she parted her lips, darted a pink, glistening tongue across them. "You're the only one here I can trust. The only one anywhere." Abruptly, she got to her feet, strode to the stove, careful to stand so Leclerc could see her tremble. Spilled liquid splattered on the stove, fouled the room with the charred aroma.

Leclerc said, "What's wrong? Why are you so upset?"

"It's all this constant talk of war and power. It means people being hurt." She faced him, eyes brimming. "You'll beat them all. I know you will. You'll be beside Gan, make the Three Territories strong for him. And I'll belong to an old man who cares more for his horse than he could ever care for me." The tears cascaded. Jaleeta kept her chin high. It was very uncomfortable, but the effect on Leclerc was marvelous.

He rushed to her. She raised a hand, stopped him. "No, don't come close. You mustn't be trapped in my problems. It's not fair."

"We have to do something." Leclerc shifted from foot to foot. His hands twitched in abortive reaching motions.

Weighing the moment, Jaleeta decided to proceed. To control him, she had to strip away all other influence. Tears of Jade had made that clear. The old woman's mistake was undervaluing Jaleeta. She blinked past tears. "You mustn't. You can't. You'll make Gan think you're disloyal."

"We'll work around him. We'll find a way to discourage him, make him see what a mistake Emso is."

"It's not just Emso. Kate Bernhardt. One of your own people. I've seen how she looks at you. And you look at her the same way, even though you pretend not to. I've seen you. I can't come between you."

"Between . . . ? There's nothing . . ." Leclerc blustered. Erratic hand movements graduated to wide arm-swinging. His face reddened. His gaze broke under hers, slipped away, came back.

Jaleeta was startled. There was more there than she suspected. Probably more than Leclerc suspected, she told herself, and almost smiled at the perversity of it. Only when she confronted the fool with his true feelings was he able to acknowledge them. And then only to deny them. Men. If they weren't so stupid, they'd be much more entertaining. She repressed a sigh. All the more difficult, too. Pleading, she asked, "You're sure you don't care for her? Is that the truth?"

He raised his hands, wanting. She took a full step forward, entered the enclosure defined by his arms. He gripped her shoulders, tentatively, then more firmly. She found his gaze comically intense, the pupils dilated to black pits of yearning. And deceit. Jaleeta wondered which lie caused that reaction.

It made no difference. Not now. Not anymore. When he pulled her to him, she met his urgency with pressures of her own. He was clumsy, as bad as Lorso, but far more gentle. Considerate. Nevertheless, there was passion.

Heat from the stove behind her rolled across her back as her blouse fell to the floor. A corner of her mind played with the difference between that warmth and the flames working within her, rising to consume all her thoughts, all her concerns.

Then he scooped her up, surprisingly strong, carrying her toward a door. She fumbled at the buttons of his shirt. Eyes closed, she thought of the moonlit figure of Lorso, gleaming with sweat, heavy muscles writhing, bunching silver in the darkness. The stableboy. That tree-trunk neck, the straining bridge of muscle from the elbow down the forearm as he pulled on the girth.

The bedroom was dark. She half opened her eyes, reveling in the insinuations of clouded vision, things seen dimly. Everything was suggestion, glossed with a delicious unreality. Closing her eyes once more abandoned her to other senses. The air was thick with man smell. There was a feeling of roughness and heavy motion, mixed sensations of warmth and strength and violence. Then she was on the bed and he was with her and she was alight with need, with delight, with taking.

Images continued to flare across her mind. Lorso. The stableboy. Leclerc.

Something else raged behind all that, a frightening thing. Then it was free. The image she dared not admit.

Later, beside the still, deep-breathing Leclerc, she rose on an elbow and stared down into the slack features. The sleeping face was infuriatingly unreadable. Had she called out? Had she spoken the name of that hard, disinterested face? Even now, sated, secure in conquest of this man, that other face fired her blood anew. Rolling the broad vowels, her tongue stroked the name into whispered, yearning sound. "Nalatan. *Nalatan*."

Chapter 64

The wind poured up the Inland Sea, a thunder that piled up green-gray water into frenzied walls. Crisp with the tang of salt water and the threat of snow, the wind drove its waves at impossible pace. Unable to meet the demand for speed, the waters stumbled, fell, shattered in white, roiling anonymity.

On the surf-roaring shore, huge logs leaped and crashed like straws. Trees, some so old that people spoke of them in awe, called them First Church witnesses, bent and groaned submission.

From the roof of Ola's castle, Gan and Sylah watched. The pulse of the storm transmitted itself to them through the vibrating rock of the massive walls. The castle murmured nervousness in its straining beams and timber-barred doors. Together, man and woman drew back from their shared crenel. They dabbed at rain-blasted eyes, loosened the drawstrings on dryjacket hoods. Gan shouted over the wind. "We may not have to worry about the Skan. Or Windband. This wind may blow us all inland to my own country."

Sylah's laughter was snatched away before it could be heard. She cupped a hand to Gan's ear to shield words. "I want to see Clas na Bale's face the day you tell him he has to live inside stone walls."

She wished the words had been blown off. Scattered. Better yet, never spoken. To mention that name was to release the waiting flame in her heart. Worse, reminding Gan of Clas' freedom only emphasized his own obligations.

Gan tried to hide his hurt, but the thoughtless thrust was too true, too deep. As he pretended unconcern, her mind raced with realization of exactly who this young man had become. A king, Murdat, and not much older than the Wolves he led in combat. A husband and father, denied all but the most fleeting of moments with wife and child. A religious protector, and a man of such quiet, unostentatious faith that one would never suspect its depth. A good man, faced with enemies without and within.

With the chill of autumn came the dead leaf rustle of fear among his followers. Whispers, like cold slime, oozed through the Three Territories. Strange men, not Peddlers or Messengers, not even recognized traders, appeared in villages to wonder aloud about the wisdom of dying to advance the ambitions of an upstart kinglet from the other side of the Enemy Mountains. Such men stayed nowhere long. There seemed to be an abundance of them; they were reported along every road and track. They spoke of accommodation. They suggested compromise. And peace.

It was the sort of attack Gan was least equipped to confront. The statecraft necessary to contend with rumormongers and manipulators clashed with his image of himself.

More than anyone else, except for Neela, Sylah understood how much Gan Moondark resented what he must be. His next words expressed her thoughts. "Clas na Bale. He's free on the prairie. Yet I know he'd give anything to be here. I know how he misses you. We're buying him the time, in a way. Windband can't attack the Dogs and us at the same time. He's safe, Sylah, yet I know how he'd like to be by my side when the war comes."

"Maybe it won't happen."

"Don't waste our time. Let's get in the corner, more out of the wind. I need your advice. This is the one place where I can be sure no one will see or hear."

It was the first time Sylah ever heard Gan allude to spies. The fact chilled her far more than the storm.

Once they were better positioned, he continued in the same vein. "I learned things while you were away on your quest for the Door. Being Murdat's no different than being Nightwatch. Attention to everything around you; that's the way. That's what keeps Nightwatch alive and the tribe secure. So I send out people the way I used to send out my dogs. They discover things I can't. The difference is, the dogs and I trust each other; we never lie. With men, it can be different." His smile was crooked, knowing. "I'm told Moonpriest has moved to the coast, just south of where the Mother River empties. They say there's a restricted area by the sea, guarded day and night. To enter that place is to die."

"Can you learn what's happening inside?"

"Moonpriest and his workers have to eat. Those who buy provisions talk, especially if there's enough gold to loosen the tongue. They describe things like wheels with paddles that turn in the wind. They say Moonpriest has brought in shiploads of slaves to mine every known godkill for copper. They say Moonpriest has many of the new catapults and trained crews. He has a wallkiller, like the one you saw in Kos. It throws stones that blaze when they break, and the people who see it die, even if they're untouched."

"Burning stones? No one will believe it."

"Not so. The man who came back with the information believed. He's gone. North. As fast as a good horse could carry him. He stopped here barely long enough to collect his fee. I paid him extra to keep his mouth shut. The one thing I know about such tales is that the wilder the story, the more likely it is to be believed."

"Can you trust him to be silent?"

Gan threw wide his hands in mock helplessness. "The nomad who spoke to him swore him to secrecy. How can I, who paid him to betray confidence, suspect him of disloyalty?"

There was loathing and self-loathing in the words. She led the conversation in a safer direction. "You said you were seeking advice. I know nothing of mysterious weapons, new tactics."

"Who does? Except Moonpriest. And Leclerc, I think."

"Have you talked to Leclerc about these things?"

"I'd like to." In response to Sylah's questioning look, Gan grew more confidential, as though the wind itself listened. "I'm concerned about him. He's withdrawn from all of us. The three women who joined Church are his people. When's the last time he spoke to them?"

"When he demonstrated his new pump. He talked to all of them."

Gan shook his head. "Not once, Sylah. Except the Bernhardt one. She went to his home. She stayed only a while, and left in anger." He gestured away her swift distaste. "I didn't spy. It's ordinary gossip. His servants talk to other servants, and they talk to Neela. She's worried about Bernhardt."

"I understand. I knew something was bothering Kate."

"I've always considered Conway and Tate my eyes and ears where Leclerc is concerned. He's not like them, he's not like you or me. I like the man, but he's different. Tate and Conway understand him. I don't."

Sylah sighed heavily. "Nor do I. But there's no one else to turn to, if you hope to learn what's in Moonpriest's mind. We must go to him."

The smile Gan turned on her melted her heart. It was the one she knew of old, the eager, hopeful expression of youth rising to challenge. He pulled his hands out of his sleeves, reached out for hers. His touch was firm, warm. " '*We* must go to him.' What a loyal friend you are, Sylah. You've been at my side at every step."

"You help Church, just as I do. We help each other."

"If you say so. But few in the Three Territories would be so quick to share responsibility. And fewer yet who wouldn't demand some measure of authority, in exchange."

A fierce gust, heavier than anything before, slammed against the castle wall. Tearing through the open crenels, it roared like a mountain stream. Gan and Sylah both ducked in instinctive reflex. When it was passed, they looked at each other, burst out laughing. Gan rose. "That's our style, Sylah. Outside, where the storm rages. Afraid of the danger, afraid of missing the action. You're a warrior."

He was prepared for her pain. Calmly, he went on. "It was a deliberate statement, because you have to realize it's true. I know how you agonize over the incident in the market. Taking a life is a terrible thing. Yes, even for one such as I, my friend. But you did what Church, the Teachers, and all your friends would demand you do. We will not have you taken from us."

She got up to stand next to him, leaning into the wind. His speech touched her more than she dared admit. She tried to put a light face on the matter. "I only fight to make right the things great oafs like you break."

He grinned relief. And mischief. "And that's not as hard as war?"

"Don't be clever with me. Do you want to know what I think must be done, or would you rather tease me?"

"The latter, actually, but I don't have a choice. You have a suggestion?"

"Be direct with Leclerc. Tell him exactly what you've heard, ask him exactly what he thinks. Ask him how he can help defend against whatever Moonpriest may be up to. While you're doing that, send another man to verify what the first one learned. Why are you looking so smug?"

"The second man left two days ago. He's from one of the border tribes just south of Jalail. He owes me a favor."

Sylah nodded approval. "Good. But what I have to say next may offend. I think you should watch Leclerc. I'm ashamed to say it, but I've seen too much, learned too much, Gan. As you say, Leclerc has always kept his distance from us. There may be a reason. We're too vulnerable to exercise blind faith."

The wind slowed noticeably. The roar was a sibilant ripping sound now; it made Sylah think of fine, wet cloth shredding to pieces on the wall's rough stone.

Gan clamped a hand over his mouth. Head bowed, he pondered his problem. At last, hand at his side again, he said, "I can't ask Emso to befriend him. Emso's so loyal to me he fears Leclerc may do something magic and frighten the people into turning against me. And he despises change. He calls it all magic, and bad, and rejects it. What about Bernhardt?"

"If she's attracted to the man, that asks too much of her."

"You're right, of course. It was a foolish idea. But if there's the smallest grain of truth in anything I was told about Moonpriest's new warmaking equipment, I have to know how to defeat those things. Leclerc's the only man who can help. I wish I could be more certain of him." He checked, struck by a thought, eyes suddenly wide. He laughed aloud, then, "I know. I know. Have you seen the way he stares at Jaleeta? His eyes bulge every time she gets near him."

"That may be the worst idea you've ever had. Jaleeta's far too ambitious, Gan. I promise you, anything she learns, she'll decide how much good the information is to her before she worries about helping anyone else."

"I'm surprised at you. She's a child. I was uncertain of her at first, but despite her courage, she has no vision. Her only ambition is a husband and children. She told me so. And Neela, too."

The unexpected sharpness took Sylah aback. Her tongue stumbled. "She's not interested in the common good."

"You women really are different. You compete without even realizing it. Jaleeta's no more ambitious than any of the rest of you. Her misfortune is to be beautiful. If she's using her weapons carelessly, it's because she's young and inexperienced, not because she's bad. I think she's the perfect choice to help me know what Leclerc's plans are. He'll tell her things he'll never tell the rest of us."

For a long moment, Sylah continued to look out into the storm. Far down the sound, the rain was even heavier. It advanced northward in a vibrating mass. It was as if the sea rose to join with the falling sheets. She heard her own voice, far away, saying, "If you're going to set Jaleeta to watch Leclerc, at least set someone to watch Jaleeta."

Glowering, Gan looked away, then back. "Oh, all right. But who? You're complicating things."

"Nalatan. She rather likes him. And he's too much in love with Tate to be influenced by a little flirt."

"See? I told you. You really don't like her."

Coloring, Sylah stretched to her full height. "You were an arrogant, puffed-up boy when I first met you, Gan Moondark. It's extremely disappointing, after all my hard work, to find all I've gotten out of it is an arrogant, puffed-up man."

It was Gan's turn to look uncomfortable. He grumbled, "I was only saying I don't think you're being objective. Women aren't always, you know."

"Men are? You're being funny again, aren't you? You're not? Well, I am amazed."

"If you want the truth, I don't like any of this. I hate it. Watching people, waiting to catch them saying or doing something wrong . . . Ugh! It makes my skin crawl. I don't think Nalatan'll go along with you."

"I wouldn't blame him if he refused. I have to ask." She put a hand on his shoulder. "We're in a bad world, Gan. You're only doing what you must. It may be unpleasant, but it's the right thing. Don't hate yourself."

"Nor you, Rose Priestess. War Healer. Old friend. Distrust—call it caution, if you will—comes no easier for you than for me."

Sylah tossed her head. "Never mind *old* friend. Friend is perfectly adequate. Now hurry, or we're going to be missed."

They were laughing as they dashed through the door leading to a flight of stairs descending into the castle. Sylah longed to stop halfway down. She wanted to comfort Gan, to tell him how much it hurt to hear the hollowness in his laughter, how the echoes of needless guilt rang in the confines of the cold, dank passageway.

It would have embarrassed her to know Gan was wishing he could say the same thing to her.

Chapter 65

"You can't ask me to do that."

"It's not spying, Nalatan. Just talk to her, listen to her. She admires you. She'll help us understand what Leclerc's doing."

"Can you hear yourself, Sylah? What you mean is for me to gain her confidence and repeat everything she tells me."

Sylah's stomach wound itself tight. Nalatan said nothing she hadn't said to herself. Hearing it from another made it worse. She walked to one of the massive chairs before the fireplace in the abbey's great room and sat down heavily. "I do hear. And I'm ashamed. Forgive me."

Nalatan picked up the fireplace poker, stirred the blazing logs. Sylah had to smile; the thick iron rod was as long as a man's leg, with a vicious-looking claw hook. She'd used it often, and it was a two-handed struggle, especially if the hook snagged and had to be worked free. In Nalatan's hand it darted and twisted. His rugged, honest face was relaxed now. Its integrity was a reproach.

Nalatan broke the silence. "Do you fear Leclerc that much? Or is it the girl?"

The question came in the soft drawl of Nalatan's desert home. Sylah was quite aware that he fell into that pattern when he meant to be formal. She was stung. "I fear neither. My training tells me the girl is untrustworthy. The man is powerful. He knows things we can't imagine which he shares with us openly. Or does he?"

Nalatan jabbed the hook into a burnt log. Charcoal grated, a gritting, slithering sound. Skin crawling, Sylah gripped the chair arms. Nalatan said, "I am still Church's man, despite being cast out, as you. I'm also your friend. I assume the privilege of warning you. Church cannot refuse to defend herself in any way she can, but she must defend against what is known, not what is suspected. Would you throw away your good name? Because of an untrustworthy girl? A lonely man?"

"You're very kind. I'm proud you call me friend. I needed your wisdom."

He chuckled softly. "Wisdom. I haven't gone crazy yet, so some people think I'm wise and understanding."

Both knew he referred to Tate's long, silent absence. There were no words for that situation. He drew the poker out of the fire, examining it as though the scars of its rough forging carried answers. He placed the middle of the shaft across his thigh, handle in his right hand. Stunned, Sylah watched him grab the hook end with his left. Diamonds of sweat broke out on his forehead. Lips bared teeth in a smile of torment. Perspiration ran tiny creeks down his face. Straining cords lifted under the flesh of his neck, distorted it. Slowly, inexorably, the bar bent.

Sylah was sure she smelled burnt flesh. She started to reach for him, to shout at him to stop. She checked. What Nalatan was doing to himself baffled her. Still, there was a faint edge of understanding, a hint of ethic that defined itself by challenge and pain.

He pitched the ruined bar away. It clanged on the stone hearth, setting off an entire chorus of echoes within the great hall. When he rose from his kneeling position, the knee of the leg he used as an anvil cracked like a whip. The pressure mark left by the rod was still visible in the woolen trouser.

"There's my wisdom." He stared deep into her eyes, moved his chin to indicate the poker. "And here." He held up the left hand, welted red blisters striping the palm. "Without her, this is what I have left. Strength. Endurance. I endure."

Something warned Sylah to say absolutely nothing. He walked away.

Nalatan was grateful she remained silent. His mind was too dangerously poised on the edge of fear to tolerate intrusion. The fury in him threatened to turn him into something like the pitiful animals that contracted the frothing disease. He'd seen the affliction twice. The memory haunted him. Pitiful, maddened dogs, they staggered and whined and snarled and bit anything. Anyone they wounded was equally doomed.

Customarily, Nalatan exhausted the rage living in him by exhausting himself. Daily he trained with the Wolves, moving from group to group, exercising any who cared to test themselves. It was the perfect outlet. He could play at killing, yet never face the consequences. None of the eager, resolute youngsters comprehended the bright menace behind a peculiar blink of his wide eyes. None knew the significance of suddenly flared nostrils. They never knew those signals normally preceded a killing thrust or slash. They never knew how difficult the decision to stay the blow.

Today the clash of steel and shouts of male excitement drew him as the sound of water pulls the thirsting.

The equipment room on the edge of the training field was a long, squat, unpainted building, marked by a single door at each end and frequent windows at regular intervals. The interior was as spare and grim as the exterior. Coarse cloth sacks on wall hooks held a man's regular clothes. Practice armor, if not being worn by the assigned Wolf, was stacked in proper order under an empty sack. The weather was fair, following the previous day's storm, so the windows were open. A fine breeze swept the building. Dust caught sunlight pouring in the windows, defined it, turned it into precise, glowing beams.

The sweat of hundreds of overheated bodies literally steeped the raw wood construction. Showers and soaks behind the place freshened the men. The building simply aged. Nalatan never saw it without thinking all the ugliness exactly suited its purpose. It was a shrine to men hacking the life from other men.

He shrugged on a thick cotton jersey, then the heavy leather jacket with its protective bands of thin steel. Leather trousers, striped by more steel laths, guarded his legs. Next was the leather-lined Olan steel helmet. He despised it. It was hot. The flap that covered the back of his neck and ears blocked out some sounds while creating a distant sort of roar that interfered with others. Grudgingly, he tied the lacing under his chin, conceding that the contraption had saved him several headaches. Probably some scars. Finally, the handguards, clumsy things like gloves, but far too thick for that name. Combined leather and steel bent so a man could grip a spear or murdat, but no one ever called them flexible.

Pulling on the left one scraped the fresh burn on his palm. He winced, more chagrined than pained.

His personal weapons leaned against the wall. Unused for long weeks, he thought they looked forlorn, neglected. Almost guiltily, Nalatan lifted sword and parrying bar. Alone in the sun dazzled haze of the building, he remembered dancing with them. A hot, celebratory day. Tate watching him. A musician stroking heartbeat rhythms on a drum. Sand pulled at his feet there, Nalatan remembered; a man couldn't dance on such footing. The love in him laughed at it and said, Then he'll fly: There's nothing can stop him. And Nalatan did. Because she was there.

The sword in his right hand chimed cadence against the metal bar as he walked outside. Men called to him, smiling at a friend. He felt himself smile back, heard himself answer their greetings, respond to their hard humor.

They couldn't see the drooling, raging beast inside.

A tenner approached, a companion of long standing. "I've got a new man in my ten I think you should meet. A Fin man. That's one of the old Harbundai baronies, you know? He likes to talk about fighting the Kwa. He's got some scars."

Something tingled in the back of Nalatan's head. He said, "Oh? Let the boy watch while I practice with someone skilled."

The tenner's eager expression wavered for a moment, but came back. "The youngster saw you coming this way. He asked if the parrying bar was a cane. The whole ten heard him, Nalatan."

Nothing could be more dangerous, Nalatan told himself. Challenged by a brave fool. Men waiting to cheer. Nalatan cursed the thing that made him ache to strike out. "Bring him on."

"What weapons for him?"

"Anything he's strong enough to lift."

Leaves caught in a whirlpool, the entire body of training Wolves circled Nalatan. The tenner had to force his way through, his recruit following. Nalatan sighed at the sight of his challenger. Tall, packed solidly, but with the still-forming muscle of youth, he was as nervous as he was proud. The result was a twitchy aggressiveness that reacted on Nalatan's frayed nerves like salt on a wound.

The routine rules of the match droned. Nalatan measured his man.

The challenger came fast, overriding rudimentary technique with boldness. Nalatan parried, noting that the man stabbed; most farmers slashed like they were cutting brush. Casually, Nalatan feinted with his sword and fetched his foe a sharp rap on the helmet with the ball on the end of the iron bar.

The man's knees buckled. His eyes opened comically wide. A trickle of shining saliva eased out of the corner of his mouth, dripped on his jacket.

Nalatan said, "Better if you practice what your Wolf leaders show you. You're brave, but you're not ready." He turned away, breathing a bit easier than he had since talking to Sylah.

It was the sudden hush that warned him. The whisper of the sword passing over his ducked head actually preceded the first horrified shout from the crowd. Nalatan continued to drop. Once flat on the ground, he rolled swiftly, springing to his feet with the bar in defense, the sword ready to strike.

Roaring, the younger man leaped to close the gap between them.

The beast in Nalatan screamed delighted release. The collision of steel on steel was sweet, exhilarating music. He retreated, parrying, striking just often enough to assure no opportunity for a well-executed thrust. The young man's confidence soared higher with each moment.

Little by little, the recruit's awareness of his predicament broke through his ignorance. The thing in the back of Nalatan's mind was a storm, howling.

The circled watchers hummed expectation. At Nalatan's first step forward, they jeered, heaping scorn on the man who'd lost the initiative. Nalatan forced him backward. Weakened by furious effort, baffled by Nalatan's style, the man's sword flailed wildly, barely arriving at a point in time to deflect one blow, then needed at another place immediately.

Nalatan toyed with him. Sword thrusts came just short. The bar hummed and whirled. The ball cracked against the man's helmet, his legs, boomed on the bullhide shield. Finally, coldly, Nalatan brought the parrying bar down on the other man's sword arm.

The young face twisted with pain. He stumbled backward, forced the sword up to defense with both hands. Swaying, knees threatening collapse, he waited, too young and brave to acknowledge defeat. Words came in heaving gusts. "I'm still standing. You haven't won if I'm standing."

The thing inside Nalatan ruled now.

Nalatan circled, studying. It was a deliberate selection of target, and the calculation silenced the crowd. Collectively, they held their breath.

There were unshed tears of frustration, resignation, and plain fear in the young man's eyes. Still, he faced Nalatan, circling, limping.

"Nalatan!" The voice was feminine, lilting. "You've never looked better. All finished with this demonstration, are you?"

Slowly, Nalatan rose from his fighting crouch. His gaze never left his opponent. The bar was poised, the sword leveled. "Neela?"

"I was riding past and saw the excitement. I was sure you'd be in the middle of it, so I came over."

Retreating one careful step, Nalatan said, "Is it over, boy?"

The tenner leaped into the circle. Positioning himself in front of his recruit, he directed his words over Nalatan's head, to Neela on her horse. "The youngster's too winded to talk, Nalatan. He's seen enough. We all have." The last was a plea, and the tenner's gaze dropped to meet Nalatan's when he said it. Men, Nalatan assumed, were ten-mates hurried to drag the youngster off before his mouth got him in more trouble.

Acknowledging the crowd of Wolves, Nalatan said, "Remember what you saw. Attack wins for units. Defense wins for individuals. Never forget." He turned to Neela, barely restrained his surprise at the sight of Jaleeta, beside her on another horse. Neela's bright smile welcomed, as always, her fair beauty a complement to the bright afternoon sun. She dressed warmly in a heavy woolen cloak. It was dark blue, shot through with threads of darker purple that caught the light, so the material seemed to ripple at all times. Her hood, brushed back from her head, framed the golden helmet of her hair.

Darker, compelling, Jaleeta's smile was quieter. Nalatan thought of whispers, of songs so faintly heard one wondered if they were real. She wore her hood pulled forward, so only stray locks of glistening black hair slipped free. They trembled in the breeze, bold against the off-white hood atop her earth-brown cloak.

"I was looking for you," Neela said. "Gan asked me to tell you he'd like to meet with you. Can you come?"

"Not until I bathe and change. I'll join you at the castle."

"We'll go ahead, then. I'll tell him you're coming."

Jaleeta loitered. Nalatan avoided looking in her direction. The pressure of her gaze wore at him. When he turned, she was waiting. Her free right hand rose slowly, tucked in strands of wayward hair. A smile misted across her features. Her gaze ripped through his composure.

The demon that shrieked its need to kill the brash youngster was suddenly alive again. Now, however, it whispered. Enticed. Spoke of stealth and mysteries, of secret, soft darkness. It sang of languor like honey, of lust like torrents of flame.

Jaleeta's smile gleamed wider. Hungering.

Chapter 66

Nalatan stepped out of the equipment building into a startlingly beautiful sunset. Jagged Whale Coast peaks glowed flame. Closer, fields and forest and the blunt geometry of Ola bathed in softer golden tones. The few puffy clouds overhead were charged with ever-changing hues of warmth. None of that affected the coldly crystalline air.

To his sorrow, Nalatan had discovered that clear days were treasured events in this country at this time of year. The climate of the Dry was harsher, but there were times when he found the determined gray of the Three Territories like a shroud for the living.

At the first, brush-shielded bend in the road, Nalatan was startled to come almost face-to-face with the tenner. The leader's ten men ranged behind him. Nalatan's hand automatically dropped to his sword. Stiffly, the tenner gestured, openhanded. "Didn't mean to come on you unaware, Nalatan. Just wanted a moment. We all saw how upset you were today when Botul here let his mouth get ahead of his brains. I thought you'd kill him. I'm glad you didn't. I never should have passed along his foolish words. I wanted to see him brought up short and hard. That's my job, but I saw a chance to let you do it for me. That was wrong. So don't hold what happened against him. He's a good man. It wasn't his fault."

For several heartbeats Nalatan said nothing, for the simple reason he didn't know what to say. Finally, he addressed Botul. "You're as brave a man as I've ever seen. Talented. Determined. You'll beat me someday. But this one"— he nodded sharply at the tenner—"is braver than both of us combined."

The entire ten goggled. Nalatan went on. "He's a true leader. He's taking blame for you, Botul. And for me. Beyond his skill with a weapon, or his muscles, or even the curses he so lovingly lavishes on you while he turns you into proper Wolves, what makes him a leader is the sure knowledge that he'll do what's right. Anything you learned from Botul or me you could learn from two wildcow herd bulls. If you learned anything important, you learned it from this man, just now." Nalatan twisted away past the slack-jawed tenner before the man had a chance to speak. He maintained his fast pace until he reached the open ground separating the town from the castle.

By then the sunset touched only the westernmost clouds. The castle walls loomed darkly. Servants appeared at several points, carrying torches. They moved along the ramparts, flames dimming and flaring as the bearers passed the gaping crenels and raised merlons. Metal fire-baskets hung by the castle gates and around the wall. It was very pretty, Nalatan grudgingly admitted. As a warrior, he knew how a night attack would appreciate such illumination. He was glad Gan insisted there be no lights after the first watch.

A guard met Nalatan at the door to the main room of the castle and escorted him to the small room off to the side. Gan sat at a long, heavy table. His chair was of light, almost honey-colored, wood, figured with dark, curling stripes. It had carved leaping tigers for the arms, with ivory teeth in open mouths, glowing red carnelians for eyes. Atop the chair's backrest snarled a larger tiger's head carved in high relief.

Despite the roaring fire in the fireplace off to the left, the room was cold, and Gan had added a thick wool sweater over his normal garb. Clearly executed by some friend or admirer, it was bright red, with diagonal opposed murdats in yellow on the front. Seeing Gan bedecked in anything so bright raised Nalatan's eyebrows. Beside and a step behind Gan, like a grim shadow, stood Sylah. Her expression showed she hadn't forgotten, or learned to be comfortable with, her earlier conversation with Nalatan.

Others occupied the room. Leclerc leaned against the fireplace wall, enjoying the heat. He was dressed in dark, sturdy wool. The remaining guest sat at the end of the table farthest from Leclerc. Emso smiled on catching Nalatan's eye, and Nalatan wondered at the forced friendliness of it.

Gan said, "I wasn't sure you'd be here so soon, Nalatan. I intended to review the meeting with you later. Now that you're here, we'll all discuss the news together." Leclerc drew close quickly. Nalatan noted that Emso merely shuffled about, remaining in the same place. Nalatan also noted Emso's homespun woolen shirt, marred by yarn of indifferent spinning, with wide variations in the size of threads. Numerous nubs, where broken strands had been tied back together, exploded from the surface like fuzzy buds. Toggles of carved bone, rather than buttons, closed it. His leather trousers were neat, somewhat better made. The effect was an insistent ordinariness that became, perversely, ostentatious.

Oddly, Emso's grizzled beard was well trimmed. More, for the first time in Nalatan's memory, there was no shaggy hair hanging down his neck.

Sylah's voice broke Nalatan's inspection. She said nothing he hadn't already heard; Moonpriest's wallkiller threw strange jars, Moonpriest's men shot huge arrows from catapults, Moonpriest killed men with lightning. The tales lacked shock value after a while. Nalatan already thought of them as stories to frighten recruits.

Leclerc was much more interested. Standing on the same side of the table as Nalatan, he edged ever closer to Sylah. Such intensity surprised Nalatan. Leclerc was no warrior, as Tate and Conway were, but he was brilliant. He didn't swallow wild tales.

Sylah finished. Leclerc straightened, a shadow of frown rippling his brow. For several heartbeats, no one stirred, caught up in Leclerc's concentration.

Emso's harshness rasped across the silence. The grizzled warrior still maintained his separation. "Magic. It's coming against us, Gan. It's a test. Look at what's happened. When we fought Altanar, the magic was given to us. Lightning weapons did us no harm at the battle of the Bear Paw, when Altanar controlled them. When Altanar's armies could have stopped us, the strangers gave us the lightning weapons to defeat them. When Altanar's walls stood in front of us, it was a stranger who gave us magic to break the gates."

Gan frowned. "There've been no spells, no chants or charms. Our friends know how to do things we don't."

Emso took an awkward backward step. The move edged him into greater darkness. "Moonpriest brings light from the sky to kill his enemies. The snakes of the desert poison them. He has new weapons. Tears of Jade calls demons from under the sea. Can't you see it? We're not just fighting, we're being fought *over.* There are powers we can't imagine, Gan; strange powers, good and evil. When we were in the right, good protected us, helped us."

Gan's voice was metallic. "I don't think I've become evil."

Sylah spoke up. "Emso, I understand. And agree with you. The war against Moonpriest and Tears of Jade is a battle against evil. We're fortunate to have a man as skilled as Leclerc to help us confront them."

Dismissing her without a glance, Emso continued to confront Gan. "It's the things we can't see, or won't see, that threaten us the most. All I'm asking is that you look at our problems the way you used to, hard-eyed and hard-minded. We named you Murdat. You're the weapon that freed us. But no weapon stands against a witch. As a friend who'd die for you, I'm asking you to think about what's happening to us."

"Did all of Windband move to the seacoast?" Leclerc's jarringly inappropriate question startled everyone. Gan stared at him as if he'd sprouted a horn from his forehead. Nalatan was round-eyed with disbelief. Emso's knuckles gleamed white where he squeezed the handle of his murdat. Sylah looked relieved. And amused. It was she who answered. "The reports say so."

Still distant, Leclerc nodded shortly. "Why would he move? Why change camps in the cold and wet? What's so important about the coast?" He rubbed forefingers at his temples, then wandered to the fireplace.

Intrigued, Gan rose, came around the table. Beside Leclerc, he said, "Yours are inland people. Moonpriest was one of you, once. Why is he attracted to the sea?" He turned to Sylah. "Is there anything in Moondance that speaks of the sea?"

"Only the moon mother's power to call the tide."

Muttering so softly the words were practically incomprehensible, Leclerc spoke to himself. "Think, Louis; use your mind. Moonpriest's crazy, not stupid. He's got a static electricity generator. All this other mumbo jumbo is probably some offshoot. The so-called wallkiller's no problem. My catapults will knock that big pile of junk out of action in no time. But why move? What's that maniac up to?" Breaking off the self-aimed conversation, it took him a moment to focus on Gan. His question was plaintive. "How long before Conway and Tate get back? I need them."

Emso moved sideways to the failing edge of the firelight. "They're already being tested, just as the rest of us will be. There have been storms in the mountains, earlier and fiercer than anyone can remember. They're trapped between unknown intruders and killing weather. If they were sent as gifts from the good power, then we should understand their loss is a sign."

"A sign? A *sign*?" Leclerc swiveled around slowly, unsteadily. "You're saying if my friends die it's a sign? It's a tragedy, you idiot. You can't imagine what a loss they'd be. You don't have the brains to begin to . . . to . . ."

Gan grabbed the stammering Leclerc by the upper arm, whirled him around, slammed his back against the stones of the fireplace wall. "No more." Gan's words grated. "No man insults Emso in my hearing. You will forgive what he said and the way he said it." Keeping Leclerc pinned with one hand, Gan looked to Emso. "You're speaking of this man's people. You'll forgive his outburst."

While Leclerc repeated "yes" and "of course," without stopping, Emso's jaw twitched in bitter silence. At long last, he managed, "I said more than I should." Then, surprisingly, he broke into coarse laughter. The sound further wounded the tense unhappiness in the room. He broke it off abruptly. "It's always that way. The least important thing becomes the most important, the least considered words the most clearly heard." He saluted, the clenched fist raised to the right jawbone. Gan released Leclerc, and without thinking, Leclerc returned the salute in the same manner. The action earned a raised eyebrow from Gan, followed by a broad smile.

Resentment sparked in Leclerc. He saw the smile as condescension, the renowned warrior pretending to acknowledge the scruffy thinker as equal. That tiny flare found eager fuel in the sense of humiliation that came from being manhandled and scolded for daring to speak out. Leclerc told himself he was imagining melodrama; Emso would never harm him. Still, when he stole a glance at the fuming older man, who continued to cloak himself in darkness like some dreadful portent, the hair on his arms tingled.

Gan turned back to Emso, walked the length of the table to stand in front of his old friend and companion. He said, "I know your heart. And you know mine. We fight in the name of those who need us. We rule because we feel it's an obligation. You know the prophecy that drives me."

"I fear it." The truth of that was plain in Emso's voice and features. "Your mother said you would always face two paths, one to glory, the other to shame. You must always move forward, always choose. I taste the air on this path and it has the foul grease of disgrace on it."

"So be it." Gan's words were uncompromising, but they were spoken gently. "I can only die. Men like us don't live with shame."

Sylah stormed toward the pair, fists clenched in front of her. They were ludicrously ineffectual weapons aimed at the men suddenly turned to confront her. The tough, hardened faces grew alarmed. Sylah was a thing of quaking fury. "Is death all you understand? You measure life by the way you leave it. You make me sick. I will hear no more of glory or shame. You will live. For your wife and son, even if you lose all else. And you, Emso. Are you mad? Gan Moondark needs you. Perhaps you'll never find it in your heart to accept me, but never speak of this man and disgrace at the same time. So long as you stand beside him, nothing will harm his honor."

By the time she finished, Gan was grinning. Emso, on the other hand, visibly blanched. When Gan attempted to speak, Emso drowned out the effort, seemingly not even aware Gan was talking. The words were uncharacteristically high, coming with staccato rapidity. "You're right. He has his fate. That path is mine, as well. Whatever happens, no one will ever question my faithfulness. Everyone knows these things. Especially you, Rose Priestess."

Sylah said, "I've caused you much pain. I never wanted to. Someday you'll see. I'm right."

Emso shook his head. He faced Gan. "I'll be off. Before I go, though, I'll tell you words you must not forget. The first is *magic*. The other is *witch*. What else is Tears of Jade? What else is Moonpriest? Ask yourself why such strange powers come against us. Ask why now. Remember; only you can choose your path."

He left, the rustle of the rough cloak making a sound like smothered language. The breath of his hurried passage set the flame of the exit sconce dancing. The ensuing pall hurried the departure of the rest. Leclerc was first to excuse himself. Nalatan offered to walk along with Leclerc. The shorter man accepted gratefully. Once the meeting room's planked door closed behind them, Leclerc glanced up at Nalatan. "Do you believe all that talk of witches and magic?" The light in the long hall came from fat candles cupped in widely separated sconces. Their flickering seemed to trap the question in midair. It hung there, heavy with possibility.

Nalatan laughed. At the same time, he made a surreptitious three-sign. "I'm—I was a monk, remember? I answer as Church would have me answer."

"No, no. Answer as Nalatan. Tell me the truth."

"I believe in power for evil, just as I believe in power for good." Nalatan was surprised to feel comfortable speaking of these things to this man. "I believe people have great powers in them. I've seen men watch without flinch while their own limbs were amputated. I've seen people hate so strongly the power of it sickened and killed others. Take Sylah, who fought harder than any man to find the Door. She's a Rose Priestess, a War Healer—but she led warriors. Conway, with those huge dogs; he brings death like a winter storm. My Donnacee. We followed a Priestess into battle. She demanded it, because Church needed the secret of the Door. And we obeyed her. That's controlling power."

"The power of the mind." Nalatan turned sharply at the amusement in Leclerc's voice, but the man's smile was introspective. Leclerc continued. "You wonder about the why of things. That's important. It's basic, is what it is. Perhaps that's why I like you. I sense curiosity. I have the feeling you were born to be more than a fighting machine, just as I . . ." He stopped abruptly, then resumed, ignoring his own interruption. "I confess I wish I could be a warrior like Conway, or you. I can't. But I can do other things. I deserve better treatment. Well, never mind. I'll tell you this, though: simple strength isn't going to beat Windband and the Skan. Maybe Gan needs Emso. He certainly needs me. More than anyone realizes." For some reason, that struck Leclerc as funny. He laughed long and loud. Nalatan wished there was enough light to study the face of a man who could warp the sound of merriment, make somber stone echo with buried loneliness.

Chapter 67

Darkness mocked Nalatan. Restful scents of sea and land taunted him. His mind was a cauldron of inchoate thought. Inevitably, everything resolved to images of his wife. In her absence, memory polished every moment of their time together, until thinking of her was a bright, blinding thing that delighted and pained unbearably.

He flung aside the blankets on his bed and rose. Cold wind from the sea drove through the open window. He welcomed its waking shock; better to be fully awake and cold than warm and groggy. He had no trouble finding his clothes. The position of everything in the room was too well known, and he'd spent too many similar nights. He smiled faintly. The castle guards hated his night forays. They were good, conscientious men, but merely troopers, for all their training. It upset them to know that someone came and went among them unheard, unseen. After having spoken from the dark a few times and startled a few guards absolutely witless, he tried to explain to them about the skills trained into a warrior-monk. He only offended them further. Now he made it a point to reveal himself quickly when he found it necessary to prowl away his sleeplessness.

Once out of his room, with its wide-flung window shutters, the rest of the castle smelled of herbal-scented soap and damp stone, with a lingering taint of burnt candles. It was all very clean, if a bit dank, but in his nostrils it stank of confinement. Hurrying outside, Nalatan savored the stiffness of the sheep-cropped grass underfoot and the weight of the whispering north wind. Far away, a dog howled. An even thinner call answered. Nalatan listened with a longing that had no name.

Benches marked the grounds, each carefully sited to provide the best view of some aspect of the buildings or plantings. In the dark, that was no benefit. He chose one at random.

When he saw the figure creeping along the wall of the castle, he doubted his eyes. When it moved again, he instantly cast off lovelorn cares, gripped his sword.

Stealthily, the other person pressed along the wall. Nalatan wondered: One of the servants? A lover bound for a tryst? The figure moved awkwardly. The right arm, only dimly observed, was raised, bent at the elbow, held back at the shoulder. The left hand was extended, feeling, scouting. A man, then. Armed. Who? A rogue guard? A spy, leaving to report?

Nalatan dropped low, the better to silhouette his quarry. Together, the two men paralleled each other through the night.

A pair of guards threw open a door mere paces in front of the man against the wall. Torchlight flooded out in a golden wave, puddling on the stone walkway and flanking shrubbery. The prowler huddled in those bushes. Nalatan determined to cut them back the next morning.

Flat against the short grass, Nalatan watched the guards exit, slam the door behind them, and stride away. They turned toward Nalatan. Chatting, chuckling, the pair walked within his arm's reach. He stifled a wild urge to leap up and whack them both from behind on their gleaming helmets.

The man in the shrubbery waited patiently before rising again. Nalatan's opinion of him improved. Whoever he was, he understood night work.

The figure took no logical course to an exit from the castle grounds. The stables were ahead, a bit to the right. No one would attempt to flee on horseback, however. There'd be no getting through the gate.

The Violet Abbey. Nalatan's gaze went to the steep, sharp roof pointing at the stars.

Sylah.

A Church fanatic, making a move to murder Church's most hated foe. They'd tried once already. Nalatan winced at the ignominy of it, a man stalking a sleeping woman, a Priestess.

Then the man was away from the castle wall. He moved low to the ground. Nalatan lay on his stomach to watch, tracking now as much by sound as sight. When the other man moved, so did Nalatan. Once the sound level dropped, so did the hunter, becoming part of the earth. Just as Nalatan prepared to move closer, to apprehend the killer before he reached the abbey, the man nearly escaped. Suddenly he was moving away from the abbey, toward the sea and the rear wall of the castle grounds. Confused, Nalatan hurried to follow.

Intent on what the man might do, rather than on what he was doing, Nalatan's concentration slipped. All at once, he realized that the only sound in the night was that of his own movement. Instantly, he lowered himself to a taut, coiled squat. He settled there, with no option but to wait. Had he been heard? Or seen? How skilled was this other man?

Senses singing with stress, Nalatan waited. Slowly, he swiveled his head, trying to get an image. Instead, a strong, unmistakable scent rolled over him. The stables. There was a sound, as well, like an immense exhalation. The stable door, opening and closing.

Nalatan remembered a rope outside the high hayloft window. Hoping against hope that it was accessible, he scuttled to it. A tug indicated it was secure at the top. He warmed his hands in his armpits until the stiffness of cold was gone, then hauled himself up. He swung through the loading port onto the loft floor. Stretched out on the soft, welcoming hay, luxuriating in the warmth, he waited for his breathing to steady. Then he moved to explore.

Flame burst to life immediately below. He nearly ran. In the moment, he realized he was standing directly over the tack room. Below him, dressed in black, someone moved about in the cubicle. Strung blankets covered the walls. It was a clever arrangement. The man had light, but the thick blankets were a perfect shield. The figure defied identification.

In the darkness outside that tiny square, something moved. The light died in a puff of breath. From the front of the barn came the sound of the high, wide door swinging on oiled hinges. This time there was a thump when it closed. The newcomer was unaccomplished.

"Hello? Is anyone there?" Nalatan's neck hair rose in alarm. Jaleeta.

A horse snuffled, stomped irritably in its stall.

Jaleeta made a tight, squealing sound. A deeper, gruff male voice said, "Be quiet, child." In sickening certainty, Nalatan recognized Emso.

From his position on the edge of the loft floor, overlooking the ground-level section of the barn, Nalatan slowly eased back against the mounded hay.

Nalatan, the man who disdained to ask questions and report the answers. A confirmed spy now, a skulking, dark-crawling thing, perched above two fools guilty of nothing more than ordinary lust and foolishness. Jaleeta, feeding an old man's folly. Emso, chasing after youth as though it could be transferred from the owner to the needy.

A degrading scene, about to be fully played out for Nalatan the noble. He despised himself. The tiny light flared again. Nalatan faced the other way.

"It's worse than I feared," Emso was saying.

Nalatan cocked his head to the side, listening. Those weren't words associated with lovemaking.

"Gan said something about Leclerc? About giving me to him?"

All it took was a mere bending of the body, and Nalatan was looking at the tops of their heads. They almost touched beside the flickering flame.

"He said nothing about you. I told you: He doesn't want people to know he uses human lives to reward his favored servants."

"Then what? What's so terrible?"

"Moonpriest's magic weapons. When Leclerc heard about them, he promised Gan to defeat them."

There was a long pause, and Nalatan realized it was because Jaleeta was thinking. It was a faculty he hadn't connected with her until that moment, and it was an unnerving revelation. He remembered the penetrating way she looked at things, the quickness of her answers. It occurred to him that there was more than one fool in attendance on Jaleeta that night. He resolved to reduce the number by half.

Jaleeta's long sigh preceded her resigned submission. "I'm doomed, then."

"It can't be. He's little more than a Peddler. I'll tell Gan myself."

"Tell him that you want me?"

Emso choked. "Me? I don't . . . I mean, I couldn't ask you to . . . That's crazy!"

"Is it? You can't imagine it? You can't close your eyes and see us? Together?"

"Of course. But it's impossible. You said it yourself. Gan wants you to go to Leclerc."

"Because he believes Leclerc's magic can defeat Moonpriest's, isn't that right?"

Emso nodded hesitantly. Jaleeta pressed ahead. "And we need a victory by Moonpriest to bring about the merging of Church and Moondance, to assure Gan allies with Church to rule the Three Territories. Isn't that right, too?"

Up in the loft, Nalatan watched Emso's head bob erratically. The lamp flame was like shining oil on the older man's cheekbones. There was a small scar on the right side. The smoother skin there caught the light better, glittered jewellike.

Cajoling, leading him into agreement, Jaleeta said, "What if Moonpriest knew what Leclerc intended to do to defeat him?" In the murky light of the enclosure, her hand emerged from a voluminous sleeve like a blind, white cave-creature. Long, delicate fingers seemed to undulate as she reached for Emso's face. "We mustn't provoke Gan, not to resentment, not to suspicion. I will do what I must, and you must help me. We must be brave together."

He grabbed her hand, kissed the fingertips. "Do what? You just said there's nothing we can do. I won't let you throw yourself away on that man, not for all the magic secrets in the world. I'll kill him first, if I die for it."

Gently, firmly, she extricated her hand, resumed fondling his features. Nalatan shivered, imagined her pulling Emso's soul out of his body with those slim, wraith hands. Her voice chased the picture. "I'll learn Leclerc's secrets. He wants me. He'll tell me what I want to know. I'll tell you. You'll tell the Violet Abbess. Her Priestesses can go anywhere, even to Windband. True Church will win, Emso. You'll save Gan's soul, save his kingdom."

Emso pushed her hand away. The gesture was solid, convinced. The voice that followed was craven. "What you say betrays Murdat. Moonpriest will never let him live. If I help the Abbess this way, I betray my friend."

"Church wants Gan Moondark back, not killed. Once everyone sees that Gan can't defeat Windband, all of our friends will confront him at once. He'll compromise. He won't let his Wolves die for nothing, he won't let himself be overthrown. Church wants him to rule the Three Territories in her name, advised by all the other friends of Church. You're not betraying him. You're doing what a friend is supposed to do. You're saving him."

"Church cannot be divided. But I've fought beside him from the beginning."

The last was a plea, and Jaleeta was properly sympathetic. To Nalatan, she appeared to flow forward. She pulled Emso's head down, nestled it against her shoulder. Her free hand ran fingers through his hair. "You're the most loyal friend he has, Emso. Possibly the only true friend." The graying head stirred, but Jaleeta held it firmly in place, continuing to talk in the same singsong tones. "Sylah betrayed Church, and made Gan her protector. We know she wants only to destroy our culture, make women what they cannot be, raise children to do the secret things only nobles and Church have the right to do. Now Gan fights Church. The Black Lightning and the White Thunder—where are they? Why is Lanta with them, and Nalatan is not? If Sylah weren't witch enough, she has Lanta the Seer to plot with her. And poor Nalatan. The black one abandoned him. Lanta works with her and Conway; all plot to bring other powers against Church. Evil powers. Admit it, Emso; you've thought the same thing. And Leclerc, my specified husband. You've seen how he looks at Gan; he'll help him only so long as he must. There's only you. Bring Gan back to Church. Make him listen to those who can make the Three Territories great. Only you can do it."

Wind hissed between the gaping boards of the barn, moaned in knotholes and cracks. Cold struck Nalatan, through flesh to bone. When he moved to massage himself some warmth, the hand on his sword hilt was locked in unconscious rigor. He pried the fingers free.

His head hurt worse than his hand, horror melding with cold. No man should be destroyed so utterly, so falsely, as Emso. Nalatan knew he must stop her, whether he was called spy or no. She killed the way the merciless Dry drained the strength of a victim, drop by drop. She would leave nothing but a loathsome, brittle husk, and people would call it traitor.

Liar.

And there was that odd look and manner of Leclerc's when he spoke of his own worth, and his rightful status.

Liar?

Sylah did enlist Gan in her cause.

Liar?

Donnacee should have returned by now. Gone with the Seer. After swearing no one but Conway or others of their tribe could be allowed to know the holy site.

Liar?

Chapter 68

Deeply perturbed by the galling insecurity created by the activity below, Nalatan missed some of the conversation. Jaleeta's chiming laughter brought him back to the present with a surge of near-panic. He didn't know what he'd failed to hear, what amused her. She went on.

"Our women are raised correctly. After all, the Apocalypse Testament tells us, 'In man is the strength of Church. In woman is the life of man. From her comes that which is tomorrow for man. From man and Church must come support for her.' How can a woman be protected if she isn't supervised? It's for her own good. We respect men who know that. We please them."

"You quote from the Testament. You're so young, and you understand so much."

"I know only what's right for me."

Nalatan winced at the brutal irony of the words.

Jaleeta and Emso still embraced, but Emso sat straighter now, gazing into

Jaleeta's eyes as if finding the world hidden there. Her words rode the pale cloud of her breath. "Spend the rest of the night here with me. We may never have a time like this again until you've saved Gan, and we can tell him about us." She kissed him lightly, and then was apart from him, sliding away to the limit of his grasp. With his hands barely in contact with her shoulders, she raised her own to her throat. Tantalizing, she untied the lacing of her cloak. Falling like rippling water, it pulled away her hood. Freed skeins of black hair swirled alive in flame-glow. Under the cloak was a blouse. White hands danced against dark material, opening buttons.

Emso made a low groaning, deep in his chest. Jaleeta smiled at him. Nalatan tried to look away. He might have, but for Jaleeta's smile at Emso. There was nothing of conspiracy in it, or promise, or even anticipation. Nalatan told himself it was the angle of his view, yet he couldn't rid himself of the sensation that her expression was raw triumph.

The widening blouse created a dim, ivory wedge of flesh. Slowly, controlling, she revealed, pulled Emso deeper and deeper into her thrall. Looping her fingers under the edges of the completely undone top, she spread it wider. Half-moon aureoles appeared, dusky contrast emphasizing the rounded perfection of milk-white breasts.

She flung herself backward. Emso floundered, empty hands clenching empty air. "What was that?" Jaleeta's wondrous breathiness was gone, taken over by shrill alarm. "I heard something! Someone's out there, Emso. I heard them."

She pivoted, bent forward to listen as she re-dressed. She managed to get between Emso and the tiny lantern. Overwrought, taken completely by surprise, Emso thrashed and floundered like a man in spasm. Desperately, he struggled to reach the lantern to snuff it. Clumsily, Jaleeta blocked every move. He literally flung her aside. The light disappeared. Utter silence filled the barn.

Nalatan knew no sound interrupted Jaleeta's performance.

He dismissed that latest perfidy, concentrating all his senses on tracing Emso's investigations around the barn's interior. When Emso made his way back to the tack room, Nalatan refused to return to his peephole.

"Wait here," Emso told Jaleeta. "I'm sure there's no one outside, but I'll look. I'll come for you. We'll go back to the castle together." Jaleeta evidently attempted argument, because Emso pressed ahead hurriedly. "I won't let you go alone. Not now. Not ever. We have a pact now, you and me."

Nalatan was glad he wasn't looking. Watching Jaleeta gloat might make him do something foolish.

When Nalatan let himself out of the barn, there was enough darkness to conceal his movements, but the last of the stars were surrendering to the new day. He hurried home. Instead of to his room, however, he went to the baths adjacent to the castle kitchen. The cleansing shower was room temperature—cold. Opening the spigot near the bottom of the large wooden tank overhead, he wet himself down, soaped up, scrubbed, and sluiced off suds at breakneck pace. With a bucket, he scooped hot water from a copper cauldron over a slow fire, pouring it into a barrellike soak. After replacing what he'd drawn from the cauldron, he added cooler water to the soak to bring it down to proper temperature. A few splashes from a ceramic jar infused the hot water and the steam rising from it with the crackling sharpness of sage.

Few people in this part of the world looked kindly on sage as a scent. For Nalatan, it brought back childhood memories from the Dry. This morning, however, was no time for reminiscence. The present was too powerful.

He closed his eyes and leaned back against the rough cedar staves. He thought about Emso; what a fool he was, and what a good man he was when he wasn't being a fool.

He thought about being lied to.

It rankled. Jaleeta was nothing like Donnacee; there was no comparison. Still, lying was lying.

The thought that spying was spying scratched at his brain like a cat sharpening its claws. He shifted uncomfortably.

Love certainly made him do some foolish things, Nalatan considered. Why should Emso be condemned for something that happened to every man? Should a lifetime of honor be crushed under the weight of a moment's infatuation? And all brought about by a woman's lies?

Lies only a spy could know about.

Nalatan examined his present surroundings. The unaffected stolidity of stone and huge, aged timbers soothed him. There was permanence represented there, a visible patience.

There was no danger in keeping quiet about Emso; not for a while, at least. Once Emso realized that the entire scene in the tack room was no more than bait, he'd shed her like a duck shedding water. Nor would Leclerc corrupt himself for the pleasure of a few flattering words and a peek at some skin.

Overestimation. Women always overestimated their influence, one way or another. Sooner or later.

Nalatan heaved himself upright, stepped out of the tub. Steam billowed around him, a sequestering haze that accompanied him to the cabinet full of drying cloths. As he rubbed his body, he made his decision.

It would be wise to watch Emso. Not to spy, exactly, but to assure he made no missteps that couldn't be corrected. Jaleeta was always about. It'd be no great chore to throw a look her way from time to time, as well. The important thing, really, was to protect Emso. Gan was in no danger; Emso would come to his senses long before that moment arrived. Emso's reputation was gravely exposed, however. That must be attended to.

Still naked, Nalatan dipped a polished copper mirror in the hot water to keep it from steaming up. Propping it on a shelf above a bench, he lathered well and shaved. His razor was one of the knives he wore strapped to his biceps. He frowned. The dulled edge bit. That was carelessness.

The chore finished, he dressed and made his way to the dining hall, passing through the kitchen, rather than around it. He liked the kitchen. The one at his monk's village was austere, a place where raw things got cooked. It wasn't that the leadership didn't appreciate good food, or that they felt eating poorly was a proper penance for some unknown sin. They simply never bothered to train any cooks, and the brotherhood didn't encourage much criticism of anything.

Loitering along, he momentarily forgot his problems. Huge cauldrons billowed steam laden with delicious soup-stock smells. Expansive griddles sizzled a patchwork quilt of aromatic smoked bacon. Banter from the industrious kitchen help flew around him, good-natured scolding for intrusion on their territory. The chief cook, a large, florid woman, made a great show of sniffing at him when he passed. "You've been in the soak again, haven't you? You reek of sage. People use it to stuff chickens, not bathe in it."

The cook had almost unlimited privilege. After all, she ruled the world of appetite. Nalatan decided to be uninsulted, sneered, continued on his way.

Some few steps later he snatched up a hot griddle cake and darted out the door. Grinning, munching his trophy of wheat, oat, and corn flours, he settled on a bench at one of the trestle tables. Pitchers of milk, pots of honey, hot pepper sauce, salt, and other condiments created neat islands of promise along its length.

He ate a full stack of the cakes, with bacon and eggs, telling himself that a day's work required a hearty beginning. Once finished, however, the good spirits faded under the memory of the previous night. He hurried outdoors, leaving a surprised cook silently extending his customary second mug of tea.

Nalatan went directly to the stable to saddle his horse. Thin light from a low autumn sun struggled to suggest warmth as he emerged. To the west, gray clouds advanced stolidly, promising more snow. There was a hard, wet taste to the air. Nalatan looked to the east. The walls of the castle blocked vision, shut him away from the depressing sight of the clouds shrouding the Enemy Mountains. He tried not to think of his wife and the choked passes between himself and her.

Occasional shelters jutted from the interior of the castle's defensive walls. Rough wooden sheds, they were places for the off-duty watch to sleep and for stockpiling missiles, drinking water, and the myriad other accoutrements of combat. Nalatan tied his horse inside one, and made his way up to the battlewalk. Folding his legs under himself, back against the wall, he waited.

The best hunters aren't merely the best marksmen or the best trackers. Those who kill most frequently enjoy a more important talent. They anticipate.

Jaleeta had spoken of friends who would help Gan rule. Emso asked for no names.

Nalatan imagined Emso's night after leaving Jaleeta. Poor man, he thought; his brain must have looked like a drop of water on a red-hot plate. Sputter, spatter, pop! Waking would be the pop, when a bleary-eyed, sleepless Emso would decide he had to talk to someone about his situation.

Nalatan wiggled about, got comfortable. If Emso failed to appear before it was time to begin the rest of the day's activities, nothing was lost. If he rode out, however, it would be interesting to see what direction he took.

As it happened, Nalatan almost missed him. Emso left the castle and headed for the stables, but he turned aside. Nalatan mounted, galloped to reach the western gate before Emso was lost to sight. He arrived to see Emso on the road to the dock. Wasting no time, Emso engaged a fisherman in a spirited, gesticulating conversation. Directly, the man's small balancebar, with Emso as passenger, cast off. They went north.

Nalatan puzzled over that. Where would Emso go, by sea, to find a sympathetic ear? Most of the coast close to the castle was the hold of Baron Ondrat. Nalatan shook his head; there was a time when he'd have suspected Ondrat first. Ondrat saved Sylah, though. Nalatan resented the loudmouthed criticism for Gan that flowed constantly from the Baron, but how could you fail to respect a man who saved someone as important as Sylah?

A bit ashamed of himself, Nalatan acknowledged that he'd originally positioned himself on the wall to observe the approach between castle and Violet Abbey. He'd really expected Emso to head that way. The assumption almost ruined his chance to see what actually did happen. There was a lesson there.

Nothing was ever what it seemed to be, Nalatan told himself, and longed for the simpler days of a monk.

Emso had to be sailing all the way up to Baron Mull's land. He was a known malcontent. Not as vocal as Ondrat, but not a hero, either.

Nalatan reviewed his performance since Sylah had spoken to him about watching Jaleeta. Without even trying, he'd embarrassed himself painfully and learned nothing he was willing to discuss. He couldn't even carry out a good stalk anymore; he'd almost lost Emso because of an overconfident guess.

It was all a matter of being cooped up in a stone box, playing treacherous games. Sitting around. Waiting. No one had a right to ask him to live like that.

Chapter 69

The trail to Leclerc's wandered south through towering forest. Hacked-out fields formed infrequent breaks in the dark mass. Clearings seemed to cower under the patient determination of the waiting trees. As the mounted group passed, farm stock—cattle, horses, or llamas—lifted heads to watch.

Oddly, there was more snow this far south. The previous night's deposit blanketed the two-cart-wide track up to the horses' cannons. Pale, choked sunlight pouring over white cloaked trees and softened earth forms created an ethereal luminescence. Haystacks, miniature versions of the occasionally visible Snowfather Mountain, dotted meadows. Smoke rose from chimneys, angling under a sharp wind to join the darker gray of the sky.

Nalatan and Gan rode side by side, ahead of the others. Nalatan glowered at his surroundings. Gan caught him, and laughed. After a quick glance over his shoulder to assure he spoke without being overheard, Gan said, "Beautiful, isn't it? I don't like it, either."

Smiling wryly, Nalatan said, "Those clouds aren't the sky, they're a lid."

"Exactly. I try to look straight ahead. When I look off into the forest, with all that fuzzy, unending white, sometimes I feel it's closing in on me."

Making a face, Nalatan gave an exaggerated shiver.

They shared a moment of laughter, and Gan went on. "I'd like to see the Dry sometime. Is there really no water?"

"Some places. You have to know where to find it, that's all." Nalatan cut his eyes to Gan. "Can I ask you something?" At Gan's nod, Nalatan said, "I would never bring this up, but I need to talk. With one who'll understand. This isn't our place. So I ask you: Is it really worth it? This Murdat thing, and the Three Territories? I understand about your mother's prophecy. Still, do you mean to expand beyond the Mother River? The Sea Star Islands? I've never heard you say so, but I've seen your face when you look at maps, or out over the Inland Sea."

Gan's good humor was strained. "I won't go looking for new wars, if that's what you mean. But I'll defend what belongs to us."

Nalatan nodded. " 'Us.' You really believe your territory belongs to everyone who lives there. It's an interesting idea."

"It's a truth."

"If you say so. If you make it so." Nalatan was polite.

Chuckling softly, Gan said, "You don't believe a conqueror can be concerned about people's happiness? How do you balance that against Church's determination to recruit people away from any religion but Church?"

It was Nalatan's turn to tighten. "Church doesn't recruit or expand with swords and arrows."

"Really? Then what purpose the brotherhoods of warrior-monks?"

"Purely defensive. We protect Church."

"Against people who have no intention of being recruited." Gan grinned, placating. "I can win battles. It's not enough. I want to build a country where everyone can, indeed, believe one view is as good as another. Any Church I support must be tolerant."

After a while, Nalatan spoke. "That would, indeed be a thing of glory. No one's ever seen such a conqueror."

"They have in Harbundai. In Ola. They will elsewhere." Gan's declaration was an unabashed mix of hard arrogance and the vulnerability of a man who understands how many people yearn to see him humiliated.

The sound of someone approaching ended the exchange. Forging through the snow, Neela's horse came abreast, blowing clouds of steaming breath. Coldar nestled inside her voluminous cape. The tiny, apple-cheeked face peered out in wide-eyed uncertainty. This was new scenery, exciting, but unknown.

Sylah remained slightly behind. A tender smile touched her almost distant mien when Gan brightened at the sight of his son and wife. Then, however, she caught Nalatan's quick look back at Jaleeta. Sylah was shocked by the force of his distaste.

After a short wait, Sylah pretended to adjust a stirrup strap. She used the opportunity to surreptitiously observe Jaleeta, and realized there was no need for subterfuge. Jaleeta's yearning was so firmly fixed on Nalatan that nothing was likely to distract her.

Sylah turned away. Straightening, she suffered a rush of blood to her head, felt a touch of dizziness. In that moment, no more than a heartbeat, an inexplicable picture flashed in her mind. The young Chosens, the future Teachers, looking up at someone. The innocent faces were stark with terror. The cowled figure raised its head, and from within the depths of a shrouding hood, Jaleeta smiled malice.

The image was gone. Still, Sylah's heart raced. Never before had she so ardently missed Lanta. Lanta would know why the thought of Jaleeta wanting Nalatan drew Sylah's mind to such a dreadful, unrelated imagining.

Movement ahead caught Sylah's eyes. Gan was replacing the silver whistle he carried on a chain around his neck. Determined to break out of her suddenly somber mood, Sylah joined Neela. She forced a light tone, saying, "There's something untrustworthy about a man who commands dogs with a whistle no one can hear."

"You can't imagine it." Neela's feigned exasperation failed to disguise her pride. "If we have an argument? Wherever they are, they go sit next to him. Then they watch me, telling me he's *always* right. It's infuriating."

Sylah's dark feelings refused to fade. She felt driven to pursue the matter of Jaleeta. "An all-too-popular concept. Most women believe it. I understand Jaleeta holds to the old ways."

Neela grew serious. "Poor Jaleeta. If she hadn't been submissive, she wouldn't have survived the Skan. In her mind, submission is survival. That awful Violet Abbess only confirms the idea."

Sound broke Sylah's thoughts. Far away, so distant it was bare suggestion, something called. The group faced east as one. Horses' ears flicked. Shara and Cho broke point to look toward the Enemy Mountains, ruffs bristling, tails up. The sound came once again, wavering. Longing.

Gan was transported. "My brothers. They greet." The women glanced his way, then looked to the distance again. Nalatan's attention remained fixed on Gan, so it was only he who saw the sudden shift to concern. Only Nalatan heard Gan's whispered, "I know, brothers; I know. The short days come quickly now, and the long darkness favors the stalkers. I am warned. Hunt well, brothers."

There was a final howl, much closer. It ended abruptly. The sighing forest closed on the silence. The dogs relaxed. Gan resumed the march as if nothing happened. It caught the women off guard. While they lagged, Nalatan said, "I've heard the tales. They're true. The wolves speak to you."

Gan's gesture indicated confusion. "Not words. A feeling. I understand."

Nalatan elected to say no more. The moment, and the few words, confirmed the war in Gan's breast. Nalatan looked into the eyes of a ruler, and saw the horizon-breaking stare of a prisoner. Falling off the pace, out of Gan's sight, Nalatan shook his head. He couldn't interfere; no man's wisdom was adequate to such a task. Gan would find his own way. At his own peril.

Thick smoke billowing from Leclerc's chimney was a welcoming banner. Turning off, the four riders approached the house between neat rail fences. To Nalatan, Gan said, "The sea's not far through those trees west of Leclerc's fields." He pointed, and a skittish yearling colt on the other side of the rail fence pretended fright. It whinnied and skylarked off, kicking up clouds of snow, twisting and cavorting.

Coldar whooped delight. His struggles to turn and follow the colt's progress threatened to disrobe his mother. The excitement was enough to pull the colt right to the fence. Every breath was a gout of fog, and wads of snow clung to its shaggy winter coat. Steaming and dripping, stark white mottles melting against rough black pelt, it shot a muscular quiver along its body. Dislodged snow flew.

Whatever dignity the son of Murdat might have been expected to display broke under that assault. Demanding hands forced their way up and over the collar of Neela's cape. Her head, jerked forward and down, was inches away from ten greedy fingers grappling empty air. "My!" Coldar yelled, and when the colt remained on the wrong side of the fence, he yelled louder. "My!"

Gan beamed fatuously. Neela pushed Coldar's hands back inside the cape, ignoring yowled protest. Glaring at her husband, she said, "A born leader, this one. You heard that? His best word. 'My.' "

Gan managed to look innocent. "What's wrong with wanting a horse? Did you want it, too?"

He avoided her boot, kneed his mount forward. Nalatan kept pace. He marveled at his friend's ability to shed the wolves' warning, to enjoy himself so hugely. Gan interrupted his thoughts. "Do you think Leclerc would sell the horse? It's not a Dog war-horse, but it might develop well."

Nalatan grinned wickedly. "I'll argue about the future. Discuss religion. Or war and peace. But if you think I'm getting in the middle of a discussion between you and your wife over a horse for your child, you're a greater fool than your enemies say you are."

"And you're too clever by far."

Leclerc stepped out to greet his guests. His smile worked nervously. "I'm glad to see you." A stablehand raced around the corner. When he reached for Gan's war-horse, Gan pulled the animal back. "He'll hurt you, son. I'll come with you to stable him." White-faced, the youngster retreated, bumping into Nalatan's mount. Flustered, he whirled, grabbing for the reins.

Leclerc stepped down off his porch. "I want to show you what we've been doing in the new workshop. Gan, can you join us there? It's attached to the barn."

Gan agreed, riding off with the stablehand. Leclerc led his guests. The new workshop was a long log construction. There were no windows.

Inside, reflector-equipped oil lamps created a surprisingly bright, warm atmosphere. At least twenty men toiled at benches lining the walls. At the far end of the central passage, facing the rear door, stood a catapult. By the time the group reached it, Gan caught up to them. He walked around Leclerc's product, stroking, touching. "Sylah says the wallkiller throws a missile as large as a man." It was as much question as comment.

"Let me show you what we can do." Leclerc was almost smug. He moved to the door, threw it open. "Imagine that sawn-off tree trunk out there is the wallkiller. We're on the walls of Ola. The tree's about the wallkiller's range, I believe. I may be off by a bit, but not much. Anyhow, watch what happens." He gestured.

A grinning, eager crew hurried forward. Everyone else stepped aside.

The men loaded a heavy dart in a sliding trough on the center beam of the device. While they cranked a windlass, Leclerc pointed out the features of the weapon. "The dart rides in that trough in the center, of course. See how there are three sections to the crosspiece here in front? Now, watch how those cords in the two outer sections of the crosspiece frame are tightened by the windlass. The stuff dripping out of the cords is corn oil. We take tendons, separate the fibers, and weave them into rope. Then we soak them in corn oil. Every few shots we re-oil the rope; the tension squeezes it dry."

The leader of the catapult crew looked to Leclerc expectantly. Leclerc nodded. With a small mallet, the man tapped the upper section of the trigger, causing it to pivot and release the taut cord. The sliding trough leaped down the centerpost track, slamming to a stop. The catapult shivered like some gaunt, furious insect. The thick-shafted dart whistled across the intervening field, literally a blur. It struck the log. The snow cap atop the flat end leaped into the air, cascaded to the ground. Moments later the sound of the impact reached the workshop.

Sylah heard herself say, "That noise. Like a butcher's cleaver."

No one else spoke for quite a while. Nalatan broke the silence. "How often can you hit a target that small? That's a known distance, and this is a prepared position."

"Anything stationary we'll hit after two ranging shots, at most. We'll destroy any wallkiller, with its crew, before it gets off two missiles."

Gan grunted approval, adding, "If we could only stabilize them aboard ship."

Leclerc said, "We have men practicing constantly. The Skan are in for a nasty surprise. One of these darts will open a terrible hole in a hull, sweep away a dozen rowers, weaken a mast so it breaks. This weapon and your fast boats will make your men the same as your Dog horsemen, only seaborne."

Gan finally smiled. "That's my goal. We'll have it."

Surprisingly, Leclerc's intensity only deepened at Gan's enthusiasm. He hurried explanation. "That's not enough. I think I know how to use Moonpriest's secret; the killing lightning."

"If you know the secret, you know as much as he does. He doesn't have magic. He's just a man, after all."

"Oh, yes. He's a man. But if he's doing what I think he's doing, he's found a true magic. Come back to my house. I've shown no one. It frightens me."

It was a silent group that left the workshop.

Chapter 70

Leclerc lowered the small, covered object to his large dining table carefully. Movements and expression indicated unusual weight. Everyone seated watched suspiciously. Except Coldar. Innocently untroubled by Leclerc's reference to magic, the child reached. Neela yanked him back.

Leclerc reassured her. "It won't hurt him now. It's not dangerous."

"Now?" Gan's question was a threatening growl. He moved to prevent any more exploration from Coldar. With that, the boy intuited some of the mystery attached to the shrouded thing. He sank back against his mother's breast, not precisely afraid, but uncertain.

Leclerc explained hurriedly. "Conway told us of Moonpriest's moon disks and the Man Who Is Death. Moonpriest claims he's harnessed lightning. He lies, but he clearly controls the power that makes lightning."

Blank stares spurred Leclerc. He whipped the cover away. What stood revealed was far from threatening. It was round, with two metal components, a massive center piece inside a tubular outer piece. The entire thing was as long as a large man's spread fingers, and about half that in diameter. Axlelike extensions protruded from the central core. The ends rested in holes cut in sturdy triangular legs of oak a good thumb-joint thick. The outer component was nailed to the legs.

There was a large geared wheel attached to the outer side of one of the legs; a crank handle extended from it. Its teeth meshed with others cut into the smaller diameter of the core extension where it protruded beyond the bracing leg.

Examining the device, Sylah suddenly recoiled, eyes wide. "Outside the tube this gray iron part is just a plain shaft." She pointed, accusing. "When you look at the inside, from the end, it has those things, eight of them, like petals, coming off it. The design is a *flower*."

Leclerc bent to look. When he straightened, his face was red. "I never noticed that. It's got nothing to do with Church, Sylah, or you. It's a coincidence. Those aren't petals, they're lobes. They're that shape so I can wrap all that copper wire around them. Look, the inner side of the tube around the shaft has wire-wrapped lobes, too. It's the lobes passing each other that generates the electricity."

"Generates what?" Nalatan overrode Sylah's continuing unease.

"Electricity. An invisible force, all around us. Like heat from the sun. No one actually sees the heat."

Nalatan was dour. "I see heat waves. I see birds soar. We know warm earth makes air rise."

"And you see lightning. This makes a small lightning. It starts here, inside the outer shell, with this little magnet." Leclerc paused, reconsidering the last word. "In my land, that's what we call iron that wants to point north. Like a north-needle. The magnet is what starts the whole thing. Anyhow, when I turn this handle, the wire-wrapped lobes cut the force that makes a north-needle want to point north. That generates electricity. Think of the sun striking a surface, heating it, making the air rise, just the way you described it. Invisible lines of force from the sun generate heat. This uses invisible lines of force to generate electricity."

Leclerc trailed caressing fingers across the shining copper wrapping, the sturdy iron casing. He described how some of the generated current was fed to the outer coil. He mumbled his way through how a piece of carbon acted as a resistor, controlling the flow. The outer coil, magnetized, contributed to greater output.

Gan's rigid suspicion almost unnerved Leclerc. He babbled. He grabbed the copper grips attached to the wires leading from the end of the device opposite the handle. "Here's where it all comes out. Jackpot." He missed the way the strange, new word warped puzzlement to outright distrust.

Leclerc let go of the stubby wires, turned the handle. Everyone else edged away. A grudging smile tugged at Sylah's lips. Raw courage was the lifeblood of her companions, yet when confronted by a whisper of magic, they reacted exactly as young Coldar.

The machine whirred. Nalatan said, "You're sure this isn't witchwork?"

"No more than building a dam to hold back water for irrigation."

Neela, ever practical, said, "I see nothing."

"You don't see lightning until it strikes." Leclerc continued turning the handle. The grinding whine seemed to voice the group's increasing tension.

Shara and Cho exploded into furious barking outside. Heavy clawed feet scrambled on the wooden porch.

Neela folded protectively over Coldar. Gan was beside her instantly, sword drawn. His chair crashed across the floor. Nalatan rose, whirled, faced the door; he too had his sword out, but his parrying bar poised to smash the device on the table. Jaleeta screeched and scuttled to crouch behind Nalatan.

Sylah's heart threatened to batter through her ribs. Nevertheless, she remained utterly still, projecting complete calm. She imagined the old Iris Abbess exhorting, steadying her.

Stunned, Leclerc goggled stupidly. He recovered like a man waking. Rushing to the door, he flung it open and charged out.

Bernhardt's horse ambled down the entry path. Its ears were pitched forward, attentive to the dogs. As Bernhardt drew closer, Sylah marked her outward dignity. Behind that composure, however, marched far stronger forces. There was yearning. And assurance. And apprehension. But the bedrock of Bernhardt's emotions was sadness.

Turning resentful attention to Leclerc, Sylah noted his surprise and anger, his embarrassed glance at Jaleeta. Sylah clenched her fists painfully, using hurt to forestall railing at him.

"I decided I was needed here, Sylah." Bernhardt's voice was firm against the rough wind. "I brought these." She held aloft two of the books from the treasure of the Door.

Sylah choked. "You came alone? With *them*?"

"They're needed." Everything about Bernhardt begged Sylah for understanding.

Sylah swallowed. There would be time later to discuss this incredible error. For now, a sister needed compassion. "You must feel very strongly. You took a brave risk."

Gan was less charitable. Sylah was taken aback by his cold, formal fury. "My friends—two of them your tribesmen—risked their lives to help Sylah find that treasure. I stand accused of heresy for siding with Sylah in her belief that it will make Church better, make us a better nation, a better people. You took it on yourself to risk it without the simple courtesy of discussion? You insult."

Neela nudged him. He continued to glare. Bernhardt dropped her gaze to the ground, seemed to shrink within her voluminous Church robes.

Leclerc said, "They're needed because they can help me defeat Moonpriest. I told Kate I had to see them."

Sylah blinked astonishment, her gaze sparking from Kate to Leclerc and back again. Wonder of wonders, she thought: Was there ever a better day for lies and undercurrents? Not only was Leclerc lying like a fish merchant, he hated doing it. Sylah glanced at Jaleeta. Composed, the younger woman feigned disinterest. Her body betrayed her. Thumb and forefinger methodically pinched a blouse cuff. Her torso pitched forward; the intrigue was that the covert belligerence was aimed at Leclerc, not Bernhardt.

Bernhardt covered up a flush of confusion with a look of pure gratitude. Then she grinned appeal at Gan. "I know it was wrong to just walk out of the abbey with them. I only brought the chemistry and physics. I thought no one would suspect. I'm just a Priestess, riding by myself."

Gan was still angry. "That alone is dangerous. There are tigers in the forest, Kate. Winter makes man-eaters of some. Hunger has made even some men desperate, far more dangerous than tigers."

Bernhardt lowered her gaze, made no reply.

The stablehand saved her further scolding. He dashed around the corner, one eye on the dogs, and took Bernhardt's reins. She dismounted swiftly, eager to get the conversation onto any other subject. Everyone withdrew into the warmth of the house. Jaleeta unobtrusively sought Leclerc's side. When she brushed against him, he bridled like a colt.

Memories, images of Clas na Bale, burst through Sylah's carefully objective observations. Tender, exciting memories of similar moments, secret contacts shared by lovers. Hands brushed, shoulders touched; the inconsequential bumps of human proximity, but for two particular people, a private shiver. Of promise. Of anticipation.

Longing threatened to overwhelm Sylah. For one terrible instant she hated Jaleeta as she'd never hated any other woman.

Jaleeta asked the question in everyone's mind, eyes bright with false innocence. "How can Sylah's treasure help you defeat Moonpriest and Windband? Or the Skan?" Sylah was a bit nonplussed when Jaleeta's expression turned haunted. Truth softened the words that followed. "I hope it can. I can't be captured by the Skan again. I can't."

Neela threw an arm across the younger woman's shoulders. "You're safe with us."

Jaleeta flashed her a wink of a smile. Her thankful simper was for Leclerc.

He reacted predictably. "I promise no one will take our castle."

Nalatan said, "Bold words. Assume you destroy the wallkiller. What can you do about weapons that kill without drawing blood?"

Uncomfortable, Leclerc looked to Bernhardt. "It's got to be electrical. But how? He can't have reliable batteries. He can't transmit enough power to enough people. Is he depending entirely on terror?"

"I have some ideas."

Jaleeta spoke again, sweetly astonished. She cut her eyes at Leclerc. "About weapons? But everyone says you and Anspach and Carter won't even carry a shortknife."

Leclerc looked questioningly at Bernhardt. "You worked on improving crops, soils, stuff like that. That's not war."

Jaw set, Bernhardt said, "I worked in appropriate technologies. I know about basic electrical generation and application. Basic chemistry, too. Probably more than Moonpriest. How about you?"

"Maybe. I mean, yes. Me too. Probably, that is. I probably know more than him, too. So what's he got, you think?"

"We ought to discuss it between us. When we've got a plan, some sound answers, we make recommendations to Gan. Our job is to give him a response, not clutter his mind."

Gan laughed. "Listen to her. She may not be a warrior, but she understands what a leader needs." He slapped her on the back hard enough to touch off a wince. Still, her eyes never left Leclerc's. Gan continued. "Pay attention to this one, Louis. She's deeper than we know. Your tribe produces truly remarkable women."

Acutely embarrassed, Leclerc covered the moment by bustling about the generator. "We haven't seen this work yet. Who wants to turn the handle?"

Everyone but Bernhardt looked at him as if he'd asked who could fly. He rushed on. "Kate, you do the honors. I'll show what happens. Go slowly; this puts out an astonishing charge, considering the size and my crude handiwork." He pushed the wired grips closer. Whirring, whispering, the generator performed. Tiny bits of blue fire spat across the gap. Leclerc joked with Gan. "Hear it? It's telling us we have a friend." He put his finger on top of the wires and whooped at the quick jolt.

After seeing Leclerc survive, the others dared the wires. Yells, yips, and hilarity proved the quick adaptability of all. Still, apprehension lingered. Except for Gan. A taint of unease tightened the corners of his eyes, soured his smile. "This thing tickles. Maybe you can make it sting. I need weapons that kill. This is useless."

"What use is a bucket of water? Drink from it, it quenches thirst. Hold a man's head in it, he drowns."

"Conway says Moonpriest's lightning roars. It has a large blue flame, not little specks. Where it touches, men die. This is nothing." A belated try at manners fell flat. "I appreciate what you've tried to do."

"Like men, Gan, what's most dangerous is the least obvious. This will do what I say."

"Turn the handle." Gan glared. Leclerc's mouth fell open, and Gan repeated himself. "This can hurt me? Prove it."

Leclerc waffled. "It's untested. I don't know how strong it actually is. But it's deadly."

"Show me strength." Gan's jaw jutted. Antagonists now, he and Leclerc matched stares.

Bernhardt interceded. "This is unnecessary, Gan. Louis, we can run some tests."

Gan shook his head. "Not now, Kate Bernhardt. If I'm to make plans, I must have faith in those who make claims. If there's power in this toy, I must see it."

"Damned well you will, then." Flushed, Leclerc grabbed the wired grips, separated them. Immediately, he leaned into the crank handle. The small generator whined delight at increased speed. It tasted power, longed to express it. Even Gan was thoughtful, as though the altered sound warned him of his folly. "Go ahead, grab the leads," Leclerc said. Stress and anger made the words a snarl.

Gan reached. Contacted. For an instant, he was rigid. His back arched, head snapped back. Then so swiftly it was part of the same action, he lifted. As if thrown by a giant hand, he flew across the room, crashed into the wall. Impact rattled the windows, shook the house. Neela screamed. She raced for her fallen husband, a howling Coldar clamped to her bosom. Jaleeta retreated, flattened herself by the door. Nalatan raised his sword. Bernhardt threw herself in front of Leclerc.

"No." Gan's croaking order stopped the warrior-monk. Carefully, Nalatan stepped back, head swiveling to keep both Gan and Leclerc in view. Gently, firmly, Leclerc pushed a resisting Bernhardt aside.

Gan's eyes wavered. He rose sloppily. Leaning against the wall, he said, "It didn't kill. Certainly hit." His lopsided smile was sheepish. "Can you improve it? And speak loudly, please. There's a bell in here." He tapped his head with the heel of his hand, looking bemused.

Nalatan eased his sword back into the scabbard as Neela wrapped herself around her husband. Her glare at Leclerc was poisonous. Coldar continued to snuffle. With his father upright again, he was more curious than concerned.

Leclerc said, "I've got some ideas. I still say I'm giving you a weapon that'll clear attackers off the walls. Are you all right?"

"Fine. Now. There may be killing power in this, after all." He gestured warily at the generator, and Neela yanked his hand back. Gan continued to smile, but his next words carried significant consideration. "You said something else I'll remember, my friend. You said 'most dangerous when least obvious.' I'm indebted to you for your wisdom. Twice. I apologize for my stubbornness."

A relieved Leclerc was generous. "Friends can disagree and remain friends." He put his hand on the machine. "Power." The word was a hymn. "This is power."

Gan nodded. Stepping forward, he extended a slow, determined hand. The flesh around his mouth paled. Sweat beaded on his lip. But he touched the generator. "Make these for the Three Territories, Louis. We must have them."

"You will, Gan. Bigger and better."

Gan nodded, watching the generator as if expecting it to join the conversation. He went on. "You're a good man, Louis. A blessing to us. You've given us so much." He looked deep into Leclerc's eyes. "Without you, my path would already be over. My wife, my son, would be slaves. Someday I will find a way to thank you. That is a promise."

Bernhardt stepped forward. "We need some answers from you and Nalatan." Gan's eyebrows flew upward at forceful demand from such an unexpected source. Bernhardt continued. "We have to know the city's, the castle's weak points, the strong points. How would you attack? Why? Tell us what a warrior can be expected to do; we can advise you on a reasonable defense and attack."

"What does that have to do with the new weapons Moonpriest is supposed to have?" Gan's earlier bantering with her was gone, replaced by solid earnestness.

"Make us see Moonpriest's mind work. Make us think like Skan."

Neela stopped rocking the still-upset Coldar and sniffed. "That no one can do."

Leclerc reverted to the genial host. "Well, we'll never get it done on an empty stomach. I've got soup, cheese, fresh bread. Let's eat, then talk." He started for the kitchen. Jaleeta leaped to follow, cutting directly in front of Bernhardt. To Leclerc, she said, "I'll help you get everything ready," then, over her shoulder, looking directly into Bernhardt's stricken eyes, "The rest of you keep out, now. Louis and I insist. Be comfortable. We'll bring the food as soon as it's ready."

Leclerc's gaze, too, went to Bernhardt. It broke quickly, sliding down to Jaleeta, now beside him. He smiled.

"Brainless fool." Sylah didn't realize her muttered imprecation could be overheard until, from the corner of her eye, she saw Bernhardt's head turn her way. Instantly, Sylah looked to see who else might have caught the mistake.

Bernhardt's low voice answered the unspoken question. "Don't worry; I'm the only one close enough to hear. And he's not really brainless." Her wry smile acknowledged the decision not to contest the other half of Sylah's judgment.

"Are we the only two who see what's going on? Is she really all that clever?" Sylah led Bernhardt to a window, pretended to look out over the snow-laden branches of the orchard.

"We're the only two who see she's a woman. To everyone else, she's a brave, beautiful, unfortunate girl."

Time passed silently. The voices of the others mumbled behind them, occasionally spiced by Coldar's now carefree, childish laughter. Finally, Sylah half turned, watching Bernhardt with a sideways, speculative look. "What fools. We stand around this table, talking of saving kingdoms with strange and dangerous tools. We'll be cursed for our power, Kate, called terrible things. There's the terrible irony. You understand this force Leclerc can unleash. But what do we do about your happiness, my sweet friend? How do we protect the soft-hearted, like Neela, while we rescue the soft-headed, like your Louis?"

"Oh, Sylah." Bernhardt's eyes glistened, her voice wavered. She was back in control immediately, forced a tight chuckle that was almost genuine amusement. "If Louis was really mine—and you're a darling to say what you said—I think the first word that would come to my mind would be 'kill.' How's that for a sweet, Priestess-y Church attitude?"

Both women laughed, softly, sharing.

Sylah hated it, because she heard the pain, the longing, the absolute truth in Kate Bernhardt's misery.

CHAPTER 71

"THAT WOMAN! SHE HAS NO SHAME." JALEETA PRACTICALLY THREW POTTERY SOUP BOWLS onto the carved wooden tray. Leclerc grabbed her wrist as she prepared to fling plates, as well. The pottery had a sturdy, workmanlike attractiveness, with its glossy yellow-on-blue fish scale motif. Still, he doubted the thick ceramic would take more of Jaleeta's abuse. Leclerc asked, "What woman? Who?"

"Who?" Pitying disbelief replaced agitation. "You men. A conniving woman makes a fool of you, and you grin and say 'thank you.' "

"What're you talking about? You mean Kate, don't you? She's working with me. There's no conniving."

Gently, Jaleeta covered Leclerc's restraining hand on her wrist with her own. Smooth as oil, the imprisoned wrist rotated. Leclerc's grip was transformed, his fingers intertwined in Jaleeta's. "You're such a good man, Louis. You think the best of everyone. Can't you see she's working against you, setting a trap?"

"Trap? Against me?"

Jaleeta sighed, pulled away. She studied him quizzically. "What makes you so blind? She loves you. You saw that, at least?"

"Loves? No. That's . . . Well, I mean, no, she . . . Who said . . . ?"

"Stop it." The command snapped. Jaleeta continued whispering. "You even missed that. Kate Bernhardt loves you. You do know about women disappointed in love?"

Leclerc shied away, mumbled, stirred the soup.

Jaleeta went on. "She knows I want you and you want me. She's mad with jealousy. And she has help." Leclerc twisted to look over his shoulder at her. She was waiting. "If someone truly walked off with the treasure Sylah risked her life to find, would she just dismiss such a crime? Would she let you defend the thief after Gan himself accused her? Of course not. Sylah and Bernhardt planned for Bernhardt to come here with it. Sylah pretended to forgive her."

"Why would she do that?"

"Because Sylah can see you're more intelligent than Gan Moondark, that's why. But she controls Gan. She wants you to remain the loyal helper. Only you and Bernhardt know the magic of the book things, so she arranges for Bernhardt to bring them here. Kate Bernhardt wants to make you hers. If she takes you from me, the three of them—Kate, Sylah, and Gan—will own you forever. I'll have nothing. Except a grandfather for a husband." She ducked her head almost in time to hide a tear.

"That's monstrous. They're not that ruthless or cruel. Kate Bernhardt's a fine woman. No one who interests me, but no one who wants to enslave anyone, either."

"So I'm monstrous? Ruthless? Are you interested in me, Louis? Does that mean I want to enslave you? Because I would be your slave. With joy." Fat tears wobbled down Jaleeta's cheeks, oddly water-green in the tinted light streaming through the crude window glass.

Slowly, tenderly, Leclerc kissed her. Jaleeta was unresponsive. When he backed away, her eyes were open, fixed on his. She resumed where she stopped. "They need to control you, Louis. You're too strong to be free."

Leclerc threw back his shoulders. "We'll tell them we're getting married. What can they do about it?"

Her wise smile ignored his bravado. "More to the point, Louis, what can you do?" The sudden reversal confused him. Jaleeta pressed ahead. "Gan would give me to you, if forced. But I won't spend my life looking over my shoulder, waiting for his vengeance."

"He wouldn't dare." There was a loaf of bread on a wooden slab on the table. A long, serrated knife rested beside it. Leclerc snatched it up.

Jaleeta came to him. Taking the hand holding the knife in both of hers, she lifted it. Her expression was resigned, almost placid. She guided the point of the blade to her breast. Bright steel dimpled the soft beige leather. "Take Bernhardt for wife, if that will help you become the leader you must be. Just never let them give me to Emso."

"No one's going to belong to anyone." Leclerc's words came as if dragged through gravel. "We'll fight."

Freeing one hand, Jaleeta raised it to trace the hairline at his temple. "In here is your weapon, Louis. Your future."

"Our future." He dropped the knife on the table. She stepped into his embrace, returned his kiss with a straining, climbing passion. When they separated, sweat was a sheen on his brow.

"Someone'll come, catch us." Jaleeta stepped back. Catlike, immaculately unconcerned, she raised the knife over the bread as Neela opened the door. Jaleeta called gaily, "You're just in time. We need someone to prepare some cheese. Where is it, Louis?"

Stammering, Leclerc indicated a door set into the logs of the wall. Neela opened it. The storage cabinet was a wooden box that extended outside the house. Daylight entered through small ventilation holes in the outer container. The inner one, also fitted with a tight lid, was a finely woven cedar-bark basket. In response to Neela's quizzical look, Leclerc said, "It's a food storage. It's roofed to protect it from rain and direct sun. It's vermin-proof, cool in the summer. In the winter, heat through the cabinet door keeps it from freezing. The holes let air circulate."

While Neela rummaged, Jaleeta lavished praise on Louis for his ingenuity. Moments later, carrying a wicker tray loaded with sliced bread and wooden boxes holding various cheeses, Neela turned at the door to shoot a conspiratorial grin at Jaleeta. The younger woman dropped her gaze to the countertop, immediately shy. Neela was chuckling softly as the door closed behind her.

Ladling soup with an unsteady hand, Leclerc said, "We've got to be more careful."

Eyes narrowing, Jaleeta spoke to his back. "Just before the door opened, you were going to fight for me."

"I am. Was. You know I would." The soup bowl in his hand clattered against the copper kettle.

Jaleeta used the bread knife as a pointer. "If we waver once, we die, Louis. You, quickly. Me, the lingering death-in-life of a slave."

Patting her back he murmured assurances. "Trust me. You'll never belong to Emso. I'll fight for you. Never doubt."

They delivered the remainder of the meal. Gan took the lead in the conversation. He restricted it to inconsequentials, tactfully leading it back to mundane matters whenever the discussion tended toward warfare or weaponry. By the time the last morsel of a dried-apple cake was consumed, the adults were relaxed and little Coldar was sound asleep.

Through it all, Sylah found herself drawn to Kate Bernhardt. There was an inescapable dignity about her that demanded admiration. At one point, the two fell into a quiet conversation of their own, initiated by Bernhardt's repeated apology for risking the books.

Sylah smiled. "I'm going to be blunt, Kate. I know exactly why you brought the books. I'd have done exactly the same thing, if I were in your place."

Squirming, Bernhardt looked away.

Sylah said, "It's something we all go through." Bernhardt's swift look of surprise and disbelief almost destroyed the confidentiality of their moment. Sylah hurried on, voice low. "It was the same with Clas and me. I knew he loved me long before he did."

"I don't know what I know anymore. There was no Jaleeta there when you were falling in love with Clas, was there?"

"What woman needs a flesh-and-blood rival? We imagine competition whether it's there or not."

Bernhardt's forlorn glance at Jaleeta showed how little she thought of that argument.

"Kate, this will pass. Louis needs time with you. He'll discover for himself that you're everything Jaleeta pretends to be, and isn't. Her beauty stuns men, but it hides an ugly mind."

"You're really not angry about the books?"

"I didn't say I wasn't angry. I said I understood. I guess I even approve." She sighed, affected resignation. "It's very difficult being around frustrated love."

Bernhardt smiled appreciation. That quickly fell away. She was penitent. "Especially difficult for you. You're separated from your husband. I'm a self-centered fool; you're too kind."

"I'd like to think we're both a shade more complex than that. In fact, I'll tell you something about yourself that the brilliant Leclerc would have seen long ago, if he were half as smart as he thinks he is. You're more than he deserves, Kate. If he loses you to that devious little bit of brightness, you'll find someone better. And if it happens, I'll make it a point of personal pride to laugh in Louis Leclerc's face."

Out of sight of the others, Kate reached to take Sylah's hand. Linked fingers clasped quickly and separated.

Leclerc returned from the kitchen. He carried an iron candle-holder made of two iron rings joined by four vertical bars the length of a man's finger. A flat disk in the center of the lower disk held a squat candle. On the table, the upper ring formed a stand for a bright copper pitcher full of honey-sweetened cider. Thyme contributed subtle aroma to delicate steam tendrils. Once copper mugs were filled and everyone gathered around the table, Gan broached the subject of Moonpriest.

"No weapon wins wars. Men do. Men who believe. Louis, I'm forever obligated to you. You've given us weapons to defeat Moonpriest's weapons. But Moonpriest has beliefs, and his men hold to them. Only when I expose the falsity of those beliefs does Moonpriest fall."

Defensiveness edged Sylah's response. "Church makes every effort to unmask him. We fight too, as hard as any."

Bernhardt said, "Are we going to quarrel?"

Gan managed a rueful smile. "I meant no criticism. I was trying to point out that truth and faith are our strength. Perhaps Church knows something the rest of us should know."

Sylah shook her head. "I'm restricted to what I can learn from travelers, tradesmen, traders."

"Peddlers?"

Sylah tightened her back muscles against the chill that danced up her spine. It was impossible that Gan could know of the connection between Peddlers and Church. "I haven't spoken to a Peddler since spring. And he knew nothing."

Lazily, Gan looked away from Sylah, back to Leclerc. "What do you make of Moonpriest's relocation to the seacoast, Louis? Can you see any advantage to it?"

Nalatan interrupted. "He'll hug the ocean as he advances north. You can't attack his right flank."

Leclerc said, "I don't think tactics has anything to do with it. It's more than that."

Gan's mockery was friendly. "What's more important to men than tactics?"

Leclerc grinned, but he held doggedly to his argument. "He needs the sea for something. I have to think what it is."

Gan's brief humor fled. His response was slow, judicious. "He's intelligent. Dangerous. Nevertheless, I fear him least. The Skan are the enemy." He rose suddenly, startling everyone. Striding to the window, he swung an arm wide. "My Wolves can't be everywhere. As long as I live, I'll never forget watching that sharker track us north along the coast when we moved to confront the Skan fleet. We've made strides in our ability at sea. We're still land people. Where there's a coast, a sea people has advantage." He spun away from the window, addressed Leclerc and Bernhardt. "Your people aren't like my tribe. You don't have the lust for personal glory that drives us, sometimes destroys us. But give us life in the battle to come, and dozens of tribes will sing your names in the firelight nights long after this mere Dog warrior is burned and unremembered."

Leclerc went ashen. Bernhardt spoke for both of them. "We'll do our best."

"Excellent. I ask nothing else."

Outside, once mounted, Jaleeta drifted apart from the others. She drew Leclerc to her with a smoldering, insistent look. "I'm afraid for you, Louis. You saw the way he promised you all the glory? You and that woman? Now can you doubt that the two of them mean to snare you? They're working together."

"You said she was working with Sylah."

"It's the same thing. Sylah, Gan; Gan, Sylah; it's all Sylah's Church, and glory for Gan." She relented, abandoned the whiplash tone. "Please, be careful. Don't let them take you from me." Then she was gone, galloping, looking back, waving, dark and exotic against the glowering sky and enfolding snow.

Alone, the couple sat in Leclerc's main room for a long time. Desultory conversation struggled, the words lifeless as falling leaves.

A husband and wife team now looked after the place for Leclerc; this evening they came and went as though it were commonplace for them to work around a couple bent on estranging each other. When Leclerc introduced them to Bernhardt, the wife, Larta, insisted Leclerc's female guest stay with them in their adjacent new house.

Kate and Leclerc were sharing amusement at Larta's determined propriety when the stablehand came to report all secure for the evening. Leclerc hurried to the window, complaining, "We get so much overcast there's not enough sunshine to bother a mole, then evening comes at noon. Lousy climate." He stomped to the fireplace, pitched in a length of wood.

"It's almost winter, Louis. The days are supposed to be short."

"I guess I ought to bless it. As soon as this weather stops, the war starts."

"Takes a lot of the welcome out of spring. Are you as worried as I am?"

"Scared spitless." He turned from the fire, finally involved in real dialogue. "Truthfully, Kate: Do you think we can carry this off without Tate and Conway?"

Bernhardt sputtered, "Without? Are they all right?"

"I don't know. There's no word. There was early snow in the mountains. Heavy."

"You think Conway and Donnacee are in trouble?" She rose, pacing.

"Bad feelings, Kate. Nothing more. But I wonder; can we survive without them?" He moved to light candles. They could have been performing an arcane ritual, the dark-robed woman pacing from light to darkness and back while he darted from point to point.

"Words. Silly words," Bernhardt said. "If they're warriors, so are we. We define ourselves, justify ourselves."

Leclerc stopped abruptly. He threw the taper into the fireplace, faced Kate. "What's that supposed to mean?"

"We're all complex. Are we cowards if we're not actively in combat?"

Leclerc's gaze drilled past Bernhardt's solemnity, seemed to seek an answer far beyond her presence. "You make me look inside myself. It infuriates me. You make logical decisions for romantic ends. How do you do that? What magic makes you sense the questions *my* heart asks *my* head? I dreamed of coming out of the crèche into a world of adventure. Well, I'm here. My contribution is mass destruction. You tell me if I'm a warrior."

"The better warrior wins. Your skills will decide the battle." Bernhardt settled in one of the soft, leather chairs. She tucked her feet under her, compressed herself into a compact, comfortably warm ball. Firelight emphasized her features, illuminated the high, smooth brow, the broad, strong sweep of long cheekbones. Darkened eyes seemed to retreat. Slightly knitted brows lent power to the slightest change of expression.

Leclerc spoke into the flames, consigning the words. "After I win this battle for Gan, why shouldn't I be accorded the same honors? Is my contribution less than his because it's based on intelligence instead of muscle?"

"Is your responsibility less than his if we lose?"

Leclerc sounded like he choked. "Damn. Thank you. You did it again, didn't you? Made me answer the question I refused to ask myself."

"There's a quote, like, 'Victory has a thousand fathers; defeat's an orphan.' After you've won, the people who want to use you will crawl out of the woodwork. They're the cowards, Louis. The people who use other people for personal gain."

"Well, you can quit babbling about not knowing which path you'll choose. You're a romantic. You'd rather die than back down." He laughed, a sound that suggested loss, rather than humor.

"Promise you won't forget me." The small joke hung in the air between them, too dangerous to touch, too important to ignore.

Leclerc said, "I couldn't do that if I wanted to."

If Bernhardt's phrase was a spark, Leclerc's blunt honesty fanned it. He came to stand in front of her. "You said you had an answer for why Moonpriest moved to the coast. Can you explain now?"

Bernhardt heard the accentuated last word. He was accusing her of refusing to speak in front of Jaleeta. She exulted in the knowledge. Let him resent. "Moonpriest needs a source of electrical power generation."

"Why leave the gorge of the Mother River? The wind's practically constant, and high velocity. Not to mention the waterpower available. And why does he need electrical current?"

"He's positioned himself to march north. At the coast near the mouth of the river he can still use windmills or waterwheels. What if he's creating capacitors?"

"Capac . . ." Leclerc couldn't bring himself to finish the word. He stormed across the room, threw himself about in circles, gesturing. "That technology died with us. If you could build one today, what would you do with it? Put together a radio, tune in on the past? Capacitors. Why not a Ouija board?"

Bernhardt grimaced. "A Ouija board in this world? Not unless you have a secret desire to be barbecue. But a capacitor wouldn't be impossible."

"You think so? Where'd you get your information? You were an agronomist."

"We worked with a lot of appropriate technology; solar power, wind generators, waterwheels. I didn't get into all of it, but I remember some. Did you know something that can only be a battery existed in the ancient world, long before anything like electrical power was understood? Some say it was a goldsmith's secret; they used it to gold-plate things."

Leclerc's patronizing was overshadowed by grudging respect. "There's a lot of difference between a dinky electroplating charge and a mankiller."

"Don't be obtuse. We know there's plenty of copper. First, you hammer that into thin sheets. Separate them with cloth, impregnated with beeswax. Induce a charge, hook it up on some kind of backpack. A simple lead to a spear, and zap!"

"Maybe. Maybe." One hand stroking his jaw, Leclerc retreated toward the table holding the books. Absently, he picked one up, fondling it, turning it over and over while he ruminated on Bernhardt's theory. "Not a spear. One contact point won't do it; no circuit. Two capacitor terminals. That'll give me two voltages, so we get a circuit. You want the current to effect as much tissue as possible, but what you have to have is a complete electrical circuit through the body. Two gapped tines, then. A pitchfork, the tines insulated from each other, and each attached to one capacitor terminal." He held his hands up, thumbs touching his chest. "Ten inches apart." He frowned, shook his head. "It won't work. One shot, and the weapon's useless."

"One shot's all you need. A rank of spearmen, weapons leveled, advance on another body of warriors. There's contact. Ten, fifty, a hundred capacitors discharge. All at once. Every man touched by a wired spear falls dead. Not some. All. Dead. It's a recipe for panic."

"But the capacitors are drained."

"Normal arms back up the spearmen. And those two-pronged things aren't exactly courtesy cards, are they?"

The tone of the last swung Leclerc around, concerned. "This is hard for you."

"I hate fighting, I hate thinking of poor Jones as our enemy. I hate remembering science so we can kill people. Sometimes I hate me. We are doing the right thing, aren't we?"

"Absolutely. There's a lot about Church I don't like, especially the Church that's opposed to Sylah, but this Moondance thing is plain evil. Still, what we have to guard against is tyranny. We can't make someone like Gan invincible."

Bernhardt was suddenly wary. "He's the most honorable man I've ever known."

Turning away, Leclerc muttered under his breath, " 'For Caesar was an honorable man.' "

"What? I couldn't hear you."

"Nothing. Thinking about weapons again." Facing her, he was sad. "You don't deserve all this, Kate. This world's too harsh, too cruel."

"Well, I'm here. I don't intend to leave soon, either. Anyone who thinks different is in for one helluva fast education."

Leclerc burlesqued shock. "Profanity. Not acceptable. And the forbidden 'l' word. You talked about learning. Super naughty."

She stuck out her tongue. "I never said 'learning.' Anyhow, that's another reason why we have to win. The Three Territories is just the beginning. Our little girls are the new Teachers. The first thing we teach is equality."

"Someone always demands to be the most equal. A leader's a necessity. Can you be sure your movement won't be usurped?"

"Yes, I can." Bernhardt's granite certainty filled the room. "All of us, Chosens and Teachers, swore a blood oath. The new Teachers will emulate the old. We live as Teachers, free, or we die as Teachers, free forever. Simple, no?"

"Terrifying. If I'd known, I'd have forbidden any such oath. It's too dangerous to even consider." He knelt before her, one hand on hers on the chair's arm.

"You'd forbid me?" Bernhardt's eyebrows lifted like warning flags.

"Stepped right into that, didn't I? All right, so I'd have argued against it. I don't want to think about you being hurt." The words finished on an edge of wonderment. Leclerc looked as if he wasn't sure where they came from.

Bernhardt rose, forcing him to stand back and get up himself. She said, "Don't think about it, then. Concentrate on winning. People depend on us."

"You're right. It's just that . . ." He made a face. "I'll get Larta. She'll take you to their cabin. Tomorrow we'll start trying to make that capacitor. If it can be done."

"We can do it. We'll be a good team."

Both turned away, pretending the words had no other significance.

Chapter 72

The thick, clinging scent of the solitary candle burdened the room. Jaleeta couldn't place the aroma. Herbal, but with no suggestion of bright meadows or nodding blossoms. This was the perfume of shadows, of shaded hollows. Something lurked where that scent was born.

Jaleeta glanced at the other woman, more than half afraid her thoughts were being read. Church forbade the practice, Jaleeta knew, but she also knew the Violet Abbess. At best, the woman had a flexible attitude toward Church's rules.

It was unfair, Jaleeta told herself again. She'd come straight here to report the meeting at Leclerc's. Remembering the older woman's response brought renewed color to Jaleeta's throat: "If Gan Moondark and his friends choose to resort to witchery, so much the better for Church. But why come to me? Emso and the Barons need this information. I'm not involved. Are you sure no one saw you?"

The candle was almost a finger-joint shorter since that speech. The Abbess' ceaseless opening of the shutter to peer out into the night was not only unnerving, it made the room cold. Jaleeta shivered inside her furs.

"You shake, child. Why so nervous?"

"I'm cold. You keep looking to see if anyone followed me. They didn't. Can't we have a fire?"

"A properly trained mind would throw off this little bit of chill."

"When I should have been trained, I was a slave." Discomfort and indignation made Jaleeta bold. "Anyhow, Sylah's women and all the Chosens get cold or hot or hungry or thirsty just like everyone else."

The Abbess was surprisingly mild. "As usual, you ignore the obvious. Church affords its best mind training only to those it considers likely to need it."

"Who selects them?"

Archly, the Abbess stared down her nose. "Inquisitive, aren't we? A dangerous characteristic. Especially for one flaunting her body for men as ruthless as Emso and the manly Nalatan. Oh. Didn't like that, did you? You imagined I wouldn't know of your flirtations? Never mind. To answer your question, the woman Church called the Harvester makes that selection. Our beloved Harvester is now Sister Mother of all Church. I was one of her selections. Now you know my secret." She patted Jaleeta's knee.

"I know another one, I think."

Jaleeta's tone and sly, sidelong glance amused the Abbess. The older woman said, "I've been too critical of you. You did well to bring me the information of the meeting. Still, I can't get involved. Church must remain on good terms with whoever wins this fight between Gan and his enemies."

Jaleeta was blunt. "I think that's another secret. I heard that a missionary Priestess traveling north stopped here a few nights ago. She came here from Church Home with instructions for you, didn't she? This decision to avoid involvement comes from Sister Mother, doesn't it? Did I guess right?"

"Quick. Very quick, you are. If your guess were correct, you'd know something very much none of your concern. Did you know people are killed for silly mistakes like that?"

"I do. I also know your friend, the one who can give you the best eyes inside Gan's circle of closest friends."

"Quite possibly too quick, my child. Remember, no one tolerates a show-off for long."

Good sense prevailed; Jaleeta lowered her gaze and repented. "I get excited, Abbess. I want to do well."

"Then assure that your information reaches the right people. You're not to mention me. You understand?"

Jaleeta nodded. "Yes."

The Abbess smiled approval. "Excellent. No questions. Because you're obedient, and because I truly like you, I'll explain. I must appear neutral, but Church actually assists Moonpriest. He and the beloved Sister Mother have just made a religious peace. We're to cooperate with each other, allowing free practice of either faith. That means we oppose the Skan together, as well. Not until the right moment, however. So you must be, as you so cleverly put it, my eyes inside Gan's circle of closest friends. Do be careful to report everything. I'll know if you try to keep something to yourself, dear. That could lead to uncertainty, to doubt. Let me show you why you must be completely open with me."

The Abbess rose, walked to the door. A push generated a grating squeal. Jaleeta gritted her teeth; she'd been unaware of the cowled Priestess standing guard—or witness—just outside. The Abbess addressed the figure, the tone commanding. The figure hurried off. The Abbess remained at the door.

Fury raged in Jaleeta. Her first thought was to inform Gan of the Abbess' multidirectional treachery. That would protect herself and get rid of this dangerous work. The notion passed as quickly as it came. The Abbess was too powerful to be toppled by one push. Gan considered the Violet Abbey enemy ground; confirmation of that conviction was worth little. Calming, Jaleeta reconsidered. Spying for the Abbess was no great hazard. If caught, Neela and Gan would believe the Abbess forced a helpless girl to inform. More, anything learned in the Abbess' service could likely be used to personal benefit. Best of all, if Gan somehow survived the net drawing tight around him, knowledge of who plotted against him would be excellent currency to buy favor.

The logic of it was quite satisfying.

Gold-orange light from a lantern crept along the wall outside the door. Anticipating, the Abbess leaned out. Jaleeta saw her greeting smile in profile. Obsequious, servile, there was nevertheless something predatory there.

When the familiar figure carrying the lantern stepped into the room, the name exploded from Jaleeta, a raven's croak. "Emso."

He continued on into the room, unmindful of the hovering Abbess, even when she plucked the lantern from his hand and summarily extinguished it. "It's me," he told Jaleeta, "come to hear what must be heard. I need you." He was on her before she could recover, hands gripping her upper arms, so close that everything but shining, demanding eyes were outside her vision. His breath was fetid with beer, cabbage, fat. There was sweat; not the hard smell of exertion, but a stale, acid thing that reeked fear and exhaustion.

A shove moved him backward with surprising ease. He winced, looked hurt. "I need you," he repeated.

Smoothly, the Abbess glided to his side. "Emso is the last hope for Gan Moondark's soul. The Apocalypse Testament tells us: 'The first evil act of humankind, be it the smallest spark or the mightiest blast, can be defeated, must be defeated. The start of the fire of evil is aberration. The conclusion of the fire can only be eternal destruction.' " In the close, dim confines of the room, the woman's voice took on rolling sonority. When she finished, Emso stood taller. Uncooperative knees and twitching fingers gave lie to his show of control.

Jaleeta inhaled, startled by awareness she was holding her breath. Simultaneously, the full import of the Abbess' words struck her. There was nothing personal in Emso's declaration: He merely wanted help. The pounding of her heart slowed.

If they wanted religious reasons to whittle away at Gan Moondark's strength, Jaleeta knew exactly what they should hear. She described the new catapult with complete honesty and accuracy, then added, "Leclerc said they slaughter the animals for the bowstrings in a special ceremony. Secret acts. He wouldn't describe them."

Emso interrupted. There was firmness in him, now. "Who does these things?"

"Leclerc and the woman. Bernhardt? I almost forgot her name. She's so plain, keeps in the background."

Emso growled in his chest. "She's fooled everyone. We all knew Leclerc was dabbling in forbidden knowledge. She fooled us all."

The Abbess said, "Go on, dear. Tell Emso what else you learned."

Jaleeta edged sideways, positioned herself by the candle. Not too close; she remembered Tears of Jade, how the old woman stayed at the dim edge of light, using shadow and contrast to confuse the eye. Movement caused the small flame to sway, heightening illusion, spurring imagination. "Leclerc captures invisible power from the air, the power of lightning. Moonpriest uses it to kill unbelievers. He turns a handle, like this. The thing is made of iron and copper, but it whispers. I couldn't understand. It's a different language. It spits fire, blue fire, and makes a noise like a whip. If you touch it while it's weak, it makes you jump. Leclerc says it kills when it's strong. Nalatan asked what it did; Leclerc said it was like the sun."

The Violet Abbess made a three-sign. Her lips fluttered in silent prayer. Emso's eyes bulged. Cords stood out in his neck. The Abbess' words came on labored breath. "The sun? He said this power is lightning *and* sun? The sun is life. Nalatan was a Church warrior-monk before the evil black one seduced him. Now he listens to an unclean one speak of the sun, and does nothing. He, too, is evil."

"Stop." Emso's order thundered. "You walk too close to the part of Church that is man's alone, forbidden to woman."

Contrition swept away the Abbess' rage. "I forgot myself, faithful Emso. It's too easy for a woman. We're weak, excitable. The things Jaleeta reveals are too strong for a woman's mind to accept. Forgive me."

"Of course." His eyes remained fixed on Jaleeta. "Gan made no objection to this blasphemy?"

"He said nothing."

Anguish scarred Emso's face. Ponderously, he turned to the Abbess. "It's worse than I feared. My friend. Tell me how to save him. I beg you."

Under control once again, the Abbess was judicious. "Forgiveness will be his with repentance and return. His arrogance is his curse. He must abandon the false and evil, humble himself, come to Church. You will save him."

Eagerness threatened to overwhelm Emso. "You know this? A Seer told you?"

"Church forbids, save where Church is concerned. If he is to be saved, only you can do it."

Jaleeta bowed her head. It hid her smile. She remembered the terrible night on the shore of the nameless Sea Star island. Cold wind slid across her naked back. Hot, shaming firelight exposed her to lusting eyes. Jaleeta saw Tears of Jade's pointing finger again, gnarled, dry, ugly. She remembered the leather line the Skan tied around her neck to lead her to the sharker. They used it to lead her, display her, through their village.

Gan Moondark would never know such humiliation. But he would know defeat. He would know the agony of seeing one life snatched away and a life of another's choosing crushed down on him. He would choke and chafe on a rawhide leash, too. One of many strands, cruel with knots of betrayal. His best friend would bind him.

Chapter 73

Snow fell on the Three Territories for three days and nights. Animals took to dens or sat huddled under whatever cover they could find. Country folk sheltered alone in their homes, worrying in quiet voices, retelling the ancient tales of years that knew no summers and winters that eliminated humans from some lands for generations. Where people clustered in settlements, they trudged through storm and drifts to share misgivings, finding perverse solace in exchanged and reinforced fear. Voices spoke harshly of uncivilized horse riders from distant lands who interfered with established tradition. Others muttered of even stranger people who came with mystical weapons of unimaginable power, unknown to any but themselves.

The name of Teacher, which shone so brightly in the summer sun, became to many an imprecation.

The word *witch* acquired heretofore-inconceivable currency. Those who previously never dared speak it now used it with common familiarity. In dimly lit taverns it slipped, whispered, from many tongues, drifting from ear to ear. It brushed frightened listeners with gray-moth wings, poisoned minds everywhere it touched.

For many simple folk, the word *witch* and the disastrous weather combined into one magnificent opportunity. Those people blamed everyone's specific misfortune on dark powers. After all, the snows proved evil was unleashed. Empty, boring lives were instantly filled with the sweet savor of influence.

Leclerc and Bernhardt labored in isolation, unaware of turmoil or defamation. In fact, they were only aware of the storm to the degree it interfered with their passage from building to building within Leclerc's compound. They noted the depth of the trenches through the accumulation, remarked on it, and kept working.

The smith and his assistants melted copper, poured ingots. Those were hammered and reheated and hammered again to form the necessary sheets. Leclerc demanded perfection. The smith failed to produce it. Hand forming resulted in imperfections—waves, dimples, ripples. Worse, there were frequent minute, hairline cracks.

The work of a full day ended up back in the crucible. Three times.

Leclerc and the smith worked two nights and a day on a project. Not even Bernhardt was allowed to participate. The morning the job was done, Leclerc woke Bernhardt, pounding on his housekeeper's door. "Got something to show you. Are you dressed?"

"Of course. Come in." She was saying, "I'm finishing eating," unnecessarily, as he practically flew through the door. He grabbed her by the shoulders and lifted her to her feet. Crockery clattered on the table when she bumped it. Leclerc was oblivious. "It works, Kate. We got it, Smitty and me."

Bernhardt was delighted; she pretended irritation. "You mean I finally get to see this marvelous thing that's going to solve our problems and make the whole world a better place? It's about time."

Leclerc laughed aloud. "I couldn't show you until now. I didn't know if it'd work." He sobered a bit. "I saw how disappointed you were getting. I didn't want to add to that. This is sort of a present."

Bernhardt flinched, hoping he wouldn't see. Thoughtfulness was the thing she feared most. A kindness, a warm look, a friendly touch—those things could destroy her. She warned herself constantly that overt display of her feelings would send him scurrying. No matter how much it hurt, her only hope was to let him find her. Standing there in front of him was a woman in love, as clear as the sun in the sky, and all he saw was an obstacle to his need to get his hands on Jaleeta. Damn Jaleeta.

"Aren't you coming?" Leclerc was three paces off, looking over his shoulder.

"Don't rush me."

"Women. Complain about waiting and when it's over, you won't hurry."

Drawing her cape around her with an imperious flourish, Bernhardt said, "My wait's over. Yours just started."

Tramping single-file along the packed snow trench to the workshop, they joked easily, comfortably. Leclerc threw open the door. The machine in the middle of the room was waist-high, very sturdy. It looked quite simple. Bernhardt wasn't sure how to react. Leclerc's enthusiasm was enough for both of them. "Isn't she a beauty? Smitty worked himself and his boys ragged cutting those gears, let me tell you. There's not another one of these in the world, I'll bet. You want even sheets of copper? Just watch."

He rushed to the machine, which was essentially two steel rollers, one above the other. Turning a handle, Leclerc made adjustments, and inserted a bar of copper between the rollers. Then he cranked another, larger handle. The rollers turned. The copper bar advanced. Coming out the other side, it was visibly thinner and longer. Leclerc brandished it. "This is a roller mill, Kate. We can turn out sheets of copper thin as paper. Steel, too. To dimension. No warts, wiggles, or wobbles."

Bernhardt rushed to him, hugged him, then took his hands in hers. The copper, heated by its ordeal, formed a shared, warm center. "I'm so proud of you. The rest of us would never have thought of it. It's what we need, isn't it?"

Leclerc was suddenly modest, almost shy. "Well, it's not the whole answer, but if Moonpriest doesn't have one of these, his capacitors will be pretty unpredictable. Ours'll be almost standardized, long, long sheets of very thin copper. We'll put take-up rollers in front and back of the mill. I'll run the metal through one way, rolling it up as it comes out. Then we'll roll it back the other way. Smitty has an annealing oven set up. Without heating, this stuff gets brittle and breaks. With this system we end up with fewer seams, too. That boosts efficiency. It'll be heavy, but it'll pack a real wallop." His smile turned wry. "I think. We haven't really made anything work, yet."

"Today's the day."

"Right. Let's get at it. You'll take care of the waxed cloth? Supervise the work crew to put everything together?"

"The sooner the better. I'm excited. The men are coming; I saw them in the distance."

By late afternoon, the man Leclerc called Smitty beamed as Bernhardt and three assistants completed the first capacitor. Two more assistants and the head beekeeper stood a bit farther away.

Two men carefully unrolled thin copper sheets about a foot wide onto a table. A third assistant covered that with fine, waxed cloth. The cotton was pressed under another copper sheet. Bernhardt assured that a tag end of cloth about an inch long extended beyond the metal, both in width and length.

Strain pulled at the faces of all; the metal crinkled at the slightest twist or distortion. When it did, everyone froze. All remembered Leclerc's stern lecture about the ruinous effect of breaks and wrinkles. Bernhardt and two assistants wound the copper/cloth/copper combination in a tight coil. The overlapping cloth was folded to insulate one copper strip from the other.

Heaving, Bernhardt and her helper upended the device. The completed roll was about the same diameter as its height. The top and bottom cloth ends were bent over. Melted wax sealed them down. Two protruding, thick terminals marked the top. An assistant strapped the capacitor to a packframe and carried it to Leclerc's generator, which was firmly bolted to a workbench. Another man connected the terminals to the generator's outlets. He was clearly afraid. Nevertheless, he grinned at Leclerc, too curious to surrender to fear. At Leclerc's nod, he leaned into the handle.

Soon, Leclerc stopped him, then demonstrated how to connect the leads of a two-tined spear to the capacitor. He warned about keeping the wires far apart. "If they touch each other, the weapon dies. Touch a man, he dies." The cold certainty impressed the crew. They were all very attentive.

With the capacitor on its packframe strapped to his back, Leclerc was prepared. A copper plate slung on a stout pole by a leather rope was the target. A copper wire trailed from the plate to the ground.

One man asked Leclerc to wait. Puzzled, he paused. The youngster dashed past the frowning Smitty. Taking a polished iron disk from a pocket of his leather smith's apron, the boy centered it on the copper plate with a string looped through a hole drilled near the rim. Turning to Leclerc, he made a three-sign. "A make-believe Moondance talisman, Louis Leclerc. For Church, strike it." He ran back to his place.

The small group raised a cheer. Leclerc straightened, embarrassed yet stimulated. No one ever cheered him like that, no one clapped hands, set up a heartbeat rhythm to celebrate him. He hefted the spear, suddenly feather-light. The heavy capacitor was a mere pressure, no burden at all. He feinted, parried. His tiny audience yelled encouragement. Smitty's deep voice demanded, "Kill! Kill! Kill!" By the third repetition, it was a chant from the workers. Leclerc thrust.

Energy released in a crack. Dazzling blue, a jagged jewel of raw power spat into the face of the target. Smoke curled from a small, ugly pit in the seared metal. The burned-black hole lifted flesh-simulating metal edges up and out. Wisping steam and smoke rose from the wire contact with the earth. Tiny deposits of copper dimpled the fake moon disk's shine.

After hoarse cries of astonishment, the group cheered and applauded, louder than ever. They crowded around the blasted plate, admiring. Tentative fingers traced the torn surface. Awed looks admired the generator, the capacitor. Finally, the men looked away, past the confining walls. Speculative.

Later, putting away tools, cleaning up, Leclerc noticed Bernhardt's troubled expression. Leaving the clustered men, he went to where she worked alone, scraping spilled beeswax off the construction table. "Tell me about it," he said.

"About what?" She continued to push the metal scraper, not looking up.

"Whatever's bothering you. Are you feeling all right?"

"Certainly." She checked, gaze fixed on her hands. Straightening slowly, she dropped the scraper, faced him, jaw set. "That's a lie. I'm sick. You should have seen yourself, posturing with that spear. It was awful."

"I was playing. We've worked hard all day. Everything I do, you make it mournful. It's not inhuman to relax, Kate. Or be happy."

Color drained from Bernhardt's face. Coal-dust smudges, bold and harsh, stood out. "Pretending to be fighting, pretending to kill someone. Don't you ever talk to me about humanity. Or happiness."

So far, the argument was quiet, if passionate. Nevertheless, the workmen knew what they were seeing. At a signal from Smitty, they eased out the back door and fled home. Neither Bernhardt nor Leclerc noticed. For a long moment, he resisted the urge to respond. His feelings overrode his judgment. "That's your trouble, you know? You don't know what being alive is all about. With you, everything's theory. Wacky abstract notions of niceness. You ought to join the rest of us sometime, find out it's a flesh-and-blood world. The people who wear that stupid moon thing are out to kill us. No arguments. Just slaughter."

"So killing them is good? We make a game of it? Score points? Penalties for murdering women and children? And what of you? What might happen to you?"

Leclerc stormed over to the post and kicked it. It uprooted and fell to the ground. The copper target landed on its edge, resonating. Dirt swallowed that when the plate fell flat. Leclerc picked it up in both hands. With the strength of fury and frustration, he scaled it. The whirling edge gouged a white scar in the peeled log wall. Once more the hollow boom throbbed, only to go mute when the plate crashed to the floor. When Leclerc turned to Bernhardt, his eyes were round, his face red. "I didn't wake up in this forsaken world just to pass the time. If you want to spend your second life wiping snot off orphans, fine. I've got better things to do. I'm going to be somebody this time. I'll be more important than Conway or Tate or . . . any of them. If that takes winning a war, and that means killing, then people are going to die. You hear that? I will have *power*."

The tirade ended with his hands clamped hard on her shoulders, shaking her back and forth with each word. When he released her, there was no force in the act, yet Bernhardt felt thrown away. He stepped back, chest heaving, waiting, eager for her to strike out, retaliate.

She couldn't. If she tried to speak, the tears would come. Stupid, female, infuriating tears. The words were there. She knew exactly how to show him where he was wrong. Why couldn't he understand that war didn't just mean other people fighting, other people dying? War meant danger to the man she loved. She'd said that as clearly as she could. Under the circumstances.

Silent reproach disarmed Leclerc. "Kate, forgive me. Please. I don't know what's wrong with me." He held her gaze long enough to get the phrase out, then looked away, studied the wall beyond her. "Sometimes I think I've got my life figured out, know right where I'm going. The next minute I'm too confused to move. It's tearing me apart." There was so much more he wanted to tell her. How when she was in his dreams, he always felt good about his work. There was strength, not just power. He didn't understand how she got inside his mind, wove his dreaming into different cloth. He studied her, intent, wishing he could ask.

Bernhardt smiled nervously under that scrutiny. "We all expect too much from you, put too many demands on you. Including me."

"That's not true. You're always there, supporting. Look what we've done here. I'd never have gotten this crowd working as a team the way you did. Other people tell me what I have to do. You help me do it."

Bernhardt felt her cheeks warming. "That's why I came here. We better go eat. Larta's going to be upset if it's cold."

Later, after determining that Kate had no objections, Leclerc sent Larta home. The older woman managed a conspiratorial wink for Bernhardt before she hurried off. Bernhardt smiled and winked back. She wished she had reason for it.

The meal passed more comfortably than Bernhardt expected. Leclerc was unusually attentive. She told herself he was making amends. They avoided anything military. When Bernhardt discussed the curriculum for the burgeoning Teachers, Leclerc listened. He made suggestions rationally, without condescension or bombast. Nor did he defer. She remembered how she used to regard him as a false macho, one of those poor souls who equates manhood and guns. She sighed. Today's unpleasantness suggested there was some of that even in the intellectuals. Glands, or something.

Louis picked up the books, gestured with them. "Whatever curriculum you decide on for the Teachers-to-be, ours is in here. I'm a pretty competent tinker, but this is technology. This is progress. For the entire world. Have you thought of that, Kate? Really thought about it?"

The import of the question made her mouth dry. Her nervous swallow turned into an embarrassing gulp. "We've started something profound, haven't we? Us. Moonpriest. We've unleashed terrible power. Electricity's just a tiny part of it."

"We didn't exactly do all of it, Kate. Sylah and Conway and Tate dug up these books, remember. I mean, we share the responsibility. It's not all ours."

Bernhardt's heart flooded with sudden, warm tenderness for the anxious man across from her. She wanted to tell him how clearly she understood, how painfully the weight of so much influence pressed on her own conscience. The man she heard now was the man she wanted. That man, revealed, was the man who wanted her, too. Needed her. Sympathetic words came easily. Automatically, in fact; in her distraction, she wasn't really sure what she said. Tone was far more important, and she was certain she got that right, because she saw his appreciation.

The only word in her own mind was Hope. It sang.

BOOK III

Renewal

Chapter 74

The second storm convinced everyone that this winter would never be forgotten by any who survived. Gan Moondark transformed his Wolves to service units to distribute stored food reserves. Supply and rescue became another tactical exercise.

Early on, it became apparent the militarization of the effort was a wise move. The infiltrating Mountain People and Kwa allies were as afflicted by the storms as any. Late arrival in the area precluded adequate stores for winter. Harsh weather drove game downhill, where milder temperatures and lessened snowfall permitted feeding, however scanty. The Kwa and the Mountains who hunted for those creatures to survive either followed them down or starved. Gan's people congregated in the lower lands.

To the invaders, humans were no less prey than other animals. Many a first-year Wolf bloodied his sword on those winter supply missions.

Nalatan rode with them. Action diminished loneliness. In the rising of dawn, he felt Donnacee's soft waking. Nightfall brought reminiscence of skin that glowed dark life, familiar, ever mysterious.

Well outside his hearing, men murmured of this laconic companion, who smiled so seldom, yet was ever helpful. They whispered further of a man who rushed to battle as to a feast, who fought with a silent ferocity that frightened friend almost as much as foe.

Marching home from a sweep south and east of Ola, a detail of the Jalail pack found Gan waiting for them on the road to the city. He sat his horse slightly ahead of his ten outriders, dressed in a heavy mink cloak. A round, flat-topped white sheepskin hat contrasted handsomely with the dark, glistening fur. He saluted the hundred-man commanding the unit, listened to his report. Gan praised him and his troopers, then kneed his horse off the road, making room for men who longed far more for warmth and shelter than any commendation.

When Nalatan pulled out of the column, Gan greeted him warmly, then, "You see how my Wolves look at me?"

Nalatan blinked slowly. "You're their leader. I see respect."

Gan's snort cut him off. "You lie poorly. They pity me. As do you, and you think you hide it."

Nalatan colored. "Worry when men seek to take your place, rather than feel sorry for you because you're chained to it."

Gan laughed at that, although bitterness sharpened the sound. "I take your point. Why do we enjoy combat, Nalatan? Why seek such a terrible thing?"

"Most neither seek nor enjoy. Most can't wait to hang up their weapons. They fight in the hope there'll be no fighting for their sons. Men like you and I are born to it. The One in All seems to have a need for us."

"Theology?" Gan's tone teased.

Nalatan was sly. "Someone has to take the blame. His shoulders are broader than mine."

"That's not religious depth, you fraud. That's dodging responsibility. You're becoming tricky enough to live inside walls."

"A truly vicious characterization." Nalatan bowed deeply. "You honor."

The day was sliding into evening when they arrived at the walls. Neela and Sylah rode out to greet them.

Sylah wore her normal black, rode a black mare. Neela, without Coldar, sat astride her Dog horse, Copper. The animal's bright rufous coat complemented her golden-blond tresses. Nalatan glanced at Gan, noted the love and admiration in his eyes. A small flame of jealousy reached to scar camaraderie.

The women greeted them in a swirl of embraces, despite the awkwardness of horseback. Nalatan savored perfumed soap and applied scent. Quickly, he moved away, aware of how rank he must be, despite daily snow scrubs. While they made conversation, riding to the gate, he fantasized about a soak.

"I need your help, more than ever," Sylah said to him, shattering his vision of calm restfulness.

He guessed. "Jaleeta again?"

"Yes. She's seduced Leclerc."

"Louis?" It was on his tongue to correct her, to name Emso.

"You needn't look so shocked. I'm not merely gossiping. This is no simple, grubby affair. Leclerc is important. Too important."

Nalatan was sufficiently recovered for sarcasm. "It's especially naughty to sleep with important people?"

"She does nothing without a purpose. Nothing."

"Louis knows his duty. She's no witch, to twist his mind around."

"Would you stake your life on that?" The very mildness of Sylah's manner rattled Nalatan. "She needn't have vile powers. She's young and beautiful. If she has ambition and ruthlessness, that's enough. As a man, would you agree?"

The last came with a hint of smirk, and Nalatan faked a huge wince, happy to escape the serious tenor of the discussion, if only for a moment. "You ask a man married to Donnacee Tate? You must hate me a great deal. But even if everything you say is true, I can't pry and squeeze information from people. You know that."

"We had this conversation before. I'll repeat the important part. She'll come to you; I'm sure of it. When she does, listen, please."

They parted in a confused babble. Nalatan went on alone, deep in thought. It seemed that wherever he turned, he was either doing something wrong or being asked to do something he considered wrong. The bathhouse beckoned sanctuary. At least lolling in a tub was risk-free.

Naked, he kindled and stoked the firebox under the rectangular stone tub and filled it with a bucket from the covered cistern. He sat on a sturdy little bench to scrub down. He worked on the long, jagged scar down his back, a childhood souvenir from a slavers raid. Tension always made it ache. Rinsed, he sank into the steaming soak. The fire was dwindled to coals, the water just right. Scented oils were within reach. He was liberal with his favorite sage. With his head resting on a wooden ledge at the tub's end, even his ears were submerged. He closed his eyes, drifted.

Unexpected noise brought him upright in a splashing, thrashing rush, reaching for his sword. It was merely the door to the women's soak, a hinge squealing complaint.

Soon after, Nalatan hauled out. He dipped a clean cloth in cold water, wrung it nearly dry. Rubbing down with it curtailed sweating, and made it more difficult for the unseens that caused colds to settle on him once he went outdoors. Straightening his pullover shirt, he was aware of the woman on the other side of the plank wall. She was humming. It was pleasant, with a mischievous lilt.

In his room, he folded and stacked the clothing he'd worn on patrol. Donnacee scolded when things weren't neat. He surveyed his work. Neat. Unnatural. He shrugged, transforming the small movement to a larger reach for the box under his bed. Opened, it was full of oily sand. Nalatan scooped a depression, dropped his rolled-up chain mail in it. Brushing and stirring, he enjoyed the unthinking rhythms. Little by little, the circular links lost their grime and small rust specks. The latter left minute black stains. Nalatan frowned at them. Mail should be bright. Challenging. He hung up the shirt, closed the box, and began sweeping up the odd grains of sand.

He almost missed the faint scratching at his door. When it came again, he opened it.

Jaleeta said, "I thought you'd come directly here." She smiled up at him, dark hair, dark eyes gleaming. A cream-white deerhide cloak, drawn tight at the throat, overlapped in front, reached the ground all around her. The beautiful face seemed to float on its own snowbank.

Nalatan's throat tightened. "Is there something wrong?"

Laughter chimed, delicate bells of amusement. "No, silly. I wanted to talk, that's all."

"Talk? With me? Why?"

"Because you were a monk, and know Church. Because you're married to a woman who's different, and not ashamed of it. I need your experience."

He shook his head, hand still gripping the door's edge. "When Donnacee returns, you should speak to her."

"I will." The smile teased. White teeth gleamed. "I'm young, Nalatan, but I know this much: To hear about women, listen to men; to hear about men, listen to women. There's much you can show me."

Nalatan told himself he heard no gloss of suggestion, cursed himself for imagining things. He said, "I don't know—" and Jaleeta interrupted. "You don't know how to be polite, I think," she said. Another smile dared him to be offended at the small joke. He stepped aside. Jaleeta pushed the door closed behind her.

Untying the robe, she folded it carefully across the back of the only chair, inspecting the rest of the room. She wore a white blouse, the collar trimmed in green. A fine leather vest featured a dozen small abalone buttons, each gaudy as an oil slick. A dark green woolen skirt with appliques of black-and-white killer whales reached down to calf-high boots. She inhaled deeply, straining the already tight vest. "A man's place." She turned, a lazily swirling circle. "You were oiling that chain mail. I smell it. There's sand, too; from the sea. Not that freshwater dirt. And you used the soak."

His eyes narrowed, and she laughed at him. "I was on the women's side when you bathed. I saw you go in."

Alarm drummed in Nalatan's head. "What do you want?"

"*Want.* Such an interesting word. We confuse it with *need.* Or *wish.* Troublesome. What I want is advice. I'm pursued by two men. I want neither."

"What is that to me?"

The blunt disinterest nonplussed Jaleeta momentarily. "It could be much to you. The men are Louis Leclerc and Emso. If one ever thinks the other is about to claim me, Gan Moondark loses at least one of his most important men. I will be responsible, through no fault of my own."

"Then tell Gan."

Jaleeta shook her head. She stepped closer. Her voice lowered to huskiness. "He wants me for Emso. He swore me to secrecy. He suspects Emso negotiates with the malcontent Barons."

This was worse than lying. This was a malicious attempt to lure three honorable men into a blind duel. Nalatan wanted his hands around that smooth, columnar neck. And yet the concept of his hands on that skin was not all violence. He swallowed. "You propose we deceive Murdat?"

"Never." She extended an admonishing hand that came to rest on his. "We must all protect him. I don't think we should tell him everything, but we're not going to lie. What I want of you is very easy; be more attentive to Gan."

"Gan?"

"Don't you see? That way you'll always be close when Louis and Emso come around. It'll be almost impossible for one of them to be alone with me."

Jaleeta was closer. "When Gan and Neela aren't there, you could stay with me. I don't think I need protection, but both Louis and Emso can be—threatening. I know you're married, but she's not here. I could be female company for you. I need an honorable friend. Please?" Her lips were parted, shiny wet. She leaned toward him. Open buttons of her blouse formed an arrowhead gap pointing to delights he didn't dare imagine.

He moved to the door, half-stumbling. When he turned to face Jaleeta, his expression shocked her erect, hand to throat. He said, "You lied to Emso. About Gan. You're lying to Leclerc. I know everything. Get out."

Jaleeta believed him. It never occurred to her to plead innocence or bargain for understanding. She attacked. "Which knothole did you spy through? Sneak. Liar. Who will you tell? You think anyone will believe? And what if they do? Inform on Emso, and the shame kills him. Inform on Leclerc, and Gan will make him take me for wife—and Emso will kill him."

Nalatan's head swam. She was right. But she was wrong. Evil. "Gan will send you away."

She laughed, and Nalatan heard the same delicate bells as before. "Those fools will seek me out. They want me, Nalatan. Like you."

"I don't. You shame."

"What shames you is knowing what you want to do." Jaleeta advanced, slowly. Nalatan shouted inwardly at himself to simply flee. But he stared, transfixed. "Come, Nalatan. Desire me. Join with me. I promise you everything. I am pleasure."

Scent laved him, crisp plant essences. Suddenly his mind wrenched him away. He remembered the rich, warm hay smell of the barn. She used her body exactly this way there, too. Emso. Ruined.

Revulsion froze lust.

Something warned Jaleeta. She retreated the smallest step. "You'll help me. It's you I want. As you want me." She gripped the vest's opening, one hand on each side. "What if I tore this bit of leather, scattered these tiny buttons around your room? Cried rape? Gan would exile you like a rabid dog. And Donnacee; what of her?"

Nalatan backed away, slammed against the hall wall, ludicrous, unable to retreat, too afraid of himself to advance. Jaleeta walked past him with one last thought. "You will help me rise, Nalatan. To keep Gan alive, to keep his friends alive. And you'll be glad. We have much to enjoy, you and I."

It was some time before Nalatan trusted himself to reenter the room. He sat down in the chair with the boneless crush of sacked grain. Little by little, his color improved. Standing, he flung open the shutters, flooding the room with frigid air. The first gust slammed shut the heavy door. Seated again, he closed his eyes. His breathing slowed, steadied. Muscles eased.

When at last he reopened his eyes to the glowering, cloud-rushing sky, he was totally changed. He strode confidently to Gan's reception room, where Gan sat alone at his ornate table with his dogs. He greeted his visitor with a smile. "I was just thinking I need someone to talk to."

"No, Murdat. Not just conversation."

Gan sobered. "What have you learned?"

"Nothing definite." Nalatan tasted the lie, dirty. He hurried on. "On patrol. There's unrest. The Wolves look over their shoulders. They're unsure of some. They talk of men in high places." Sweat started. The dogs regarded him curiously.

"The dissident Barons." Gan leaned back in his chair. "Emso has come to trust the Ondrat one completely, visits with him. Even in this winter's weather, Ondrat's men watch the coast for Skan."

"I know Ondrat saved Sylah, but—"

Gan's laughter interrupted. He walked to the fireplace. "You and Emso: His suspicions go down, yours go up. With you two watching my back, I can concentrate on the enemies in front of me. I'm a lucky man."

Nalatan swallowed. "You should know. Jaleeta. Both Leclerc and Emso are interested in her."

"Oh, I know that." Gan turned from the fire, winked broadly. "She tells Neela everything. The two of them embarrass her. She's far too young for them. Just the other day she was saying she visited Leclerc. Lectured him about what a fine woman Kate Bernhardt is. Matchmaking. They have to do it. Women, I mean. Men are blind in these matters. Men need facts, not moonlight tales."

"I have to leave here." The words boiled out of Nalatan.

Sympathetic understanding quickly replaced Gan's surprise. "I forgot, Nalatan. Talking about all this. It's pointless to go after Tate, you know. The snows are unbelievable. She's safe, hidden away, waiting for better weather. And I need you."

"I wouldn't know where to start looking for her. She may still be on the sunrise side. But I have to get away from Ola. Outside walls."

"If you don't search for Tate, then what?"

"Moonpriest. I can find out what he's doing."

"A far mission, my friend. Dangerous." Nalatan's blank stare made Gan smile. Dryly he continued. "Can you do that and return in time to meet Tate?"

"I can try. But I need to get away."

"Perhaps. Perhaps." Gan drew into himself. After a long pause, he sighed. "When will you leave?"

"As soon as I saddle a horse." Nalatan stepped away from the fireplace. "I'll go east. No one will miss me until tomorrow, at the soonest. By then, I'll be far south."

Gan's chuckle was rueful. "Almost unseemly haste. A man could think his hospitality was being rejected."

"Never that. But it's for the best. For everyone." He gulped, wished he could pull back the last.

Gan merely nodded. "Our secret, then. The official story is that you've gone on your own. I don't know where. Until I speak to Tate." They shook hands.

At the evening meal the following day Neela said, "You're going to have to say something about Nalatan's disappearance, Gan. The rumormongers say he deserted you."

Jaleeta choked explosively. Neela raced to pat her back. When Jaleeta recovered, her smile was nervous, disconcerted. "I heard nothing of this. I was with the Chosens all day."

Gan was condescending. "I'm not interested in rumors."

Neela's look was shrewd. "No? Then you know something."

Flustered, Gan tried brusque denial. They argued with the good humor of two people who are not only fairly certain of the eventual victor, but don't really care if there is one. Neither noticed Jaleeta's near-manic intensity.

In the end, Gan said, "Oh, all right. But it's not to go outside this room. He said he wanted out of Ola, so I asked him to do something for me. All very simple."

"Then why all the secrecy? And rush?" Neela was disdainful. And a bit skeptical.

"I'm glad he's gone."

Gan and Neela started, stared at Jaleeta. Her face was splotched red. When she realized the others were watching her, she looked down at her lap. Then, "I went to talk to him yesterday. He always seems so lonely. I was just being nice. He . . . He's not the way everyone thinks."

Neela and Gan exchanged stunned looks. Neela put her arm across the other woman's shoulders. "He didn't do anything, did he?"

"Not really. He grabbed me. Said things. He stopped chasing me when I got outside. Where people could see."

Gan said, "You should have told me," trying to keep sick anger out of his voice.

Jaleeta looked away. "He's your friend."

Her face was still red. Gan was impressed by the tight-lipped determination. Pain and humiliation made her look more angry than embarrassed. "Exactly what did he say?"

Neela jerked upright. "Gan!"

Jaleeta's look, full of disappointed understanding, destroyed him. He apologized. Neela led the younger woman away, who mustered a small, brave smile.

Alone at the table, Gan shook his head. Sometimes one could look straight at the darkest deception, and see nothing but bright honesty. It made a man think.

CHAPTER 75

CAPRICIOUSLY, THE ABNORMAL STORMS TURNED TO CLEAR, COLD DAYS LITTLE MORE THAN A moon after Nalatan left. When a man from an outlying timber camp rode into Ola with the news that Tate, Conway, and Lanta were on their way to the city, an impromptu celebration blossomed.

Bedraggled, trail-grimed, all three reacted as if clubbed when Gan led a welcoming party to greet them. A particularly flustered Tate was brushing at her clothes, arranging her hair, rubbing mud off her boots on her horse's flanks long before she could recognize anyone. As the oncoming riders closed, she scanned faces with increasing anxiety. Appearance was forgotten. She rose in her stirrups.

Gan and Neela exchanged glances. As much as they relished welcoming home a friend, they dreaded breaking the news of her husband's absence. More than anything, they hated the unbearable secret hidden in their hearts. Together, they raced ahead of the crowd, determined that Donnacee should learn of Nalatan's mission to the south from no one but themselves.

Tate continued to look past Gan and Neela, her smile fixed and strained now. When her friends reined to a stop in front of her, her expression questioned. And feared. Rapidly, Neela broke the news, finishing, "He had to get out, away from walls, he said. And no one thought the storms would stop. He'll be wild when he gets back. He missed you so, and now this."

Tate tried to be calm. "I understand. I really do. We spent the whole time in tight little snow caves, practically buried alive. I know about walls." Then her resolve almost cracked. "It's just that I looked forward to him so much. It hurts, Neela. Bad."

Neela spun her horse around, put herself next to Tate, threw an arm around her. "Be strong, Donnacee. Please. The people need heroes now, and they're welcoming three of them home. Help us."

Tate gripped the pommel, straightened. "I'm all right. Let's do it." She moved ahead, forcing the others to hurry to catch up.

The threesome were allowed to bathe and sleep the rest of the day away, but at nightfall, celebration demanded them. No one commented on Tate's dispiritedness. In her presence. When the night was half over, however, Gan made excuses in the town for his friends and withdrew with them to the castle. A smaller party ensued. That was when Tate drew Gan aside. They sat in a dark corner, large mugs of beer in hand, and she regaled him with their adventure. She pressed Tinillit's case, asking Gan to grant them land. He agreed readily. It was in her mind to tell him of the weapons cached in the passes, but the pact protecting all such equipment forbade. For all that, she had ideas of her own about those mountains. *Her* ideas.

At one point, they fell quiet for some time. Tate looked out onto the crowded floor. Couples danced to stringed instruments. Most reminded her of guitars, but some were much slimmer, some much deeper. The rhythm section was a man in the middle of a circle of graduated drums. He played melody on them, as well. The music was lively, merry.

Facing Gan again, Tate said, "After the second storm hit, it kept snowing for weeks. We had snow huts. At first, living in my personal little white box, with more snow coming down all the time, I thought I'd go crazy. I mean, in there I was warm, but so alone. Outside was cold, storms. The huts weren't built to entertain guests, believe me. If I wanted company, I crowded in with Lanta and Conway. Not to mention the dogs."

"It must have been very difficult," Gan said.

Tate was watching the party again. "Sometimes I was so jealous of Conway and Lanta it scared me. You and Neela, too. How do you help envying happy people when you're miserable?"

"I've never known anyone who wasn't guilty of that, one time or another. I know you can't let it control you. We're not worried about that, are we?"

She smiled broadly, then rose. Before he could move, she bent across the small table and kissed his forehead. When she sat down, he was smiling, but surprised. She said, "That's for saying 'we.' You really are a sweet man."

He glared mock fury. "I am Murdat, warrior, ruler of the Three Territories."

"You're a big old pussycat." She sniffed, turned away. He chuckled softly, and the silence that fell over them this time was companionable.

"One more question, Gan, and then I'm through here for the night." She looked deep into his eyes. "You know what I'm going to ask, don't you? So tell me—why'd Nalatan really leave? The whole story."

Nervous fingers tapped the table. Gan drained the last of his beer. The mug thumped heavily when he lowered it to the table. "I told you, Donnacee. He said he had to go, that he felt closed in."

"Where was he going before you asked him to scout out Moonpriest?"

Gan glanced around. "Careful. No one knows that. I don't know where he was going. We'd already agreed he couldn't find you, because he didn't know where to look."

"He wasn't going somewhere definite?"

"He didn't say."

Tate shook here head, stood up slowly. "Strange. Man says he'll wait here for me, then changes his mind. I can see why he'd want to go, but why didn't he have a place in mind to go *to*? Doesn't make sense."

Gan waited until she was through the door and into the hall before he dabbed the sweat off his upper lip.

When Leclerc and Conway called on her early the next morning and insisted she join them to view Leclerc's latest accomplishments, she accepted with alacrity. They rode out the snow-packed trail, savoring the day.

Kate Bernhardt greeted them from the porch. Tate waved happily, thrilled to be with yet another of her friends. Inside, Kate offered fresh bread, a large crock of pale butter, and blackberry jam. After the cold ride, food and hot tea disappeared quickly.

Leaving for the workshed, the women fell in behind the men. Tate gave Kate a quick hug. "We lived on dried fruit, dried vegetables, dried meat. Some game and forage. Pemmican. Other stuff. I dreamed of hot bread and melted butter. If I'd dreamed of jam this good, I'd have started walking, blizzards or no. Oh, that was good, Katie. I love you."

Bernhardt glowed. "I'm glad you liked it. It's all new to me. I live with Louis' housekeeper. She's been teaching me."

Tate squinted. "Live *with* the housekeeper?"

Kate missed the import. "A husband and wife keep up the place for him. I have the attic space in their house. Her name's Larta, and . . ." She stopped as if she'd hit a wall, then turned, crestfallen. "With the housekeeper. And her husband. Not exactly the way I'd have it."

It was Tate's turn to be abashed. "Oh, Kate. I thought I was being funny."

Bernhardt linked arms with her, explaining the triangle that was her, Jaleeta, and Leclerc, ending, "Even so, I want to marry the man, not just sleep with him. Is it possible for us to be old-fashioned? Considering certain weird ramifications?"

"You be anything you want. I'm on your side."

They were entering the shed then. Leclerc said, "Let's show them what we can do, Kate." Like a proud parent, he led Conway and Tate to the rolling mill that produced sheet copper. Then he took them to the storage shed to show off completed, stacked capacitors. Conway whooped. While Bernhardt explained manufacturing details to Conway, Tate and Leclerc discussed technique.

Conway's voice carried over. "Show us the generator, Louis."

Leclerc hurried them back to the workshed. They played with the generator like children. From there they walked to the first of the new buildings. The unseasoned, untreated wood was studded with golden drops of sap, and the building was rich with the smell of new-sawn lumber. It was uncomfortably warm. Smiths worked at furnaces, at anvils. Younger men, some literally children, served their apprenticeship at workbenches and at bellows.

Conway gestured at men pulling copper wire through a series of smaller and smaller holes drilled in a steel plate. "They're making wire. For another generator?"

"A much bigger one." Leclerc frowned. "We're having trouble casting the shaft.

It's not just a matter of making something bigger, we've learned. We're breaking new ground here, technologically." He flashed a twisted smile. "Rebreaking new ground, at least. There's nothing in the Door books to cover this kind of metallurgy. But we'll get it. Come on—one more thing to see." Cheerful again, Leclerc took them to the last building, another new one.

Men and women worked on catapults. Noticing the pairing, Tate looked a silent question at Bernhardt, who explained, "The smiths won't admit women to their craft. Just won't. Maybe the iron settles in their heads; I don't know. Anyhow, we're training women here."

Tate nodded satisfaction. "Armorers. That's what they're called. People who make weaponry are armorers. They should know that."

Kate beamed. "They will."

On the way back to the farmhouse, Conway indicated the distant barn. "You still make your black powder in there?"

"No. Too dangerous. I needed a place to store the materials and work and still keep the secret to myself. I've got a sort of bunker, just over there. See the stovepipe coming out of the low mound? The door's hidden under snow now."

"Whoo!" Tate burlesqued great excitement. "A secret laboratory. You really have become the Defense Department, haven't you?"

Leclerc laughingly shooed her inside the house and complained about lack of respect. When he followed with a pompous demand for an increased budget, the others booed heartily. When they were serious again, Leclerc launched into a technical monologue about the larger generator, adding, "More power opens the possibility of different weapons. It's exciting."

Bernhardt said, "You should see him. Always with his nose in those books."

Tate and Conway both started. Indignation sparked Conway's questions. "Books? Here?"

Guiltily, Bernhardt said, "I brought them. He needs them."

Not wanting to spoil the atmosphere, Conway softened his initial manner. "Is that safe, Louis? I mean, we hear about raiders, and all. This place is no fort, you know? What about the red book; it's not here, is it?"

"Well, yes, actually. They're all hidden. When I'm not using them. Buried, out in my bunker."

Tate made a rude noise. "With the black powder? Come on, Louis."

"Well buried. Safe. I guarantee it."

Bernhardt worked to smooth things over. "They really are well protected. And he does need them. He's got some wonderful plans. Not just weapons, either."

Leclerc was eager to lighten the conversation, as well. He grinned at Tate and Conway. "My greatest fan. And the one with ideas, as often as not."

Deferentially, Bernhardt contradicted. "We don't always agree. We're really different about what we think Moonpriest is up to."

Leclerc made a wide gesture of dismissal. "He moved to the coast. We've heard reports of windmills. It's nothing. He's probably got belt-driven saws to cut timbers for his wallkillers, or some such. It's nothing."

Bernhardt argued with quiet tenacity. "I think he's making hydrogen."

Tate made a face. "Beg pardon?"

Bernhardt went on. "We know his moon altar works on electricity. If he's built windmills, that steady source of power could be to electrolyze water, break it down into hydrogen and oxygen. If he's capturing those gases, he can throw genuine bombs with that wallkiller thing. I'm glad you're here with plenty of ammunition."

"If, if, if," Leclerc objected. "Too many ifs. Our catapults will smash his wallkillers, no matter what they throw."

Shortly afterward, riding back to Ola, Tate asked Conway, "Did anyone say anything about Leclerc and Jaleeta last night?"

"Who? Oh, yes; the girl who got away from the Skan. All the single guys know about her, for sure. Her presence in the Three Territories gives a whole new resonance to the term Wolves. I guess Emso's eyes glaze whenever she goes by, but no one mentioned Louis. The guys said she's Old Church. She's a For, and a lot of them are that way. Demure. Obedient. She sticks pretty close to Neela. Or the Violet Abbess. Spends time with the Chosens and our friends. They love her. Aside from that, there wasn't much said about her."

" 'Aside from that?' " Tate snorted laughter. "You got everything but her dental record and glove size, you twit." Then, hating it, she asked the question she dreaded might have an answer. "Was there anything about Nalatan? Why he took off the way he did? Didn't he say anything to anyone but Gan?"

"Not a word that I heard about. You know how he keeps things inside. It's no surprise, considering. He needs room, Donnacee. He's no city-dweller. We knew that."

They clopped along without further discussion after that. In her heart, Tate blessed Conway for saying "We knew that," just as she'd kissed Gan for including himself in her troubled mind. At the same time, she cursed Matt Conway, her best friend, for a forced heartiness that offended worse than an outright lie.

Had he heard something he wouldn't repeat? Or was he simply trying too hard to be reassuring?

Why had she asked?

A wolf howled in the distance. Response floated back across the crystalline night. Tate heard the calls as inexpressibly sad, and she raised her chin as if she would answer. Instead, she whispered, "Hunt well, Gan's brothers. Hunt well, and know one envies you your terrible innocence."

CHAPTER 76

THE FAINT KNOCK STARTLED TATE. SHE FLIPPED A BLANKET OVER THE DETAIL-STRIPPED WIPE on her bed and called out, "Who is it?"

"Jaleeta."

Tate said, "Who?" then recovered. "Come in, please." She rose to meet her unexpected visitor.

Tate had no way of knowing Jaleeta had on the same clothes she'd worn to visit Nalatan. The shorter woman posed in the hallway, off-white cloak contrasted with dark stone. Contrasting black boots shaded into the background, adding to the impression that Jaleeta floated, rather than stood. Tate studied the face above the supple leather. Dark brows and eyes and full red lips further accentuated skin white as milk.

Mentally inventorying her own appearance, Tate resisted the urge to look down at the mess she'd made of herself that morning. Greasy hands, grimy fingernails; surely the utmost in fashionable squalor. Insouciant frayed cuffs on the rough, stained sweater that featured a cunning hole at one shoulder to daringly expose the baggy homespun shirt. And, of course, scruffy old Wolf field trousers, the kind with the weave so hard the troopers called them ironbutts. All that, and a madcap, simply crazy, frazzled do-rag to crown the ensemble. Enchantment.

Tate smiled sweetly. "Come on in, Jaleeta. It's nice of you to visit."

Jaleeta returned the smile, swept past. Tate sat on the bed, gesturing her guest to the chair. Jaleeta seated herself, then, "We've never really gotten acquainted. I've heard so much about you."

"I've heard a lot about you, too. Hoped to see you at last night's party."

"I don't like parties. The men—the ones my age—are . . . what's the word? Frivolous? A woman likes to feel a man has a steady, concerned side. Exciting men usually forget there's more to life than excitement."

It was said with such offhand candor Tate laughed in spite of herself. This was, after all, the woman complicating Kate Bernhardt's life. Tate said, "Women usually wait a while to discover that. At some cost."

"It seemed important for me to learn quickly." Jaleeta made a wry joke of the allusion to her past.

The attempt sat poorly with Tate. Something suddenly jarred. Jaleeta was not only entirely too beautiful, she was far too complex. Tate thought of the lithe seals that frolicked in the Inland Sea. Their swift appearance and disappearance gave them an almost sinister grace, a capacity to make the mind distrust the eye.

Jaleeta continued. "I hope you're not angry because I didn't ride out to greet you with Neela and Gan and the others. I really didn't want to."

"Why not?"

"The thing about your husband. When he left, I was afraid you'd come home before he got back. I just felt so terrible. It's silly, I know; I mean, I never even spoke to your husband. Not really."

Nerves tingled at the back of Tate's neck. Hair rose. There was a hitch in Jaleeta's words, an inflection. Tate said, "It was the most disappointing moment in my life. I understand, though. If I'd been thinking, I'd have known he'd have to get out of here. Neither of us can stand being enclosed."

Animated, Jaleeta stood up. "I knew that's what you'd say. I'm so pleased."

"Pleased? About what?"

"That he left because of that. That's what Gan told me, and I wanted to believe him. The other was depressing."

Again, a tremor ran through Tate. "What other reason could he have?"

Quickly, as if waiting to answer, Jaleeta said, "Only one. Of course. Everyone's heard how devoted you are to each other. But she said it wasn't so."

Tate ground her teeth. "Who said what wasn't so?"

"The Violet Abbess. She had some long talks with Nalatan. She said he was very concerned. It's the new weapons. He started to worry if they were anti-Church. He must have heard it from Emso; he's always complaining to Gan about the new things. Nalatan's whole life was Church, but everyone knows how much more you mean to him. Even if the new things bothered him, he'd never leave for that reason. After all, didn't he tell Gan himself what his reason was?"

"Nalatan talked to the Abbess? You know that?"

Eyes wide, Jaleeta sat back down. "She told me. You're not going to tell her I said anything, are you?"

"Damned well told I am. We're not talking about lost baggage, girl. Whatever it was that sent my husband out of here, you depend on me finding out."

"I didn't mean to upset you," Jaleeta fluttered. Tate noted, however, that the eyes that met her own were composed, focused.

After a perfunctory washup, changed to a dark blue quilted shirt and lighter blue pants, Tate pulled on a green blanket-thick cloak. To Jaleeta, she said, "Things got away from me, there. Sorry."

"Certainly. I didn't explain well. All I want is to be your friend, and I was clumsy. It's my fault."

Tate mumbled something. The walk to the Violet Abbey was without much conversation and devoid of incident, save one puzzling moment. They passed a detail of Wolves, shepherding yet another wagonload of supplies from the docks to the needy, and the young leader idly glanced at the two women hurrying past him. Idly, that was, until recognition struck him. He sat bolt upright, clearly startled. His belated salute slapped the side of his head. He blinked foolishly, continuing to stare after Tate returned the salute.

Surreptitiously, Tate peered back over her shoulder. The unit's pennant was the stylized owl of Mull. One of the dissident baronies. She made a mental note to ask Emso about discipline in that organization.

A Priestess ushered Tate and Jaleeta into the Violet Abbess's quarters. The gaunt, older woman sat in a rocking chair in front of a blazing fireplace, blanket across her lap, embroidery hoop in hand. The scene reeked of staging, yet the welcome seemed genuine. As her guests pulled up chairs, the Abbess put aside her work and rang a small bell. The Priestess returned. At the Abbess' urging, Tate accepted a cup of tea, specifically requesting chamomile for its soothing properties; she warned herself that this was no time or place for temper. The tightness in her back muscles, the feeling of preternatural alertness, was like readying for combat. Tate remembered a fight with a sharker captain, and intuition warned her that she was in similar danger, despite tea and comforting hearth.

The servant Priestess brought three plain ceramic cups and a two hammered silver pots enfolded in down insulators. Tate admired the waxed wooden tray with handles carved in marvelous likeness of leaping dolphins. With the servant gone, the Abbess poured. Handing Tate her preference, she said, "The first thing I want to say is that Church is truly sorry to learn of your difficulties. Nalatan is a fine man, as you are a fine woman."

Tate sipped, eyeing the Abbess over the rim. Then she said, "Your Sister Mother tried to kill both of us. She'd enjoy watching us burn. So tell me what you know of Nalatan."

Coughing discreetly, the Abbess dabbed her lips with an exquisite lace handkerchief no larger than a man's palm. "You are all they say. But don't misjudge Church, my dear. All who come to Church are forgiven. Never forget that. Nalatan remembered. It's that simple."

"Not a chance." Tate drank tea, shook her head.

"Oh, I doubt he's on his way back to the Dry, but he was terribly concerned about fighting for Gan Moondark. He's not alone, child. Many are disturbed. Those who break Church tradition are broken by faith."

"I'm not your child. And I'd like to hear you reconcile 'forgiven' and 'broken by faith,' when we have more time." Tate put her cup on the tray, got to her feet. "If you don't have anything definite, I'll leave now, Abbess. Thanks for your help."

From the corner of her eye, Tate saw the Abbess' gaze flick in Jaleeta's direction before she continued. "There is one other thing." Tate stopped, turned. The Abbess was tight-mouthed, as though she'd bitten something incredibly bitter. "You may hear rumors about Nalatan. About another woman. He spoke to me of them, asked me to speak to you in his stead. It's very distressing, but he asked me. He wanted to assure you the tales are untrue, and he wanted you to hear it from another woman, one he trusts and hopes you'll trust."

"There's no other woman. And he'd go to Sylah, not you."

Chin rising, eyes flashing anger, the older woman still spoke calmly. "He came to me. Your husband is finding his way back to his roots. I believe our conversation is over."

"Forevermore." Tate whirled as quickly as she could, caught Jaleeta's avid, fractional smile an instant before the younger woman managed to turn it to frowning concern. To Jaleeta, Tate said, "You've enjoyed this, haven't you? I owe you one, sweetlips. I can't figure out exactly what your game is, but when I do, we'll have another cup of tea and I'll teach you about messing with me."

The Abbess hissed anger. "Never use the forbidden word here. This is a holy place."

Numbed by the inanity of the remark, Tate could only laugh. On her way down the narrow stone passageway her guffaws echoed off the walls. Once in the cold daylight, however, the shallow humor faded quickly.

Had Nalatan actually gone to a woman like the Abbess?

There were good reasons to believe it could happen. Nalatan's background. Loneliness. Strange surroundings. Worst of all, forced to live with the burden of a wife who left him to pursue her own secret agenda. Still, it didn't feel right. Once more, Tate found herself thinking of water, of looking down at something obscured and distorted.

She walked a long time, thinking, until a tumbling, headlong stream blocked her way. It shocked her to realize she had no recollection of her route, and when she looked back at the walls of the city, the distance surprised her.

Just as she started to return to the castle, a harsh, descending cry drew her attention skyward. An eagle soared overhead. Wings stiff, it banked, stooped.

Pumping once, it increased speed. The last Tate saw of it, it was dropping on some unknown prey. Awed, she felt the bird's arrogant pity for all trapped, earthbound creatures. She remembered the eagle from the day the Violet Tender died, and the one that glared into her eyes, into her mind, up in the Enemy Mountains.

Gan looked up from his table when the Wolf guard admitted her. His smile disappeared immediately. He shook his head. "You can't imagine how much you remind me of Nalatan right now. He wore exactly that expression . . ."

"When he came to tell you he was leaving here. Well, me too."

"You couldn't possibly catch him."

"I'm not looking for him. I'm going off by myself, to stay with the Smalls."

"Who?" Gan refused to believe his ears. "We need you here."

Tate hipped herself up on the table, looked across at Gan. "Something's going on, Gan. It's all over your face. Some troopers saw Jaleeta and me together this morning; they gave us a very strange look. Now I think I know what it was all about." She waggled the finger under his nose. "You ought to see your face. You heard the whispers that prune-faced Abbess told me about, didn't you? My man wouldn't cheat on me. That's a fact."

"What whispers? Who called Nalatan a cheat?" Gan appeared genuinely startled.

"It's not important. The point is, like him, I have to get out of here. There's something I want to do."

"Do? You're risking your life. For what?"

Tate held his gaze with her own. "It's nothing I can explain, but I'll tell you this: If what I have in mind works, it'll benefit you. If not, no loss."

"That's very mysterious. Tell me, do your friends know of this decision?"

"No, and they won't hear about it from you until I'm long gone." Tate got off the table, straightened to go. Gan raised a questioning eyebrow. The expression suggested little cooperation. Tate continued. "I got to thinking today. It dawned on me, I've gotten into a lot of trouble since I came here. Maybe I'm not the contributor I think. I couldn't save my poor dogs. Or my horse. Dodoy saved my life, remember? And Sylah, when that tiger came at us."

"What's wrong with you?" Gan's sharp anger brought Karda's head up in a surprised jerk. "Sylah says the tiger was dead when it hit the ground. Your dogs and horse were the gifts of my tribe. They were bred to live in danger and die in service. That's their world. And mine. And yours. Or so I believed." He paused. "No. I'm right. I know you for what you are. You're the one who's uncertain."

Tate smiled weakly. "Maybe. But I need to think. I won't get anything done looking over my shoulder at that Violet old crow or that snip, Jaleeta."

Gan tensed. "Jaleeta? Why her?"

"A feeling. She irritates me."

Twin red spots showed up on Gan's cheekbones. "You misjudge her. Nalatan may come back while you're in the mountains; how will you know?"

"Tell him to head for the main pass, but don't send him if it makes you shorthanded. In that case, though, please send a runner, or something." She laughed lightly. "Just don't leave me out there in the woods without one fine reason, you hear?" Then, almost instantly, she was quiet, hesitant. "Don't you dare tell him, but I really do want him to come after me. But I really have to find out if he will. I guess what I'm hoping is that we can have a marriage like yours and Neela's. You all are a team. We have to learn how to be one."

Gan moved away from that subject. "You think these Smalls are so good they'll see someone coming for you?"

"Absolutely. That's one reason why I'm going. They've got some interesting skills. Will you apologize to everyone for me, once I'm gone? I don't need any good-byes."

The request hung between them long enough for Tate to nervously shift her weight from foot to foot. Finally, Gan nodded. "I will. Do what you must, but remember, please, how much your friends love you. Nothing foolish. Promise me that."

"No more foolish than my friend, Gan Moondark."

Gan smiled ruefully. "Small comfort in that."

She kissed him on the cheek and was gone. Gan looked after her for a long time, then reached for Karda, scratching his ears. "What have I done, boy? I do love her, you know. Have I become part of her pain? If Nalatan is unfaithful, have I made things worse? If he's hurt her, he's hurt me; what do I do about that?"

Chapter 77

A brilliant sun burned down on the Skan coast, its warmth stark contrast to Lorso's chill mood. He walked the rocky beach alone. Limp notwithstanding, long strides carried him north until intervening hills hid the fort and village of his people from view.

Staring into the sea, he saw kelp tendrils sway and imagination made them Sosolassa's slithering tentacles. Tearing his gaze from that, he concentrated on the wave-battered rock of the headland ahead, and was imagining the throne of Sosolassa, where the god watched his white-rotten, decaying slaves dance attendance on him.

It was such thinking that required Lorso walk alone. His thoughts permitted no confidant. Lately, questions keened in his mind, more insistent, more dangerous than stormwitch song.

If others besides Tears of Jade spoke for the god in the past, what assurance was there that only one should speak for the god in the present?

Lorso stopped abruptly, looking around as if his mind's words roared over the surf's crash. Walking on, he determined to focus better. Experience told him he planned best when he took time to concentrate.

To settle himself, he examined his surroundings. Normally, he paid little attention to the concept of beauty. Beauty this land had, however, in almost overwhelming abundance. Trees, darkly green, cloaked towering mountains. Snow masked the taller crests. Just ahead, a rivulet leaped from a cliff face. The silvered froth of it tumbled eagerly to the cobble beach, raced to embrace the mother sea. Crystal-green combers rose high, charged the beach. Sunshine dappled their spume-crowned heads, blasted shifting, dazzling light patterns through their heaving bodies. They threw themselves at Slavetaker's feet, roaring. Brotherhood.

Lorso struck a fist to his chest, over his heart.

It was evening when he escorted a sour, reluctant Tears of Jade into the All. He felt the eyes of the god, reassuring, and he took the speaker's platform with confidence.

Once the gathered Navigators were quiet, Lorso spoke of Moonpriest's unexplained move to the coast. He complained of the restricted area, where even Skan allies were forbidden entry. Suspicion and anger slicked across an audience heretofore neutral and curious. Lorso thought of oil on water, the way it spread and spread, wringing color from above and below, altering everything it touched. That was what he must have.

To regain Jaleeta.

Words flowed from him, soft-spoken, reasonable. What magic did Moonpriest work? he asked. What friend changed an agreed-upon battle plan without consultation of any kind, then insisted it only reflected a different route of advance? What friend denied landfall to friends? What friend allied Moondance with Church, with no confirmation or collaboration for the Skan? What friend said nothing of religious alliance with the true god, Sosolassa?

As Lorso expected, it was Tears of Jade who asked the first question. "What suggestion do you have, Slavetaker?"

He heard her distrust. And warning. There was another thing, though. Indecision? Fear? No, not fear. Perhaps.

Lorso surreptitiously dried his palms on his coarse woolen trousers. "The great prize is the people of the Three Territories. Kos cries for slaves. Moonpriest blathers of religious converts, meaning manpower for his banners. Every man claimed by Moonpriest is a loss to us, and a man we can be sure we'll have to fight in the future."

Tears of Jade sneered. "I asked for suggestions. You give me facts."

Lorso concentrated on the Navigators. "Baron Ondrat must strike at Gan Moondark's back. Only if we guard against Moonpriest can we assure that the Skan take a proper number of slaves from Ola and Harbundai."

A Navigator said, "But you mean to take Olan slaves."

"I said Ondrat must understand. He need not understand the truth." Enthusiasm lifted Lorso's voice. "Imagine Moonpriest advancing from the south. Moonpriest expects us to come from the sea, take the defending Wolves from behind. Instead, we claim the weather is wrong, our sharkers aren't ready. To keep Moonpriest's confidence, however, we raid Ola and Harbundai, thereby gaining slaves at little or no risk. When Moonpriest is at the walls of Ola, we enter the battle from seaward. Moonpriest will wake to find the Skan holding the castle. We surrender it to him, of course."

A growl of angry disapproval rose from the Navigators. Lorso met it with a broad grin. "We surrender it after negotiations. During those talks our sharkers raid the entire Inland Sea, taking every man, woman, and child they can find. We leave Moonpriest to rule over nothing, to recruit from infants and stragglers."

The gathering howled delight. One Otter Navigator leaped into an exuberant dance, chanting a war song. Another joined him, and another, until all of Otter moved in a tight, rhythmic circle. Laughing, clapping, the other Navigators gathered around. Lorso stepped from the platform into his shoes and joined the crowd.

A moment later, a man tapped his shoulder. Turning, Lorso saw Tears of Jade, eyes glittering, standing on the platform. Several others noticed her at the same time. Discreet nudges, whispered warnings, moved through the crowd. The dancing stumbled to a halt. The singing faded.

Into the expectant silence, Tears of Jade sent her withered, withering rasp. "Skan warriors! Have I not preached that we must destroy Gan Moondark and the witch who calls herself Sylah? Who among you planned to destroy our enemies? None. Until Slavetaker. My son. Share my pride. He is ours."

She extended both hands, tottering. Lorso ran to her embrace. Her arms gripped like hawsers, all gristle and bone, startlingly powerful. Her muttered words were clear. "You will be the greatest of our people. But you must never forget that we—you and I—serve the Skan as the will of the god."

Lorso's mind whirled. The mistlike sense of something like apprehension was in her voice again. He was sure of it. Almost sure. Wasn't he?

"Take me home," Tears of Jade said. "We must talk."

Seated by her fireplace, flames from kindling mottled one side of her face. On the other side, a glowing charcoal brazier merely touched her with a russet glow. From inside her sleeve, a gnarled, bent finger aimed at Lorso. "I know what you want."

Lorso's throat closed. He couldn't breathe. He wanted to speak, knew he couldn't.

Voice tight with impatience, Tears of Jade went on. "Fear the god. Or sink to serve him." The dry, clawlike hand withdrew into the sleeve. When it came out again, it sprinkled something on the charcoal. Smoke writhed up in thick coils. It stank of burnt sea-flesh and ocean water. Lorso's stomach rolled. Tears of Jade's voice crackled. "Do not resist. The smoke is to attract the god. He must have free access to your mind."

Instead of ordering Lorso to fetch water, the old woman rose painfully and did it herself. Sweat tickled Lorso's back, his underarms. He took the opportunity to ease away from the smoke, draw fresher air. Tears of Jade mixed her concoction, handed it to him. Her expression told him he must drink.

Lorso knew of many men who sampled his mother's mixtures in similar circumstances. He remembered nothing good.

The brew was vile, sickly sweet. Lorso gagged violently, pitched up out of his chair. Liquid and saliva erupted. The clinging spray landed on Tears of Jade's robe. She staggered back, flailing thin arms, bony hands, screeching anger. Lorso grabbed a drying cloth, brushing at her while she continued to berate him.

It was the work of a heartbeat to empty the cup. In the dimly lit cabin, the liquid disappeared on the pounded earth floor. To be safe, Lorso stood on the stain. Apologizing profusely, he pretended to down the concoction.

The duel wasn't over. Lorso shivered, wondering what his reaction to the liquid should be. When Tears of Jade noted his movement, her gaze sharpened. Lorso continued to shiver.

Tears of Jade smiled. "Breathe in the smoke, my son. Slavetaker. The smoke and the tea together bring the god. You'll see. What joy you'll know!"

Lorso forced himself to put his head into the fumes rising from the brazier. It hurt his eyes, but his mind remained clear. Tears of Jade droned, telling him to think of the sea's smooth rocking, of lulling ground swells.

Lorso sat back down heavily, still shivering.

Tears of Jade purred on. Then, startling him so badly he almost lost control, he heard the voice of the god. Terrified, he peered through slitted eyes. The voice came from her, resonant, even as it bubbled and hissed. "You are chosen to lead my slaves, the Skan people. You will avenge my spirit woman, Tears of Jade, by killing the betrayer, the one named Jaleeta. Know fear, Slavetaker. Obey. Do you understand?"

"I understand." When Lorso tried to open his eyes, he felt the smoke pressing on his face, blinding, smothering. Woe swept his mind like a tide. The god had spoken directly through his mother.

Jaleeta.

He wanted her. As he wanted nothing else.

The voice of the god burbled in Tears of Jade's ancient mouth once more. "Go now, son of my spirit woman. You have heard my voice, my demand. Obey. *Obey.*"

Lorso shambled outside. The cold night bathed him in freshness, blew rags of fog from his mind.

He spilled out the drink, but she said the drink and the smoke worked together. He saw her thin, desiccated lips, her aged, browned teeth when she spoke.

When the god spoke.

No human had such a voice, such speech. If speech it was. Lorso shuddered, remembering. The god spoke from her mouth. Potion. Smoke. Where was the reality?

He straightened, whispered fiercely, "You are Lorso, who owns Jaleeta. The man who tricked the spirit woman."

He walked to the harbor's edge where the massed sharkers waited to strike Gan Moondark. He squatted, bathed his face in the cold water. At his feet, the water was a swelling, seething blackness, shot through with glints of stars. "Sosolassa. I will give you the man and the witch. Jaleeta is mine. I have served you better than any man. Even a god has obligation. I take what is mine by right."

Rising, he looked out where sea and land were only dark, suggestive masses, things of portent. Until his feet were safely on the road paralleling the harbor, he walked backward facing the sea. Watching. Watching.

The sharker slipped through the channel in the night-cloaked marsh. Long, slender oars whispered entry into still water. Greased leather pads sighed. Whirlpools swirled briefly in the rippling wake. Bordering reeds rustled sleepy irritation.

Soon the wide-spanning oars touched the enclosing vegetation; they rose to the vertical. Four men lay down on the sides of the hull. Using stubby paddles, they propelled her. A sharp hiss from the bow watch changed course to the right. Moments later, the sound of the water against the hull told of a quicker current. The transition point where marsh ended and river began was at hand.

Landfall was a gentle crush of earth against wood. Then cold, hostile silence.

The signal light was quite distant, far away on the flat shore. The bow watch responded to the light with a fox's wailing bark. Skan warriors lowered themselves over the side, silently disappeared into the scrubby growth.

The men approaching from landward made noise. Footsteps slurped in mucky soil. Weapons clanked. Someone stumbled, splashed, cursed aloud. Aboard the sharker, teeth gleamed in predatory, scorning smiles.

Lorso sniffed the air. Dismissing the rich brew of tidelands, he concentrated on what else the faint inland breeze carried. Cattle, in plenty. Horses. The faint tinge of smoke, with a minute flavor of cooking. Fish. Potatoes. Something unexpected plucked at his mind. He tensed, hand on sword.

Sweat. He swallowed laughter. Despite the night's biting cold, the men coming to meet him stank, sweating profusely.

The first call came as question. "Lorso? Is it you?"

Perversely, Lorso refused to answer. Three men, silhouetted against the stars, shifted about anxiously. The next attempt was querulous, moving quickly to bluster. "Lorso? Where are you? Who's there? Speak up. I see your boat."

"Right here." Lorso rose, well within striking distance, savoring their fear. "You are Baron Ondrat."

"Yes. Yes, I am. Baron Ondrat. I'm proud to meet you. These are my personal bodyguards. This marsh can be dangerous. Smugglers. Slavers."

"A wise precaution." Lorso cut across the babble. This incompetent was to be an ally against Moonpriest? On the other hand, cunning got Ondrat this far. He was bad steel, but used properly, he might cut well enough.

The Baron said, "I've arranged a small cabin, on higher ground. It's much warmer, with good food. The maps are there." Unctuous. Too smooth.

Lorso cleared his throat. That signal told his men to attack at the first sign of aggression, either by the Baron or himself. He said, "Our agents made agreement. Talk aboard my sharker."

Ondrat was contrite. "It's but a short distance to the cabin. I'll send a man for the maps, join you on your boat, as agreed. I meant only hospitality."

Lorso considered a moment, then shrugged. "Warm and well-fed sounds good, Baron," adding, "We must be quick. My sharker must be hidden by dawn." Ondrat couldn't know that Lorso's last phrase instructed half his crew of thirty to follow covertly.

Entering the cabin, Lorso instantly regretted his decision. Candles blazed everywhere. The room was far too warm. Scented smoke clotted his nose, deadening smell. Worse, his night vision was destroyed.

When the food came, it was mostly wildcow and pork—no fish whatever—

and steamed vegetables. Ondrat hadn't even the brains to determine that Skan hardly ever cooked vegetables and rarely ate red meat, even when it was cooked properly crisp. This stuff came in limp, bloody slabs. Somehow, Lorso got through it all. Only the beer was decent. He risked a meager taste. His head remained clear, even if his stomach growled. Lorso started mildly enough. "Your shore watchers are comfortable with the way they meet our scouts? We can continue the arrangement?"

Ondrat used a cloth to wipe his mouth. "My people complain that your men are too silent. They frighten the watchers." He laughed hugely.

"Another question; we lost a man some time ago. We hear rumors of a Skan balancebar wrecked on your coast. Is there anything to it? Why was there no report from your watchers?"

"There was no wreck, no man. We'd protect such a survivor, of course. You know the Skan are hated by everyone but us. Any discovered elsewhere would die quickly."

"Perhaps not that quickly. It takes more than hard feelings to kill us."

Ondrat forced a grin. "Shall I tell the watchers to be alert for him?"

"No need. Sosolassa holds him by now." Lorso considered telling Ondrat of the Skan vengeance on Domel's family. Terror had a salutary effect on potential traitors. He decided Ondrat wouldn't handle pressure well now. The example of Domel's disgrace would keep.

Spreading a large folded cloth on the cleared table, Ondrat beamed at Lorso. Guttering candles transformed the white linen into a spread of soft gold. On it was an illustration of the castle. Archers peered through crenels. Carefully drawn catapults aimed heavy bolts. Leclerc's pumps stood at the ready. A counterattack force lurked in the waterfall garden. Two more hid behind the abbey buildings.

Lorso ran his right hand across the surface of the picture. Ondrat watched with a sort of appalled fascination, as a man might spy on another caressing his lover. When Lorso grunted deep in his chest and crushed the center of the painted castle in a triumphant fist, Ondrat shrank back.

Slowly, almost reluctantly, Lorso replaced the cloth, smoothed it out.

Ondrat made a gesture meant to assert his own claim. He put a fist on a corner of the map. "Slaves from Ondrat have worked on this castle for generations. I know it better than the usurper, Moondark.

"Now, assume you're King of Ola. The bulk of your men are gone, resisting Windband. Describe your defenses. When and where do you expect attack? Where are you weakest? Why?

"Fortunately, I know exactly how Gan Moondark means to defend. We'll make him regret his mistakes."

After Ondrat's summary, Lorso was sorely tempted to ask him to detail what improvements he'd make. For a man unaccustomed to defending a fortified position, Gan seemed to have considered everything, even to external positions that would cause an attacker to deploy early, exposing him to the long-range fire of the catapults.

Little by little, Lorso determined the interior organization of the castle. When Ondrat wondered why that was so important, Lorso explained with a chilling smile. "Your Skan allies assure complete victory, Baron. I have to know where Gan will hide his wife and brat. Rats in a nest, Baron; kill all, or suffer them again. Where will the witch, Sylah, try to hide?"

"The War Healer?" Ondrat blinked rapidly.

"Her magic is nothing to Skan warriors. We're protected by our god."

Ondrat automatically started to point, pulled back the finger as if burned. He used his chin to gesture. "There. In the Iris Abbey." He shook his head, waved dismissing hands. "No, I'm wrong. She'll take her Chosens and Priestesses and her alien friends inside the castle. With Gan and the others. Yes. She'll fight."

"The better to kill them all at once. The escaped Skan slave—where does she sleep?"

Ondrat braced his wrist on the edge of the table to damp his trembling. He indicated Jaleeta's quarters. "She's practically in Gan's bed." The lame joke elicited a disapproving squint. Ondrat reacted swiftly. "She's very influential with Gan's closest friend; we know in advance every move the Wolf units make. Then there's Leclerc, the magic. He follows her like a calf, tells her anything. I've heard whispers that the Black Lightning's husband left Ola over some misadventure involving her. Now the Black Lightning's gone too, and no one knows if either of them will ever be back. Watching Jaleeta is like watching poison work."

Lorso dared not respond immediately to Ondrat's nervous chattering. Poison. Tears of Jade used that word, long ago. When he straightened, the others were watching him, fearful. He stared at them, one at a time, making them see Slavetaker. The day was coming when the memory of that face would turn their guts to water. He said, "I go to Windband. One moon from this night, you and our other Olan allies must be constantly alert for the arrival of more sharkers than any man has ever seen. Our massed fleet will leave harbor like Sosolassa himself rising to claim his slaves. We may have no time to warn you of our coming; Moonpriest has hinted at excessive ambition."

Warily, Ondrat said, "We recall other sharker appearances. What's this of no warning? Or Moonpriest's treachery?"

Lorso inhaled. Thoughtfully. First this self-important piece of dung hinted at Jaleeta's involvement with other men. Now he wanted to quibble over the Skan attack. "Trust us. No matter when Moonpriest starts his advance, your Skan allies will arrive before he reaches your borders. We claim no Olan land. But what we want north of you, we take. Slaves. Property. Livestock. Anything."

"You help us against Windband. If it's necessary?"

"During the war, certainly. After that?" Lorso shrugged casually. "Without access to all the Inland Sea, free of interference from your For pirates, we risk too much to reach your territory to the south. I realize that's where Moonpriest will attack you. Sorry."

Almost groaning, Ondrat said, "We can agree to your access. Myself and the other Barons will find a way to deal with Wal and his For. In exchange for protection."

Affable, Lorso reached over to clap a hand on Ondrat's shoulder, then rose. He started rolling up the map, hesitated. His gaze wandered, focused on a point beyond the wall. Ondrat watched curiously. Lorso shook his head, apparently dismissing a vagrant notion.

"What is it?" Ondrat asked.

"I thought I might have a solution to your problem, but it's not possible. The Skan want only peace and trade with Ola. Our hatred is for Gan Moondark and the witch, Sylah, their empire and evil religion. If Gan were overthrown early enough, we'd have no need for further presence here. Unless you called for help against Windband, of course."

Pale, hands up as if expecting a blow, Ondrat pushed back against his chair. "The Wolves are too loyal, too strong. I'm a warrior, Lorso, and I consider myself a brave one. But I'm not a fool. I won't strike at Gan Moondark until I'm certain he's weak enough to kill."

"Wisely said, my friend. The easiest fool to kill is one who thinks he's clever. Be patient. Gan Moondark is finished. We'll burn him, his family, and all his loyalists. Soon." He stretched. "And now I go. Secrecy is our greatest weapon; the sun must not find me in your waters."

"We'll show you the way." Ondrat got up, gesturing to his guards.

Lorso's quick wave stopped them. He was out the door before anyone could move, the door closing with a barely audible thud.

The trio in the cabin watched the door. One exhaled, grating against the extended silence. "Demons. Skan are demons," he said.

Ondrat backhanded the man. "Quiet!" His whispered command was gravelly. "What if he's listening? You'll get us killed."

The guard spat. Red-flecked spittle marred the wall. Sullenly, he said, "We are three to his one. And five more a shout away."

Seeing the near-derision in the face of the other guard, Ondrat put on a knowing, superior expression. He drew himself to full height. "I didn't mean he'd kill us, you brainless wart. If we kill Lorso, we lose the support of the Skan. Then Windband defeats Gan Moondark. That's how you'll get us killed. Can't you understand anything?"

Outside, prone, almost touching the wall, Lorso stifled laughter that edged close to hysteria. The fish was in the net. It was a good feeling.

Silent as the bone-chilling fog piling up in the hollows, he worked backward on his stomach, melted into the night. When he heard the faint rustle of his warriors falling in behind him, he allowed himself to mouth the words rattling in his mind. "The easiest fool to kill is one who thinks he's clever."

Tears of Jade shielded her eyes against the flat rays of the setting sun.

Since shortly after the midday meal, she'd waited in her sedan chair, watching, waiting for Lorso. Ever since the vision of him as man-ship, with the crew singing his name in something like reverence, her mind twisted uncomfortably while he was at sea. Something was happening between him and the world, something that excluded her.

That could not be.

But his mind was no longer the same. It maddened Tears of Jade to know of subtle, insidious changes she couldn't identify, much less control. Of course he lusted after the woman; that was the stone to hone his steel. Of course he yearned for complete independence; that was the measure of strength. Tears of Jade must dictate where that sharpened edge was applied, how much strength drove it.

Suddenly, the sharker was clearly visible. Her introspection had allowed it to close unnoticed. Furiously cursing her chair slaves, she ordered them to stand away while she clambered out.

The glare of sun on sea hurt Tears of Jade's eyes. She closed them. In the instant, the god claimed her. There was no chance to struggle. The sharker was the same as in the previous vision. The same man-boat, the same rhythmic chant. But the Lorso face at the bow was cold, ice and steel. It looked into Tears of Jade, into her mind. The face knew no fear of her.

Below her, the true Lorso looked up to her from his deck. He waved. She waved back. There stood reality. Everything was as it should be.

Chapter 78

Nalatan had never been so far off the ground in his life. There were mountains in the Dry, and sheer cliffs that sucked the breath out of a man and made other parts of his body behave badly. They were solid, though. Dirt. Stone.

People were not meant to be in trees. No matter the base was too huge for two men to reach around; the part Nalatan presently clung to was barely as big around as himself. The branch underfoot was considerably smaller. Sea breezes pressed gently, but determinedly. The trees responded by swaying gracefully. Back and forth. Back and forth. Nalatan swallowed hard. He reflected on the ignominy of being discovered because of upset stomach. He felt like an incompetent bird.

A shout startled him. Craning about, he caught movement, far below. Another Windband patrol. It took all night for him to penetrate Moonpriest's forbidden area and climb his tree. He'd hoped that, once inside the perimeter, security would be relaxed. No informant warned of patrols that crisscrossed the entire area. Still, it was very unlikely he'd be seen. Unfortunately, his view was less than perfect and he had no idea what he was looking at.

Perched on a bluff above the beach and pounding surf, tall poles held up things that looked like oar blades. They rotated in the wind, their groaning and squealing carrying all the way to Nalatan's perch. Outside the excluded area, those who'd heard the eerie complaint blamed it on demons.

Whatever the towers and paddles did, Nalatan knew they were somehow connected to the incredible copper towers ranged behind them. Already growing green with salt-mist patina, they were three-pronged, like huge forks. Partially hidden in a trench paralleling the bluff, they required water. Slaves hauled goatskins up scaffolding steps to empty them into the central tube, which was by far the taller of the three. Other slaves seemed to be drawing off something from the two flanking tubes. Whatever they were getting—and they were as constantly busy as bees at a blossom—went into large round containers.

Slightly north of the trench holding the copper towers, a small stream flowed through a lush little valley. Nalatan noted that the waterskin bearers disappeared in that direction, which explained where the water came from. Not that any of it made the least bit of sense.

There was a wallkiller on the flat ground of the meadow, half again the size of the one he'd seen in Kos. The counterbalancing stone weights were huge, the throwing basket immense. Nalatan imagined that monster's missiles hurtling at Ola's walls. At Donnacee.

Nightfall was most welcome. Nalatan started his climb down dissatisfied with what he understood. He took some solace in knowing he'd seen, however. Donnacee would make sense of it all. Along with Leclerc and Bernhardt and the others.

The others. Jaleeta.

Nalatan slowed, stopped. The image of that beautiful, wicked face made his hands anxious on their purchase, his knees weak. A few words from that enticing mouth, and he had no life. Who'd believe he ran away to avoid her?

His hand slipped. Grabbing, clawing, he felt dry, crumbling bark tear loose. He clutched the trunk with his knees, wrapped arms around the trunk. An angry squirrel scolded. Bits of dislodged bark pattered on the forest floor. He hung motionless, not breathing. No one shouted challenge.

As soon as he had a solid branch underfoot, Nalatan looped his climbing rope around the tree. Trembling hands looped the free end under his belt. At every branch, he had to release the rope, pass it under the obstacle, then secure it again.

The last part of the descent was even trickier. With no branches for holds, Nalatan angled out from the great trunk, keeping the line tight. Flipping the rope in tempo with short, stiff-legged steps, he walked down to solid, wonderful earth.

He moved swiftly through the forest. The guards were slack; all locals had long since fled the area. More, the unburned bones of trespassers were prominently displayed on roads approaching the site. Moonpriest's punishment was swift, brutal, and extended beyond death itself.

Murmured conversation halted Nalatan. A man demanded quiet. Someone laughed. Nalatan crawled ahead. The drone of conversation fell behind. When it disappeared entirely, he rose to stand against a tree, blending with it. Patiently, he sensed the darkness. When he was satisfied, he resumed his journey.

Shortly after dawn, a hunched, hooded figure on horseback approached the point of Nalatan's escape. Four lounging guards rose jerkily, standing away from their fire. The rider ignored them, scanning the ground. Reining in, he pushed back his hood with a left hand that hung at a peculiar angle, the fingers clawlike, immobile. A mangled, hawk-fierce visage glared down at the guards. The right eye was covered by a black patch. Fox cleared his throat, spat. "Who had first watch?"

A man gestured. "We all did. It was quiet. We kept each other company. Bentek took next watch."

"I said first watch. What did you see? Hear?"

"Nothing. I said, it was qui—"

Snorting surprise and pain, Fox's horse leaped forward. The nomad speaking had no chance, took the full weight of that charge, flew backward in a yelling heap. Trying to rise, he collapsed again under clubbing blows from the flat of Fox's sodal. Blood oozed from ugly split-skin wounds.

Fox dismounted haltingly. His movements on the ground exposed a twisted right foot. The remaining three guards huddled away from their companion.

Pointing with the sodal, Fox shouted at the trio, "Here. Ten paces from your lazy, stupid hides. Someone passed last night, before dew. Where were you?"

"Here, Fox. Awake, on guard. There was no one." It was the first speaker, wiping blood from his eyes.

Fox spit on him. He turned to the others, the wrecked foot causing him to swoop. "Can't you see the sign? Footprints. Here."

The men looked guilty. One muttered, "We thought we heard a noise. It was first watch."

Fox remounted. "Get your horses," he told the cowering trio, and to the disgraced senior man, "You, too. The intruder dies, or you do."

The sight of pursuit pounding down the valley behind him tightened Nalatan's stomach hard enough to drive out the hunger pains. Even as he ran for his life, he marveled at how the leader of the five read tracks. Nalatan forced more speed. If he could reach his horse, the advantage was his. His pursuers were on weary mounts.

The horse was where it should be, none the worse for the experience of spending a night in an abandoned house. It followed Nalatan outside calmly, until it sensed his excitement. It capered like a goat in the rank growth where a vegetable garden flourished in better times. With Nalatan aboard, it leaped to a full gallop as if enjoying this strange, different world.

Nalatan silently blessed it. Now all he had to do was reach the river ahead of his pursuers. And hope the River who was supposed to haul him across the Mother River was true to his word.

Far behind, Fox halted his group. Studying Nalatan's tracks, he pulled at his chin, deep in thought. When he spoke, it was essentially for his own benefit. "No ordinary man. Too fast, too much stamina. What, then?" Silent for a long breath, he exhaled slowly. "No Kossiar. No fish-stinking River, either. Headed east. Runs like a cursed Dog warrior; he'll want across the river." He pointed at the guard leader. "You. Come with me. You three follow the tracks. Can you do that?"

They nodded vigorously. Fox sneered at their eagerness, whipping his lathered horse into a gallop north and east. With a helpless look at his friends, the leader hammered off after him.

For Nalatan, the first appearance of the river was an elation. Brown-green, its misted surface suggested warmth, a relief from the drifted white remains of the winter storms. Nalatan was congratulating himself when he saw the two riders quartering a field far off to his left. This couldn't be pursuit. No one would cut an angle after him. How could they?

Someone had outguessed him. They had a clearer route to the waiting River and his sailer than he did. He needed time to get on the sailer, cast off, get out of arrow range. He slapped his horse's rump. It vaulted forward, tripped. Rattled, it bucked furiously. Nalatan didn't realize he'd been thrown until blurred vision revealed the back end of the horse disappearing into brush. Silvery horseshoes glinted derision.

He ran. Crashing through brush, vaulting downed logs, scrambling up crumbling gully walls, he conjured images of Moonpriest's vengeance. He heard Conway's horror of Moonpriest's rattlesnakes. He remembered the description of the moon altar, the unspeakable lightning that cooked a man.

He braced against a tree, breathing hard. The riders were in constant view now, on the trail paralleling the river. The floodplain was grazing land. Just ahead was the clump of brush where the River hid with his sailer. Open ground from the tree line to the sailer's cover meant exposure. Interception.

Unless the riders would pursue him into the forest, negating their mounted advantage. Nalatan dashed out into the open, faked astonishment at the seeing the oncoming riders. He retreated at a run.

A voice shouted for him to stop. It was so stupid Nalatan looked over his shoulder. To his delight, one rider galloped after him, alone. The second, wheeling his horse in frustration, screamed orders.

Nalatan almost felt sorry for the eager victim. Dodging through the trees, Nalatan lured him farther from the road. Soon the nomad was in a narrow draw, forging through a grove of young alders, some so close together horse and rider had to select passage around the clumped trunks. Choosing the place for confrontation, Nalatan wondered what could make a man so anxious to prove himself that he abandoned his wits.

Nalatan feigned a limp. The nomad screamed a war cry, lashed his mount into a weird tree-dodging charge. Nalatan whirled, ran back the way he'd come. The nomad, surprised, managed a clumsy cross-body swipe. Nalatan parried the sword with his bar, drove the iron ball full into the nomad's face. The man tumbled out of the saddle, one foot stirrup-bound. Frightened, the horse ran wildly through the trees. Briefly, the nomad tried to get free. After hitting a few tree trunks, he flopped about brokenly. Thoroughly spooked by its macabre hindrance, the horse stampeded away.

Nalatan hurried back toward the river. His second enemy waited, far enough into the grazing ground to keep a long stretch of the river road under observation. Sitting there, this man made Nalatan think of a bird of prey, knowing it's seen, uncaring, certain of its prowess.

Nalatan walked out of the forest east of the rider. Almost leisurely, the mounted man moved to apprehend. Nalatan broke into a trot. If he reached the river, his accomplice might see him swimming and sail to his rescue. He was relieved to see his foe carried no bow. Nevertheless, that pleasure faded quickly as the rider drew a sodal. In the gray light there was no glitter, but a cold, composed gleam.

Nalatan checked his grip on the parrying bar, drew his own sword. It looked embarrassingly short contrasted to the long sodal.

The horse stretched out, galloping. The rider's hood blew back. Profoundly scarred on the left side, a black eye-patch stood out against the flesh. There was something vaguely familiar about him, but Nalatan dismissed all thoughts save avoiding the near-lancelike sodal. The first pass was classic, exactly as the brotherhood master taught; the iron bar deflected the sodal. Nalatan raced on. He gained a few paces before the horse was charging on him again. Once more Nalatan avoided the sodal.

The river beckoned.

The rider changed tactics. Advancing at a slow trot, the sodal was high, ready to thrust or slash. He maneuvered between Nalatan and the river.

Swords and parrying bar clashed, the battle-song of steel shattering the peace of the meadow. The rider shouted hoarse, guttural curses. Nalatan answered with a war cry.

The sodal's tip bit into Nalatan's chest, spun him, dropped him facedown. Reflexes born of unstinting training made him roll, even as shock tried to assimilate the fact of blood cascading down his chest. The sodal plunged into the turf, flipped up a clod. A part of Nalatan's mind registered dangling grass roots flying over his head.

His counter was pure instinct. Rising he dropped his sword, swung the parrying bar with both hands. The sodal deflected it. The iron ball cracked into the horse's skull. The one eye Nalatan could see rolled up. Momentum carried the stunned animal onto its nose. From such a composed, fierce fighter, the shriek of utter terror as the horse rolled was strangely excessive.

The animal rose, staggered off drunkenly, completely addled. The rider thrashed clumsily, uncoordinated. The frightened River, mooring line in hand, made a three-sign, watching Nalatan race toward him. Together, they leaped onto the long, slim sailer. Light as a leaf, its rib-and-hide construction supple as the fish it resembled, it arrowed into the current under the force of their impact. The River hoisted the triangular sail. The tiny boat, almost swamped under its burden, still sped away from shore. Far downstream, men on the deck of a moored sharker glanced at the sailer and went about their business.

Neither man spoke until they were well out into the water. The River said, "You're bleeding."

"I know." Nalatan stuffed a piece of shirt in the hole as he spoke. "Hit a rib. Maybe broke it. It'll heal."

A cry from shore brought them both upright, staring. The one-eyed man stood on the bank, sodal raised. Behind him, three riders hurried to join him. He ignored them. "Nalatan! Next time, I kill you. I swear it."

"Who are you?"

"Donnacee knows. Ask her about Fox Eleven. Tell her I come soon."

Nalatan grabbed the mast, hauled himself upright. The thinking part of his mind refused to accept that the dandy, straight Fox he knew was this twisted scrap. His soul heard nothing but the name of his wife. Nalatan's words grated, metallic. "Turn around. Take me back."

The River shook his head. Nalatan raised the parrying bar. The River's eyes grew huge. He swallowed. "You'll just drown if you kill me. Him and his friends will kill both of us. I'm not fool enough to go back there."

Nalatan lowered the weapon. From the receding shore, Fox called again. "Nalatan! Ask her about the only real man she ever knew."

Nalatan stared away, at the far side of the river. It surprised him to discover that hatred was such a physical thing. He removed the cloth from his wound, half expecting to see something vile and frenzied leap from the punctured flesh. But there was only blood.

Chapter 79

Nalatan woke with senses at full efficiency, muscles ready to respond.

A rooster crowed derision.

Nalatan smiled. He deserved to be laughed at. Louis Leclerc's farm wasn't the dark forest. The snug bed wasn't any carefully hidden den. Luxuriating in the sheer comfort of it—linen sheets, soft mattress, quilted down covers—he stretched hugely. At the rooster's ringing insistence, he rose, flinging aside the bedding, anxious to get the day under way. He hurried to get into fresh underclothes and heavy wool trousers, grimacing at embrace of the frigid material. Thick wool socks and serviceable, scuffed boots followed.

A brightly glazed water jar and basin rested on a wooden cabinet. Snorting, splashing, Nalatan washed. Lathering to shave, he blinked at the hollow-eyed mask staring back from a polished silver mirror. He made a face at the gaunt man; Nalatan had a wife who'd fatten him up. The ugly rascal in the mirror would have to fend for himself.

Leclerc supplied razor and strop. Nalatan drew the fine steel across the leather rhythmically, caught up in thoughts of Donnacee. He remembered Leclerc's minute hesitation when he asked if she was back in Ola. It nagged. But if she were there, Leclerc wouldn't say he didn't know. He wouldn't dare.

Nalatan was grinning when he came out of the small bedroom. Leclerc and Bernhardt were already at the table. The housekeeper watched from the kitchen door. All returned the smile. Bernhardt came to him, hugged him, kissed his cheek.

Louis laughed aloud. "You've embarrassed him. Shame on you, Kate."

Her smile was mischievous, fixed on her guest. "It's his own fault for being so rugged and handsome. I just couldn't help myself. I'm so glad you're safe. We've been worried. It's been a long time."

Leclerc said, "It's also time for me to tell you exactly what the situation is with Donnacee."

Nalatan looked up, tense. Leclerc paled, but his jaw was firm. Words rattled out of him. "You asked if she's in Ola. I told you I didn't know. I thought it best to let you get some rest before giving you the details. She and Conway got here just after you left. She went back into the mountains. She told Gan there was something she wanted to do. Like you, she didn't want to stay inside walls. For all I know, she's come back. But I don't really think so."

Still as death, Nalatan held Leclerc's gaze until the other man could stand it no longer. Louis looked away, waving his hands. "Gan tried to talk her into staying in Ola."

Rasping, Nalatan asked, "She was told I'd be back soon?"

Bernhardt answered, "She knew you'd be back, yes."

Inhumanly remote, Nalatan swung his head her way. "You were there?"

"Well, no."

"Then you don't know what was said. Or not said. How long was she in Ola? Who else 'advised' her? What's been said about me?"

Bernhardt quailed under that look, and Leclerc rose, moved to stand beside her. "No one advises Donnacee. No one's said anything about you. Certainly Kate didn't have anything to do with Donnacee's leaving. You're frightening her. Stop it."

At the crisp demand, Nalatan jerked. He looked to Leclerc, seething. What he saw shamed him. The smaller man, a protective arm across the stricken Bernhardt's shoulder, stood firm. Fear painted his face.

Nalatan sagged. He looked down at the table. When he linked the fingers of his hands, he was sickened to realize the right hand had been on the hilt of his knife. He said, "Forgive me, please. This is bitter news." While they murmured reassurance and Leclerc resumed his seat, Nalatan phrased his next questions. "Did you see her before she left? Did she speak of her reasons to anyone but Gan?"

"It was very sudden," Bernhardt answered. "She only said good-bye to Conway because he saw her leaving. She told him exactly what she told Gan."

"Not like her." Nalatan shook his head. "She lived in Harbundai. Inside the walls. She lived here, in Ola. Without complaint. Something happened."

Leclerc said, "She said there was something she had to do. By herself, with the Smalls."

"Smalls? From the Enemy Mountains to the south? Here?"

"Not here, exactly. Smalls came north." Leclerc briefly told Nalatan of the events of the Tate-Conway-Lanta trip.

When the name of Fox was mentioned, Nalatan rose. "That filth. Moonpriest's war chief. Did she injure him?"

Bernhardt winced. "He's dead. Conway tied him to a horse and set it free."

Quieting, Nalatan sat down again. "He recognized me from the fight at the Door. I wondered what happened to him. He's crippled now; left hand and arm almost useless, right ankle broken, left eye gone. But he lives. He made me believe he hurt her. Is she injured?"

Leclerc nodded. "Not by him. A rock fell on her hands. She's fine now."

"I should have been there. She wouldn't let me."

Again, Bernhardt tried to catch Leclerc's eye. The man rigidly refused to look in her direction. He said, "We're a different people, Nalatan. Not like you, or Gan, or anyone else. She'll come back when she can."

"I let her go. I wasn't here when she came back."

The housekeeper picked that moment to reenter, carrying a wooden platter heaped with griddle cakes. Beaming, she announced, "The cook at the castle said these were your favorite, Nalatan." The tableau registered on her. Her face fell. The happy, brisk step stopped.

"Thank you." Nalatan struggled for manners. The confused woman put the tray on the table, hurried away. Nalatan put cakes on his plate, buttered them, poured dark-gold honey. Forking up a bite, he gestured with it. "The body needs food. I won't get anything this good for a long time."

Apprehensive, Bernhardt asked the logical question. "Why not?"

"Because the ride back to the Dry is hard, and I burn everything I cook."

"Not so fast." Leclerc affected casualness, helping himself to cakes from the platter. He let Nalatan wait while he prepared them before going on. "I sent riders to the castle while you ate last night. I asked Gan to come here."

"That's nothing to me. You've told me what he said."

"He sent fresh riders back immediately. He wants to talk to you."

"I have my own wants. None of them are here. Not anymore."

"Nalatan," Bernhardt chided gently. She came to him. He continued to eat, ignoring her. She persisted. "I know you're angry about Donnacee. I don't blame you. She didn't think you'd be back so soon, that's all. If you leave, how will she feel when she finds you're gone? And Gan's your friend. At least hear what he has to say. It may not even be about Donnacee."

Leclerc agreed. "It probably isn't about her. If that was it, wouldn't he ask you to come to him? He's coming here for a reason."

"To see the things you make." Nalatan pointed, almost accusing. "Sylah's books are here."

Flinching, Leclerc was defensive. He pulled the offending volumes from their shelf, put them on the table as if making an offering. "Only these two. And the red one, of Conway's."

"The one he said we must never mention. But he gives it to you, out here, unprotected."

Leclerc ran his fingers across the cover. "There's something here. I have to figure out what it is."

"I don't care." Nalatan started to rise.

Bernhardt's hand on his shoulder stopped him. "This is ridiculous. You and Tate are as bad as Conway and Lanta. You've made life miserable for each other. You're in love, yet you impose these foolish requirements on each other. It's destroying you, and I want you to stop it. You're brave. Do it."

Nalatan looked utterly baffled for a moment, and then he resumed eating. To Leclerc, he said, "I owe it to Gan Moondark to tell him what I've seen. I'll wait for him." Then, for Bernhardt, "I appreciate what you're doing. It's too late. But before you criticize me and Donnacee, look at yourselves. Our fault is pride. Very well. Now judge yourselves." He left a silence that ached like a wound.

They were all pleased by Gan's early arrival, meeting him in a solemn row on the roofed front porch of Leclerc's house. Securing his horse to the hitching rail, he addressed them formally. "I know you, my friends. Nalatan's return should be a happy event. What troubles you?"

Sensitive protocol was involved in the response. As owner of the home, it was Leclerc's right to answer first. His primary responsibility, however, was the satisfaction of his guests. Leclerc deferred to Bernhardt with a glance and nod. She, in turn, gestured at Nalatan. He cleared his throat. "My wife returned to the Enemy Mountains."

Gan marveled at the complexity of inference, of tonal shading. Only someone privy to his and Nalatan's last conversation would understand all the forces at work. Gan felt he had a foot on the finely balanced trigger of a deadfall. "I told her you agreed to carry out a mission for me. She was disappointed to have missed you. I believe she used the anger as excuse. She has a project, she said."

Head up, nostrils flaring, Nalatan struck directly at the heart of his concern. "What's been said of me, since I left?"

"I listen to rumors. I don't repeat them. Besides, I have greater problems."

Bernhardt edged closer to Leclerc. "Come in. We're all freezing out here. I'll get tea. There's trouble?"

Inside, sitting down at the table, Leclerc reopened the conversation. "What's happened?"

"Slave raids. Windband and Rivers, east of here. Striking north of the Mother River."

"At least they're far away. There aren't many people there, either." It was Bernhardt, coming from the kitchen with steaming teapot and cups. The prickly scent of blackberry leaves and wild ginger warmed the room.

As the pot moved from hand to hand, Gan destroyed Bernhardt's sanguine view. "Moonpriest torments me. If I don't react, I'm seen as weak. If I do, I have to march men all the way there to attack small, fast-mounted raiding parties. If they wait for me to arrive, which is unlikely, they'll run and circle and run some more until they exhaust my stolid Olan Wolves. Worst of all, the men I send reduce our defensive strength here."

Leclerc shrugged helplessly. "What's the answer?"

There was something much like relief in Gan's smile. He glanced at Nalatan, tantalizingly suggestive, too quick to read. "Following me this morning is a full hundred of the Ola Wolfpack. We march to attack the raiders."

Nalatan said, "What of Moonpriest? Will he attack when he hears you're gone from the castle?"

"Too early, I think. Anyhow, the prospect of a hundred Wolves will make him nervous. The slave raids aren't specifically intended to pull me out. He needs the manpower to move supplies and for laborers to support his attack."

Leclerc said, "You're sure he's coming, then?"

"He'll come. Early spring."

Leclerc leaned back in his chair, contemplative, staring at mist whorls like a man reading portents. "I need silver. Quite a bit."

Bernhardt was astonished. "You never mentioned silver."

Leclerc shook his head, concentrating on Gan. "We have some?"

Gan held out open hands. "Whatever you need. Go to Emso. He's in charge while I'm away. He knows where the stores are."

Leclerc grimaced. Bernhardt said, "Leave that to me."

Coldly, Gan said, "Emso acts for me. Tell him I said you're to have all the silver you want. Without questions."

"Questions!" Leclerc slapped his forehead with his palm. "No one's asked Nalatan what he learned on his mission. What fools we are."

No one argued the point. Nalatan described his route south, told of falling in with River People who provided support. Until the matter of the triple tower structures came up, Leclerc almost dozed through the recital. At that, however, he sat bolt upright. Bernhardt's attentiveness rose, equally.

Leclerc heard the description through, then drew Bernhardt off to the side. "You were right. Windmills for power. Electrolysis of water. Large ceramic spheres. Exactly what you predicted. Hydrogen."

"And oxygen. Use the wallkiller to start fires, then throw the spheres full of flammable gas. Bombs. Larger fires. Now aren't you glad you built those pumps?"

He hugged her. "Oh, we're a pair, we are." Then, sobering, "But how do we defend against gas bombs?"

"Destroy the wallkiller. And educate the people. Any explosions should be low-order, do no more damage than a large rock. Beat the fear, defeat the weapon."

Leclerc agreed. Choosing words carefully, they explained to Gan and Nalatan that the towers "changed" the water, which was then put in the spheres. The latter were probably designed to be thrown by the wallkiller; where they landed, they would start fires. The two warriors made three-signs. They asked no questions. Miracles from the aliens might be frightening, but they'd also become commonplace.

When Nalatan stood up, Gan did the same. Nalatan waited, wary. Gan said, "We have to talk." They stepped outside, bundling up against the cold. Gan's dogs wagged heavy tails in greeting. Immediately aware of the tension between the two men, they quieted, crowding close to Gan, intent on Nalatan. He ignored them.

Far away, the war drum of the Olan Wolves rumbled advance.

Marshaling his thoughts, Gan cast back to Donnacee's last conversation with him. She said she wanted Nalatan to come after her, but she made a specific point of saying Nalatan shouldn't be sent if his loss would be missed. No man was better suited to interdict Moonpriest's slavers.

Gan was uncomfortable with that rationale. He decided to move the considerations to another level. "You'd be surprised at how much the Chosens have learned since you left. The Church women enlisted Jaleeta to help them. She's very good with the children. Very gentle, very forgiving."

The idea of Jaleeta having to forgive anyone was darkly amusing to Nalatan. Sarcasm glinted off his answer. "A well-hidden talent. But I shouldn't say that. I really don't know her."

Gan hated the answer. It smacked of strong dislike. It was far from evidence of anything. But disturbing. It could mean anything.

For his part, Nalatan didn't care. The whole conversation was a waste. Donnacee was gone. Again.

He wished he could hate her.

Gan decided he had no more time to waste on emotional tangles. There was no one as good as Nalatan to stop Windband's raids. He said, "I need your help."

Nalatan was dubious. "I'll be blunt. I feel no trust from you. I'm not sure I can be your friend any longer. I won't be your enemy. Let me go home."

"My cavalry is plowhorses. The riders are apple pickers and clam diggers; tough, loyal, and likely to fall off. Help them, or the raiders will butcher them."

"Bad luck. I think you blame me for Donnacee's leaving Ola. Tell me why."

"Only when I have you together. When we return to Ola."

"What if I'm killed?"

"Then no rumor will concern you."

"Very clever. What if you're killed?"

Gan wheeled around slowly. His gaze was level, steel cold. "My work isn't done. But if it should happen, avenge me. Do you value our friendship that much?"

Grinning crookedly, Nalatan moved to return inside. Over his shoulder, he said, "You're a born king, aren't you? Devious as a frog in muck."

"Flatterer. You're with me, then?"

"Until we return to Ola. After that? It depends on you."

The column wound out of the forest where the trail bisected Leclerc's farm. The two men on the porch moved toward each other, looked to the roaring, demanding drum.

CHAPTER 80

"HE WANTS WHAT?" EMSO JUTTED HIS JAW, REMINDING SYLAH OF A PARTICULARLY VICIOUS dog that guarded a meat stall in the city's market. The animal couldn't be tempted to touch a scrap from its master's counter. Nothing else—including the legs of passersby—was safe.

Beside Sylah, Bernhardt pulled back her shoulders. "You heard. Silver. Gan approved it."

"Where is he, then? And why didn't Gan speak to me?"

Emso's suspicion provoked Sylah beyond manners. "You doubt Church. You insult."

Uncertainty eroded Emso's truculence. "What does Leclerc need with silver? I have a right to know. I'm responsible to Gan for all supplies."

Bernhardt spoke up again. "Gan said he gets anything he wants."

Emso considered retort. He bit it back when Neela entered with Jaleeta. "I wasn't arguing against Gan's decision."

Neela's eyebrows arched. "Argument? What trouble is this?"

Sylah answered, "Kate brought a request from Louis. The misunderstanding was my fault. Emso was doing his job."

Emso didn't bother to thank her. To Neela, he said, "In the past, he's always wanted copper. There's plenty of that in the godkills. Now it's silver. Why not gold? And it's all for magic."

"That's not true." Bernhardt's eyes darted, nervous. Still, her voice was firm. "What Louis does is intelligent, not magic. He'll do more, too. You'll see. This is just the beginning."

Grumbling, Emso insisted on leading the way to the treasury. When it became apparent where they were going, Neela and Sylah exchanged glances, then stopped. Puzzled, Emso waited for explanation. Neela supplied it. "That way is where King Altanar imprisoned Sylah and me. We go no closer."

The other women murmured sympathetic understanding. Emso told Bernhardt, "Most of it's in ingots, about so." He described a form with his hands. Bernhardt closed her eyes, then opened them again. "Two of those, I think. If I remember my weights at all."

The others looked blank, and Bernhardt grinned foolishly, sweating, hoping no questions followed. Emso broke her tension. "I'll get them." He hurried off.

After he'd taken a half-dozen steps or so, Jaleeta called, "Wait." She said to the other women, "I don't want to look at those terrible cells, but I want to know you, completely. I can't, if I don't know about your suffering. I have to look." Her look begged for understanding.

Neela smiled appreciation. "It's not necessary. There's really nothing to see. Just a bad place."

Sylah's sarcasm was subtle. "What a becoming sentiment. By all means, have a long look."

All Bernhardt saw was Jaleeta, manipulating.

Around the corner and down a long, dank corridor, Emso pointed to a gap in the bottom of a thick-planked door. "That's where food and water went in to the prisoner. Water in a flat bowl, like for a dog. This was Sylah's cell." He removed the securing beam, threw open the door. Jaleeta clapped a hand over her nose and stepped back. Not before she smelled it, however. Something fetid that spoke of human waste and sweat and ineradicable fear. The stench permeated the very stones.

Emso stepped into the cell. He came out quickly, holding two rough ingots. Not until the door was barred again and he was several paces down the hall did he exhale and draw in long, relieved breath. Beside him, Jaleeta was unnaturally quiet.

On rejoining the other women, Jaleeta embraced Neela tightly. "What a horrible, horrible place. I thought I knew how strong you are, but I never imagined."

"It was harder for Sylah."

"How could it have been?" Jaleeta looked up into Sylah's distant reserve. "It must have been unbearable."

Thoughtfully, Sylah said, "What makes trial memorable isn't survival, it's the use we make of it. Fire and hammer alone can't make good steel. The mind of the smith determines. Women, especially, must make better steel of ourselves, always. Or be slag."

Neela said, "You always speak for my heart. My sister. Thank you."

Bernhardt grinned. "I know a place where you'd have fit in *so* well. But thanks from me, too."

Jaleeta continued to watch Sylah, whose expression and focus on the younger woman never changed. Jaleeta finally looked away. To Emso, she said, "Let's get away from here."

Neela took her arm. Emso led the way. Bernhardt and Sylah brought up the rear. In response to a mime from Bernhardt that suggested strangling Jaleeta, Sylah frowned stern disapproval before snorting a most un-Churchlike giggle through her nose.

As soon as Bernhardt was gone, Neela went to her quarters to attend to her household and her son. Sylah, restless, elected to wander idly in the castle. She ended up in the great hall, where Emso was scheduled to conduct government business. She held to the darkest corner, telling herself it was merely a precaution to avoid the appearance of spying.

She watched Jaleeta as an owl watches a mouse.

Gallingly, there was nothing to see. Proper as possible, Jaleeta remained distant, watching Emso with a cloying adoration that made Sylah's palms itch. When the petitioners were disposed of, Emso came out from behind the bar between dais and crowd to sit on the edge of one of the massive firepits. Jaleeta joined him, close, but still infuriatingly proper. When they were interrupted, Jaleeta made a pretty departure, all half bows, smiles, and simpers.

Sylah fumed.

Emso left shortly afterward. Sylah saw him to the official business room, with its huge table and fireplace. Past the guard, he sat at the table, lost in thought. Sylah relented. He looked so very alone, so achingly out of place. She wished there were some way to comfort him. By then, it was time to return to the abbey.

At his table, Emso brooded. The plain fact was, he didn't completely trust Wal's boats or the fishermen of Ondrat and Mull to detect sharkers. There was too much water out there. Nothing forced a boat to stick to a trail, or look for a ford. Fishermen in particular were more likely to run and hide than sound an alarm. Emso unconsciously wrinkled his nose. It wasn't natural to take to the water. It wasn't natural to trust those who did.

After the midday meal, he rode to Ondrat's castle. If anything, it was more disheartening than before. With the onset of winter, the midden heap moved closer to the walls. Leprous with patches of snow, it was presently inundated by squalling, scavenging bird life. Like angry puffs of dust, they rose and swirled when pigs assertively rooted for dainties. From a distance, several dispirited cows watched the proceedings. Scraggly wisps of hay littered the snow in front of them. Hipbones rose from their hindquarters as clearly defined as castle turrets, sign of their sparse rations. One mooed plaintively at Emso. He looked away, rode through the unguarded gate.

Ondrat was at table when Emso was ushered in. The Baron appeared to be barricaded behind a huge ham, bowls of vegetables, a massive tureen of steaming soup. He was alone. Rising, with one last draft from a tankard, he came around the table to greet his guest with great gusto. When he got to "brother warrior," Emso decided he'd heard enough.

"I need something from you," he said, interrupting. "A small force, no more than thirty men. They'll take orders directly from me. Hard duty, but extra coin for all, more for those who excel."

Tugging at his ear, cocking his head, Ondrat was very reluctant. "Any other time, I'd hand over twice that many, and pay them myself. Serving you would guarantee I'd get back the best trained men in Ola. The Territories, I mean. Or is this work so dangerous they won't be coming back?"

"Perfectly safe. No danger at all. What do you mean 'any other time'?"

"Life is hard here. Some of my people are literally starving. They eat bark, grass, leather. All my troops are foraging. All not requisitioned for duty as Wolves, that is."

"I want men. A safety precaution. Gan's gone on a patrol. He took some of the castle guard. We're not shouting it in the streets, you understand? I want to reinforce the men I have left. I want them from you, because you're a man I can trust. The less known about any of this, the better."

Ondrat's voice dropped almost to a whisper. "I'll find a way to get the men. My people will go without, if need be. Gan Moondark is our hope for the future."

On the way out the gate, Emso congratulated himself. Negotiation wasn't as difficult as Gan made it look. He smiled to himself; apparently, being a leader involved a little flair for acting. You made the easy things look hard, and the hard ones look easy. Poor Ondrat. He'd never know he could have suggested twenty-five men, or even twenty, and made his opponent happy.

The same cow bawled at Emso again. It was lying down now, and the effort seemed to tire it completely. It shivered, as if dislodging imaginary flies, and rolled onto its side. Stark ribs heaved. It shocked Nalatan to realize the beast was literally dying before his eyes.

There was nothing he could do. He forced his gaze straight ahead, rode on. Three ravens launched themselves from a branch directly ahead of Emso. They drifted past on their way to the cow, so close he could see the grained bare skin of their legs, hear the oddly clattering pass of chill wind through feathers. Jet-eyed, avid, they ignored him utterly on their way to vigil.

Chapter 81

Jaleeta watched the Chosens run toward her, and dredged up a friendly smile. Then, putting on a glum look, she pointed at the Violet Abbey. The children understood immediately. A game ensued. One made a sad face like hers, pretended to open a book. Another rubbed her stomach and smacked her lips, miming Jaleeta's usual gift of a sweet.

Jaleeta turned away, continued her walk. The children couldn't know the significance of her hidden, dismal expression.

Gan's departure was only a short while past, and already Emso's behavior was erratic. Even the arrival of Baron Ondrat's men to reinforce the castle garrison failed to help.

Outwardly, nothing was wrong. Yet Emso grew morose. Tirades directed at guards were fiercer than ever. The new Ondrat men took it particularly badly, their undisciplined sullenness so pronounced the other Wolves avoided them as much as possible, kept one eye on them at all times.

Neela was sure she understood. She counseled Jaleeta. "Emso's a lonely man. You can make him smile. Try to help him."

Jaleeta stopped in her walk to avoid a small detail of Wolves, marching across her path. Eyes properly averted, she still managed to keep them in sight. The straight, young bodies and their pounding cadence reminded her of Nalatan. She smiled, remembering how she'd planned to survive musty old Emso's fumbling by imagining Nalatan in his place.

Somehow, that duplicity got twisted inside her head. At first, she meant only to think of Nalatan while enduring Emso. Soon, however, she was imagining Nalatan wanting her and being denied. That idea grew darker; she saw Nalatan denied all pleasure. Pain was substituted. For every good thing that happened to Jaleeta, Nalatan suffered the more. Eventually, Nalatan's pain was paramount. It became her delight. Thrilling.

She didn't want that in her mind. She couldn't rid herself of it.

The troops moved on. Jaleeta resumed her progress.

If Emso was normal, none of those disturbing visions would have ever happened. There was no manhood in him, after all. When they were together at night he was terrified of being discovered, closing doors, drawing shutters, snuffing candles. During daylight he sought obscure corners, croaking about "propriety."

For the first secret meeting, Jaleeta went charged to do her sexual best. She was rejected with whiffling fluff about marriage, children, and the embracing sanctity of Church. By the time she conceded defeat, she was twitching like an alder leaf and possessed of a raging headache. Worse, he withdrew farther every day. When he wasn't inspecting the guards, he was either looking out to sea for Skan or to the south for Gan's return. He hardly slept.

Arriving at the Violet Abbey, Jaleeta asked for the Abbess, and was ushered in as if expected. The older woman signaled the attending Priestess to bring Jaleeta tea, then motioned for Jaleeta to sit with her in front of the fire. Jaleeta pulled up a rocking chair like the Abbess'. Its ornately carved headboard illustrated a robed Priestess blessing lambs. The Abbess' own chair had arms and headboard carved to indicate sprays of the abbey's namesake flowers. The blossoms were inset chips of amethyst, luminous in the soft firelight.

"What is it this time, child? It can't be Nalatan." The Abbess chuckled. "It really was clever to spread that rumor of his lechery among the True Church believers. Many distrust him completely now, and Tate's lost respect, as well. Is the rumor true?"

Jaleeta opened her mouth. An imperious hand stopped her. "Say nothing. You'd lie, and I'm too weary for useless disagreements."

Petulant, Jaleeta said, "I brought news. I come for advice."

"Of course, my dear." The Abbess sipped in silence as Jaleeta took her cup from the returned Priestess. When they were alone again, the Abbess turned away to put her cup on a small polished brass table. "I'm glad you came. I think it's time we were completely honest with each other, don't you? No, you don't. Let me help you decide." She edged her chair closer to Jaleeta, intense.

Jaleeta took advantage of the older woman's movement to interject, "I've been honest. I've worked for Church."

"We all lie. We have no time for it now, however. Too many things are happening too fast. If we're to achieve our ambitions, we must work together."

"I have no ambitions."

Calmly, the Abbess raised an admonishing, waggling finger. When she jabbed with it, the movement was so quick there was no chance for Jaleeta to comprehend the action, much less avoid it. The pain that exploded in Jaleeta's head was such a surprise that it overwhelmed the injury for a brief instant. Then her right eye was a live, searing coal. She curled in a tight ball, clutching herself. Over the sound of her own astonished hurt, she heard the Abbess' dispassionate voice. "Time is short. I can tolerate no evasions, no deviations. I shall be the Harvester. You will help me. In exchange, we shall arrange for you to enjoy the power and influence you so lust after. Do we at last understand each other, child? Are we sharing now?"

Jaleeta mumbled an affirmative, broken by a sob.

"Do sit up straight," the Abbess said. "We can't talk with you hunched over that way. And stop crying. You'll look a fright when you leave, and everyone will know we've had unpleasantness. We're not going to have more, though, are we? Such a bright girl. That's one of the many things I like about you. Now, can we rely on Emso for anything?"

Jaleeta gritted her teeth. Facing the Abbess, she refused to wipe tears or hold a hand to the stinging eye. When she tried to open it, however, it was too much. She said, "Why ask me? You seem to know everything already."

"You're resentful. Try to overcome it. There are worse things than a touchy eye. Is Emso capable of commanding the garrison? Does he act like a man considering betrayal?"

"Emso cares only for Gan Moondark. Never think otherwise."

"Thank you. And the witch, Leclerc? He can be used?"

This was the most dangerous ground. Emso was a tool. Leclerc was magic. Whatever happened, he must belong to Jaleeta. Yet this deceitful old woman saw lies as easily as other people saw sun or moon. Jaleeta was suddenly afraid. Afraid enough to want to please. "He can be used. The apostate Priestess, Kate Bernhardt, loves him. I think he loves her, but he wants me. We must not lose him."

"We won't. We must step very surely, however. No one dares harm me. One mistake, however, and they'll have you. Let these men learn of the games you've played with them, and they'll put you in a stable, just like another horse. We don't want to think about that, do we? Are we sharing now?"

"Yes. We're sharing. Everything."

"I'm so pleased." The Abbess rose awkwardly, favoring joints too long immobile. Jaleeta stood, as well. The audience was over. The Abbess leaned on her shoulder on the way to the door. Before Jaleeta could open it, the Abbess added, "I've always been the only one you could depend on. You should have seen that. Gan despises me, but he honors my life protection. Church is woman, and woman's only salvation is submission. We accomplish only through cunning and deviousness. Confrontation is the tactic of the overlord; deflection is ours. Men believe steel commands. We know that guile bends all metals, and beauty is the greatest guile of all. Learn about Emso, Leclerc, about anyone you think may help us. Inform me."

"What if the Skan come while Emso's like this? I must not be taken by them. Don't think they'll spare you. Sosolassa cares nothing for Church."

"Never mention false gods on holy ground. And don't fear them. I'll hide you from your vengeful Skan. So long as you're true to me."

Jaleeta eased out from under the hand on her shoulder, pushed open the door. This wicked, cheating Abbess had tricked her, somehow gained an upper hand. Jaleeta was driven to salvage some sign of respect from her. In the hallway she spoke over her shoulder. "Are we sharing?"

The Abbess' jaw tightened. Muscles twitched. She nodded pleasantly, however. "Indeed we are. Be sure of it." She pulled the door closed. A flash of irritation marred her features. She was contained quickly, relaxed. Making her way to a window, she assured herself that Jaleeta was returning to the castle. That done, she rang a delicate silver bell. She told her attendant Priestess, "Have my horse saddled and brought around. I need a little exercise. And solitude. No outriders."

A short while later, Ondrat hovered around his guest, helping her off with her rich, black cloak and its green-and-violet trim. She took possession of one of the two massive chairs in front of the huge fireplace, holding her hands out to the flames. "This weather." She sighed, let the sound express her feelings.

"At least the snows have stopped. And soon it will be spring."

The Abbess looked up sharply at Ondrat's pleased tone. He went on, smug. "We'll be rid of Gan and Sylah."

She looked away to hide irritation. First Jaleeta with her self-importance, and now Ondrat, reeking superiority. If he weren't such a frightful fool, he'd be comical, she told herself, then straightened abruptly. Ondrat was a murderous fool. One mustn't forget that. "As the One in All wills."

"I think we can be a bit surer than that."

She made her smile flattering. "You've done something clever and you're keeping it a secret, aren't you?" She poked a playful, accusing finger. The gesture reminded her of Jaleeta. For one sweet instant, she savored the image of Ondrat spinning in a crazed, blind circle.

Ondrat said, "We're in a position to welcome Moonpriest as an equal, not someone begging help. Our future has been handed to us."

"Really? By whom? More importantly, why?" The Abbess saw concern twitch Ondrat's features, and wished she'd spoken with less asperity.

Recovering, Ondrat was severe. "I have questions for you, first. What evidence do we have that this Moonpriest means to allow Church primacy in Ola? Does alliance mean equals, or subordinate and superior? Gan Moondark isn't Church's only enemy; has Moonpriest ever struck at any others?"

Surprised, the Abbess looked to the fire, gave herself a moment to think. Those questions had already troubled her; she never expected to hear them from Ondrat. She said, "The alliance was approved by Sister Mother. Questioning it would be a sin. As for Moonpriest's honor or his intentions, no one can know."

"One can be suspicious. And prudent. It's in my mind—and our power—to control Ola before Windband moves. You can present the witch Sylah and the apostate Gan Moondark to Sister Mother as gifts of celebration."

Without her training, the Abbess would have known only the bland tempting voice. Shame subtly disfigured Ondrat while he mouthed the words. She knew he planned murder. She loathed his lie even as she reveled in its advantage. Sylah's execution by someone other than Church meant Sister Mother's hands would be spared that blood. Still, she must discover his plan. "You have suborned the Wolves?"

"Of course not. But we're in position to strike at the heart of the Wolves, when the time comes."

"The troops you sent Emso? The other guards watch them as if they were the enemy."

"Woman, don't presume. I'm aware of the disrespect shown my gallant men. If you want to know more, don't interrupt."

"My enthusiasm overrode my manners, Baron. Please forgive me."

Ondrat continued. "I can bring our northern allies, the Skan, to Ola. I can be in the castle, in command, when Moonpriest arrives."

Stunned past comment, the Abbess goggled. Ondrat grinned and paced across the fireplace, basking in that light as broadly as in self-approval.

The Abbess' mind flew from consideration to consequence while she steadfastly maintained her look of awe. She phrased her question to draw him. "You said you would be King of Ola. What of Harbundai?"

"Given to the Skan. Those northern scum have lorded it over us since Gan and his witch friends overthrew Altanar. They chose the anti-Church; let them suffer for their blasphemy."

A well-phrased reply, the Abbess thought, and determined to remember it. "You trust the Skan? Why would they leave you anything to rule over?"

"To keep Windband in its place. They fear Moonpriest's ambitions for Moondance." He stopped and whirled, thrusting his face in the Abbess' so unexpectedly that she sank back in her chair. "And the best part is this: I know what that crippled devil Lorso really has in mind. He doesn't want to put his warriors ashore here to fight us and Windband. He wants to raid, the way he and his back-stabbing savages always do. He thought he was so clever, sniffing around about the castle's defenses. He plans to sneak inside, that's what. He's not even thinking about occupying Ola. He just wants to deny it to Moonpriest."

"The time is now. Immediately."

Ondrat managed one word. His voice cracked on it. "Now?"

Ice claimed the Abbess. She was a clear winter stream, freezing solid. Logic and understanding capped her, protected the racing emotions deeper within her.

Harvester. She would be Harvester.

Ondrat cleared his throat. He repeated "Now?" in a gruff bass.

"Gan is gone, with the apostate Nalatan. Emso is weak. Exhausted. The Black Lightning is disappeared, hopefully dead. Conway and his whore are almost always gone, distributing food. Leclerc is at his farm, too preoccupied to know anything until it's too late."

"Gan." Speaking the name drew color from Ondrat's flushed features. "He'll come back. After us."

"You'll have his wife and child."

"Hostages?"

"Let's say assurances of good behavior." The Abbess rose, drew her cloak around her. Taking time to be precise, she arranged the hood and its drawstring. Only when ready to step into the cold did she face Ondrat. "Once again, I apologize for my earlier intrusion into the concerns reserved for men. I'm deeply grateful you allow me some consideration in dealing with Church's grievances."

Ondrat's jaw still hung slack when the Abbess disappeared in the dark hallway.

Chapter 82

Conway scanned the forest flanking the narrow trail, thinking how much he must resemble a turtle. The heavy sheepskin hat gave his head a round, indistinct form exactly like Lanta's smaller version. Also like her, he wore a sheepskin coat over layers of clothing. The finishing touch was the coat collar, which buttoned just under his nose, so only peering eyes were visible.

He wished he felt as invulnerable as the turtle. Instead, he had the sensation of being a fat target. The squeal of leather tack and saddle seemed abnormally loud. The shuffle of the fifteen horses making up the small relief unit took on the irritation of loud laughter. The Wolves maintained perfect trail discipline, not talking, watchful. Still, he had to swallow the urge to turn and warn them to be quiet.

Beside him, Lanta spoke softly. "Did you see something? You're nervous."

Pulling aside the collar, he answered, "It's very difficult being in love with a woman who knows what you're thinking before you get a chance to say anything." She laughed quietly, and he went on. "I haven't seen anything. The dogs are edgy, though. There's something around, and they're not happy about it. I think we're being watched."

Serious now, Lanta nodded agreement. "I think it's Smalls."

"I thought of them. They wouldn't be down here. They keep to the high ground."

"I still think it's them."

"Why?"

She shrugged, the movement practically absorbed by mounded clothing. "I just do."

"Well, that settles it, then. What else could it be?"

Lanta's response was to stick out her tongue and button up her collar, retreating behind it and a great silence.

The small column approached the base of a cliff when Conway spotted something ahead that shouldn't have been there. He raised a hand, waving it side to side. Wolves trotted off the trail into outward-facing readiness. The senior man rode up quickly. Conway stood in his stirrups, pointing. "Look there. Tracks, coming down off the mountain by that cliff face. They've torn up this meadow. Looks pretty well used."

The young Wolf studied the scene. "Something wrong with them. The tracks, I mean. See?"

Chagrined, Conway saw what the other man meant. Temperature changes had thawed and refrozen the snow cover, obscuring any certain reading, but it was obvious the trail was made by snowshoes. Conway told the Wolf, "Get your troopers into a couple of wedges, in column. The Priestess rides between them. I take point with the dogs. Snowshoes means either Mountain People or Smalls."

Lanta's voice was an invisible smirk. "Smalls. I told you."

The Wolf grinned. Conway said, "I almost hope she's wrong, just so I don't have to listen to her brag."

The Wolf continued to grin as he turned his mount. "If it's all the same to you, Matt Conway, I hope she's right. I've seen enough of the Mountains to last me. I never saw a Small, though. And I won't have to listen to her brag, either."

"Get back to your men." Conway's rueful smile covered any bite his tone suggested. Still, for all the lightness, it was a wary, intent group that edged abreast of the cliff.

"Yo! Conway!"

Conway recognized Tate's voice instantly. So did the dogs. They dropped to hiding positions. Tails wagged, nevertheless. Conway looked to the base of the cliff to see Tate on horseback, edging out of a dense fir thicket. She was a good fifty yards away, he estimated, on ground higher than the meadow. He waved, and she returned it.

Advancing at a slow walk, she called out, "You're too bunched up. One good Marine with a dozen eggs would turn you all into an omelet. Can't I teach you people anything?"

"Nothing about how to greet a friend, that's for sure. We were admiring your tracks. Who's with you?"

"No one, now. They're back up in the high country."

"Smalls?"

Even at distance, her grin dazzled. "That's how I knew to intercept you here. They watched you ride in with the supplies, let me know your route back to Ola."

She was close enough to eliminate shouting then, and Lanta spoke up. "You waited for us? Why?"

"We'll talk about it. First, how were things in Ola when you left?"

Conway was direct. "Nalatan came in, but he went back out with Gan, Donnacee. Big trouble down on the river. Slavers. Gan asked him. There wasn't much Nalatan could say."

Tate's smile wavered, but it held. She went to Lanta first, exchanging hugs, then to Conway. After embracing him, she pulled back. "I told Gan to keep Nalatan close if he needed him. I shouldn't be surprised that he asked him to help on this chore. But I am. Is Gan trying to keep him out of Ola? This whole thing was a mess, going in. It's beginning to smell really bad. I'm asking you two to help me. That's not easy for me."

Conway said, "A lot of people know you're in one place and your husband's in another. Of course there's talk. You want us to repeat all that garbage? I told you what I know. I won't tell you what I don't know."

The dull silence of the snow-heavy valley eventually forced a response from Tate. She startled Conway with a sharp, false smile and an offhanded manner so artificial it made his throat catch. "We'll sort it all out, me and Nalatan. For now, I want you to send this detail on into Ola. Be my guests this evening. We'll go home tomorrow morning."

Lanta blinked. "Stay here? Why? Is it safe?"

"No Mountains or raiders. Can't be sure about animals." Tate's good humor was partially returned. Something was amusing her.

Conway addressed that fact. "You've got something up your sleeve. What is it?"

"Later, after the troops are gone." She winked broadly. "Secret stuff, buddy. You won't believe it."

He laughed. "Donnacee, you're unbelievable. Okay, I'll pass the word."

While the puzzled Wolves drew away down the valley, Tate regaled her friends with stories of the Smalls. The loneliness of her stay with them was clear, but so was her appreciation of their hospitality and ingenuity. "There are families now, whole communities. They're surviving this winter on dried food, several varieties of pemmican, frozen game. They'll need valley land for farms."

Conway was grim. "Between the Kwa and this killer winter, there's plenty of available cropland. The Smalls will be welcome."

Not long after that, Tate flashed a smile full of conspiracy and accomplishment. "You wait here," she said. "Promise you'll stay right here until I come back. It'll be a while, so no cheating."

So sworn, Conway and Lanta waited. Curiosity grew to uncertainty, then concern. Conway was pacing irritably, muttering about taking the dogs to hunt for her when the shrill whistle swelled across the wilderness. Momentarily confused, Conway and Lanta searched in all directions. It was the dogs, craning up, that directed their gaze to Tate. She waved from high atop a cliff face that stood bare and broken against the more gradual flanking slopes with their dark forest.

Lanta was nervous. "I wish she'd step back from that edge." Then, "Oh, good. She did. What can she be doing up there?"

Conway's answer was choked off by the appearance of a large, bluish-gray triangle. It edged forward, limned against the black-and-green of trunks and branches. The object trembled, then grew with astonishing rapidity.

Billowing, arrowhead sleek, the thing plunged off the edge.

The whistle shrilled, triumphant. Tate's voice followed, a paean of delight, excitement, life.

Lanta's attempted scream broke free as a strangled rasp. She threw herself at Conway, staggering him, clasping him as if that contact were all that was left of reality.

Conway embraced Lanta without taking his eyes from the swallowlike grace of the hang glider. The descending flight was a series of cautious arcs across the cliff face. In the stillness of winter-silence the For cloth ruffled confidence. Taut rigging contributed a harsh whisper.

Tate shouted at her transfixed audience. "What d'you think, Matt? Lanta? Is this something?" In her exuberance, she lost concentration. A wing dipped, and an unscheduled swoop sent her voice caroling upward on the last syllable. She was back in command immediately, however, and wild laughter rang exhilaration.

Lanta found her voice. "Come down! You'll be killed! Donnacee, come down. Please."

Conway threw back his head, laughed as loud as Tate. He shouted at her. "You're a genius. A marvel. You're going to break your damnfool neck."

Her landing pass swept her over Conway and Lanta almost close enough to touch. She was laughing again, exultant, vibrant. The dogs crouched and growled. Conway rose on tiptoe, stretching almost enough to make contact. Lanta continued to cling to him, but now her expression was tempered by relief. She watched, awed, as Tate lowered her feet, stumbling to a sprawling, falling stop in a snowy welter.

Tate was free of her rigging when they arrived. Conway swept her off the ground in a whirling, shouting bear hug. As soon as he put her down, Lanta piled in, scolding, laughing, so excited her words were an incomprehensible froth. The dogs, infected by the hilarity, galloped around the trio, barking, tumbling each other. At Conway's call, they came to him, flopping down in the snow, tongues lolling, every panting breath a puffed cloud.

Calming, Conway inspected the hang glider. He stroked the frame, puzzling, and Tate explained, "Remember those Small blowgun-spear things? Split bamboo, Matt. I asked them to make me some big pieces. Laminated. They use animal glue. Stinks like fury, but it holds."

"I can tell it holds," Conway interrupted dryly, shaking his head.

Unperturbed, Tate went on. "You know this For material. Can't tear the stuff with a team of horses, I swear. It seemed like a good idea, so I tried it."

Lanta said, "That's what you've been up to, living out here? Without a Healer anywhere? What if you fell?"

"I started slow. Easy slopes, soft snow to fall in." Tate shifted her attention back to Conway. "I can't get over how easy it was, Matt. It all just fell in place. That's why I never said anything to you; I figured I'd make a fool of myself, and I didn't want you knowing how badly I failed."

"Well, you can forget failure. Wait till everyone else sees it. What a sensation that's going to be."

Abruptly, Tate contradicted him. "No one's going to see. Not yet. I've thought about it, Matt, and I want you and Lanta's word you won't say a thing."

"What? Why not? With this we—"

"We can what?" Tate faced him, lips tight, eyes narrowed. "Once I leave the ground, I pretty much go where the wind and gravity send me. From the walls of Ola I don't have enough altitude to even crash with class. We have to keep this a secret until we can use it to good effect. If I can make one, so can Moonpriest. That's why I asked you to send those troops on ahead, why the Smalls scouted out this valley."

Conway rubbed his jaw, looked longingly at the hang glider.

Tate moved to Lanta, draped her arm across the smaller woman's shoulder. She continued to address Conway. "Think about this, too. We're already considered witches, or close to it. The first time we're seen flying, we're branded. No matter how many people we train to do the same thing, we'll be the ones who brought this witch's tool to our friends. If you think people call names now because of the secret of the Door, or because of Leclerc's developments, wait until they learn we can fly."

From the corner of his eye, Conway caught Lanta's surreptitious three-sign. He answered Tate, "We can't just let something like this go, though."

"Absolutely. When we use it, we do it where we can win big. Big enough to offset the fear that comes with it."

Lanta squeezed Conway's arm. He glanced down, and she said, "Donnacee's right. If you use this . . . this thing and defeat an enemy, many will say you're magic. They'll fear you, but be glad you're on their side. If you just show it to them, the way Donnacee showed us, they'll be frightened and confused; they may run away. If you use it in battle and lose, friend and foe alike will call you witch. You and everyone known to you will be destroyed."

Bitterness warped Conway's grin, made it cruel. "So we'll be forgiven and loved if we win people's battles for them, and cursed if we lose."

Lanta took Tate's hand in hers. "Church's Healers have lived with that knowledge since the beginning. Warriors know it in their hearts always. It's time you admitted it to yourself, Matt Conway."

"It shouldn't be that way for you. You only help others."

"I do what I believe is right. That's enough to create an army of enemies. Anyhow, I say Tate's right. We say nothing about . . . What is that thing, Donnacee?" Brisk, Lanta faced the hang glider squarely, pointed an unflinching finger.

"I call it a hang glider." Out of Lanta's line of vision, Tate rolled her eyes for Conway's benefit, then added, for Lanta, "And you're a champion. Want to see how it comes apart for carrying?"

Absently, Conway joined in, too disturbed to be properly impressed by the intricate bindings and flexible strength of the device. With the suspense and initial excitement of Donnacee's revelation over, he found himself unable to reconcile lying to her. It was inescapable that she hear the rumors of Nalatan's involvement with Jaleeta. Tate would reject them, as did anyone who knew him.

But she'd hear them. The pain would be excruciating. Such wounds infected easily.

Chapter 83

Steady rain pelted the trio as they broke free of the trees for their first glimpse of Ola. Behind Tate, a packhorse carried the dismantled hang glider in a long tube.

In unspoken accord, the riders stopped, looking at the distant city.

Lanta said, "I think I like it better this way, uncertain, gray against gray. The outlines of the buildings are all misted soft. It looks as if it might disappear. Maybe nature wants to absorb all that strict stone and mortar, the way it did the godkills."

Tate and Conway exchanged glances, each trying to hide hurt at their profane knowledge of how unimaginably greater cities died. Tate answered Lanta, "The rain does change the way things look. I used to think it was just grim, but it has its own beauty. It's not flagrant; you have to look for it."

While the two women chatted amiably about subtle color and the effect of flat, universal light, Conway tried to concentrate on the effect of warming weather on mobility. The snow was gone now, but streams and rivers were rising. Lowlands would flood. After a while, the waters would recede.

Moonpriest would come.

Conway caught himself remembering Windband. He remembered eyes watering and nostrils smarting, assaulted by the stink of homes burning, of death pyres. Far, far back in his mind, he heard the war cries, the screams. His mouth went dry. Not dry enough to kill the taste of battle, of smoke, of fear, of air redolent with blood.

Shaking his head, Conway dislodged those images, only to confront something much more immediate, something he genuinely dreaded as much as facing any enemy.

Tate knew as much about hurt as any other fighter. What was coming was worse. It was the obscene pain of known, but unproven, snickering behind one's back. It was the smiling face that sneered when it thought it was unobserved, the polite voice that sought darkness or an intervening wall before it dared express its true character.

"Tate, we've got to talk." Both women faced him, his tone bringing alarm to Lanta, but a twisted, anticipatory knowing to Tate. Conway glanced at Lanta, caught her silent plea. He said, "I'm not letting her ride into that mess unready."

Tate said, "This is about Nalatan, isn't it? Is he all right? Is he hurt?" Voice and manner made lies of the questions, made it known that she feared something deeper, more damaging, than physical injury.

Conway stalled, swinging his horse around so he faced Tate, his knee almost touching hers. It didn't use enough time. Nothing would. He said, "When he rode out without any explanation, some people wondered about it. Some made up stories to suit their own standards."

"Stories?" Her interruption stopped him. He met her eyes, but her focus wasn't for him. He felt her gaze grind through him, reach for the distant city, seeking. There was hatred in the look, lethal, and Conway shivered, not knowing exactly what its target was. She altered her question. "Or story? How many versions?"

It was an odd reaction, disturbing. Conway said, "Who cares? It's lies."

"Poor Matt." She touched his cheek, consoling. "Lots of rumors means lots of uncertainty. One rumor means a root somewhere. A lie, perhaps, but a central lie, one that everyone agrees on. Maybe for a reason."

Nothing was going the way Conway expected. Hatred he understood. Or anger. Sadness and sympathy were totally out of place, even if directed at himself. "When you hear, you'll know it's a lie, and there's no reason whatever. The rumor says Nalatan made a move on Jaleeta, and when she turned him down, he left. See how stupid it is? Just don't lose your temper. And don't let him, either, when he comes back."

"Of course. I'll be fine. I should have expected something like this, really. Nalatan and I set ourselves up pretty good." She touched his cheek again, and Conway had the inexplicable feeling that somehow she was reassuring herself. When she turned to Lanta, she made an effort to brighten. "What do you think, Lanta? Are men a problem, or the cause of all problems?"

Lanta found a smile. "It depends; some days it's one, other days it's the other." Unwilling to see the matter end with the most important aspect ignored, Lanta brushed aside inconsequentials. "He loves you. What lie, what tale, can darken that?"

"Stay close to me, Lanta. I'm going to need you. You'll never know why, or how much, but I'm going to need you."

"And Nalatan."

Conway's heart leaped as a flash of Tate's old spirit crossed her features. She answered Lanta, "Don't worry about that. More than anything in the world, Nalatan."

"Good." Lanta looked to Conway. "You were right. It's good we got that talked out. Let's go get a hot bath and a good meal. My memory of both is fading fast."

Their welcome at the castle was joyous. When Janet Carter and Sue Anspach came racing through the rain from the Iris Abbey, Tate leaped from her horse to embrace them, the three staggering about in a joyous whirl. Similarly, Neela came outside to exchange effusive hugs. Lanta's hand sought Conway's when Jaleeta appeared. Tate greeted her politely. Emso followed. Tate flustered him completely with a huge hug and a kiss for both cheeks.

In an aside to her husband, Lanta said, "That's very disturbing. On first sight, he was nervous, almost frightened. For that moment when he was with Tate, he was like his old self, pretending to be such a bear. Now he's like he was before. And look how he edged over to be close to Jaleeta."

Out the side of his mouth, Conway said, "He's uncomfortable being in command. That's normal. Jaleeta's standing out of the rain. So's he. That's normal. And us sitting here in this downpour is very not normal. Can we put the horses up and get on with our lives?"

Lanta sighed, kneed her mount forward. Conway had to scramble to catch up.

When he did, she said, "You'll certainly never die from a blow to the brain. If I can just keep the rest of you healthy, I should be able to keep you around forever."

Forging slightly ahead, Conway leered back at her. "You said something about a hot bath. Let's go together; I'll explain why you want to keep me around."

Jerking around, Lanta looked over her shoulder, then made a hushing noise at him. "You're making my face red, and Tate's right behind us." When he turned to check, she added, "Last one to grain his horse has to scrub his wife's back," and when he looked up, she was gone at a gallop for the stable.

The day was ending when someone knocked on the door of their quarters. Lanta was in the closest of the room's three leather-sling chairs. She opened the door, greeting Sylah and Tate. While Lanta embraced Sylah, Tate eased past, came to where Conway stood by the fireplace. He said, "I figured you for a week or so of uninterrupted sleep. Did you get the hang glider secured? How'd you explain that carrying case?"

"It's slung from the ceiling in my quarters. Barely fits, diagonally. I told them it's full of poison spears. No one'll mess with it."

"So what brings you and Sylah here?"

"Trouble. She'll explain."

Conway turned expectantly. Sylah and Lanta waited. After a short, warm greeting Sylah grew serious. "I'll be direct. We have some very serious problems. I'm most concerned about our Emso. You saw him earlier?"

Lanta said, "I did. Matt was somewhere else."

"I was not. I just didn't see anything that . . ." He stopped, looked at three pitying expressions. He surrendered gracelessly. "He seemed a little tense, I guess. Sort of edgy, maybe."

Tate said, "He's tight as a kite string. You didn't hug him. He hasn't had a bath forever."

The other women nodded agreement. Conway said, "So he's nervous, then. He's got heavy responsibilities. He's still Emso. If we support him well, he'll be fine."

"He's lost, Matt." Sylah shook her head as she spoke. "He never accepted the new Teachers. He's allied himself completely with the old Church."

"I can't believe that. I mean, he was right here when that old sow Harvester tried to kill Tate. And you. And me."

"Let me come back to that. There's something else. You know Kate Bernhardt's in love?"

"Kate? No. That's great. Some good news, at last. But what's that got to do with Emso?" His eyes bulged. "She's not . . . ?"

Sylah blinked slowly. When she continued, she was very patient. "Louis, Matt; she's in love with Louis. And I believe he loves her. The complication is Jaleeta. She interests him."

Conway said, "I think I can see this coming," and Sylah leaned back, expressionless. Conway proceeded. "Jaleeta's got Emso and Leclerc hating each other. Because Emso favors the old ways, he's against Leclerc's new weapons. And all of us. Everyone's heard about Moonpriest getting close with old Church. You smell some sort of deal, don't you? You're afraid Emso's going to try to strike a bargain, protect Gan from us, Windband, and the Skan, all at once."

Rising, Lanta ran to throw her arms around him. Looking back at Sylah, she said, "Didn't I always say he was smart?"

Grinning ruefully, Conway continued to address Sylah. "Do you have any evidence? What we've just done is awful. Emso is Gan's best friend. He'd die before he'd hurt Gan. We're branding him traitor. Because he and Leclerc are all wound up over this Jaleeta. Because he's old-fashioned. Bad things, maybe. Not treacherous. What have we got?"

Tate said, "What kind of weapon uses silver, Matt?"

He blinked. "Silver? I don't know. What?"

"I don't know either. But Leclerc asked Gan for some. He made Emso give him two ingots." Tate held out her hands, indicating size. "That's a lot, man."

Sylah picked up the conversation again. "I do have something, as you put it, Matt. She's a Priestess who lives in the Violet Abbey, and risks soul as well as life to glean what she can for me. She's quite sure Emso is involved in a plot involving the Violet Abbess and Baron Ondrat."

"Ondrat? He saved your life, Sylah."

"Or eliminated those who failed to take it."

"That's too convenient. This Priestess of yours comes to you with scraps of conversation, and you build a plot out of it. Louis asks for silver, and you suspect him. Of what?"

Sylah remained calm. "That much silver would assure a man high social position in an Ola run by someone like Baron Ondrat. An infatuated man might be tempted to invest something in his own position."

Conway gently disengaged himself from Lanta. "This is unacceptable. Unsubstantiated charges, suspicion, speculation—the four of us will be at each other soon. I'm going after Gan."

Lanta said, "We'll send a Messenger."

Shaking his head, Conway flatly rejected the notion. "I trust no Messenger with this sort of thing. I'm going, and that's that."

The tip of Sylah's tongue darted across her lips, shining in the firelight. A hand in her lap twitched. She said, "You'll confront him? Tell him everything?"

"I may miss lovers' signals, and I don't have your intuition, but I know how a man like Gan thinks. You all work on your schemes and subtleties. I'm coming back with him and we're going to hammer this the way we would any other barrier. It may not be pretty, but we'll straighten it out."

The women shifted nervously. Sylah rose. "Ride hard, Matt Conway. I think we've little time. You know we have many Ondrat men on the castle guard now. We have Jaleeta inside and the Violet Abbess and Ondrat outside. If any part of what I suspect is accurate, the danger increases daily."

"You really think Emso would overthrow Gan?"

"Of course not. But I think a confused Emso would make it very easy for someone to overthrow Emso. You see?"

"Too clearly. I'll leave at first light."

Sylah swept forward, kissed him lightly on the cheek. "The One in All protect you, Matt Conway."

Automatically, Conway responded, "And you, my friend," before the implications struck him. He flinched. Sylah laughed. "I doubt we're in that much danger. We have the Wolves, after all, and our own Black Lightning."

Tate lingered, aimless. Conway went to her as Lanta saw Sylah down the hallway. Tate stood at the fireplace, hands on the mantel, body hanging down so she appeared to pitch forward at the fire. Her cheek gleamed. When Conway came to her, she tilted her head and looked up at him from the corner of her eye. "Aren't you going to tell me why you didn't say anything? Why Sylah didn't?"

"About what?"

"Nalatan. All this talk of 'who-did-what' and who's chasing who; nobody mentioned Nalatan and Jaleeta. Or me. It's like I wasn't even here."

"That's not so. Don't make things worse than they are."

She chuckled, metal grinding on stone. "How's it get worse? Y'know, just before I left here, I told Gan I was worried about myself, how I'm always getting into some jackpot and having to be rescued. Then there's the other thing, how I was so locked in on finding a black husband. Then I fell in love with Nalatan, told myself everything was all right. But I had to push it, go off on my special mission. I know he didn't fool with that tramp, Matt. I know it. But there's this thing eating at my brain. It tells me I can't make it as a warrior 'cause I'm a woman, I can't make it as a woman 'cause I'm all messed up in my head, and I can't make it as a human 'cause I'm a black one. That's just about three strikes, isn't it?"

"What it is, it's three bags full. I won't even talk about full of what. Listen to me. I'm depending on you to take care of our friends. You. No one else. I trust you. Hell, I love you. I'm bringing your husband back here. He's a good man. I'm telling you one time; you ruin your marriage, I'm through arguing with you. You've proven yourself to everyone but you, and I'm tired of waiting. Get on board or get on the road. Is that clear?"

While he spoke, she sagged until he ended talking to the back of her head. Face obscured, he could barely make out her answer. "You don't know what it's like, Matt. You just can't know. But don't worry about me. I won't let you down. I won't lose him either. Not this side of the burning." She straightened slowly. When she faced him, her eyes swam with tears pride refused to admit. She said, "I love you, too, you mean, miserable jerk. Don't you know anything? You're supposed to hold me, make me feel good. Who tore out your heart and promoted you to Commandant, anyhow?"

Conway took her by the shoulders, turned her toward the door. "Go get some sleep. You're so punchy you talk like a girl."

She took a halfhearted swing behind her, managing something like laughter. "You be careful, you hear? Don't you dare leave me here alone." She turned with real plea in her face. "I mean that. Don't you dare."

"No fear. Cupid never fails."

"You really are hateful."

He closed the door softly.

Chapter 84

The sea rolled the sharker gently. A following sea hoisted the carved sternpost and rudder high. The long, supple hull squealed softly, the sound of small children, far away, delightedly terrified. Each marching wave continued forward to lift the bow; the whitebear's head snarled at the night.

Amidships, under an inadequately tanned, brine-soaked hide, Ondrat squatted on the heaving deck and swallowed continuously. Bedded coals glowed fiercely in a square ceramic firebox centered on the sand of a shallow wooden container. Warmth was snatched away by the wind that drove the waves. Ondrat drew no relief from the embers, but got full benefit of the cookstove's fumes. Cremating fish grease did nothing for a stomach aching to demonstrate its distress.

Lorso sat on the deck, upwind of the coals. The soft glow picked out facial highlights; high, smooth brow, axe-edged cheekbones, slim nose. Primarily, the light transformed his eyes. Deep-set in shadowing sockets, they were reduced to prickling points of light. He rode the ship's motion in flexible partnership.

Ondrat cleared his throat. "She wouldn't come. No argument would persuade her."

"Argument? What woman argues with a man's orders?"

"A woman much like your own spirit woman, I think." Ondrat saw the instantaneous wadding of muscle in Lorso's jaws, and cursed the roiling stomach that made him so miserable he ignored prudence. He cursed the Violet Abbess, for good measure, before adding, "She emphasized how much she wants to confer with you, but her fear of water forbids her coming out to your boat."

The sounds of the boat enveloped the two men. Lines chafed. Wood squealed and groaned. Water slapped the hull. "Very well. I'll come to your castle. You understand what will happen if my sharker is discovered?"

"There's no danger." Ondrat knew Lorso had no fear of discovery. The word he meant was "betrayed." Sweat tickled Ondrat's spine. There would be betrayal, in plenty. But not yet. He made a covert two-sign.

Lorso slipped out from under the hide, gave orders. Then, "Come stand with me. You'll need your night vision when we reach this hiding place of yours."

Ondrat suffered the sodden cold with mixed emotions. It knifed through his clothes to freeze his guts and made him feel less seasick. He studied Lorso. Lame leg braced against the shield wall, the Skan steadied himself with one hand while the other clasped his sword hilt. He leaned forward into the night. Stone, Ondrat thought; the man is nothing but stone. He shivered, and only the least part of it had to do with the cold.

Unerringly, the fisherman acting as guide for Lorso led the way into the alder-shrouded slough where the sharker was to hide. Looking to the stars, Lorso said, "We've plenty of night left. We'll stay in the main stream." To his second-in-command, he said, "Take a few men and inspect. Keep the fisherman here until I return. Guards out, upstream and down, as well as inland on both banks." Lorso's smile when he turned to Ondrat dared him to take offense at security measures on his own territory. Ondrat accepted it, grinned wildly, hating.

As they entered Ondrat's darkened fort past a startled, stammering guard, Ondrat dismissed the incident airily. "We have no security concerns this time of year. Winter keeps everyone but a few harmless raiders inside where it's warm."

Within the confines of his hood, Lorso permitted himself a dark, feral grin.

Ondrat blithered on. "I want to thank you for agreeing to this meeting here, and especially for coming alone. Allies need trust more than weapons."

"Yes. I asked myself, 'Why would Ondrat trick you?' and I had no answer. If I brought an escort, we'd be so outnumbered we could only die bravely. And if you capture me, my people will be very offended. You need us for friends, not enemies. Isn't that right?"

"Exactly." Ondrat shoved open the door to his great room, bustling in behind his guest. A lone figure was seated at a large table before the hearth. The fire's glow was a tentative bubble that reached out into the darkness. Where it touched was warmth, life. Beyond its reach darkness waited, compressed by invisible walls.

Lorso stopped. "That is her? Who guards the other doors? Where are they?"

"The Abbess and I personally barred all entries but this before I left to meet you. No one can hear."

Like an animal on strange ground, Lorso advanced on the Abbess. Having afforded her one swift, dismissing look for identification, he swung wide into the gloom, hand on sword. Bent almost to a crouch, his limp giving him a sinister, rolling motion, he made his way past the table, then circled back.

He found the Abbess watching him from her chair with amused tolerance. Without rising, she extended a hand. "I admire your caution, Lorso, even as I assure you there's no need for it. Of all people, I'm the last who can afford to be seen with a Skan war chief."

"Slavetaker, not war chief. My other name is Slavetaker. And among my people, it is I whose soul is endangered by our association."

"I'm sure. But religion isn't why we're here, is it? There are more earthly matters at hand."

"Ondrat's message said now is the time to attack, and we must meet to coordinate. The Skan attack when they decide."

"But you're here, so obviously you feel there's reason to talk, don't you? Baron Ondrat says you should come now because Gan Moondark is away."

"So he said. I told him before, the Skan care nothing for Ola's politics. We want Gan and his family dead. Your sister, Sylah; dead."

"Sylah must die. If Neela and her child can be captured, we—Baron Ondrat—must have them. As hostages."

"Because you fear him. No, the Skan will kill Gan and be done with him."

Ondrat coughed, pitched his voice low, forceful. "Gan's absence is a blessing, Lorso. Conway, the one called White Thunder, rides after him. The man guarding the castle is a weakling, unnerved by responsibility. He seeks counsel only from two people. The Abbess is one of them; she can practically put him in your hands."

"Who is the other person? Can we eliminate him quickly? Is it the witch who makes Gan's magic, the Leclerc who lives on the farm to the south?"

Beseeching, Ondrat looked to the Abbess. Her thin-lipped glare made it clear what she thought of his ill-considered revelation. Her rigid silence made it equally clear he must answer. "I wasn't going to mention her. It's Jaleeta, the girl who escaped from your people. He pants after her like an old dog. She flatters him. It's disgusting. He's besotted, really. I know you must hate her. So do we. If she survives, we'd be glad to hand her over to you."

Lorso's voice, directed at the thick table was sepulchral. "Our god demands we punish those who hurt us. Do you remember I asked you about one of our boats that might have made it to your shore? We never found the man. His entire family serves Sosolassa now. Weighted, sent to the sea bottom. Tears of Jade sang the song of curses. Those spirits will forever lurk just under the sea's surface, waiting to pull others down. There is no worse thing for a Skan. Domel's blood is gone from our people. Save one man, a fishing slave. To remind others." He gazed deep into the eyes of the Violet Abbess. "So we take revenge. So we please our god."

She blinked. "And happy he must be. If he wishes Jaleeta, he may surely have her. We don't care. Do we, Baron?"

"Not at all. Good riddance. Little slut." He wheezed.

Lorso's head sagged again, almost as if he were too weary to continue. He made a wet sound, not quite a sigh, not quite a hiss. Ondrat and the Abbess avoided eye contact with each other as assiduously as they avoided staring at Lorso. His voice, when he spoke, was as heavy as before. "This is what will happen. I return here on the night of the third day from now. On the night of the fourth day, the moon will rise halfway through the night. The Skan will attack early."

Ondrat interrupted. "You mean later. You won't be able to see if there's no moon."

Lorso made the strange noise again. The Abbess glared at Ondrat. Lorso continued. "My sharker will lead, of course. You will prepare the hiding place for us. We will lay up there the fourth day and prepare to attack. If Gan Moondark is returned by then, he dies with his family. Or the woman and child die without him. If Sylah lives through the battle, she leaves with me. And Jaleeta." He looked up. His eyes were wild, drifting; it took an effort for him to focus on Ondrat. When he did, he centered on some point within the Baron's skull. "Your men will strike when they hear Skan war cries. Not before. The witch and Jaleeta must live, must be given to me." He rose. "Be ready."

He was halfway to the door before either the Abbess or the Baron recovered, the looming blackness swallowing the sound of his heels on the stone floor. The Abbess gestured furiously at Ondrat, clucking her tongue as at a shying horse. After a false start he bolted after Lorso.

Carefully bracing her elbows on the arms of her chair, the Abbess leaned back luxuriously. Chin resting on tented fingers, lost in contemplation of the ever-changing pattern of fiery coals, she smiled.

* * *

Domel understood Baron Ondrat's insistence on secrecy in political matters. What troubled him was the distance that suddenly yawned between himself and his benefactor. He could date its beginning quite accurately.

Three nights ago.

There was a visitor that night. Someone extremely important. The flurry of security activities—which included a guard on himself, Domel noted sourly—was extraordinary. As was the after-dark arrival of the Violet Abbess and her predawn departure.

Domel trusted his instincts. He no longer trusted Baron Ondrat. Never trusted the iron-eyed old bitch who called herself Abbess.

So he presently sat in his quarters putting together a knotted line of leather horse tack, stolen from the stables. It was quite strong. It had to be; it was at least three body-lengths to the ground from his window.

Before being politely but firmly confined to the quarters this morning, Domel saw Baron Ondrat was going quietly wild with more security efforts, preparing for another visit. The cook, always grateful for an appreciative audience, grumbled to Domel about having to ready food for impossibly late guests. He also wondered about anyone who insisted on vegetables that were either raw or pickled and wanted no meat, but fish. To Domel, that meant only Skan. And that meant betrayal.

Darkness presently crawled across the fort while he worked. A small leather bag held soot. He scooped some out now, blackening the line. There would be no pale line descending the wall to betray his departure.

Domel made a great show of going to bed. He pressed a wooden wedge under his door, then smeared face and hands with more soot. Securing the line to a heavy table, he pitched it out the window. Dropping, knot to knot, was easy. He leaped lightly to the ground, and in moments had scrambled to the back end of the great hall.

At the peak of the roof was a triangular entry. In summer it was covered with a wooden screen, allowing air circulation. Now, in winter, it was fitted with solid wooden doors. Men normally reached it by ladder. Domel tested the rough corner of the stone building. There were protrusions and chinks, enough for toes and fingers. Reaching high, he tested his first grip. He lifted himself. A knuckle cracked under the strain, unpleasant warning that aging tendons and joints flirting with arthritis were not the preferred tools of stealth. Domel gritted his teeth. He couldn't get younger; if he didn't discover what was happening in the great room, he might not get older.

Fingertips burning, feet threatening to cramp, Domel reached the roof overhang. To reach the window required a sideways maneuver, feet against the wall, hands clamped atop the roof. Domel took a deep breath, launched himself. Moccasins scrambled for scant purchase. Weary hands grabbed, pressuring for holds. He edged toward the window.

He was trembling when he reached it. Panting, he danced frantically, feet searching for the tiny sill under the window. Finding it was wonderful, exhilarating. With most of his weight solidly on his legs, he bent to grab one of the two door handles to pull it open.

It refused to move.

Domel tugged harder. The hand on the roof slipped. Fingers jammed through the sturdy wooden hoop. When his falling weight pulled full force on them, he groaned at the pain. But held on.

Dangling over the courtyard, he reached high, sought the other handle. Pulling himself up, he saw the small wedges securing the door. They were tight, but he got them free. After that, it was a matter of hanging by one hand, pulling the door free, and scrambling, wriggling, squeezing through the hole. Stretched out on the massive tie beam just inside, he closed the door behind him.

For some time he simply recovered.

Below, the Violet Abbess and Baron Ondrat argued. Voices echoed off the walls, one mingled with the other to create a rising, falling surf of angry, indistinguishable sounds.

Cross struts linked the tie beams. Domel hurried along the timber nimbly. Directly above the couple, words were clear, bouncing off the massive flat chimney. More, Domel was far beyond the revealing light of the fire. Lying flat at the junction of tie beam and pole plate, he wedged himself into the angle formed by the rafters.

The Abbess was saying, "You must calm yourself, Baron. He said he'd be here; he shall."

Ondrat's deeper voice, rough with tension, contrasted with the Abbess' coldly controlled anger. "But he's late. Can't you understand anything? If he's late in the attack, we lose the benefit of darkness."

"How can he be late? He specified no time. He's the one who has to avoid Wal's sea patrols and curious fishermen. The worst that can happen is that he'll be killed. We'll simply fall back on our original plan."

"What if he's captured? He'll tell everything. We never should have agreed."

"I asked you once before, Baron; please don't keep saying 'we.' This whole scheme is yours."

Ondrat stomped into the darkness. When he returned, he was calmer. "I worry about the Wolves. Once we strike the castle and Ola, every man in the barracks will come after us."

"Really, Baron. No conquest can go unchallenged. Still, all we need do is hold the castle until Windband arrives. The Wolves will be trapped between our walls and Windband's riders. They'll have to surrender."

"Who knows how long before Windband moves north?"

"Perhaps a Messenger to Moonpriest, explaining that you'll rule in the castle in the next two days, would move him north a bit more quickly."

Ondrat was thoughtful. He mauled the side of his nose with a forefinger. Musing, he said, "I like that. I'll see to it immediately. There's a Messenger lounging about here now. They sense trouble, I swear it." He rubbed his hands, held them to the fire. "And when Windband advances, it'll give those filthy Skan more to think about. The more distraction we offer them, the better I like it. What savages they are. Domel's family; they did nothing, and still suffered abominations."

The Abbess' dark hood bobbing affirmation made Domel think of a bird stabbing its beak at prey. "Drowned, like unwanted kittens. What did he say? 'The song of curses.' I wonder what that means."

"Don't forget the fisherman, the one enslaved. Someone must have liked him, to let him survive."

The Abbess' hand crept out of the sleeve, tapped the table. "The man's a great liability, Baron. What happened to his family could be extended to his protectors."

"I only kept him alive because he seemed to have some value for Church." Ondrat grew thoughtful. "Lorso might pay for him."

Unctuously, the Abbess said, "Remember, we kept him because of Church. If you sell him, there should be some consideration involved."

Domel heard no more. Images shrieked across his inner vision. He'd never been a loving husband or father. He paid little attention to his children, less to grandchildren, practically ignored the rest of his kin. But they were kin.

He wondered who was left alive, to labor blind, testimony to Domel's disgrace.

And now these lying landscum spoke of selling him. A Navigator. *Selling.*

The song of curses.

Given to the god. A god that couldn't beat a man in a fair fight at sea. A god that used a twisted, evil cheat to get his revenge.

Saturated with hate, Domel heard no more until the huge door to the great hall boomed open. Even that sound barely registered. It was the potent, trenchant smell of the sea that thrust him back into the present.

Lorso strode into the red-gold firelight.

Domel felt Lorso's words, his presence, as clearly as he heard.

The Skan plan of attack was simple. A detail of Ondrat's men, pretending to be ordinary travelers and relatives of the city dwellers, must infiltrate Ola on the following day. They would take individual lodgings. Shortly before sundown, the combined dissident forces of Krevelen, Byrda, Mull, and the rest of Ondrat would move on Ola. Those warriors must be in position to charge the city just after nightfall.

Lorso's sharker would reach the narrow beach below the castle a little later. The seaborne raiders would signal the attack with fire arrows. The Ondrat men in the city must be in position to kill the Sunrise Gate guards and admit the rebels. Simultaneously, Ondrat's men assigned to the castle guard must attack their Wolf counterparts.

"What of your men?" Ondrat asked. "What do they do?"

Lorso answered slowly. Domel smiled at the offense in his voice. "We scale the seaward castle walls. We'll be inside in time to finish what your warriors start. Where will the lightning weapons be?"

"There's only one." The Abbess spoke up. "Conway's off to fetch Gan home. Tate may be anywhere."

Lorso faced her. "Will Gan and Conway be here tomorrow night?"

She shook her head. "Impossible."

"I don't like that word." Lorso was thoughtful. "Request a meeting with this Emso. Ask for the Black Lightning to attend. And Sylah."

Dryly, the Abbess interrupted. "You're putting together a guest list."

"Excellent. A party. Tell Emso you have something wonderful to announce. Gather all of them in one place."

"I can't." The Abbess' hands fluttered, moths against fire.

"You will." He turned back to Ondrat. "We have until dusk tomorrow. You know where my sharker is. Come, if you have questions. If not, I'll see you in the castle—King Ondrat."

Domel craned to watch. Obscure in shadow, Lorso's interrupted gait became sinuous, wavering progress. Once again, Domel fancied he smelled the sea.

The door boomed shut.

Domel's mind took him from that room, carried him home to thundering surf. Clear green water that bathed the feet of lush, cloud-snaring mountains. Forests of silence so profound that the smallest birdcall lingered, fixed in a listener's hearing. Domel mourned that he'd paid so little attention.

Baron Ondrat and the Abbess renewed their vocal hacking at each other, primarily casting about for lies to induce Emso to invite the intended victims to the party.

Retracing his steps, Domel arrived at the far wall. Head and shoulders outside, door in hand, he was distracted. Someone pounded, a bass, drumlike sound. There were shouts. Curses. With his back to the excitement, attempting to refit the obstinate little door, Domel bent awkwardly to see. An armed guard erupted out a ground-floor door of the wing where he quartered. He sprinted for the back entry of the great hall, directly below.

Domel froze.

The guard hammered on the door. Ondrat himself opened it. Light spilled out. The cowering guard mumbled, held up something. Ondrat's hand reached out, grabbed the man by the jersey, and jerked him inside. Trailing on the ground, snaking into the building behind the disappeared guard, were the perfectly distanced knots of the escape line.

Chapter 85

Trapped, Domel retreated inside, hid among the timbers. The Abbess scurried out behind a roaring, cursing Ondrat.

The noises of pursuit seeped through the walls, picked at Domel's nerves. He held fast to his shadowy perch. There was no alternative. Time passed. Slowly.

Something furtive moved down below. Sound suggested haste. Domel chanced leaning over the edge of his beam. Rats, big as cats, moving with fat, rolling assurance. Thin, almost inaudible squeals laced the room. Flurrying games became near-mayhem when the leaders reached the table's rich leavings.

Such boldness pleased Domel. It inferred complacence, meaning few security patrols checked that area. Then the door flew open. Rats scattered, a torrent of skittering, blurry forms that disappeared into darkness. Ondrat's disgusted scorn echoed. "Do you think the renegade Skan scum had dinner in here with us, you fool? I've been in here all night. Get away. Search where he might be."

The door closed. Domel ignored the returning rats. Wedged in his space, he considered his situation. Unarmed. Trapped. But very much alive. And reasonably safe. Unless he tried to escape.

For him, there was no escape. There was revenge.

In the morning, servants bustled about, sweeping floor and table with the same broom. Domel remembered the rats, and smiled happily down on Baron Ondrat at his morning meal. A steady stream of armed men reported. Again, Domel was impressed. There was fear in the Baron, and plenty. He had that stiff, twitching action. Every time a door opened or a shout penetrated from outdoors, his whole body turned to it, concentrated on it. Yet he functioned well, decisive and explicit.

Domel wondered how long that strength would last. There was a sense of brittleness in it, like steel, too rapidly ground to razor edge. Blades like that cut flesh admirably; they splintered on other steel.

When the castle fell silent, Domel knew darkness was near. Much later, he rose carefully, massaging chilled, stiffened joints before trusting himself on the huge tie beams. He crossed to the river rock chimney. It provided holds if one was careful.

Once on solid ground, Domel considered the matter of outer clothing and a weapon. He decided to try the kitchen. There were knives, if nothing else.

The cook sat at a small worktable. Domel crawled through the open door. He advanced, hiding behind the long workbench in front of the hearth and stove. Selecting a massive skillet, he leaped, crushed the unsuspecting man's head.

The cook's heavy wool overcoat and hat fit well. Domel pulled them on, then helped himself to the cook's favorite cleaver. With a blade almost as long as Domel's forearm, very thick along its noncutting edge, and sword-sharp on the other, it was a formidable weapon.

Outside, night held the walled village utterly still. A dog's bark was a raw wound of sound. Domel fidgeted. Deserted streets and darkened buildings assured him that most men had already left for Ola. He crept to the wall. A guard stirred in the darker shadows where stairs led to the battlewalk.

The heavy cleaver proved a fortunate choice. The guard's metal helmet would have turned a lighter weapon. As it happened, it collapsed under Domel's two-handed blow. Too loud. Racing, Domel reached the battlewalk as running footsteps and shouts closed on the sound. Dropping the cleaver to the ground outside the wall, Domel followed it. He had the weapon in hand and was running seaward before the first torch was lit.

He found the trail leading to the fishing village easily and followed it at a steady trot. Balancebars were conveniently lined up on the beach. It seemed to take moons to heave one into the water. The temptation to simply luxuriate in the feeling of a boat under him was irresistible. He stroked the gunwale with one hand, shifted the tiller back and forth with the other.

A querulous cry spiraled up from the cluster of fishermen's houses.

Domel hastily raised his sail. The little boat responded smartly, hoisting its extended bar, swooping out to deep water. Lying on his back Domel watched for a sharker silhouette. The stars provided him a direct course, avoiding coastal indentations. The straighter route risked meeting Lorso. Time necessitated it.

When the lights of the castle were visible, Domel sat up, hauling the sail drum-tight. His little boat throbbed as if it understood that this was no fishing trip, that adventure was at hand. It snapped at the swells, split them furiously. When the mast groaned, it was a throaty growl of pride.

Overhead, stars glittered with wild intensity. Wind whipped Domel, burned his face. He reveled. Plunging a cupped hand in the black, frigid water, he drew it out filled, swabbed his face. The smell and taste of the sea infused him, its chill mingled with windburn and blood fired by emotions too powerful to express.

This was the world as it should be. His muscle, his boat. The sea.

Ola came too quickly. Regretfully, he heeled over for the beach north of the castle. Sail full, he slammed onto the coarse rock and sand. The hull shrieked across the grinding, hostile surface. Momentum ripped Domel's grip free of the gunwales; he flew forward, somersaulting over the side. Next to him, the mast cracked, moaned, crashed down. The boat rolled, settled. It made a sound like a shuddering sigh.

Domel put a hand on the hull, levered himself upright. The wood was stiff, inert. It's dead, he thought. One chance to be completely alive. Then finished.

He ran from there.

At the northern gate, he called to the guards, "You! Up there! Let me in. I have to see Emso."

A head appeared, a spot against the stars. "In the morning. The gate's closed for the night."

"You're going to be attacked."

Another head appeared. "Who're you? How many are with you?"

"I'm alone, you fool. Does it take a whole crew to make you understand there's an attack coming? If you want to be ready for them, open this gate and let me in."

"It's closed for the night. Those are the orders."

"Listen to me. The Skan are going to shove your orders down your throat and open your stomach to pull them back out. Can you understand that? Get me to Emso."

"Skan? What d'you know about Skan?"

"I'll show you my tattoos. Is that enough?"

There were more words, much quieter, and Domel knew there was at least one arrow aimed at him. He held very still. The gate creaked open, the two halves coming at him like the spreading lips of a huge mouth. Torches revealed four archers, arrows drawn to the head. A fifth man stepped from behind them, sword drawn, advancing cautiously. He peered into the darkness behind Domel while using Domel's body as a shield. When close enough, he said, "Give me your sword."

Domel extended the cleaver. "This will have to do."

Expressionless, the young Wolf took it, flipped it over his shoulder. One of the archers scooped it up. The man facing Domel said, "The tattoos?"

Taking off his coat, Domel rolled up a sleeve, exposed the characteristic geometric red-and-black figures.

The Wolf backed away. His sword remained aimed at Domel's midsection. "Come with me. I'll take you. He better be glad to see you."

They were inside then. The gate rumbled shut. Domel went on. "Hurry. They come before moonrise."

Another Wolf joined the first. They put Domel between them, their swords in the hands away from him. They picked up the pace to a fast walk. Yet another Wolf, this one obviously an officer, took over when the two younger men brought Domel to him. Now they moved at a fast trot into the castle itself. Halting the group at a door, the officer told the Wolves, "Anything tricky, and I want him hitting the ground in pieces, you hear me?"

The Wolves saluted. One looked at Domel with quiet determination. The other was tense, eyes wide, white around the lips. Domel concentrated on him.

The officer came out with Emso right behind him. He said, "It is you. What?"

Domel was shocked at his appearance. Never meticulous, Emso was so poorly shaven he looked almost mangy. Greasy hair was carelessly combed. Domel was sure the clothes he wore were a week old. They had a smell that was more than mere dirt. They were sour, acrid.

Emso repeated, "What?"

"The Violet Abbess asked you to gather tonight with her and your friends. Are they with you now?"

Emso's eyes glazed. He made a three-sign. So did the Wolves. Domel saw the tense one's knees bend, and he prepared to dodge. Emso said, "How could you know this?"

"Would it be best if we went inside, talked to everyone? You won't want to repeat some of the things I have to tell."

Emso considered for a moment, then gestured for Domel to follow. Over his shoulder, he told the Wolves to stand by at the door.

Innocent, welcoming curiosity warmed the faces of the Black Lightning and the two women flanking her. One wore the robes of a Rose Priestess; Domel knew she must be Sylah. The striking blond woman, then, had to be Gan's wife. His real attention was reserved for the Violet Abbess and Jaleeta. Their expressions were priceless, horror to be relished. "I am Domel, a Navigator of the Skan."

"Kill him!" Jaleeta leaped to her feet, hands outstretched toward Emso.

Emso half drew his murdat. Domel spoke quickly. "That one is the agent of Tears of Jade, spirit woman to Sosolassa, god of the Skan. She allies herself with this Violet Abbess to overthrow Gan Moondark and replace him with—"

"Liar. Liar." The Violet Abbess rose, shouting accusation. "Pagan. Anti-Church." She turned on Emso, shrilling, "Kill him. He fouls Church's name, her servant. Kill him, or be damned forever. I demand it."

Pale, dazed, Emso wavered. The murdat inched upward, exposing more steel. Domel shouted over the Abbess. "Emso. They mean to kill us. Then Gan. His wife and child. Sylah. Everybody. Listen to me."

The Abbess screeched interruption again. Jaleeta hurled herself around the table and into Emso. She strained to yank his murdat clear, grunting with effort.

Emso swayed under the assault, looking at Domel with a mixture of hatred and agonized uncertainty.

Sylah's voice rang clear. "Domel. You spoke of an attack."

Domel continued to focus on Emso. "Before moonrise, the Skan will be inside your walls. Ondrat men here will strike down your Wolves. Other men from Ondrat, Mull, Byrda, and Krevelen wait now, just beyond the walls of Ola. When they see the fire arrows of the Skan, they rush your gates. Other Ondrat men, already in the city, wait to murder your men and open them." He transferred his gaze to Jaleeta and bared his teeth in a smile he hoped she understood. "The one who leads this attack is named Lorso. We call him Slavetaker."

Jaleeta's hands rose to her throat. Her "No" was keening terror. She backed against the wall. Emso stepped in front of her, but she pushed him aside, unwilling to have her view of Domel obstructed.

The Abbess was sterner. She advanced on Domel. "Liar. Emso, I forbid this filth. Church demands his life."

Sylah challenged her. "Hold your threats, woman. Emso. Test this Domel. Form the Ondrat men into one unit in one place. Alert the Wolves in their barracks. If he lies, you've lost nothing. If he speaks true . . ." She let her look at Jaleeta and the Violet Abbess speak for itself.

"It's a trap." Jaleeta sounded as if she were choking. She gained strength as she continued. "I lied to them, Emso. To protect you." She came forward, clung to his sword arm.

Domel glanced at the Abbess. She appeared to be near fainting.

Jaleeta went on. "You know the Skan sent me. They sent this man, too. I promised the Skan I'd help him. While you send your men to the Sunrise Gate and reinforce the castle walls, the Skan and Baron Ondrat will come at the North Gate. I had to be sure of the plan before I could confess without ruining everything. Please don't hate me."

Emso looked down at her. The urgency of his need to believe made him tremble. He looked to the Abbess. "You knew about Ondrat?"

She sneered. "Of course not. Would he confide in a woman? Or Church? Especially a Church that needs you and a reformed Gan Moondark to protect her?"

"Reformed?" Sylah's question cracked across Emso's yearning. "Gan Moondark needs no reform. Emso, you may be killing all of us."

Tate finally stood up. All eyes went to her. She walked to the wall, picked up her wipe leaning there. She brandished it. "Emso, do what you believe is right. I'm going up on the west side of the roof. Just in case."

Instead of exiting directly, Tate chose to go to the other side of the table, close to Emso. Stopping in front of him, she saluted in the fashion of the Wolves. His attempted smile was awful, the salute infinitely weary. Over his shoulder, Tate saw movement.

Until that moment, she'd managed to avoid Jaleeta. Now the younger woman stared directly at Tate. Fear disfigured her beauty, but it was merely background for clear, cold malice. Angling behind Emso, away from any line of vision, but Tate's, Jaleeta smiled. A tiny, hardly visible movement of lips, a minute crinkling around the eyes. Cruel.

Shaken, Tate found her way out of the room.

With an inarticulate, broken sound, Emso half ran, half stumbled to the door. He physically pulled the three Wolves inside. Keeping his back to the room, he spoke to the officer. "Send a runner to the barracks. Everyone move immediately to defend the Sunrise Gate. Send another runner to alert all Wolves in the city that we've been infiltrated. Expect an attack intended to open the Sunrise Gate from inside. Take the Skan prisoner with you. Wait for me where the north and east castle walls meet. *Go!*"

The officer stepped past Emso, grabbing Domel. Pushing the Skan ahead of him, he sprinted to obey. Emso continued to keep his eyes averted from those behind him. "You two Wolves take the Violet Abbess and the woman named Jaleeta to the old dungeons. One is still empty. Keep them there. Do not harm them. Release them to no one but me."

The Wolf who worried Domel spoke. "The fight, Emso. We won't even see it."

"What you're doing is more important. Don't question it."

"I question." The Abbess moved toward the door. Without turning, Emso flung out a blocking arm. He told the Wolves, "Bind her, if necessary. Do not harm her. Ignore anything she says. Do you understand?"

Both men saluted. He looked away as they herded their charges out. When Jaleeta sagged, the Abbess caught her. Arm around the younger woman, she fastened a venomous glare on Sylah and Neela, then walked out, head high.

Emso said, "Sylah. Neela. Are you listening?"

Both assured him they were.

He lifted his head, seemed to speak through the stone walls to someplace far beyond. "When I'm dead, you'll hear many things from others about me. Some truths. Some lies. The usual things. I swear one thing only. Please remember. My wrongs grew out of love. Not ambition. Not envy. Whatever else they call me, please, always tell them they must also call me the man who loved Gan Moondark more than life. You promise me this?"

Neela said, "You won't die. You can't. We need you." Sylah kissed his cheek. "Go with a good heart, old friend. We promise. We will speak as you ask, because we know it is truth."

Chapter 86

From the roof of the castle, Tate frowned out over the mist creeping south down the Inland Sea. The wall torches were extinguished. She wore black, nonreflecting leather. The wipe rested easily in the crook of her left arm. A finger touched the trigger.

Overhead, stars were diamond-bright. The low fog edged ever closer, smothering lowlands, absorbing normally dependable features.

Somewhere under that mass was a sharker.

Tate looked south. Where Nalatan was.

Jaleeta. The way she looked from behind Emso. Tate marveled at hatred so strong it superseded terror. Jaleeta even found pleasure in knowing Tate saw her enmity.

Another realization came to Tate. Jaleeta's actions weren't those of a woman who believed her life was over. That malevolent smile included challenge, a determination to turn even this potential catastrophe to advantage. Jaleeta intended to live. To win. To assure that Tate lost.

Tate wandered toward the southern wall, staring off into the blackness. In the mist-shroud far below a seal barked, splashed. Down on the beach raccoons brawled over something. Their squalling cries always made Tate think of nasty little children.

She tried to dismiss resurgent suspicions and worries, tried to imagine where Nalatan might be, picturing him riding north, passing things they'd seen together on the return from the Dry. She wished he stood beside her, wished none of this foolish separation ever happened. But what she'd done was for a purpose, for the benefit of all. Surely he could understand. He was the one who was just being hardheaded.

Suddenly, sickeningly, Jaleeta's image was back. In Tate's mind, the heartless smile was broader.

Shouts erupted behind Tate. A man screamed hoarse dismay. The sound ended as if broken. Instantly, the night was shattered by the sounds of battle. War cries soared. The castle warning drums boomed redundant alarm; every available man was already on the battlewalk or at his counterattack position.

Tate ran to the north side of the roof. A fire arrow arced across the sky. It appeared to come from the juncture of the city wall and the higher castle wall. Even as Tate wondered which wall was compromised, she heard combat erupt below her.

Her aim at the join of the walls was distracted by clatter on the roof behind her. She turned, expecting to see an arrow. Instead, it was a much heavier object, more like an extra-thick axe handle. Tate jumped, startled, when it began to move rapidly toward the crenellated wall. Then she saw the thick line dragging it sideways. Following, Tate drew her murdat.

The stick spanned one of the crenels with room to spare. Moving several paces to the side, Tate cautiously peered down. Two men already scrambled up the line, literally walking the wall. A third steadied it at the bottom. Tate hacked at the line.

Sparks flew.

Unbelieving, she struck again, then again. Something gleamed, and she understood that a leather-encased chain attached the bar to the climbing line. She reached out and down to sever the line. The closest Skan was ready. Hanging on with one hand, he engaged her with the sword in his other. An arrow from the man on the ground shattered on the crenel a handspan from Tate's head. Shards and splinters stung her cheek. She jerked back instinctively. The Skan gained ground, got a knee into the merlon between crenels, thrust at her.

The red-orange muzzle flash of the wipe revealed a face twisted with desperate exertion. The expression had no time to alter. The round flung the man off, sent him tumbling into empty air. Tate leaned out to blow the second man off the line before he could safely drop to the ground. The third darted into covering darkness.

When she pulled back from the wall, another Skan was on her, sword raised. She dropped straight down, rolling into him. He tripped over her. Firing at him as she rose, Tate pushed against the roof, driving herself backward. Yet another Skan's sword stroke whispered fury at its miss, slicing the night where she'd been. A shot dropped that man; a second shot finished the other. Running to the south wall, Tate found another grappling bar, the line slack. She pulled both lines up.

The battle below her was going badly. Ondrat war cries mingled with Wolf howls and the high, screaming yells of Skan. Somehow, the traitorous unit had entered the action.

In such a swirling, dark melee the wipe was as dangerous to friend as foe. Tate slung it across her back. Pistol in one hand, murdat in the other, she ran to help.

Curled in a trembling ball, Jaleeta pressed against the legs of the standing Violet Abbess. The older woman, in the open doorway of the dungeon, held the two young Wolves at bay with an icy dignity. Her extended hands rested on each side of the opening. Bathed in the wavering light of two smoking torches fixed in wall standards, she exuded authority. "You will not close us in this foul pit. I shall stand here until freed by your master or your death. It's all one to me. But you will not imprison us in darkness and filth."

The more earnest young man argued unhappily. "It's not that dirty, Abbess. It's just for a little while. Emso ordered us."

"Church orders you." A pointing finger made the man flinch. Moving slowly, pivoting, the Abbess included the more highly stressed individual. "Emso ordered you to use no force."

He lost the staring match almost as soon as it started. He told his friend, "This is dumb. We can't make her stay here. Why should we stay? Our friends are fighting. Dying, even. They need us."

The first one clenched his jaws. He shook his head, attention riveted on the Abbess. His companion shifted his weight, a barely perceptible move that distanced him. The unburdened foot scuffed backward quickly, jerkily. Hearing the sound, the first one turned to him, quizzical.

The tense one said, "I'm leaving."

"You can't. We were ordered."

"Stay then. If I'm killed, I won't care what Emso says. If I'm hurt, he'll be sorry for me. And if nothing happens to me, I won't have to tell everyone I missed the fight guarding an ugly old woman and a sniveling girl."

The Abbess' eyes narrowed to slits. She held her tongue. Only the wiry twitch of a pulse at a temple betrayed her anxiety.

The high-strung guard fled. The shouts of his companion echoed uselessly. The remaining Wolf told the Abbess, "You ruined him. Emso won't care what you say. You should be ashamed."

Jaleeta rolled over on her side, moaning. She struggled to all fours. Retching, coughing, she vomited in the direction of the Abbess. The older woman dodged, yelling, gathering her robe. Jaleeta, hair hanging down, continued to hack and spit. She backed away from her mess, beastlike, clumsy. "They'll kill me. Rape me. I can't stand it. Don't let them get me." Then, gasping, "Water, please. Throat. Hurt."

The Wolf unfastened his leather water-bag quickly. Eyes perfect rounds, he bent to her. Jaleeta reached blindly, felt it, grabbed. She drank, rinsing and spitting. Another spasm racked her. She extended the bag as it did, the erratically wobbling hand sagging under the weight. The Wolf bent to take it.

He may have seen the shortknife in her left hand that slashed murderously across his stretched, exposed throat. If he did, he still had no opportunity to avoid it. He straightened in one spasmodic lunge, both hands clutching the gaping wound. Blood spurted between the fingers. Eyes still living watched with the glazed disbelief of the dead.

Jaleeta rose, stepped back against the wall. The left hand, holding the knife, remained extended, defensive. With her right, she raised the water bag for a cleansing mouthful, spat. Her expressionless gaze remained fixed on the slumping warrior.

Summoning impossible strength, the young man stepped toward the Abbess. He extended reddened, begging hands. The flow was a sickly, slack thing already. He tumbled forward in wasted hope. His collapsing embrace left terrible accusation staining the front of the Abbess' robe.

She stepped back, staring down at him.

"You stay here, if it pleases you so." Jaleeta dropped the water bag, headed down the corridor. In an afterthought, she bent down to collect the dead man's murdat. She wiped her shortknife on his jacket and replaced it in her sleeve.

The Abbess hurried behind her.

Outside was chaos. Opening the door admitted the full fury of battle-sound. In the light of burning buildings, cursing, shrieking knots of men surged and swirled across the grounds, killing and dying. Two steps into the night, the Abbess checked, hands to her ears. She shrank back against the wall.

On the wall, desperation lifted Emso's voice above the din. "Jaleeta! Here!"

Directly in front of her, Jaleeta watched a Wolf ram his murdat halfway through an Ondrat warrior. The ensuing scream added impetus to her dash for the stairs leading to the battlewalk. Once there, she was slammed against the stone wall, Emso shielding her with his body. Within moments, she cursed her choice. Emso's pocket of defenders was small, and it was being forced away from the stairs. Ground level offered at least relative safety; a counterattacking Wolf unit was winning its struggle just outside the great hall. Movement beyond them caught Jaleeta's eye. She looked to Chosens being herded into a castle side entry. She was certain Neela was among them, and the tall Priestess gesturing at the others could only be Sylah.

Suddenly, she was aware of something on the battlewalk floor, beside her. Domel, hands and feet bound, lay with his back against the wall. The officer who'd brought him to this point lay beside him, an arrow in his chest. Domel grinned at Jaleeta, a grimace of acceptance. And triumph.

Whatever Domel said to her was lost in the roar of battle. Scuffling along the wall, keeping Emso in front of her, Jaleeta realized the Skan controlled the battlewalk from both directions now, and were forcing Emso's group away from the stairs.

Death—or capture—was inevitable.

Jaleeta darted out from behind Emso, tried to reach the stairs. Embattled Wolves blocked her, ignored her pushes. Screaming Skan sensed complete victory.

A voice rang above the conflict. "Don't kill the woman! Don't kill her!"

Lorso.

Jaleeta felt her mind erupt in white-hot heat. Her heart seized. She couldn't breathe.

Until she understood. It was all so simple.

She searched the struggling mass in front of her, located Emso, called to him. "Emso! Here." He pulled away from the fight, hurried to her, reaching. Jaleeta grabbed the outthrust arm at the wrist. Pivoting, bending at the knee, combining her weight and strength with Emso's momentum, she pulled the arm across her body. As Emso's grizzled, shocked mask of incomprehension flashed in front of her, falling from the battlewalk, she screamed as loud as she could, "Lorso! Help me! I'm here, Lorso! Save me!"

Startled Wolves glanced over their shoulder. One shouted, "Emso fell. She pushed him." He rushed at her. Lorso leaped through the gap, struck the man down as he raised his murdat.

Ranks broken, the surviving Wolves leaped off the battlewalk. Grabbing Emso, they dragged him against the wall, formed a defensive semicircle.

An eerie lull fell across the battle. Here and there, individuals continued to duel. They grunted, animals preying on each other, while metal clashed with metal. The Wolf formation by the entrance advanced methodically, forcing back Skan and Ondrat men. Figures scurried into the darkness.

On the battlewalk, Jaleeta talked for her life. "I knew you'd come. I told Tears of Jade, 'Lorso won't let me die among those people.' She made me come. I couldn't tell her about us, but I told her I was a Skan woman, forever. She said I had to do this, or she'd hurt me, hurt my mother. But I knew you'd come. That's why I pushed that one off the walk. That's Emso, Gan Moondark's favorite. I killed him for you, my Lorso. For the glory of Slavetaker."

"Gan is here? His wife and child? Sylah?" Lorso's hands were at her throat, thumbs centered, pressing.

Just as she shook her head, the Skan with Lorso ran down the ladder to attack the Wolves who'd jumped to escape them.

Lorso turned away from Jaleeta. He raised his sword, prepared to command. She grabbed his arm. "There's no time. You were betrayed. The Wolves from the barracks will be here before you can kill Sylah and Neela. There's one you want far more than either of them."

Lorso, paused, unsure. Jaleeta rushed on. "The man Leclerc. He has magic, but he's weak. A puny man, Lorso. Take him back to Tears of Jade. Make him use his magic for us. I've seen it, Lorso. Powder that breaks rocks, spears that kill with blue fire."

"Blue fire? Like Moonpriest?"

She shook her head. Below them, the battle slacked again. In the distance was the sound of howling coming at a rush, and the massive pounding of a war drum. "I told you the Wolves were coming. Yes, the lightning, like Moonpriest. He has a lightning weapon, too. Slavetaker could make him show how to use it."

Lorso barely hesitated. His fleeting smile was enigmatic. He shouted, "Skan out! Skan out! To the boats!"

Immediately, his men took up the call, streamed toward the wall. The abandoned Ondrat men yelled dismay. Those who attempted to follow the Skan were summarily beaten back. The Wolves, unconcerned with the politics of the situation, went at the distraught Ondrats mercilessly.

With Jaleeta slung over his shoulder like a sack, Lorso dropped down a Skan climbing line. Off-sword hand wrapped in Jaleeta's hair, he directed his men's withdrawal.

A few Ondrats fought to the end. Most surrendered quickly. The quiet of post-combat swept the grounds inside the walls. The moans of wounded and dying ebbed and flowed. Tentative voices called the names of friends. Officers and small unit leaders shouted for order. Yet, compared to what went before, everything was crushingly lethargic. Men seemed afraid to add or detract from anything around them.

Into that, Sylah and the other War Healers of both abbeys brought their soothing, whispering voices and their ministrations.

On the battlewalk, Domel finished slashing his bindings. He rolled to the edge, indistinguishable among the human wreckage. "Emso," he called, carefully face-down. A moment later, a groaning voice said, "Here. Who calls?"

Domel smiled. That was something better left unanswered. "Are you able to fight?"

"My leg. It could be broken. Are they coming back? Who are you?" Growing recognition sharpened the last question.

"They mean to take the magic one called Leclerc. Jaleeta's showing Lorso the way. If you can warn him, you better. Or see his skills turned against you and your Gan. Good luck. You're a good warrior."

"Wait! Wolves! To the wall! Catch him. There's a Skan there."

Domel slipped through a crenel, dropped rapidly down one of the Skan lines. He was far away, shrouded by the night, long before anyone reached the battlewalk.

As soon as the fire-arrow tore the night, Baron Ondrat drove the rebel forces at Sunrise Gate in a frenzied effort. If the gate wasn't under control by the time the Packs arrived, the game was lost. He literally screamed orders, exhorting his men to rise above themselves.

The Wolves opposing him fought with the desperation of men who know their effort is key. Many were Olans, and they remembered well the cruelties of the old reign. Others were from baronies where liberty was an equally rare wine. They understood that the Three Territories was their sole hope of freedom. Knowing the Skan and traitors fought their friends inside the castle, they gave no ground, dying where they stood.

At the howling of their onrushing brothers from the barracks, and the thunder of their drums, they found the energy for hoarse cheers. Those fighting inside the walls attacked. The infiltrators, expecting to cut down a few unready guards, were surprised and ineffective. The defenders on the battlewalk poured arrows into the rebels, who had barely a handful of ladders. Wolves met the few brave souls who climbed them.

Baron Ondrat relinquished his position in front of the rebels, got behind them, pushing them ahead. Slowly, almost imperceptibly, he worked his way all the way to the rear. A few paces beyond the last rank, with no one to see but the ground-littering casualties, he slipped away. Trotting across the meadow that was the cleared area around the city walls, he complimented himself on his foresight. He even smiled, thinking what his fellow Barons would pay for a seat on board the balancebar waiting at the fishing village near his fort.

Life among the Skan would take some getting used to.

He swung aboard his horse, whipped it to a gallop.

A sack of gold would soften anyone. Even a Skan. More than that, however, the Skan traded with the Nions. Nions loved gold.

Clever men all loved gold. Clever men also avoided dying beside inferiors.

CHAPTER 87

TATE'S FIRST REACTION TO THE SKAN RETREAT WAS NEAR-HYSTERIC RELIEF. SHE DREDGED UP the last of her energy to engage an Ondrat warrior who seemed intent on salvaging the honor of his barony single-handed. Rasping, almost sobbing, Tate demanded that he surrender. The man answered with a two-handed descending slash that hammered her sword tip down to earth. In the instant when both weapons were grounded, she drove the crown of her head directly into his nose. Cartilage crunched. A knee into his crotch doubled him over. Measuring, she drew back the murdat and swung. The flat of the blade took him just at the top of the ear, a sound like dropping a ripe melon.

Tate slumped to a sitting position against a wall, legs splayed ahead of her. She almost beat her victim to the ground. He snored hugely. Tate closed her eyes.

When she opened them, Sylah was standing over her, looking afraid. "Are you alright?"

Tate said, "Never better. We'll get him in the next round."

"What?"

"Nothing. A little punchy. No, no; forget that." Tate tucked her feet under her, reached out to Sylah for a hand up. "Tired, that's all. How are the troops?"

"Many injured. Many dead. There are fires. In the Violet Abbey, in the castle."

Gritting her teeth, Tate said, "I'll get men on Leclerc's pumps. Where's Emso?"

"Organizing the remaining men, I expect. I've been too busy . . ."

"Don't you dare apologize. You're holding us together, you and your Priestesses. Got to run—fire's calling. See you." Tate managed a long pull on her water bag as she ran to the nearest pump. Checking the hoses, calling for help, she had it working quickly. Some Wolves had already practiced on the machines; they led teams to operate the other pumps. The fires, restricted to the Violet Abbey and the castle's northern side, were stubborn. Tate continued to look for Emso. The image of him calling to Jaleeta refused to go away. She tried to deny the sound of that cry. It was more than a man seeking to protect a fellow human. Tate ruefully considered that she'd become particularly sensitive to emotional undercurrents. Her problem was a failure to react properly.

A Wolf she recognized dropped off the pump handle as she was passing. Another man crawled up to take his place. Tate went to the one resting, asked if he'd seen Emso. Surprise raised singed eyebrows, revealed whites startling in a soot-blackened face. "Didn't you hear? He ordered a large detail to Leclerc's farm, told them to guard it. His leg's broken; he had some Wolves help him to the stable, and he rode out a little after the others. He told me you were in command until he gets back."

"Why didn't he tell me that? I've been fighting fires. We don't have any security on the walls, do we?"

"I stationed men there. You were busy. There aren't many. More like lookouts than defenders. A lot of men went down."

"You did a good job. Get some rest. I'll see about relieving the watchers. Now that I know Emso's left me to run this lash-up, I better get with it."

Hurrying to the wall, Tate looked back at the fires. They seemed to be under control, at least. Most importantly, they were no danger to the dungeon area where the ammunition was stored.

Thinking of that made her check her own supply. It also made her stop to consider why Emso would send survivors from a battered force to take on additional guard responsibilities. She decided it was because he finally realized how important Leclerc was to the Three Territories.

It was a long time coming. Emso was a fine man, despite his cranky old-fashioned attitudes. She hurried up the steps to the battlewalk, hoping Leclerc and Emso would finally patch their differences.

Emso listened to the triumph of the Wolf packs. The cries tore at his soul.

Fool. Old fool.

The steady rhythm of horse hooves repeated the words mercilessly. Not that he deserved mercy, he told himself. A traitor rejected that consideration the instant he stepped onto the path of betrayal.

His memory dragged him back to the wall, where he sheltered she who brought him to his end, and shame burned in him. The truth was plain when he ordered her imprisoned. Yet when he saw her endangered he was helpless. He had to save her, protect her. Even be victimized by her.

With his good leg, Emso heeled his horse, demanded greater speed. He hoped Ondrat cowered in his fort, hoped the gate was unguarded. Emso allowed himself a grim, tight smile. He didn't believe Ondrat would stay and fight with his men. As soon as defeat was apparent—or even likely—Ondrat would run; Emso was sure of it. He was equally sure Ondrat would go to his den, prepare to negotiate.

The jarring of the faster pace made the bones of the broken leg grate unpleasantly. There was the other stuff in the saddlebags, as well. It wouldn't do to damage that. But the important thing was to kill Ondrat. Frowning, Emso admitted he wasn't certain he could best Ondrat standing on one leg. He straightened in the saddle. Ondrat must die; there was no alternative.

A full, clear moon bathed the fort's walls, creating a pattern of vertical silvers, grays, and blacks. In the middle of it, the entry yawned sinister invitation. There were absolutely no lights in the village.

Emso approached very slowly, warily. His mount sensed Emso's nervousness. It tossed its head constantly, but gave no other sign of excitement. Emso silently blessed it.

Emso entered the gateway, murdat bared. No challenges, no sound of running feet. Eerily, sounds came from some of the buildings he passed. They were small, scratchy noises that made Emso think of burrowing animals scrambling to escape a predator. He dropped forward on his horse, blending with it in the dark, offering as little target as possible.

The door to the castle was as open as the gate. It sighed gently on bulky hinges when Emso prodded it with the tip of his murdat. He dismounted, smothering a cry when the heel of his broken leg struck the ground. Securing the horse to a hitching post, murdat in hand, he hopped through the door, cursing his awkwardness.

In the farthest of the two large chairs in front of the fireplace, Ondrat waited. He was angled so he equally faced the door and the low glow of dying embers. Emso advanced quickly, using the murdat as a prop until he could reach out and balance with one hand against the hearth. By then the bared sword lying across Ondrat's lap was clearly visible.

Emso said, "I see you expected me. I was afraid you'd run. Stand, Baron, or die where you are." He leveled the murdat.

From the darkness, a disembodied voice answered, "Too late. He owed me, as well. I collected first."

Emso whirled, ready. "Domel? Is that you?"

Again, from the dark. "Yes. If you'd taken the time to inspect on your way in, you'd have seen the two dead guards at the gate, and the man just to the left of the doorway here. You should thank me. The way you're crow-hopping about, you wouldn't have made it past any of them."

Bridling, Emso waggled the murdat. "If my walking bothers you, come over here. We have our own affair."

Domel materialized, wraith-silent. "I understand how you feel. Better than you know. I'll accommodate you, if it's what you want. You're crippled. I'll kill you."

"Perhaps. It's not important."

Lifting his own weapon, Domel aimed it at Ondrat. In the ruddy luminance of coals, the moving steel took on a sliding, graceful life. "He'd tell you otherwise. I'd agree with him. Killing a thing like Ondrat is correct. For one of us to kill the other—or for us to kill each other—is mere killing. Both of us have covered ourselves in shame and regret. That's why I killed Ondrat. He was part of my disgrace."

"No less than mine. And you helped them shame me."

Domel sliced the air with his sword. His voice was as dry as the whisper of the blade. "Will you tell me that it wasn't in your mind to eliminate me, once Gan Moondark's present problems are under control? Or if it appeared the Skan were about to defeat you? If that young woman hadn't pitched you off the battlewalk, you'd have sold me back to Lorso or killed me like a trussed chicken."

"I may have."

Snorting, Domel took a step closer. "If you feel you have to fight me, I won't disappoint you. My own goals are larger. I can never recover my name and honor, but I can assure that those who took them will never forget me."

"Well, tell me. What will you do? If you get past me."

"I don't want to get past you. Help me."

Bitter laughter rocked Emso. He leaned heavily into the stone hearth. "Help you? Into the Land Under."

"Exactly."

Domel's equanimity silenced Emso's lingering chuckles. "What's that mean?"

"Everyone in the Three Territories will hear how Jaleeta tricked you." Ignoring Emso's suddenly raised murdat, Domel walked easily to Ondrat's side. Shoving a dead elbow out of the way, he sat comfortably on the chair arm. "Unlike you, I mean to die striking at the root of my troubles."

"You mean me. Or Gan."

"Don't be so proud. I mean my own people. The Skan."

"I don't believe that."

"Then listen. A Skan fleet lies in our main harbor. I think Lorso ordered this raid to capture Jaleeta. If so, the main attack must be imminent. I intend to harm those sharkers, rob the Skan of their glory, as they robbed me of my reputation."

Emso lowered his weapon, rubbed a jaw pensively. "Gan's spoken of something he calls the Journey. Men salvage honor in a suicide ride into the tribe's enemies."

Domel waited, silent. Emso sighed. "We're a pair of old fools."

"Then I die as a brave fool. A revenged fool."

Sheathing his murdat, Emso said, "I guess you have a boat ready?"

Rising, nudging Ondrat's body with the tip of his sword, Domel said, "He did. He doesn't need it now." He replaced his own sword, reached to help Emso away from the wall. He nodded at the leg. "Broken?" When Emso grunted, Domel took it as an affirmative. He said, "At least the one who tricked you was young and beautiful. Mine's ugly enough to send the salmon back downstream."

Emso let Domel take some of his weight. "I wish we'd met in a different situation. I think we could have been friends."

Domel was dry. "After my people finish with us, we'll have a long, long time to get acquainted."

Remembering the rest of his mission to Ondrat's barony, Emso halted. Turning away, he hopped back to the hearth, as Domel watched, puzzled. Emso took the big ash shovel from its hanger, scooped coals out onto the floor, against the wooden wall. Domel added kindling and firewood from the fireplace supply. Hungry flames rose swiftly. For a fleeting moment, their brightness added vibrant color to the faded, tattered banners festooning the wall. Then the ancient cloth withered, was devoured, and there was only fire.

Domel said, "Why do we burn such vermin?"

Emso looked at him, feeling weightless, as if the growing draft of the fire could suck him off the ground, consume him. He thought of a smith's furnace, how the light lured the mindless moths from darkness, inhaled them into consuming heat. In his mind, he saw himself; a single hissing spark. He said, "I must," and as Domel helped him on his awkward passage into the night, he wondered what question he'd just answered.

Chapter 88

Gan looked up as Conway and Nalatan approached from opposite directions. When both were beside him, he asked, "Are the men all right?"

Nalatan answered, "The rear guard's doing as well as could be expected. They're worn out, Murdat. We should rest."

"I agree." Conway's answer was hoarse with exhaustion. "The point was wobbling in his saddle like a drunken man. His tenner says they're all like that. If we don't get some sleep, we'll be useless when we reach Ola."

"The surprise of our return will outweigh that. We're the only ones who know how weary we are." There was no point in his saying that the Skan might already have crushed resistance in Ola. That thought drove them all from the outset. Still, what began as a dash degenerated to an endurance event. Without extra mounts, short of food, sleeping only when the lack of it tumbled them out of the saddles, they barely maintained military capability.

Gan tried to lighten the mood. "At least we've got relief coming. The River People volunteers aren't far behind us." The effort went ignored.

Conway said, "You'd think someone on these farms would have some information. I've got a suggestion. We're making good time now that the moon's finally high. It's not far to Leclerc's. He'll be there, unless there's been a real problem. Let's pull in there. If he knows there's trouble at the castle, we press on. If not, we sleep in the barn and the workshops and get a good start in the morning. We lose very little time, and we come into Ola fresh enough to do some good, if we have to."

The idea wasn't unique to Conway. Gan wondered about it before moonrise. Shelter from the enervating cold would help the men. Hot food after a few hours' sleep would restore them. But Conway's "little time" could prove crucial. Even catastrophic.

Then Nalatan said, "If the Skan are coming, they're either here already, or they won't come until tomorrow night. As Conway said, the moon's high. They'll time their attack to start when dark's heaviest, so they can close on us without being seen. Once the fight's under way, they'll want the moonlight to coordinate the attack or withdrawal, if it's necessary. We all know that."

Gan was short. "What if the Skan are attacking as we ride? The sound of it wouldn't reach Leclerc."

"Tate would send for him." Conway was certain. "He and Bernhardt know how to use the lightning weapons."

Gan considered, then nodded decisively. "We turn off at Leclerc's farm. I'll decide what to do after I see him."

Soon after, Gan abruptly reined in. Nalatan and Conway did the same. Gan's sharp whistle halted the advance guard. Rising in his stirrups, as though the extra height would somehow make things clearer, Gan listened. Nalatan cupped his hands behind his ears, swiveling. Conway watched, disgusted. His senses were nothing like as sharp as his companions', and he resented it. Finally, impatient, he spoke out. "What?" It was a demand.

"Lightning weapons. Two." Gan looked to Nalatan for confirmation. The monk nodded. Another whistle from Gan rallied the unit around him. There were forty-two men, counting Gan himself. Still upright, he addressed them. "Louis Leclerc is being attacked. I'm taking the point. Any man whose horse falls, follow on foot. Any man who feels unable to fight, dismount now, give your horse to another."

A young voice, resentful, rose from the slumped riders. "We may fall down. We won't fall out. Why are we wasting time?"

Gan was grateful for the darkness that covered his first flush of anger at the insubordination, and the embarrassment that replaced it. "Excellent attitude. Bad mouth. Follow me, then. And the One in All be with all of you."

The silence of the march disappeared, replaced by voices harshly urging dispirited, nearly blown mounts.

Shortly after that, a sinister orange glow limned trees silvered by the full moon. "Fire," Conway said. Nalatan grunted. He unlashed the parrying bar from his saddle, checked the fit of his sword in the scabbard. Then he did the same thing with the knives in their holsters at his biceps. For his part, Conway fixed the bayonet to his wipe, jacked boop and wipe rounds into the chamber. Ahead of them, Gan already had his murdat in his hand, controlling his horse with the other.

Conway fell back behind Nalatan, then whistled his dogs in to flank him. Footsore, limping, Karda and Mikka paced beside the horse, too weary to even look up when Gan whistled in Shara and Cho.

When the column broke clear of the confining forest, it compacted, forming a shocked, dismayed mass.

Leclerc's farmhouse was completely engulfed. Smoke pillared into the night, obscuring stars. The workshops were afire, as well. Skan war-cries carried a malicious ring of certainty, despite the distance. As the small group stared, lightning weapons blinked fire from one of the workshops. Gan wheeled his horse. "You. Ride for Ola as hard as you can. Get help. *Go.*"

More constrained, he told the rest, "Charge on my command. The fire will expose them. Pick your first man on the approach. I figure at least forty Skan there. Good hunting." He moved out at a walk.

Conway wanted to scream at him to gallop. He ate the words, even if the urge continued. It was too far. The horses would collapse long before they got there.

As it was, Conway could feel his mount's legs stiffening, see the head and ears pitch forward, down. Moonlight afforded enough illumination to observe the other horses. They were as used as his. We hit them with our best shot, he told himself, and then we're on foot. Good hunting, indeed.

Loud cheering broke into his considerations. He looked ahead, squinting, to make out a group of Skan, new arrivals, running across the field between the buildings of Leclerc's compound and the tree line to the west. Conway ground his teeth in speechless frustration. Miserable odds had just multiplied.

A hand signal from Gan spread the men into a line formation. Any other time, it would have been ludicrous. Horses stumbled. Men rolled around in saddles. The line wavered like a windblown row of wheat stalks. Gan signaled a canter. The Skan were erratic silhouettes against the flames.

Another signal brought the troops to a trot. A horse stumbled into the one next to it. Both went down in a weak, flailing jumble. One Wolf rose, chased after his companions in a shambling run. Another horse dropped, quivering as if shot. The fourth crashed headfirst, pitching his rider. The man rolled upright, pressed on.

Conway shouted, an involuntary outburst of fear as Skan crashed through the workshop door. One shot followed, muted by the walls. To Conway, it had a forlorn, weak sound.

The heat from the burning house was palpable. Gan brought the Wolves to a gallop, angling to keep to the dark. Conway, abandoning discipline, flogged his horse, desperate to reach his friends. The animal tried, but it hadn't the strength. Breathing in ragged, sucking gulps, it barely kept up with the charge.

It was the scream of a fallen, leg-broken horse that warned the nearest Skan. By then the Wolves were on them, cutting down men like cornstalks. Conway rode through to the far side of the building, reins in his left hand, wipe in the right. Karda and Mikka raged beside him.

By the time the Wolves were beyond the burning workshop, turning to charge again, the newly arrived Skan were kneeling, firing arrows. The Skan inside the workshop streamed out. Four of them carried a body.

Only one. Conway screamed the names of his friends, slapped his horse's rump. The spent animal managed a halfhearted leap, then played out entirely. Spraddle-legged, shaking, it simply stopped. Its nose was almost touching the ground, and frothing sweat bathed it from chest to loins.

Vaulting out of the saddle, Conway snapped a round at the group carrying the captive. They were behind the archers now, racing for cover in the forest and the sea beyond.

Nalatan, also on foot, caught Conway's arm just as he broke into a run. When Conway tried to shake him off, Nalatan only held harder. Conway turned, shoving viciously. Nalatan stumbled back. He remained calm, even in the face of threatening growls from the excited dogs. He said, "Easy, Matt Conway. Those archers will kill you and your dogs before you can close with them. Look, to the left; Gan's already got some of our men returning arrow fire. See there; he's moving the rest to outflank the Skan archers."

"They've got a prisoner."

"I saw. Come. We'll go around to the right. Keep down." Without waiting for argument or agreement, Nalatan was gone. Crouched low, he moved with a gait that made up for its near-comical appearance with speed. Conway followed, keeping the dogs close.

Within the trees, Nalatan said, "Use the lightning and the dogs only if you must. Silence is our best weapon."

The forest behind Leclerc's house extended a considerable distance, ending abruptly at high, sheer bluffs. There were interruptions in that vertical face, places where landslide created steep avenues of exit inland. Part of the Skan raiding party now fought furiously to cover the escape of their captive-taking companions while the latter hurried to one of those routes. Consummate warriors, the Skan let Gan's exhausted, clumsy men come to them. They slashed from behind trees. Some lay in small depressions or under sprawling ground cover, reaching up with swords to disembowel men too tired to search effectively.

For once, Conway's night skills matched Nalatan's. Necessity demanded. Between them, they were a baleful force. Skan died under thrusting bayonet and crushing parrying bar. Inexorably, however, it became clear that the Skan were succeeding. The surviving Wolves united at the mouth of a declivity leading to the beach. In the bright moonlight, four sharkers waited offshore. Amidst tumbled driftwood logs, Skan warriors screamed defiant taunts at their enemies above. Another group, much smaller, crouched at the limit of the piled timber. Between them and the sea was a broad expanse of moon-silvered beach.

Conway said, "That small bunch has to be the one with the prisoner. They're getting ready to go. We've got to move."

Somber, apologetic, Gan answered, "We've eleven wounded. Even with your weapon, even with the dogs, we can only kill some of them, and die."

Helplessness threatened to destroy Conway. He squeezed the stock of the wipe so hard it felt his skin must split. "They came for Leclerc and Bernhardt because they've heard what they can build, the weapons they can produce. Let them get away and you're doomed. Believe me. I've seen it."

Gan said, "We can't save them. We can hope the other of your friends survived. We'd do better to go back, search for that one, and the treasure of the Door, if it wasn't burned."

Sharp embarrassment touched Conway's mind. He'd forgotten entirely about the books. Leclerc even had the red book, the one with the crèche locations, all the identities. If that was burned, the last link with the old world was gone.

So much knowledge. The final break.

Conway said, "I'm going down there. Whatever happens, it's worth it to me."

For the second time that night, Nalatan stopped him. "My skills are better. You and the lightning weapon will allow me to reach the ones carrying your friend. We each have our place."

"I can't do that. Tate . . ."

". . . is who she is. I am who I am." Nalatan's interruption was without heat, but it snuffed out possible further talk. Silent, feral, he disappeared downhill.

Chapter 89

A disheveled Wolf skidded a lathered horse to a stop, shouting, "Where's the Black Lightning! They need her."

Supervising the last of the fire-fighting effort from the roof of the castle, Tate heard. She ran to the front of the building, calling down.

He pointed. "The Skan! They attacked Leclerc's farm. He sent me back to get you."

Tate understood. Jaleeta. She told the Skan—*her* Skan—about Leclerc and Bernhardt, the inventions, the weapons. Tate looked south, tried to deny the taint of flame-glow marring the night. It refused to go away.

Racing to her quarters, she replenished ammunition. Her mind hurtled through considerations. Jaleeta understood real power. She knew about the books, and knew that what Leclerc and Bernhardt built once, they could build again. It came to Tate that the greatest horror of the raid wasn't the destruction of the weapons needed for defense, nor even the killing of so many young Wolves. It was the potential desecration of knowledge.

Muttering, "So what else is new?" Tate took down her hang glider in its tube, struggled outside with it. Lungs and eyes burned from smoke drifting through the building. In the open, coughing, she called for the rider. "Exactly what's happening?" she asked.

"Leclerc told us to defend from the bluffs, then fall back. The Skan were ashore when we got there. Four sharkers. Not just crew, either. We fought back to the farm. There's too many, Tate."

"Is Emso hurt?"

"He didn't ride with us."

Shock beyond fear, beyond loss, shot through Tate. She burned with the memory of Emso calling Jaleeta.

The fool. The pitiful, treacherous fool. Tate wanted to weep, to see him dead, to hold and comfort him.

The messenger said, "Are you coming?"

Tate jerked out of her maundering. "I've got other work. Ride for Sunrise Gate. Go to the commander of the Wolf reserve. Tell him I said go to Leclerc's immediately. And send a fast rider to the Wolves pursuing the rebels. Have them come back to the city. Repeat what I said."

The man did, without error. Tate slapped his horse on the rump. "Go, man."

Before the rider completed his turn to leave, Tate was bawling for Lanta, Carter, and Anspach. All ran to her urgency. As soon as they gathered, Tate explained, "This is a hang glider." She ignored the stunned expressions of her two crèche friends. "I need you three to come with me and help. I don't have time to argue with anyone who wants to call me a witch or a goblin or some other Halloween ghoulie. Will you come, help me get airborne in this thing?"

"Whatever for?" Carter's surprise was already replaced by her normal tight intensity.

"The Skan are attacking Leclerc. They'll try to kidnap him and Bernhardt. From the air, I can shoot down at the sharkers."

Anspach shook her head. "Not in the dark. You can't have practiced enough. It's crazy. Anyhow, you can get close enough to shoot from land."

"Maybe. If I can, I will. The hang glider's insurance."

"It's a death wish." Carter nodded agreement at Anspach, continuing, "You'll kill yourself. What if the wind's wrong? You don't even know where the wind's coming from."

Tate thought fast, remembered the smoke from the fires. "Quartering from northwest," she said, so relieved she was smug. "We're losing time."

"Come on." Lanta ran for the stables. Tate caught up quickly. Carter and Anspach hesitated long enough to exchange resigned shrugs before following.

Taking Lanta's advice, the four rode south on the beach. Obstacles forced them inland occasionally, causing delay, but Tate's requirement to launch from the bluff made it the most effective route. They heard the sound of the fight long before they saw anything. A little farther and the sharkers appeared, stark against the moonlit water. Deciding they were close enough, Tate led away from the sea, up one of the eroded gaps in the bluffs. Crumbling soil broke down under the horses' hooves, and the grade was far too steep. The women dismounted, hauled the unwieldy bundle up the slope by main strength. Scrub-growth handholds ripped palms and fingers. Imbedded rocks offered treacherous footing that collapsed under full weight, leading to twisted ankles and skinned legs. But they persevered.

Unwrapping the hang glider's components, they discovered that moonlight was unsatisfactory construction illumination for three people totally unfamiliar with the device. Again, they managed.

A bull-like voice down the beach bellowed instructions. "Sharkers! Send the small boats! Stay offshore! They can't send the lightning at us without risking the prisoner."

"Prisoner." Anspach voiced their fear. "Just one."

Tate said, "We can save whoever it is down there. Quickly, quickly."

They lifted the triangular airfoil. Tate hurriedly inspected lashings, condition of the cloth, the underslung bar. Wind caught the material. It pulled eagerly. Carter said, "It's like a huge bird, ruffling its feathers." Then, after a momentary pause, "You can do it, Donnacee. I know you can."

Lanta and Anspach echoed her encouragement.

Between the edge of the forest and the bluff was a narrow strip of weedy growth. It was just wide enough for the hang glider to pass. Tate said, "I have to run north, into the wind to launch. Here goes."

Gunfire stopped her first step. She stumbled to a halt, turned to look south with the others. Hidden in the trees of the bluff, revealed only by a faint flash of muzzle blast, someone fired at the beach.

A fierce, throat-ripping war cry split the night.

Tate stiffened, fists at her sides. "No. No, Nalatan, don't. No." It was full of resignation and guilt and plea.

Furious shouting boiled up in the night. Metal clashed, the unmistakable impact of sword on sword. A man screamed. Through his agony came the ring and scrape of steel battering steel again, another man shouting. The initial screaming faded to weak cries for help. Then the sword duel stopped.

Nalatan's voice pierced awesome silence. "Where is the coward, Lorso? Run away so soon?"

The wipe cracked.

Nalatan called again, "Lorso. My friend of the lightning weapon just took another of your men skulking in their driftwood fort. They can't help you. Come, show them what sort of man you are. *If* you are."

Tate ran, raising the point of the hang glider. Turned. Off the edge.

Fell. Fell.

With the sound of stuttering collapse, the black wedge was a diminishing scar across moonlight-gleaming beach. Carter gasped. Anspach clutched her. Lanta spoke. "Up." She barked the word, amazingly deep and demanding from the tiny frame. "Get *up*, you bewitched rag. Don't you fail her. *Don't you dare!*"

Wind gusted. Caught the hang glider as Tate twisted into a southern turn. The material fluttered loudly. Anspach whispered, "She's coming back this way. Steady."

Carter said, "You're breaking my ribs. Yes, she's going to do it. She is."

Now Lanta was silent. Only she knew that if she opened her mouth, it would be to cry for happiness.

Tate pulled and pushed and jerked herself around under the noisy, swooping wing. The providential increased wind gave her lift when she needed it most. From behind, it gave her speed she was hard-pressed to handle. She strained to discover exactly what the situation was on the beach. Where Nalatan was.

Everything was shadows. Moonlight made varied blacknesses, cast a weird shimmer over wet beach and sea. The world was a shifting ambiguity.

Small boats headed for the sharkers. One was turned back. From above, Tate heard conversation with magical clarity. "Slavetaker is not insulted by landscum. Slavetaker's men are not forced to die like pigs in a pen."

"It's a trap, Lorso. They'll send the lightning at us."

"We've seen the lightning thing miss. They won't chance killing their friend." The small boat was almost on the beach. A man leaped out. Another man rushed to meet him in the water. Nalatan.

From Tate's viewpoint, the match was a hideous uncertainty, a conspiracy of light and movement that revealed only peril. She saw, and did not—could not—see.

She dropped the nose of the hang glider. It closed on the struggling pair.

Tate brought the wipe to bear. The men were too close. Hand-to-hand, knee-deep in the surging, glistening water. Grunting, panting exertion came to Tate as the straining of beasts.

Too fast. Tate plummeted. Too steep. She let the wipe hang by its sling, hauled up the nose of the hang glider, circled out to sea. Low, fast, she skimmed toward the sharkers. Terrified shouts marked her approach. Her passage overhead left a howling chorus in its wake. She banked so low individual rocks glinted at her, beaconlike. She swept down the beach, suddenly filled with a joyous power. From the corner of her eye, she was aware of more muzzle flashes. The alternating sounds of wipe and boop seemed an exotic, irrythmic music sent to celebrate her strength. Away from Nalatan and his foe, men ran and screamed. Some charged headlong into the sea. The men in the last small boat paddled furiously toward shore, calling a name.

One of the pair struggling in the water staggered, retreated toward land. He dropped to his knees.

Nalatan. *Nalatan.*

Tate was sure.

The enemy raised his sword. The small boat was almost on them.

The murdat was in Tate's grip. She screamed, a primal, hating challenge. The man attempting to kill Nalatan turned at the sound. Tate had time to marvel at his ferocity; he moved to strike, not avoid, the apparition streaking at him.

Leaning out and down, Tate slashed. The murdat bit hard. She almost dropped it. The hang glider shuddered, seemed to hesitate.

She was past, falling to her right, looking at the black, reaching sea. For a sickening instant she had a sense of demand from that expressionless void, as though she'd taken something from it, and payment must be made.

Fear generated overcompensation. The hang glider whipped sharply landward. She crashed into the piled driftwood. Laminated bamboo absorbed enough impact to prevent her serious injury. She tumbled free, running, calling Nalatan's name.

He answered. It was the finest, bravest, most wonderful of sounds. Only then did she acknowledge the battle continuing around her. Up ahead, Gan roared orders, exhorted. Wolf howls echoed from the bluffs; they were shabby, exhausted squalls, but they carried victory. From the sea, frightened voices called names and shouted querulous orders. A wipe blasted. Tate wondered who fired. And who was the prisoner. And if that prisoner still lived.

A small group retreated shoreward, splashing through water almost to the waist. Whoever fired the wipe covered the retreat. The last of the small boats was almost to the sharkers. Three of the latter, oars sculling lightly, were already turned north. One drifted, abandoned. Fire in her bowels illuminated the sail.

Closer now, Tate saw a figure supported in the midst of the shore-bound group. Calling Nalatan, she ran faster. Someone broke into an answering run, answering shouts. Nalatan. Calling her name. Coming to her.

The indomitable warrior and daredevil fell into the needed, needing embrace of her husband and cried like a child.

Those nearby, some wounded, all bone-weary, each battle-tested, saw that Nalatan, that deadly man, wept as well. Conway, whose own throat was unaccountably restricted of a sudden, noted how no one found it opportune to laugh at this deplorable unmasculinity.

* * *

Dawn came gray-cold under sodden cover that left no horizon. At the foot of the bluff, the remains of a driftwood pyre marked the resting place of the dead, foes no longer.

A smaller fire blazed in the center of the gathering on the high ground. Men sprawled, sleeping where they fell. Carter and Anspach drifted among the wounded, murmuring encouragement, assurance. With most of the human damage under control, they insisted Lanta join her husband. The three couples huddled close to the flames with Gan, finally able to review the night's events.

Gan spoke across weariness, the words almost slurred. "If the Three Territories survives, we owe any success to Louis Leclerc. And you, Kate Bernhardt. I'll forever thank the One in All for your survival."

Bernhardt blushed, inclined her head toward Leclerc. "He's the one. He made us store everything in his bunker, made me stay in there with it. I'm sorry we lost some catapults. But without Emso's warning, we'd have been completely surprised. The Wolves he sent bought us the time to save the other weapons."

Leclerc wore a large bandage on his head. He smiled wanly. "It's been a night of heroes. You can't imagine what it was like, lying in that boat, knowing I was about to be a slave. Even after Nalatan killed their leader, I was a goner if the rest of you hadn't dragged me free. I'll never be able to thank you enough." Despite heavy robes and the fire, he shivered violently. Bernhardt pressed closer to him. He smiled appreciation, managing to look sheepish at the same time.

Tightly, Conway said, "The books, man. You saved them, too?"

The question offended Bernhardt. She answered tartly, "They're buried under the floor of the bunker, even safe from fire. Louis insisted."

Conway continued. "The red one, as well?"

That brought Leclerc's head up sharply. "With the others. Why so interested in that one?"

In truth, Conway's response was the product of fear. That book's lists of dead people and places was almost a talisman. It symbolized a self Conway barely remembered, and missed as one mourns an alienated brother. He mouthed phrases to dismiss the matter.

While that was going on, Tate turned within her husband's encircling arm to whisper up to him. She deliberately sat on his right. His left eye was a mere slit. Looking like a poisonous flower, a swollen red-centered bruise disfigured that whole half of his face. She said, "See Kate and Louis sitting so close? The way they look at each other? They learned something, 'Tan. We've got a romance on our hands."

His smile was perfunctory. His speech was odd, altered by the battered jaw. "There are things we have to talk about. Rumors. Accusations. When there's time."

She squeezed his hand. "I know what's been said. I love you. That's all that counts."

Nalatan shook his head. "Of all the answers you could have made, that's the one I was afraid to hope for. I don't deserve you."

"I know."

He didn't even bother to look surprised. Sighing resignation, he addressed

Conway, now that the latter was finished talking to Leclerc. "Lorso's not dead. At least, he wasn't. If his men hadn't struggled so hard to get him in the boat, they could have kept us from getting Louis out."

"You didn't kill him?" Tate straightened. "I thought I hit him. I thought you . . ." Nalatan's manner stopped her. He looked away. She would have sworn she saw sympathy. "What happened, then?"

"His hand." Nalatan held out his own right arm. "It's severed. For such a man, it's worse than dying."

"Good." Surprise greeted Lanta's comment. She met it boldly. " 'Slavetaker,' they call him. A hundred lives, ten hundred hands—he can never experience as much pain as he's given. If he comes to Church, I must forgive him. Not before. His kind of cruelty lives in the eyes of all my orphaned Chosens."

Leclerc laughed softly. "I understand. Oh, do I."

Gan rose. Knees cracked loudly. When he stretched, a shoulder did the same. The group was laughing when a man called from the forest. A young Wolf, practically sleepwalking, escorted another man, almost as tired. The Wolf said, "He says he's a River. Been to Ola. They sent him here." He swayed.

Gan told the Wolf, "You're off watch. Sleep," and turned his attention to the stranger.

The River was blunt. "Moonpriest comes. Windband began crossing the river three—no, four—days ago. Moonpriest made a promise: 'Moon dark after next, the man called Moondark is no more.' "

Conway watched the faces of his friends go flat. Gan said, "Even if he and his Skan allies take my head, they lose. My heart will live on in the breasts of my friends, as theirs does in mine. Now, let's get to Ola, pull that old wolf Emso off the trail of those rebels. He'll be sorry he missed the fight here."

Within his enfolding arm, Conway thought he felt Lanta flinch. He was certain of one thing; Tate refused to look in Gan's direction.

Chapter 90

Tears of Jade stood on her accustomed rise, waiting. Leaning on her ceremonial staff, she hugged it in a transport of delight.

Everything was perfect.

Everyone knew of Lorso's clandestine recruitment of volunteers for his raid. Shaking with laughter, Tears of Jade struck the ground with the base of the staff. The silver bells chimed warning. She muttered a quick apology to the god. His cunning—expressed through his spirit woman—was no object of levity.

Shuffling painfully, she moved to where the collected sharkers were visible. Nestled in line, one against the other. Pointed bows, sharp, like rows of teeth. She saw them rending a leaderless land. Slaves in masses. Loot.

Perhaps she needn't be quite so stern with Lorso. Punishment must be inflicted, of course. No one, not even Lorso, deceived Sosolassa's spirit woman, and deceit was in Lorso's heart.

As Tears of Jade always intended.

She smiled, savoring the terror of the slave sent to inform her that Lorso had secretly sailed to destroy Sylah and Gan. An unusually clever touch, for Lorso. He assumed her rage would be so great she'd have the messenger sent to the god.

Lorso could be quite perceptive. Sometimes.

Jaleeta. Tears of Jade preened, still lost in memory. Jaleeta. What a masterstroke. Poison that men fought to taste, would kill others for. Then kill themselves.

Now Jaleeta was the victim. If Lorso did as he'd been told. A twinge of doubt, not even a fully realized thought, fluttered across Tears of Jade's consciousness. Impossible. Today was good. If Lorso's unapproved raid succeeded in eliminating Gan Moondark and Rose Priestess Sylah, the danger warned of by Sosolassa so long ago was eliminated. The child of sun brightness and the child of dark brightness, the twin threats to Skan domination, were destroyed.

And Slavetaker was a hero to the Skan forever. Acting without the blessing of Sosolassa's spirit woman would prove to the tribe that Lorso was the darling of the god.

Only Tears of Jade knew how she and the god manipulated all of them. So the Skan would rule all shores of Sosolassa's fateful sea.

Straightening, Tears of Jade reminded herself that she didn't know if Gan and Sylah lived or died. Still, if Lorso's raid failed, the alliance with Windband would crush the Three Territories. The problem with that was the need to share the glory. The even greater danger was that Moonpriest might make some accommodation with Gan and Sylah. They must die at the hands of the Skan, the true heirs to all power.

If Lorso's raid failed, punishment must be severe. The Skan must never think Sosolassa weak.

She forced that from her mind. The raiders' successful return would be a mighty celebration. Sosolassa would forgive the impiety of an unblessed raid. Everyone would hear it from her own lips. Lorso, favored of the god. Tears of Jade would name Lorso ruler of the Skan.

There might not be a better time. Despite the whispers, she wasn't born before the beginning, wouldn't live forever. Her lips moved, made a slash of a smile. She still thought of him as a youngster, a living, breathing vessel, waiting for knowledge and belief to be poured into him. So childishly brave, even now, sneaking off to rescue his toy, incapable of imagining the years of preparation devoted to that goal. Sailing home, he must picture himself the holy warrior, servant of the god's most dire command. Poor precious fool.

She envisioned him stepping ashore, red-faced, earnest. How does a man explain that he set out to rescue the woman he thought he loved, only to be divinely commanded to kill her? He would beg for understanding. Consolation.

Tears of Jade, ever-gracious, would grant it all. And demand Slavetaker be king.

If Gan and Sylah died, as well.

The dim image of Domel crossed her mind. A gnarled thumb rubbed the dry, dead-leaf skin of an index finger. Domel was almost a mistake. His blood, the blood of his blood, paid the god for his sin.

But today was beautiful, to favor great events. In bright, crisp sunlight, the curling surf was living green translucence. Its blowing spume was sometimes thick and heavy, like finest cream. At another view, it was delicate, the pale glisten of first breath on a freezing morning. Stark rocks of the headland trembled under the winter's sun. The light plunged obliquely into the wet, jagged surface, striking darks and lights that worked intricate, unceasing changes.

Lorso's sharkers sailed into view. Shielding her eyes with a hand, Tears of Jade excitedly counted. One missing. How many dead, then? How many more crippled, useless?

Turning away, she gestured. At the bottom of the rise, her team waited with the sedan chair. Her new driver positioned the slaves and drove them up the hill. He was charming on his little perch atop the chair's box, bright as a squirrel in oiled leather jacket and trousers. The boy showed flair, tricking out his rakish cap with bits of iridescent shell. He got full effort out of the lazy slugs on the team, too.

Tears of Jade saw it the day she'd let the young rascal drive the team to the stables; he was one who understood stock. With a proper whip in hand, he had them jumping like fleas, but far more eager to please. The boy had a future.

All the way to the harbor Tears of Jade was plagued by fleeting images of the man-boat that was Lorso. Always, the image carried foreboding. She shouted for speed. The whistle and crack of the whip provided some relief, even if the clumsy oaf at lead right front did stumble at every paltry stripe across his back.

From inside her sedan chair, she watched the boats maneuver. Lorso commanded from the bow, but he was pale, grim. He leaned heavily against the figurehead. Tensing, Tears of Jade examined the crew and the warriors gathered at the base of the mast. All, even the men busily making ready to beach, watched Lorso, their faces bright with awe. As the vision showed. Trickling ice ran down her spine.

There was something else. Something nailed to the mast. A leather bag?

Slumping back in the chair, she said, "Driver. My cabin. Gallop."

Aspects of her vision had been manifested in fact. The god was testing her. She must—*must*—discover the meaning hidden in those signs.

Impatience drew her to the cabin window soon after she dismissed her sedan chair. A crabbed finger lifted an edge of the hide covering. She peered out. And hissed alarm. Lorso was practically at the door. Hurrying, scraping across the room, she flung herself into the chair by the fire. Sharp old bones stabbed into sparse flesh. She glared balefully at Lorso as he stepped inside. "Ask permission to enter the house of the spirit woman." She growled the words.

Lorso stood aside for Jaleeta, unperturbed, right hand behind his back. "I grew up in this house. It's as much mine as yours." Jaleeta favored Tears of Jade with a tiny, knowing smile.

Tears of Jade's heart hurt. Her breath caught. "You. Betrayer. What have you done to my son?"

Lorso's laugh was ice, north wind. "I know the god, Mother. Better than you, perhaps. He gave me Jaleeta. He gave me this." He held up his wounded right arm.

Tears of Jade's eyes bulged, rolled up until the irises were tiny crescents. Jaleeta exclaimed aloud. Lorso watched, immutable. Gripping the arms of her chair, Tears of Jade struggled back from the edge of unconsciousness. Words came out mushy, in a barrage of saliva. "Tell me. Your hand. Explain."

Lorso wore a leather cap laced over the stump. He gestured with it as though the injury had been with him for years, rather than days. "I forced Gan Moondark's castle. With my men, I defeated his personal guard, drove his wife and friends from their beds, burned their castle." He waved his maimed arm. "Witchwork. The black witch attacked me, Mother. Only me. She flew. A bat. I struck her wing. She took my hand."

Although dark lines channeled his features, and his eyes blazed from smudged, smoky-looking hollows, he spoke with a solid confidence. Tears of Jade had the unsettling sensation that the son she'd tricked into doing her bidding was the one who was crippled, and that this stronger, wounded man in front of her was his formidable replacement. She said, "The witch flew? She leaped down from something."

"Flew. Circled from the land out over the sea, struck at me as other bats strike at insects. All my men saw. She rescued the other witch, the magic man."

"Gan? Sylah?" Tears of Jade snarled. She knew the answer. She also felt the need to humble this man.

Unruffled, Lorso said, "Gan was south, fighting. I don't know where Sylah was."

His answer bothered Tears of Jade even more than the foolishness about a bat. "You said Gan *was* south; where is he now?"

"I don't know."

"Do you know how much beer was necessary to make you and your crew all see the same bat?"

He stiffened. "No more of that, Mother. I told you: I now know the god. We saw what we saw. The Black Lightning took my hand. Ask the god yourself. Tea and smoke, remember? The god gave me strength. Look at me. Have you ever seen a man suffer such a wound so tolerantly? Hear this: I am what you and our god created. Entirely." Turning from the older woman, he stared at Jaleeta. She smiled at him. As before, Tears of Jade saw secret knowledge in the expression. It was the face of a woman who has won. Tears of Jade knew it well, had felt its warming thrill on her own flesh.

It was hateful to look on.

Draining weariness seized Tears of Jade. The comfort of the hearth seemed suddenly to be drawn up the chimney, leaving her cold and lost. To Lorso, she said, "You deceived me. The raid was unapproved."

He smiled. Tears of Jade's breath caught in her throat as if barbed. It was an expression she'd never seen before. "You approved it long before you sent me to capture the girl you would raise to do your bidding. 'Poison,' you called her. You, of all people, should have remembered that handling poison means some of it may stick to the poisoner."

"Do not attempt to lead my mind, Lorso; you're not the one for that task. Never have I suggested you raid—"

"You meant for me to go after her. Her mission succeeded. Gan Moondark's most important subjects distrust each other. There is open rebellion. His Wolves are weakened, ready to be beaten. You meant for her to draw me to Ola. I am your son now, as I never was before. I fought witchcraft such as no man before me, and won what I sought."

"You deceived me."

"Let's say we exchanged untruths. Then we can be mother and son once more. Work together. We both have what we want now." He reached for Jaleeta with the injured arm. She stepped inside the bend of it, pressed to his side.

In the dark cabin, redolent with mysterious scents, festooned with arcane paraphernalia, three minds probed and touched, grasped and rejected. Jaleeta broke the silence. "I am Lorso's woman. I will serve him well. I will bring him delight or comfort or what he wills. I will also serve Tears of Jade."

No terms. No obvious evasions. And, Tears of Jade told herself, no scrap of truth. Still, the words were spoken. It was a place to start. She said, "The Skan must understand that Sosolassa spoke directly to Lorso, consecrating this raid. Lorso was made to sacrifice his good right hand to prove his devotion and the god's power. He rescued Jaleeta, my assistant, for me. She is my gift to him. He is the choice of the god. Slavetaker must rule."

Yet again, that knowing, confident look on the troublemaker, the liar, the cheat. Jaleeta.

Tears of Jade almost didn't hear Lorso's good-bye. She waved, already staring into the fireplace. She remained in that attitude, pensive, until the scratching at her door broke her concentration. She flew at it in a fury, clawlike hand raised to call down a curse.

It was the boy, her teamster. Surprise choked the imprecations in her throat. The boy's words tumbled out. "Forward left leader. Sprained his ankle. I replaced him. I can't drive the team tomorrow."

The manner of the announcement alerted Tears of Jade. The boy was hiding his feelings. Part of her mind applauded his skill at it; the remainder tried to define what she saw. Anguish. Disappointment? Not another challenge; she wouldn't stand for that. She felt anger returning. Curiosity overrode it. "Why can't you drive?"

"I take my father's place, fishing."

"Tell your father I want you with me."

"He died on Lorso's raid. My mother's alone now. With us. And all I have is sisters. My father shouldn't have gone." The last came with a raised chin, unflinching blue-green eyes. Challenge, indeed.

Tears of Jade ran bone-thin fingers through his fine hair. A good boy. Bright. "Your name is Borosso?"

He nodded, wary.

"Go home, Borosso. Tell your mother your family is taken care of. I want you to work here. For me. All the time. You understand?"

He nodded again. She gripped his ear in fingers like pincers, squeezed. "When I ask a question, you speak."

Unshed tears swelled in his eyes, little glittering blisters of hate and gratitude and surrender. "Yes, Tears of Jade. I understand." Not bending away, complaining.

She released the ear, delighted. "Go, then. After this, you must call me Aunt. We're going to do wonderful things, young Borosso. Wonderful."

Closing the door behind him, Tears of Jade laughed happily.

Chapter 91

"This is as far as we go by boat." Domel dropped the sail as he spoke. Wallowing, yawing in the confused chop of the Throat, the small balancebar immediately fell off toward the sea. Domel shoved a paddle into Emso's hands, whispering, "Work while you puke. And be quiet about both."

Emso was too miserable to retort. Paddling provided surprising relief. Or maybe it was hope; the rise of land ahead was the most desirable thing in the world. He almost laughed aloud, thinking of his impending relief. From so many things. Forever.

About a boat-length from the beach, Domel eased over the side, making no sound. Emso's splinted leg splashed. Domel pushed on the hull to send it away, but Emso hung on, fumbling in the bottom. He hauled out a pair of saddlebags. Only then did he help Domel get rid of their boat.

Emso followed Domel's lead ashore. It rankled to admit it, but he'd learned to truly appreciate the sea skills of the Skan. Now, as a final touch, he would observe a raider's skills, as well.

As a Skan would observe a Wolf's determination. Demonstrated by a former farmer, former leader of the Wolf packs. Former leader. Under his breath, Emso said, "Only because I loved you, my friend. A man who hated you could never hurt you as I have."

Domel came to his shoulder. "Still sick? What's that noise?"

"Nothing to you. Keep moving."

"I may kill you myself. I can do this alone."

"You can't do either. Shut up. Lead the way."

Domel mumbled. They moved out. Emso realized the Skan was picking the easiest route in deference to his companion. He'd done that on the balancebar, too. Carping constantly about Emso's seasickness, he never failed to let Emso sleep a bit extra. He said he didn't trust landscum to follow a star. Emso knew better. Two outcasts, two nonbeings, their changed fate allowed them to accept each other as men. Emso smiled to himself. He wondered if any non-Skan ever had a leg splinted by a Navigator. He didn't think so.

A touch on his head stopped Emso's crouched hobble. Domel backed behind a log, whispered instructions. "Once we pass that big log sticking out almost to the water, we'll go inland a way. From there we can see the harbor and the sharkers; they'll be nested in deeper water. There are slave guards. Chained to posts. There should be three. We'll see the closest, so you kill him. I know where the other two posts are; I'll get them."

"Free them. They'll fight with us."

"Fight? They're slaves."

"Let them die fighting."

"I don't die with slaves. Anyhow, they know what happens to slaves who fail. Or resist. They'll never fight."

"We'll go around them."

"Listen to me. They're going to die. We'll be quick. My people will be slow. And if the slaves sound the alarm, we may not destroy any sharkers at all. What is this? They're just slaves, Emso."

"They're men."

"Kill them, or you waste your own life. And mine."

Emso sighed, looking at the moon. It was lopsided, missing a sliver. "If it has to be. But it's wrong."

They crawled to a point a few body-lengths from the first guard. Emso waited for several long breaths after Domel disappeared before beginning his own stalk. A stiff breeze rustled brush, created a rough sound cover for his awkwardness. The seated guard shifted, concentrating on the moon-bright sea. Emso struck. The heavy metal ball on the murdat handle cracked the man behind the ear. He grunted, sagged sideways. Emso caught him, clapped a hand over his mouth. "Quiet. One sound, you die. You understand?"

Returning consciousness stiffened the man. He nodded, fear-rounded eyes glistening.

"I'm going to pry free the spike holding the chain. Join us or run, but make no sound."

The man nodded. Slowly, cautiously, Emso loosened his grip on the lower half of the man's face. The frightened eyes remained locked on his. Arching his back, the sentry pulled away. He opened his mouth, screamed. The attempt was less than a yelp, a pitiful squeak confounded by the swift murdat in his throat. Emso threw himself on top of the man, crushed him to the rocky beach. They struggled horribly, stones scraping under them in a wet, sibilant clatter, the man still trying to cry out. Black shining under moonlight, his blood gave off faint steam.

When the man was at last still, Emso rolled off him. Domel lay within arm's reach. Softly, he said, "You're a greater fool than I thought. Why do you think some of them surrender, let themselves become slaves?"

"Don't you ever shut up? What now?"

"Collect the small boats. We'll tow them out with us."

Rattling rocks stopped Emso in midrise, turned him around. Domel crouched, the same as himself, facing inland. Encircling dogs trapped them against the waterline. The animals paused. In the faint light, their nervous shifting created the image of a single, erratic entity. Tense, high whines descended through deep growls. Emso made a noise in his throat, jabbed with his murdat. Most of the pack immediately in front of him faded back. Two held their ground, heads lowered, snarling. Stiff-legged, the leaders advanced. The rest followed.

"The blood," Domel said. "It excites them."

"I'll excite them." Emso draped the saddlebags over his left arm, gripping so his fist was hidden in the leather folds. Extending that shield, he clumped toward the pack, making his own wordless threat. The pair of animals ahead of him spread apart. Other dogs snaked forward. Clammy fear touched Emso's stomach. The brute intensity of the animals was unnerving, seemed more concentrated than human enmity.

One of the leaders leaped, jaws gaping, teeth gleaming. Emso thrust the leather padding. The dog seized it, shaking, growling. Emso's slash decapitated the second leader as it joined the attack. In the same motion, he stabbed the one ripping at the saddlebags. It dropped, its death shriek a jagged tear in the silence of darkness.

The rest of the pack disappeared, gone like smoke.

Domel grunted. "Good thing you brought those saddlebags. Why did you?" He was barely quieter than normal conversation.

Emso chided him. "Keep your voice down. That scream will bring every warrior in the tribe."

"Dogs fight and die all the time. No one will notice. And there's no one here to hear us. Come on; we've got work." He handed Emso a large goatskin. It sloshed. "Oil," Domel said. "There's a store shed down the beach. I stopped by." He hoisted a heavy sack onto his own shoulder. Bared teeth gleamed white. "Beeswax."

Eyes wide, fully awake on the instant, Lorso lay absolutely still, not breathing, listening. His head throbbed. The scream. Did he dream it? Did he voice it? Beside him, Jaleeta slept soundly, her breath soft, relaxed.

The dream came back to him. Staring into darkness so ponderous it was like keeping his eyes closed, he experienced it again. The terrible black bat swooping. The witch's screaming, hating face. The hard blow of the claw. The unimaginable sight of his sword dropping across his vision, his hand clenching the hilt.

Blood. Fountaining. His other hand, darting, catching sword handle and its own amputated twin. Incomprehension.

Then the pain. Yes. The god's wrath. Even as it came, blinding in its magnificence, Lorso knew it for its true purpose. The god's gift.

Lorso, smiling confidence while his frightened, clumsy crew tied the blood line tight around his arm.

Pitch, boiling in its iron pot. Sosolassa's cast image on the side of it, clotted almost to indistinguishable curves and forms by years of accumulated soot and smoke. And blood. The cautery pot. Sacred. Feared beyond words.

Lorso looked past the fire, past the drawn, frightened faces of his raiders. To Jaleeta. Her face seemed in constant motion. Lorso understood that was significant. He thought of massed kelp leaves, deep under the surface, swaying, mingling, one plant becoming all plants. All becoming one.

Pitch formed fat, lazy bubbles that crawled thickly to the surface. They opened like greedy little mouths, then collapsed to nothingness. Lorso stepped forward, brushing aside supporting hands. "Slavetaker heals his own wounds." He plunged the thing into the roiled mass. There was an almost inaudible sizzle, a feeling of immense weight pulling him deeper. Through the encrusted layers on the outside of the pot, he felt the eyes of the god watching his mind.

"Enough!" It was a crewman, an older, experienced man. Sweating, he seemed abashed at the sound of his own voice.

Lorso smiled at him. His skin seemed to be trying to slide off his body, but he held onto a distant, hard calm. He pulled the thing from the pitch, smiling down at the god, then at Jaleeta, then at the others. "I'll rest now. Jaleeta will tend to me." He pointed at the severed hand lying on the deck, where no man dared step close. "Put me in a leather sack. Nail me to my mast." He walked to his pallet. Pitch dripped where he passed.

In the present darkness, Lorso frowned. Sweat chilled him, despite piled furs, despite the sweet-scented warmth of Jaleeta beside him. He remembered the rest.

Long before the sun, he tried to rise. Pressure pressed his face into the coarse cloth. He was near panic when the voice came. Noises. Bubbling, smacking, like liquid pouring, separating, coming together. Not words. Not language. Not the self-serving jabber of a used-up old woman.

True awareness of the sea Lorso thought he knew was revealed to him; he was ashamed to realize his previous ignorance. The pulse of the seasons was instilled in his blood. He was one with clouds, wind, and sun. Other images swirled through his mind, vague promises of more things he would learn.

Tears of Jade. He saw her, and the sticky-wet sounds were louder, derisive, and Tears of Jade was afraid.

Happiness filled him. Ecstasy. The god had spoken.

Pain. A reminder. Fire crushed the injured wrist, shot through his body, blasted the air out of his lungs. He suffocated, his whole being screaming plea for breath. The weight lifted. He sucked in air, gratefully, prayerfully. Choked on the stench of his own cooked arm.

Stench.

Lorso blinked his way back to reality, rubbed his temple. Something smelled.

First the scream: Had he heard it? Now a smell: Was it real? Messages from the god?

Was the god telling him he would never know his world from dreams?

Someone was shouting. Fire. Lorso leaped out of bed, threw on trousers, grabbed his sword from the scabbard. Awkwardness lashed his fury.

At the end of the nested sharkers, Domel stood on deck before the mast and smiled. There were five lines of sharkers, fifteen vessels in each line. Fire was eating the first line, starting on the second.

Emso crawled up out of the bilge. He carried a lightproof candle box. Domel slapped him on the shoulder. "They're awake now. Listen to all that yelling."

"Is the boat ready?" Emso peered over the side. Domel nodded. Emso said, "Then let's go."

The sharkers in the other lines were igniting. Heat and wind swirled brands high in the air. When they fell on another vessel, more flame erupted. Domel laughed wildly. Emso shot him a wary look. Domel said, "They say Domel is no more, not even a name. Let them look. And know."

Skan crowded the water's edge, searching vainly for the small boats Emso and Domel had towed out. Ducking low in escape, the pair paddled hard to make the dark west shore, away from the gentle beach where the Skan gathered.

Slipping ashore, Emso and Domel kept to shadows, followed the arc of the small harbor. They stopped simultaneously to draw weapons. Emso draped his saddlebags over his head, creating a semblance of protection for his upper chest and back. Domel stripped off his outerwear from the waist up, exposing a gallery of red-and-black geometrical tattoos. When the crowd parted to make way for Tears of Jade, Domel snarled, started forward into brighter light. Emso fell in beside him, swinging the splinted leg, refusing the pain of it.

For several paces, no one noticed. The first man to see them literally screamed Domel's name. Some who heard him shouted or pointed. Others stared, dumbstruck. After the initial consternation, silence blanketed the entire gathering. Fear was a palpable surround.

Domel stepped forward. He shouted over the fire's roar, "Old woman! Look on me. You told the Skan your god destroyed me. Here I am. You told the Skan your god would send them to victory in their sharkers. There they are, burning by my hand. I, Domel, challenged your god. Defeated him. Look on me, and admit your lies."

Emso moved up beside him. "Only Domel knows my name. No other man here has enough honor to speak it."

An arrow whistled out of the crowd, flew past the two men. The sound was still in the air when Lorso's voice boomed, "No! Take them alive. They insult us, our god. I want them alive. Take them!"

Maddened Skan warriors screamed release at Lorso's orders. They charged down the beach.

Emso reached inside the front saddlebag. On his left Domel was pale, a picture of dread. He turned his sword to his throat. Emso yelled to make himself heard. "We won't be captured. I made sure." When Domel looked, Emso handed him one of a pair of things that looked like dull green metallic slingstones. Domel stared confusion.

"Grenade, Tate called them." There was no more time. Demonstrating, Emso pulled the pin, holding down the spoon. Domel did the same. Emso said, "When I tell you, let that little metal thing go. Don't fail. I'll see you in the Land Beyond."

Emso's calm assurance impressed Domel. He held the grenade in his left fist. The right readied his sword. Emso crouched a few feet away, in the same attitude. Domel couldn't know that Emso's quiet smile reflected the irony that the witchery of the aliens who'd come to Ola now deserved his eternal gratitude for one last kindness. If the strange metal thing worked.

Like surf, the Skan poured around their quarry. They parried and dodged, forbidden to kill. Emso and Domel, unconstrained, did terrible damage. A plaited leather line flowed up from the crowd, settled a loop around both men. It tightened immediately. Domel's sword fell to the ground. Emso raised his murdat to hack free. A warrior leaped forward, grabbed the arm, screamed for help.

Emso and Domel disappeared, inundated.

Tears of Jade exulted at the sight. "We have them. Now Domel will see what Sosolassa . . ."

The thrashing pile of humanity lifted, mounded. Explosions cracked, steel-sharp, second reinforcing first. Bodies flew, rising on searing red-yellow flashes that illuminated some men, silhouetted others. Concussion staggered Tears of Jade. She stepped back, tripped into Jaleeta's arms. An instant later the uncomprehending screams reached her. Calls—names, mother, the god.

The able backed away, leaving the dead and the squirming, moaning wounded. Many ran, shrieking. Some dropped to their knees in supplication. Lorso ran toward the slaughter, bellowing orders, calling for aid to the casualties.

Tears of Jade leaned into the arms of the woman holding her, forgetting her as Jaleeta, thinking only of needed help. Jaleeta disabused her quickly. She whispered softly, "Now is woman's work the most important. Now is the god most needed. The Skan are hurt. The minds of the people are dulled by pain, shaken by fear. The sanctity of the god is challenged. The strength of the mightiest leader is suspect. Now is a time for beginning, for building anew."

Bracing her walking staff, hauling herself erect, Tears of Jade turned to face Jaleeta. Bathed in the light of flames, high moon glittering in slitted, sunken eyes, the old woman exhaled heavily. The gusting breath sounded of ice-crystalled wind, of the chill mist that steals the mind, making the unwary sag into the easing sleep that never ends. Furor and devastation were dismissed. Each woman looked deep inside the other. Tears of Jade smiled and said, "Yes. My Jaleeta. Indeed we shall begin again. Build anew. Oh, yes."

Chapter 92

Except for the black-robed Sylah and Lanta, the group inspecting the defensive preparations dressed as if for a fair. No fair required polished chain mail, however, and weapons, however brightly shining, are never particularly festive. Still, there was color in plenty. Tate, as usual, set the pace. She dressed in green trousers, bloused above moccasins of leather so light it was almost yellow. Her leather jacket was cut full, but tucked at the waist, where a wide belt separated it from the trousers. The buckle was polished copper, chased with a stylized bear's head. She wore her long hair tucked inside a rakishly tilted fur cap. Over the entire ensemble, she wore a thick wool cape, as black as Church robes, emblazoned on the back with a white appliqued wolf visage. Two jade disks were the eyes.

Even Kate Bernhardt managed to introduce some variety into her semi-Church robes. More constrained than the always-flamboyant Tate, her arrangements seemed more to symbolize the spring struggling to break over the countryside.

The sleeves of her woolen outer robe were a buttery yellow, the inset panels of the lower half a rich purple. Her heavy scarf matched the latter. Looking at her, letting his eye stray to the meadow beyond the battlewalk, Leclerc smiled to think how closely her colors matched the crocus and daffodils declaring spring.

The small bandage marking his almost-healed head wound was his own most obvious fashion statement. He was dressed well, though. Kate was responsible for the new leather trousers, warm woolen shirt, and ankle-length swash of a new leather overcoat. He secretly fondled the horn buttons, wondering how she'd had the coat made up in such a short time. He turned away, unable to hide a smile. She was right beside him; she'd ask what he was smiling about. This wasn't the time or place to confess that he was just being happy because she gave him a gift. And he certainly didn't want to botch telling her again. Not after the way he stammered and waffled earlier.

He was such a jerk.

When he tried to tell himself he messed up because he was exhausted, a small voice murmured a name—*her* name—in the back of his mind. Another confession, then; he wasn't exhausted when he let Jaleeta fry his brains. Alert but stupid. That covered it pretty well.

Conway drew his murdat, pointing at the cleared field outside the city. He squinted into a strong south wind. A black-and-white striped sleeve added force to the glint of bared metal, as well as striking contrast to the bright scarlet of his cloak. The hood was back, leaving his head bare. "Wherever Moonpriest sites his wallkiller, the catapults can reach it."

Tate sighed. So much for a quiet stroll to impress the troops and boost morale. A quick glance showed the nearest Wolves looking thoughtfully at the now-threatening terrain. She could almost hear them thinking about boulders tumbling through the air at them.

Nalatan said, "The one I saw was bigger than the one in Kos. Would it throw farther?" His speech still had a thick quality, carryover from the crushing impact of Lorso's shield. The side of his face remained swollen, discolored in vivid blues, purples and a particularly ghastly green.

Tate wanted to ignore his question, throw this whole morning out the window, and tell him how much she enjoyed just looking at him, damaged face and all. His wildcowhide jacket, with that bristly copper-red body and sueded sleeves, was handsome. So were the polished black half boots, and the rich brown homespun trousers. She almost frowned at the hat. Ola wasn't so sunny a man needed a wide-brimmed thing like that. Especially one that looked like the illegitimate get of a Mexican sombrero and a cowboy's Stetson. On the other hand, no one from this world knew what either of those things was.

Brows knitted, Nalatan said, "Where are you, Donnacee? I asked if Moonpriest could bring the wallkiller I saw here?"

Heat rushed to her cheeks, down her throat. She stumbled through the answer. "Sure. I mean, yes, I suppose he could."

"Then we have to plan for it."

"Exactly," Conway agreed. His murdat indicated the castle roof. "Up there, catapults will command its supply route."

"They'll resupply at night," Tate said, "but maybe Louis can come up with black-powder warheads. That'll certainly interfere, if it doesn't stop them."

Leclerc was curt. "We don't have an unlimited supply of powder. The boop rounds may be much more effective." His own voice surprised him. He didn't mean to sound so unpleasant.

Conway continued. "Speaking of supply, we haven't seen you here since the night of the Skan raid. It's been almost two weeks. How's reconstruction? Kate says you sleep in that bunker of yours, won't let anyone else inside. Any more secret weapons for us?"

Leclerc heard his last response echoing in his head, asked himself why he was so angry. Belatedly, he said, "We're getting there."

Tate asked, "You were making larger generators; how are they coming?

"Four weeks. Three, minimum." Mean voice. Petty.

Leaning against the wall, Nalatan addressed the group. "When Tate and I rode south, right after the raid, our lead units were already engaged with Windband well north of the river. Those were scouts, but Windband is cavalry; they move fast."

Sylah entered the discussion. "Not with a wallkiller. Not with Moonpriest's obscene altar. He can't move them at horse pace."

Tate said, "Fast or slow, their objective is to pin us inside the walls, isolate us. Until the Skan make it difficult, we'll bring in what we need from the sea. Wal's got boats, and the Whale Coast has food supplies we can draw on."

They all followed as Sylah walked on. When she stopped again, there was wariness in her manner. A gesture brought her friends closer. Drawn, worried, she seemed to have lost strength. "Tactics isn't what concerns us. It's survival. It's the destruction of our mutual friend, Gan. What are we to do about him? Not even Neela can bring him out of the foul darkness claiming him since Emso's betrayal. How do we make him understand we need him?"

Lanta said, "He understands. He doesn't care. His heart's broken."

There was a force—a knowing—in her voice that ripped at Conway. Nevertheless, she looked him full in the eye, and there was nothing there but confidence and trust. It was a small thing, but he knew she made it a point to star his life with those moments. She appreciated his necessity to confront the demons of their mutual past, and his need to know she was beside him while he did so.

Sylah was saying, "Gan's never known betrayal, not of that nature."

Grim, almost forbidding, Nalatan said, "The Wolves are willing—eager—to understand. They want to share his anger. They're less willing to accept his failure to fight through pain. They're expected to take inhuman abuse and win; they believe their leader should be able to withstand human frailty. Remember, Emso betrayed them, too. They've accepted it. For warriors, treason can only affect the timing or the certainty of their dying. It won't have any bearing on the manner of it."

Sylah said, "Surely they'll fight as well as ever? What if Gan doesn't recover completely, what if he's changed?"

Tate answered, "A military unit reflects its leader's personality. Properly trained, it'll perform almost by reflex. For a while."

Defensive now, Sylah argued, "The peoples west of the Enemy Mountains, from the near shore of the Mother River all the way north beyond the mountain called The Destroyer, are one. We can't lose that. We mustn't."

"We won't." Conway's declaration was a low growl.

No one disagreed.

Sylah and Lanta exchanged covert glances. To them, the hidden doubts were blatantly revealed, the fear of one companion for another achingly clear. Sylah wanted no more of it. She said, "I've been with Gan and Neela since he was forced to flee his own tribe, since before Emso. I'll speak to him."

Conway said, "Bring the old Gan back to us."

The women embraced each other before Sylah left. After some desultory conversation, the couples drifted off, each one sure of the heart of every companion. They parted company almost shyly.

Tate remarked on it to Nalatan. "It's as if we shared thoughts sometimes, you know? Like those Smalls I told you about."

"I think you're right." She cocked her head, suspecting ridicule. He was quite serious. "You know how my brotherhood shares knowledge of the Dry, how we chant the knowing song and dream of what we know. I don't know how a man sees places where the other chanters have been and he never has, but I did it. Somehow, the Smalls must mix field skills and concentration. They confuse the minds of men and animals. They're not invisible. They make themselves overlooked."

"You've thought about that more than I realized."

"Because of the cleansing you told about, the dance the Smalls do. How many times have I wished to scour my mind? If I can't forget, why can't I at least be at peace with what had to be done?"

"It's our curse. For us, there's no pride without sadness, without horror. Maybe even regret."

He put a hand to her chin, turned her so she faced him directly. "We can't live without it. It's what drove us apart. We can't let that happen again. I love you. I'll never again let myself send you away. I won't let you send me away."

Tate took his wrist in her hands, raised the palm, kissed it. Her gaze never left his. She said, "And I love you. No jokes. No tough lady. Just a woman. I'll love you till always."

They'd wandered to a point in the chill shadow of the castle wall. Deserted for the moment, it was a mute, massive backdrop. Its very existence was an ominous message. Beyond the smiles and pledges, both were suddenly aware that "always" and "never" were frighteningly fragile conceits.

In the small waterfall garden, Kate Bernhardt pointed at a bench, feeling much as she did when facing a recalcitrant Chosen. The pupil seating himself, however, was Louis Leclerc. "We have to talk, Louis," she said, hating the prim banality. She pulled back her shoulders. "First, I want you to know how proud I am of you. Since the attack, you've been a whirlwind. But you've got to slow down. You can't work all day with the artisans and me, then hide in that suffocating bunker and work all night. You're ruining your health."

Behind her, the little waterfall's laughter mocked her. It seemed to captivate

Louis. He stared at it, just past her elbow, the faintest line of a frown scarring his forehead.

She waited for a response as long as she could, then, "At least tell me what you're doing in there. We care about you. Let us help." Her voice lowered, turned in on itself. "Let me help."

Still, he failed to speak. She tried a last time. "Please. We need you. You're no good to us sick."

He stirred, like a man waking. Indeed, when he looked up at her, he appeared as she saw him every morning when he emerged from the hole in the ground she'd come to detest. They shared the day's first meal then, in his kitchen. She suffered through every one of them, trying to bring some life into him. Those same eroded features and sunken eyes called to her now. She hated that look, always touched by it, distressed that she couldn't make it go away. It made her feel useless.

Breaking off, he looked around, spoke very deliberately. "Reality; I'm working on reality. I'll rest when I believe I've earned it, Kate. You say 'No good to us sick?' Sweet Kate. I'm trying to prove to you, to our friends, to myself, that I can be good to us at all."

She tried to protest. He held up a preventing hand, resumed staring into the mystery of the falling water, searching. Then, blindly, he reached for her. Kate linked her fingers with his.

Conway trailed Lanta and Sylah into the great hall. The cacophony of construction—hammering, sawing, shouts, the chop of mallet on chisel and the chink of steel on stone—resounded in the arching chamber. Ducking past workers into the passageway leading to Gan's informal meeting chambers, the trio made their way to that room. With Neela beside him, he waited. A wan smile, meant to be welcoming, was an obvious social grace.

Sylah was sharp. "This is no longer mourning, Gan. You embarrass. Your Territories need you."

Lingering spirit flared, brought color to his cheeks. "A wounded man needs time to heal. My wounds are worse than most."

"Your recuperation becomes indulgence."

Gan bolted to his feet. Shara and Cho, hitherto dozing beside him, scrambled upright. Gan ignored their confused rumbling. "I was betrayed by a man I trusted second only to your husband. Betrayed by an Abbess of Church, one I fed, housed. And Jaleeta. What can be said of Jaleeta?"

Neela edged away from him until she was closest to Sylah and Lanta.

Sylah said, "Is that reason to abandon yourself? What of the glory you're to bring the Dog People? The treasure of the Door is at your feet. A new world calls, and you bury yourself in wounded pride."

Red-faced, Gan broke under her unflinching gaze. He looked away, with the brute incomprehension of a mired animal.

Suddenly, literally a blur, Neela was in front of Sylah, all eyes and fury. "You will not speak to him so. He's your friend still, and it's you who embarrass for forgetting. He's never once turned his face from you, and this is how you speak to him when his heart is torn. Go away."

Contrite, Sylah made as if to speak. Neela held up a single warning finger. Her expression eloquently underscored her demand. A troubled, silent trio filed out.

Neela went to her husband, guided him to a chair. When he was seated, she curled up on the floor beside him, resting an arm across his knees. She said, "They think they own you."

He nodded, searched her features. "I haven't been able to speak of it." He closed his eyes, gathering himself. "To be an enemy, to know others plan your destruction, is a hard, cruel knowledge. It's no easier planning—or committing—the destruction of others. Good men die for bad, and that's a sickening fact. But betrayal by a friend . . . I loved him. He was with me when we rescued you. He played with Coldar, Neela; stood beside you and laughed with you while I changed the boy's diaper and tried not to be sick. And Jaleeta. I trusted her with you. Alone with Coldar. What if she'd . . . ?" He closed down on the sentence, left it.

"Deceit needs trust. Only those who won't trust can't be betrayed. Or be human. Never mind all that. I don't love Murdat, or the powerful ruler who allowed himself to be blind to an evil woman and a misled man. I love Gan. But I worry about our son."

Gan glowered. "What?"

"Do you want to continue as Murdat, or can we go back to our people? If we stay here, is Coldar to inherit your role? Will we step aside, let the people choose a chief, as the Dogs do?"

"I haven't thought about those things. Not lately. You're right, though. Once we've finished with Windband and the Skan, I'll have to call in the Barons, tell them Coldar's no princeling. The Three Territories will have a chosen ruler." He reached to her long, blond hair, repeatedly coiling it in his fist, letting it tumble free. "I stay here. My mother said there will always be two paths for me, but my goal must always be glory for the tribe."

Neela's chin rose. "Not that again. I'll not live that woman's dreams. I have my own. I expect you to have yours. Tell me what you want; I'll be beside you. I won't walk in her shadow. I *won't*."

"It's not that. The prophecy . . ."

"No!" Neela put her hands on his knees, pushed her face almost into contact with his. "Speak for yourself. Has betrayal drained your heart for high office? Fine. We'll leave now, go home. Would you rather die? Give me time to entrust our son to Sylah; I'll fall beside you. But live or die, it must be with you. Not with prophecies, not with self-pity."

Roughly, Gan stood up. Neela staggered, but she rose with him, not retreating a finger's width. He bellowed, "I won't be pitied. That's enough."

"Is it? Is it enough? What's enough? And who says it?"

The answer came slowly, burning with a volcanic anger. "I say it. No one takes what is mine. No one. I'm not beaten. Let no one pity me."

"Not even you?" She reached to put her hands behind his head, kissed him, lingering. For a few heartbeats he was stony with anger. Slowly, as if conceding unwillingly, his arms rose, embraced her, pulled her to him. When she bent back to peer up at him, head tilted to the side, her expression was mischievous, daring. "Not even Gan?"

A reluctant smile spread across his features, surfacing like something thought lost. He returned her kiss, far more passionately. He released her abruptly. Solemn, but without the previous apathy, he said, "There's been one benefit to all this, if it can be called that. There was a thing in my head, like a dream. More than once. About the ocean. Dark. A voice. Not words. It hasn't bothered me since the Skan raid. It must mean something. What?"

"I'm no fake Seer, telling hands. I only interpret my husband."

He strode toward the door. The dogs lumbered after him, waiting expectantly while he turned to face her again. He said, "What Sylah said is all true, you know."

Neela colored. "A little. Perhaps."

"Entirely. Not a little."

She tossed her head. Golden hair swirled like poured honey. Defiant, she straightened. "No matter. No one criticizes my husband. Church nor anyone else."

The young, too-wise face softened. The warrior who was Murdat revealed himself as simply a man entranced by the woman he loved. Softly, admiring, he said, "Not even you?"

Her color flamed brighter. She said nothing, stood tall and proud. His laughter rang in the stone room, echoed, called up memory and promise. He said, "We'll win. I must. Just to see what a man the son of such a woman will be."

His free, challenging laugh rolled down the long hall with him. He never saw Neela's glad tears of relief, never knew they quickly broke on concern and fear.

Chapter 93

The banners flew bravely and the war drums rumbled superb threat whenever a column of Wolves marched out of Ola. On their return, the men were met with spring flowers and the proud blare of trumps and horns. Still, for almost a moon their war had been a gritty series of cutthroat ambushes and running fights. There were innumerable variables; circumstances of engagement, time of day, terrain, weather. There was one constant; there were fewer Wolves after every engagement.

The weary, decimated packs could afford no set-piece battles. They struck without warning, fled without regret, then struck from cover again to destroy pursuit. Windband understood these tactics. They were their own. But this was forest, where horse-mounted mobility frequently counted for nothing, and occasionally was a drawback. The tough Wolf foot soldiers considered horses transportation, and fighting a job for men standing upright. They prowled the forest like their namesakes, finding cover and advantage where cavalry saw obstacle and diminished capacity.

Bloodied constantly, dying in steady dribs and drabs, Windband's savagery exploded. Word of their cruelty was wildfire, racing ahead of them. Real fire marked their advance. No habitation stood where they passed.

Columns of smoke warned the company at Leclerc's farm. Gan's arrival was stark commentary on the situation. He rode in with the Jalail pack, his own tattered red-and-yellow pennant lolling in the faint breeze. Molelike, Leclerc emerged from his underground shelter. He shaded his eyes with one hand, squinting. At the sight of Gan, he grunted understanding. "Time to leave, is it?"

"I'm afraid so."

"You can't buy me a few days? There are some things I'm not sure about."

Gan's laughter was jagged. "There are a few questions in my own mind just now. Is it something in the air, do you think?"

"Smoke, maybe." Leclerc's own smile was perfunctory. "Almost everything's inside Ola's walls already. How much time do we have?"

"Sundown. No more."

Leclerc whistled. Losing no more time, he ordered all equipment loaded into wagons. Lastly, he supervised the transfer of several large bundles from his personal workshop. When Kate playfully threatened to peek, he was firm in his refusal. Intuitively, she said, "This has something to do with that silver, doesn't it?"

His eyes flew wide; he said nothing, but turned a suspicious frown on his best metalworker. The man gestured wildly, proclaiming innocence and utter secrecy. Leclerc continued to glare, but when he looked to Kate, it was more a mix of exasperation and appreciation. Still, he made no comment.

In the evening, Gan stood with Conway on the city wall above Sunrise Gate. A melancholy vista stretched before them. The flame and smoke of burning buildings was haunting contrast to the burgeoning myriad greens of spring. Fallow fields sprouted malevolent rows of angled posts, sharpened ends aimed to disembowel any horse ridden into them. At the edge of the distant forest, horsemen flirted in and out of the trees.

Far away southwest, a drum sounded, heavy and slow, threatening. Conway jerked around, faced it. "Blizzard," he said, and when that beat stopped, he pointed more toward due south. On cue, another drum thundered a different rhythm from there. Conway explained, "They'll work all the way around to the northwest, one drum at a time. They're telling us we're surrounded."

"You trained these Blizzardmen, I understand. It's hard to imagine you living with those people. Fate leads us into some strange corners, my friend. None of us truly knows himself, does he?" It was more statement than question. "How well will this Blizzard unit fight on foot, against walls and good defense?"

"Like demons. They believe if they die fighting for Moonpriest, they go straight to a perfect world on the moon. They're supposed to be reborn with him later, and live forever. They don't like pain any more than anyone else, but they don't fear death."

"I hope they come soon. If they coordinate their attack with the Skan, I don't think we can handle it." The second drum fell silent. A third came to life. Gan frowned, turned away.

A Wolf called from inside the wall. As Gan returned his salute, the young man shouted up, "Leclerc says you're needed at the castle, Murdat."

Gan ran down the stairs. Conway sprinted to catch up. Leaping into the saddle, Gan said, "Maybe it's sharkers." They galloped to find out.

Leclerc waited just inside the great hall, with Sylah and Lanta a few paces beyond. A few candles in a pyramidal frame provided the only light. Conway's eyes were still adjusting to the change when a figure materialized from the greater darkness to take position next to Leclerc.

The man was Nion, dressed in unusual finery. His jacket was bright red. Silk, Conway was sure, with silver buttons. Low-cut shoes, black with white wingtips and balloon trousers, striped indigo blue and white. He wore a flat leather cap with a small bill; it sat at a jaunty angle, trailing a fan of three long black-and-white feathers down the back. There was also a two-handed sword, the lacquered scabbard magnificent with an inlaid dragon of colored glass chips.

Conway was surprised. He'd assumed no one would be allowed past the Skan fleet into the Inland Sea.

Bluntly, Gan said as much. "How did you pass our enemies?"

The man's grin was infectious. "Boats gone." His audience goggled. He laughed, continuing in tortured language to relate the story of Emso and Domel. On arrival at the Skan village, he was allowed to anchor in the harbor, but required to remain aboard his boat. One of the guards sent to stay on the boat and watch them had a great liking for a drink the Nion called sawa. The Nion winked. "Makes mouth go fast, head go slow, understand?"

The group understood. The Nion sobered slightly. "Man Lorso come my boat. No hand." He held up his own. "Say witch take it. Black woman. You know?"

"My friend," Gan said. "Not a witch."

"She fly."

"Not a witch. Why are you here?"

The Nion seemed to want to pursue the witchcraft thing, but let it drop. "Trade. You better friend than Skan, I think. You kill Windband, we trade. Fur, leather. Jade. You got black-rock-burn—coal, I think? We talk. If live, you."

"We'll live. And we've got something better than coal."

The Nion looked to Sylah and Lanta, then back to Gan. He said, "My people hear much about Healers. We talk that, too. But no Healer go Skan. Young woman—Lorso wife—say kill all Church. Bad woman. Now I go." He bowed, excusing himself. When Gan repeated the move, a glow of genuine appreciation touched the man's cheeks. He smiled warmly.

Leclerc spoke almost dreamily. "Trade. With Ja . . . Nions." He was suddenly alert, turned to Gan. "You'll do it? Get involved in trade?"

"My greatest dream."

Leclerc left abruptly. Conway smiled. "Now what's he up to?"

"Something very powerful, I hope." Nalatan's voice pulled the attention of all to the door. He went on. "A scout just arrived. By boat, around the encirclement. The mountain passes are still closed. No help is coming from the Dog People. Windband's main body is setting up camp."

Sylah said, "We're prepared, Gan. The abbey is a healing house. The right prayers have all been offered, supplies put by and blessed."

He thanked her. Deep in thought, he headed back outside. As he mounted his horse, he looked to Nalatan and Conway. "The One in All is being good to us. He took Emso, but He let Emso eliminate the Skan. We've been given another chance."

"A small one." Conway swung up into the saddle, met Gan's gaze.

Laughing, Gan grabbed Conway's shoulder, shook it. "Would we know what to do with a large chance?"

"I'd like to try. Just once," Conway shouted after Gan, falling in beside Nalatan. The warrior-monk's smile was tight. "Wait till you see the campfires, Conway. Their smoke is like fog. They brought their wagons, the huge covered ones. They glow in the night like candles under cloth. Even with Leclerc's lightning, I think our small chance is very small."

They didn't even reach the wall before the first leg-length catapult arrows snarled into the city and smashed against buildings. Both men rode hard to get close to the wall to defeat the angle of fire.

Darkness came with a rush. Wolves sallied through the gates, setting ambushes, attempting raids. Nomads launched similar efforts. Meanwhile, catapult bolts from both sides ripped through the night, their humming, whistling passage playing melody to the unceasing rhythms of Blizzard drums.

Conway surprised himself by falling asleep easily. He woke once to the sound of horrible screams, shakily realizing it wasn't human misery. Wheels, he decided; the wallkiller, moving into range. Near dawn, an explosion roused him. This time the cries were all too human. One of Leclerc's trip-wire mines claimed victims.

Dawn shouldered its way through the smoke of hundreds of fires. More and more, the light revealed what lay in store for Ola. Brushwood piled among the stakes lay ready for firing. Conway struck the wall of the castle in frustration when he saw the screens protecting the positioned wallkiller. Two large mats, thickly woven of branches and saplings, shielded the trebuchet. Several yards apart, suspended from thick hawsers, the mats were free to swing under impact. A catapult bolt striking the first mat would probably penetrate, but be wrenched off aim and drastically slowed. The second would duplicate the original effect. A bolt getting through would lack enough energy to do serious harm. The only part of the trebuchet visible was the sling arm at the vertical.

Flaming arrows now reached up from the Windband positions, savagely graceful. They curved, smoking, seeming to pause at their crest. Conway wondered when the world would rediscover words like apogee and perigee. Falling, the arrows feathers whistled softly. The flaming tow made a nervous ruffling. In moments, the brush around the anticavalry barriers was aflame. Conway originally suggested they be equipped with sacks of black powder. Seeing them burn up without ever being attacked made him glad he'd been overruled.

From the corner of his eye, he noted the trebuchet sling arm lowering. Gan's shouted order to the catapults to engage the target was repeated down the wall. A half-dozen bolts slammed out of their weapons, buzzing like enraged hornets. Two penetrated the mats. Conway saw the first punch through, only to dribble down the backside of the second mat and fall harmlessly on the ground. The second was deflected wide. The other four were trapped. Gan ordered the archers to save their bolts.

By then the trebuchet arm was out of sight. The Wolves, never having seen such a weapon, hunkered down behind the wall, peeking, unwilling to miss the action. The load sling was suddenly there. The shattering bang when it stopped, flinging its missile, made everyone jump. Breasting the air with a peculiar moaning noise, the large boulder was short. The Wolves, easily gauging the trajectory, shouted derision even as it came toward them. Their scorn died in mid-celebration when the rock hit the ground, gouged a plug of turf as long as a man's body, skipped back in the air, and slammed the city wall. The stone defenses seemed to buzz with the power of the blow.

Far behind Conway, a single loud explosion seemed to answer the strike of the boulder. He looked to see Tate on the castle roof. The barrel of the sniper rifle poked over the edge. She fired again. Conway had time to turn and see the puff of dust where the heavy spent-uranium slug hit the first of the two mats protecting the trebuchet. Seconds later, he heard a pained yell from the hidden wallkiller crew.

As soon as the barrier fires died out, Windband riders whipped a herd of cattle out of the forest, hundreds of head. Running, bawling, they streamed toward the walls. Some of the Wolves found it amusing. The more thoughtful watched glumly, as did Conway. The hapless animals, driven by incredibly skilled horsemen who offered almost no target whatsoever, stampeded across the front of Ola's walls. Every trip wire was pulled, every charge exploded.

Men were sent out to butcher the injured cattle and retrieve the dead. A weapon was lost; the meat would be salvaged.

That afternoon, Leclerc led a procession of two-horse teams and carts out the castle's east gate and into the city. A last wagon was larger. Coursing the city wall, Leclerc stopped at measured intervals, unhitching the carts, leaving one at each place. The large wagon off-loaded long spears at those locations.

Conway grinned down at his friend, who smiled, sent a thumbs-up, and hurried on.

The new wired spears were ready. The carts each held a generator a good three times the size of Leclerc's initial effort. As Conway watched, Louis instructed the Galmontis pack. He repeated the demonstration using the copper plate on a pole. These spears, however, were for defending the wall. Each worked directly off a cart-mounted generator, and was attached by one long, waxed-cloth insulated wire. The second wire was attached to a spike sunk in well-soaked earth.

Four men worked the machine's opposed crank handles. The spearmen were equipped with massively thick leather mitts.

The first Wolf to approach the target was unimpressed. There was, after all, little excitement in probing a sheet of metal. With the power of the larger generator, the effect was awesome. A loud, brittle crack accompanied a darting tongue of blue fire. The copper plate bucked like a live thing. Acrid smoke boiled from the gaping black wound in its center. The spearman dropped the weapon, yelling at the top of his lungs. Jets of electricity leaped from spearhead to the ground until the handle operators stopped.

Leclerc brought the pack close, let them inspect the damage. The rest of the training session was conducted in an atmosphere of attentive respect.

The second night fell. No Wolf patrols prowled outside the wall. Windband's catapults were quiet. There were the drums. Incessant. Promising.

In the shuffling, hovering darkness, preparations were made. Confidences, never before spoken aloud, some never before thought through to conclusions, were shared. Those warriors who slept at all twitched and muttered. Others lay awake, intrigued by living as only those aware of death's hovering presence can know it.

CHAPTER 94

THREE RIDERS MATERIALIZED FROM THE DIM WALL OF FOREST AT THE FARTHEST EXTREMITY of Ola's cleared fields. They advanced through a pale, rain-spattered dawn at a confident trot that soon brought them close enough for identification. Windband's drums stopped.

The man ahead of Moonpriest and Fox carried a large white flag, raised in both hands. Standing on the wall under his own pennant, Gan chuckled, drawing quizzical looks from Tate and Nalatan. Gan explained, "Someone has to carry the white signal. It's beneath Moonpriest's dignity. Fox won't touch it." He added, "You were right about Fox's injuries, Nalatan. I'm not sure I'd have recognized him. Even from here, I'd say it's a wonder he's alive."

Tate said, "Hate can do wonders for your will to live. Can you really tell how badly he's injured? How'd you know they'd be coming?"

Gan ignored the comment on his vision. "I've listened to all of you about Moonpriest. I already know Fox and his Mountain People. I expect Moonpriest to come with some trickery to make surrender look preferable to battle. Fox will come to gloat." He waved the tall pole holding his braced pennant aloft, assuring the advancing men saw it.

Wolves and civilians alike flocked to the wall to witness this moment. Wolf leaders assured distance between the gathering crowd and the three leaders.

Tate turned her attention to the battlefield, where burgeoning light revealed a deceptively pastoral landscape. Immediately, however, she grabbed Nalatan's arm. " 'Tan. Look. The wallkiller. They moved it last night."

"Into the ground." He frowned, puzzled.

"Dug in like that, they can load and fire, and I can't hit them."

Overhearing, Gan noted the problem. He looked grim. "At least it can't reach the castle or the healing house from there. The buildings of the city are at risk."

Tate said, "It'll take out the walls, Gan. We've got a problem."

"If he breaks a hole, he has to come through it. Also, he doesn't know his Skan allies aren't coming. With our rear secure we can spare a larger counterattack force."

Moonpriest was close enough to talk. He waved, quite jaunty. "Good morning, young Murdat. And to you, Donnacee. It's a pleasure to see you again."

Tate leaned through a crenel, shouting down at him. "I know you. You sent that murderous piece of rotten meat to kill me and Conway."

Fox stood in his stirrups. "Have you told your husband what pleasures we shared, black witch? Does he know everything that happened?"

A collective intake of breath from the crowd was a breeze of shock. Strangling with rage, Tate raised her wipe. Nalatan encircled her in his arms. He lifted her, turned her around. Ignoring Fox's laughter, as well as the gaze of the crowd, he spoke low, earnestly. "They stand with the white signal. Calm. Please."

Slowly, her head drooped. She closed her eyes tight; tears sparkled at the corners. "He hurt me, really bad, 'Tan. I thought I was dying. But he never . . . never . . ."

He raised a hand, touched a finger to her lips. When she relaxed, he loosened his grip. She said, "I'm all right." Her look said far more. She resumed her place at the wall, Nalatan beside her.

Moonpriest was saying ". . . no need for loss of life. We can arrange terms." He broke off at the sight of Tate, smiled broadly. "Ah, you're back. Forgive my friend. Negotiation isn't one of Fox's major strengths. As you know. I was explaining to your friend that I'm a religious, a man of peace. I'm allied with his own Church to bring the people of the Three Territories back into the fold."

Tate refused to answer, looking to Gan, who said, "Leave the Three Territories while you can."

Moonpriest's lackadaisical wave presaged trouble. The trio on the wall tensed. The man with the white cloth waved it. Another rider exited the forest at a trot. A green riding cloak covered the rider, fanning out to drape across the saddle front and back as well as below knee-length. Designed to husband warmth of both horse and rider against the lingering winterlike chill of early mornings, it was equally effective, with its hood, as disguise. Nevertheless, Gan and Nalatan exchanged thin smiles. Tate demanded to know what was going on. Gan's answer was oblique. "I thought that's where that one disappeared to."

The unknown rider was with the others by then. With a quick flip of the hand, the Violet Abbess threw back the hood. An interior facing band of green and blue flashed brightly. Nalatan grunted as if struck in the stomach. "They actually made her Harvester. That lying old woman and the Gleaner are second only to Sister Mother."

Keeping well clear of Fox, the new Harvester waited for Moonpriest's nod to address the trio on the wall. Her voice cracked on the first word, but the knifing enmity was undiminished. "Sister Mother authorizes me to grant amnesty to all who repent of following the known witch and blasphemer, former Rose Priestess Sylah. All who defend this place are cast out. Your bodies will be unburned, left for wild things to devour. You will suffer the eternal torments of the Land Under."

Without warning, her horse reared, pawing the air, eyes rolling. It whinnied, almost a scream. It took both Fox and the white signal bearer to calm it. On the wall, everyone strained to see the cause of the reaction. Then, below them, the brass-fronted Sunrise Gate doors swung open. A massive swell of surprise rose from the crowd at this indication of treachery.

Sylah and Neela galloped out, skidding to a stop a few paces from Moonpriest's group. The excited horses quickstepped, tossing their heads. Pointing, accusing, Sylah raised her voice to its fullest. "You shame Church. You shame yourself. Church is forgiveness. Solace and healing. Church is more; Church is learning."

This last was almost too much for the listeners. Many on the wall mumbled uncertainly. The Harvester made a grandiose three-sign, histrionically turned her face as if struck.

Neela forced her mount ahead a pace. "And well you should flinch. Traitor. Oppressor. Many in Church have worked with men like Moonpriest and Altanar for generations to assure women's subservience. Sometimes Church has been the fingers of the iron fist, sometimes willingly, sometimes under protest, but never bold enough to make us free. We are free here, free to learn, so we may be freer and stronger yet. Church has made it so. Murdat has made it so. The people—men as well as women—*all* the people of the Three Territories have made it so. *We will be free!*"

On the wall, a lone woman's voice rose in a high, ululating cheer. It rang defiance, pride, determination. Another took up the sound. It exploded from hundreds of throats, from every woman the length of the wall. A Wolf of the Jalail pack scrambled atop the wall, straddling one of the crenels. He thrust high the red-and-yellow pennant of his pack and raised a howl.

What had been declaration by the women alone became unity.

Moonpriest yanked his horse around, nearly bowling over the Harvester. He galloped back toward his own positions. The Harvester and signal bearer followed in a panicky flurry. Fox shook his fist at the crowd, the last to go. Whatever words he mouthed were lost in the uproar.

A great silence fell. The calls of crows and a gull's descending scream were shockingly loud. A calf bawled, and hundreds of pairs of eyes blinked, sought the disturbance. The few defenders who spoke did so in subdued tones.

Then the wolf calls floated across the quiet. Distant, wisping threads of sound, the song reached inside the defenders, spoke to each one of the freedom of the singers. For several long breaths, the world seemed to hold in place, caught up in that wild, spine-jangling sound.

That sound collapsed under the renewed thunder of Blizzard drums.

From out of the forest, horses drew odd wagons, long and slim, with high wheels. The tall front and sides of the wagon box sloped inward. Out of catapult range, the wagons halted. Horses were unhitched. Previously hidden men leaped to the ground from the rear of the wagons. They pushed them ahead, stopping in a neat line. The men leaped back into the wagons.

Gan's catapults opened fire. Few bolts struck true on a wagon front surface. When one did, sparks fountained. The wagon jerked; the bolts shattered. Conway, who'd come to the wall with the sniper rifle immediately after the wolf chorus, said, "Iron armor. I'll bet Moonpriest's catapults are inside." As if responding, the wagons all dropped their front wall. Men adjusted the aim of suddenly revealed horizontal bows. Within two heartbeats, a sheaf of arm-long bolts were coming at the defenders. They carried flaming oil-soaked rags. Leclerc's pumps were quickly in action. Nevertheless, fires started.

The wallkiller lofted a missile.

By that time, only Wolves assigned to defend the walls manned the battlewalk. They watched the spherical object come. As it closed, many remarked on its odd projections, on the combination of whistle and roar. The object seemed almost to float along, then suddenly its progress was shrieking rush. Men yelled, ducked. It hurtled over them, crashed in a street in myriad shards.

People looked, fearful. One, braver, edged forward, kicked some pieces. "It's a pot," he said, full of wonder. "A great damned pot. And empty." A nervous titter broke out of a woman, not far away. When he turned, she blushed, but her laughter continued. He joined her. Soon many others joined them, examining the pieces, making jokes.

A man on the wall shouted warning. The crowd disappeared into doorways.

The second missile struck a burning building. Mixed with the sound of breaking pottery was a dull, heavy thud. The fire billowed wildly, raged outward. It seemed to double its ferocity.

Gan looked to Tate and Conway, dismayed. "You know this weapon. How does it feed fire?"

"A gas. Hydrogen." Conway made a face at Gan's incomprehension, then continued. "The jars can start fires, but only where there's already a flame. It's like oil."

Dark anger suffused Gan's features. "More of your people's learning? I think it may cut in too many directions, Matt Conway."

There was no answer to that. Conway hurried to the battlewalk, hammered the catapult wagons with the sniper rifle. Even that heavy slug failed to penetrate the metal shielding. He waited for the front wall to drop before firing. Two catapults went down before the crews learned to only partially lower the door, fire immediately, and raise it again. Meanwhile, Conway became a prime target.

The wallkiller flung jars filled with a mix of pitch, oil, and wax. Where they smashed, a huge smear of inflammables spread in all directions, ran into cracks, seams. The catapults ignited it with flame arrows.

The city erupted in flame. Leclerc's pumps were overwhelmed. Stone-and-brick buildings, filled with wood and fiber products, turned into furnaces. More hydrogen spheres exploded, knocked down walls, accelerated fires.

Moonpriest launched a mass attack on Sunrise Gate. Windband poured from the forest in a yelling, shouting wave. Gan called to Conway, "Take the south side. They mean to hold us there with few men and the wallkiller. You and the lightning weapon can replace many, and that lets me reinforce here." To Tate and Nalatan, he said, "Stay with me, you two. The main thrust is here."

Moments later, Neela rushed up. She went directly to the wall near Gan with her double-curved bow. Fastidiously—ludicrously—she brushed dust from the flat surface of her chosen crenel. Only when she saw Gan's incredulity did she realize where her preoccupation had taken her. She shrugged, sheepish, then drew an arrow from the quiver at her back and looked to the advancing nomads.

Gan was laughing hugely when he turned to direct his battle.

Archers like Neela turned the clear ground in front of the city walls into a shambles. Windband nomads carrying ladders and line with grappling hooks screamed battle cries, sang of the glory of life eternal. They died in heaps.

Their own archers and catapult gunners drew blood in plenty. Young Wolves spun from the crenels, dropped to the battlewalk and were still. More staggered back, clawing at wounds.

In a culture that knew few mechanical objects, Tate was a machine, sighting, firing, killing. With the boop, she blasted holes in grouped nomads. The wipe smashed them to the ground as individuals. When a number bunched at the base of the wall, she dropped a grenade among them. Nalatan, beside her, worked his bow with deadly precision. When he looked at his wife, he saw past the unknowable person sowing destruction, sensed the complex of hurts that fueled her.

The attack shattered on the missiles. It failed to place a single ladder against the wall. While the survivors broke and retreated, the Wolves facing east howled victory.

They nearly drowned out alarm rising from the southern wall. Men streamed off the battlewalk. Catapults stood abandoned. Some defenders dropped to their knees, clawing at their throats, their eyes. Many more were seized by violent coughing.

Gan looked to see a top section of the wall, twice as long as a man, collapse inward. The weight of it tore out an equally long section of wooden battlewalk. The mass dropped on a wooden shelter below, one that held horses. The screams of the broken animals mingled with those of broken men.

Another wallkiller stone enlarged the damaged area.

Gan realized he'd fallen for a devastating ruse. Moonpriest sacrificed the nomads littering the killing ground fronting the eastern wall to make the defense believe it was the major thrust. Now, however, with his reduced defenders broken by this inexplicable affliction, mounted Windband warriors broke out of the forest to the south. Worse, the covering forest was closer there, meaning the enemy would reach the wall quickly.

Stomach closed in a hard knot of anxiety, he leaped down the stairs, calling Shara and Cho to him. He raced to rebuild the defense at this new threat.

Adding to Gan's consternation, Conway staggered away from the damaged wall on a dangerously teetering section of battlewalk. Gan roared for Leclerc's teams, called for the counterattack force to man the wall.

Men continued to act in the same puzzling manner as Conway. Some were terrifying to see, agonized. Their cries were horrible. Death came to few. It came very hard.

Sylah reached Conway first. She guided him to a wall, sat him against it. He fought for words, asked for water. When Tate arrived, he struggled harder, clamped down on her painfully. "Chlorine." The word was so raw it sounded bloody. "Gas. Jars. Chlorine." She stared, uncomprehending, and he practically screamed, "Salt water."

Leclerc, rushing up, overheard. He paled, struck his forehead. "Imbecile. How could I be so stupid? The triple towers, by the sea. Electrolytic breakdown of water, yes, but seawater. Not only hydrogen and oxygen, but hydrogen and chlorine. Moonpriest. That filth. He's using poison gas."

Chapter 95

The defense was wounded. The rupture was small. So, thought Gan, was the head of an arrow; it killed, nevertheless.

Traces of a bitter, burning stink lingered. Beside him, his dogs pawed at their noses, sneezing, miserable. Hot wind from the fires brought different fumes. Ordinarily, they would have been distasteful. They dispersed the other smell, however, and were welcome.

Conway, coughing furiously, struggled to rise.

The sounds of Windband's assault pulled at Gan's attention. Instinct told him the contemptuous fury disfiguring Leclerc was more important for the moment. Gan said, "This stink that makes my eyes burn and hurts my dogs—is that what hurts Conway and the others?"

"Yes. It's poison. It gets in your lungs, makes hydrochloric acid. It's like . . ."

"The air? *Poison?*"

Leclerc looked up from Conway's struggles. He felt he was seeing Gan, truly seeing him, for the first time. How old was he? Leclerc asked himself. Barely launched on manhood. Victimized by technology he had no prayer of understanding. The notion made him very sorry for both of them. "Yes, Gan. I'm afraid that's it. Some of the jars poison the air."

For the briefest moment, Leclerc thought he saw the gloss of panic tighten on Gan's features. Then the man was Murdat. "Moonpriest can't poison air where his own men breathe. We stay away from the wallkiller jars, stay close to Windband warriors." He spun without hesitation, racing with his dogs to spread that word. It was just in time. Wolves were backing away from the afflicted area. Some dragged wounded or gassed comrades. Fear sat on them all. As Leclerc watched, one threw down his sword and fled.

Sylah's distress drew Leclerc's attention back to her and Conway. The latter was on his feet, bent over in pain. He warded off Sylah's ministrations. "No time. Got to go roof. Blizzardmen. Know their tactics, signals." He lurched to a door, shouldered inside. Leclerc and Sylah watched him literally crawl upstairs.

She turned away, helpless, angry. "I can't help him if he's going to be like that. At least they—" The irritability was blown away by the crash of yet another boulder. Built to withstand arrows, slingstones, and destruction by fire, the wall was proving no match for Moonpriest's wallkiller. Three Wolves, huddled immediately opposite the impact, were ripped by shards spalling off the inside surface. Ragged, spinning like leaves, they shot off the battlewalk like bloody dolls. That section of the wall's top collapsed, taking out battlewalk.

On the roof of his building, Conway looked across the intervening clear area at the deep crescent knocked out of the stonework. Through it, he saw Blizzard attacking in their standard three columns. The outer two kept a steady rain of arrows falling on the wall's defenders. The center one, on reaching the breach, dismounted to attack it. Already, ladders were in the notch; Conway was certain they were going up beside it, as well. In the far distance, he saw previously hidden catapults churning out of the forest. Their bolts interdicted Gan's reinforcements rushing to plug the gap.

The wallkiller lobbed gas jars as well as solid missiles beyond the fighting. Fire was general. Roiling plumes of flame and smoke climbed into a dull, drizzling sky. Off to the east, a house wall collapsed on top of one of Leclerc's generator wagons as it rushed to the point of greatest danger. Conway noticed others, and the pumps, as well, bouncing headlong over debris on their way to the breach.

He held his fire while the first elements of battle-mad Blizzardmen ignored arrows and missiles to clamber through the gap. Screaming war cries, shouting their names for glory, they appeared in the irregular hole like creatures boiling up from hell itself. The drop to the ground inside was the height of a man; it lessened quickly as the bodies of Blizzardmen and Wolves piled there.

As soon as Blizzard established itself on the remaining battlewalk, they passed up shields and archers. The latter attempted to isolate the battle, raking reinforcements with plunging fire. Other nomads, totally ignoring everything else, worked at the edges of the rupture, prying at stones, pounding with sledges and wedges, struggling to enlarge the opening.

Tate's rifle roared. The shield of a nomad archer on the battlewalk jerked backward. The man crouched behind it leaped to his feet, screaming disbelief at the shredded mass of flesh where his left arm used to join his shoulder. He toppled into the maelstrom below, shrieking a name. Conway wondered who it might be.

Tate was immediately the focus of attention. Blizzardmen in possession of a captured catapult narrowly missed her. For a horrible moment, Conway thought she was hit.

Unaware of her situation, Nalatan fought at the penetration. He was destruction incarnate. The heavy parrying bar whipped like a willow wand. Where the iron ball on either end struck, bone broke, swords shattered, helmets caved in. The conical handguard punched open vicious wounds. His sword reaped a fearsome harvest. Nevertheless, he was forced back with the rest of the Wolves.

Leclerc appeared, standing at the flank of a line of spearmen protected by full leather and steel plate armor. Clearly terrified, he held his position with the fierce determination of a man past his limits. He flanked the advancing Wolves. Their twin-tined spears glinted. Burdened by the heavy backpacked capacitors, they moved with almost comic deliberation. Their fellow Wolves ran headlong out of their way. Blizzardmen, certain they were seeing retreat, charged the spearmen.

Those touched by both prongs died. The surety of the thing was eerie. There were few dramatic sparks or reactions. Nomads touched by the prongs jerked and dropped. Few even screamed. Some took the contact on a warding shield or a sword blade and shorted the circuit. As Tate once pointed out, the tines served quite well in that extremity. In short order, the survivors of the first Windband wave were fleeing.

Fresh attackers poured in, shouldered them aside.

With the capacitors exhausted, the electric attack was spent. Covering his men's retreat with the wipe, Leclerc moved them out of the fray.

Other spearmen, using the weapons attached to the new, more powerful generators, were in position on the battlewalk by then. Conway, from his roof, admired the teamwork in their effort. Men pushed the pumps and water wagons toward the action, protected by the bulk of the equipment. Partially sheltered by the same gear, the horsedrawn generator wagons and their two-man crews followed. The pumps sprayed to their farthest reach. The smell of salt water in such an environment was most peculiar, but Leclerc had pointed out that it was a far better conductor.

The nomad warriors cared nothing for that. Once they realized they were simply being wet down—something the rain had already accomplished—they continued their attack. In the melee there was no time for learned discussion. Somehow, however, there was a communal, almost psychic, awareness that a different, not-understood menace stalked them.

The new spears, spitting bright blue fire, defined that subliminal apprehension. On the battlewalk, advancing behind shields proof against anything but catapults, the spearmen advanced with stolid patience. On the ground, ten formed a line. The cracking, blasting power killed everyone the spears touched. Nevertheless, they could only advance so far, restricted by the vulnerability of the generator crews. They couldn't stop the masses of men now tumbling through the increasingly large gap. It was the situation that made Conway seek the roof. When the first Blizzard signal flag went up, he shot the flag-bearer. Without tactical instructions, the incoming Blizzardmen milled in confusion.

Off to his left, Conway heard Tate's contribution. At every blast of her weapon, another Blizzardman fell.

In spite of everything, the invaders were getting into the city. The battle degenerated into isolated groups colliding with each other, fighting until one defeated the other. Survivors stumbled off to reunite with another group. And start the butchery again.

Twice Conway caught sight of Gan. He tore through the streets of Ola, a living flame, organizing, directing, fighting. Once Conway saw him gather wandering Wolves into a unit, send them into battle. The other time, Gan and his dogs were part of the fight. The glimpse lasted but a few heartbeats. In that length of time, Gan, Shara, and Cho surrounded themselves with carnage.

In the end, the numbers of Windband hemorrhaging into Ola doomed that defense. The units on the east and north walls were in great danger of being cut off from the castle. Wolf drums and warhorns rumbled the melancholy rhythms of retreat. Conway hurried down from his sniper's post, each inhalation a flame in his lungs. He wondered if he'd be able to fight the following day.

The withdrawal was stubborn, starred with heroism. Wolves knowingly abandoned no wounded or dead. Street by street, house by house, they gave ground. At the cleared fields in front of the castle walls, they held for the generator wagons, pumps, and water trucks to cross before following. From the castle defenses, catapults covered the final retreat of the terribly reduced Wolf units.

A few berserk nomads tried to charge after the rear guard. They went down under so many arrows they and the cropped grass around them seemed to magically sprout feathered shafts. The Wolf archers were pleased to display their willingness to fight on.

Day ended with the defense confined to the castle. Ola's gutted buildings shimmered heat waves that disdained the drizzling rain. The city's treasures were reduced to a greasy black pall drifting sluggishly east. The drums of Windband mocked from the remaining city walls, as if Moonpriest pleased himself by emphasizing their failure. The gaping wound torn out of the south wall by the wallkiller was pillowed at its base by dead Wolves deemed irretrievable and Blizzardmen, embraced in a brotherhood of loss.

Fists clenched, Gan burned with the mindless waste of it. Beside him, ever aware of her husband's deepest concerns, Neela said, "It's the right fight, for all the right reasons. Those men understood."

He was silent, but he reached to squeeze her hand. Hoping to provide him some relief, she said, "Many wives of Wolves stayed behind to help Sylah and Lanta and the rest of Church's Healers in the healing house. Wal's sharkers evacuated the worst wounded to his island. His men are raiding behind Windband; the warehouses and sea access are unaffected. We're going to win."

Gan continued his silence. He seemed to be listening. Neela asked what troubled him. He pointed his chin generally southwest. "Digging. That squealing and deep groaning can only be heavy wagons. They'll move the wallkiller tonight, so it can strike all the castle. The air-poison will come."

Leaning against him, Neela said, "I'm glad Coldar is with Wal's people."

"I wish none of us were here." His belated sardonic chuckle brought Neela's head around, expectant. He continued to stare out into growing darkness. "That's a lie. I'm glad I'm here. I fear dying. I hate the deaths of my friends; there are times when I hate the deaths of my enemies, because I feel their lives were taken for nothing. Yet I'm drawn to this, as helpless as any moth. I believe my mother's prophecy is real, that I'm meant to seek glory for my people, but I'd find a path to war if my mother had never spoken a word. It is me."

A lone Windband drum pounded a slow, solemn beat. Gan and Neela faced it, ignoring the Wolves lighting the torches that illuminated the walls against surprise attack. Then Neela pulled away, the contact lingering in shared warmth, in the slow slide of his arm from around her shoulders. She said, "You have things to do. I'll see how I can help in the healing house."

He kissed her, a gentle touch, so inappropriate to the situation that she stepped back too quickly, awkwardly. Her departing smile was perfunctory. She hoped he hadn't noticed. It was out of the question for her to turn and attempt to explain, or wave. Or anything. Not when she was so entangled with frustration and relief and pride and fear that she had no idea how to express herself.

Chapter 96

Catapults dueled into the night. The heavy bolts did no appreciable damage to the stone of the castle or the other buildings clustered around it. Twice they struck the large illuminating sconces outside the wall. Both times, answering shots from Wolf weapons disrupted Windband's following cheers. Casualties were minimal on either side, but the goal of the contest was primarily to harass.

Genuine dread was reserved for the dark-rending slam of the repositioned wallkiller. At each report of the throw arm, everyone within the castle walls flinched. There were no fires yet, so there was no concern about the hydrogen jars. The boulders elicited fear. There was no attempt to concentrate on a particular area. Again, the boulders were meant to harass, terrorize. Actual casualties were a side issue.

Not so with the chlorine jars. More than the crushing boulders, the defenders feared those agonizing fumes. Each new crash stoked the panic within the walls. Merely waiting ate deeply into resolve.

Gan looked away from the lights of Windband's campfires and was surprised to see Nalatan had come up undetected while he was distracted. Nalatan said, "I come from the healing house. Four Wolves have died of the air-poison. Two wives. One Priestess; I saw her go. It's a bad way to die. Like burning alive, from the inside."

"It's how Moonpriest means to break us. He'll keep sending his filthy jars until we're used up."

"At least he hasn't started any fires in here." Nalatan indicated the town. "Still a west wind. I hope it holds."

The tone alerted Gan. "Why?"

"I'm going out."

"I forbid it."

"I wish you wouldn't. If you forbid, I have to disobey. I'd dislike that."

"You'd dislike? I'd dislike losing the best fighter in my camp. I'd dislike explaining to my friend Tate that I stood by while you threw your life away."

"It's because I'm the best you have that I'm going. They've moved the wallkiller missiles to the new sites."

"How can you be sure?"

"Smell; earlier, there was grease and wax. To silence the wheels. It's gone now. No horse noises, either."

Gan swallowed chagrin. Those were things he should have noted. Still, it was foolish of Nalatan to try a one-man raid. "What would you do?"

"The wallkiller is wood. I'll burn it. And the jars full of whatever helps fire." In the dim light, his features took on a coldness harder than the stone beside him. "Think of the other jars, Gan Moondark. Think of them smashed, air-poison drifting east. Where those who brought this curse lie sleeping. A thing to poison air is evil beyond mercy. It must be destroyed."

A catapult bolt sighed overhead, struck the castle, shattered. Splinters hummed warning, clattered on the ground. At last, Gan said, "It's a bad idea." Nalatan's agreeing nod was barely visible. Gan went on. "It's too much. One man can't do it." Nalatan said nothing. Gan shifted uncomfortably. He sounded irritable. "Who'd watch your back? Cover you? There's no one here with your combat skills."

"There's one."

Gan turned to look more closely at his companion. "I'm responsible for every soul here. I can't go prowling around in the dark like some night raider."

"No one said you should." The innocent tone was sarcasm at its highest.

"You baited me, didn't you? You learned your Church lessons well, monk. You're as devious as a weasel."

"The better to stalk the nomads, wolf-talker. I'll wait for you at the door through the south gate while you tell your wife."

"You've already told Tate?"

There was a very pregnant pause. "She's sleeps. I thought it best to let her rest."

"So I'm to tell Neela, and she'll tell Tate what happened if we don't come back. Is that it?"

"Well, yes. After all, you're Murdat, in charge of things. All that. Someone has to know where you went."

"I'm sorry I called you devious. The word falls short." Gan rolled upright. "Come on, we'll get ready. I don't relish choking to death like a snared rabbit, either."

At the south gate's small door, Gan ordered the illumination torch refueled. He and Nalatan sprinted for the exit. As soon as the basket was hauled up and the light gone, he and Nalatan let themselves out with Shara and Cho. Away from the wall, they all flattened in the grass to crawl forward. Both men carried bows and quivers of arrows, as well as close-combat weapons. Nalatan was further equipped with a goatskin of lamp oil slung on his back.

At the decreased distance, the sounds of the wallkiller crew were obvious. Muted mechanical noise suggested it was being readied. Hushed commands and men grunting in exertion confirmed it.

The crew worked without lights, but Gan and Nalatan discovered no further security. The mounds of gas-laden jars, tucked into two revetments dug into the side of a low knoll, were unguarded. Up close, their size surprised Gan. He ran his hands over them, familiarizing himself with the tubular protrusions and their hammered-in wooden plugs. A sniff at the latter revealed they'd found the chlorine first. He and Nalatan eased away.

East of them by a few paces, the unsuspecting crew strained at the arming winch. With the massive machine silhouetted against the stars, both raiders watched in awe as the huge arm crept back. The man issuing commands rode the platform. He lit a small lantern, its dark side to the castle. When he moved to inspect the machine, his actions were crabbed, but quick, assured. He bent down, swinging the lantern to eye level.

Gan and Nalatan recognized Fox immediately. Nalatan's exhaling hiss was no more than the whir of a mosquito. It was charged with a yearning bloodlust that underscored Gan's own dark-shrouded sigh.

Very carefully, Nalatan readied the goatskin full of oil. Gan nocked an arrow. They nodded at each other. Releasing the shaft, Gan shouted, "Fox!"

The twisted figure spun about almost too quickly for the eye. Not too quickly for the arrow, however. It struck his chest, the impact like a fist. He staggered backward, caught himself, dropped to his knees.

The skin was already hurtling through the air onto the carriage of the wallkiller. Oil gushed out, soaked into the checks and cracks of the wood. Gan's fire arrow whirred. Flame engulfed the timbers. Fox struggled to rise, got to his knees. Fire engulfed him. Soundlessly, he crumpled, lying in the center of the conflagration.

Gan released the dogs on the stunned wallkiller crew. He arrowed four more men. The dogs were demonic, leaping from darkness to rend and tear, then fading away. Crewmen attempting to escape became disembodied screams from the night; most such cries ended abruptly, horribly.

Nalatan busied himself at the revetments, packing black powder charges in the stacks of round jars. He lit the fuses with a coal from a small carrier. As soon as they were sputtering, he whistled to Gan. In turn, Gan used his silver whistle to bring in the dogs.

They were barely started back to the castle when the mounted patrol bore down on them.

Yelling, firing arrows as fast as possible, the nomads charged. At Gan's signal, Shara and Cho circled to the flank, then drove at the horses. Between that attack and the accurate return fire of Gan and Nalatan, the charge erupted in pandemonium. Horses reared, screaming, falling. Riders tumbled to be seized by the raging dogs. When attacked the animals simply fled into darkness. Meanwhile, Gan and Nalatan held off the milling, cursing crowd.

A commanding voice named riders, told them to keep the dogs at bay. He called for the rest to follow him. Gan and Nalatan raced for the castle, shouting for the illuminating torch to be extinguished. Confused yells answered. The torch continued to burn, exposing the two running men cruelly.

Nalatan stopped. Wheeling, he loosed an arrow. The closest nomad jerked back in his saddle, flopped loosely, the shaft protruding from his throat. The four remaining riders swerved wide. Nearby, reinforcements shouted encouragement.

The remaining riders fired arrows at Nalatan. He dodged one, called to the now-stationary Gan. "Run. Quickly. If you delay, I won't have a chance to lose them in the dark. Don't let me die here for nothing. Save yourself. *Run.*"

Gan twitched, ripped by indecision. Shara and Cho raced to him from the darkness. Once more, Nalatan demanded he leave. With a wordless cry of loss and fury and pain, Gan ran. Calling his own name to the men on the wall, he sped to the door and tumbled through with his dogs. He turned to see Nalatan dashing away from the wall, into darkness, toward the sea.

Windband was entirely awake. The burning wallkiller was a fiery stick poked at a hornet's nest. Torches flared. Horsemen raced from the forest to intercept their tormentor.

The black powder exploded. The effect of the hydrogen was thunderous. Rather than one massive blast, it seemed to build, rising to a terrible, spectacular crescendo of sound and light. Blue-violet flame balled, billowed to red, leaped into the night. Jars rocketed across the fields, exploding in a glory of fire and sparks.

From the chlorine revetment, an infinitely more insidious power oozed across the landscape. Invisible, utterly silent, it crept the dark, revealing itself only in the sudden agonized screams and rales of its victims. Maddened horses stampeded. Panicked men cried for help, for mercy, and ran blindly away.

In the middle of all of it, the towering arm of the wallkiller leaned to the side. Creaking, cracking, it crashed to earth.

Inside the castle wall, a disheveled Tate, sleep-swollen face masked in horror, stood between Neela and Sylah. Their strength held her upright. In a voice wretched with disbelief, with accusation, she begged Gan to tell her that it wasn't true, that the man left outside, alone among the nomads of Windband, wasn't her husband.

Chapter 97

Donnacee Tate howled like a mad thing until Sylah and Kate talked her into drinking a powerful relaxant tea in the healing house. Even then, she was more incapacitated than asleep. She twitched and cried out, muttered in a strange, oddly inflected language. Sylah could only wonder at it; frequently Bernhardt winced and turned away, as if she understood the gibberish. Sylah was even more confused when Anspach and Carter came by to see their friend, and Kate said, "She's regressed. It's the narcotic, I think. She introduced Nalatan to her family. She talked about football. Then she explained to someone named Maria why she had to volunteer for the crèche."

None of it made any sense to Sylah. It clearly frightened the other three women, however. They carried Tate's cot to the farthest corner of the room.

Still and all, not long afterward, when the war drums sounded alarm, Tate came upright. She staggered crazily, but, wipe in hand, forced her way past the Healers attempting to stop her and made her way to the wall.

Torches advancing through the forest wavered and blended, winked out behind trees only to burst into brightness again. They were in a dispersed cluster, constant shifting giving them and the trunks around them a mysterious, transient quality. As they came out of the trees, a Windband drum throbbed. More torches were lit. Very quickly, flames spangled a semicircle around the city. The huge drum continued the steady thub-dub of a human heart.

The original group of torches came forward. Lights went on in nomad wagons, transforming canvas tops to massive golden-light lanterns.

A spectacle with all the elements of beauty and mystery failed, however. Perhaps it was the thudding monotony of the drums, or the chill mist that drifted in from the west to smear the light. Whatever it was, the scene was menace, not grandeur.

When the advancing torches grew closer, the white signal carried ahead of the group was clear. Less discernible was the horse-drawn object some distance behind. It appeared to be a wagon, rather like the catapult carts.

Standing beside Tate, Gan and Conway were astounded when she perceived the significance of the wagon long before Gan. Her solitary word was a sigh. "Nalatan."

Gan leaned into the castle wall. "There's someone standing in the wagon. It might be him." He sounded ill.

Tate's voice was flat, dead. "It's him. To show us."

By then, the goal of the group's destination was apparent. The wall that surrounded the castle itself was slightly higher than that which enclosed the entire city. Although Windband's nomads couldn't stand on the city wall because it was swept by missiles from the castle wall's positions, neither could the defenders. The oncoming party aimed for the junction of the two walls, the point signifying Windband's triumph. Leclerc joined Conway and Gan as they followed a distraught Tate there.

A large band of nomads followed the white signal group. They clung to the darkness, a shuffling, whispering presence in the night.

When the illuminated group stopped, their torches were carefully placed in two lines perpendicular to the wall. The wagon wheeled around to face back to Windband's lines. The horses were hobbled as soon as it was centered between the lights. Nalatan was in the center of the box, lashed to a cross as if crucified. He searched the wall for Tate. She called to him, and he nodded, expressionless. He appeared uninjured. When Tate lunged forward, calling again, Conway pulled her back. He said, "I know how it hurts, Donnacee. It hurts him more to hear you suffer. Don't give that other scum the pleasure of seeing it. Hang tough. For him." She refused to take her eyes from Nalatan, but she quieted.

Moonpriest, dressed in white from turban to shoes, dismounted and walked to climb aboard the wagon. The Harvester joined him, remaining on the ground.

Craning up at the wall, Moonpriest said, "This has been a costly war for you, Murdat. And for me. My ally, the Harvester, prevails on me to make peace. I think we can come to an agreement."

Gan looked to Tate. Misery clawed his features. "He's going to offer me Nalatan. I'll give anything I can."

She looked at him. Wordlessly, she turned back to the scene below.

Leclerc slipped up behind Gan, saying, "Talk. Keep him talking. Negotiate over anything, everything. But keep him talking." He acted as if his orders were unquestionable. He spoke to Tate the same way. "Tate, get down off the wall. Muster up a rescue team. Choose your own numbers, but understand you're going to have to hit fast and hard. Wait at the south gate, have it ready to open. Don't worry about a signal. You won't have any questions."

She was cold, unmoving. "I don't know what you're talking about."

"You can help me help him, or not. I don't have time to waste. Get ready to ride out and grab him off that wagon or back off so I can find someone who will."

From the darkness, a Wolf said, "I'll go."

Tate whirled as if burned. "You'll go with me, then. Come." She literally snarled at Leclerc on her way past. He flinched, involuntarily stepped back. Still, he smiled when he faced a wondering Gan. "Got to keep her busy," Leclerc said, then, "Angry too. That's good. I just hope it doesn't land on me." With that, he rushed toward the steps, calling Conway.

As Conway moved to follow, he heard Gan ask why Moonpriest felt he needed so many warriors with him under a white signal. Moonpriest's answer was insulting: "I know you for a clever, deceptive foe. I've ridden far in front of my positions. I wouldn't want you to think I was without defense."

Praying that Gan wouldn't lose his temper, Conway ran to catch Leclerc. As soon as he did, he asked, "What d'you think you're doing, Louis?"

"I brought something from the farm. I hope it works."

Conway almost stumbled. "What's the matter with you? You've got Tate hoping you'll save Nalatan."

They were at the wagons by the burned-out Violet Abbey then. As Leclerc tore at the covering cloth on one, he snapped at Conway, "If you've got an idea, use it. I told her, and I'll tell you: Shut up and help, or come up with something better. Grab that bundle there. And be careful with it." Again, Leclerc turned away as if unable to imagine not being obeyed. He called to some Wolves in the counterattack force. "You two. Come give me a hand."

The three of them lifted a large box out of the wagon, about an arm's length square, perhaps a third as deep. Conway cradled a tripod. At Leclerc's word, they raced for the wall. Once on top, Leclerc directed his impromptu crew in putting together his device, keeping it flat on the battlewalk.

It consisted of a large dish-shaped piece from inside the square box. The dish, of polished silver, attached to the tripod. Conway said, "A reflector? What's the point?"

Leclerc ignored him, squatting beside Gan, out of sight of Moonpriest. From the side of his mouth, Gan said, "Do something. I don't understand why he's still talking. I'm babbling."

"Make him talk about his religion."

Gan glanced down. Leclerc said, "I have to have it. Do it."

Gan nodded. Leclerc scurried to Conway. He called two men carrying generator-connected spears. In a moment, he disconnected the wires and attached both to one generator, then to fittings on the back of the dish. On the inside, he placed two black cylindrical objects, like cigars with one pointed end, in clamp holders. The sharpened ends almost touched. He told Conway, "When I wave my hand, you get this thing upright, aimed at Moonpriest. Don't get in front of it. Pull that switch, right there, and yell at the generator team to really get their backs into it. You use that lever to move the cylinder on top. As soon as the generator's at speed, bring them together. They'll light off. When they do, separate them." He turned.

"No, you don't." Conway grabbed him before he could get away. "What's this thing do?"

Exasperated, Leclerc pulled free. "You've forgotten everything. It's a carbon arc light. The cylinders are a baked mix of powdered coal and pitch and a little sawdust for a binder. When it lights off, it'll be the brightest night-light anyone's seen since they sealed the crèche on us. I think."

"You've never tested it, have you?"

Leclerc's grin was sickly. "Like I said: Got a better idea?" He raced to Gan's side, not bothering to hide this time.

Moonpriest was saying, "We've delayed long enough. Surrender the apostates and witches to me: Leclerc, Conway, Sylah, and Lanta. I give you Nalatan. Everyone else will live. Refuse me now, and everyone defending the castle will be dealt with as witches. Decide now."

Gan's gaze irresistibly went to Tate. In the dim light of torches, she looked back, stone-faced. There was defiance in the tilt of her chin, but terrible defeat in the way her shoulders sagged.

Leclerc said, "Tell him he's a fraud, he has no power."

Gan blinked. His glance for Leclerc suggested insanity. Nevertheless, he faced Moonpriest. "It takes no man to murder a prisoner. You only do this thing to pretend to power you know you don't have."

"Oh, but I do." Moonpriest's pleased smirk was clearly visible. He sounded pleased to have been challenged. He called the Harvester onto the wagon with him, positioned her behind himself.

A murmur of nervous anticipation swept the wall. Archers nocked arrows.

Stepping up beside Nalatan, Moonpriest extracted the thick-bodied rattlesnakes from inside his robes. The noise on the wall turned into a moan that rose swiftly, trailed away. Behind Moonpriest, the massed horsemen made a similar sound, but this one reeked of anticipation.

Perversely, Leclerc was pleased, excited. "We've got him," he said, grabbing Gan's arm. "Tell him even a god doesn't threaten to kill prisoners under the white signal. His mother will withdraw her power. Tell him."

Doubt wrinkled Gan's brow. Nevertheless, he delivered Leclerc's suggested message in a voice dire with conviction. Moonpriest's reaction was mild to the point of amusement. He waved a languid hand at the crowd behind him, called over his shoulder, "Withdraw, Windband. Unbelievers can't harm me."

A Wolf called softly to Gan, "He's no god. He's just hiding behind Nalatan, Murdat. Let me put a catapult bolt through both of them. Nalatan will thank you. Don't let those things bite him."

Gan said, "You'd hit the Church woman. Don't chance it." Then, to Leclerc, "Well?"

"Yell. Tell him you can bring on the moon. Tell him." Leclerc called to Conway: "Get that thing upright. Turn it on."

Gan raised his voice. It resonated across the night. "The moon, as all things, is part of the One in All. No man can claim godhood from a thing that is no god. Trickster. Magician. The true Church, the good Church, is here. I will prove it. I will show you the moon on my command."

Saying, "Now!" to Conway, Leclerc signaled Tate. Men eased open the south gate. The generator moaned to life, settled to a hum of promise.

Conway closed the switch. Nothing happened. Gan stood, dramatically posed, pointing at the silver disk. Its mirror surface glowed gently in the light of flaming torches. A harvest moon through ground mist might have been that pale. As it was, this was a blatant fraud, a clumsy trick. Raucous laughter and coarse threats boomed from the darkness behind Moonpriest's torchlight.

A tiny spot of red marked the tips of the compressed coal cylinders. Leclerc said, "Don't move, Gan. We're getting there."

Moonpriest's laughter was like a whip. The Harvester's voice rose in mocking triumph. "You'll burn. All of you. My vision showed me, flames all around. Flames destroy false Church. All of you."

Along the walls, men groaned, turned to their companions. Despair—worse, damnation—was in the air. Hands worked three-signs, two-signs. Lips moved in prayer. Hearts that feared no death withered at the thought of bleak eternity.

Gan said, "You've doomed us, Louis. Whatever you meant to do, the Wolves' spirit is breaking. We're done."

The red spots on the cylinders were suddenly white. There was a sputtering, crackling noise. Speeding strands of blue-white smoke lifted.

Conway jerked the lever, separating the cylinders. The budding brightness spat loudly, turned back to a surly red.

Agonized, Leclerc shouted, "Not so fast. You killed it. Bring them back together. Separate them slowly."

From the darkness, Windband mumbled anticipation. Far off, war drums sounded their intricate rhythm. Screeching like fingernails on slate, the Harvester's laughter threaded through all of it.

Trembling, Conway tried again. The ruby glow turned white again, sent out more smoke. And brilliance. With a busy, satisfied sound, the cylinders sparked alive with blinding intensity. The disk lived, beamed directly at the tableau on Moonpriest's wagon.

The snakes recoiled on Moonpriest's arms. He, dazzled, was already throwing his hands up against the glare. Rattling wildly, the snakes flew from their purchase, fell onto his shoulders. Facing the Harvester. They struck in perfect synchrony, jaws agape, fangs lancing the horrified, transfixed features.

Tate and her rescue party thundered out the gate. They were on Moonpriest and the wagon before stunned warriors could recover. Swift sword strokes freed Nalatan, eager hands slung him across Tate's saddle. The group was returning to the gate before most of the nomads realized they'd been cheated of their captive.

Or before the rescuers realized no one had finished Moonpriest.

Under the wagon, which now held the shrieking, writhing Harvester, he screamed for help. Wolves who'd have given anything to arrow him held off, afraid of hitting the woman, even though all knew she was already dying.

That was when the full weight of Moonpriest's treachery revealed itself.

Under cover of bargaining with Gan, with the attention of every man in the castle drawn to the south wall, numbers of Windband slipped from the burned-out city to the east, across the open ground between the two entities. Now, at the unbelievable appearance of a light that exceeded the moon itself, that force rose as one.

They saw weapons that killed impossibly. In faith, they attacked. They saw their wallkiller, proclaimed an irresistible destroyer, reduced to ashes, and its deadliest capability turned against themselves. Still they attacked. Seeing their god's own symbol turn against him, however, seeing him reduced to quaking, screaming for help, was beyond bearing.

A handful of the men who accompanied Moonpriest's treacherous embassy rescued him. They slashed the horses' hobbles, leading the wagon off. Moonpriest scrabbled along, crablike, cowering under its protection into the darkness.

The distant drum, heretofore supremely arrogant, faltered. It stopped.

A Wolf raised a ragged howl. Swelling, the call soon rang from everywhere, stronger, surer.

The fields in front of the castle walls stood empty.

Silence cloaked the victorious defenders. Gan braced a forearm against the lasting stone, lowered his head onto it. He heard in that quiet the relief and loss and fearful hope that comes to every combat survivor. It is the silence of the warrior, alive, assessing cost. It is the most precious of all moments, sullied only by the knowledge that it must pass. Must be repeated.

Gan cared nothing if anyone saw his tears. He dreaded only that he might have to explain that they weren't for the dead and maimed alone.

Torches retreated into the forests sheltering Windband. Their flaring belligerence faded to listless, pale glimmers that eventually disappeared. Lamplike nomad wagons drifted across the darkness, spectral creatures seeking solace in company. Several formed a circle. Soon, there were flames within that enclosure.

"Pyres," Conway said. "Committing their dead. It's over. We've won."

There were no more cheers. Mute, the Wolves watched the fires burn, tracked more disappearing torches into the forest depths.

Neela and Sylah appeared on the battlewalk. Neela said, "Tate's in the healing house with Nalatan. He's fine. A few bruises. Leclerc's with Bernhardt. They tell me the Harvester said something about a vision. Flames."

Gan turned to look at her, wincing at her exhaustion, at the robe stained with the unspeakable detritus of tending wounded. Concentrating on her eyes, he nodded, answered, "Visions and prophecies. They seem to always stand in need of interpretation." He smiled. It was a distant, thoughtful expression.

Chapter 98

Eight days after Moonpriest's retreat, a troop of riders approached the Sunrise Gate. They were expected. Patrolling Wolves, instructed to observe without contacting, reported them long before. They identified them as heavily armed warriors.

Construction stilled as the men came into view. Nervous women hurried about, gathering up children. Those who escaped maternal concern raced for vantage points on the wall, nimbly dodging Wolves determined to send them home.

Gan, with Conway and Nalatan, ignored that byplay. Worried expressions underscored their concern for the slight numbers of Wolves climbing to defensive positions. At one point, Gan frowned over his shoulder at the city, clearly concerned for the women and children recently returned from their island safety.

There were only twenty riders in the oncoming group. The scouts confirmed that. They also confirmed that these men came from the south, and that other men were with them. The second group caused most concern. They stayed to the woods, seeming to drift along in parallel with their companions, unapproachable.

It was known that the group of twenty spoke to Moonpriest in passing. That worthy and his surviving Windband camped with River People allies on the north shore. Informants reported that Moonpriest was already blaming the Harvester's death on the apostate Church, and his defeat on the combined strength of several known witches within Ola's walls. Some of his force believed him. Many didn't.

But these newcomers talked to him, and rode directly at Ola.

Gan didn't like the look of it.

When Sylah joined them on the wall, he abruptly told her it was no place for her. She sniffed. "Twenty men? Riding up here like they were coming to market? Not very frightening."

"We don't know who or what they are. Or what sort of men Sister Mother might send, now that her Harvester's been killed. At least keep out of sight."

She tossed her head. The rich skein of black hair caught the light wind, fanned out like a wing before settling. Part hung down her back, part draped her shoulder. She reached across her body with her left hand to straighten it. The massive gold bracelet on that wrist gleamed back at the sun.

The lead rider's mount checked. It danced and pranced. Then it was charging, so swift, so unexpected, the rest were many lengths behind before they started.

Tension sang along the wall. Men tested bows. The sound of murdats leaving scabbards was like metallic rain.

The rider came on, the horse's mane streaming, tail bannered in flight.

Sylah looked at Gan, saw expressions too swift to actually register, like watching raindrops strike still water, each impression unique, each too brief to distinguish. Her own heart leaped. She spoke one word. "Him?"

His grin answered. With an involuntary cry, she was racing down the stairs, running for the gate.

Clas na Bale swung to the ground while his charging war-horse was still skidding to a dirt-throwing, shuddering stop. He swept her up in his arms, pivoted, spinning, until she squealed delight and alarm. He kissed her, and for a moment the world whirled more. Holding her at arm's length, his look absorbed her. He said, "Never again. As sure as I hold you now, I'll never let go. Not for anything."

"Yes." It was what she lived to say, the only thing she could say. And it wasn't enough. She pressed on. "We'll be together. I don't have to go anywhere. We'll live in the same place. No more quests, no more—"

He kissed her again, and it occurred to her that "yes" was quite enough.

Gan stood off to the side, waiting. Clas finally noticed him. The men embraced. All around, Wolves murmured among themselves, pointed at the strange, black square tattooed on Clas's cheek. They commented on his scars. Several expressed surprise that Gan's mentor was a bit shorter than his pupil. Others noted that he had muscles like a prairie bear.

Then Clas was beside Sylah again, an arm around her as if she might disappear without contact. To Gan, he said, "We tried to get here in time to help. I'm glad we weren't needed."

Grimly, Gan corrected him. "You were needed. We won, but we lost many. Too many. Even a group this small would have helped."

"We have this many more Dogs, including ten Nightwatch with their dogs. And twice as many Smalls."

Gan blinked. "Smalls? With you?"

Too nonchalant, Clas said, "Didn't you know? We're great friends, Dogs and Smalls. Wonderful people." Suddenly sly, he added, "Ask the Donnacee one. Fox would have told you, but Moonpriest tells us he didn't survive."

"My scouts said you spoke to Moonpriest."

"I warned him off Three Territories land. He's negotiating to leave wounded and the families of his dead with the Rivers who helped them. The Rivers aren't enthusiastic."

Sylah said, "Church will take the families. I'll send a War Healer to take care of any men they leave behind." Both men stared. She went on. "They're people. They've been misled. Now they stand a good chance of becoming slaves. I'll send Priestesses to bring them here."

"You may be right."

Clas said, "Put aside land for Smalls. Lots are coming up from the south. Most will want places in the foothills and into the mountains."

"Why didn't the ones riding with you come in now?" Gan asked. "And what about the rest of the Dogs?"

Clas shifted uncomfortably, cut a sheepish glance at Sylah. "A sort of ceremony. A brotherhood thing. For men. Tinillit's in charge. Tate knows him."

Sylah was cautious; ceremony and brotherhood had religious connotations. "The Smalls seem to know some interesting things about the mind. Rather like the way you control pain."

"That's it." Clas brightened, squeezed her with the arm already tight around her shoulders. "They can teach us a lot. They'll work with Church, too."

The rest of Clas' Dogs were in the city by then, the younger ones admiring the buildings. They mingled easily with the other packs. Some of the new arrivals were veterans of the war against Altanar. They pointed and spoke loudly, showing off their experience, swapping stories with the defenders down off the walls.

The threesome of Gan, Sylah, and Clas rode for the castle. Gan sent runners to find his closer friends, including Leclerc and Bernhardt, who were rebuilding the farm. Everyone else was gathered in the castle's dining hall when a diffident young man entered, hat in hand, to explain that Leclerc and Bernhardt had urgent need to talk to their fellow tribesmen. The couple requested that all the others join them on the farm.

The idea amused the group. Festive, everyone talking at once, they rode south. They were still in a holiday mood when they arrived. Louis and Kate, with true rural hospitality, greeted their guests from the porch, handing out hot tea. A table labored under a load of fresh bread, smoked ham, cheese, butter, and a bowl of honey cookies.

Sylah noted that Leclerc seemed to have something on his mind. She remarked on it to Lanta. Her small friend agreed. "He's anxious. Not exactly troubled, but he's eager for everyone to be relaxed. Some new proposal, I suspect."

The Seer wasn't far wrong. Soon afterward, Leclerc asked for attention. "I must do something very rude now. I have to ask all my fellow tribesmen to separate from wives or husbands, and come with me. There's something we must discuss in great privacy."

Gan rose, teacup in hand. "There's enough trust within this group to accommodate a little privacy. We'll wait here. Better yet; those who stay behind will start a fire. We'll cook outside tonight, a campfire dinner. All right?"

It was decided. The "tribal" group, on horseback, followed Leclerc and Bernhardt. The hosts refused to discuss the reasons for the journey on the way. The ride took little time, and brought them to a ridge overlooking a small valley. Where they stopped, a For cloth covered an object on the ground. Four sturdy wooden legs provided no clues. Dismounting, indicating the others should do so, Leclerc and Bernhardt positioned themselves in front of it.

Leclerc reached into a pocket. He withdrew the red book, flourishing it dramatically. "People of our time. In crèches, as we were. Gone." He held the book toward them, face out. "Remember these numbers? The doodles? They're why we're here. Radio frequencies. Low-range radio frequencies."

Conway reached for the book, looked at the numbers. "Damned low, Louis."

"They carry better. Easier to pick up. And I've done it." Leclerc lifted the For cloth. The thing under it was weird-looking.

Carter said, "It looks like an electric insect. What's it do?"

In answer, Kate and Leclerc went in opposite directions. They stepped away a few paces, then came back, each carrying a long piece of wire. Kate pointed. "Louis strung a wire—an antenna—across this valley. This is probably the crudest radio anyone's built since long before Marconi, but it's a radio. He's getting a signal."

While Leclerc attached ground and antenna wires, he described a tube about the length of a man's arm, wrapped with beeswax-insulated wire, finest any of them could remember seeing in this world. A bared strip of those coils ran the topmost length of the tube. Attached to one end of the device was a miniature version of the spear capacitors. This one was about five inches long and two inches in diameter. A separate wire attached it to the terminals at opposite ends of the tube.

A raised wooden bar spanned the length of the coil, the support for what Leclerc called a slide. The latter was a thin, pointed copper leaf, designed to move along the bar. It touched one of the fine bared wires at a time. Another fine wire led from the slider to the spark gap, which was two wooden blocks drilled to tightly accommodate copper wires. Where those wires exited the blocks, they were honed to needle sharpness. The block not wired to the slider was attached to the ground wire.

The silence quivered with repressed excitement. Leclerc's voice literally shook, as did his hand when he pointed at a small sundial. "See those three rocks, there? When the shadow strikes each of those, I get a signal. Long. If that was it, I'd say it's a machine, like the ones that kept us alive, sending a dead hand down the centuries. But I'm getting random signals, as well. Some long, some short, but always on the same frequency."

Tate said, "I can't believe this. Someone . . . ?" Implication overwhelmed the sentence.

Leclerc nodded. "Transmitting. Someone with massive power, or I'd never identify the signal. Looking for us."

"Or someone like us." It was Carter, ever practical, frowning. Leclerc wasn't pleased about being corrected, but he nodded affirmation.

Anspach said, "Do the times of reception give you any clue about the transmitter's location?"

"Not a thing. But we have the locations of the other crèches."

Conway shook his head. "We can't be certain it's one of them. If your assumption that this is a signal is correct."

Bernhardt rounded on him. "It's correct. We've checked it. Every day. Four days. It's correct."

Gently, Conway said, "Four days isn't very long, Kate."

Tate was next. "It's long enough for me. Louis gets these things right. Can we listen? It's about time." She pointed at a marker, about to be touched by the gnomon's shade.

"There's nothing to hear." Leclerc pointed at the tiny gap in the wire leading to ground. "Watch there."

Tense, crowded together, the group stared. "There!" Leclerc shouted, pointing. Tate straightened. "That? That fuzzy little blue thing? That's your signal?"

Too busy looking at the spark to be offended, Leclerc struck the air with a fist. "Right on time. As advertised."

Long after the spark disappeared, they concentrated on the gap as if still seeing something. Yearning. It was Conway who broke the silence. "Okay. It's a signal. Now what?"

Carter whirled up from her crouch, stepped back, and faced them all. She raised a hand. "Not yet. No one say anything. There are others involved. We've got to think."

Tate demurred. "Think, yes, but fast. We've got to decide: Do we go looking for whoever might be out there, or not? But Janet's right. There are others involved. For me, it's Nalatan. For her and Sue and Kate, it's the Chosens." She winked at Leclerc. "Well, maybe them, too." Louis had the good grace to color vividly as he grinned. Kate positively glowed. Tate went on. "If anyone wants to go or stay, that's it. I say we decide on the way back to the farm. When we get there, we speak out. No questions from anyone, no arguments. Agreed?"

There was a long, deep silence. Absently, Leclerc disconnected his primitive radio and covered it. He spoke thoughtfully. "I suppose it's best. Our own decision, arrived at for our own reasons. I'll go first, after we're back. If no one minds."

Hesitant glances found no objection. The silence continued. The ride back to the farm was very long, very subdued.

Still full of cheer, Gan greeted them from in front of a fire ebbing to coals. "Good timing. We can cook soon." He stopped, studied their faces. His own fell. "Something's happened. Why so serious?"

They dismounted, almost shamefaced. Tate moved quickly to be with Nalatan, and Conway moved to Lanta with hurried strides. She looked at him with alarm, but he just shook his head.

Leclerc said, "We came to you as travelers, Murdat." The title made Gan wary. Leclerc hurried on. "You know us as different from all others. You know us as people who trust you as you trust us. Now I ask you to accept a mystery. We—all of us of our tribe—have received a message, sent in a way known only to us. If such a secret is discovered outside this gathering, we shall all die as condemned witches. We are not. We are merely different. We ask you to understand that, to accept it, and to understand that this message requires us to decide what to do with our lives. We are going to tell you all, you who are so precious to us."

Carefully, making a three-sign, Gan said, "Who speaks first?" As he did, Neela eased away from him. She, too, made a three-sign, and although she drew back, deferring to his leadership, she remained close enough to come to his aid.

Clas na Bale ostentatiously shouldered in front of Sylah. Muscles bunched in his jaw when, equally forcefully, she refused to be shielded.

The talk of mystery and witches wasn't sitting well.

"I speak first." Leclerc was firm. "I've helped the Three Territories and you. I also envied you. I told myself I should rule." Gan's expression darkened. Leclerc ignored it. "I was mistaken. I'm not a leader. But I can help you be a better one. I can make the Three Territories stronger, safer. I swear you my loyalty. I stay with you."

Gan nodded, solemn. He looked to Bernhardt. "And you, Kate Bernhardt?"

Flustered, off guard, Kate waffled, hands jerking, mouth working. She blurted, "The children. The Chosens. And . . . And other stuff. I mean, I'm staying here."

Leclerc moved to her. Grim determination emphasized his awkwardness. Still, when he took her hand, it was gentle and confiding. She looked at him in amazement. He said, "If she'll have me, I'm asking her to marry me."

Kate stammered. Exploded. "How can such a bright man be so silly? Are you asking him or me? Of course I'll marry you. I love you, you fool." And she kissed him.

The applause stopped before she did, but when it was opportune, Conway told Gan, "I stay. There's a world to build here. Trade. Defense. Perhaps conquest. It's a challenge I want to confront." He saluted. Gan smiled, returned it. When Conway turned to Lanta, she embraced him. She said, "I would have gone with you. I'm glad we're staying."

Conway heard something in the words, spoken directly against his chest. "Why? What're you telling me? Is there some Church law I was breaking, or something?"

Still pressed to him, Lanta shook her head. "Not now."

He looked over her to the others, baffled. Sylah curled her lip at him in a pitying sneer. Gan snorted laughter. Tate's look made him feel he'd taken his first step into boot camp. He swung his head like a stunned ox. "What?"

Lanta stamped her foot. "I wasn't going to tell you like this. Everyone else certainly seems to have guessed. I'm pregnant."

Hands under her arms, Conway lifted her until her head was higher than his. They laughed like children. He whooped, then howled like a wolf. She put her hands to her ears, then to his mouth. Suddenly, stricken, he lowered her, clumsy with apology. "What am I doing? Are you all right? I didn't hurt you?"

Dryly, Neela said, "She fought a war a few days ago, Matt Conway. I think she can stand a bit of exercise. Congratulations, Lanta; what wonderful news." Again, there was applause. The other women crowded around her, hugging, congratulating. When the hubbub slowed, Conway drew Lanta with him to the fire, opposite Tate. As they sat down, he whispered, "I love you. I've never been so happy." She smiled, the look confiding, sharing. Then she snuggled against him.

Carter stepped forward a pace toward Gan, shrugged. "The Chosens—they need us. I mean me. I'm staying."

Anspach said, "Me, too. Those children are like my own. I couldn't leave. Not for any reason."

Sylah left Clas' side, moved to embrace both women. She was laughing aloud. "I almost died, holding my breath. You don't know how happy you made me. I'm going east with Clas. I want to start an abbey there. I was going to ask you to be the new Iris Abbess and Violet Abbess here."

Gan interrupted their impromptu celebration. "It's not like you to be last, Tate. I think I know why."

Tate sat by the fire, wipe across her knees. Like petting an animal, she stroked it as she spoke. Pointedly, she looked directly at Gan, refusing to acknowledge Nalatan, sitting beside her, shoulder to shoulder. "You're right. I'm the one who goes. I have to discover what's out there." With that, her composure broke. It was a minuscule fracture, just enough for a glance at her friends, to include them in her hidden meaning. She continued. "Glory for your people is your fate, Gan Moondark, and for a while your fate was ours. We grew in your light. Even those who stay here, though, have their own goals now. Mine is away. I don't know where. I *will* seek it. Outside walls."

Nalatan put an arm around her shoulders. Tate shivered, sighed. As if letting go of something treasured, but outgrown, she relaxed to lean against his strength.

The others seemed to leave them alone in some unstated, mutually understood agreement. Nalatan said, "We are different, we two. Different from everyone. I marvel that I found you. Thank you for saying we must go. Are you sure you did it for you? Not because I hate the walls?"

"I did it because it's what I want." She squeezed his hand. "Now I've got everything I want. Except food. Are we going to eat?" They were laughing when they rejoined the others.

The rest of the evening went smoothly, albeit a bit strangely. The tinge of melancholy was offset by other considerations—of accomplishment, of challenge, of decisions long put off and finally determined. If their laughter was sometimes a shade forced, it was never without warmth. They ended sitting around a fire of such spent coals that the pale glow nearly drowned in the light of myriad stars. For some while, they were all quiet, caught in that splendor.

Finally, Gan rose. He said, "I doubt we'll ever see a night like this again, this group. These companions. What times we've had! But there are other things to come. So let us all say one last good night as a band. Tomorrow is different. Another world to build, another world to create, another world to discover. A salute, one to another. To the love of friends for friends."

All stood. There was a salute. And embraces. Some tears. Quietly, whispering the good night Gan suggested, they parted.

The distant song of a wolf, eternally pure, reached into the hearts of all and soared, misted with dreams, to seek the stars.

About the Author

Donald E. McQuinn was born in Winthrop, Massachusetts. After moving often and eventually graduating from high school in Texas, he attended the University of Washington. He retired from the United States Marine Corp in 1971. He lives in the Pacific Northwest with his wife, Carol; they have three grown sons.